speak
the graphic novel

Laurie Halse Anderson

artwork by
Emily Carroll

speak
the graphic novel

Farrar Straus Giroux
New York

Author's note:

I wrote the original *Speak* in the late '90s, before the Internet, before cell phones, and before the awesome phenomenon of graphic novels. I wrote it to deal with the depression and anxiety that had shadowed me since I was raped when I was thirteen years old. I never dreamed that the book would be published. I couldn't imagine that people would want to read it, or share it with friends, or teach it, or turn it into a movie.

But here we are, because life can be bewilderingly wonderful sometimes.

I've watched the growth of graphic novels with excitement, and have long pondered how to transform the story of *Speak* into the graphic novel form. Art and artistic expression play a significant part in Melinda Sordino's transition from traumatized victim to empowered survivor. The story and the form seemed to be a natural fit, but only in the hands of the right artist.

Emily Carroll is that artist. Her artwork combined with my story have created a new expression of what it feels like to have your voice stolen from you, the battles that must be endured to find it again, and the triumph of speaking up.

Thank you so much, Emily, for sharing your talent and for all of your hard work on this book. Thanks also to our genius editor, Joy Peskin, and fabulous art director, Andrew Arnold, for helping us blend words and images to create magic. The entire Macmillan team has supported the novel, and now the graphic novel, with energy and passion that is very much appreciated.

I reserve my deepest thanks for two groups:

The community of educators who have boldly championed *Speak* through countless censorship challenges have helped change the national conversation about sexual violence. I salute their courage and am grateful for their friendship. My extended, blended family (including biological relatives and those of the heart) has cheered me on through years of writing, travel, some struggle, and much joy. They have taught me all that I know about the power of love to heal. My boundless love for them weaves the greatest story of all.

—Laurie Halse Anderson

To everyone seeking their voice
and reaching for their power

FIRST MARKING PERIOD

"Welcome to Merryweather"

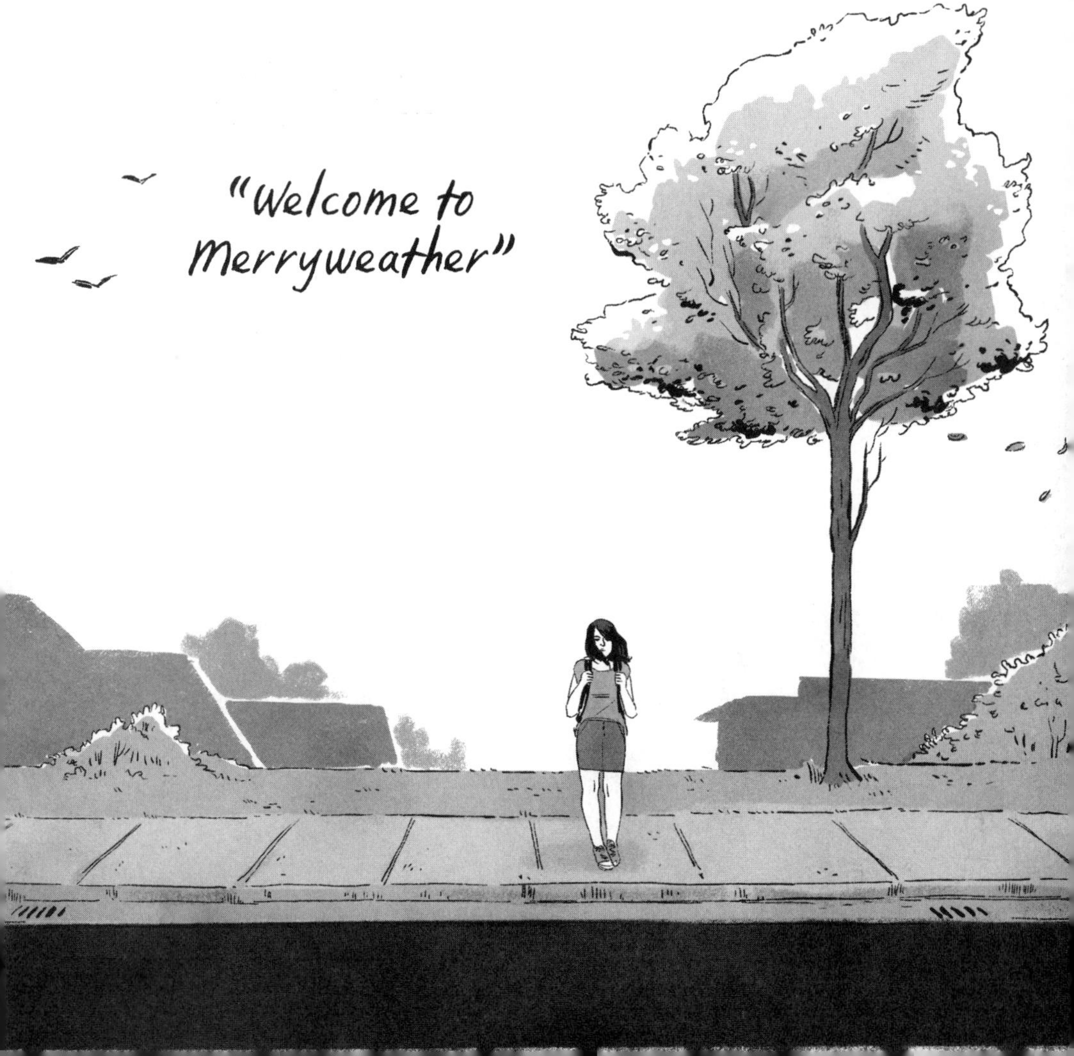

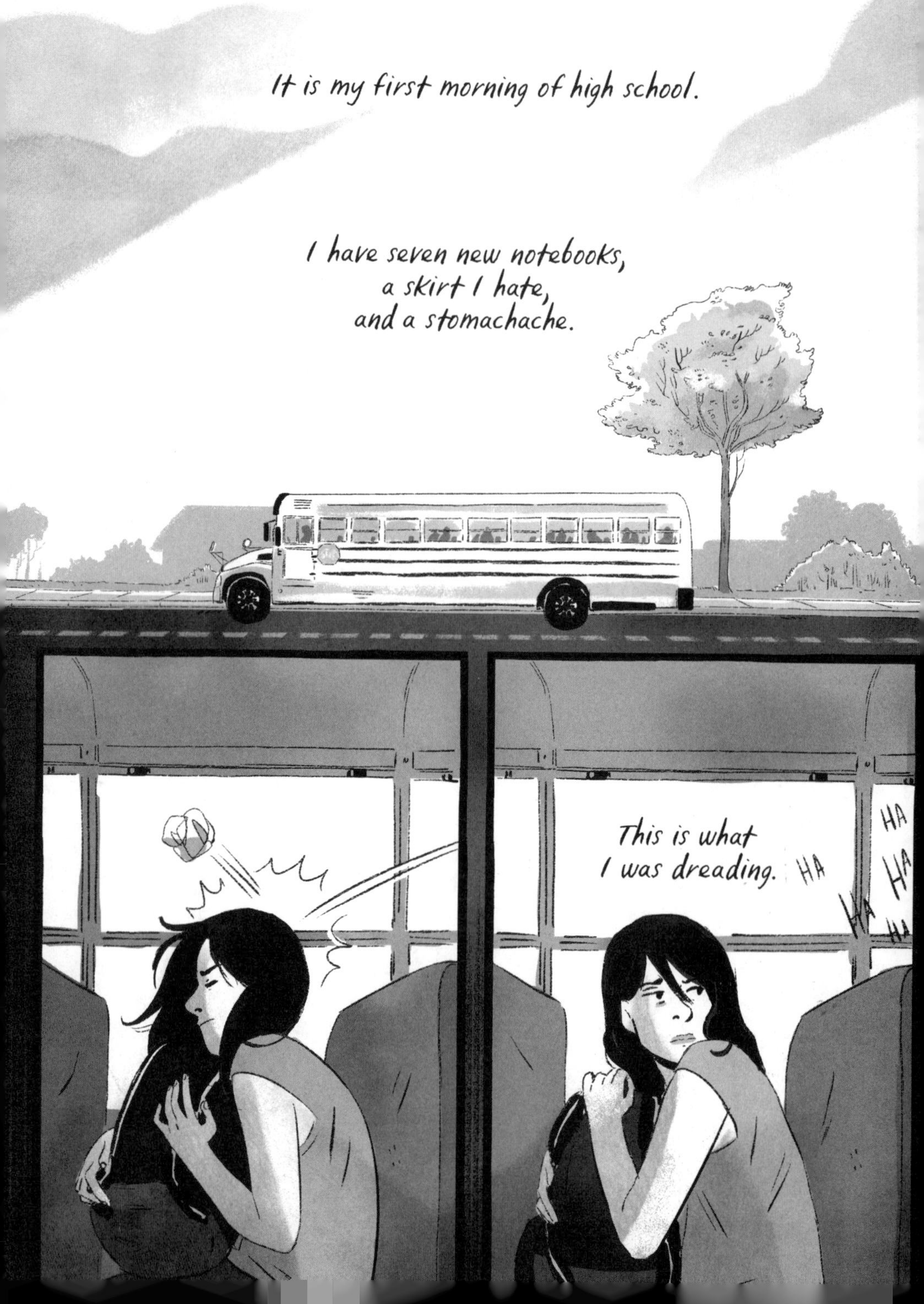
It is my first morning of high school.
I have seven new notebooks, a skirt I hate, and a stomachache.
This is what I was dreading.
HA HA HA HA HA

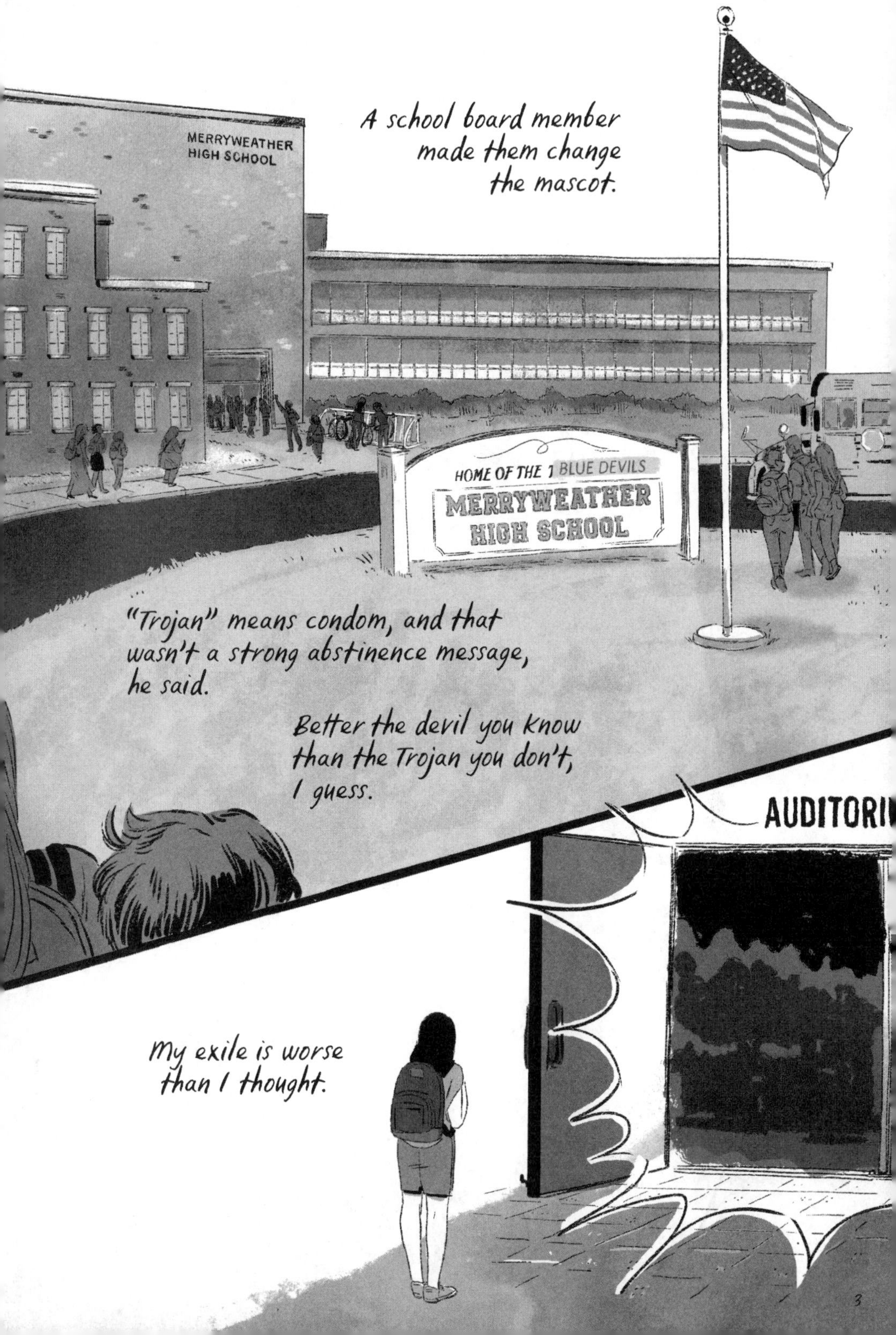
MERRYWEATHER HIGH SCHOOL
A school board member made them change the mascot.
HOME OF THE BLUE DEVILS
MERRYWEATHER HIGH SCHOOL
"Trojan" means condom, and that wasn't a strong abstinence message, he said.
Better the devil you know than the Trojan you don't, I guess.
AUDITORI
My exile is worse than I thought.

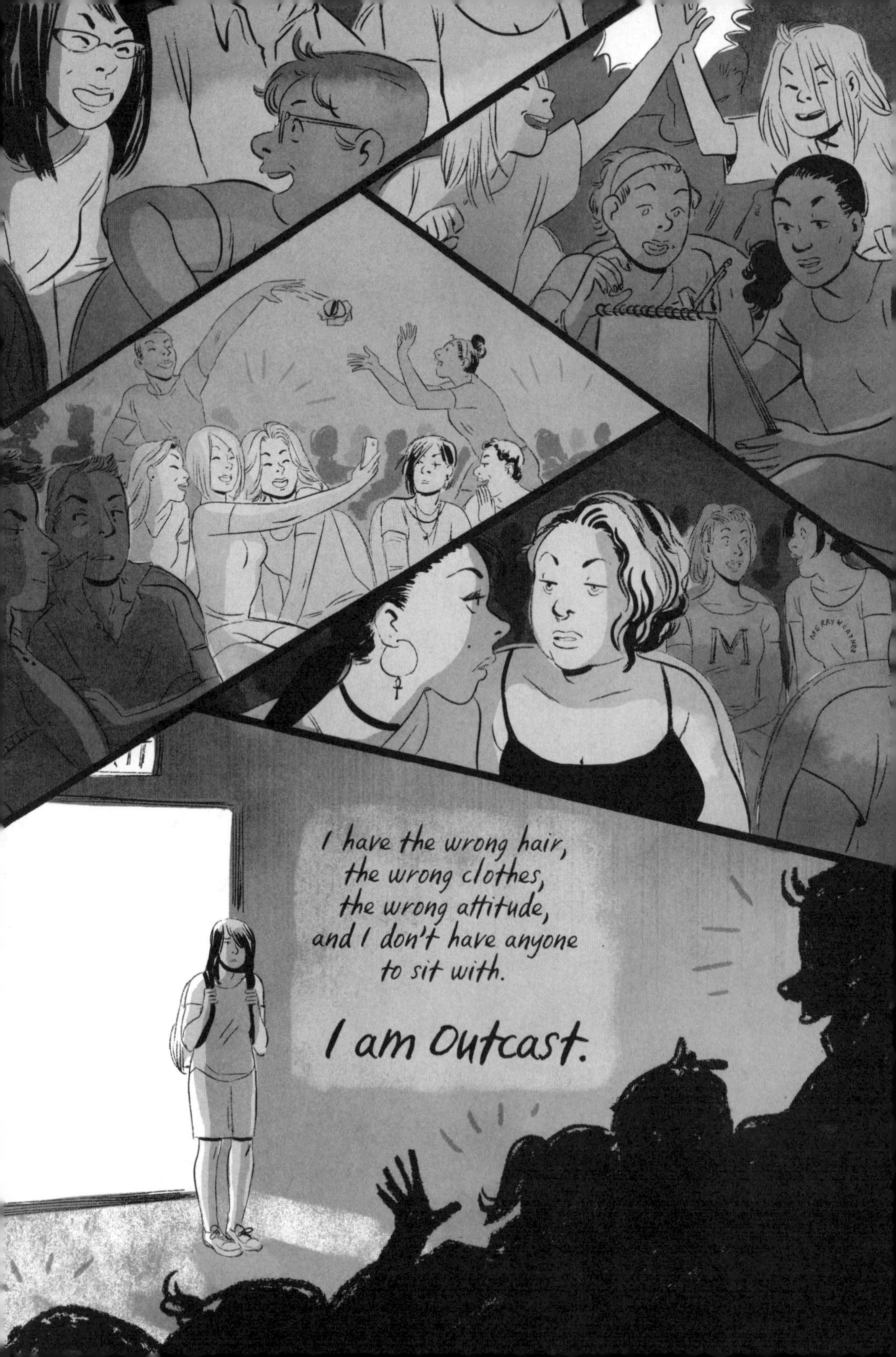
MERRYWEATHER
M
I have the wrong hair,
the wrong clothes,
the wrong attitude,
and I don't have anyone
to sit with.
I am Outcast.

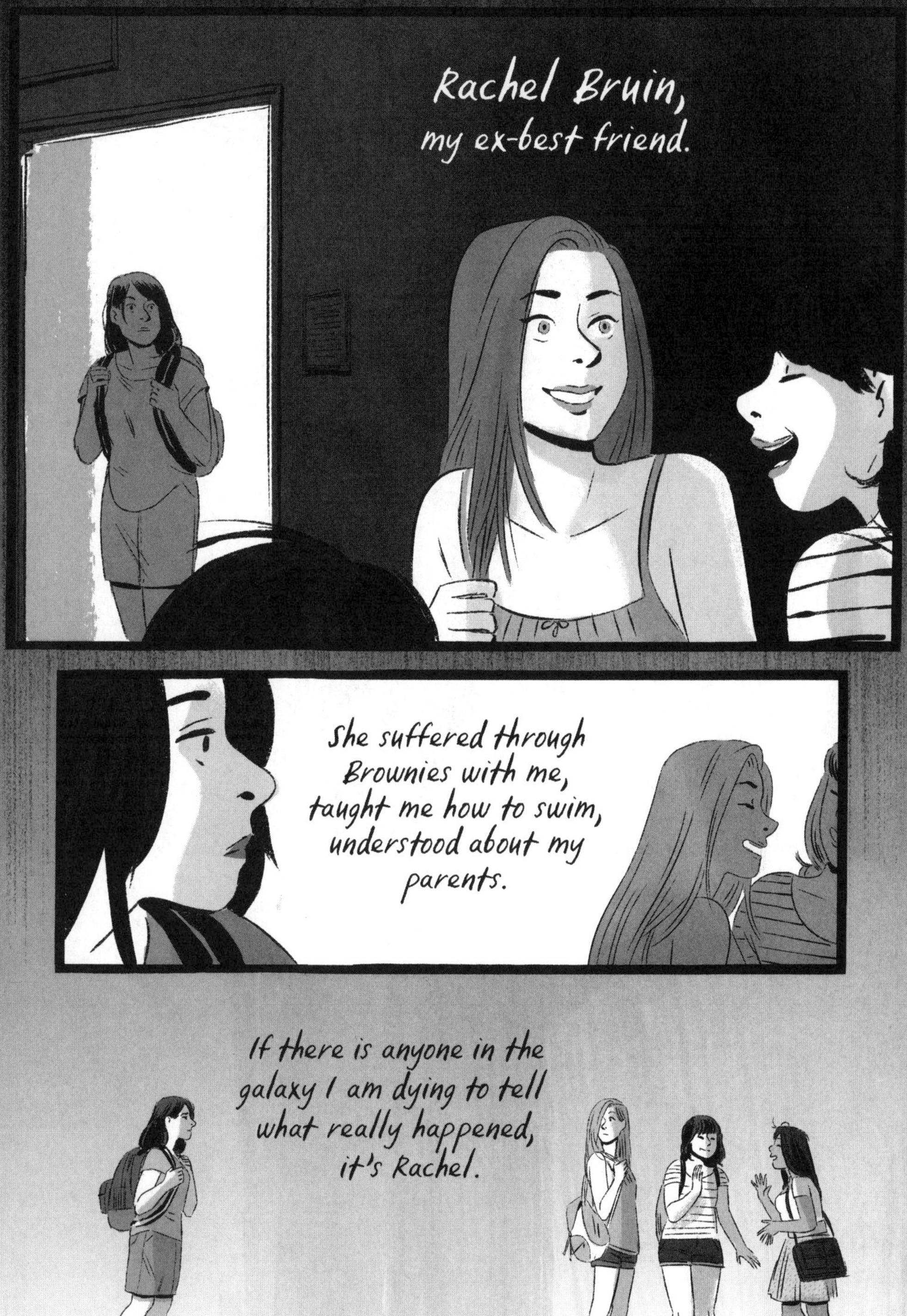
Rachel Bruin,
my ex-best friend.
She suffered through Brownies with me, taught me how to swim, understood about my parents.
If there is anyone in the galaxy I am dying to tell what really happened, it's Rachel.

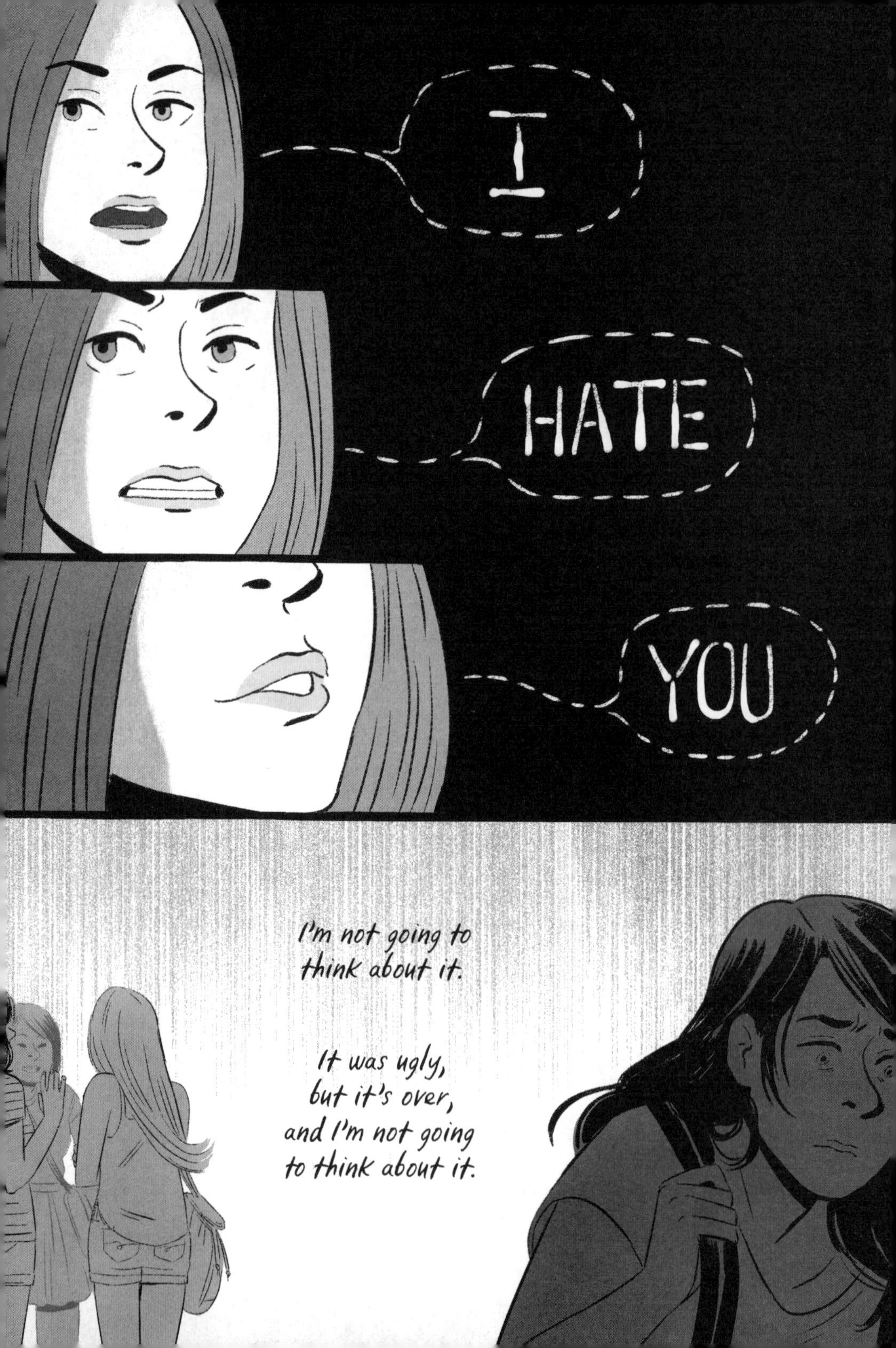
I
HATE
YOU
I'm not going to think about it.
It was ugly, but it's over, and I'm not going to think about it.

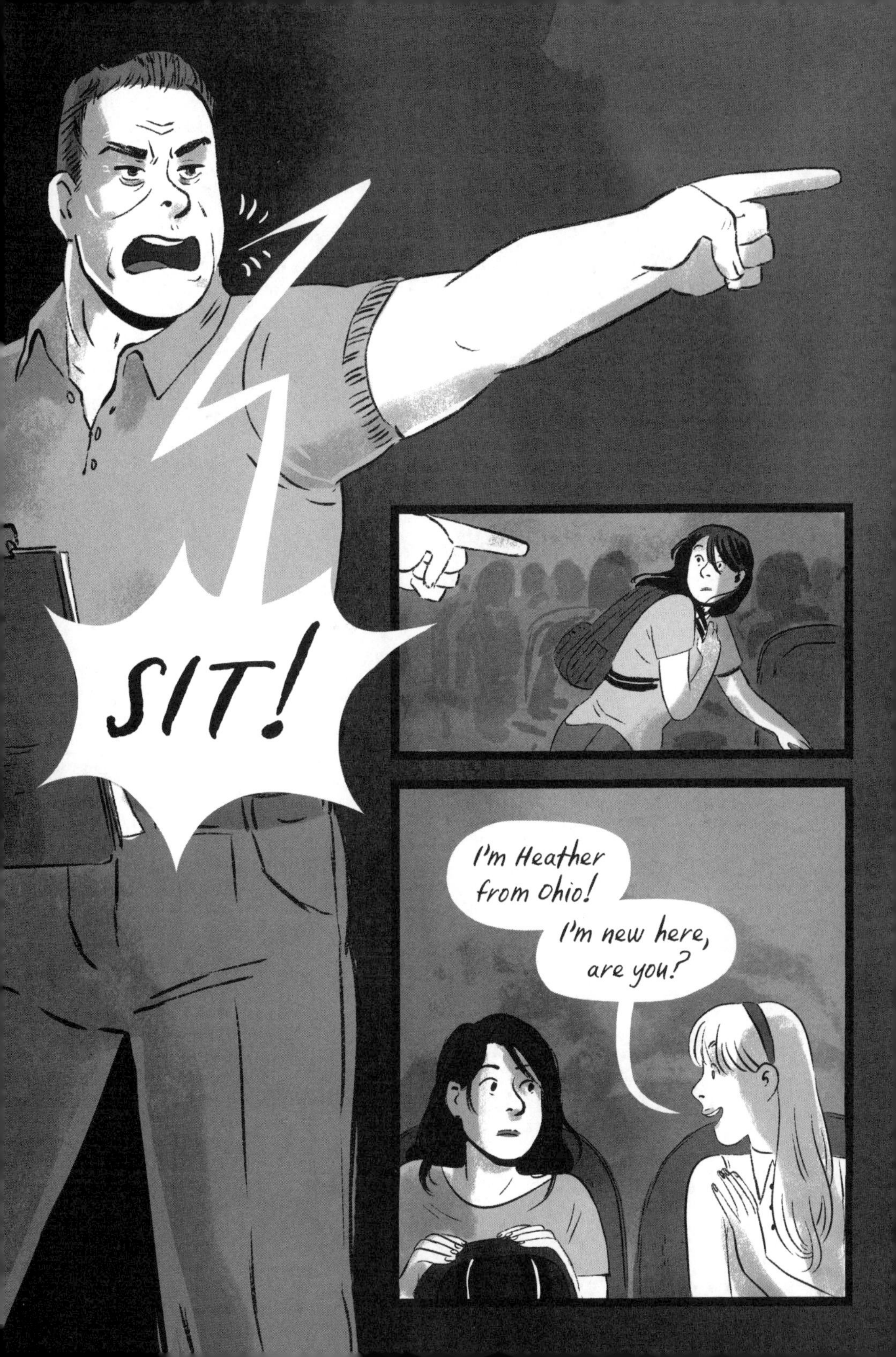
SIT!
I'm Heather from Ohio!
I'm new here, are you?

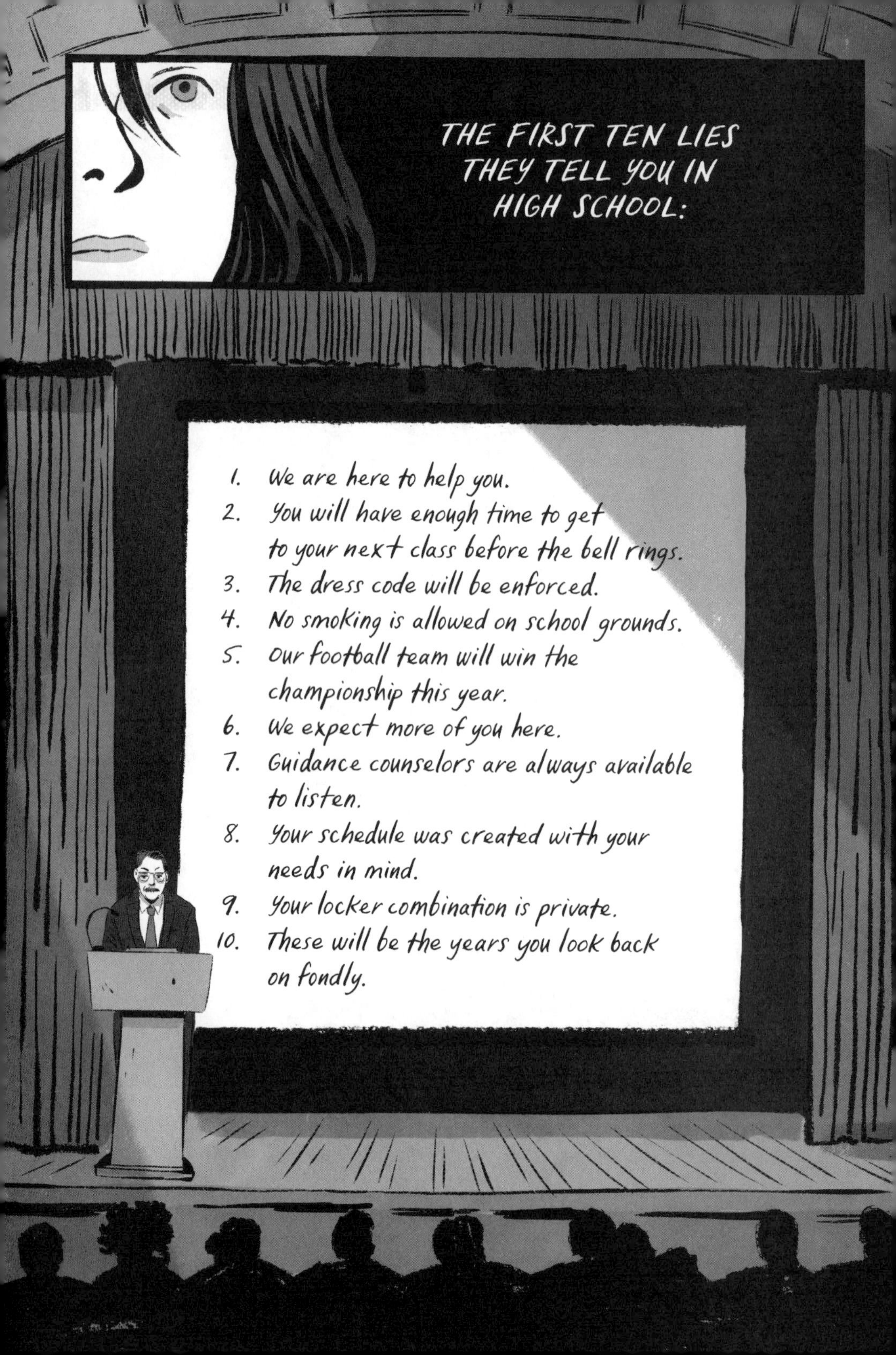
THE FIRST TEN LIES THEY TELL YOU IN HIGH SCHOOL:
1. We are here to help you.
2. You will have enough time to get to your next class before the bell rings.
3. The dress code will be enforced.
4. No smoking is allowed on school grounds.
5. Our football team will win the championship this year.
6. We expect more of you here.
7. Guidance counselors are always available to listen.
8. Your schedule was created with your needs in mind.
9. Your locker combination is private.
10. These will be the years you look back on fondly.

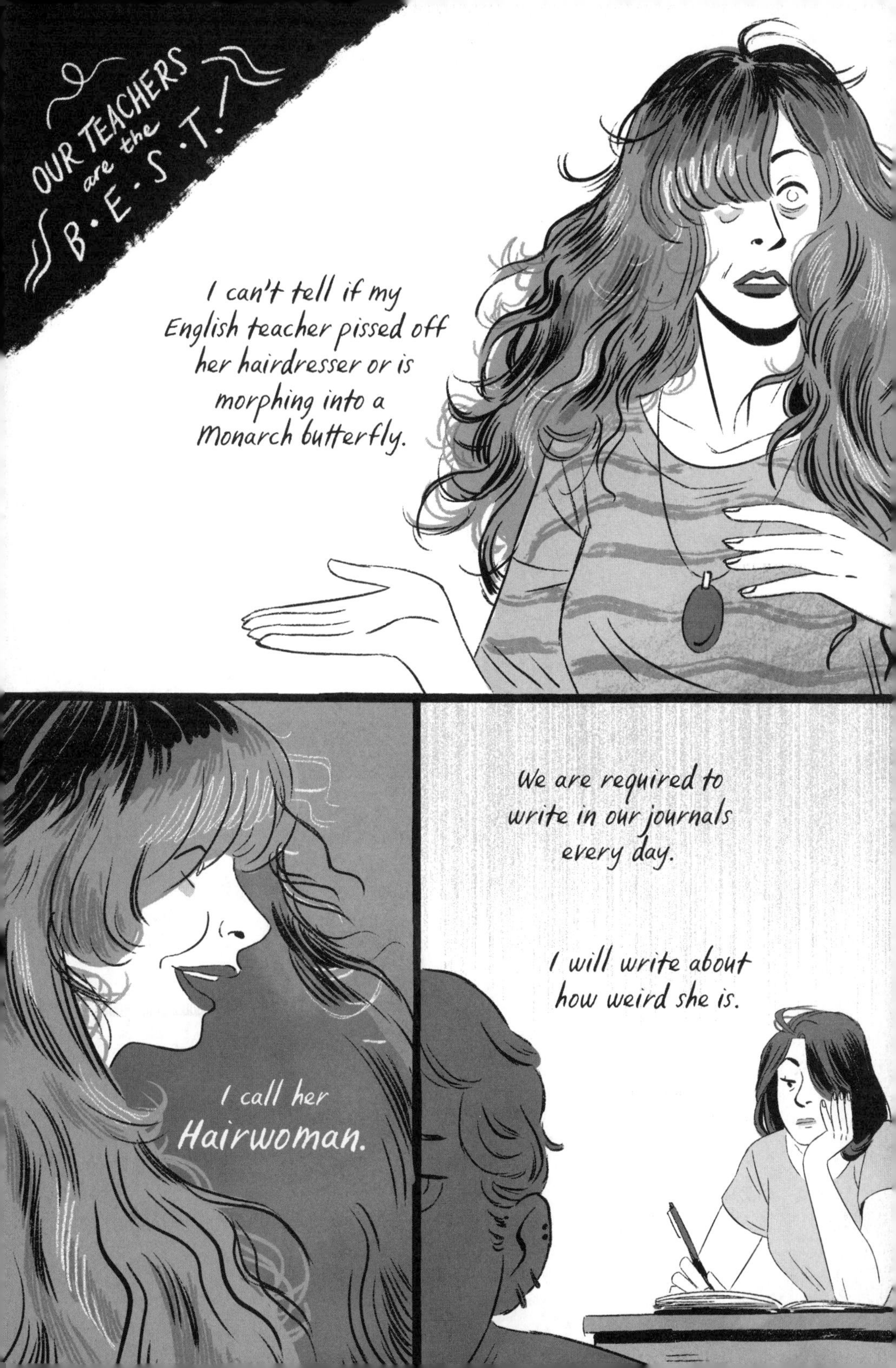
OUR TEACHERS are the B·E·S·T!
I can't tell if my English teacher pissed off her hairdresser or is morphing into a Monarch butterfly.
I call her Hairwoman.
We are required to write in our journals every day.
I will write about how weird she is.

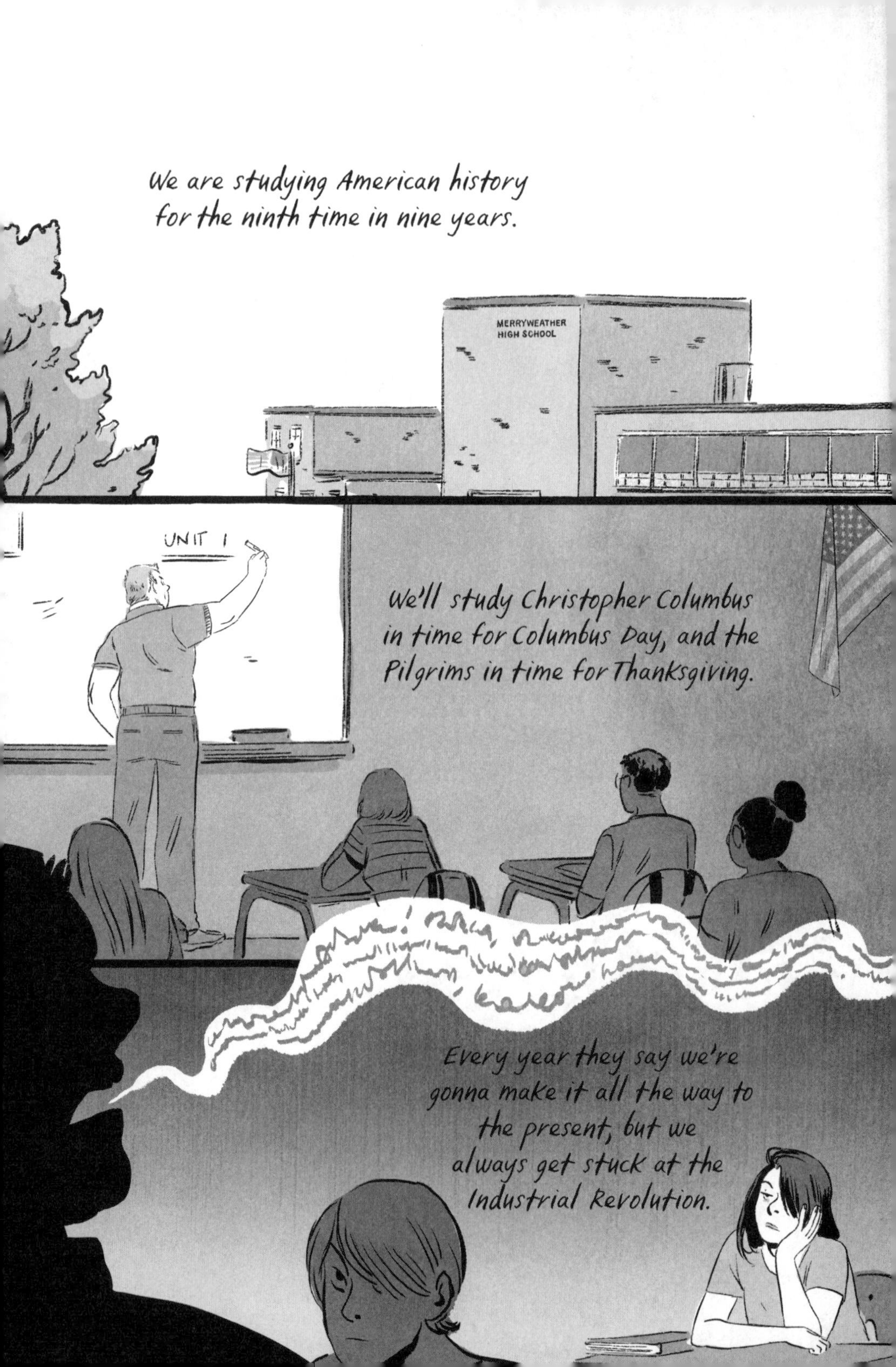
We are studying American history for the ninth time in nine years.
MERRYWEATHER HIGH SCHOOL
UNIT 1
We'll study Christopher Columbus in time for Columbus Day, and the Pilgrims in time for Thanksgiving.
Every year they say we're gonna make it all the way to the present, but we always get stuck at the Industrial Revolution.

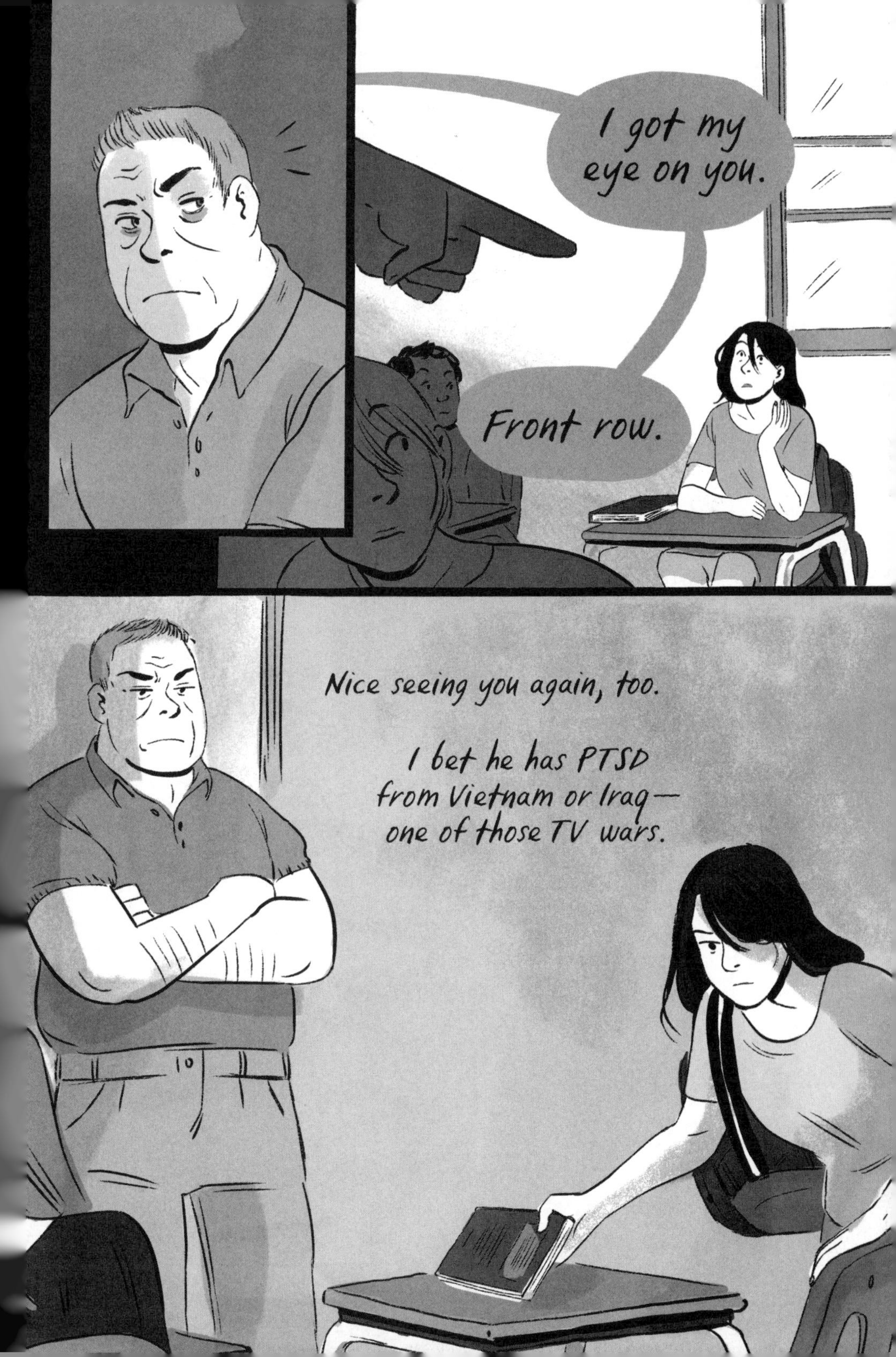
I got my eye on you.
Front row.
Nice seeing you again, too.
I bet he has PTSD from Vietnam or Iraq—one of those TV wars.

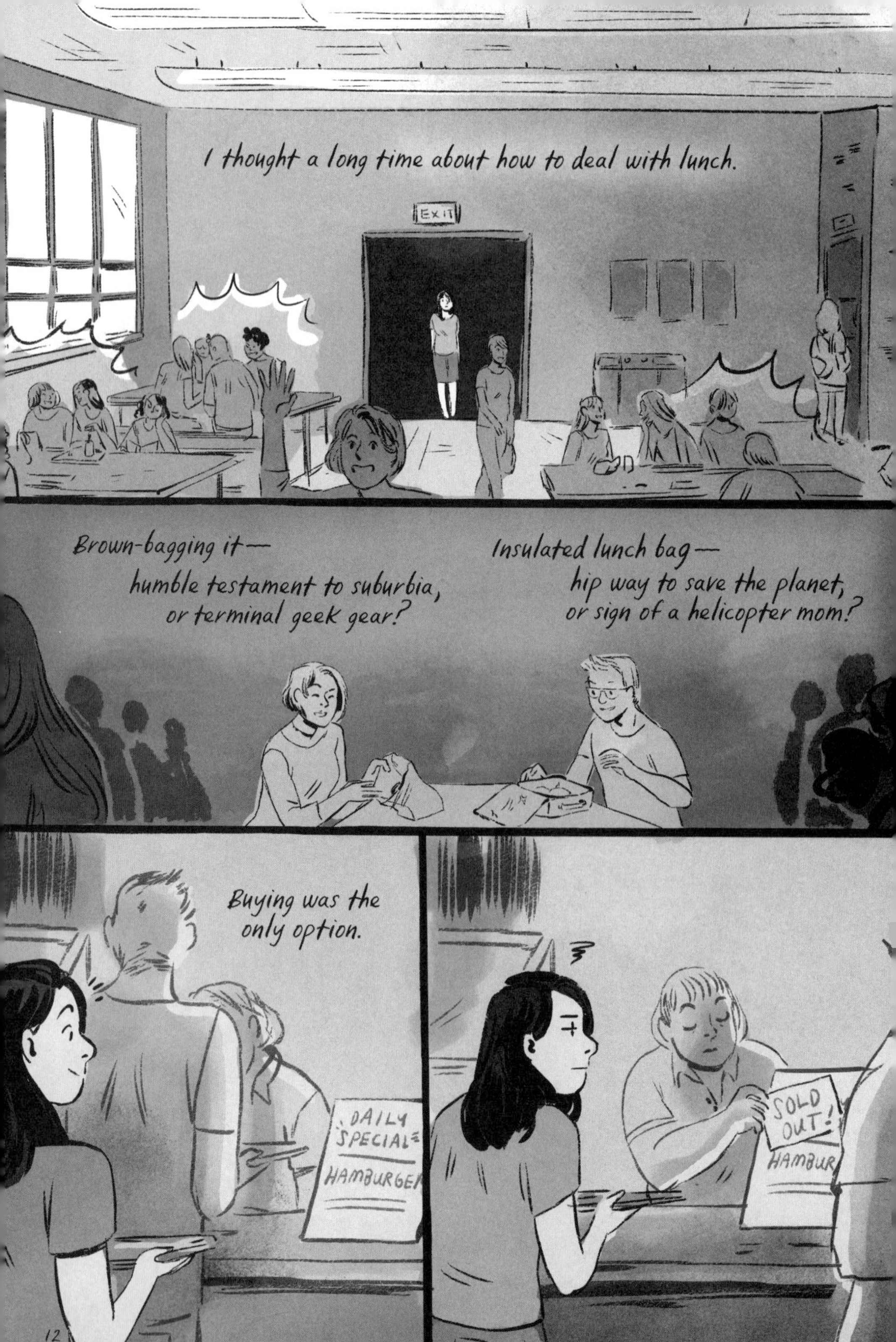
I thought a long time about how to deal with lunch.
EXIT
Brown-bagging it— humble testament to suburbia, or terminal geek gear?
Insulated lunch bag— hip way to save the planet, or sign of a helicopter mom?
Buying was the only option.
DAILY SPECIAL
HAMBURGE
SOLD OUT!
HAMBUR

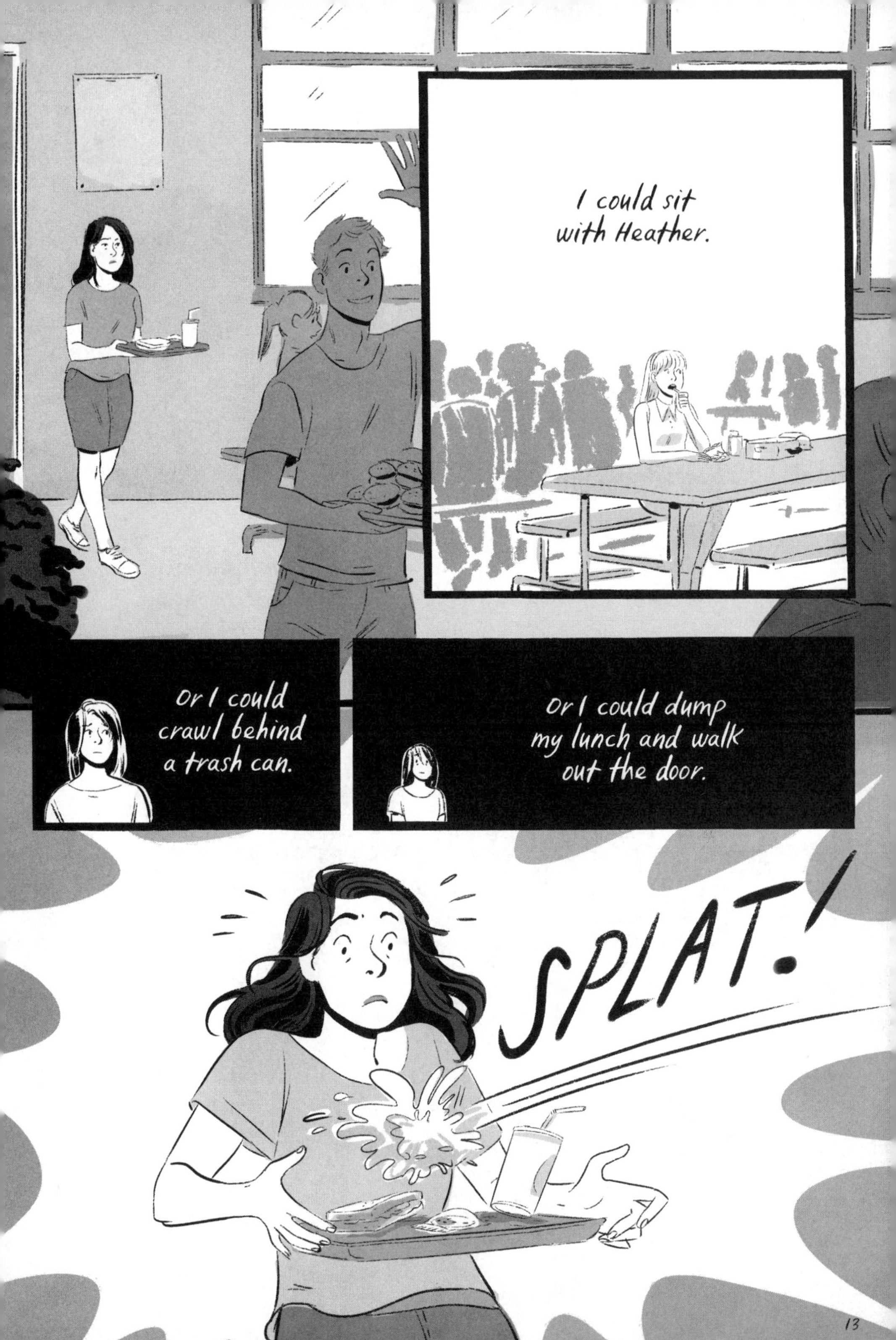
I could sit with Heather.
Or I could crawl behind a trash can.
Or I could dump my lunch and walk out the door.
SPLAT!

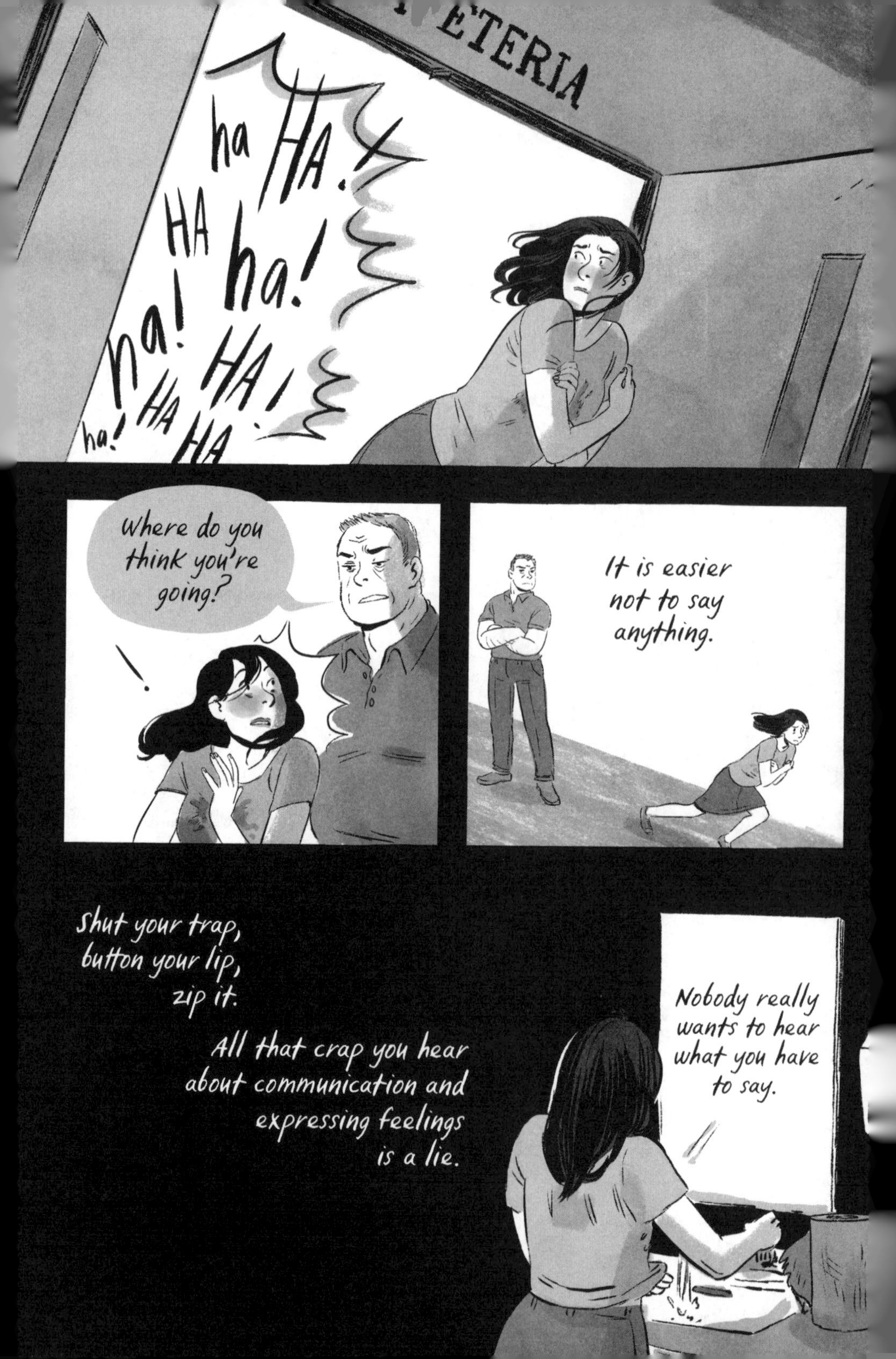
ETERIA
ha HA! HA ha! na! HA! HA ha! HA
Where do you think you're going?
!
It is easier not to say anything.
Shut your trap, button your lip, zip it.
All that crap you hear about communication and expressing feelings is a lie.
Nobody really wants to hear what you have to say.

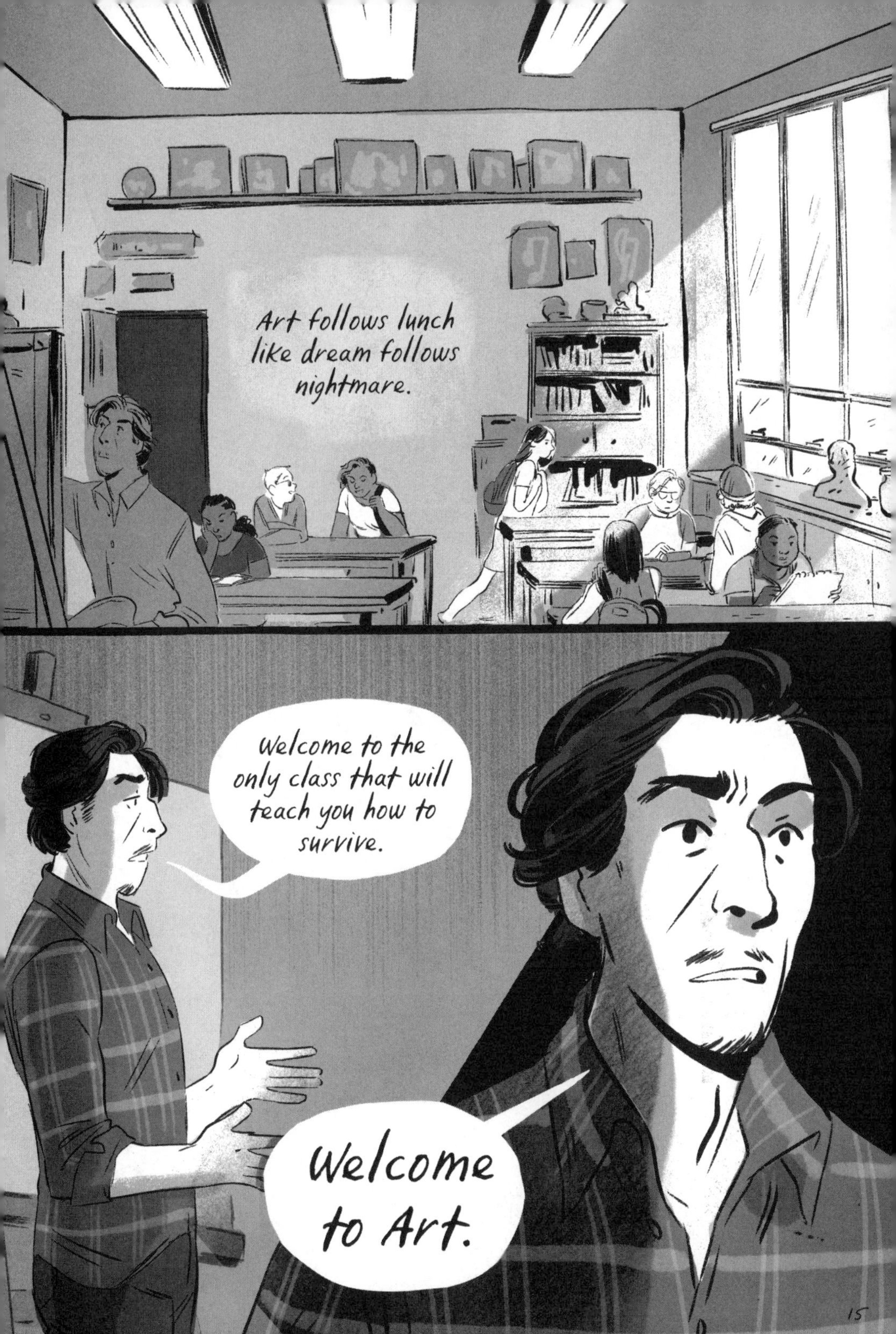
Art follows lunch like dream follows nightmare.
Welcome to the only class that will teach you how to survive.
Welcome to Art.

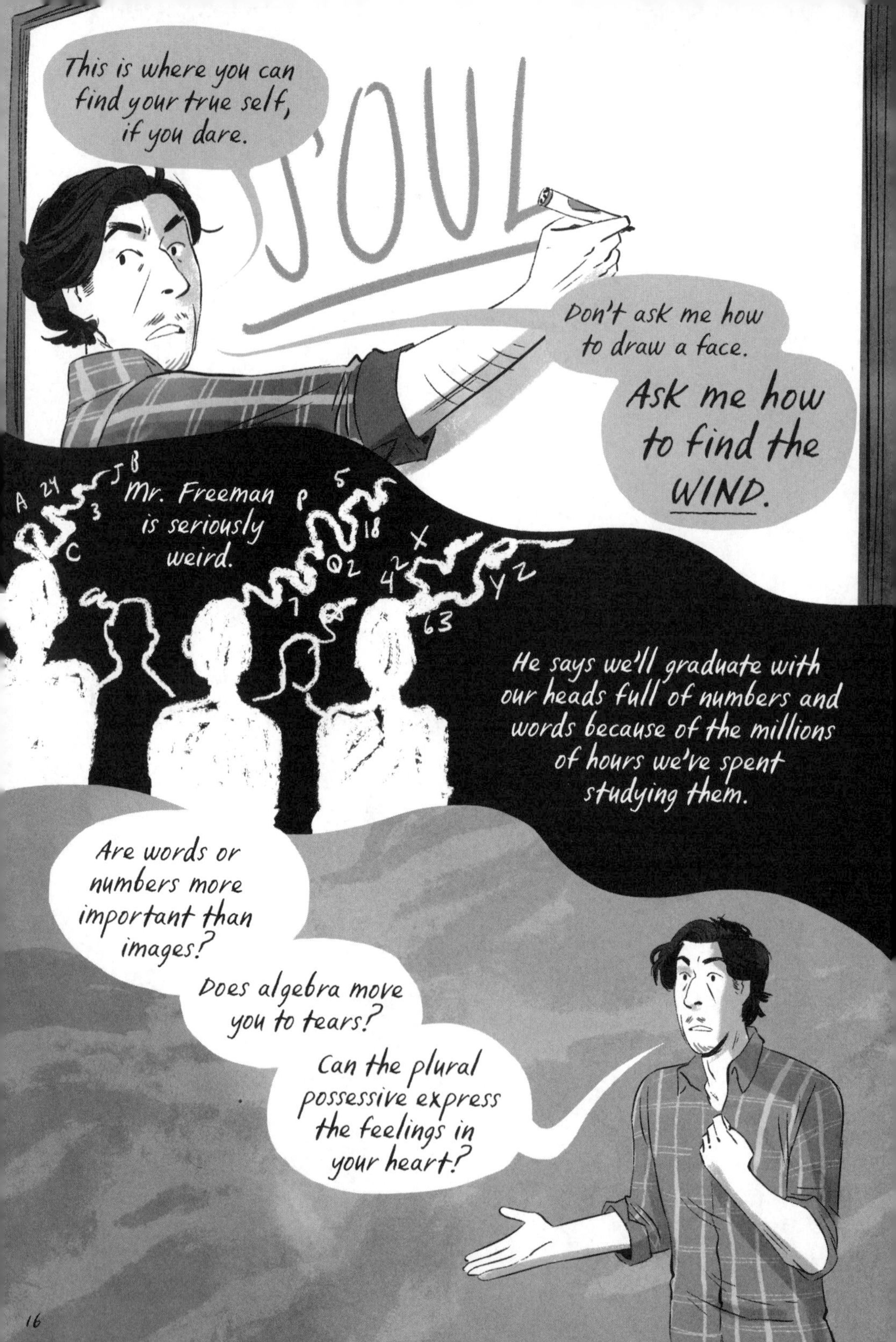

This is where you can find your true self, if you dare.
SOUL
Don't ask me how to draw a face.
Ask me how to find the WIND.
Mr. Freeman is seriously weird.
A 24 J B 3 C P 5 18 X Q2 4 2 Y Z 7 63
He says we'll graduate with our heads full of numbers and words because of the millions of hours we've spent studying them.
Are words or numbers more important than images?
Does algebra move you to tears?
Can the plural possessive express the feelings in your heart?

I stare at Ivy, trying to make her look at me.

In fifth grade, she slept over at my house every weekend.

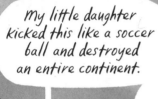

My little daughter kicked this like a soccer ball and destroyed an entire continent.

And I had a vision! What do you think it was?

That you should have bought her a regular ball?

Have you already let them beat the creativity out of you?

This beautiful, crumbling metaphor for our planet could contain an entire world of art, of humanity, of splendor...

...just for you!

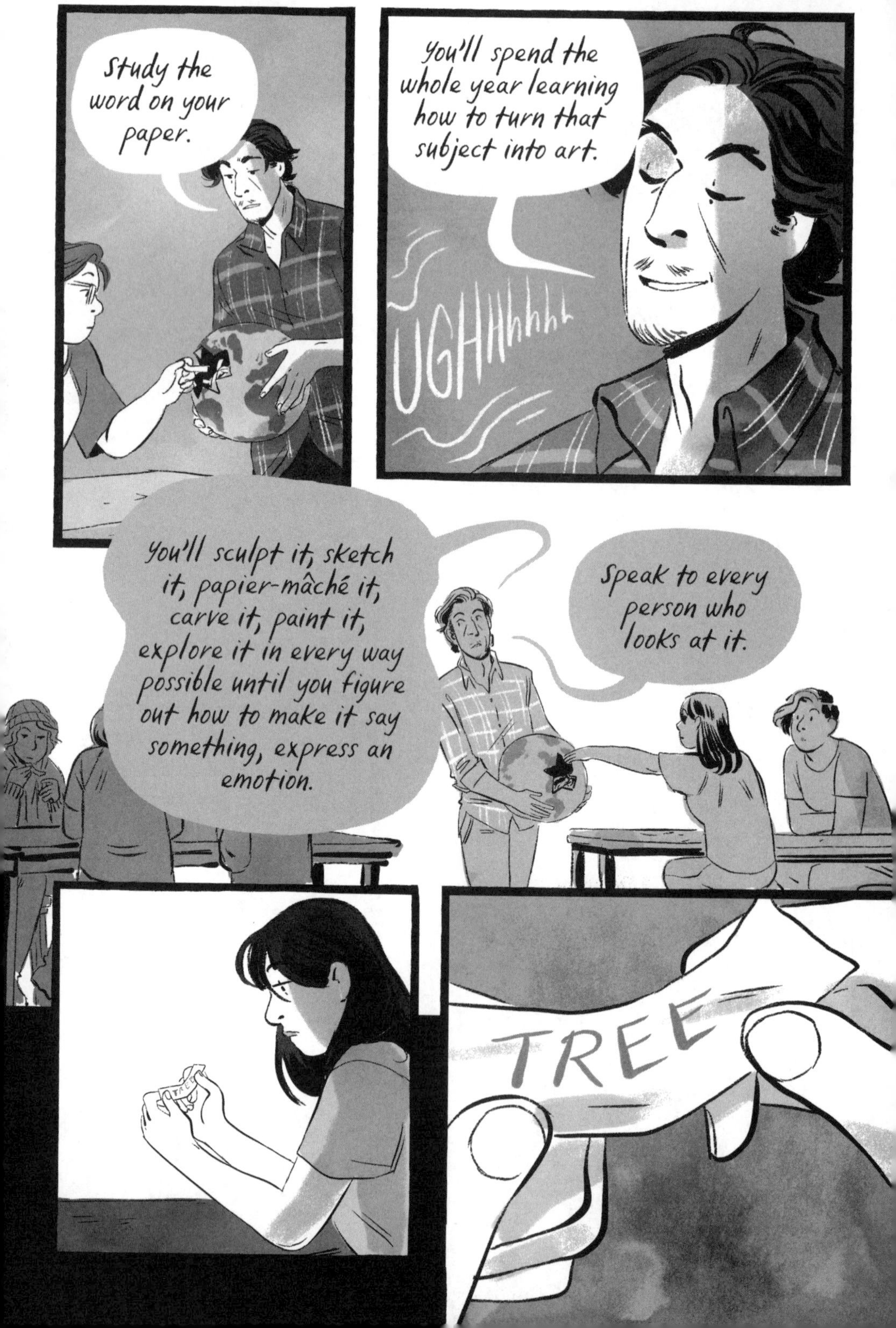
Study the word on your paper.
You'll spend the whole year learning how to turn that subject into art.
UGHHhhhh
You'll sculpt it, sketch it, papier-mâché it, carve it, paint it, explore it in every way possible until you figure out how to make it say something, express an emotion.
Speak to every person who looks at it.
TREE

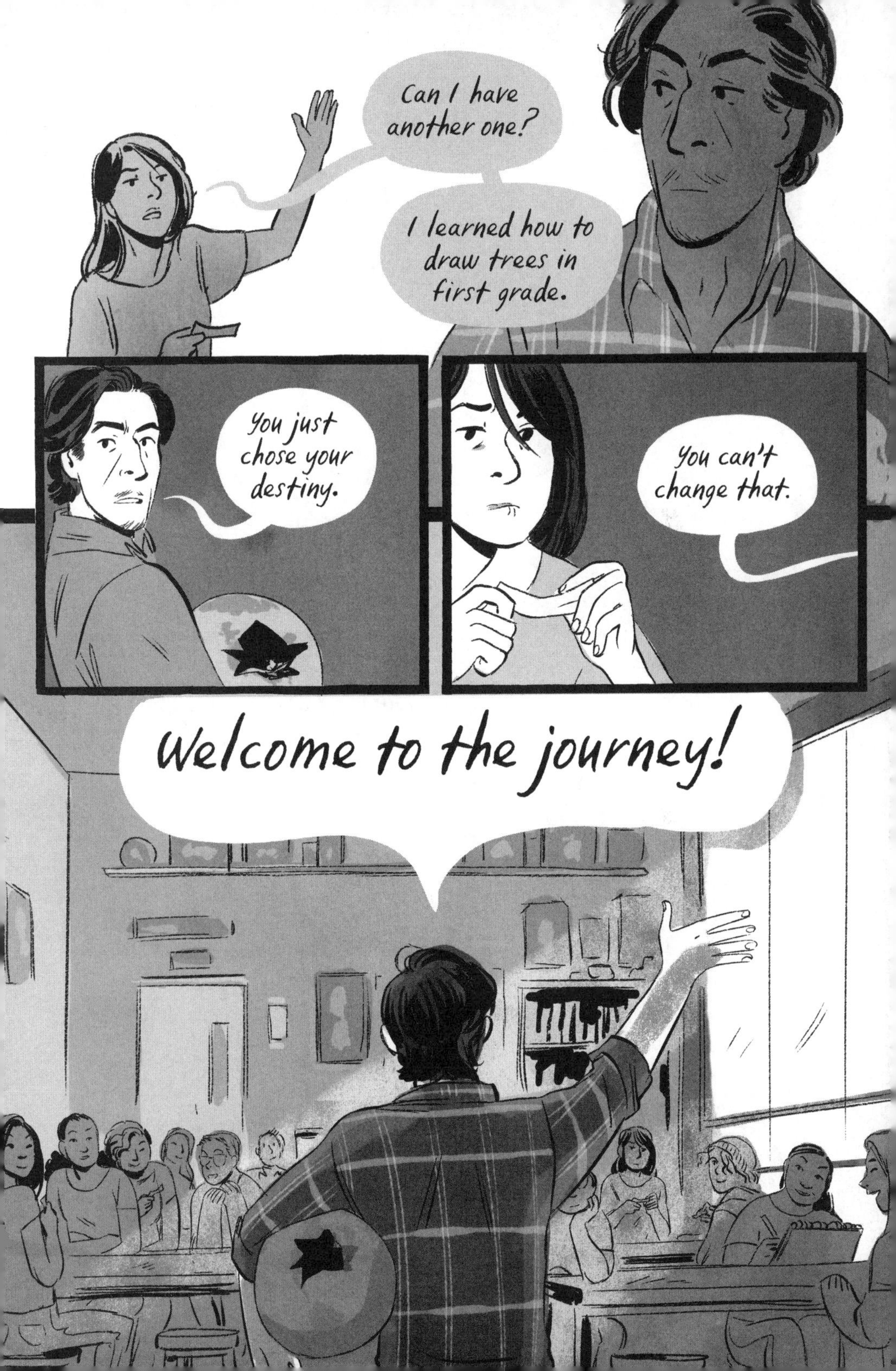
Can I have another one?
I learned how to draw trees in first grade.
You just chose your destiny.
You can't change that.
Welcome to the journey!

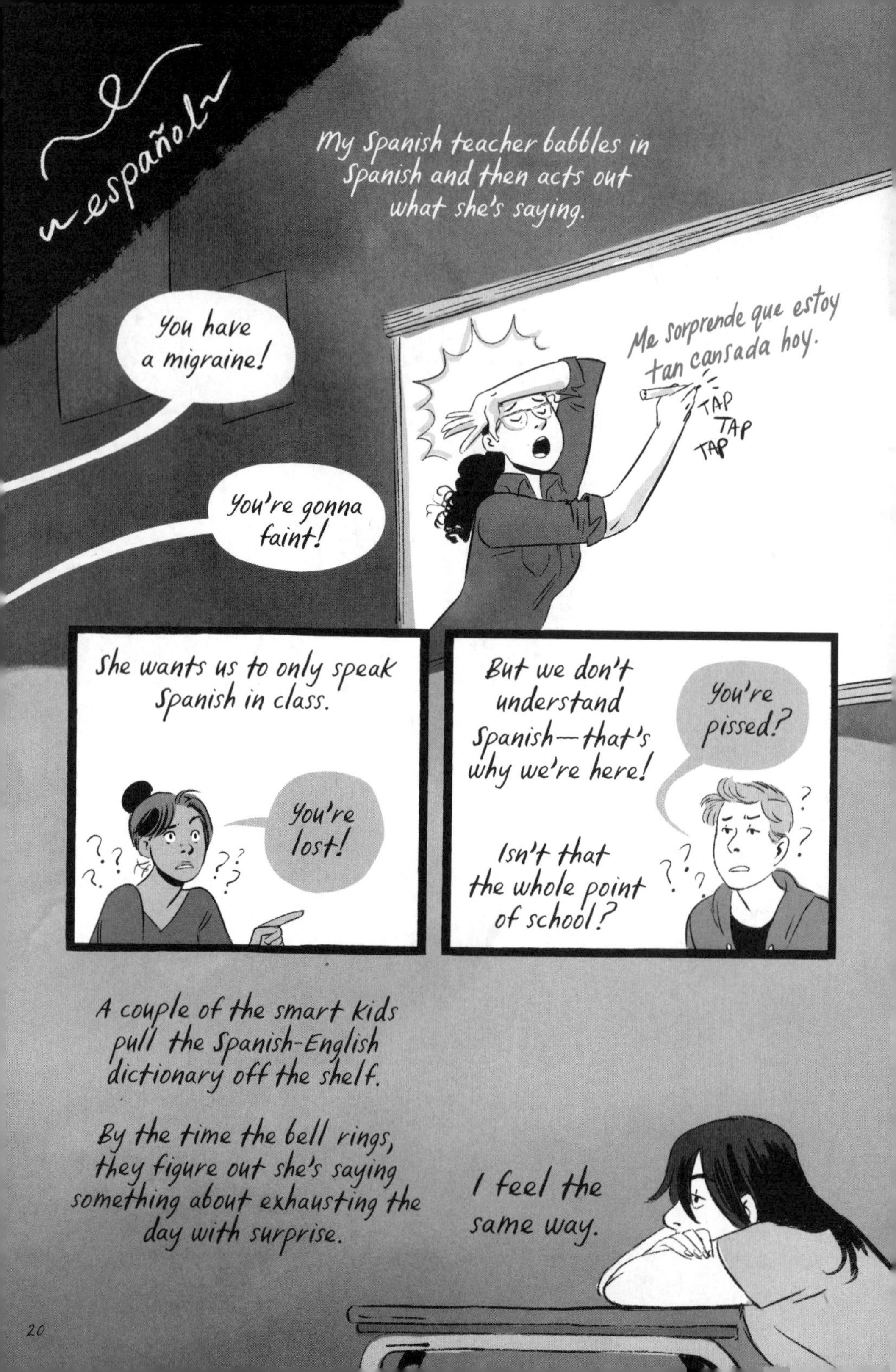
español
My Spanish teacher babbles in Spanish and then acts out what she's saying.
Me sorprende que estoy tan cansada hoy.
TAP TAP TAP
You have a migraine!
You're gonna faint!
She wants us to only speak Spanish in class.
You're lost!
But we don't understand Spanish—that's why we're here!
You're pissed?
Isn't that the whole point of school?
A couple of the smart kids pull the Spanish-English dictionary off the shelf.
By the time the bell rings, they figure out she's saying something about exhausting the day with surprise.
I feel the same way.

HOME. WORK.

I survive the next few weeks without a meltdown.

I get bumped a lot in the halls.

Tripped.

Accidentally shoved into lockers.

A few times books are ripped out of my hands.

I try not to dwell on this.

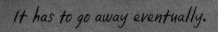

It has to go away eventually.

It's easier to get out of the building without any hassle if I stay after and take the late bus home.

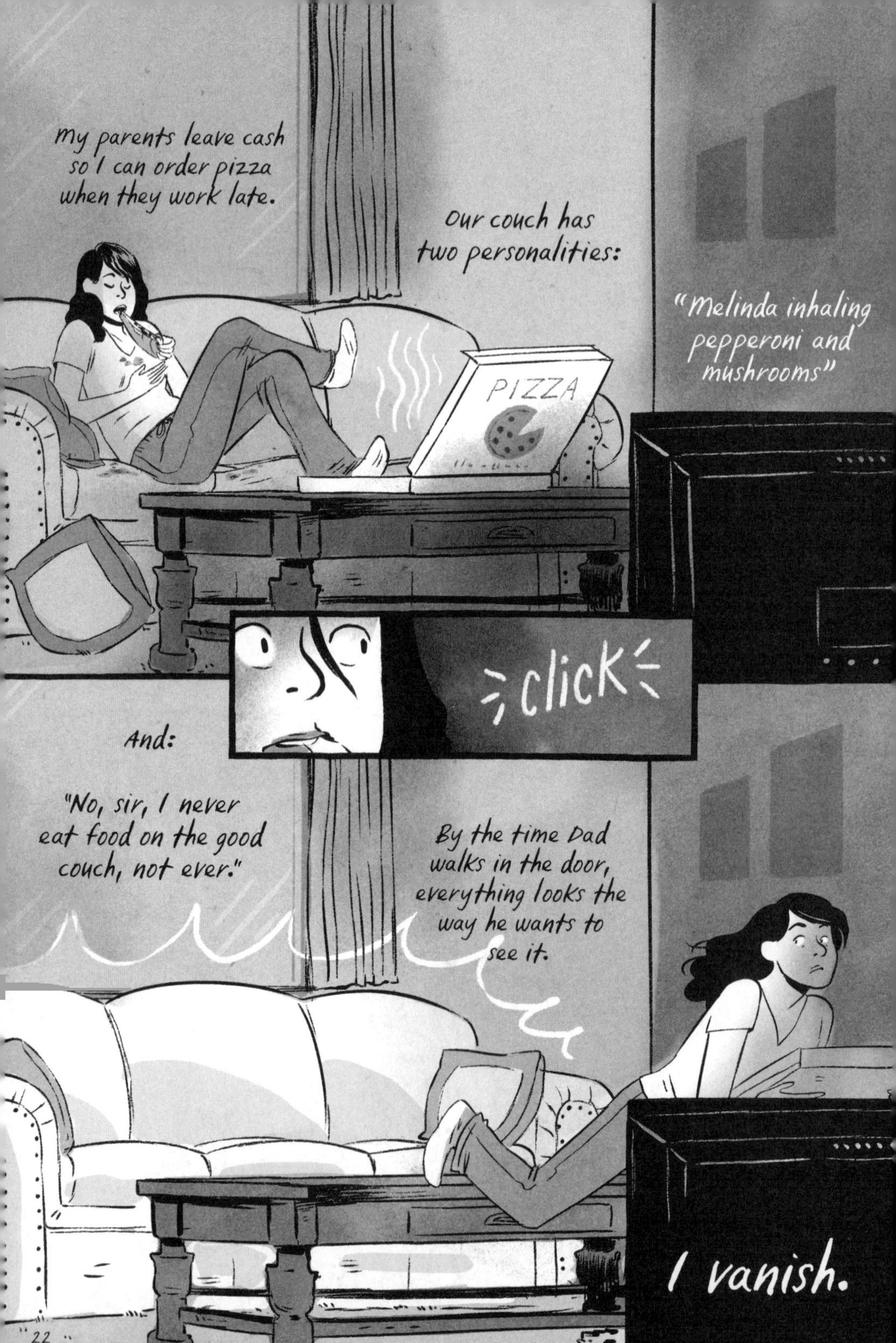
my parents leave cash so I can order pizza when they work late.
Our couch has two personalities:
PIZZA
"Melinda inhaling pepperoni and mushrooms"
click
And:
"No, sir, I never eat food on the good couch, not ever."
By the time Dad walks in the door, everything looks the way he wants to see it.
I vanish.

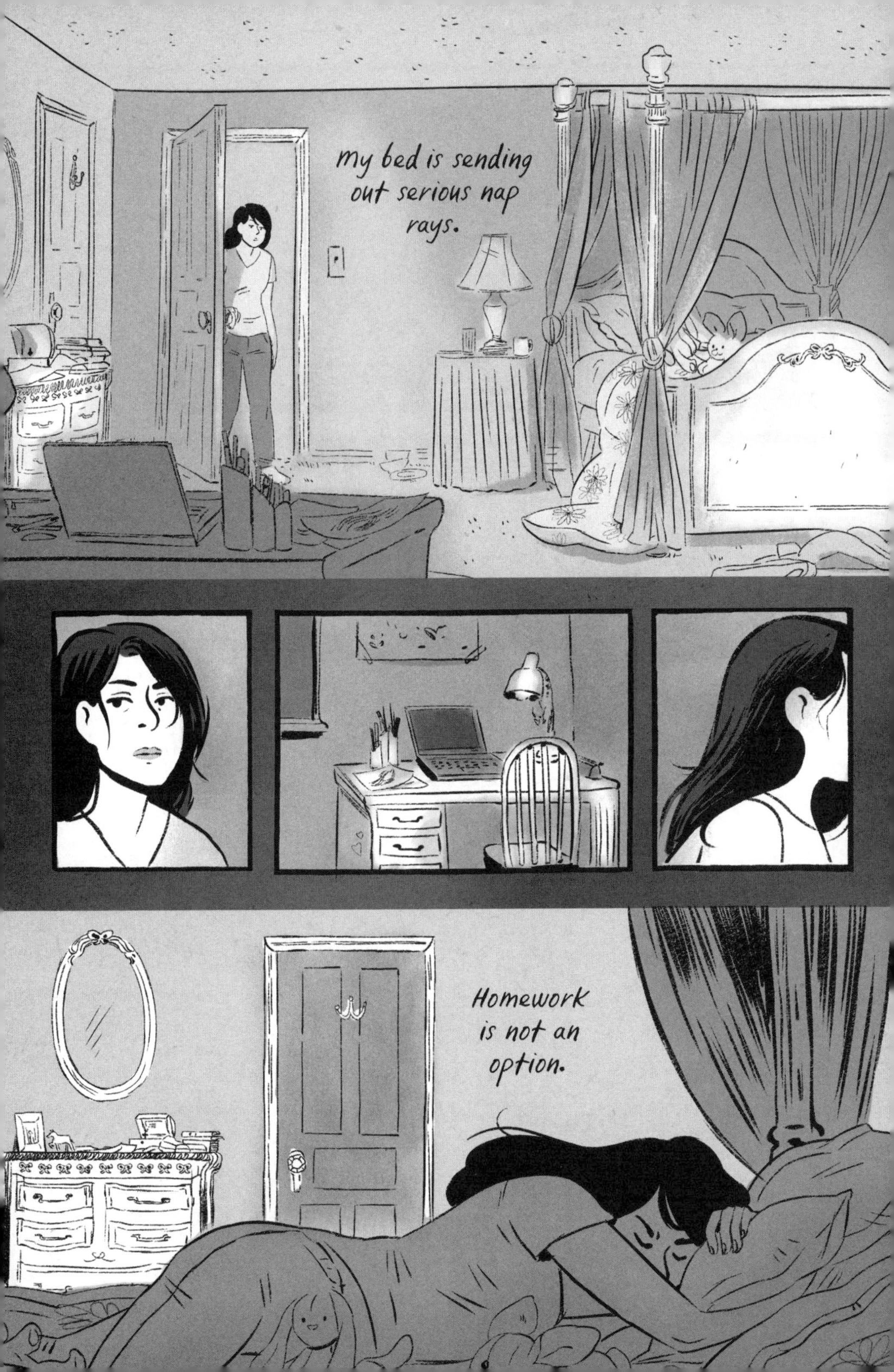
my bed is sending out serious nap rays.
Homework is not an option.

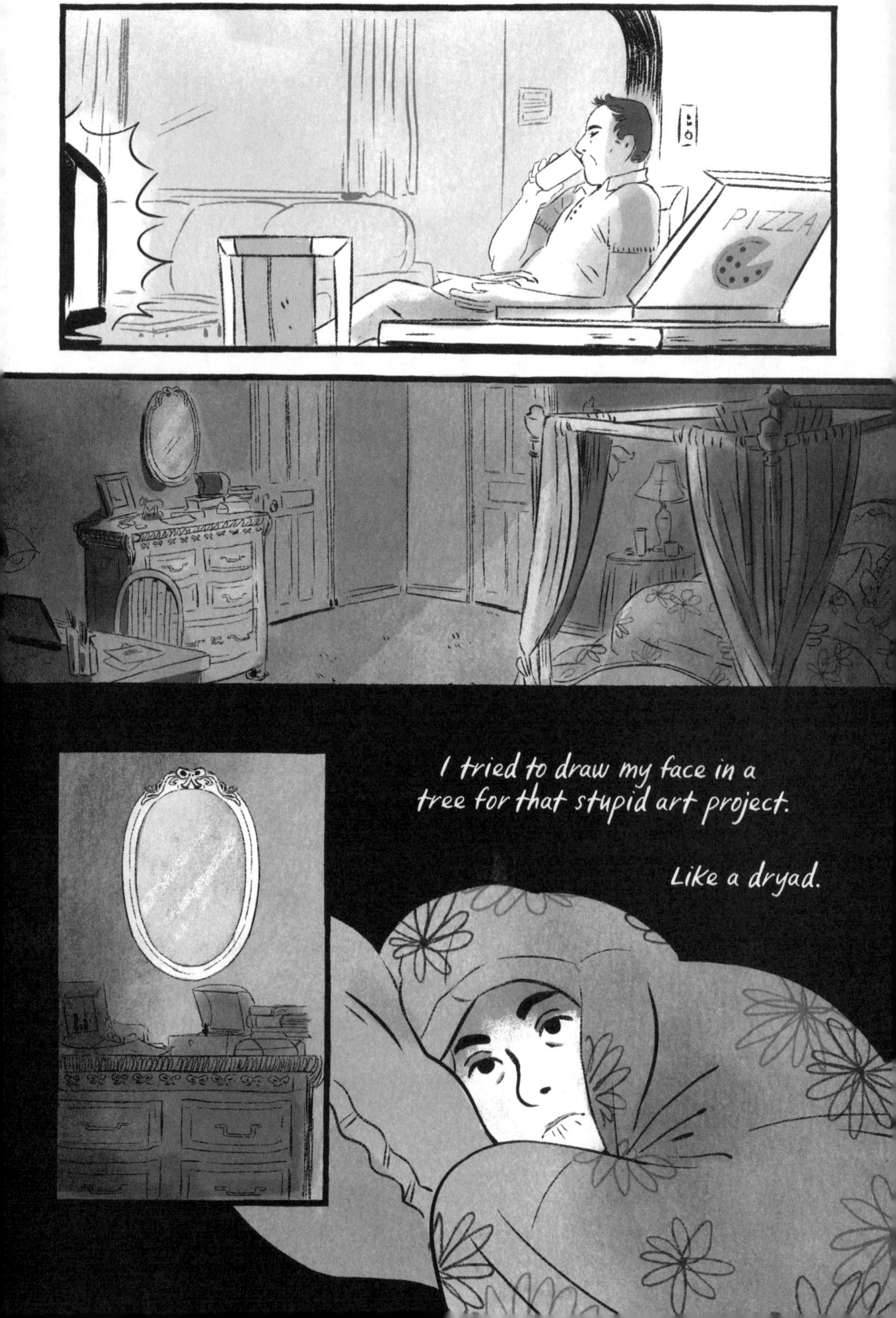
PIZZA
I tried to draw my face in a tree for that stupid art project.
Like a dryad.

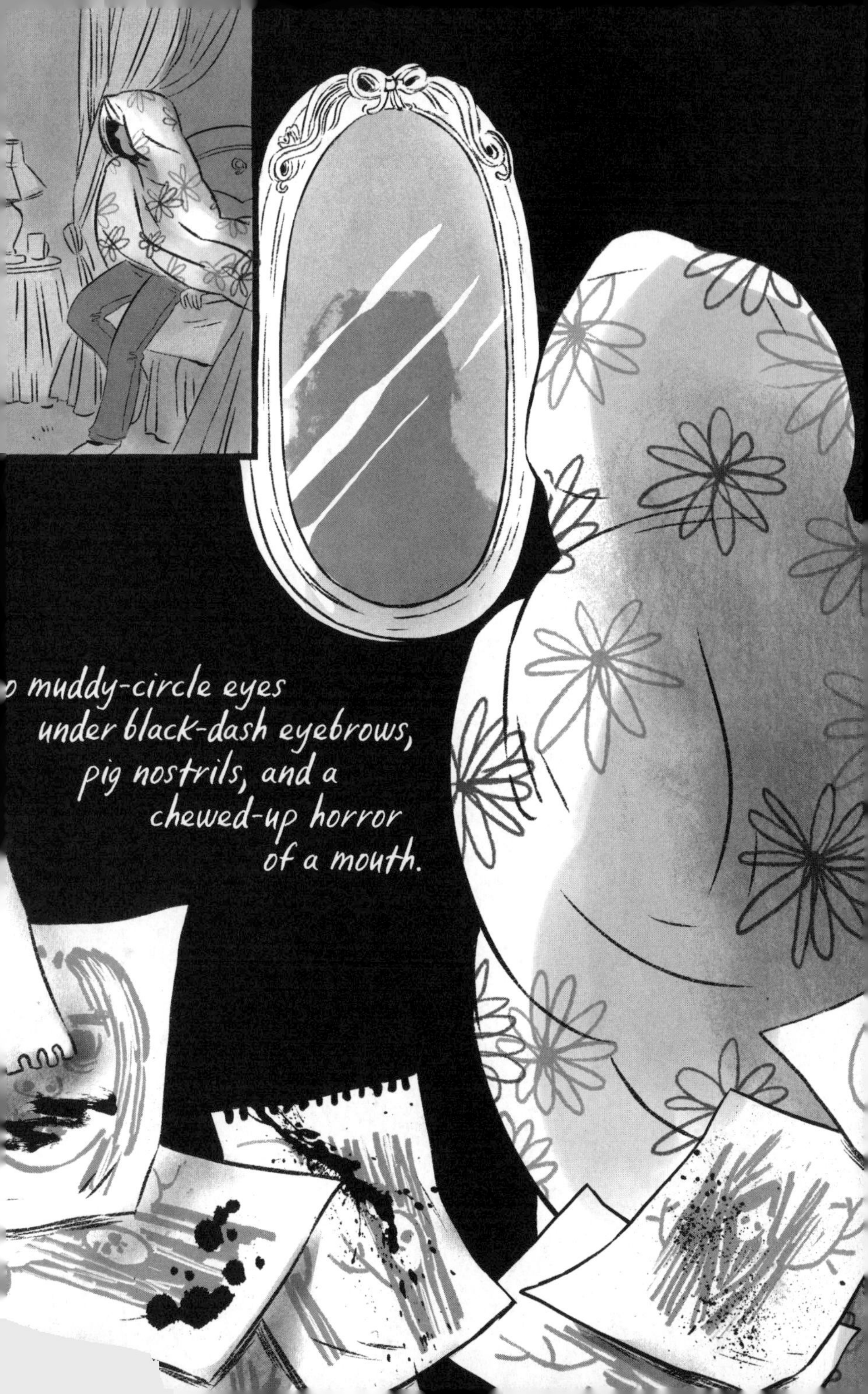
o muddy-circle eyes
under black-dash eyebrows,
pig nostrils, and a
chewed-up horror
of a mouth.

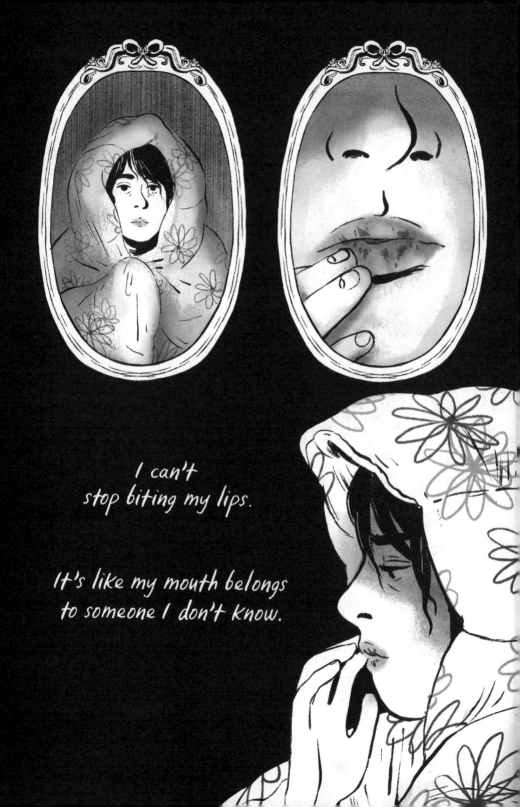

I can't
stop biting my lips.

It's like my mouth belongs
to someone I don't know.

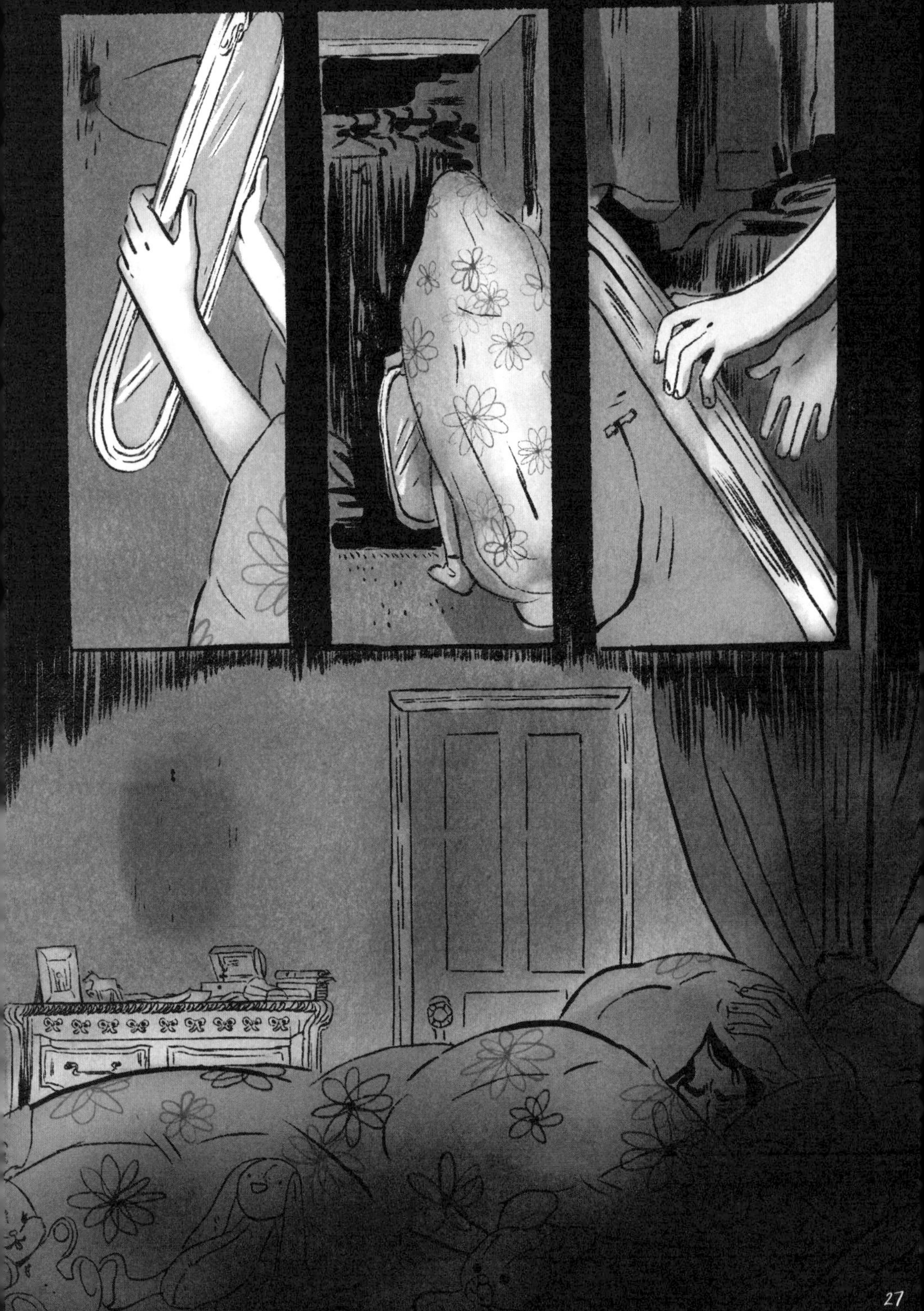

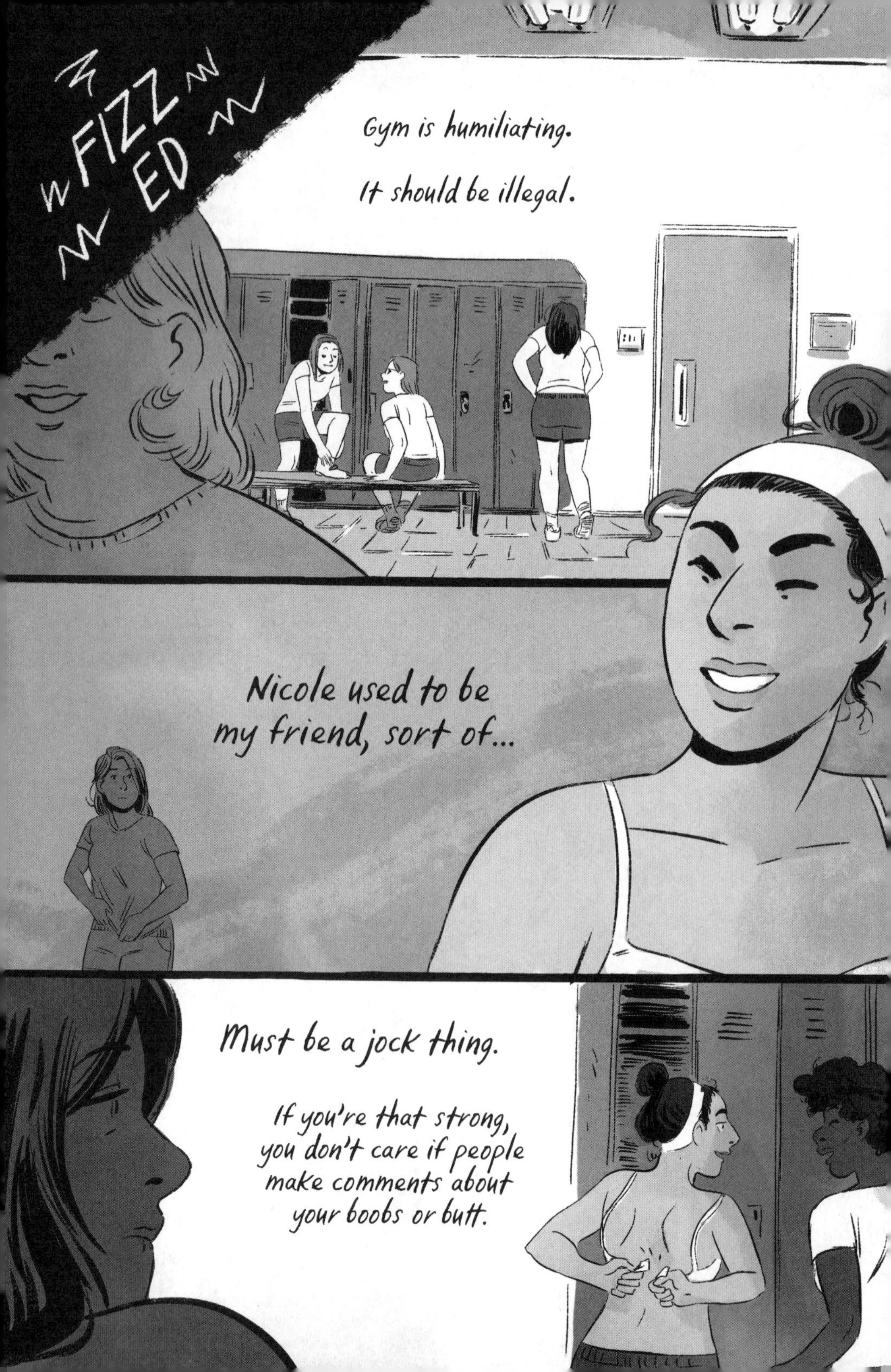
FIZZ ED
Gym is humiliating.
It should be illegal.
Nicole used to be my friend, sort of...
Must be a jock thing.
If you're that strong, you don't care if people make comments about your boobs or butt.

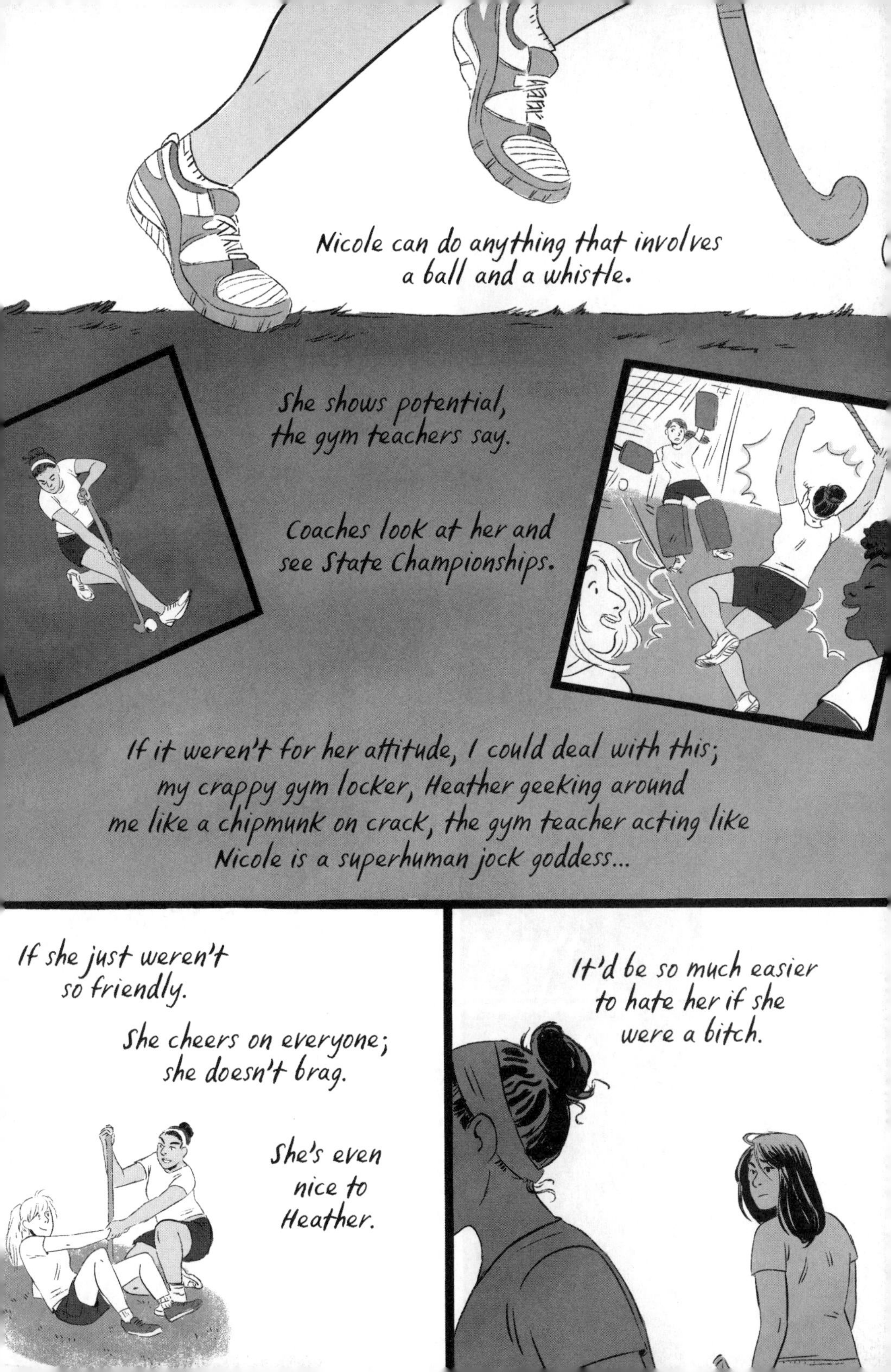
Nicole can do anything that involves a ball and a whistle.
She shows potential, the gym teachers say.
Coaches look at her and see State Championships.
If it weren't for her attitude, I could deal with this; my crappy gym locker, Heather geeking around me like a chipmunk on crack, the gym teacher acting like Nicole is a superhuman jock goddess...
If she just weren't so friendly.
She cheers on everyone; she doesn't brag.
She's even nice to Heather.
It'd be so much easier to hate her if she were a bitch.

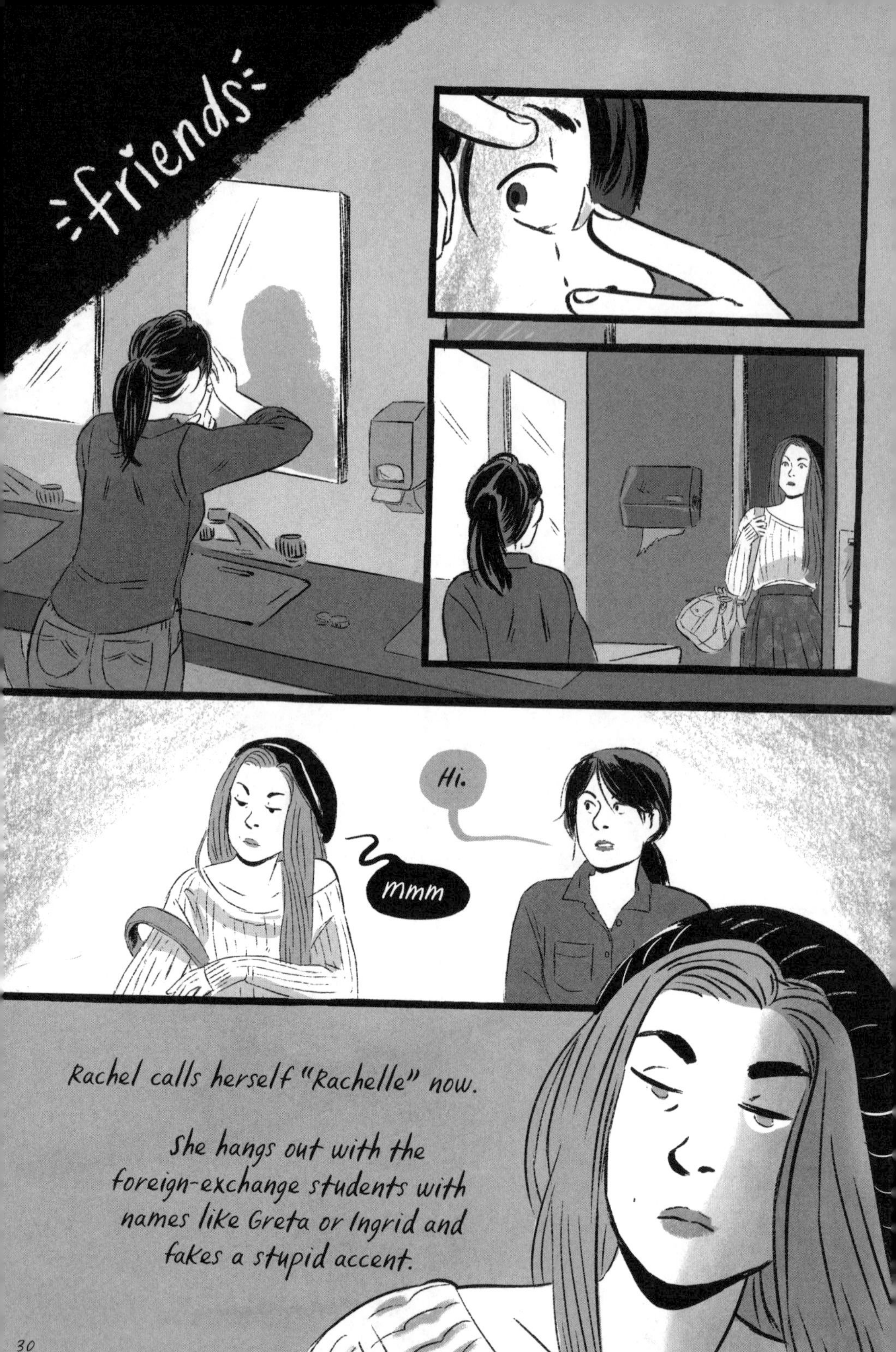
friends
Hi.
mmm
Rachel calls herself "Rachelle" now.
She hangs out with the foreign-exchange students with names like Greta or Ingrid and fakes a stupid accent.

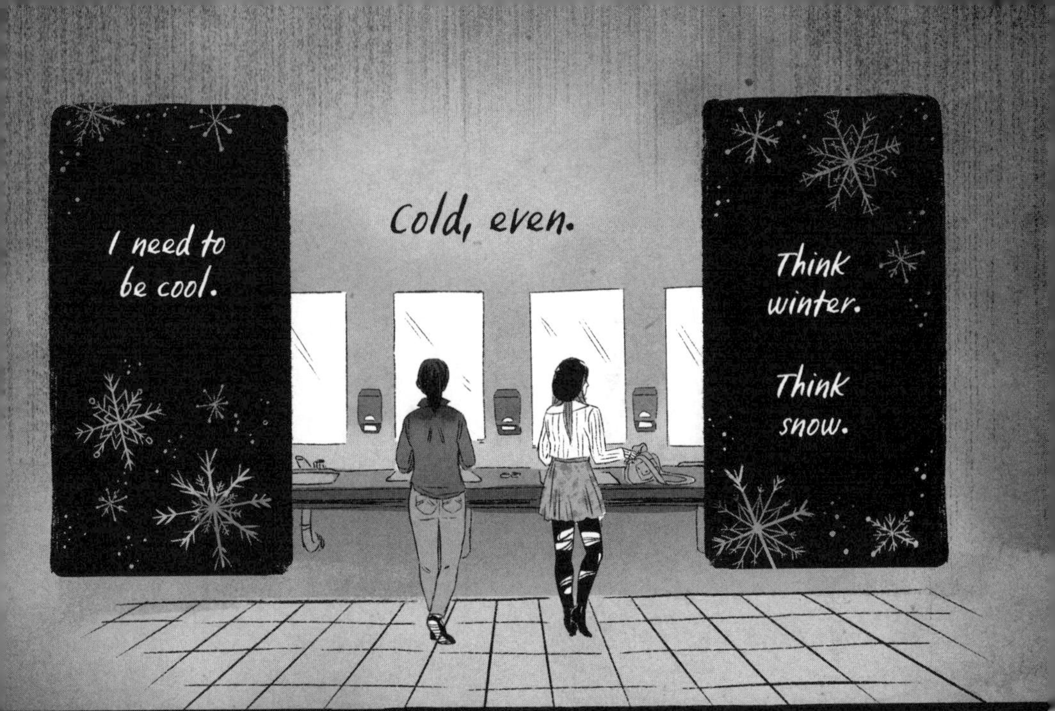
I need to be cool.
Cold, even.
Think winter.
Think snow.

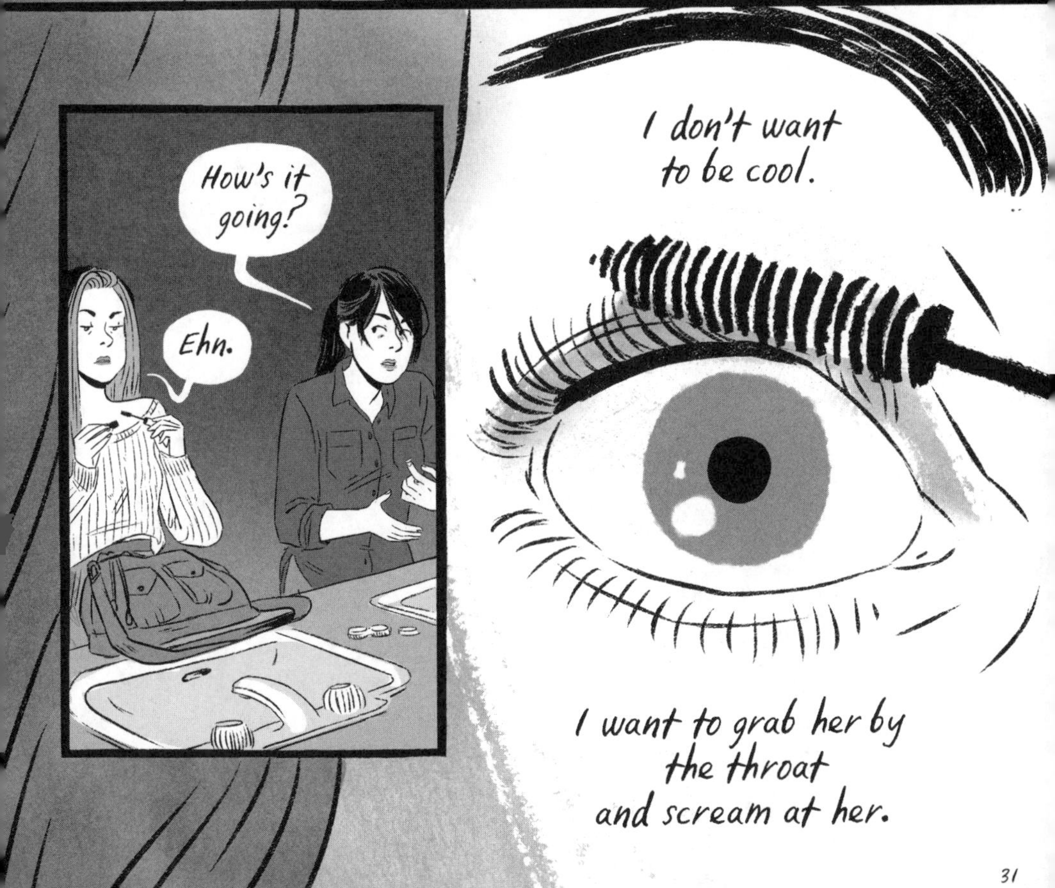
How's it going?
Ehn.
I don't want to be cool.
I want to grab her by the throat and scream at her.

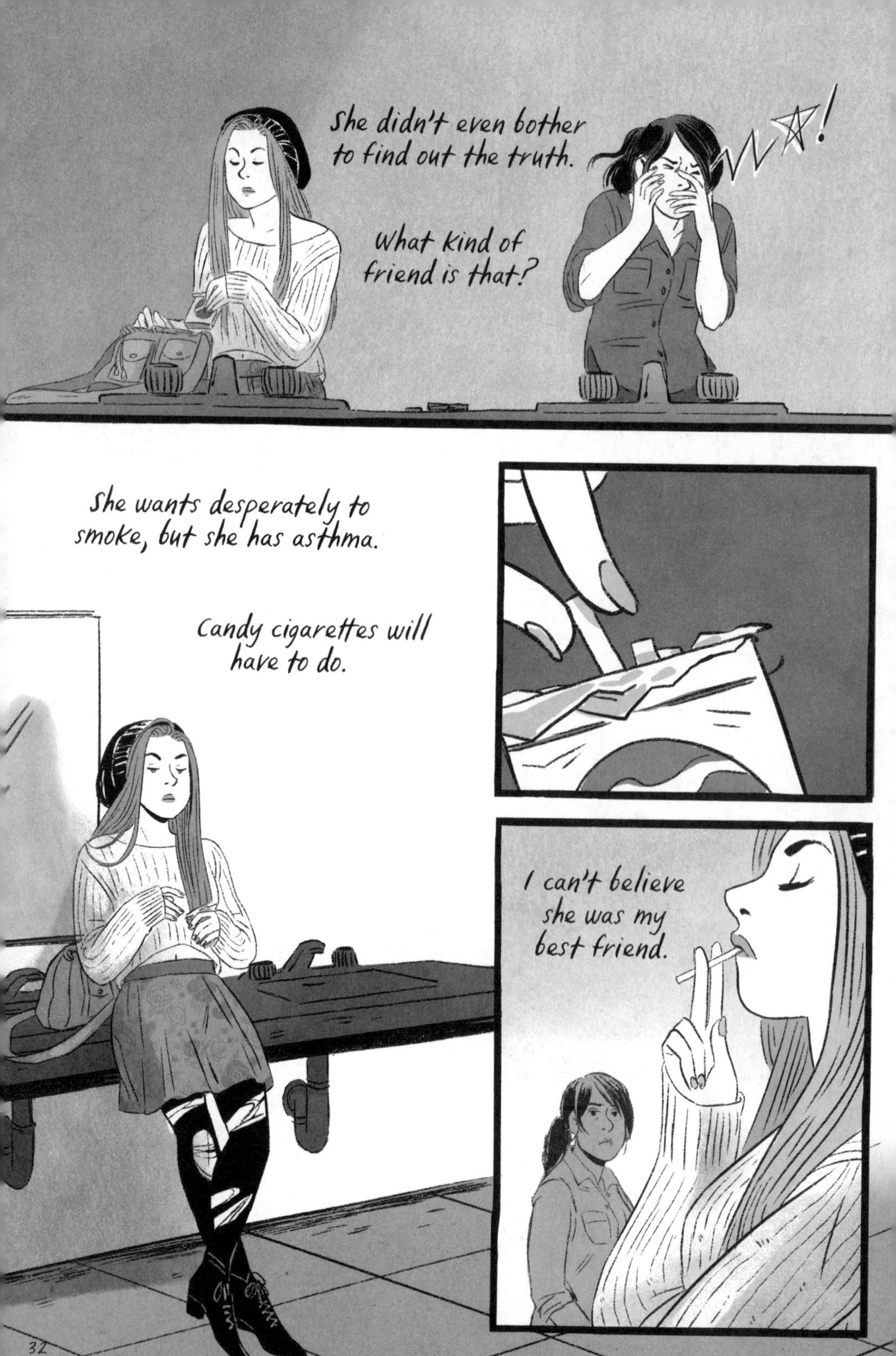
She didn't even bother to find out the truth.
What kind of friend is that?
She wants desperately to smoke, but she has asthma.
Candy cigarettes will have to do.
I can't believe she was my best friend.

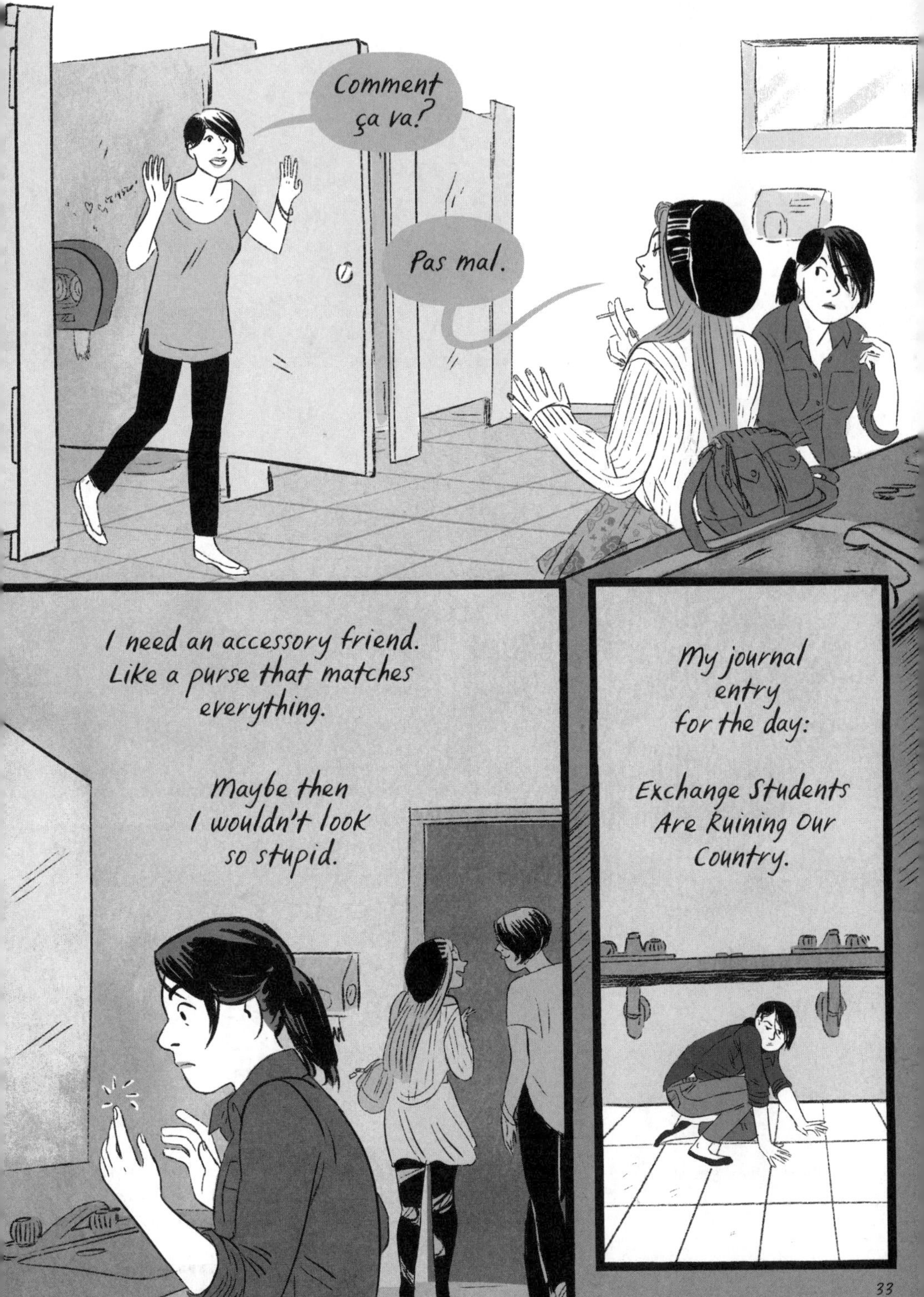

Comment ça va?
Pas mal.
I need an accessory friend. Like a purse that matches everything.
Maybe then I wouldn't look so stupid.
My journal entry for the day:
Exchange Students Are Ruining Our Country.

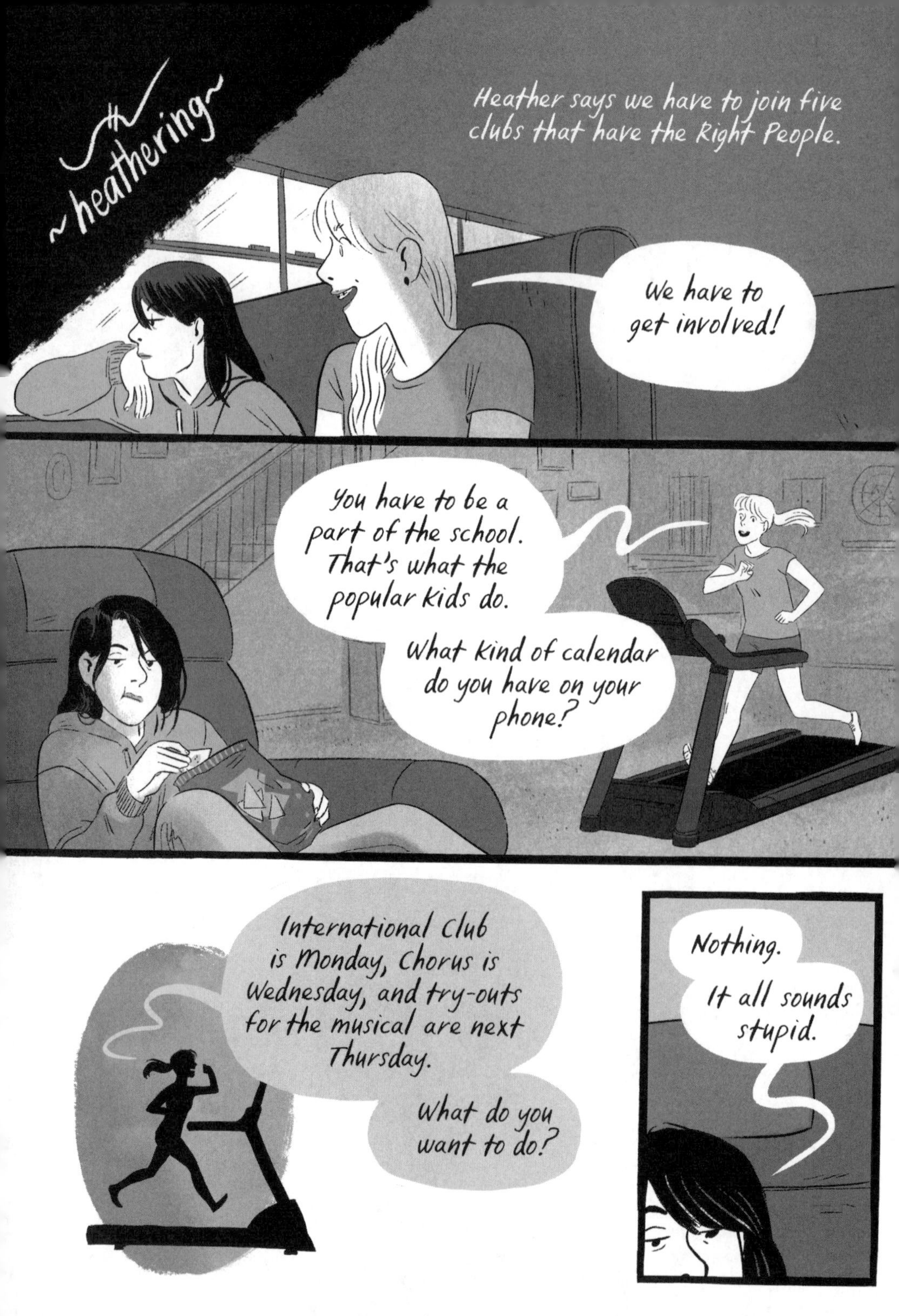
~heathering~
Heather says we have to join five clubs that have the Right People.
We have to get involved!
You have to be a part of the school. That's what the popular kids do.
What kind of calendar do you have on your phone?
International Club is Monday, Chorus is Wednesday, and try-outs for the musical are next Thursday.
What do you want to do?
Nothing.
It all sounds stupid.

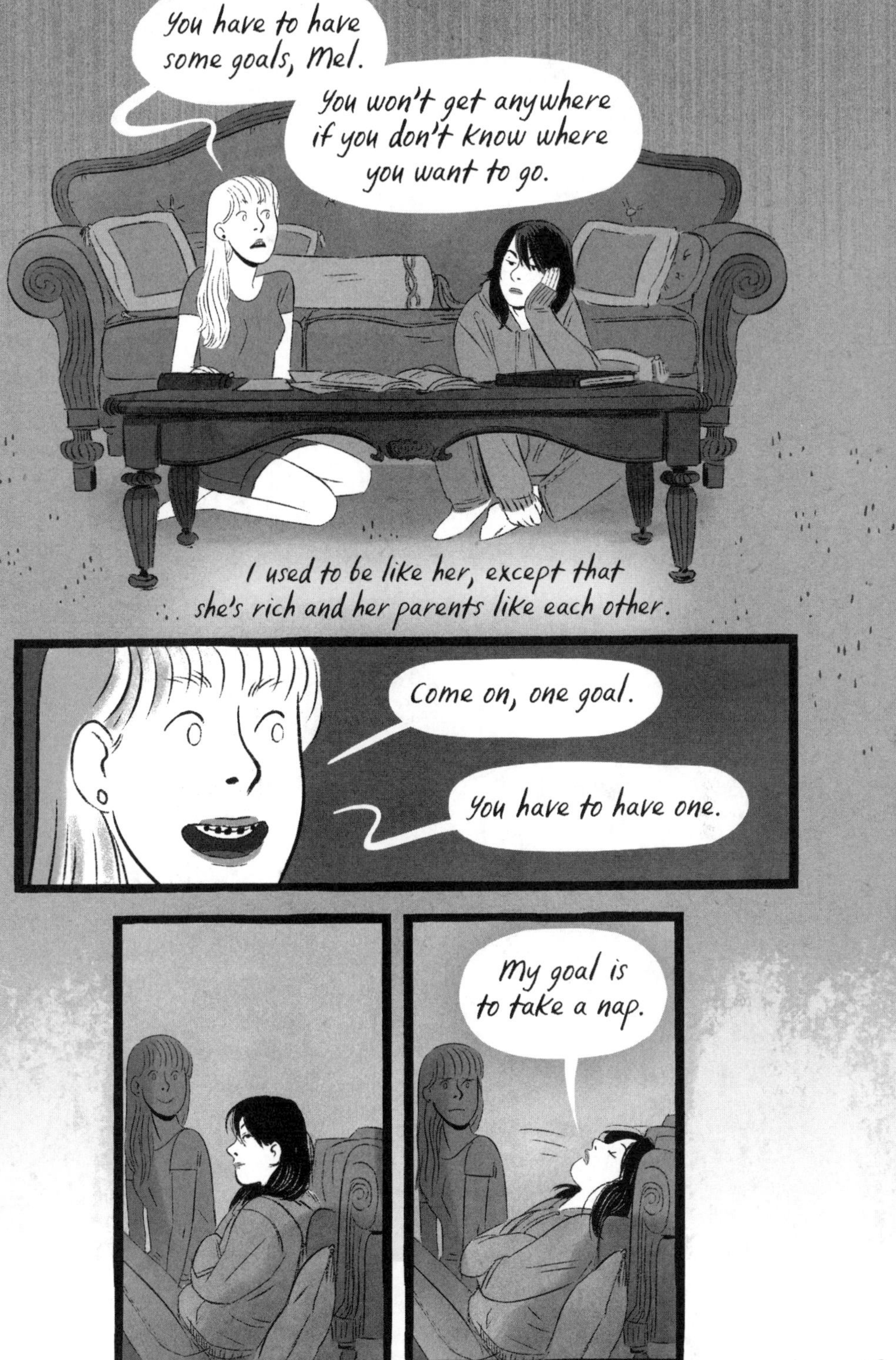
You have to have some goals, Mel.
You won't get anywhere if you don't know where you want to go.
I used to be like her, except that she's rich and her parents like each other.
Come on, one goal.
You have to have one.
My goal is to take a nap.

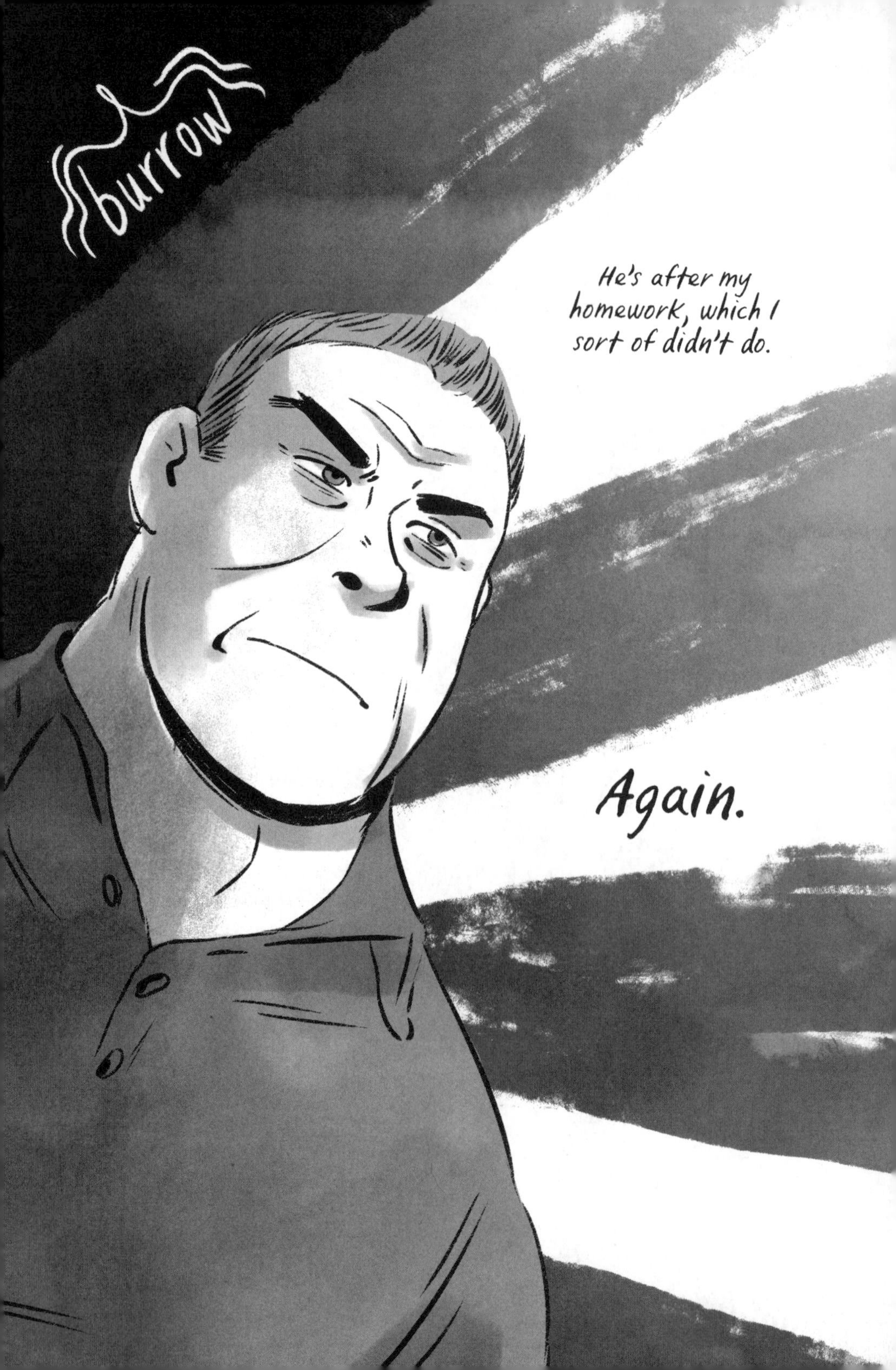
burrow
He's after my homework, which I sort of didn't do.
Again.

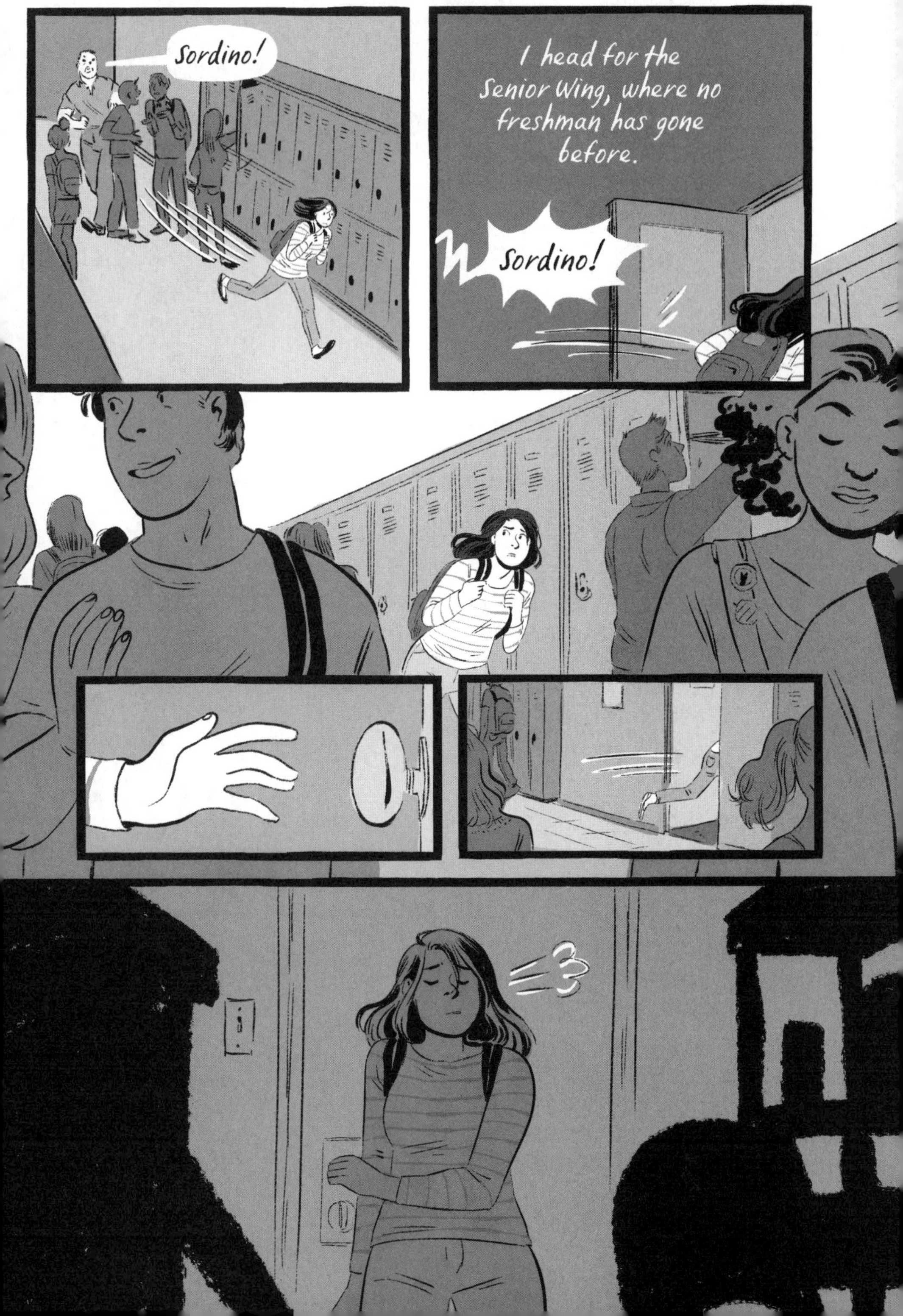
Sordino!
I head for the Senior Wing, where no freshman has gone before.
Sordino!

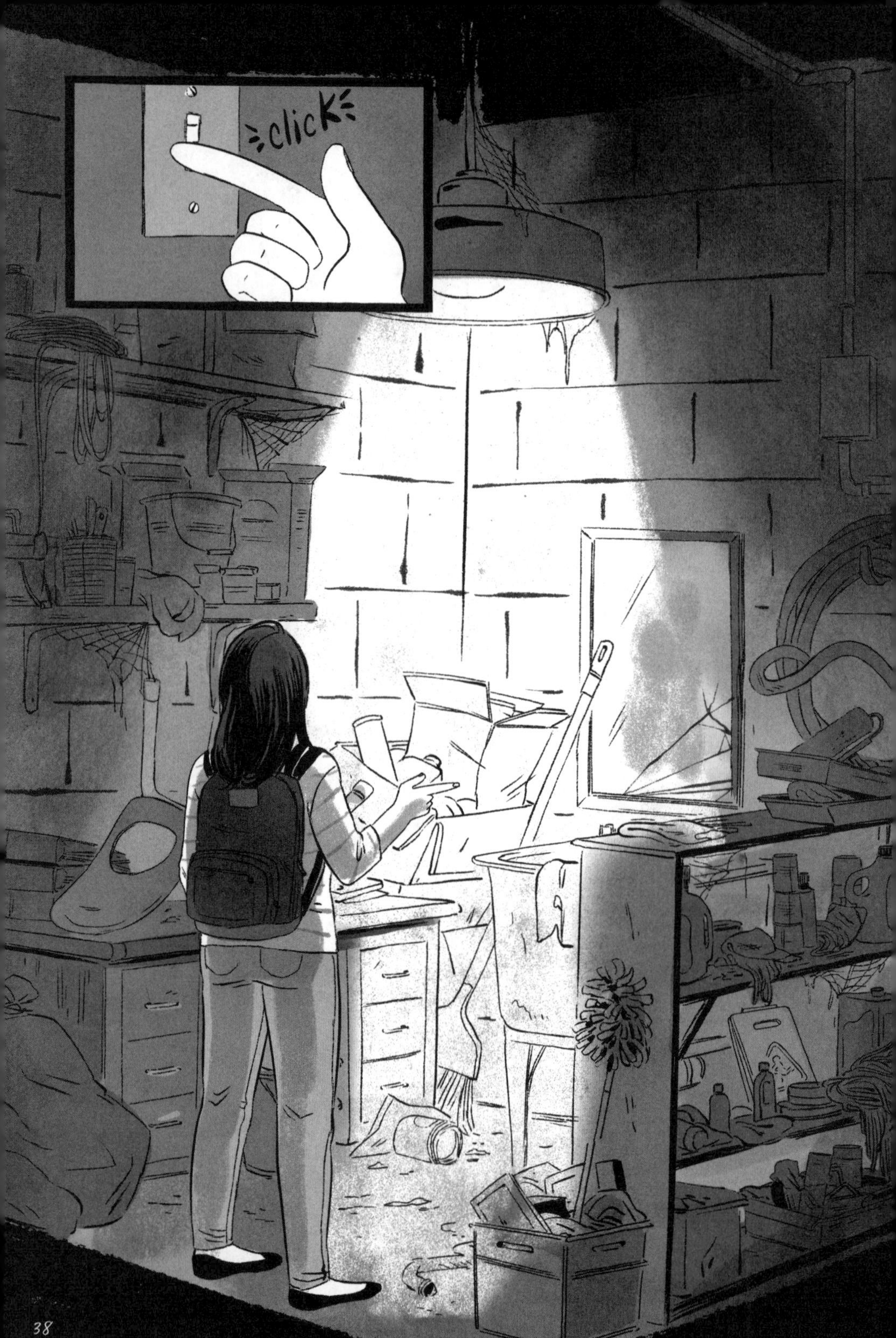
click

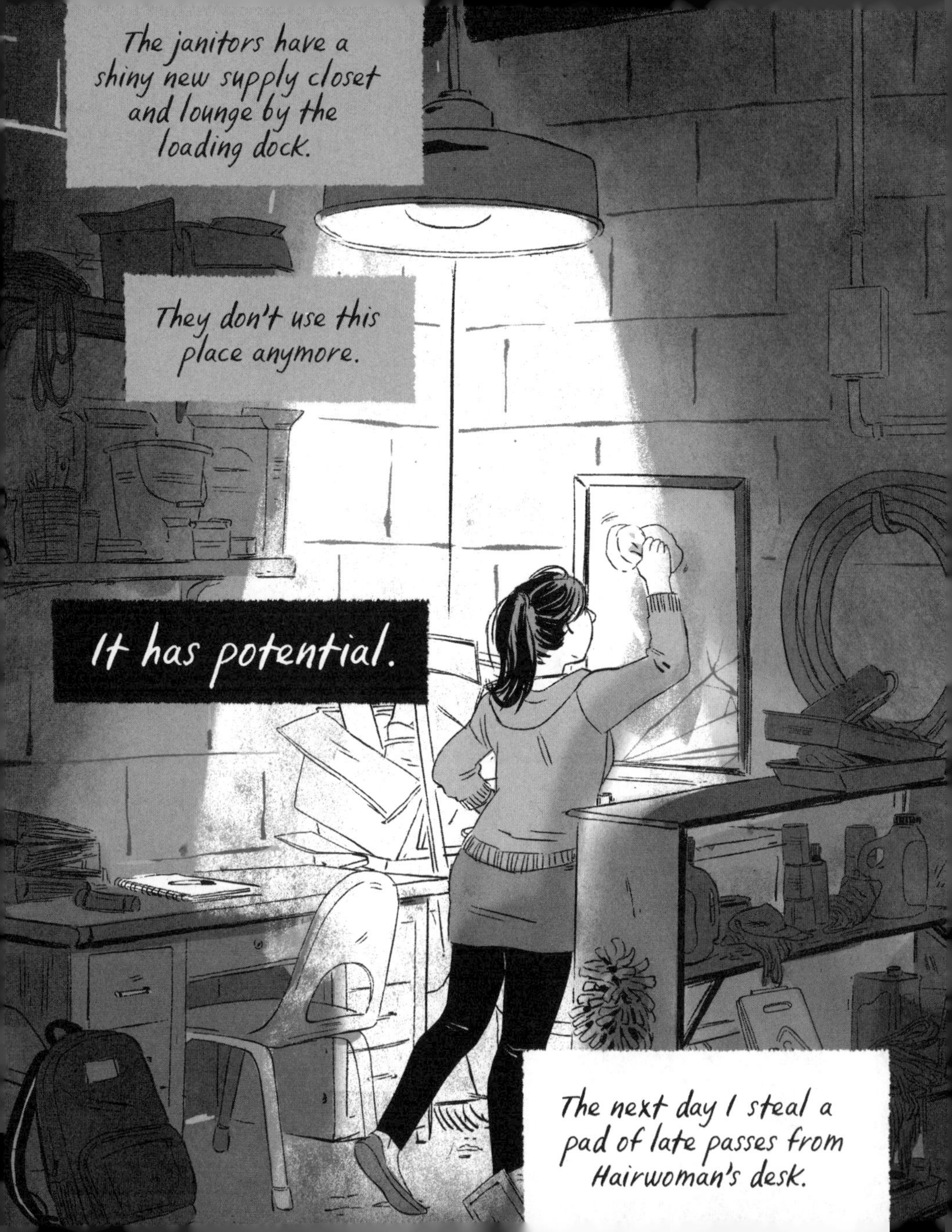
The janitors have a shiny new supply closet and lounge by the loading dock.
They don't use this place anymore.
It has potential.
The next day I steal a pad of late passes from Hairwoman's desk.

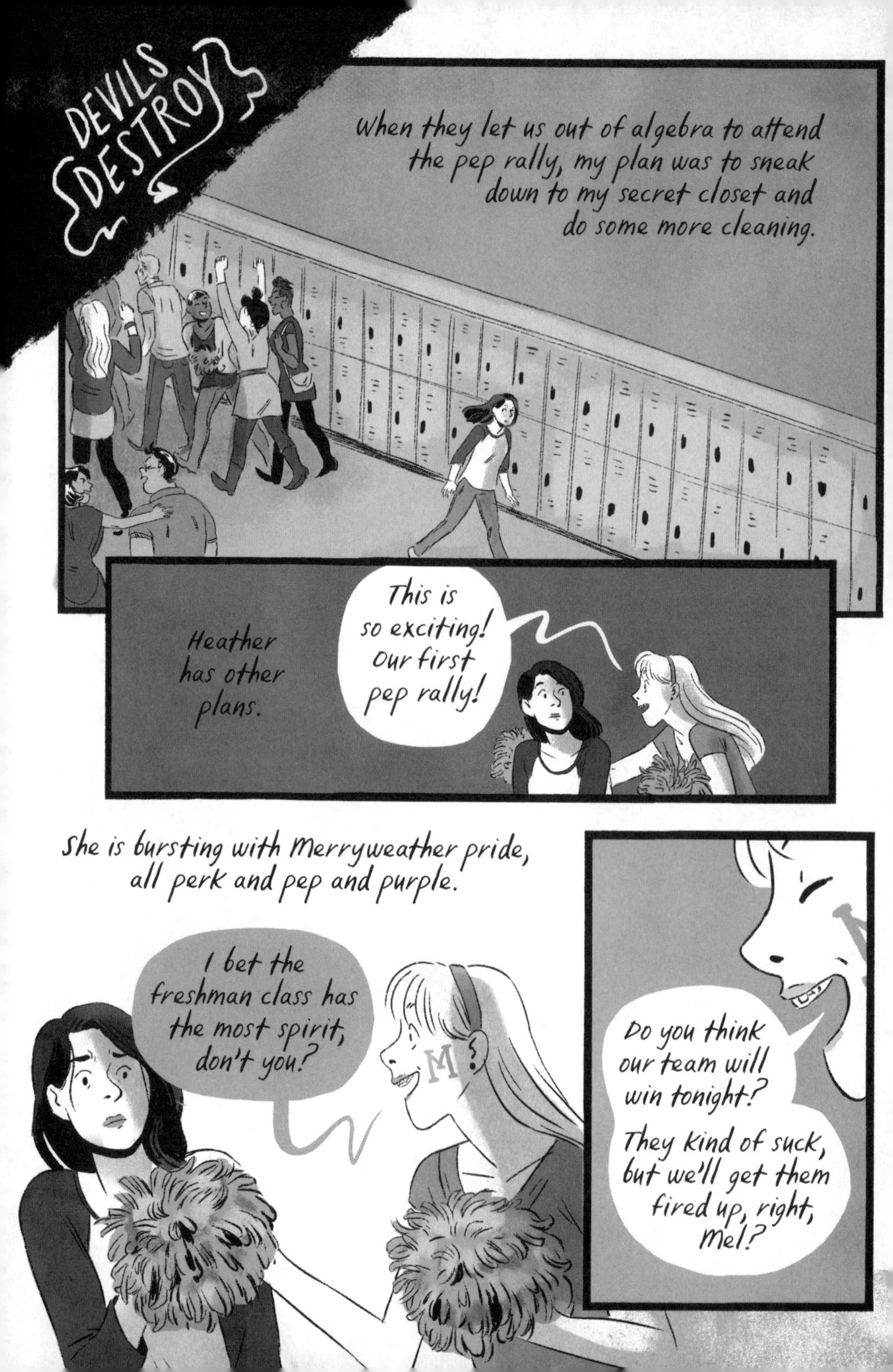
DEVILS DESTROY
When they let us out of algebra to attend the pep rally, my plan was to sneak down to my secret closet and do some more cleaning.
Heather has other plans.
This is so exciting! Our first pep rally!
She is bursting with Merryweather pride, all perk and pep and purple.
I bet the freshman class has the most spirit, don't you?
Do you think our team will win tonight?
They kind of suck, but we'll get them fired up, right, Mel?

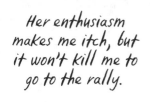

Her enthusiasm makes me itch, but it won't kill me to go to the rally.

At least I have someone to sit with.

We can sit with these guys.

They work with me on the newspaper.

We have a newspaper?

The Merryweather cheerleaders confuse me.

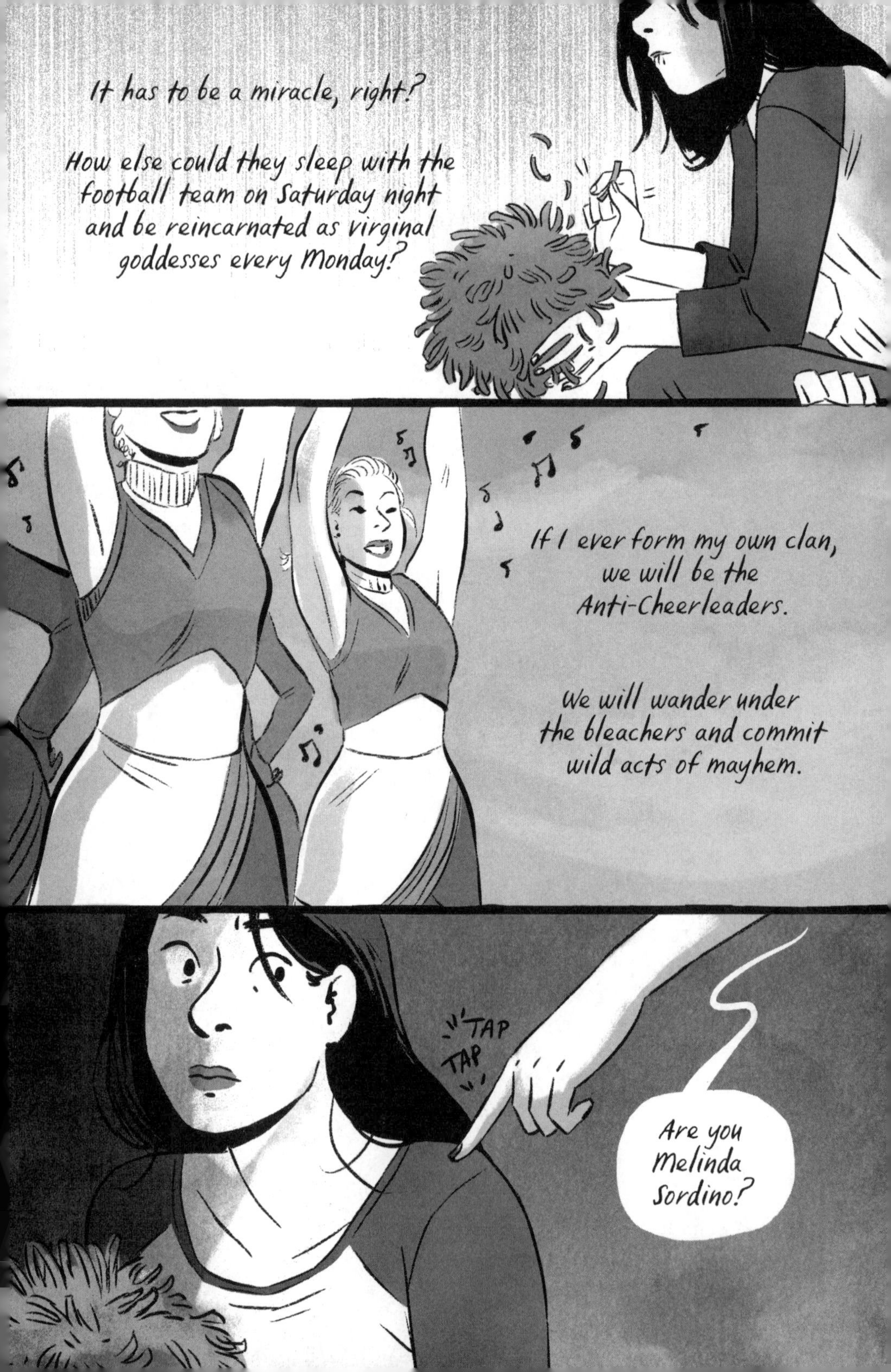
It has to be a miracle, right?
How else could they sleep with the football team on Saturday night and be reincarnated as virginal goddesses every Monday?
If I ever form my own clan, we will be the Anti-Cheerleaders.
We will wander under the bleachers and commit wild acts of mayhem.
TAP
TAP
Are you Melinda Sordino?

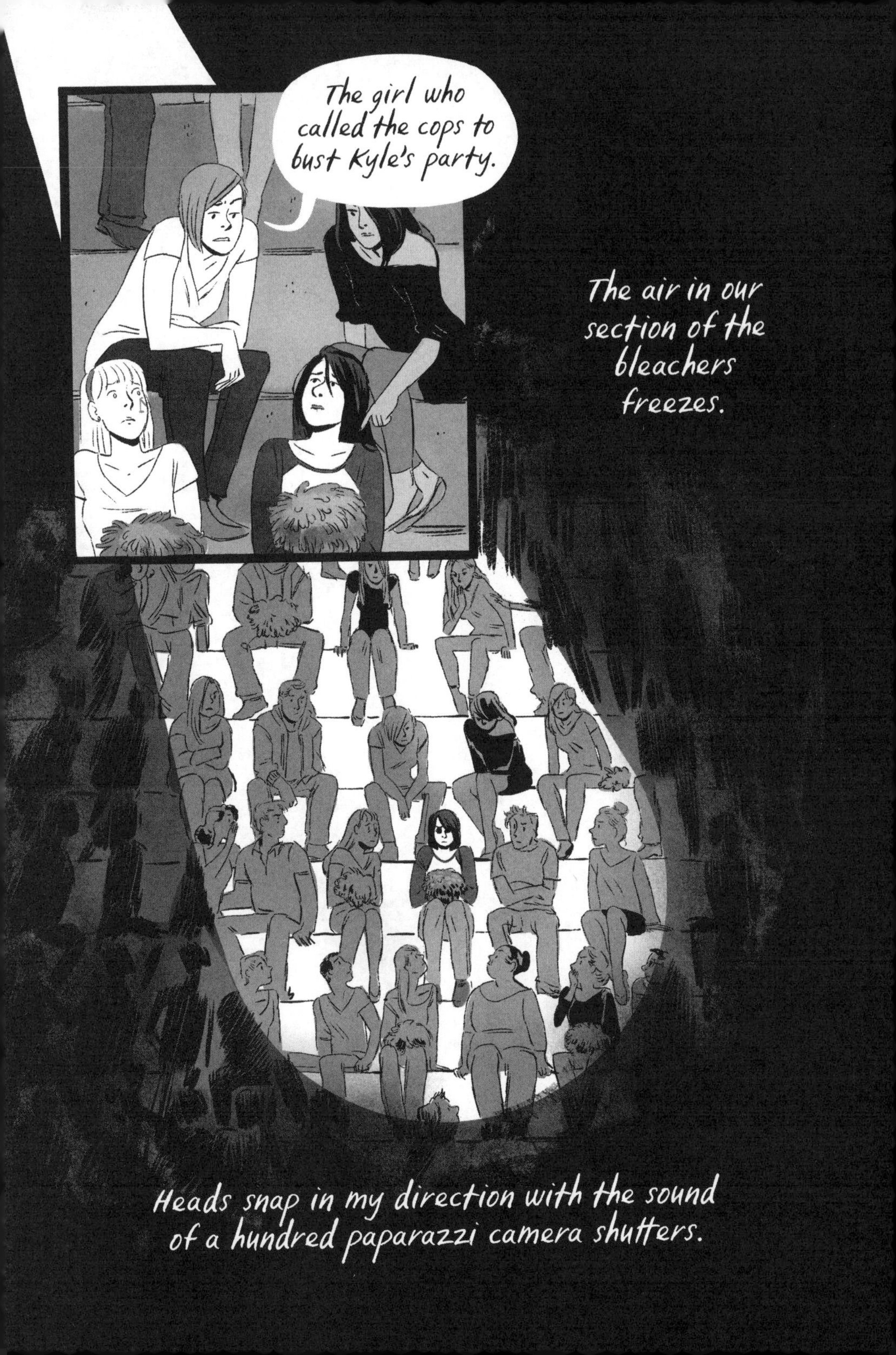

The girl who called the cops to bust Kyle's party.
The air in our section of the bleachers freezes.
Heads snap in my direction with the sound of a hundred paparazzi camera shutters.

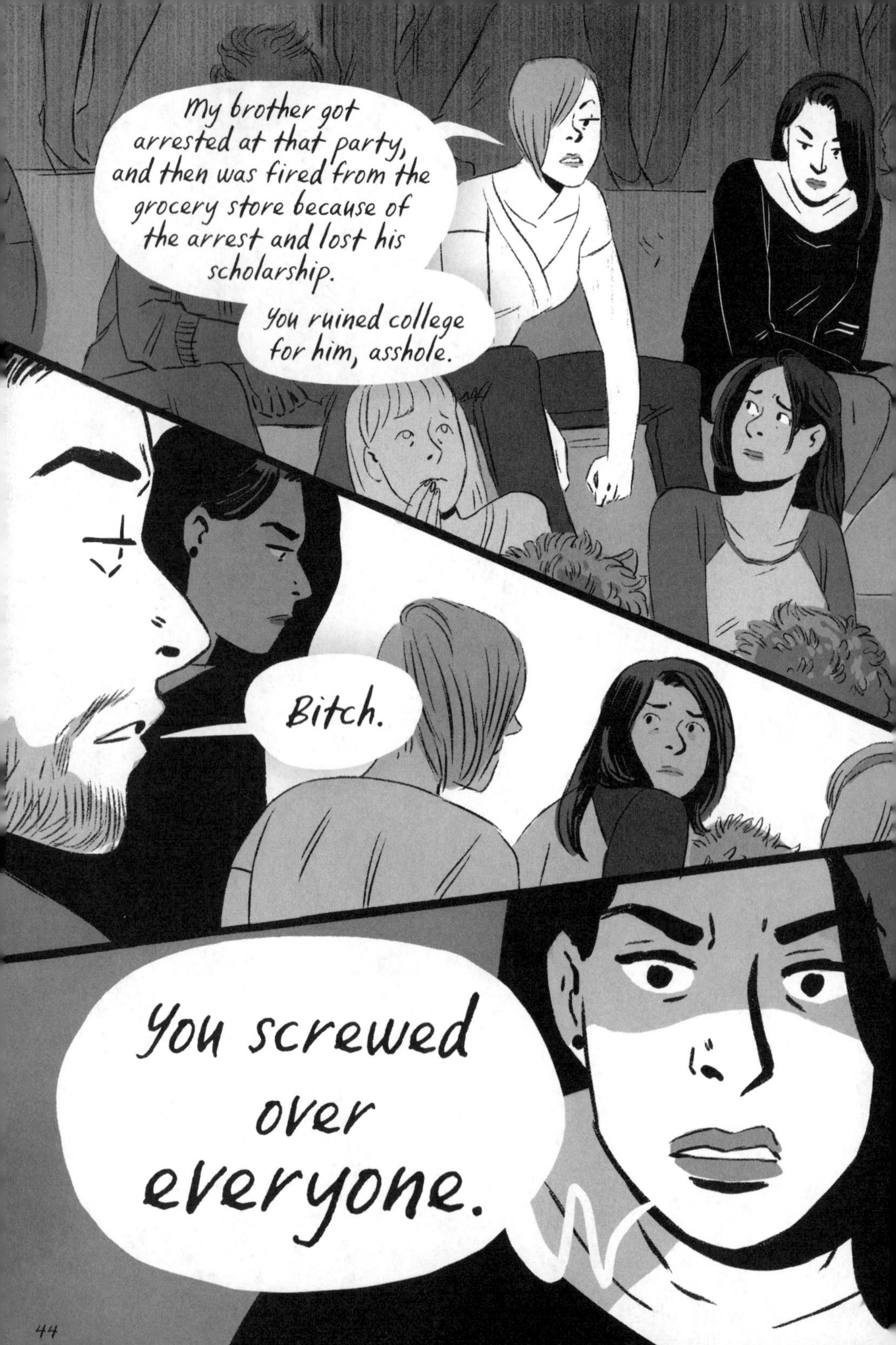
My brother got arrested at that party, and then was fired from the grocery store because of the arrest and lost his scholarship.
You ruined college for him, asshole.
Bitch.
You screwed over everyone.

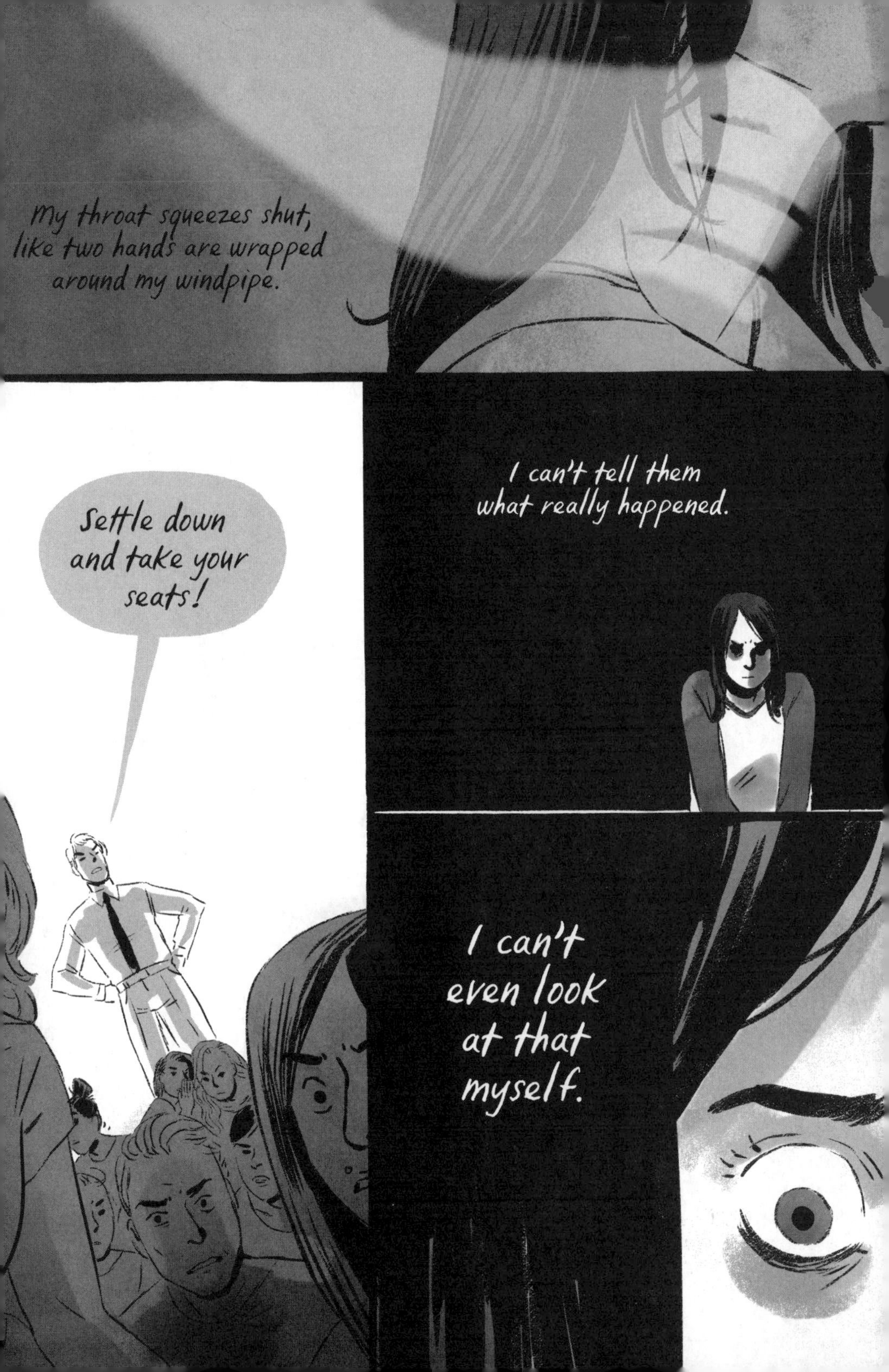
My throat squeezes shut, like two hands are wrapped around my windpipe.
Settle down and take your seats!
I can't tell them what really happened.
I can't even look at that myself.

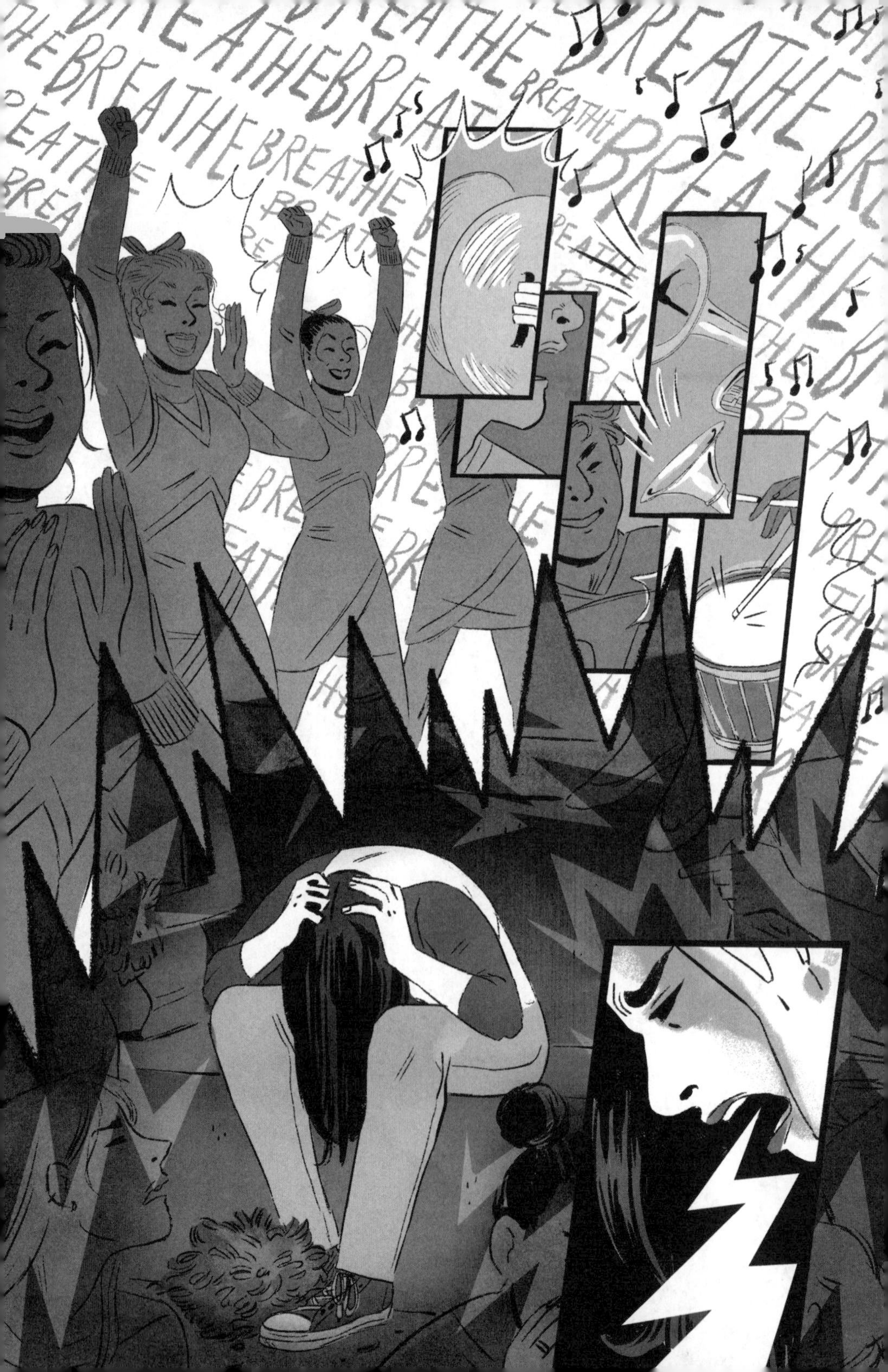
BREATHE
BREATHE
BREATHE
BREATHE
BREATHE
BREATHE

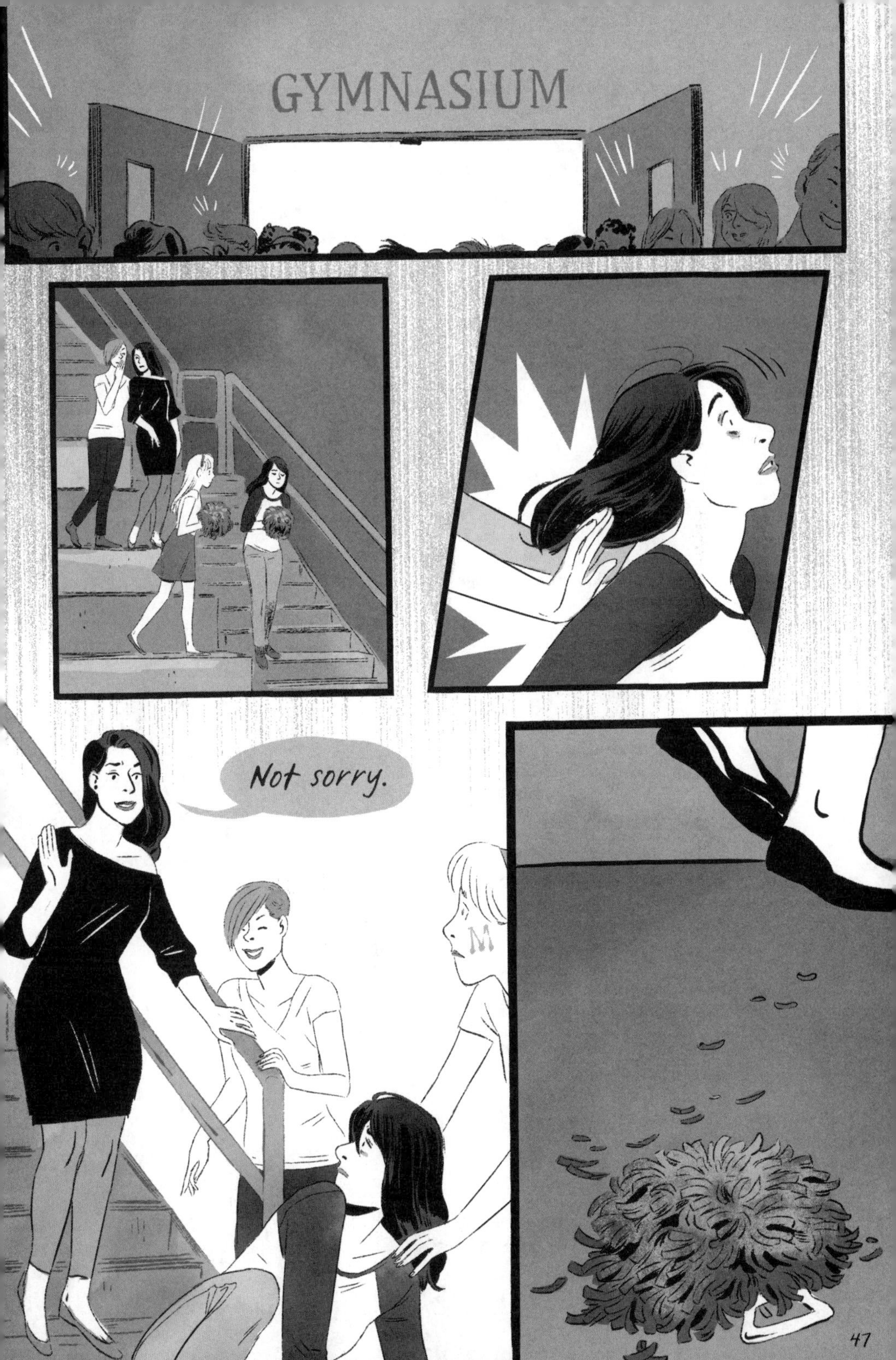
GYMNASIUM
Not sorry.
M

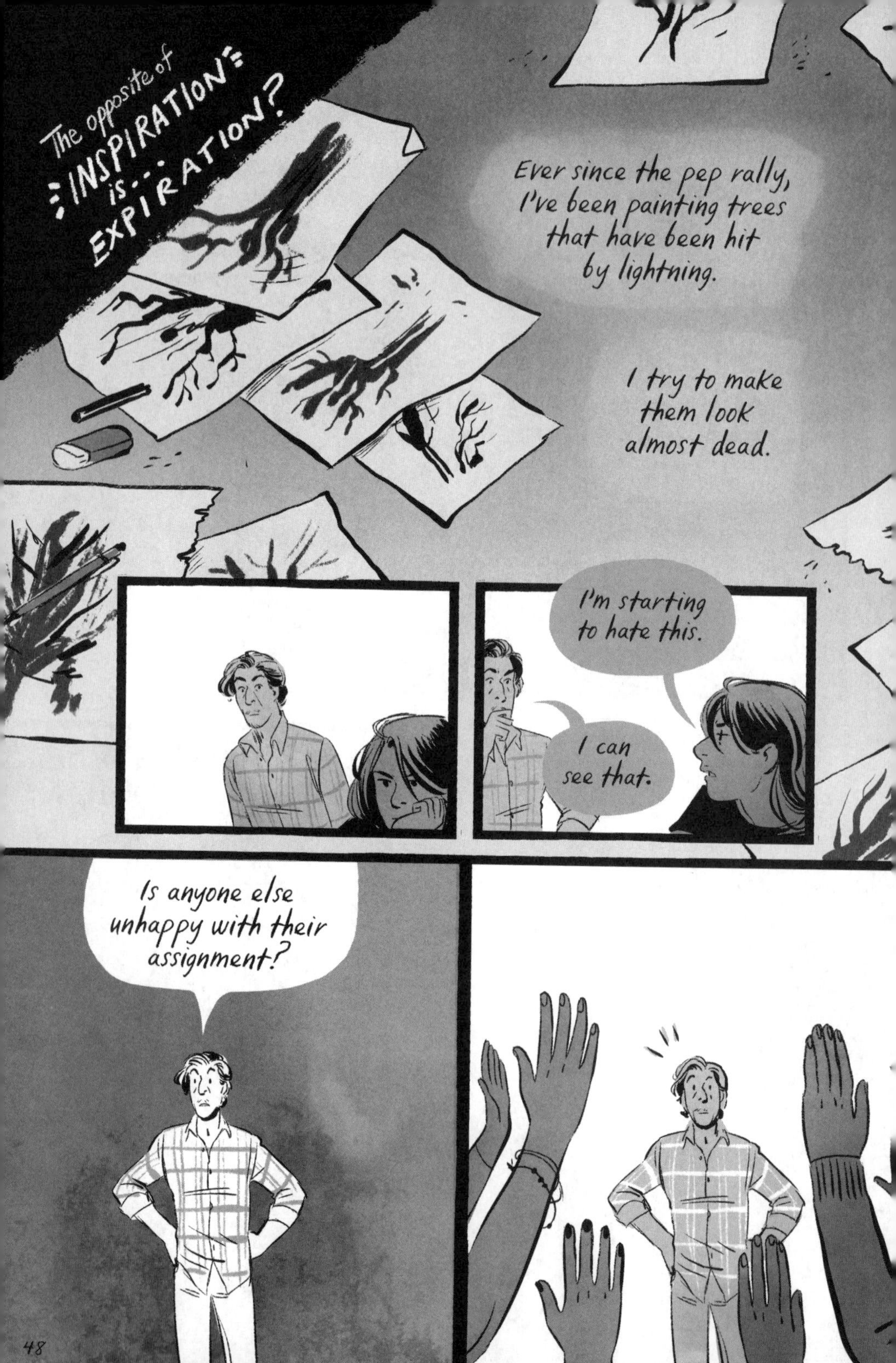
The opposite of INSPIRATION is... EXPIRATION?
Ever since the pep rally, I've been painting trees that have been hit by lightning.
I try to make them look almost dead.
I'm starting to hate this.
I can see that.
Is anyone else unhappy with their assignment?

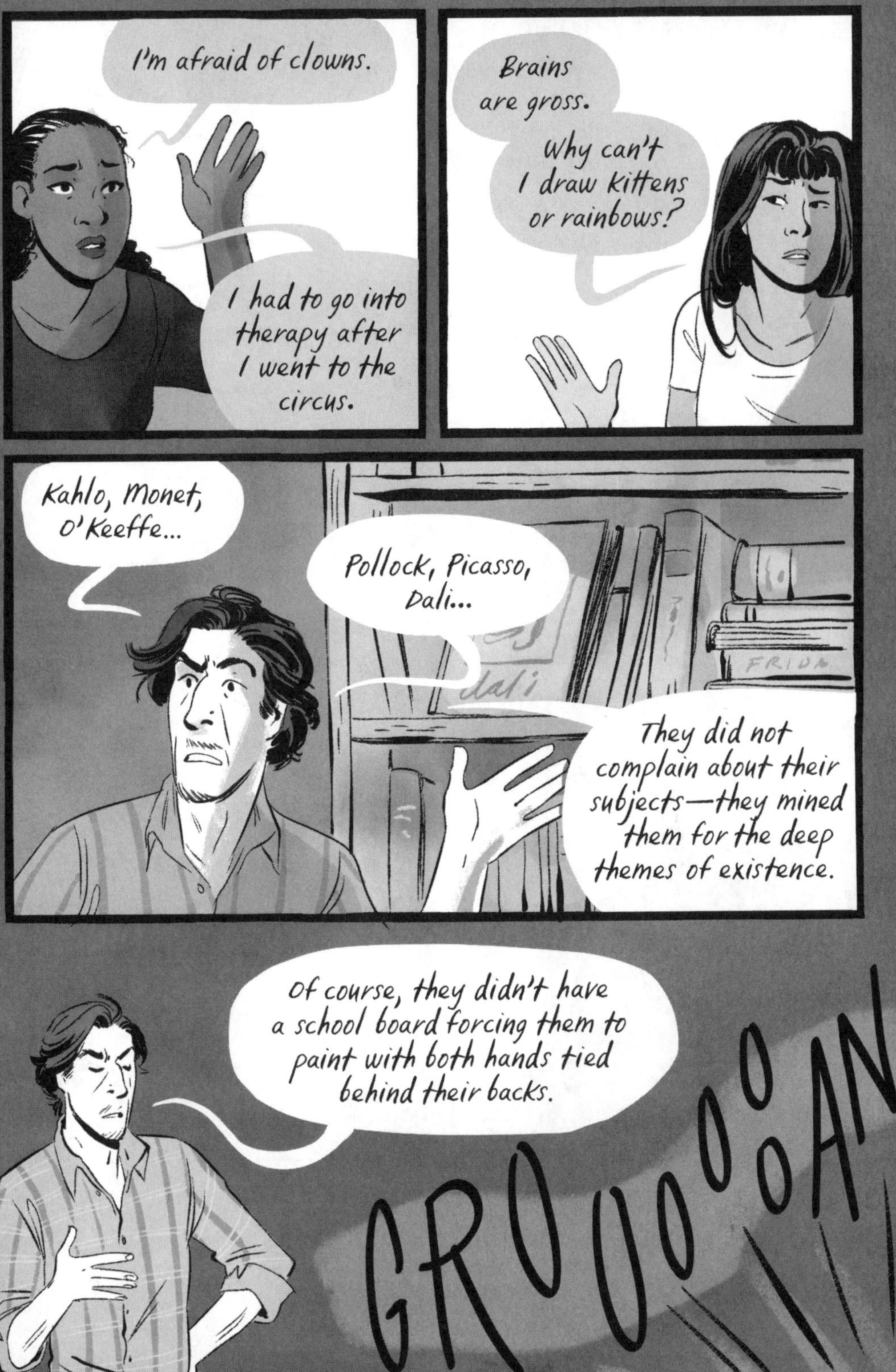

I'm afraid of clowns.
I had to go into therapy after I went to the circus.
Brains are gross.
Why can't I draw kittens or rainbows?
Kahlo, Monet, O'Keeffe...
Pollock, Picasso, Dali...
dali
FRIDA
They did not complain about their subjects—they mined them for the deep themes of existence.
Of course, they didn't have a school board forcing them to paint with both hands tied behind their backs.
GROOOOOOAN

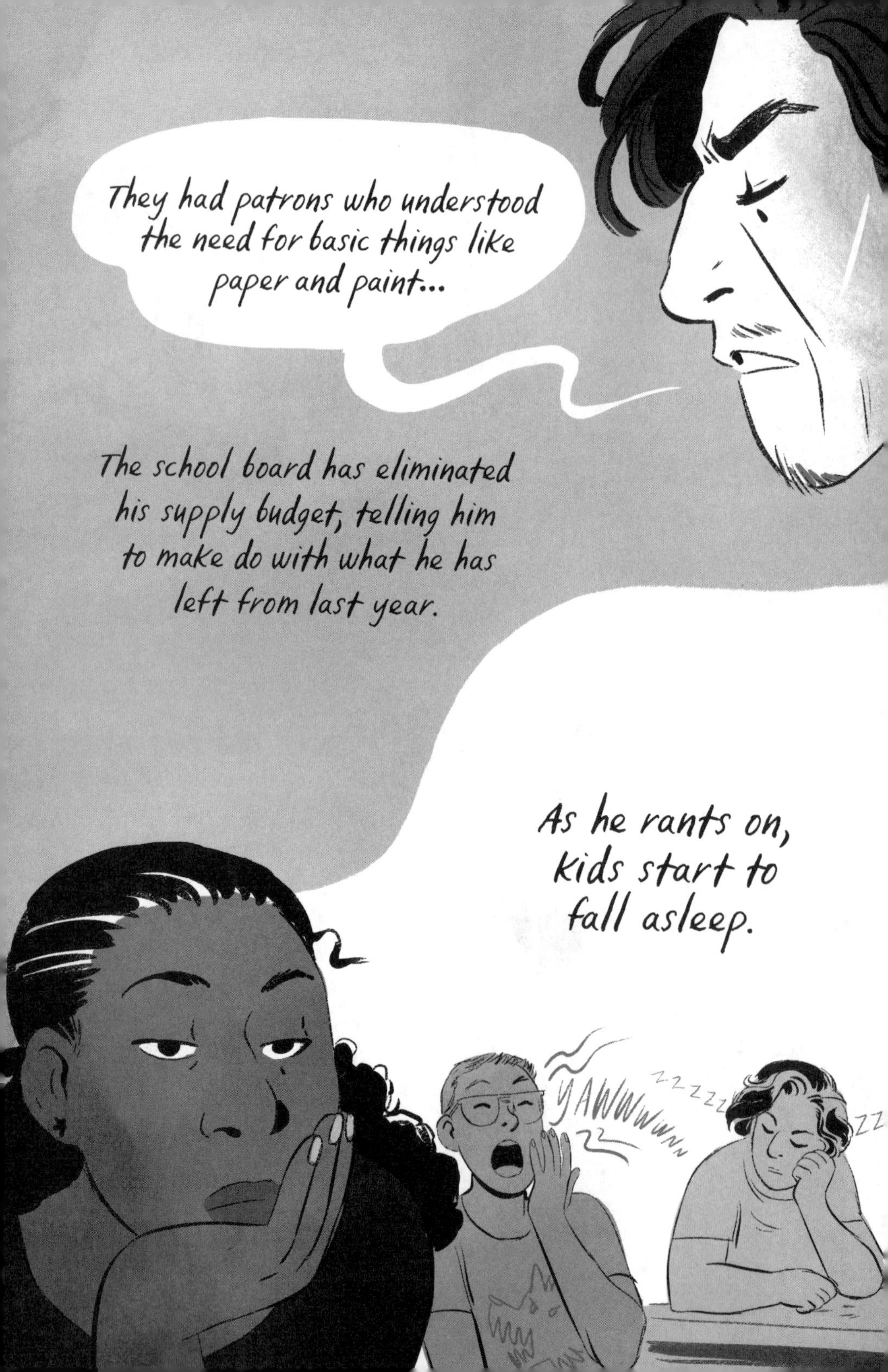
They had patrons who understood the need for basic things like paper and paint...
The school board has eliminated his supply budget, telling him to make do with what he has left from last year.
As he rants on, kids start to fall asleep.
YAWWWWNN
ZZZZZ
ZZ

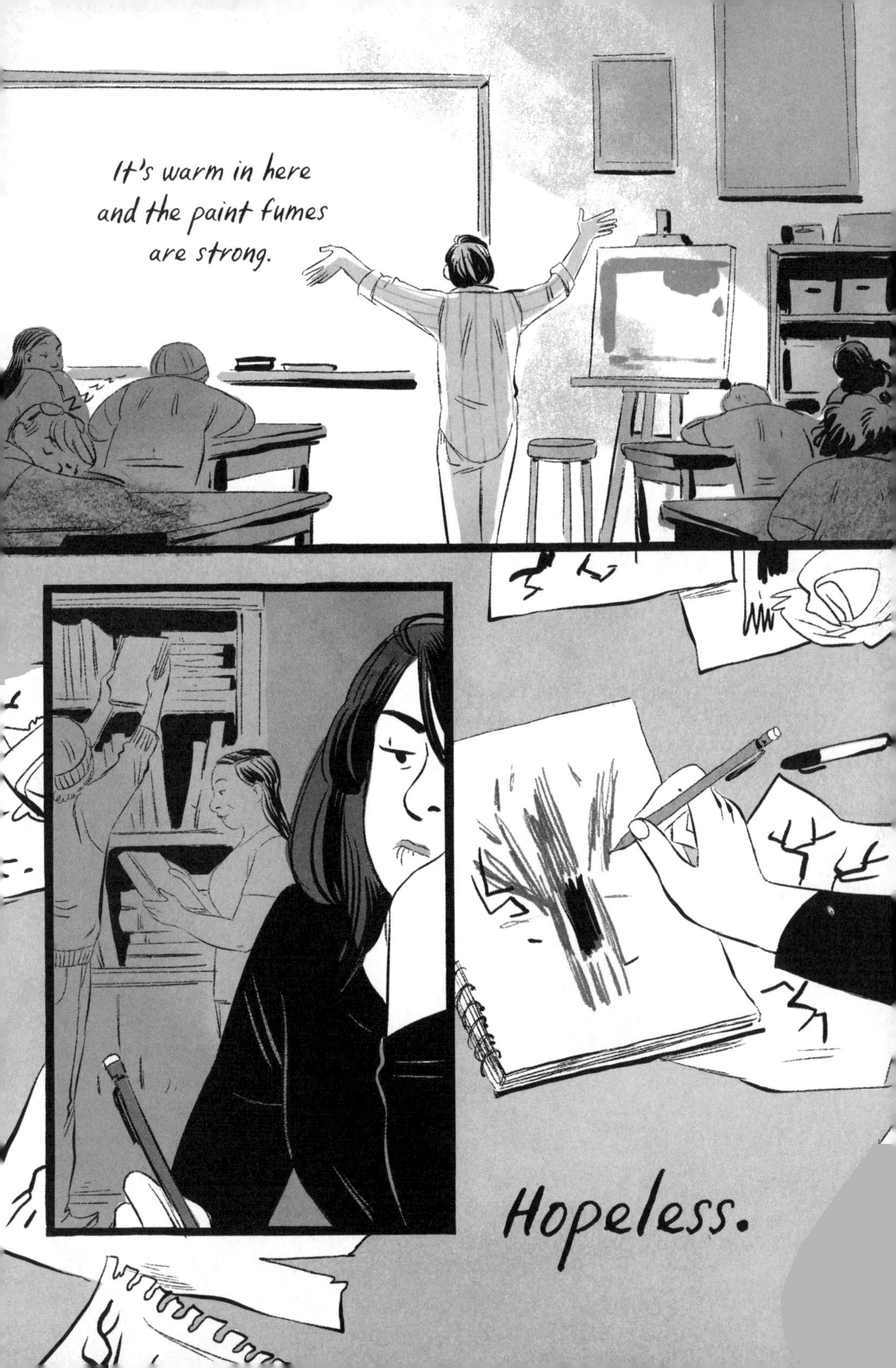
It's warm in here and the paint fumes are strong.
Hopeless.

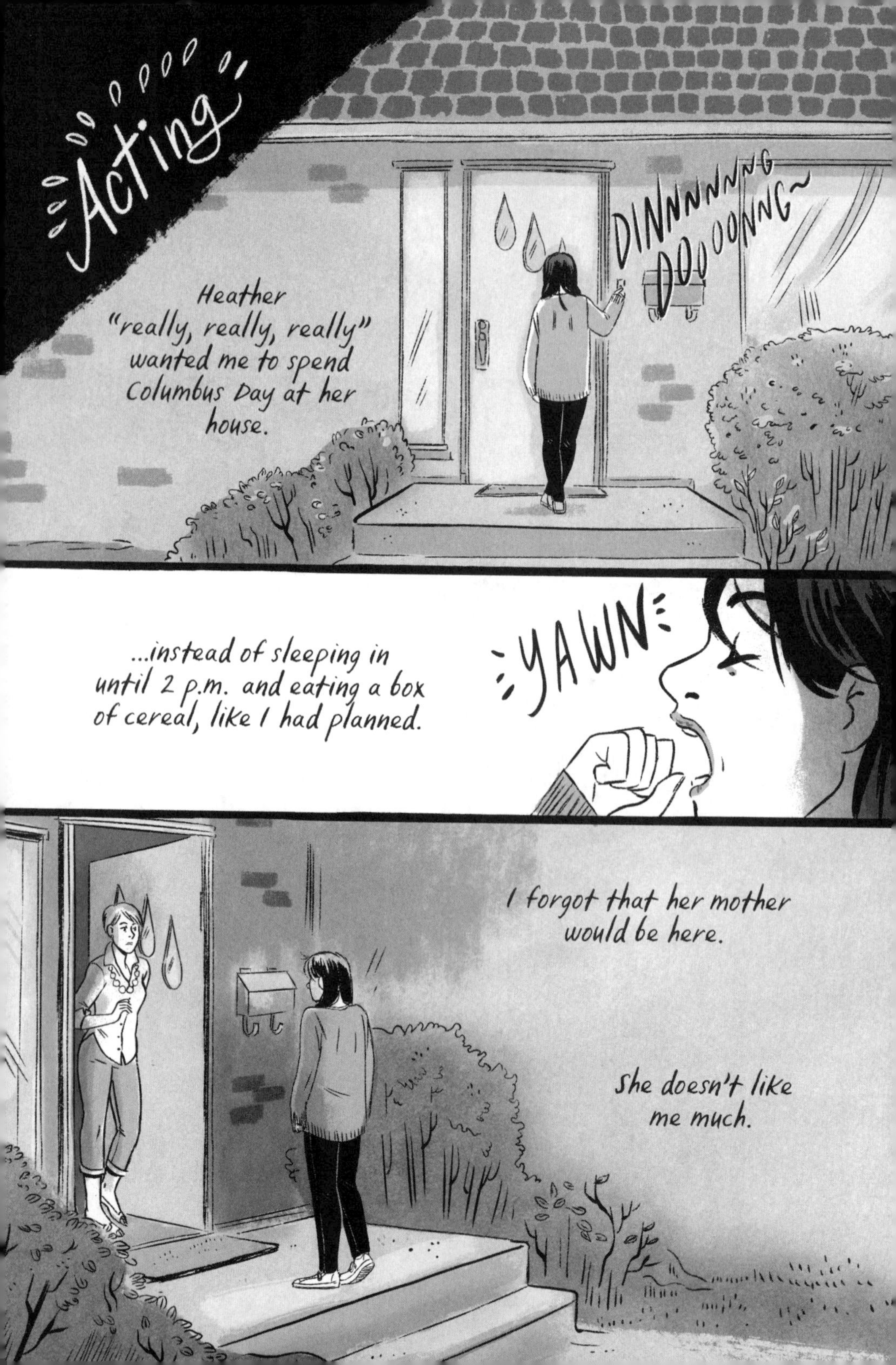
Acting
Heather "really, really, really" wanted me to spend Columbus Day at her house.
DINNNNNNG DOOOONNG~
...instead of sleeping in until 2 p.m. and eating a box of cereal, like I had planned.
YAWN
I forgot that her mother would be here.
She doesn't like me much.

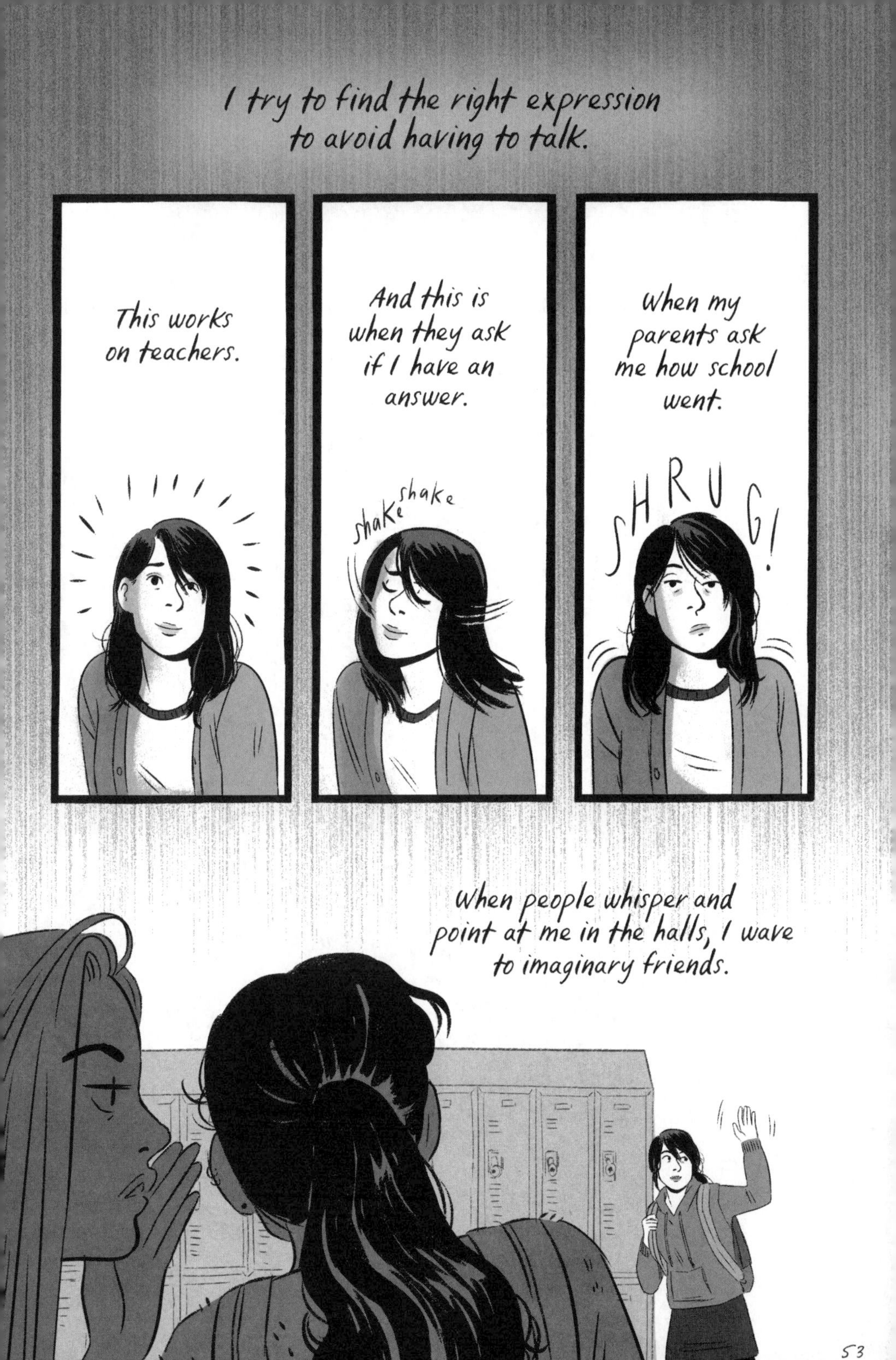
I try to find the right expression to avoid having to talk.
This works on teachers.
And this is when they ask if I have an answer.
shake shake
When my parents ask me how school went.
SHRUG!
When people whisper and point at me in the halls, I wave to imaginary friends.

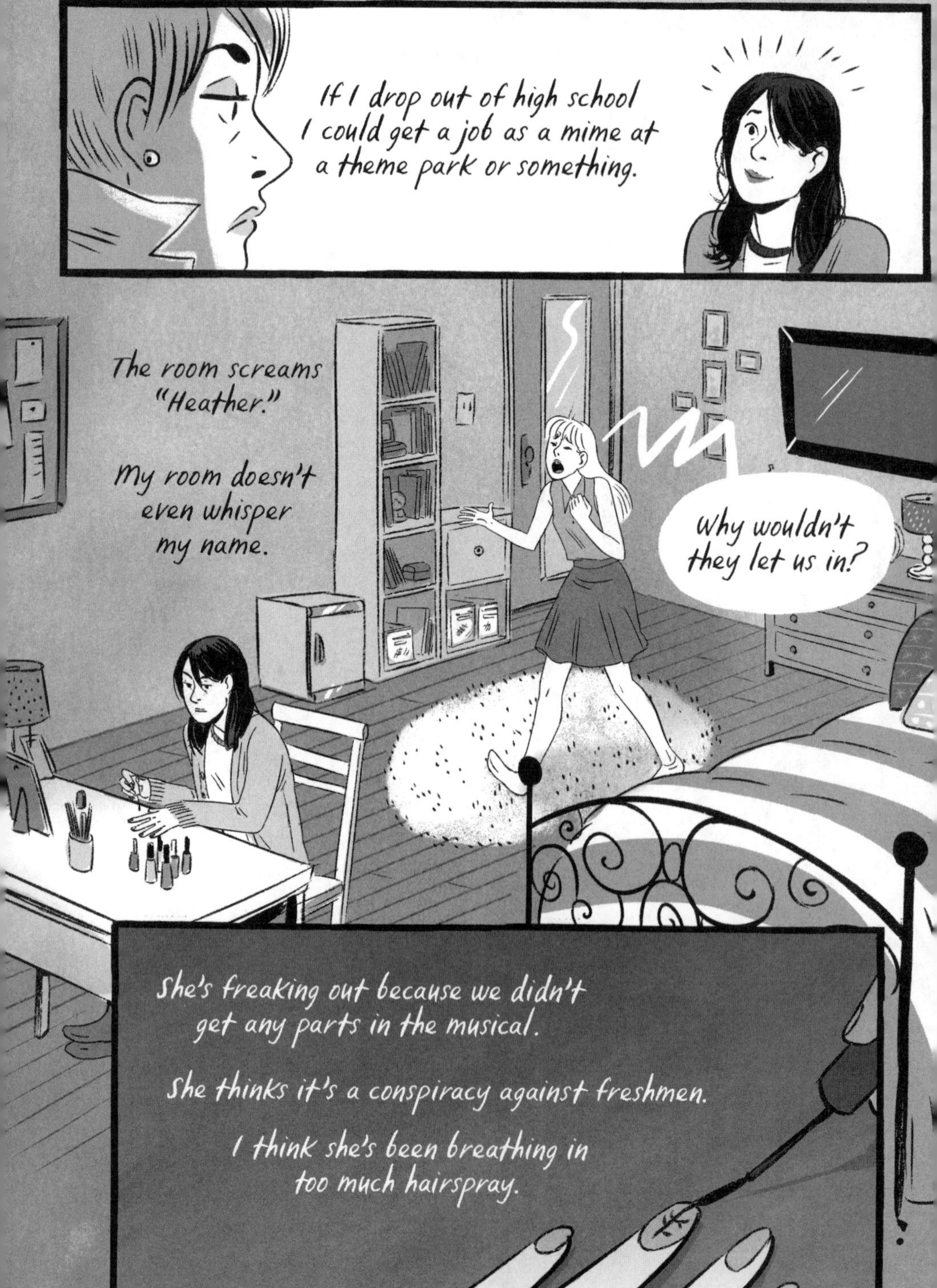
If I drop out of high school I could get a job as a mime at a theme park or something.
The room screams "Heather."
My room doesn't even whisper my name.
Why wouldn't they let us in?
She's freaking out because we didn't get any parts in the musical.
She thinks it's a conspiracy against freshmen.
I think she's been breathing in too much hairspray.

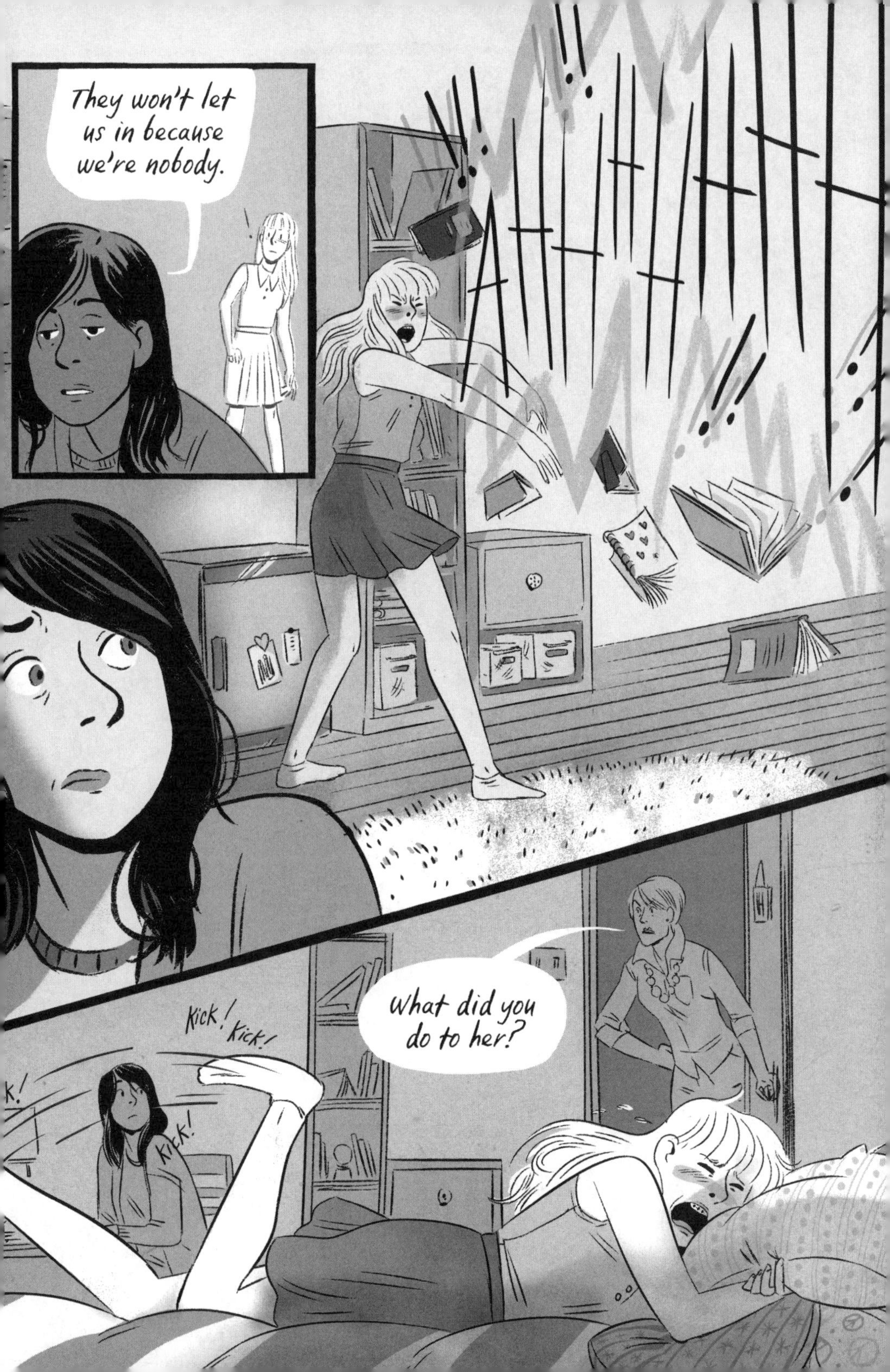
They won't let us in because we're nobody.
AHHHHHHH
What did you do to her?
KICK! KICK!
KICK!

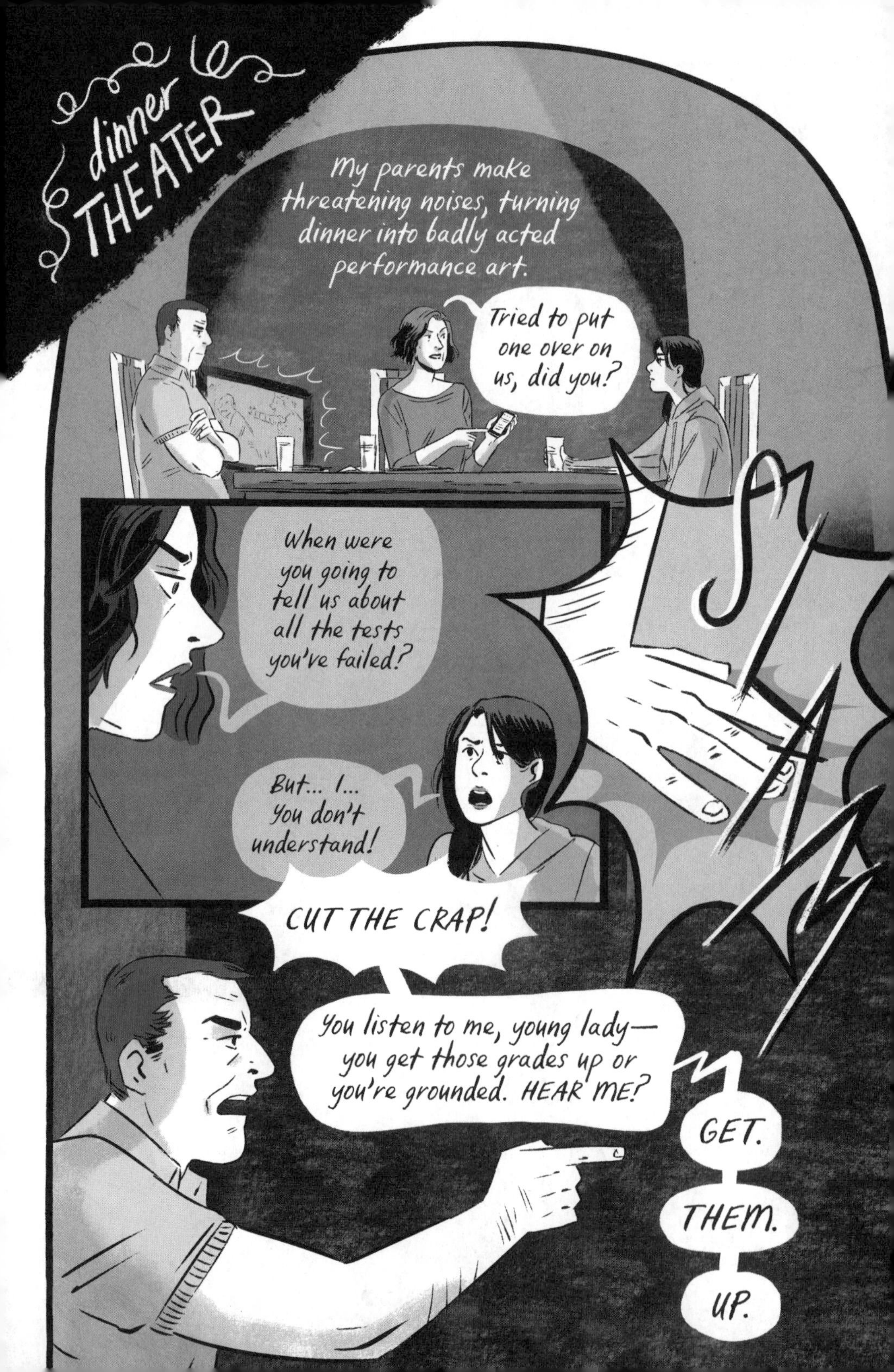
dinner THEATER
My parents make threatening noises, turning dinner into badly acted performance art.
Tried to put one over on us, did you?
When were you going to tell us about all the tests you've failed?
But... I... You don't understand!
SLAM
CUT THE CRAP!
You listen to me, young lady— you get those grades up or you're grounded. HEAR ME?
GET.
THEM.
UP.

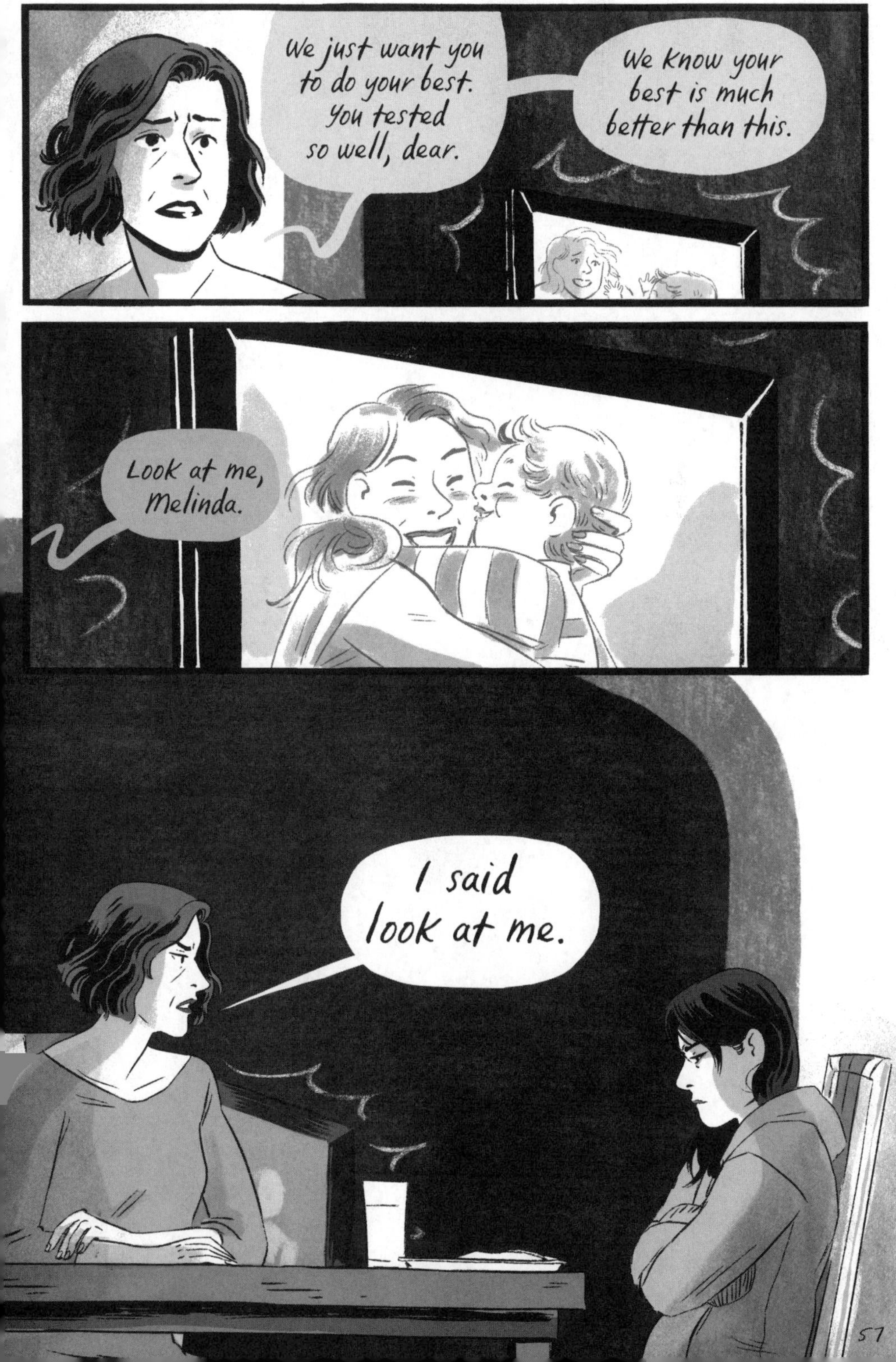
We just want you to do your best. You tested so well, dear.
We know your best is much better than this.
Look at me, Melinda.
I said look at me.

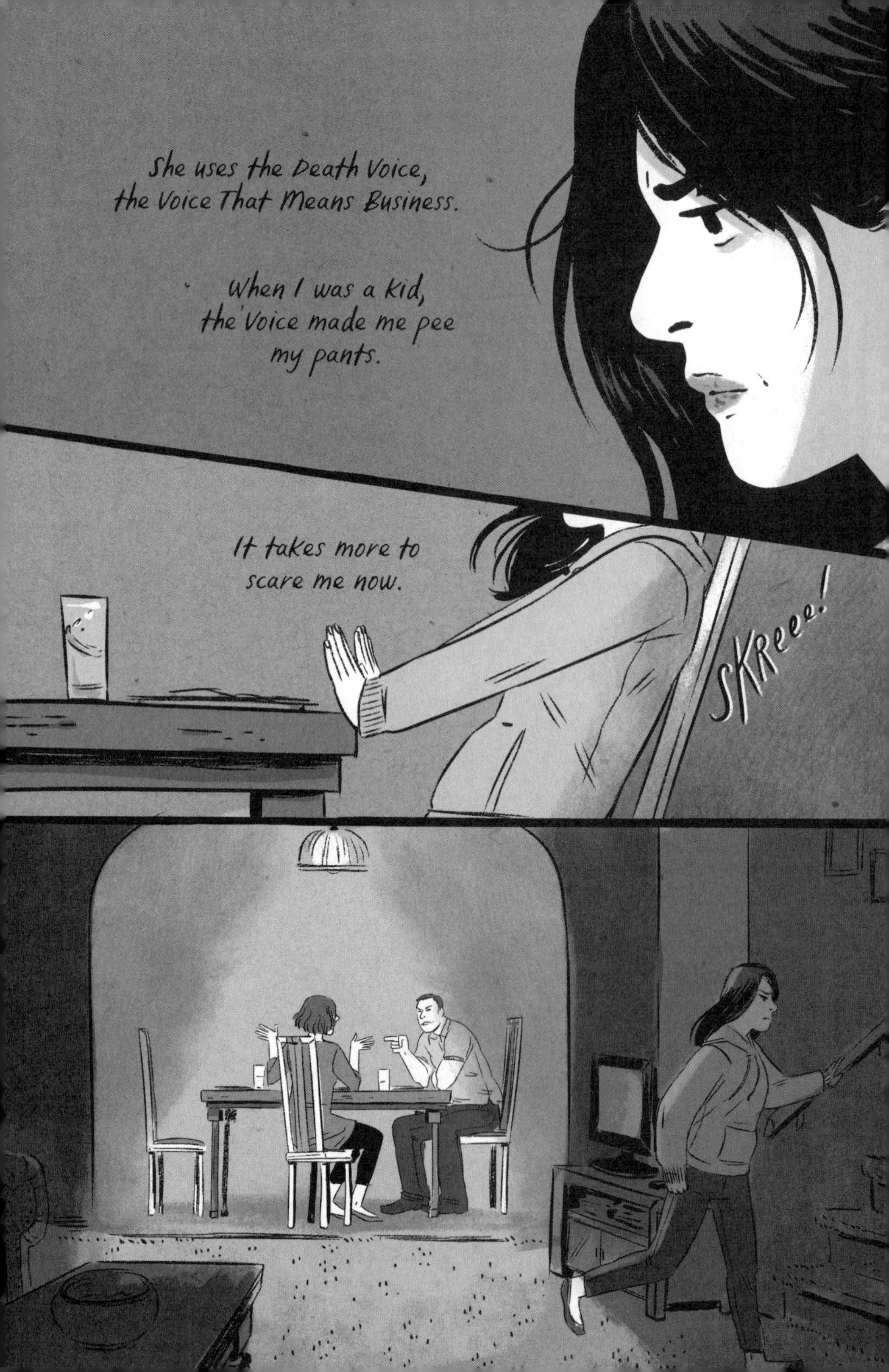
She uses the Death Voice,
the Voice That Means Business.
When I was a kid,
the Voice made me pee
my pants.
It takes more to
scare me now.
SKReeee!

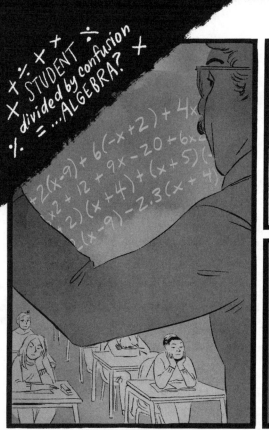

STUDENT
÷ + × ×
÷ divided by confusion
× = ...ALGEBRA? ×

Mr. Stetman
talks about algebra
the way some guys
talk about their cars.

Ask him
"Why algebra?"
and he launches into
a thousand and one
reasons.

Melinda?

• • •

FOR WHAT VALUE OF THE CONSTANT K DOES
QUADRATIC EQUATION $x^2 + 2x = -2k$
HAVE TWO DISTINCT REAL SOLUTIONS

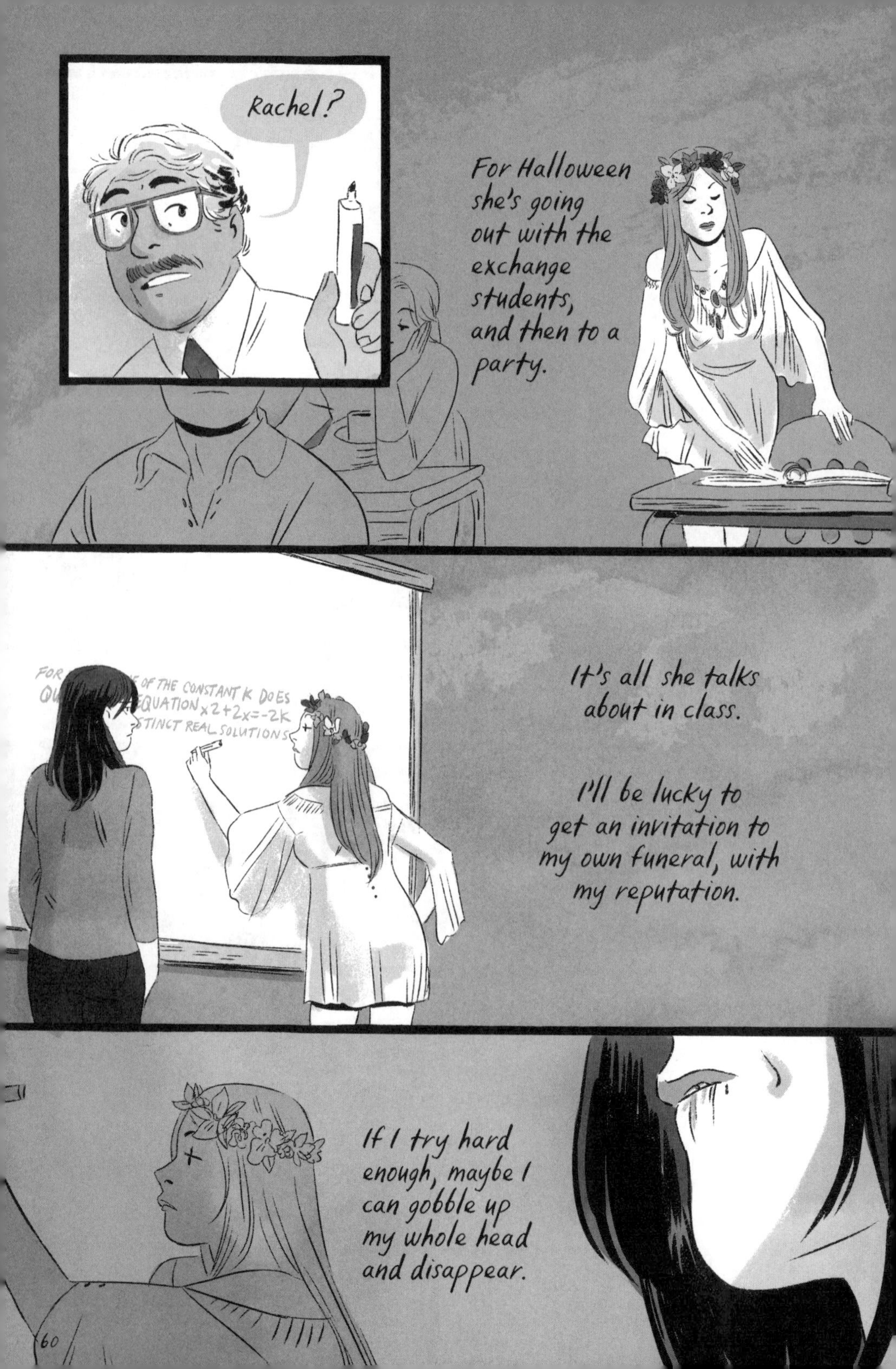
Rachel?
For Halloween she's going out with the exchange students, and then to a party.
FOR
E OF THE CONSTANT K DOES
QU
EQUATION x2+2x=-2K
STINCT REAL SOLUTIONS
It's all she talks about in class.
I'll be lucky to get an invitation to my own funeral, with my reputation.
If I try hard enough, maybe I can gobble up my whole head and disappear.

HALLOWEEN
Why don't you ever see a kid dressed up like a groom on Halloween?
TRICK OR TREAT!
Oooh, what do we have here?

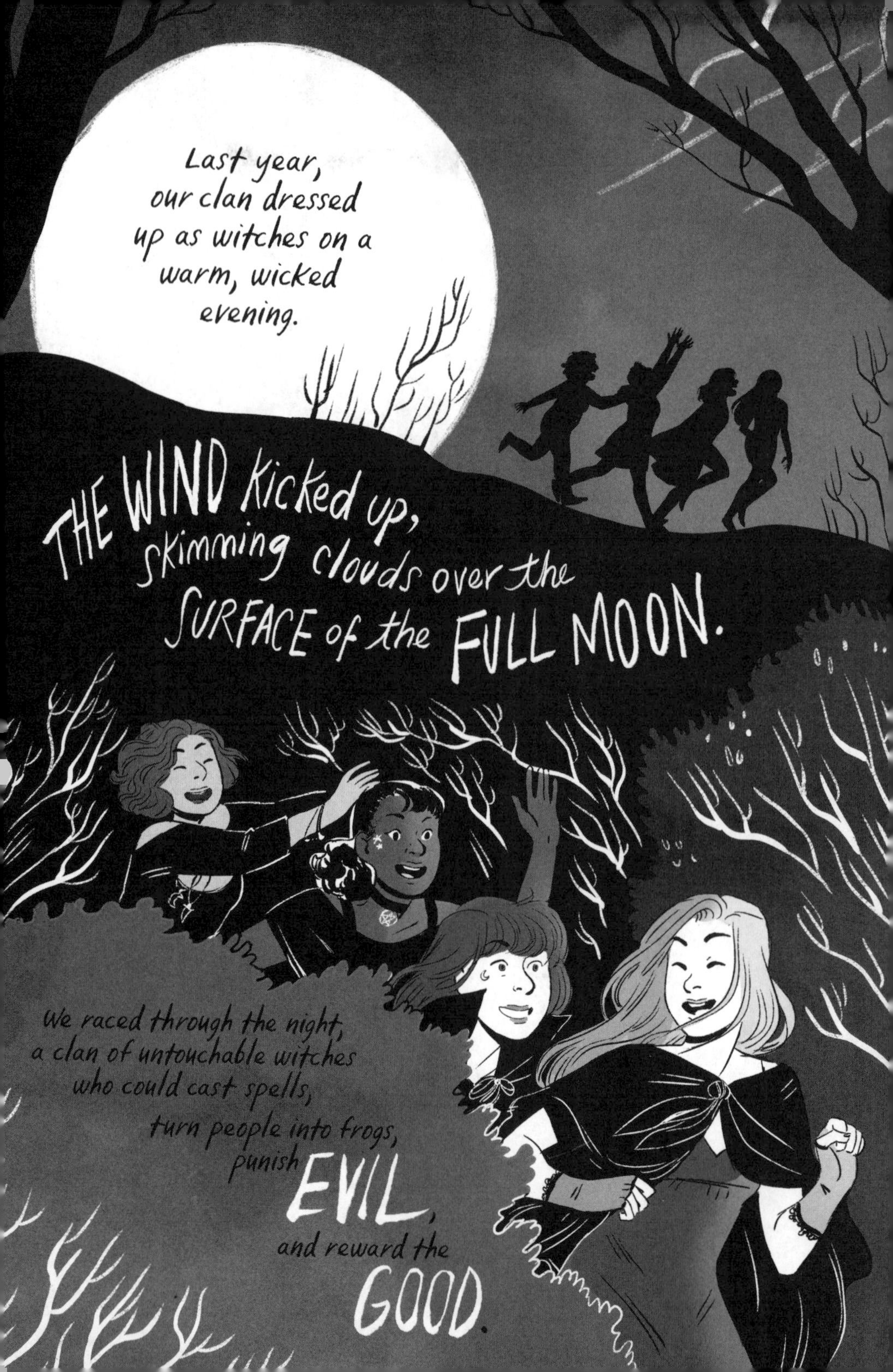
Last year, our clan dressed up as witches on a warm, wicked evening.
THE WIND kicked up, skimming clouds over the SURFACE of the FULL MOON.
We raced through the night, a clan of untouchable witches who could cast spells, turn people into frogs, punish EVIL, and reward the GOOD.

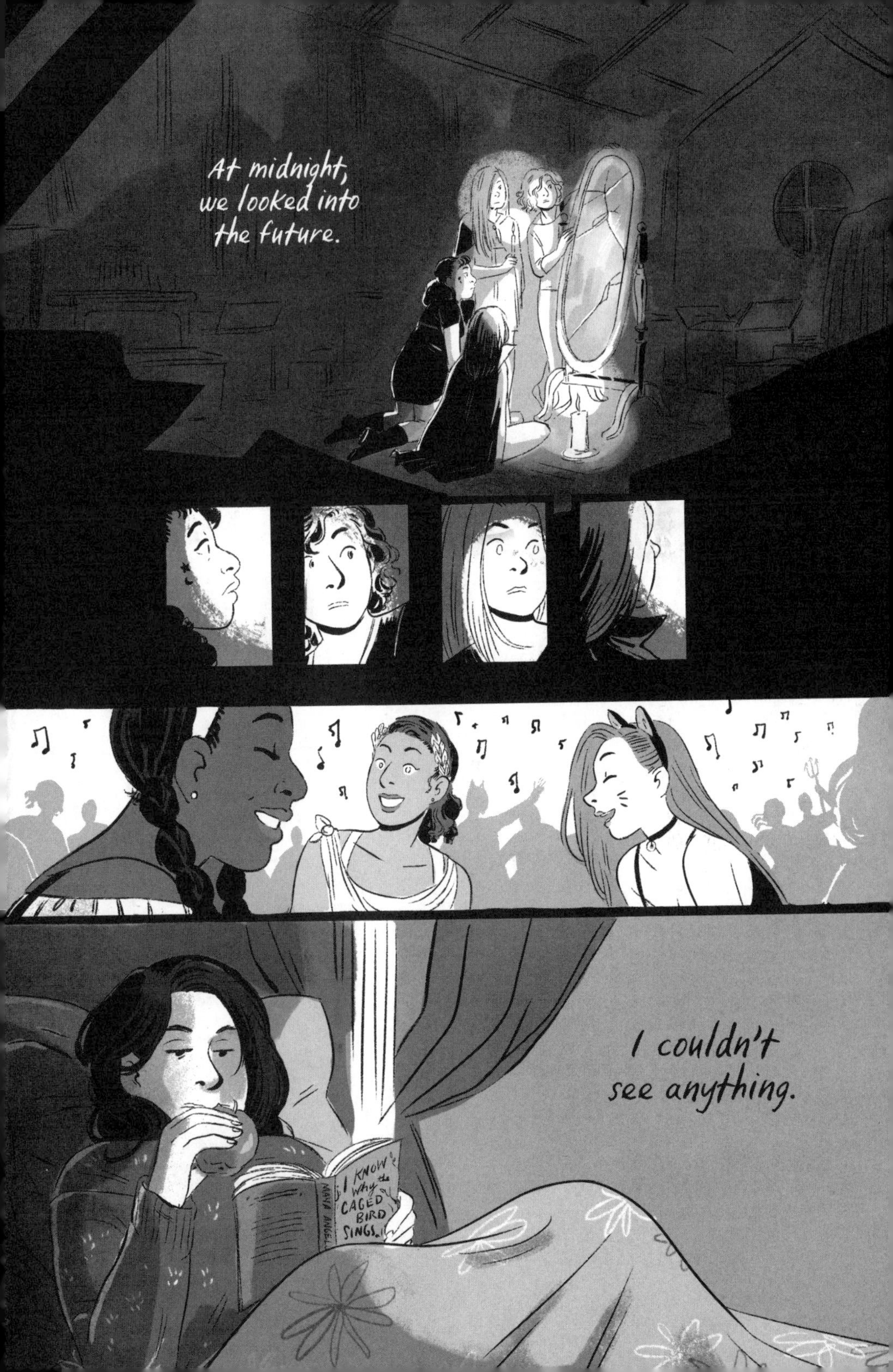
At midnight, we looked into the future.
I KNOW why the CAGED BIRD SINGS
MAYA ANGEL
I couldn't see anything.

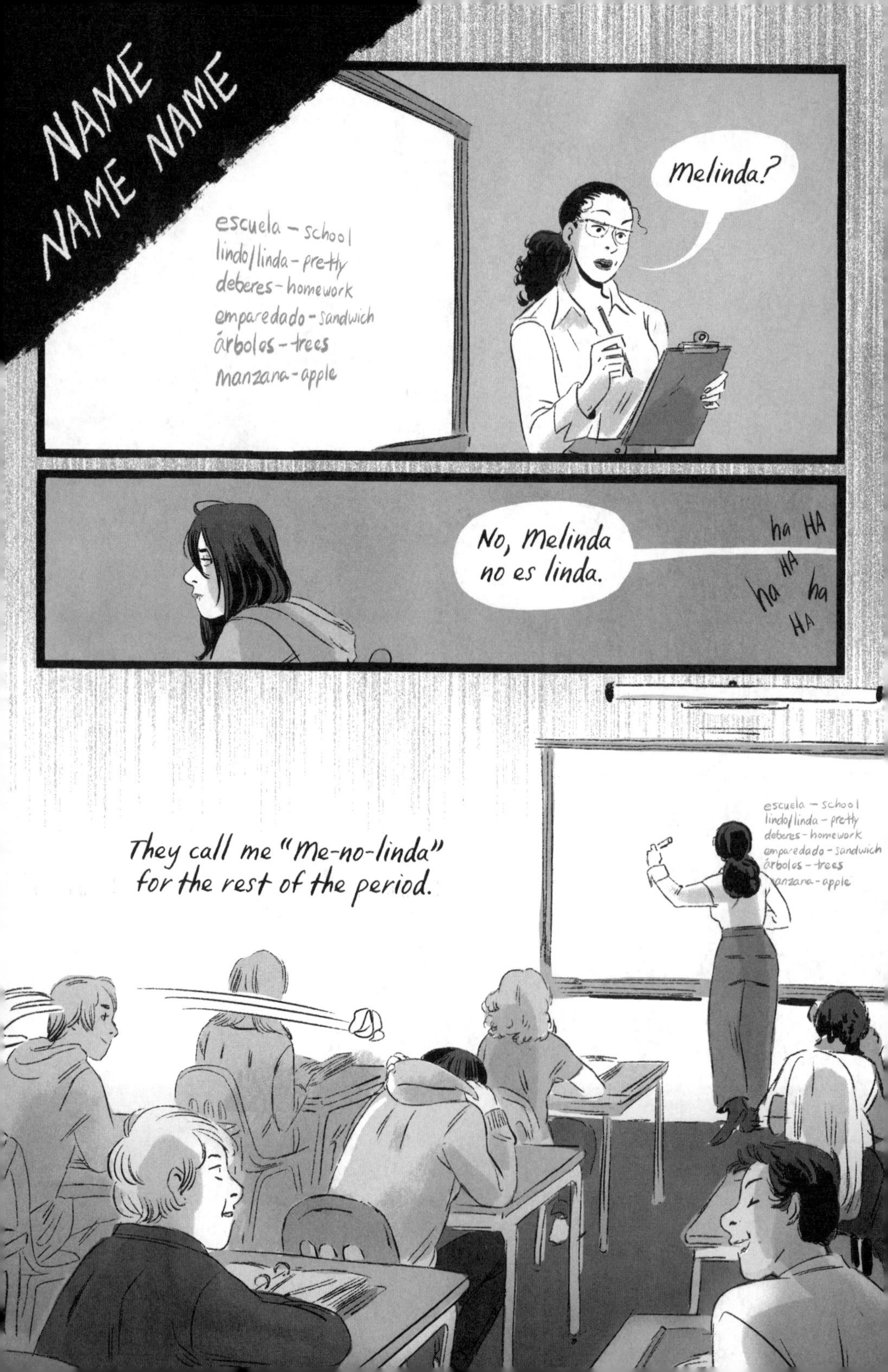
NAME NAME NAME
escuela - school
lindo/linda - pretty
deberes - homework
emparedado - sandwich
árbolos - trees
manzana - apple
Melinda?
No, Melinda no es linda.
ha HA HA ha ha HA
They call me "Me-no-linda" for the rest of the period.

Maybe I was abducted by aliens the night of that party.

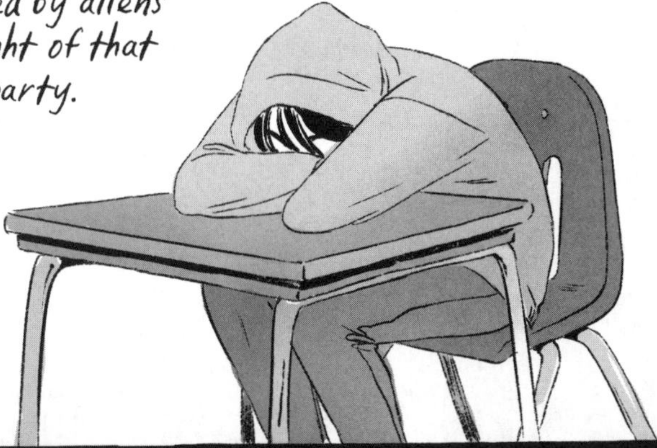

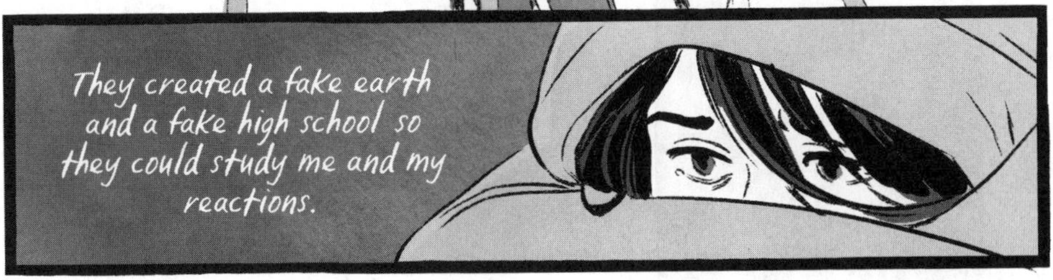
They created a fake earth and a fake high school so they could study me and my reactions.

This theory explains so much, doesn't it?

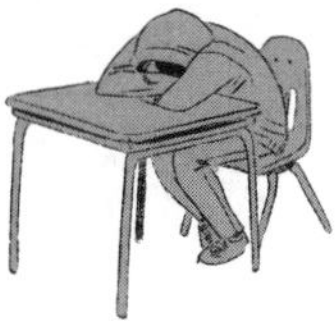

Aliens have a sick sense of humor.

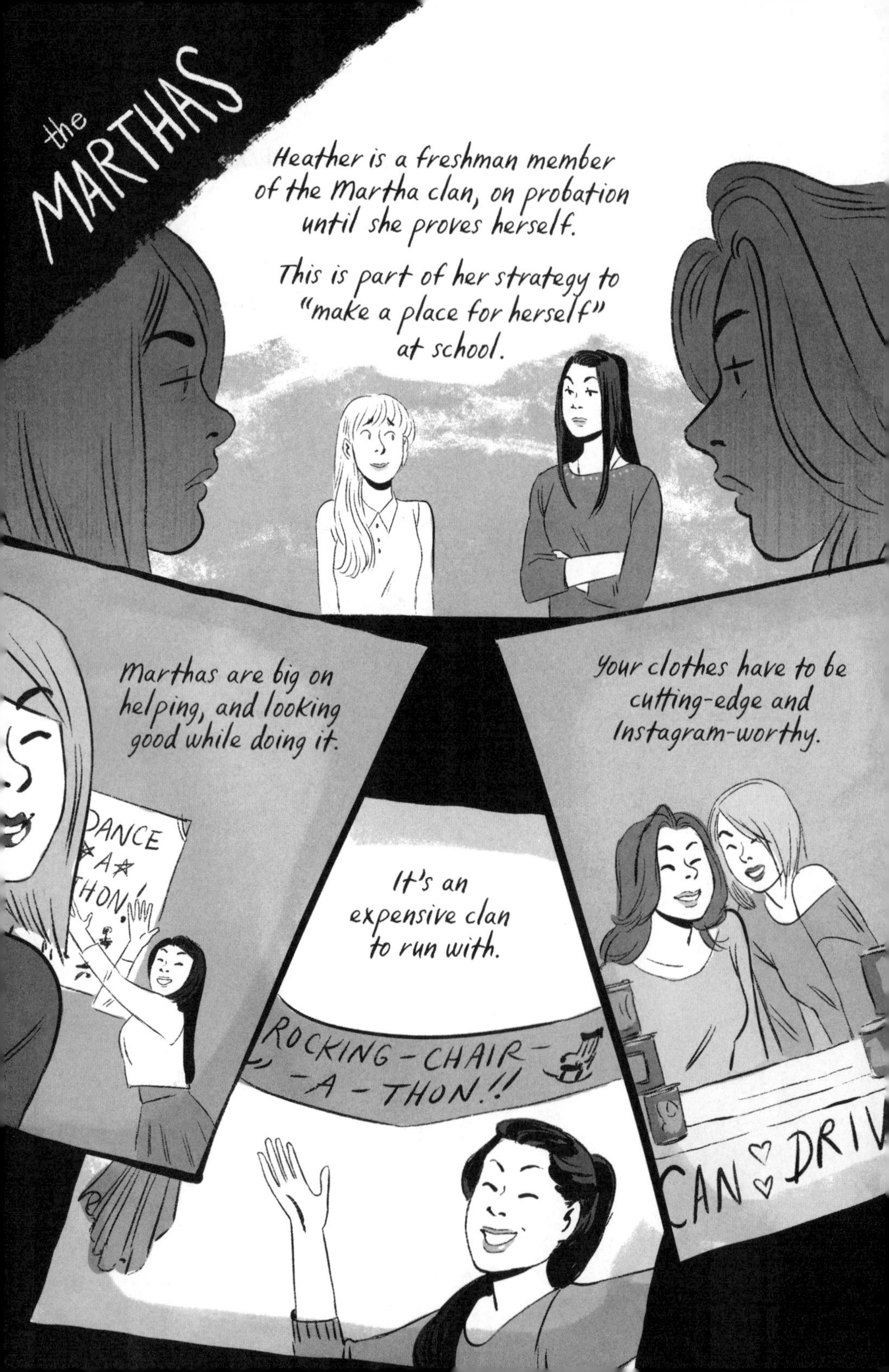
the MARTHAS
Heather is a freshman member of the Martha clan, on probation until she proves herself.
This is part of her strategy to "make a place for herself" at school.
Marthas are big on helping, and looking good while doing it.
DANCE A THON!
Your clothes have to be cutting-edge and Instagram-worthy.
It's an expensive clan to run with.
ROCKING-CHAIR-A-THON!!
CAN DRIV

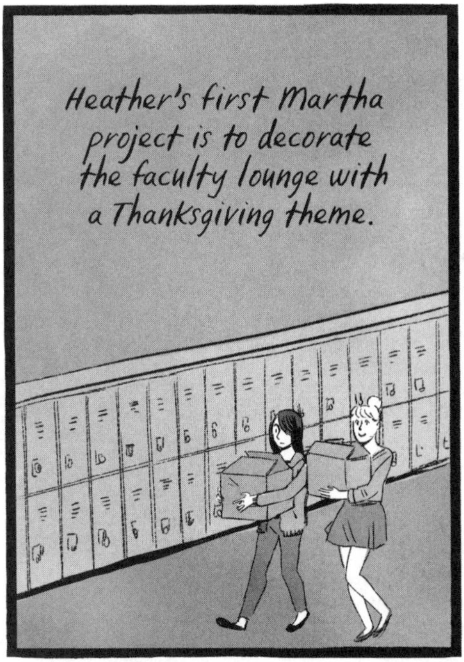
Heather's first Martha project is to decorate the faculty lounge with a Thanksgiving theme.

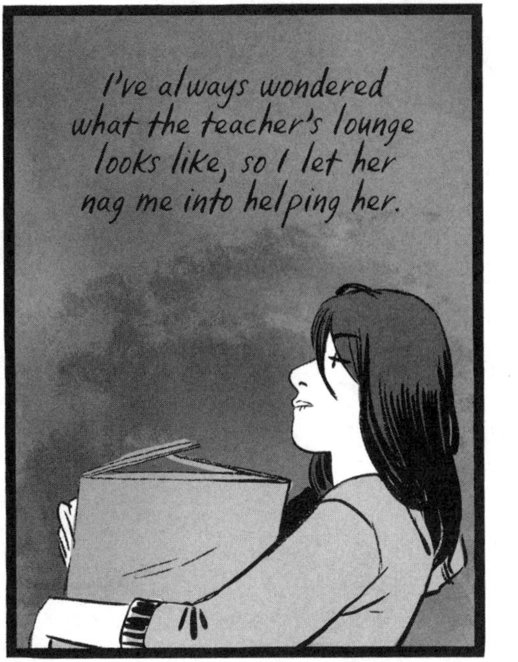
I've always wondered what the teacher's lounge looks like, so I let her nag me into helping her.

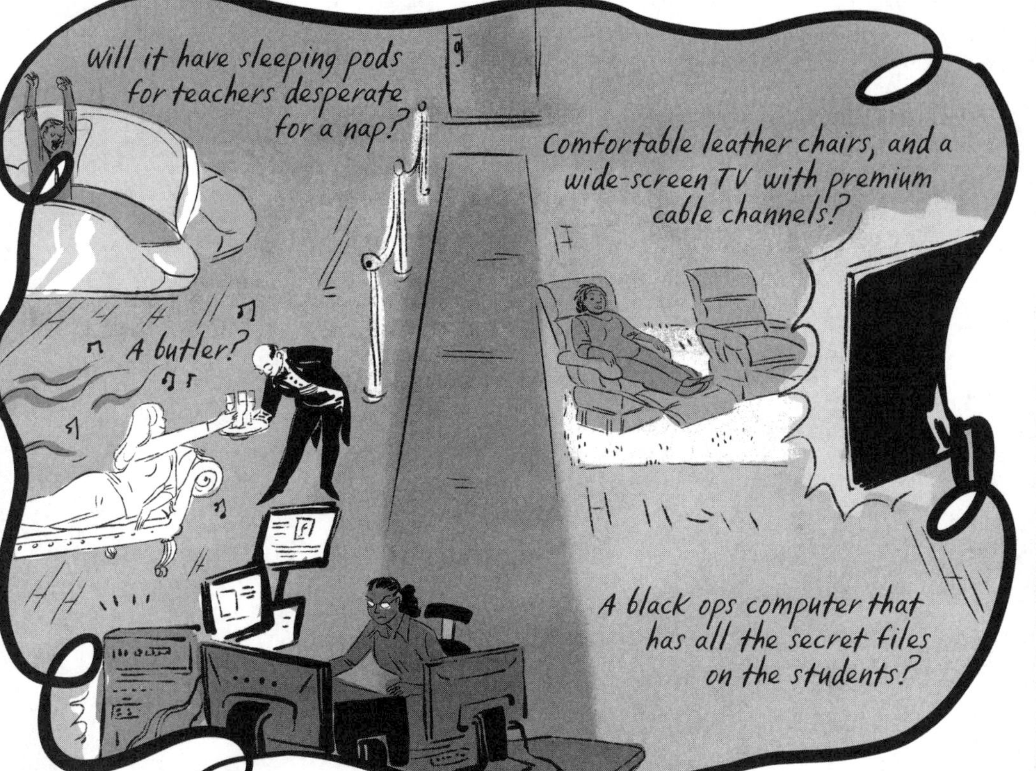
Will it have sleeping pods for teachers desperate for a nap?
Comfortable leather chairs, and a wide-screen TV with premium cable channels?
A butler?
A black ops computer that has all the secret files on the students?

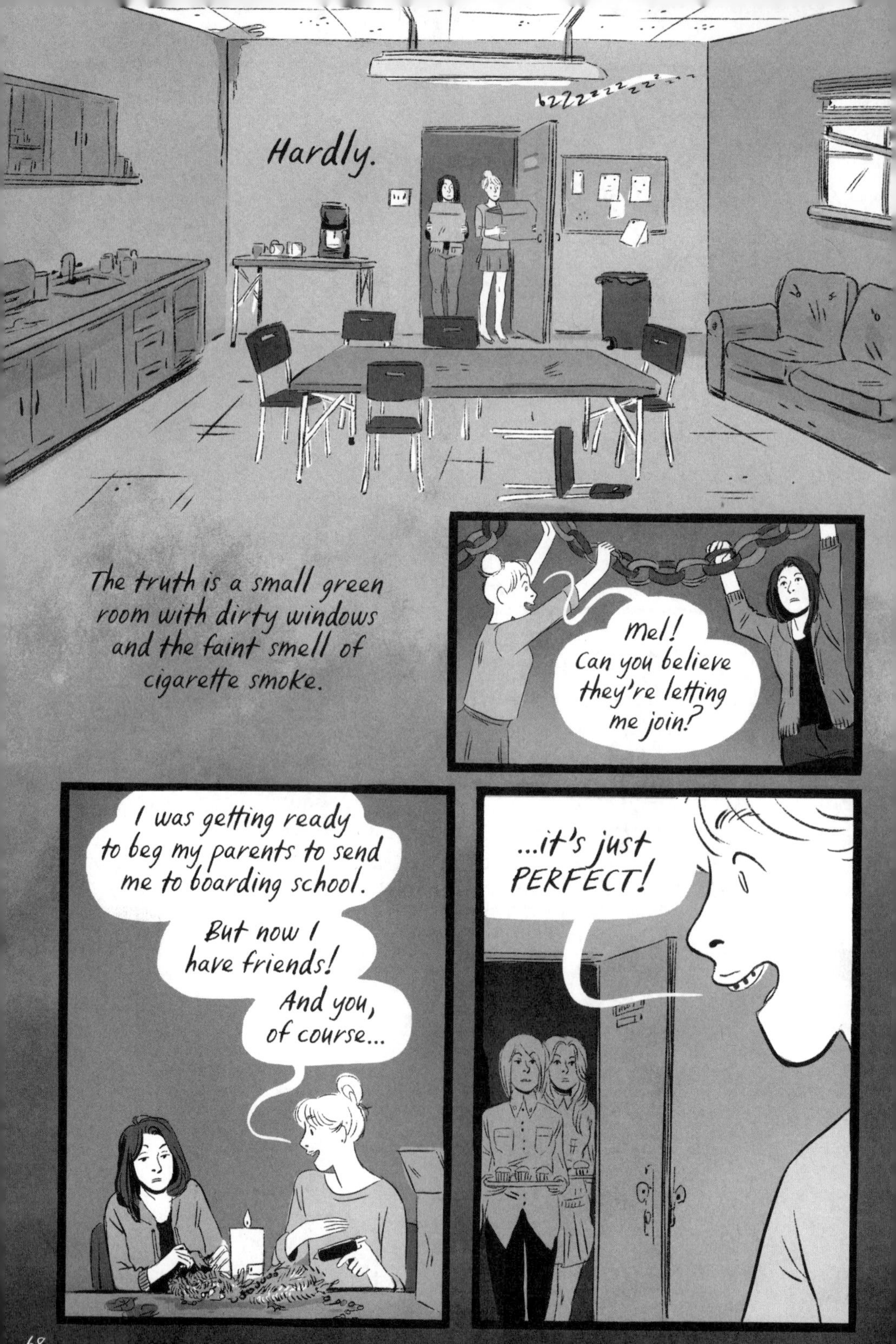
Hardly.
bzzzzzzzzz
The truth is a small green room with dirty windows and the faint smell of cigarette smoke.
Mel! Can you believe they're letting me join?
I was getting ready to beg my parents to send me to boarding school.
But now I have friends!
And you, of course...
...it's just PERFECT!

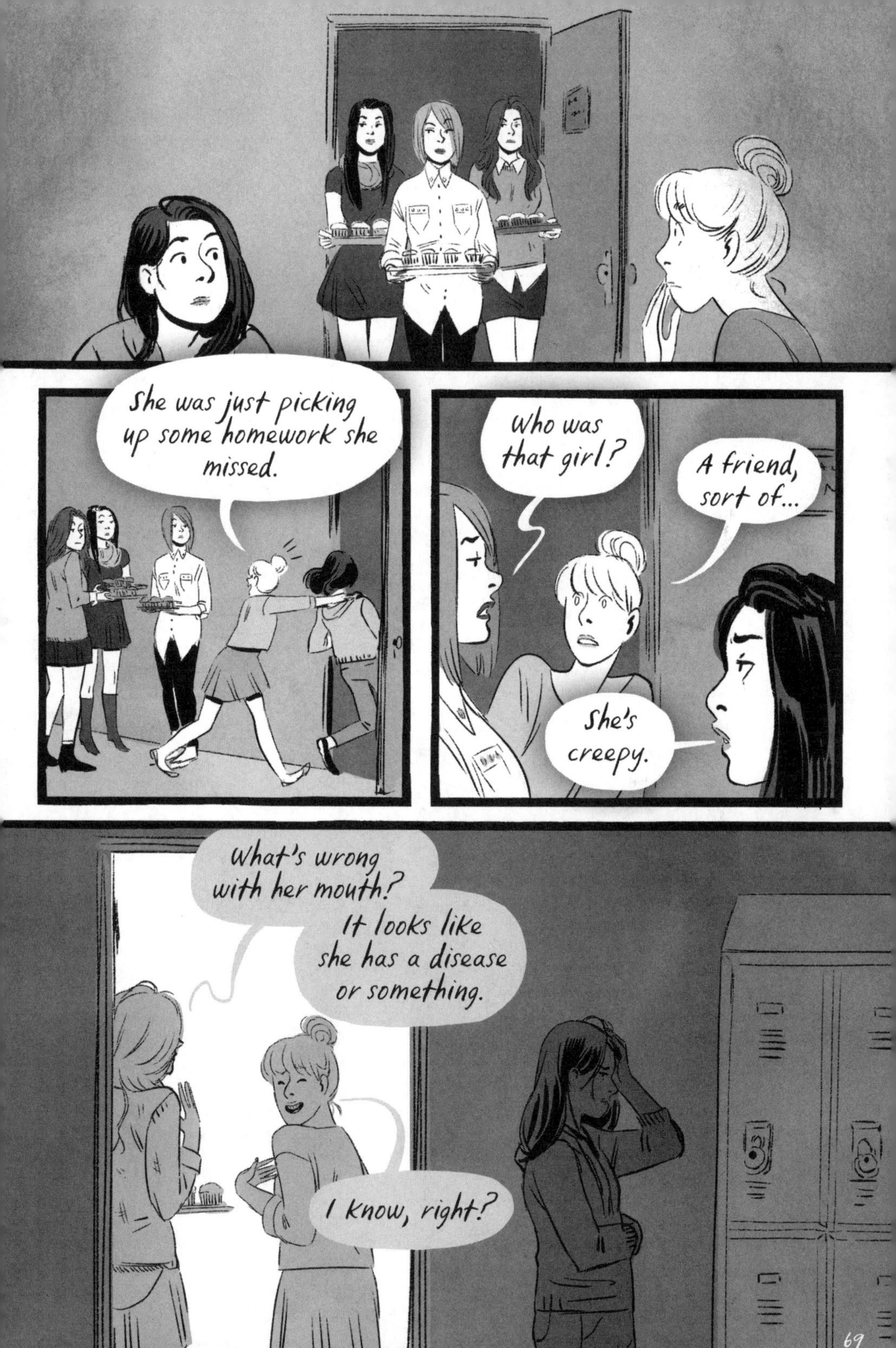
She was just picking up some homework she missed.
Who was that girl?
A friend, sort of...
She's creepy.
What's wrong with her mouth?
It looks like she has a disease or something.
I know, right?

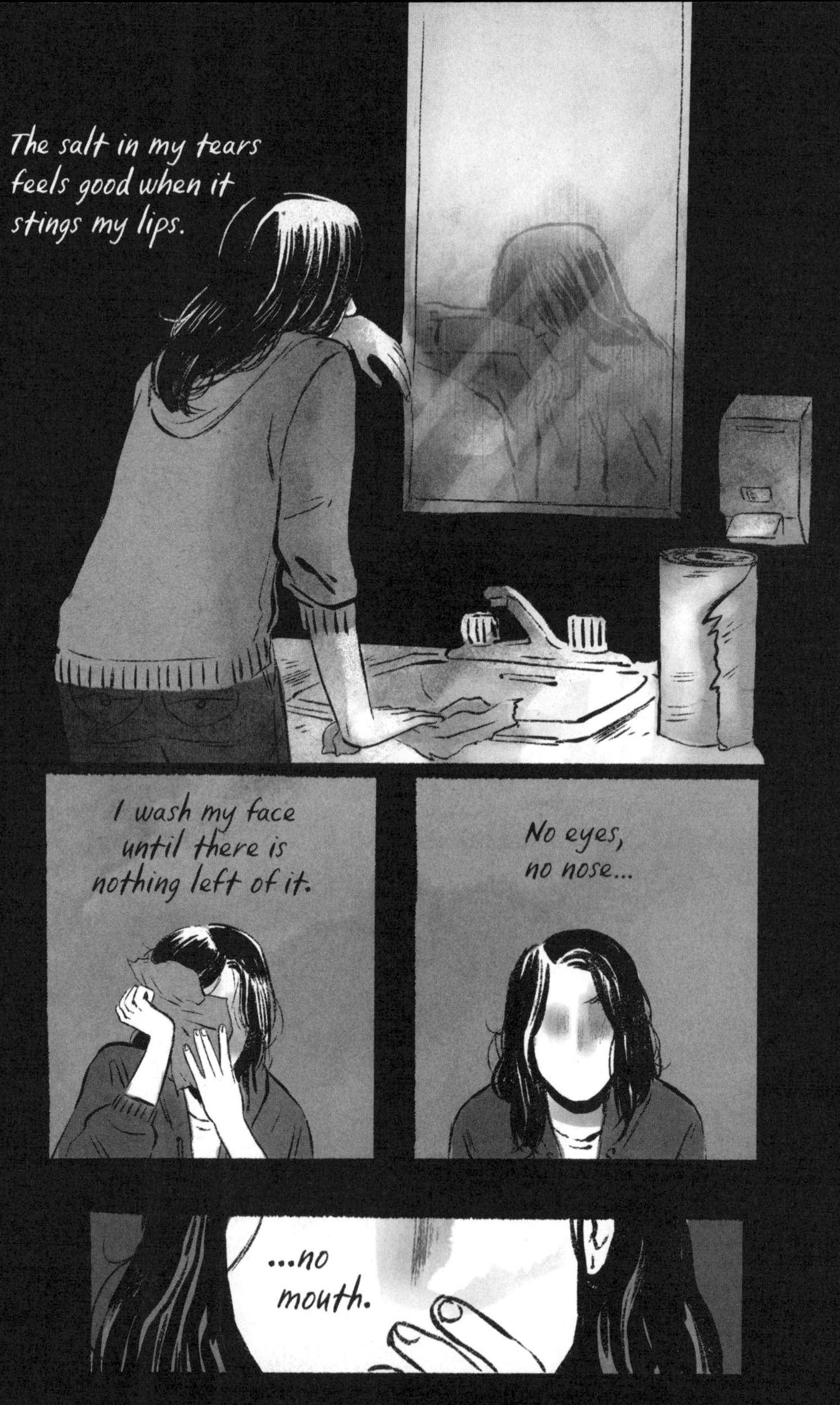
The salt in my tears feels good when it stings my lips.
I wash my face until there is nothing left of it.
No eyes, no nose...
...no mouth.

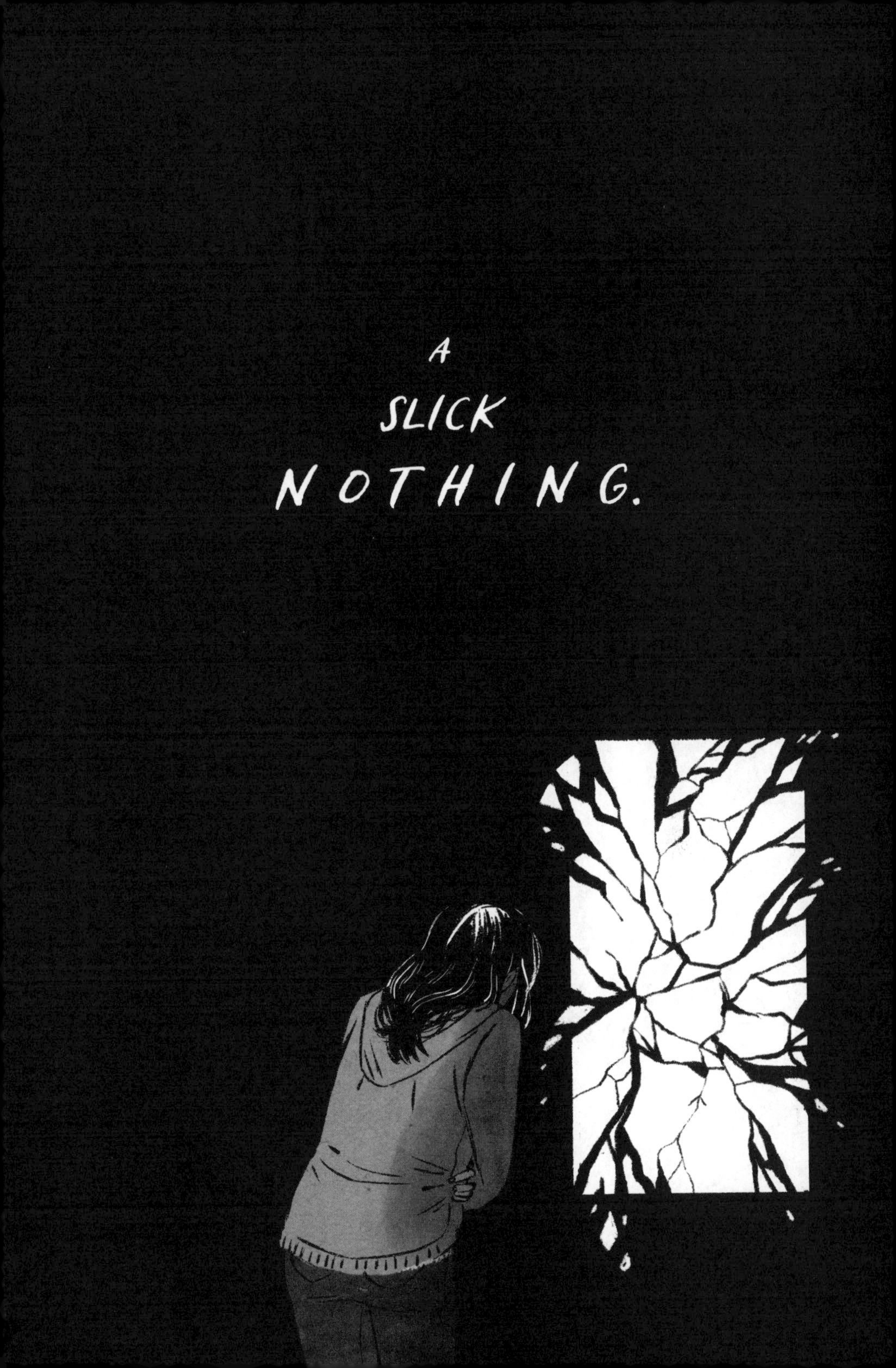
A
SLICK
NOTHING.

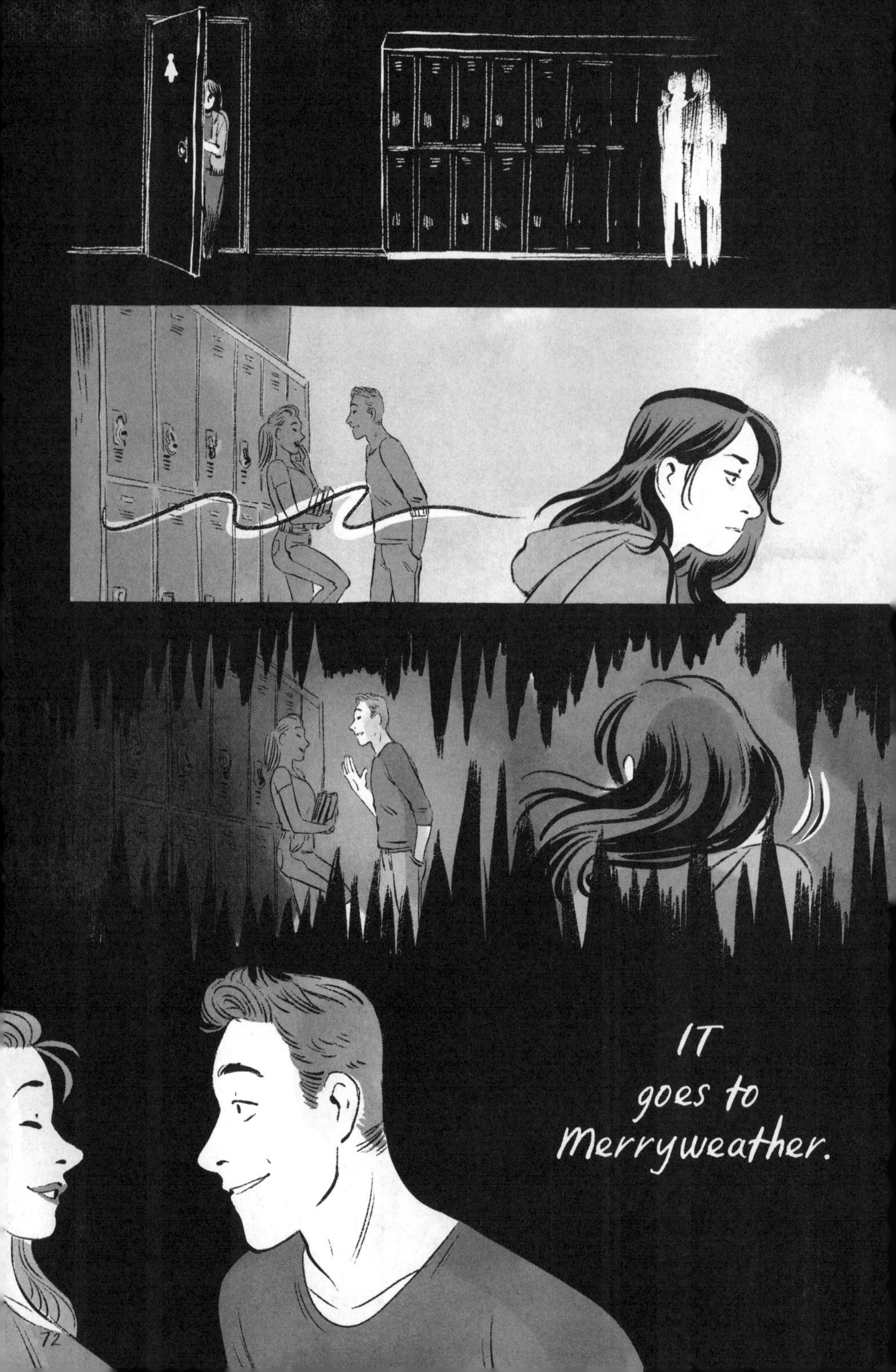
IT goes to Merryweather.

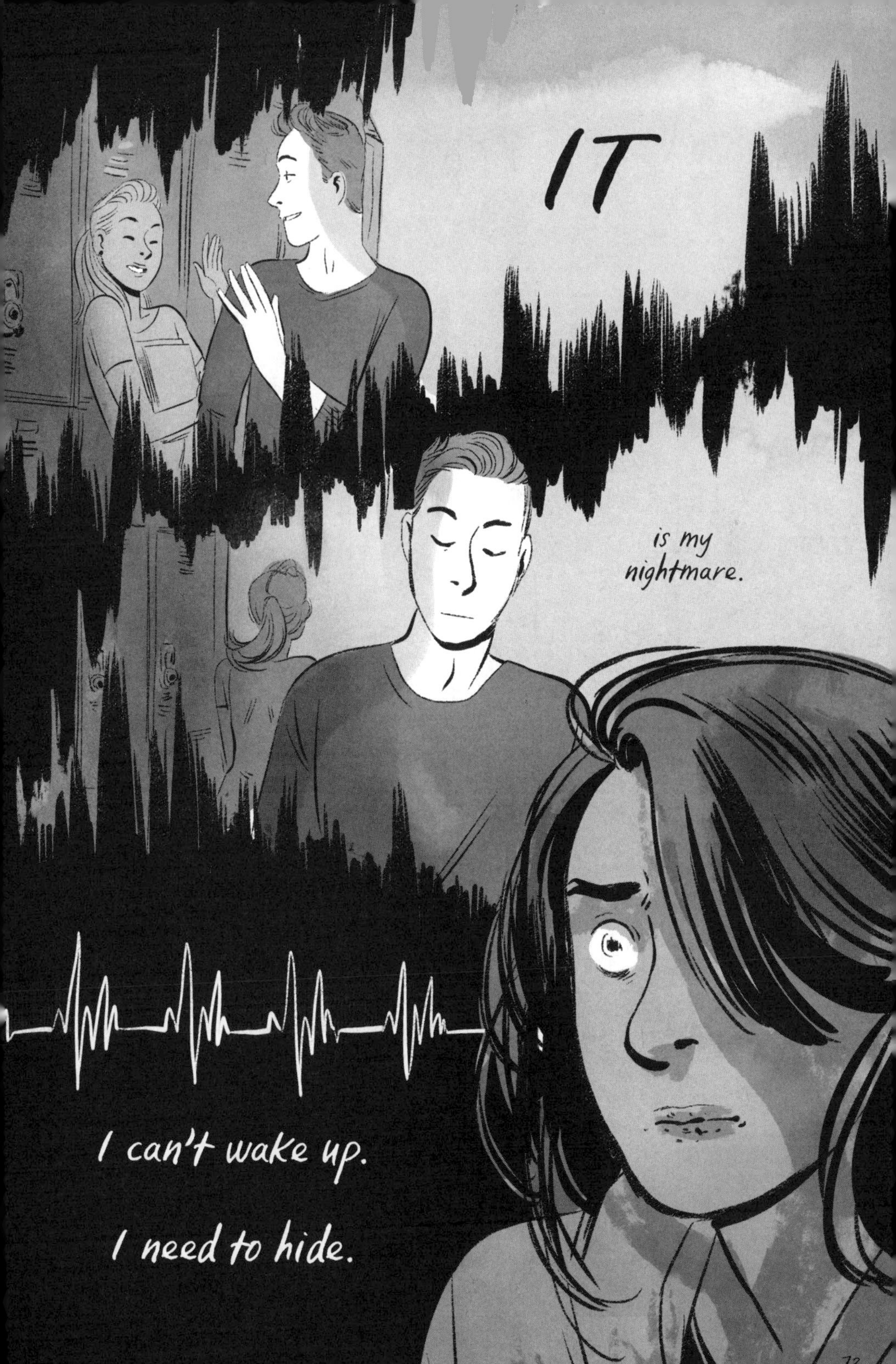
IT
is my nightmare.
I can't wake up.
I need to hide.

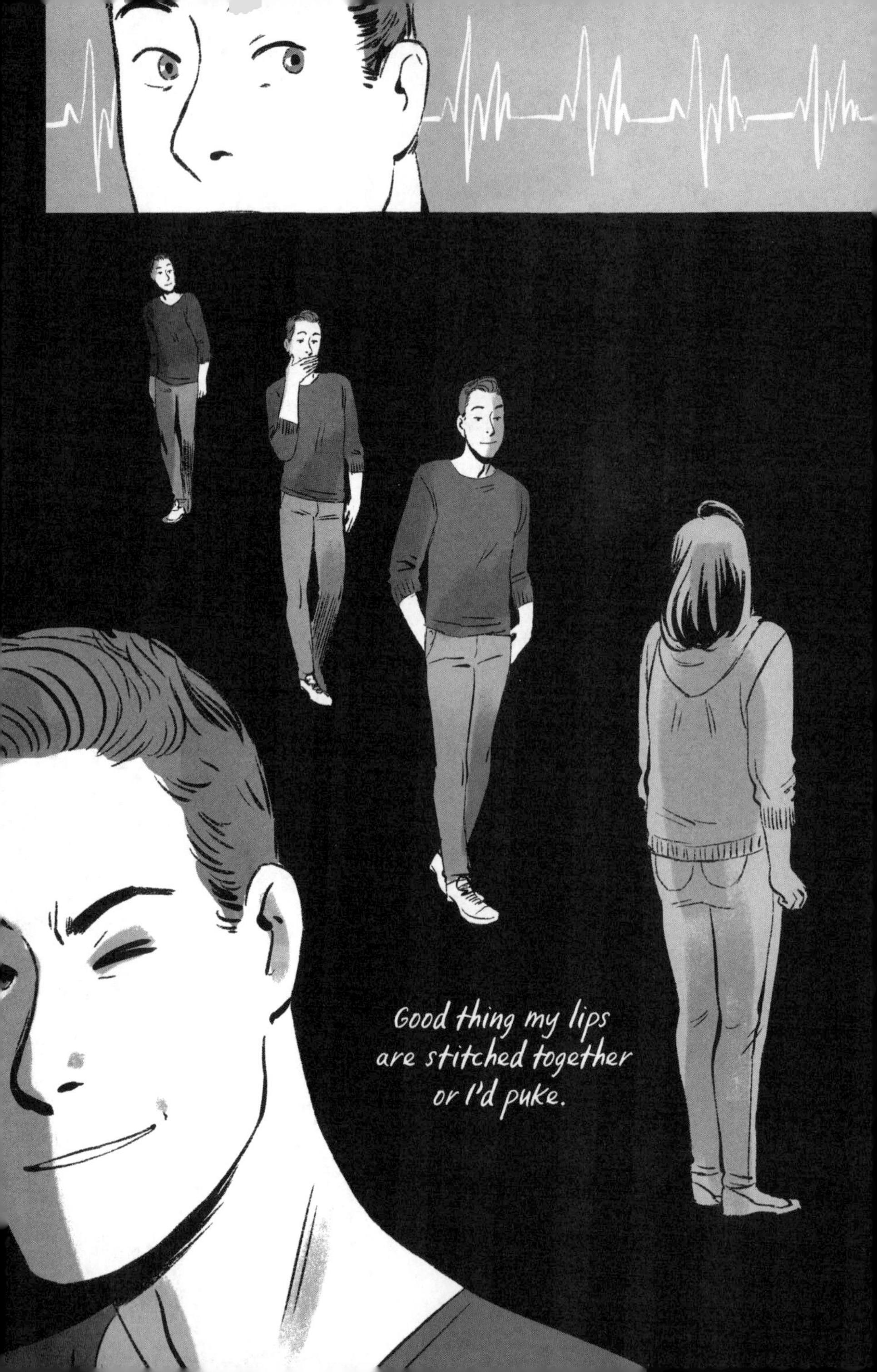
Good thing my lips are stitched together or I'd puke.

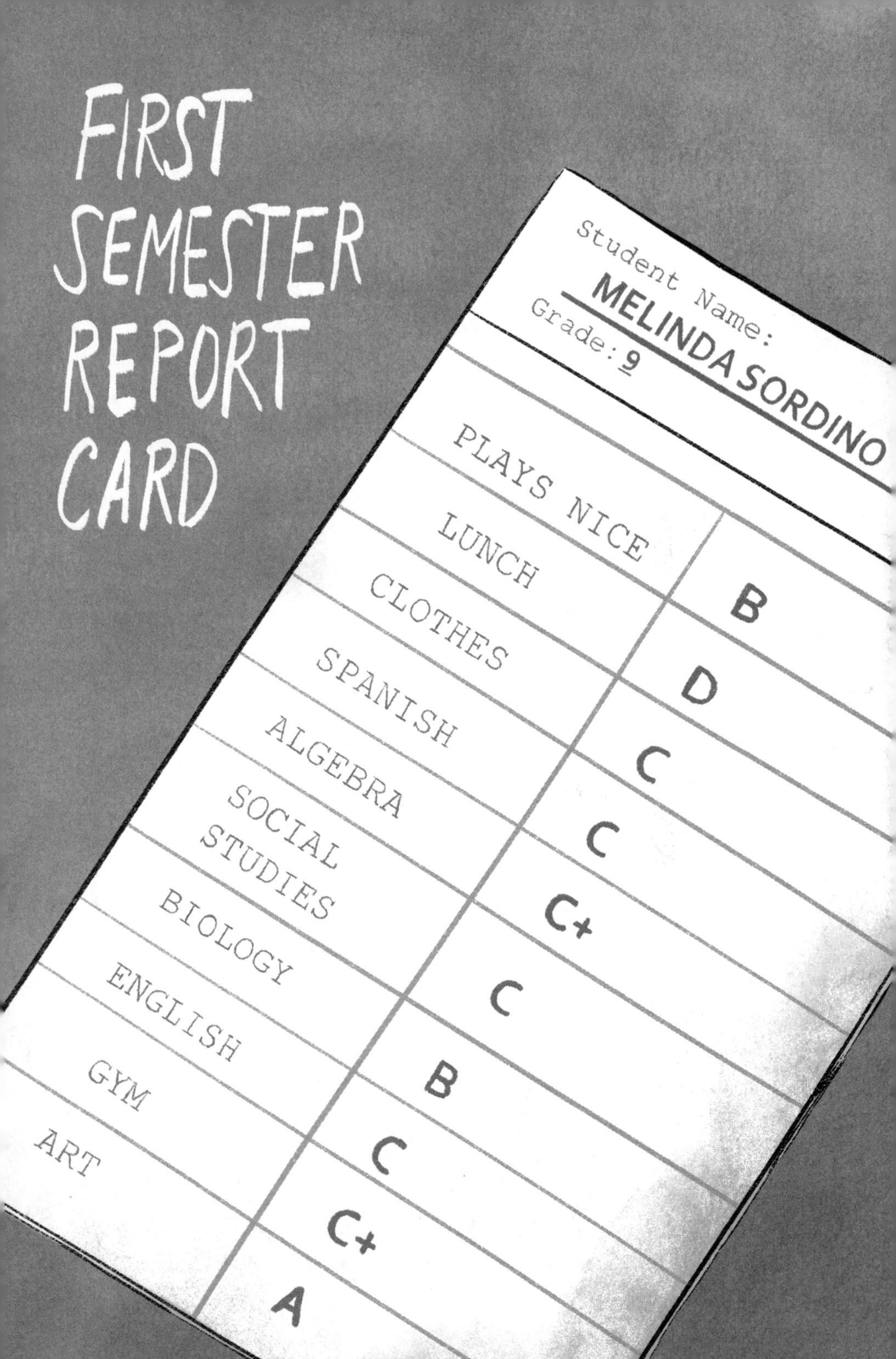
FIRST SEMESTER REPORT CARD
Student Name:
MELINDA SORDINO
Grade: 9
PLAYS NICE B
LUNCH D
CLOTHES C
SPANISH C
ALGEBRA C+
SOCIAL STUDIES C
BIOLOGY B
ENGLISH C
GYM C+
ART A

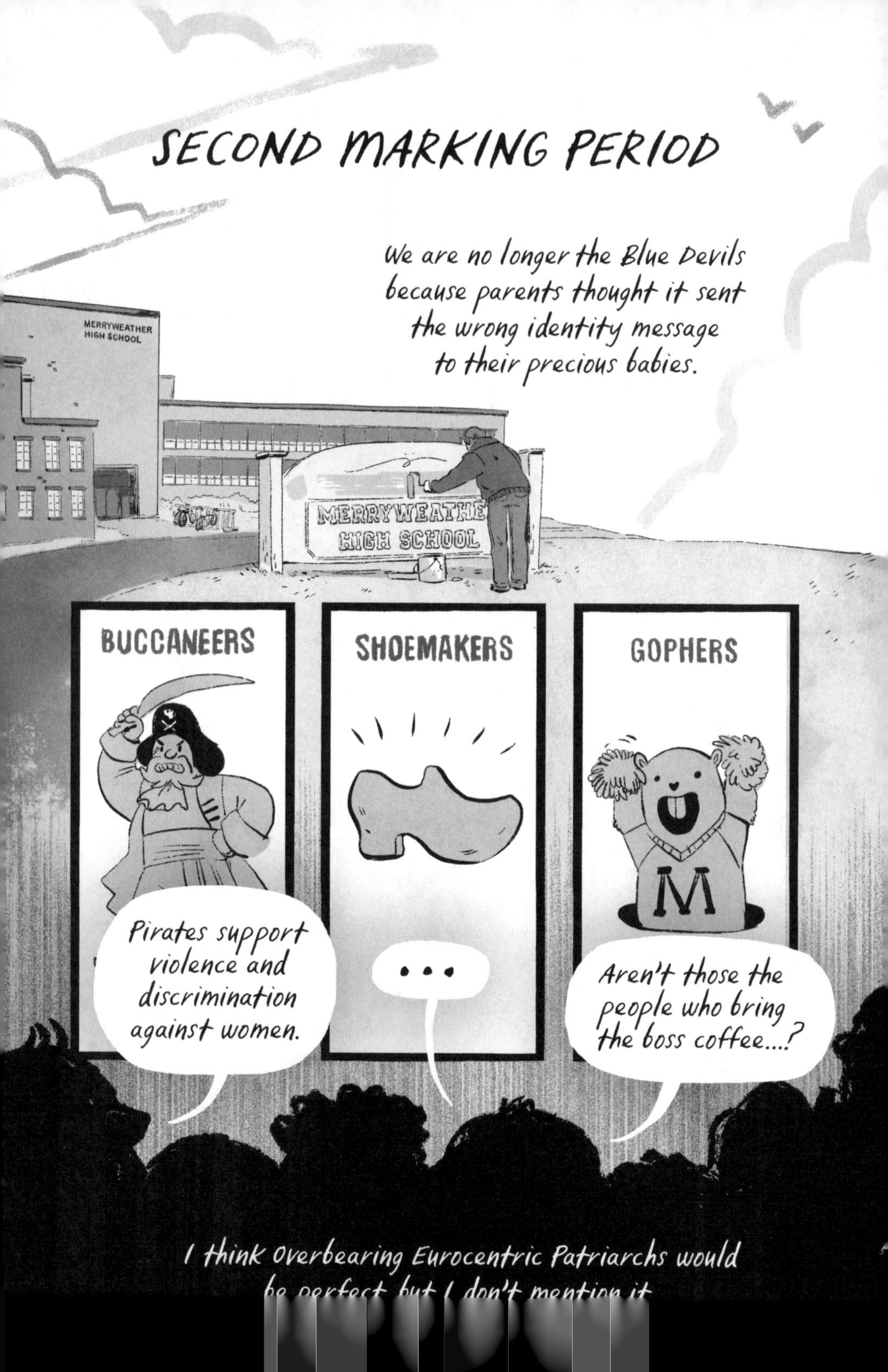
SECOND MARKING PERIOD
We are no longer the Blue Devils because parents thought it sent the wrong identity message to their precious babies.
MERRYWEATHER HIGH SCHOOL
BUCCANEERS
SHOEMAKERS
GOPHERS
M
Pirates support violence and discrimination against women.
...
Aren't those the people who bring the boss coffee...?
I think Overbearing Eurocentric Patriarchs would
[redacted]

VOTE FOR A NEW MASCOT!

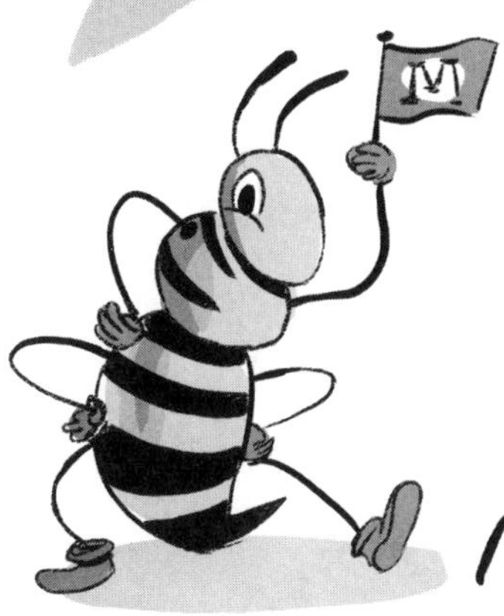

M

BEES!

Useful to agriculture,
painful to cross.

ICEBERGS!

In honor of our
festive winter weather.

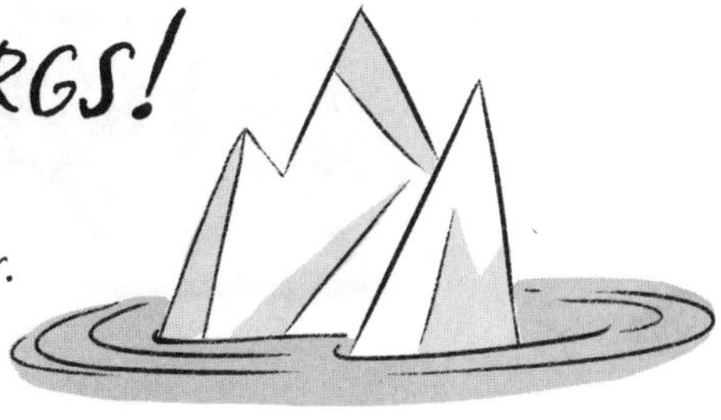

HILLTOPPERS!

Because our school
is on a hill.

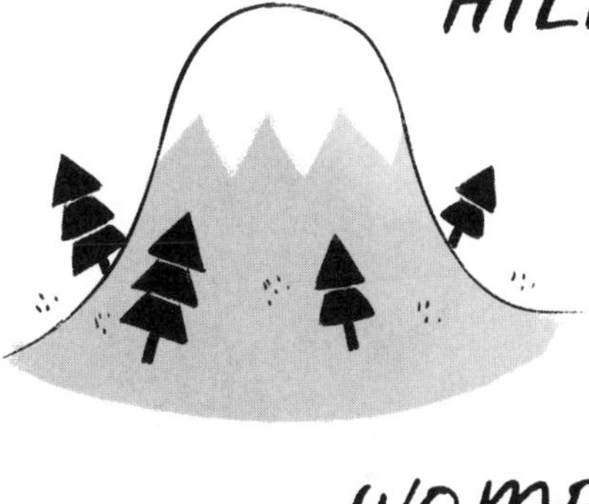

WOMBATS!

...because no one knows
what they are.

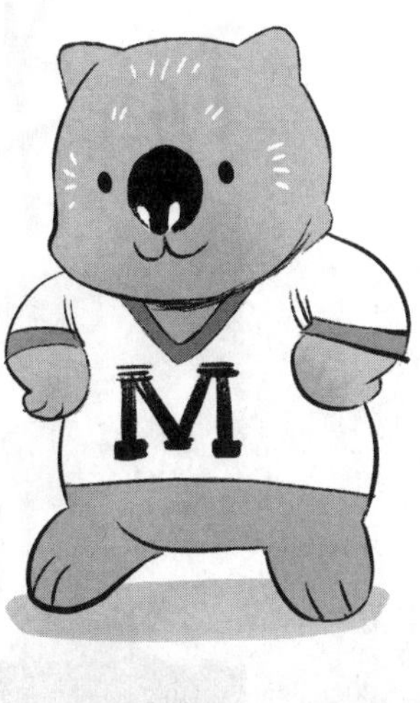

M

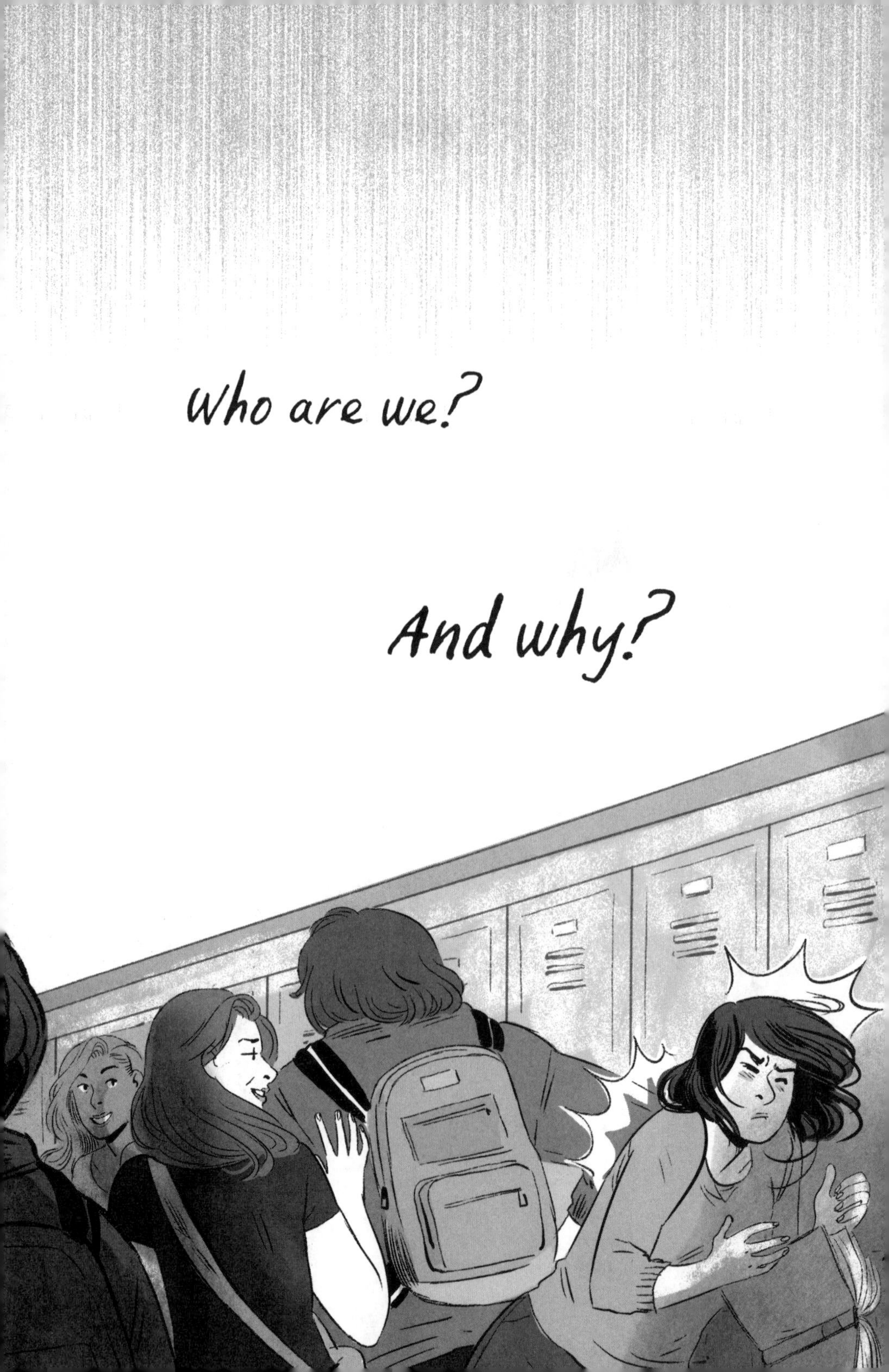
Who are we?
And why?

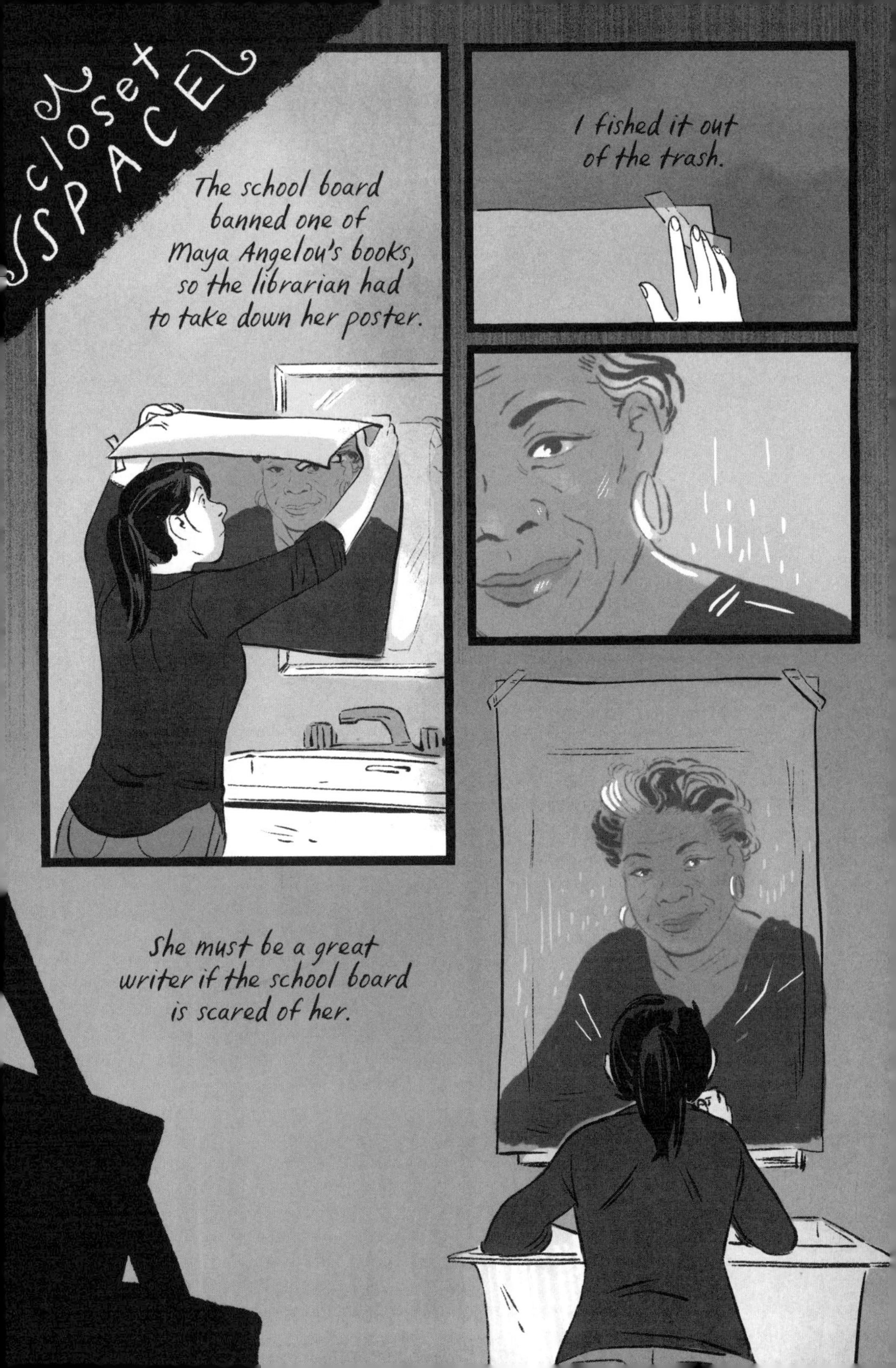
closet SPACE
The school board banned one of Maya Angelou's books, so the librarian had to take down her poster.
I fished it out of the trash.
She must be a great writer if the school board is scared of her.

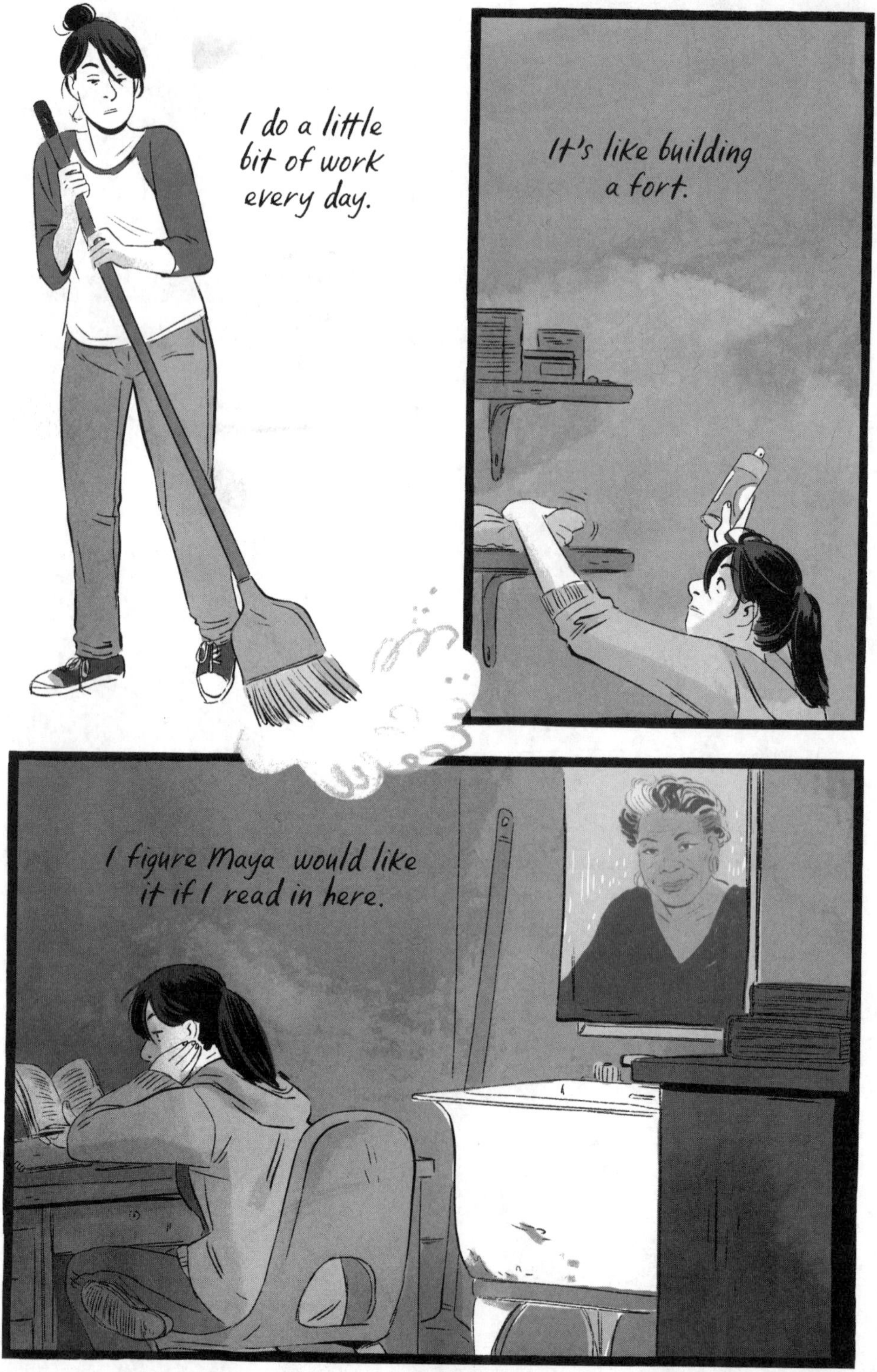

I do a little bit of work every day.
It's like building a fort.
I figure Maya would like it if I read in here.

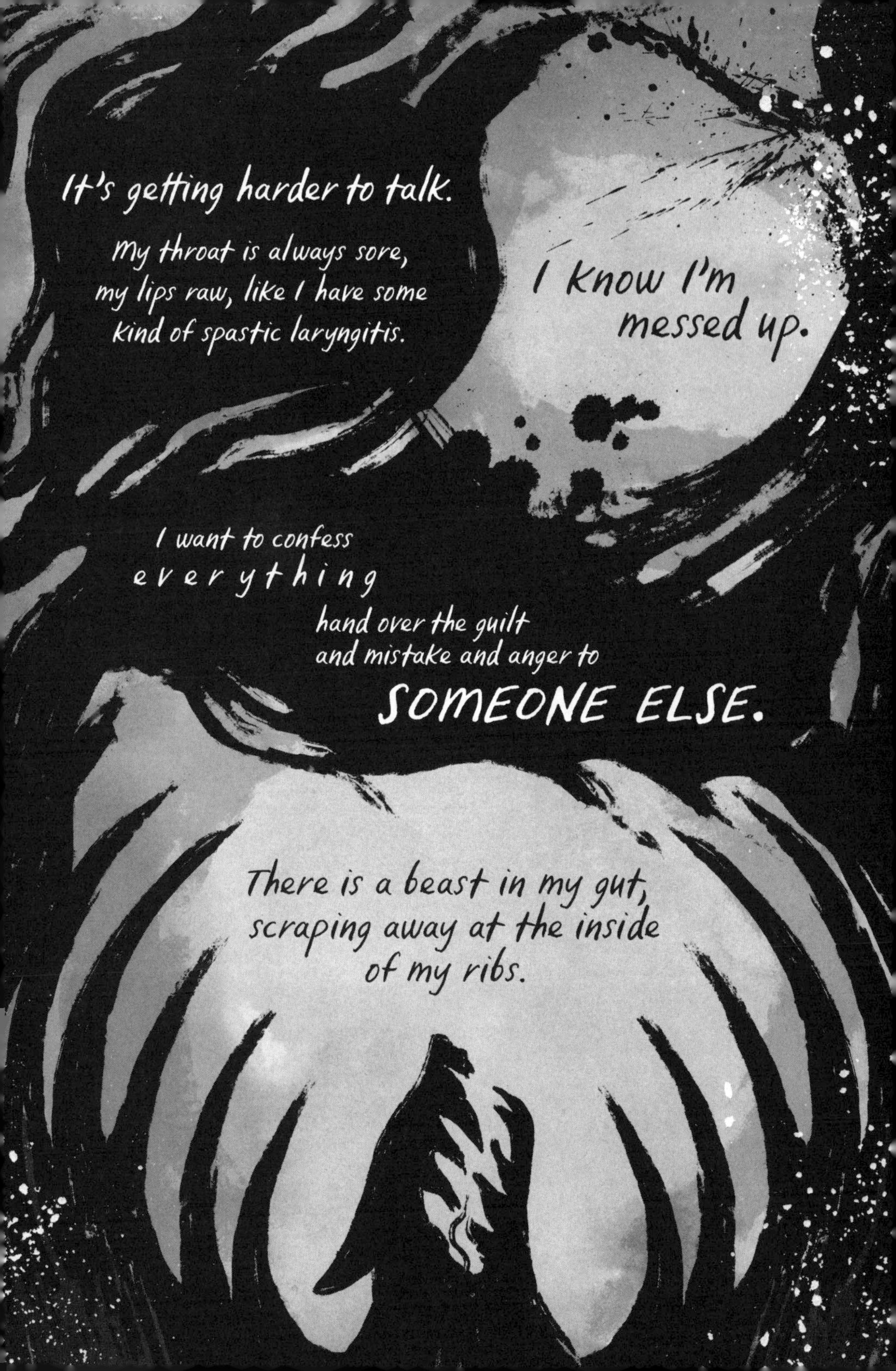
It's getting harder to talk.
My throat is always sore, my lips raw, like I have some kind of spastic laryngitis.
I know I'm messed up.
I want to confess e v e r y t h i n g
hand over the guilt and mistake and anger to
SOMEONE ELSE.
There is a beast in my gut, scraping away at the inside of my ribs.

Even if I dump the memory,
it will stay with me,
staining me.

My closet is a good thing,
a quiet place that helps me
hold all these thoughts inside
my head where no one
can hear them.

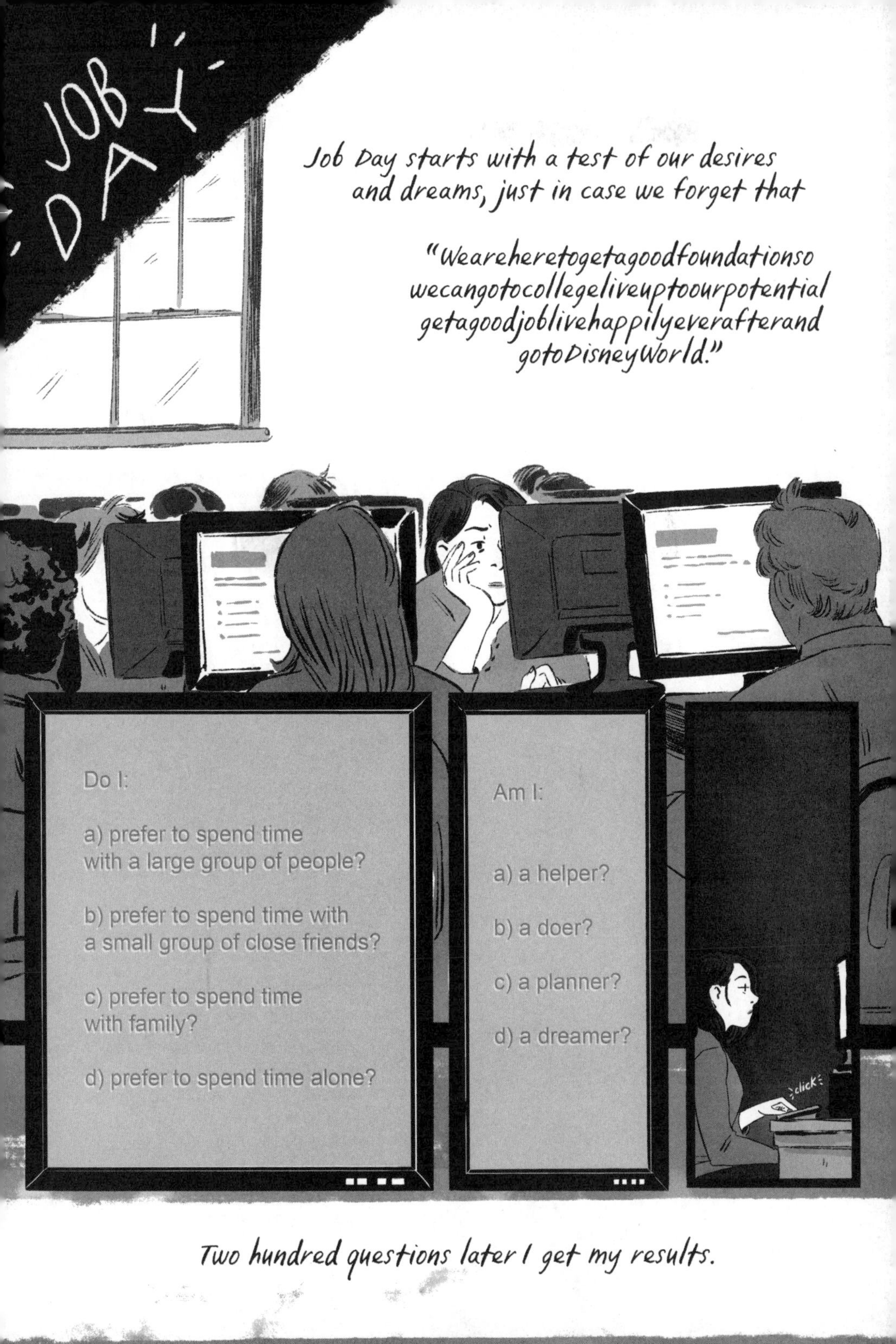
JOB DAY
Job Day starts with a test of our desires and dreams, just in case we forget that
"Weareheretogetagoodfoundationso wecangotocollegeliveuptoourpotential getagoodjoblivehappilyeverafterand gotoDisneyWorld."
Do I:
a) prefer to spend time with a large group of people?
b) prefer to spend time with a small group of close friends?
c) prefer to spend time with family?
d) prefer to spend time alone?
Am I:
a) a helper?
b) a doer?
c) a planner?
d) a dreamer?
click
Two hundred questions later I get my results.

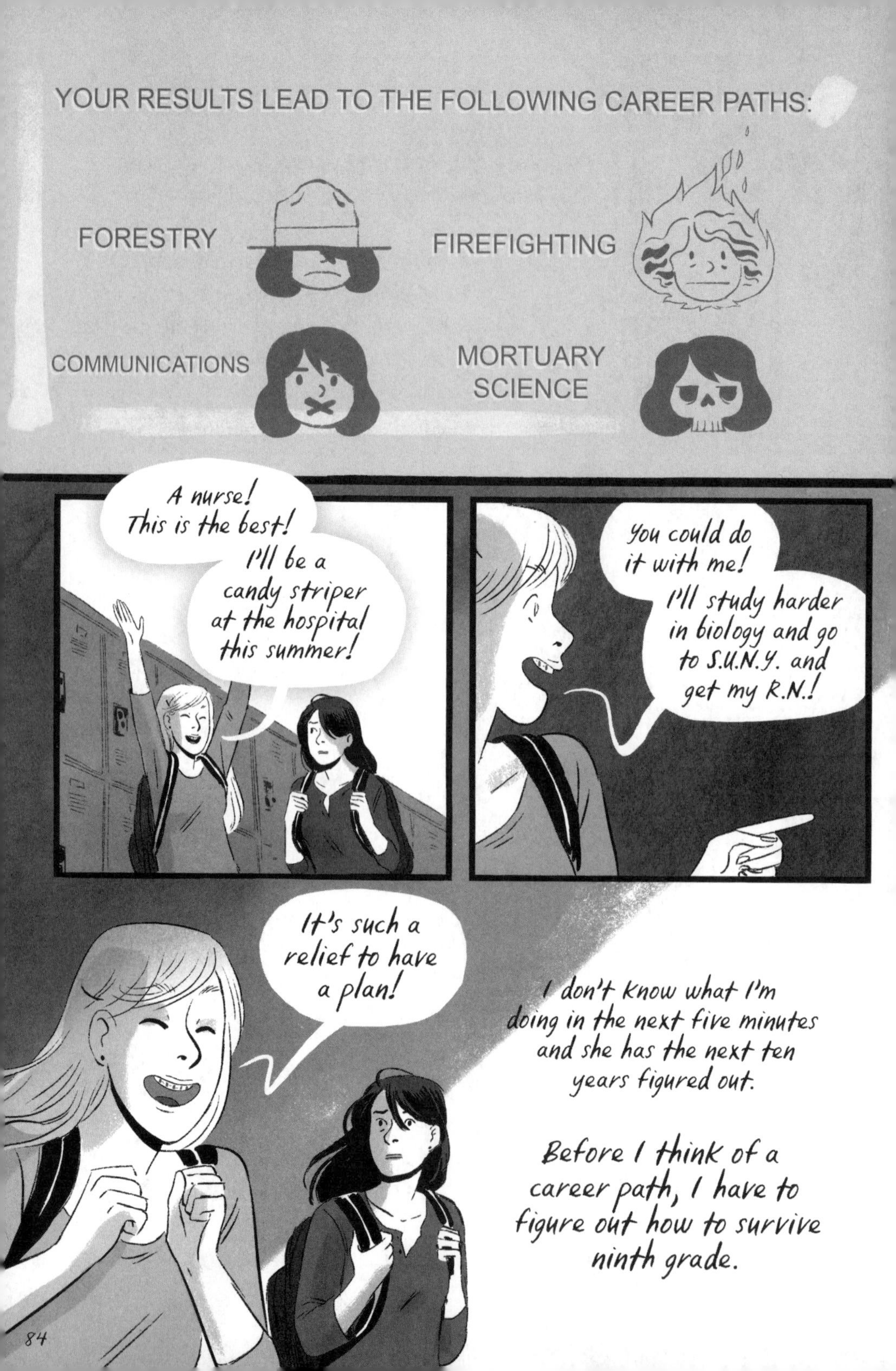
YOUR RESULTS LEAD TO THE FOLLOWING CAREER PATHS:
FORESTRY
FIREFIGHTING
COMMUNICATIONS
MORTUARY SCIENCE
A nurse! This is the best!
I'll be a candy striper at the hospital this summer!
You could do it with me!
I'll study harder in biology and go to S.U.N.Y. and get my R.N.!
It's such a relief to have a plan!
I don't know what I'm doing in the next five minutes and she has the next ten years figured out.
Before I think of a career path, I have to figure out how to survive ninth grade.

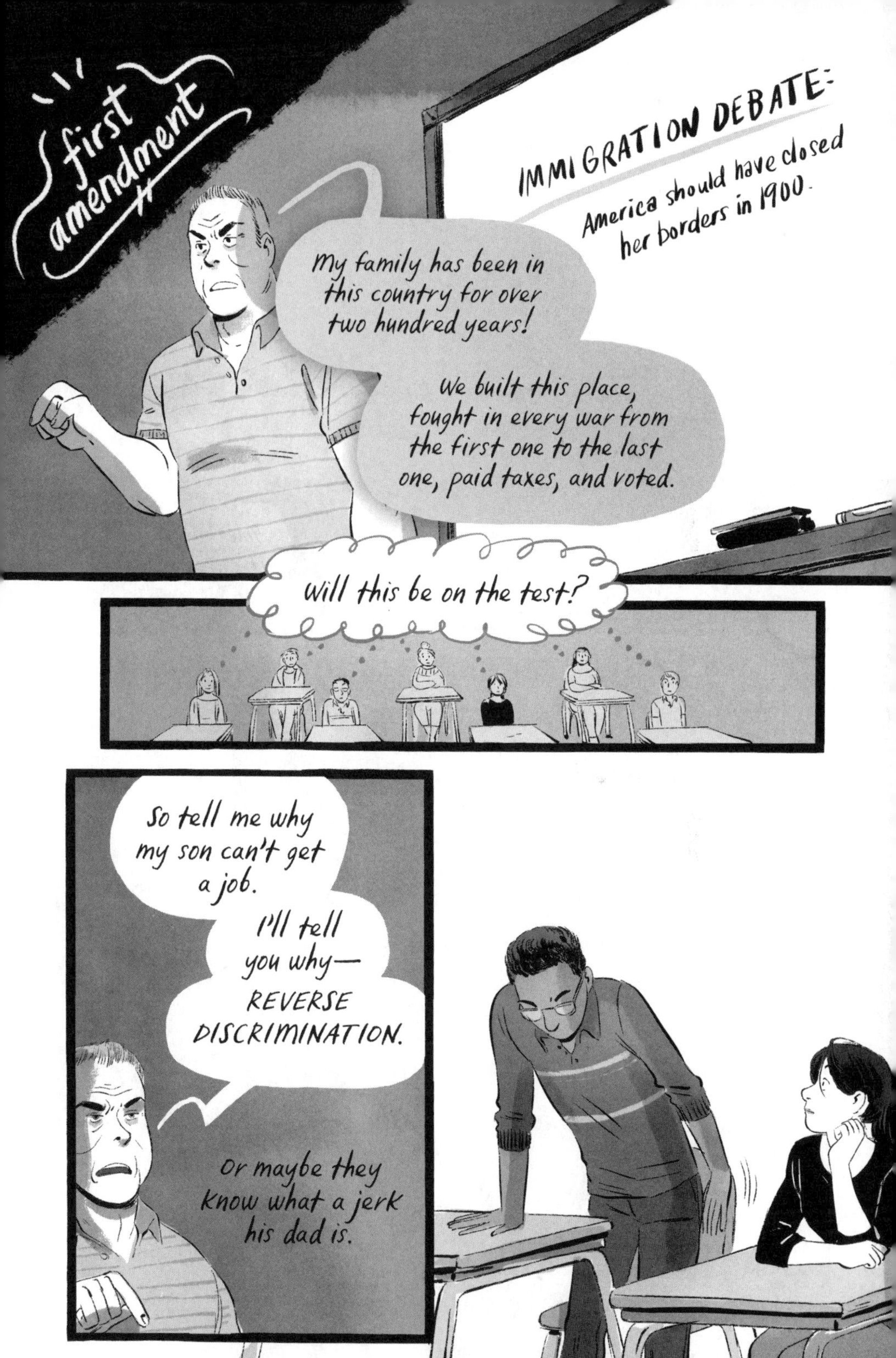
first amendment
IMMIGRATION DEBATE:
America should have closed her borders in 1900.
My family has been in this country for over two hundred years!
We built this place, fought in every war from the first one to the last one, paid taxes, and voted.
Will this be on the test?
So tell me why my son can't get a job.
I'll tell you why—
REVERSE DISCRIMINATION.
Or maybe they know what a jerk his dad is.

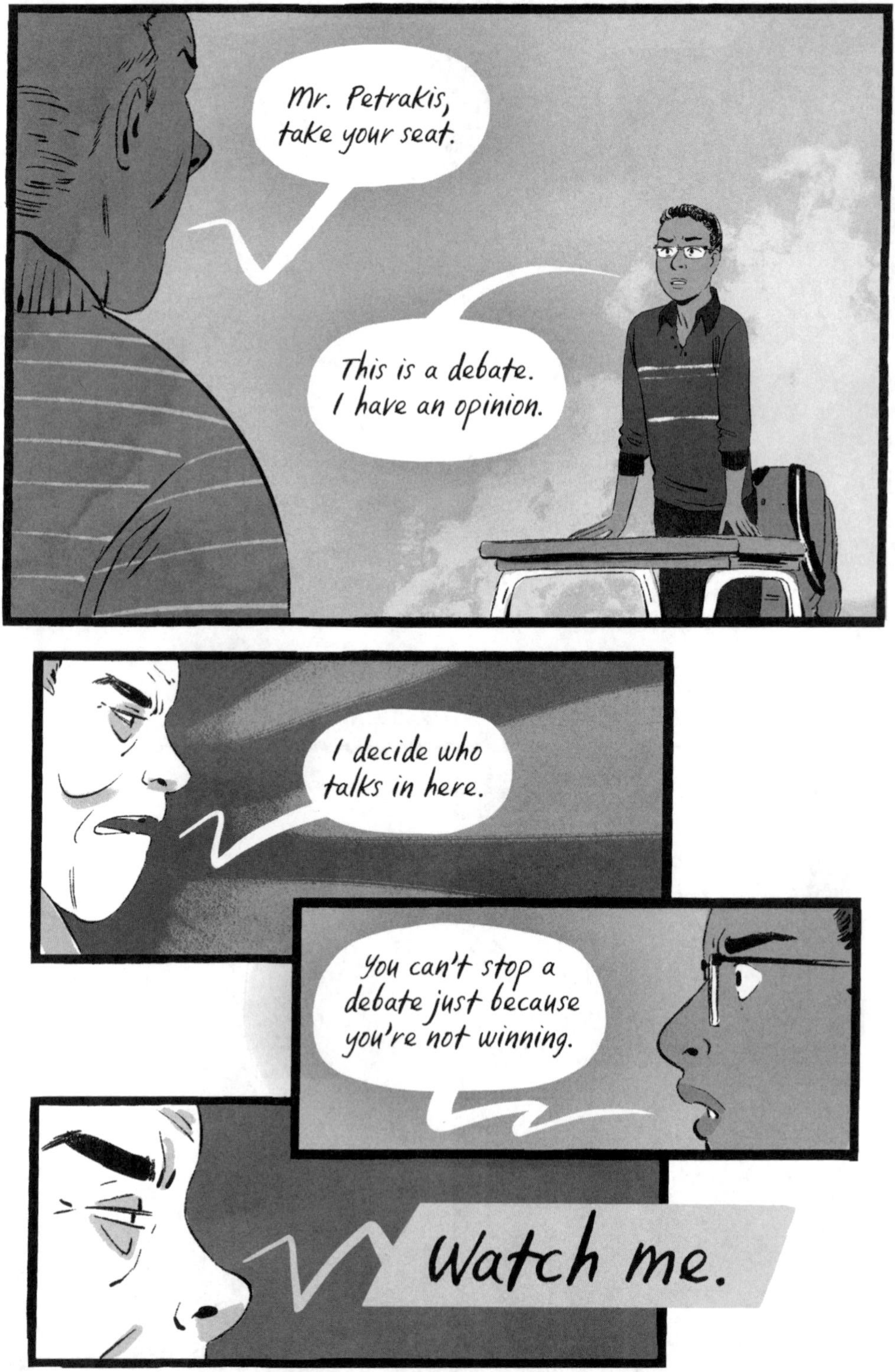

Mr. Petrakis, take your seat.
This is a debate. I have an opinion.
I decide who talks in here.
You can't stop a debate just because you're not winning.
Watch me.

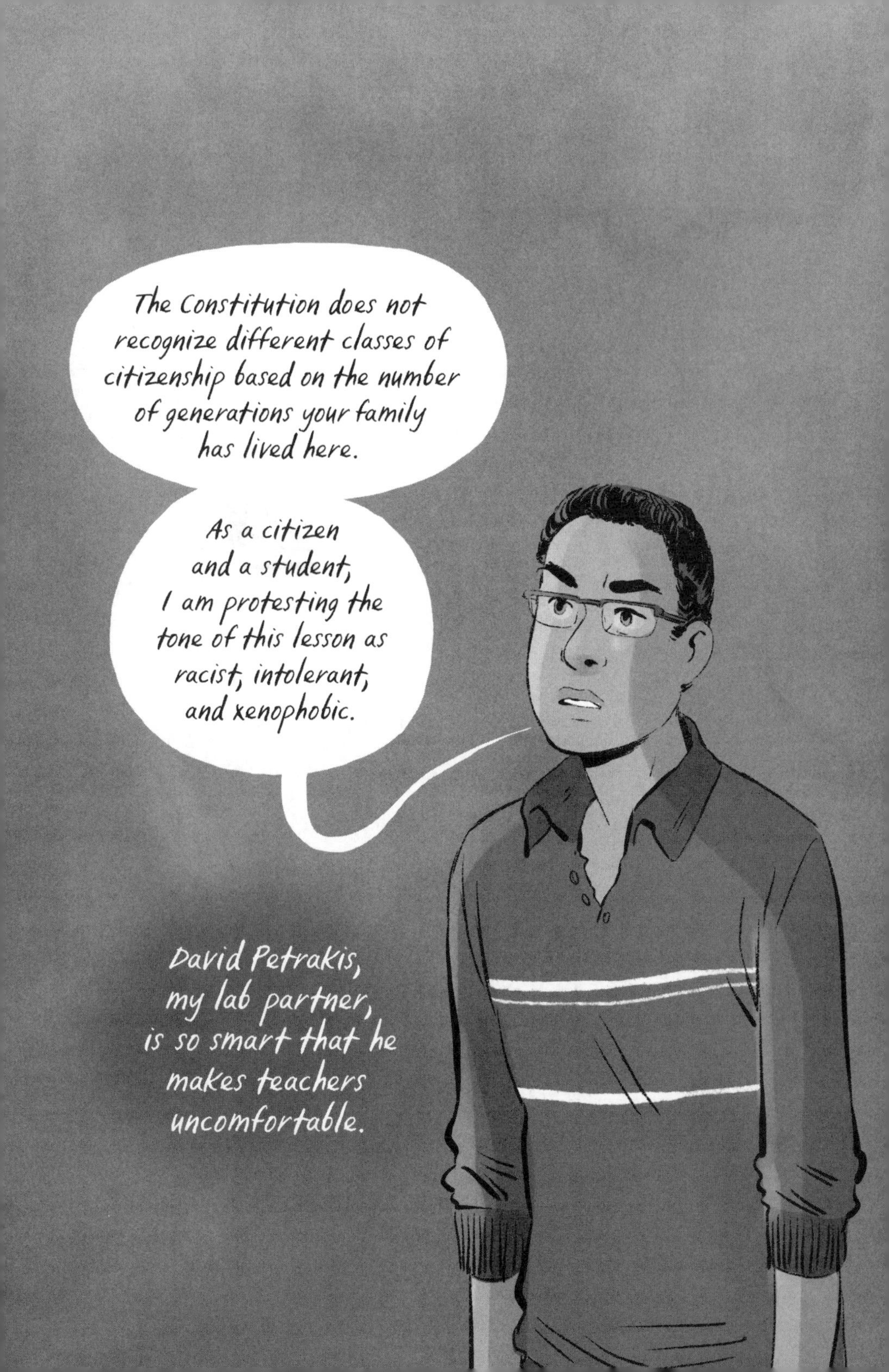
The Constitution does not recognize different classes of citizenship based on the number of generations your family has lived here.
As a citizen and a student, I am protesting the tone of this lesson as racist, intolerant, and xenophobic.
David Petrakis, my lab partner, is so smart that he makes teachers uncomfortable.

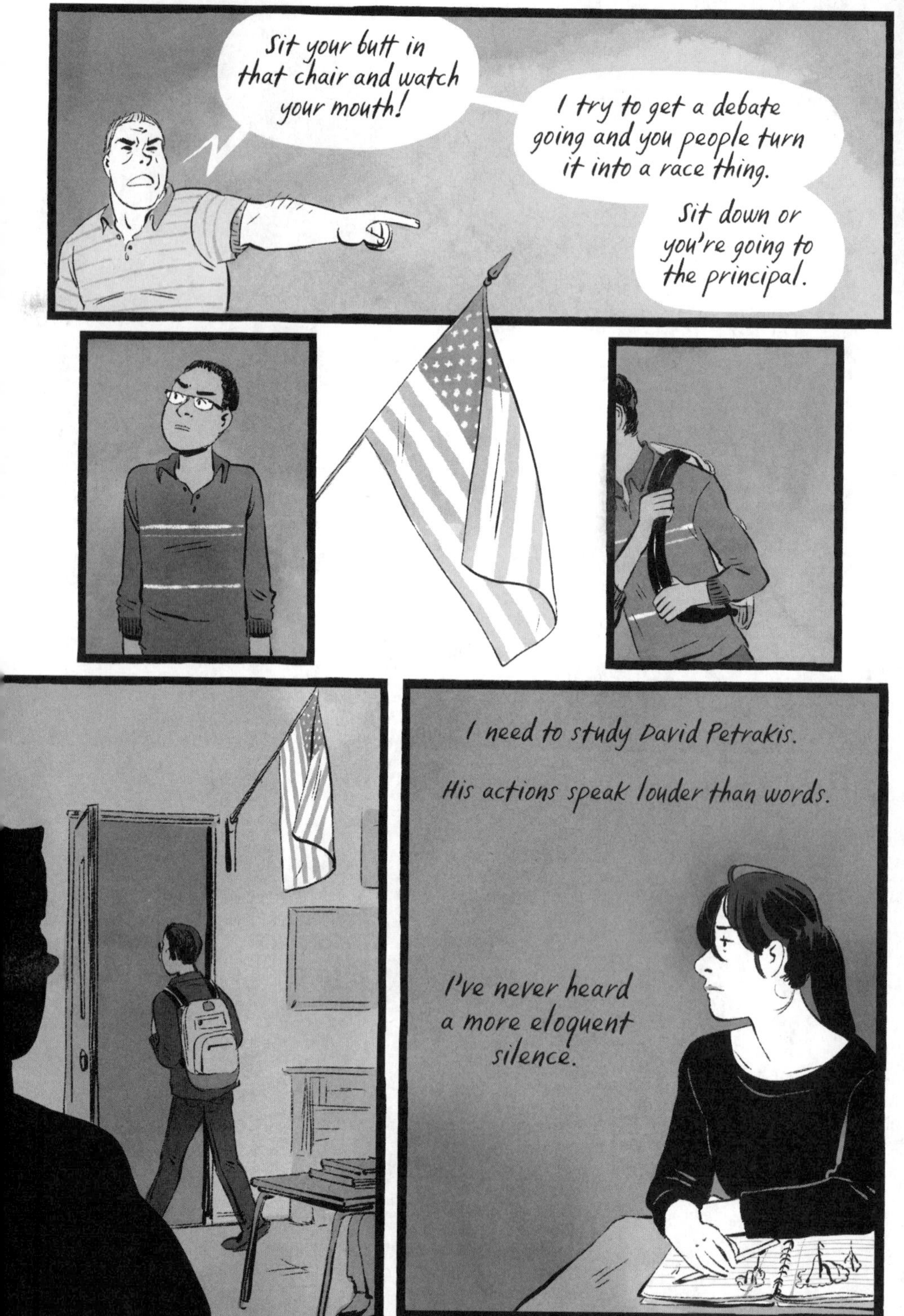

Sit your butt in that chair and watch your mouth!
I try to get a debate going and you people turn it into a race thing.
Sit down or you're going to the principal.
I need to study David Petrakis.
His actions speak louder than words.
I've never heard a more eloquent silence.

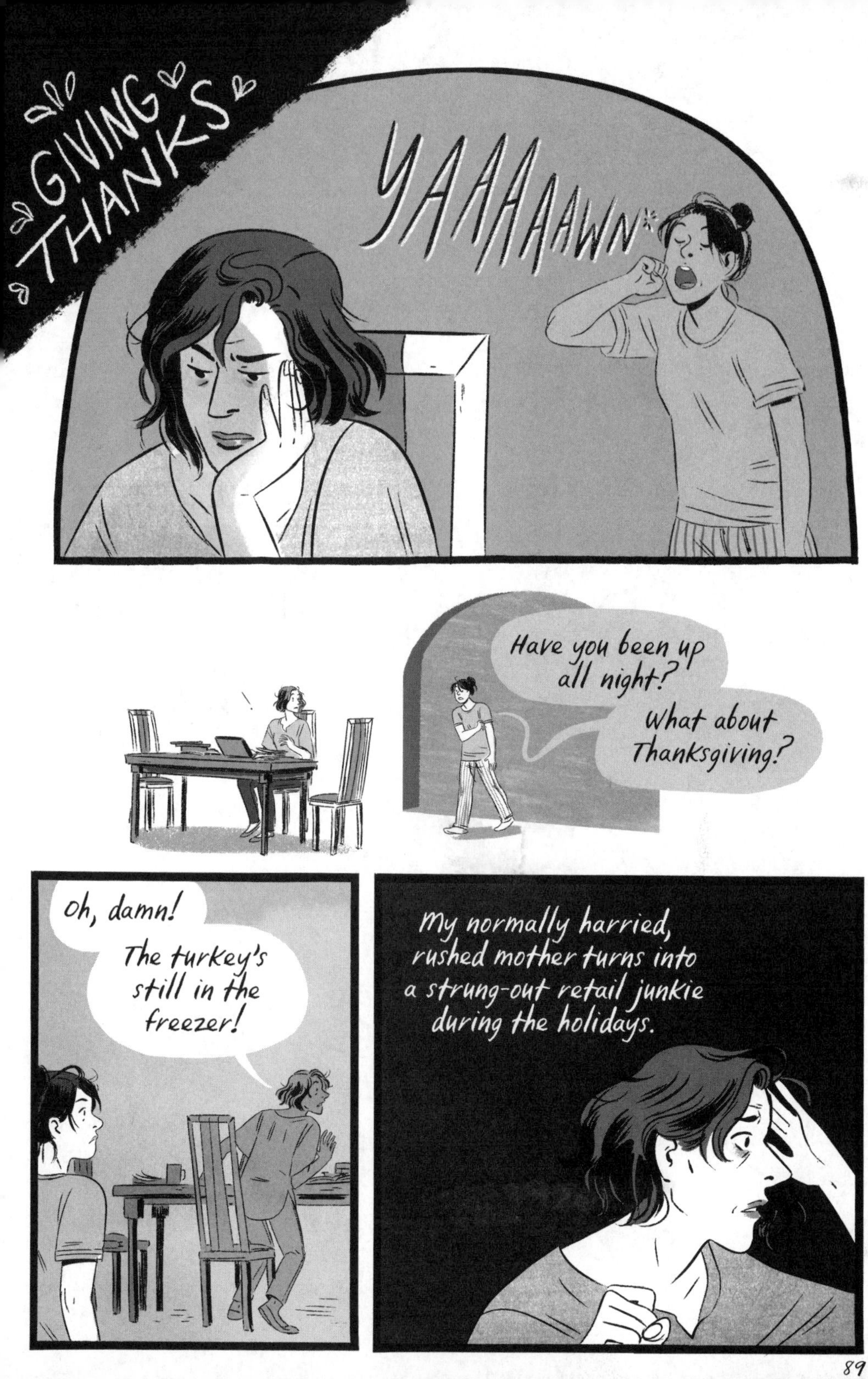
GIVING THANKS
YAAAAAWN*
Have you been up all night?
What about Thanksgiving?
Oh, damn!
The turkey's still in the freezer!
My normally harried, rushed mother turns into a strung-out retail junkie during the holidays.

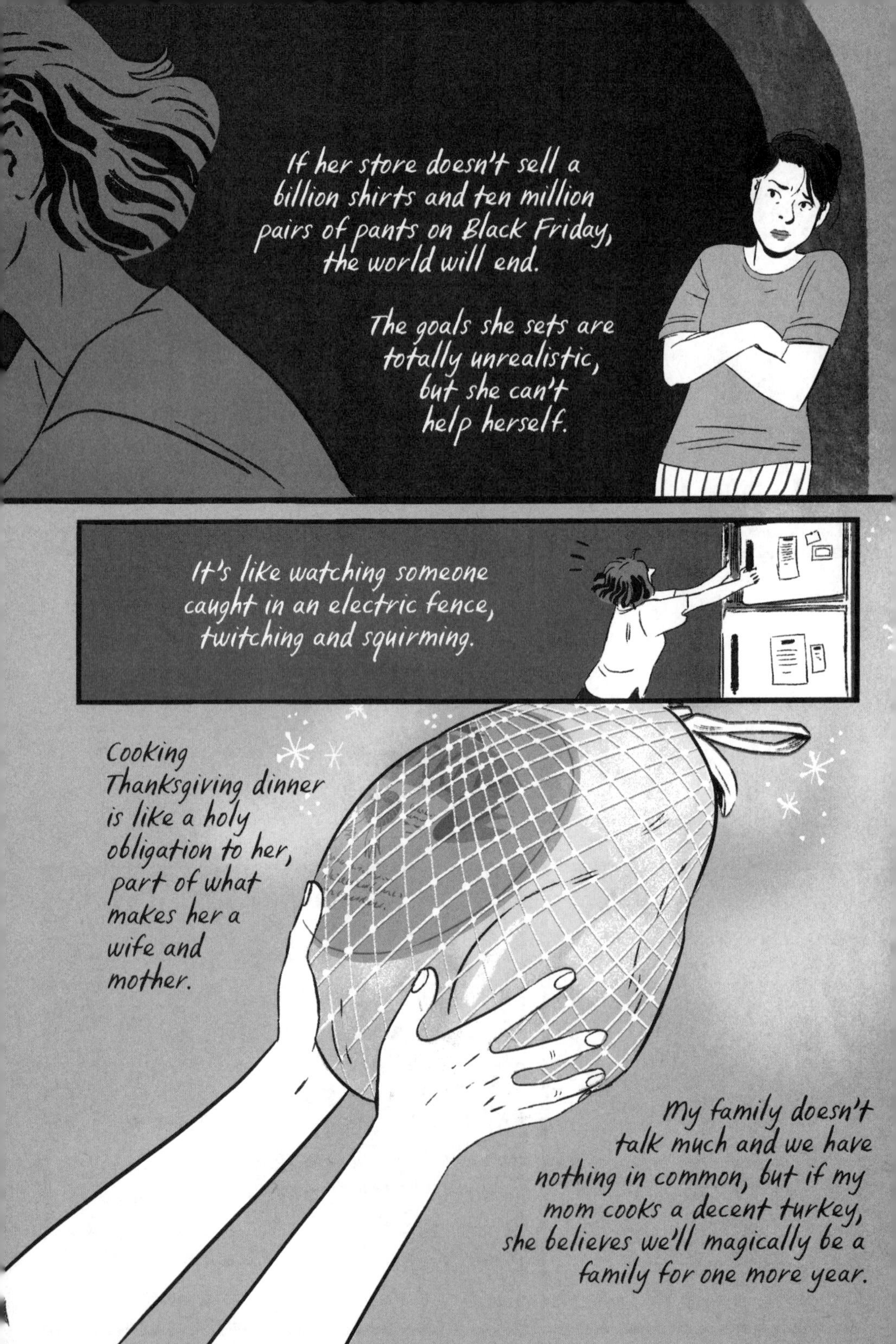
If her store doesn't sell a billion shirts and ten million pairs of pants on Black Friday, the world will end.
The goals she sets are totally unrealistic, but she can't help herself.
It's like watching someone caught in an electric fence, twitching and squirming.
Cooking Thanksgiving dinner is like a holy obligation to her, part of what makes her a wife and mother.
My family doesn't talk much and we have nothing in common, but if my mom cooks a decent turkey, she believes we'll magically be a family for one more year.

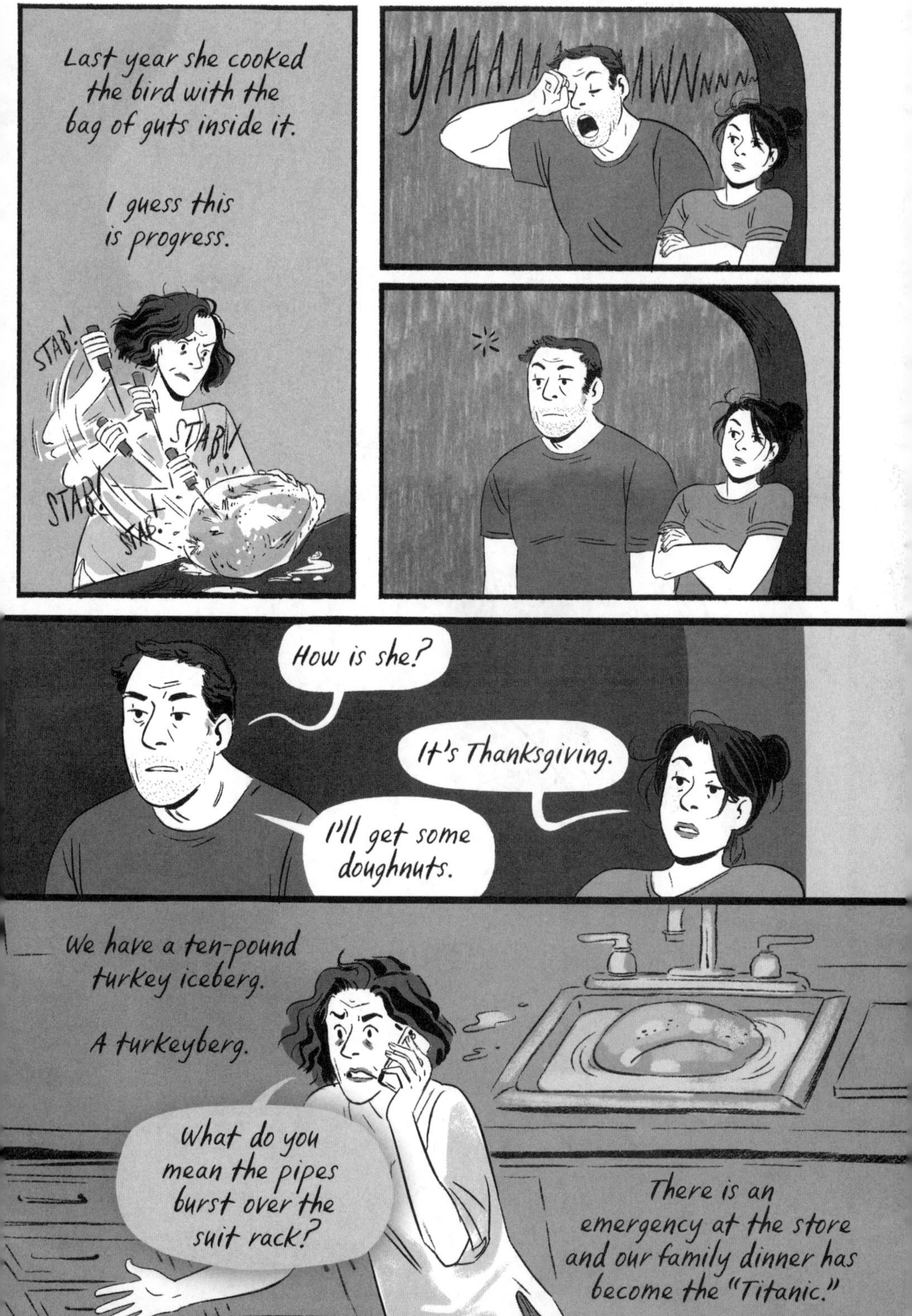
Last year she cooked the bird with the bag of guts inside it.
I guess this is progress.
STAB!
STAB!!
STAB!
STAB.
YAAAAAAWNnnn~
How is she?
It's Thanksgiving.
I'll get some doughnuts.
We have a ten-pound turkey iceberg.
A turkeyberg.
What do you mean the pipes burst over the suit rack?
There is an emergency at the store and our family dinner has become the "Titanic."

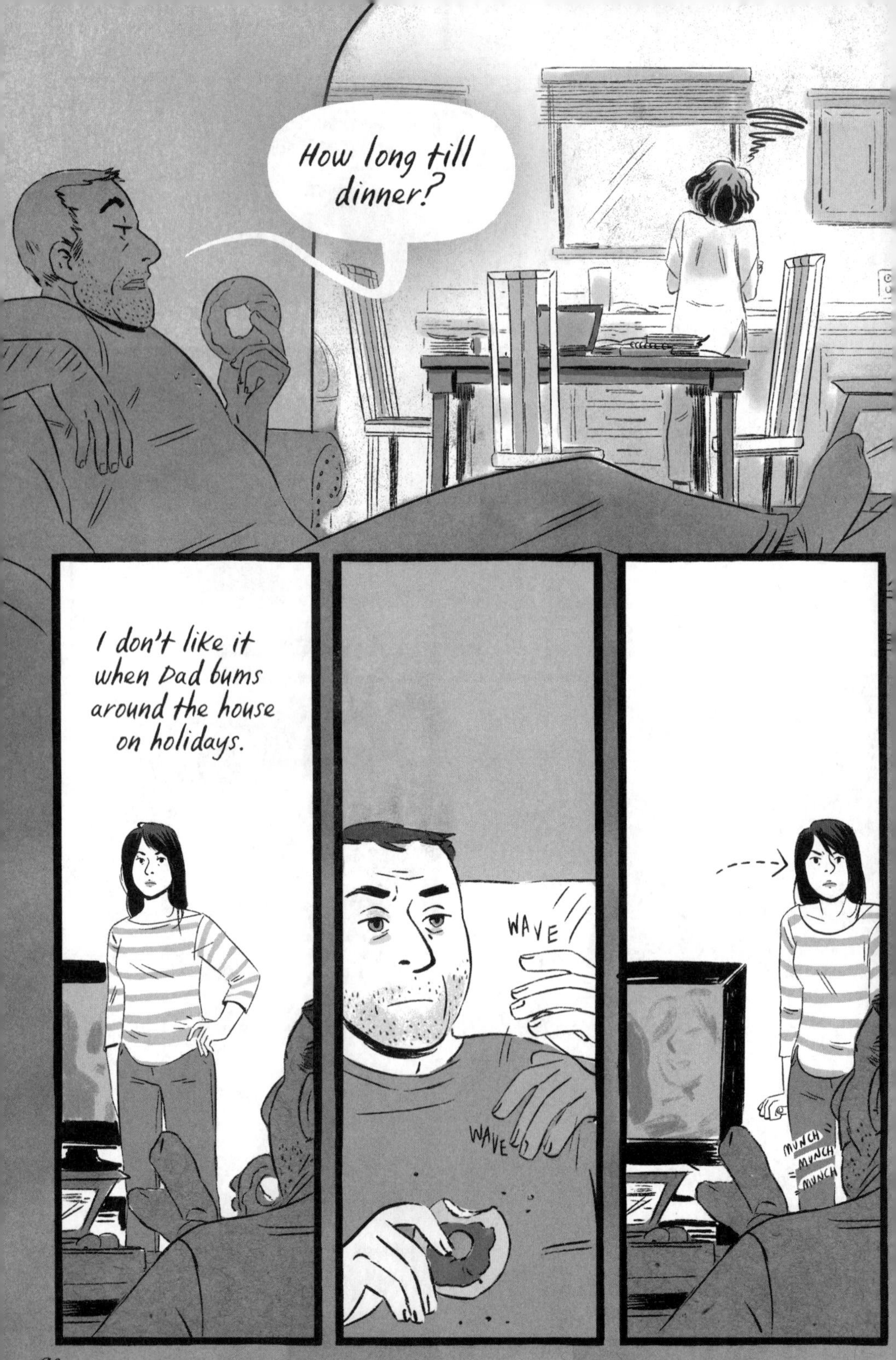
How long till dinner?
I don't like it when Dad bums around the house on holidays.
WAVE
WAVE
MUNCH
MUNCH
MUNCH

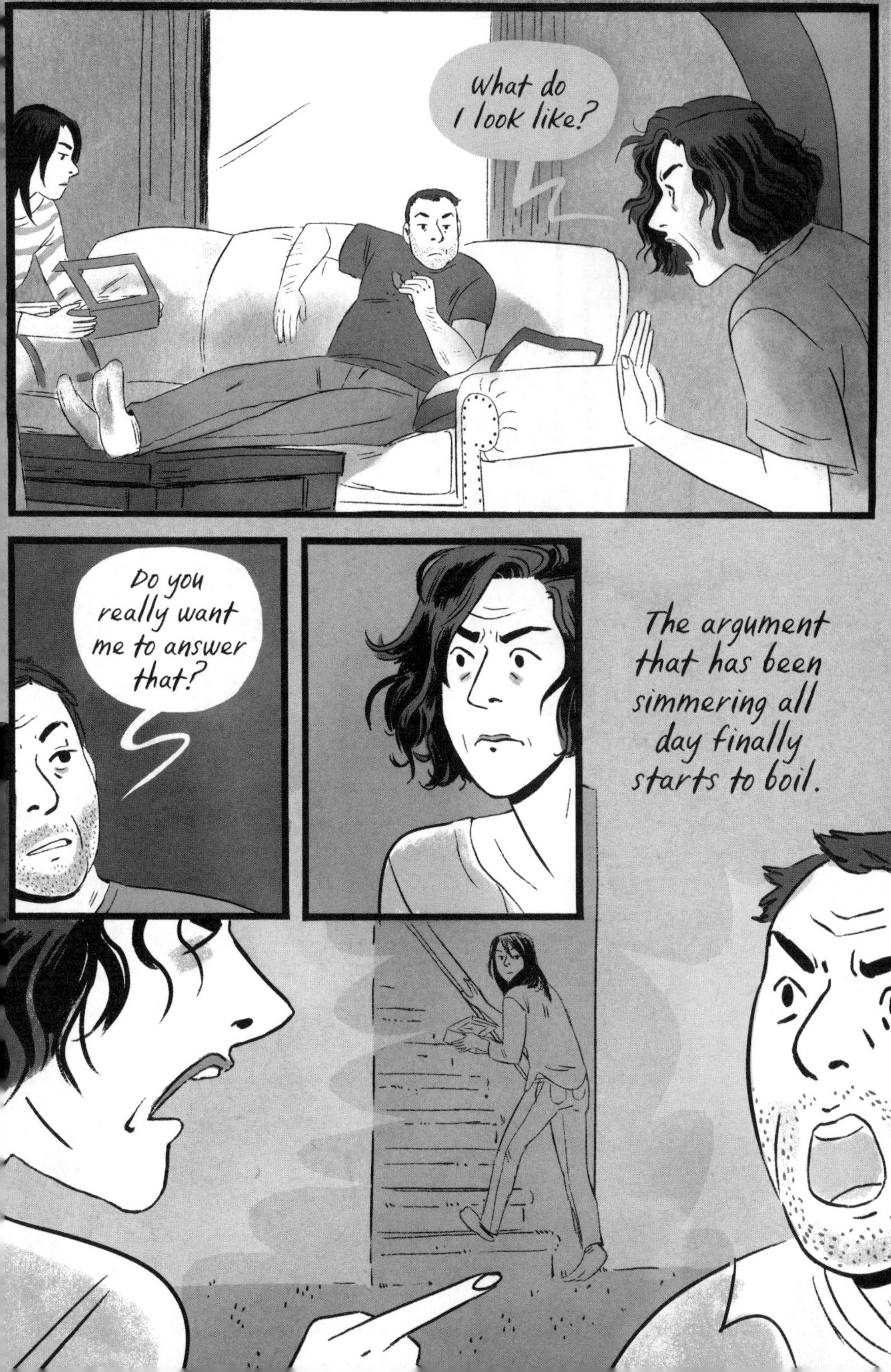
What do I look like?
Do you really want me to answer that?
The argument that has been simmering all day finally starts to boil.

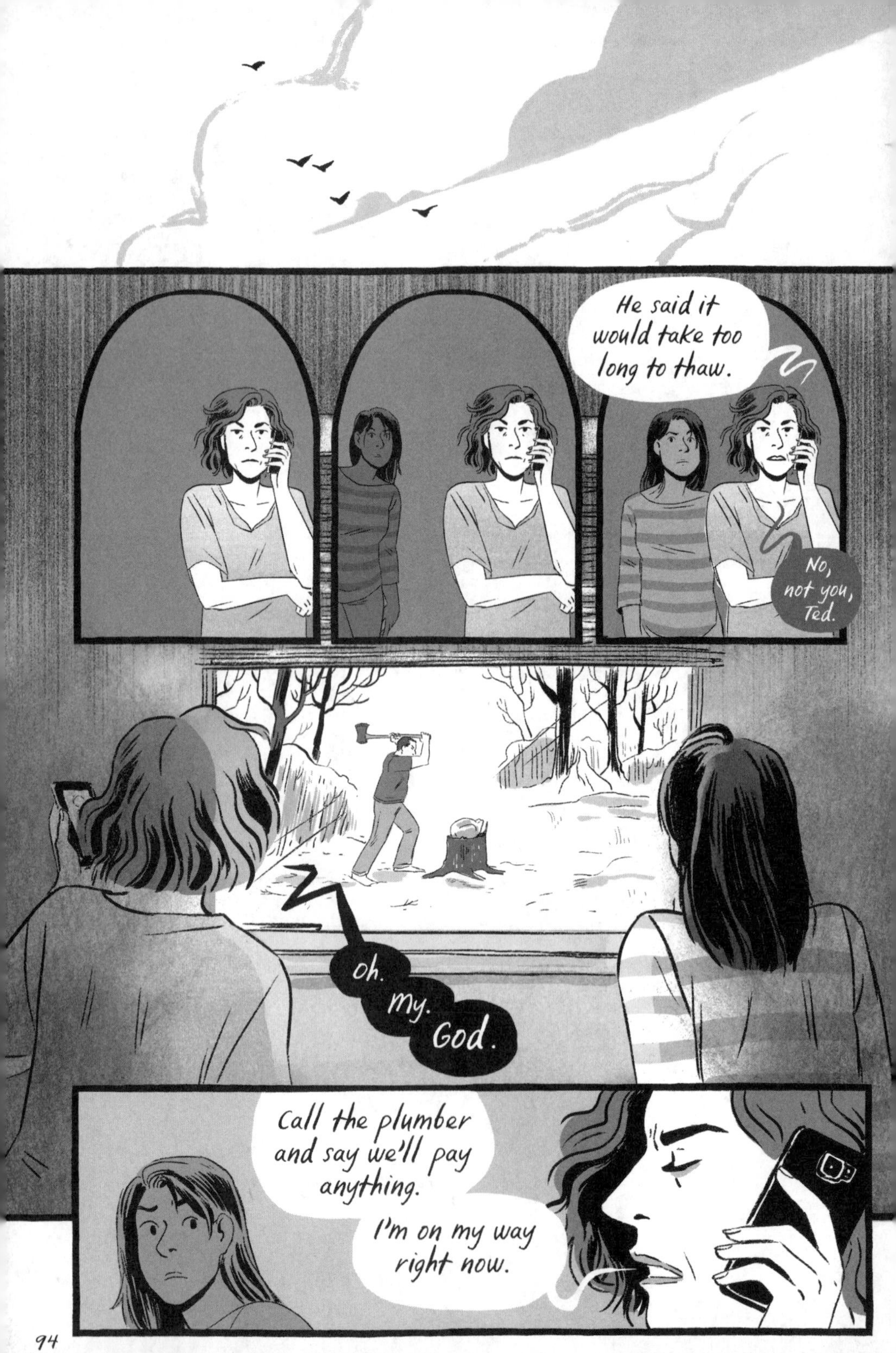
He said it would take too long to thaw.
No, not you, Ted.
Oh. my. God.
Call the plumber and say we'll pay anything.
I'm on my way right now.

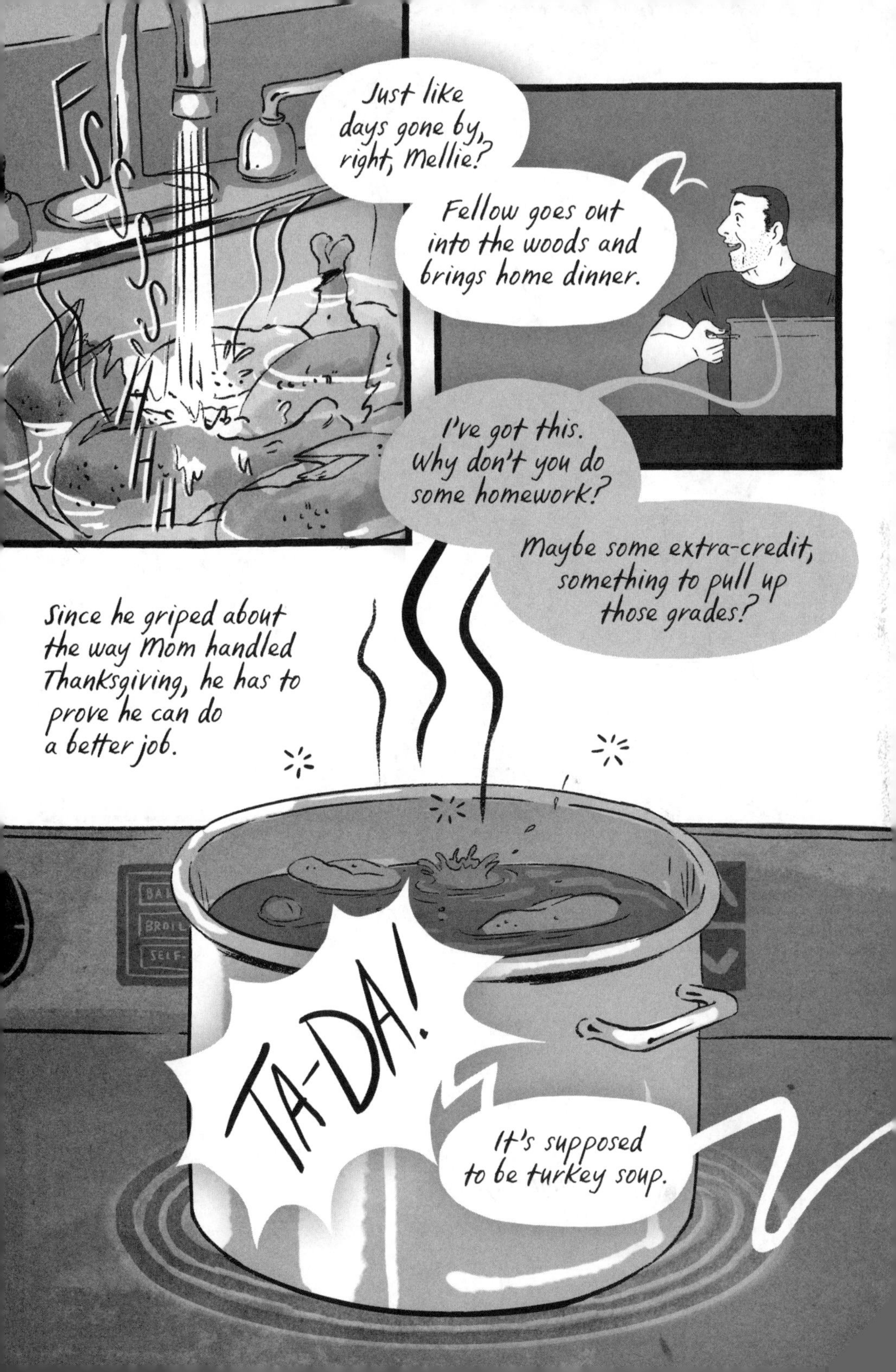
FSSSSSHHHH
Just like days gone by, right, Mellie?
Fellow goes out into the woods and brings home dinner.
I've got this. Why don't you do some homework?
Maybe some extra-credit, something to pull up those grades?
Since he griped about the way Mom handled Thanksgiving, he has to prove he can do a better job.
BAK
BROIL
SELF-
TA-DA!
It's supposed to be turkey soup.

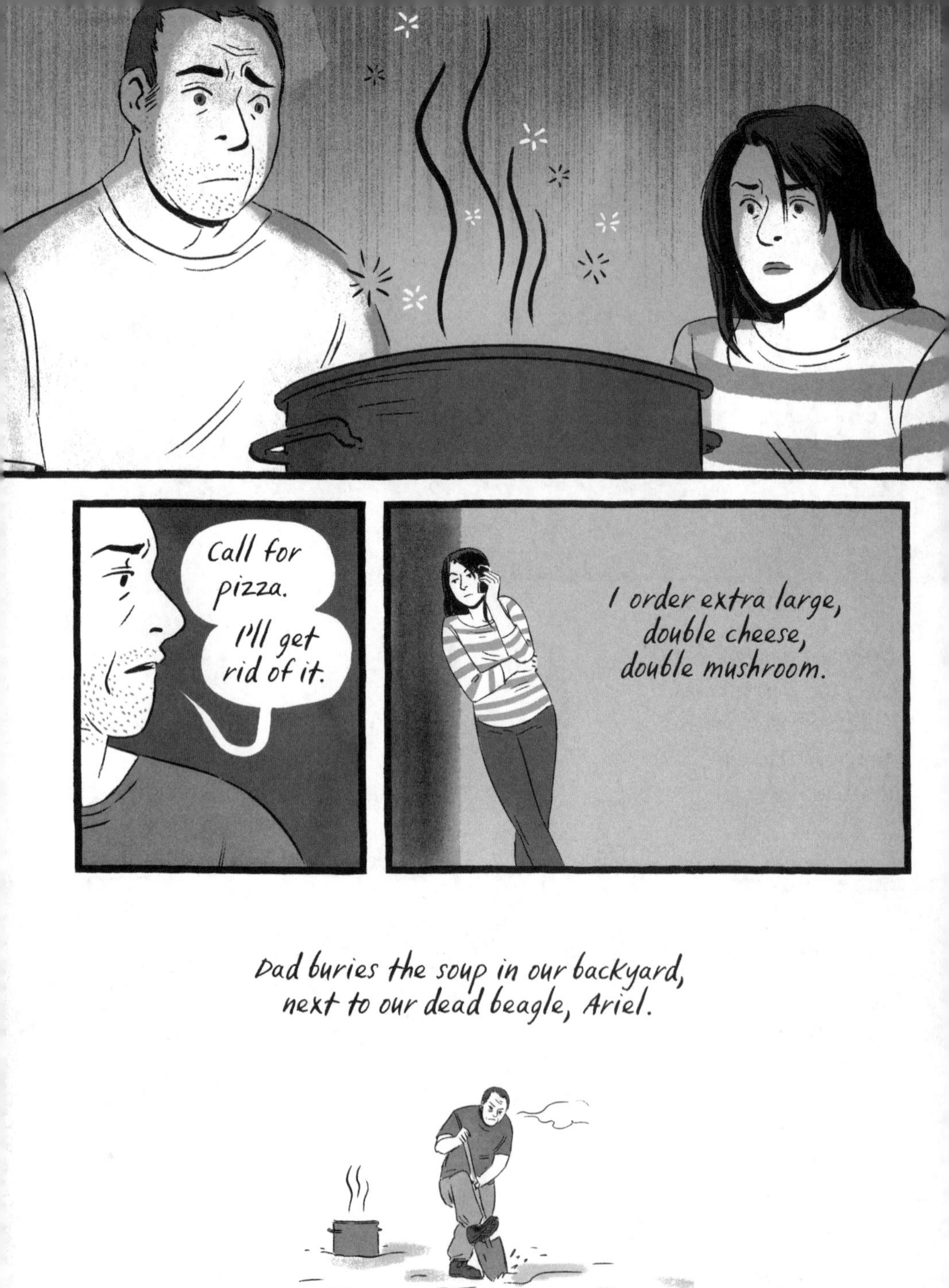
Call for pizza.
I'll get rid of it.
I order extra large, double cheese, double mushroom.
Dad buries the soup in our backyard, next to our dead beagle, Ariel.

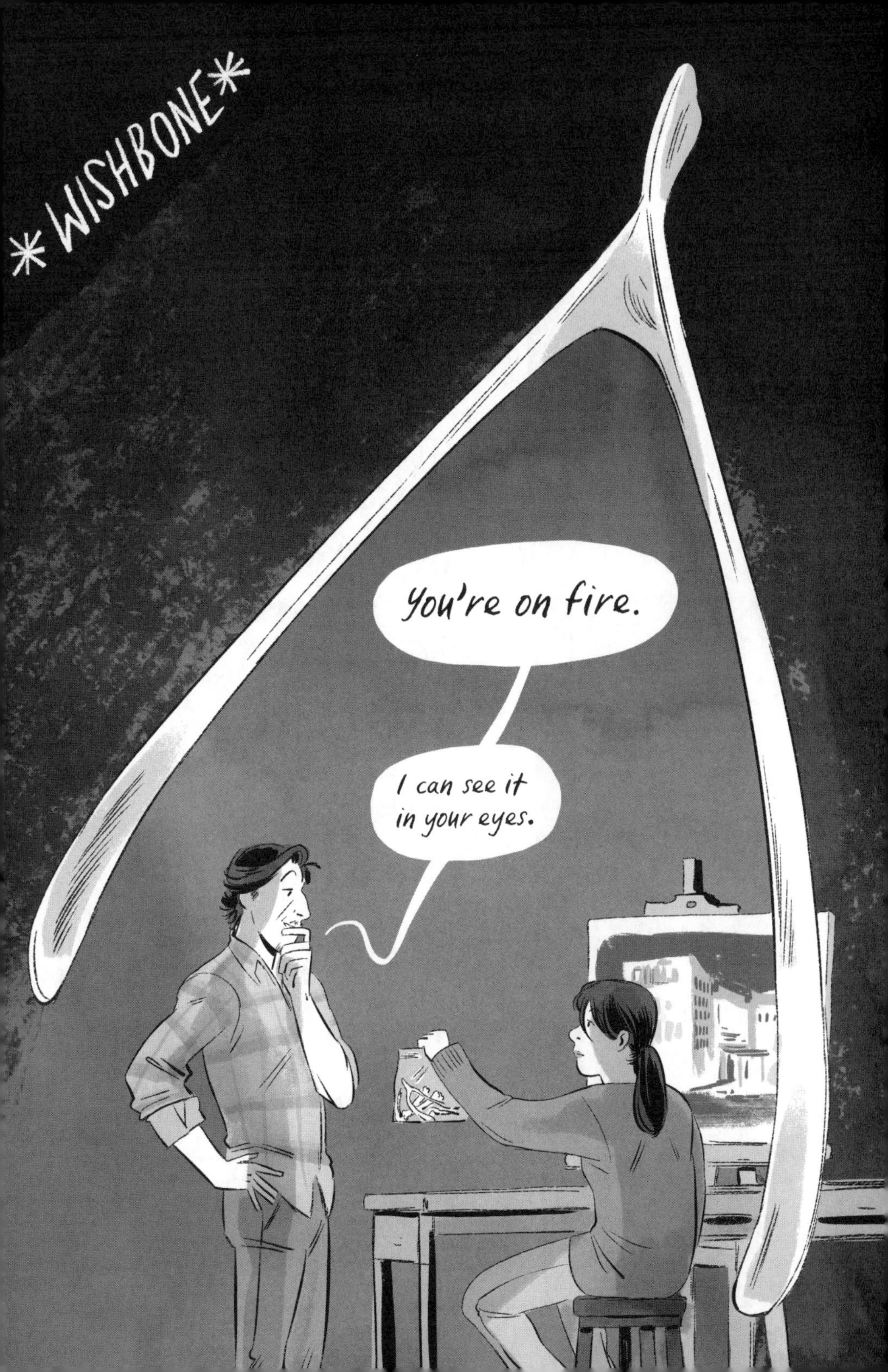
WISHBONE
You're on fire.
I can see it in your eyes.

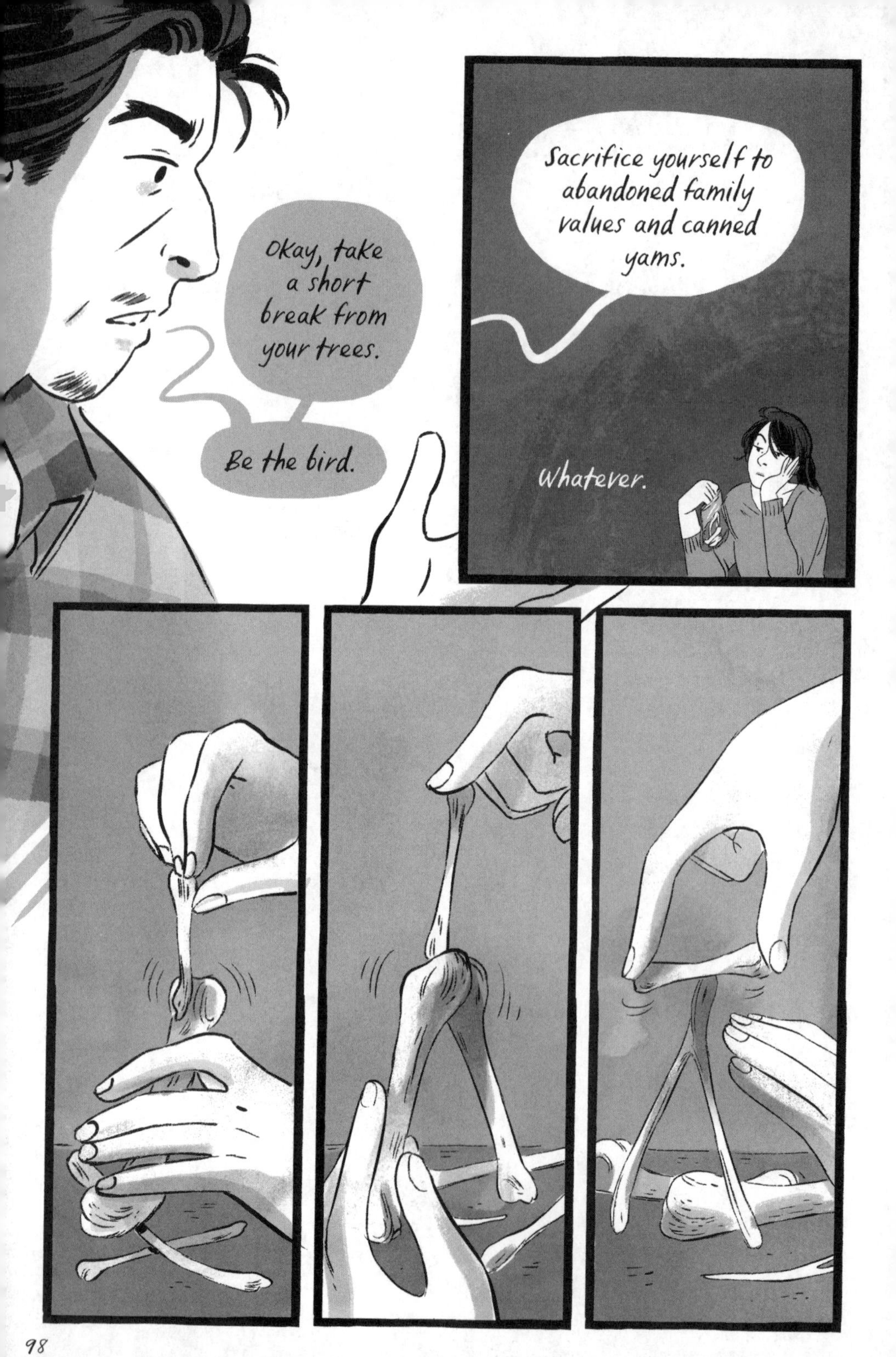
Okay, take a short break from your trees.
Be the bird.
Sacrifice yourself to abandoned family values and canned yams.
Whatever.

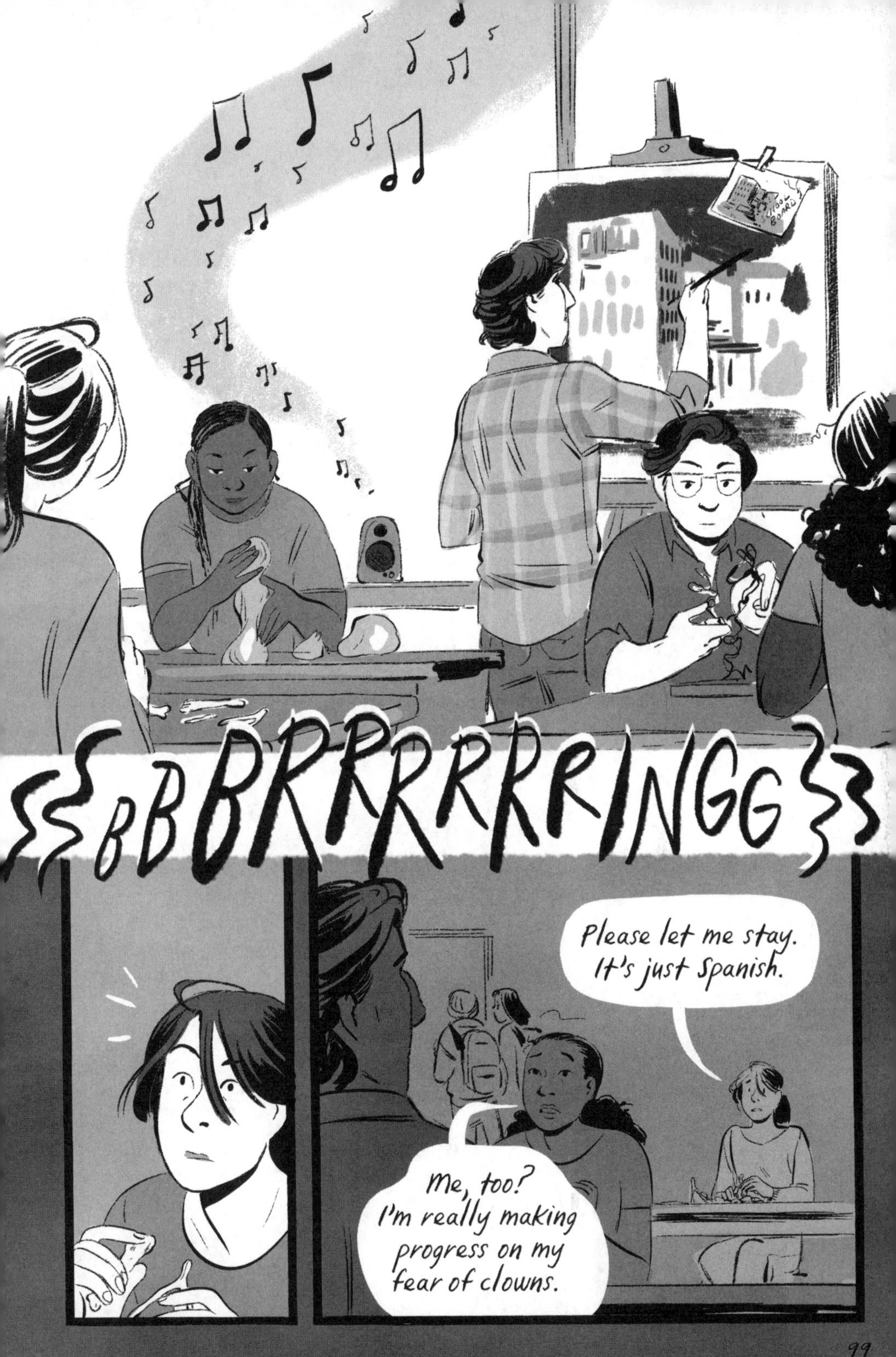
BBBRRRRRRRINGG
Please let me stay. It's just Spanish.
Me, too? I'm really making progress on my fear of clowns.

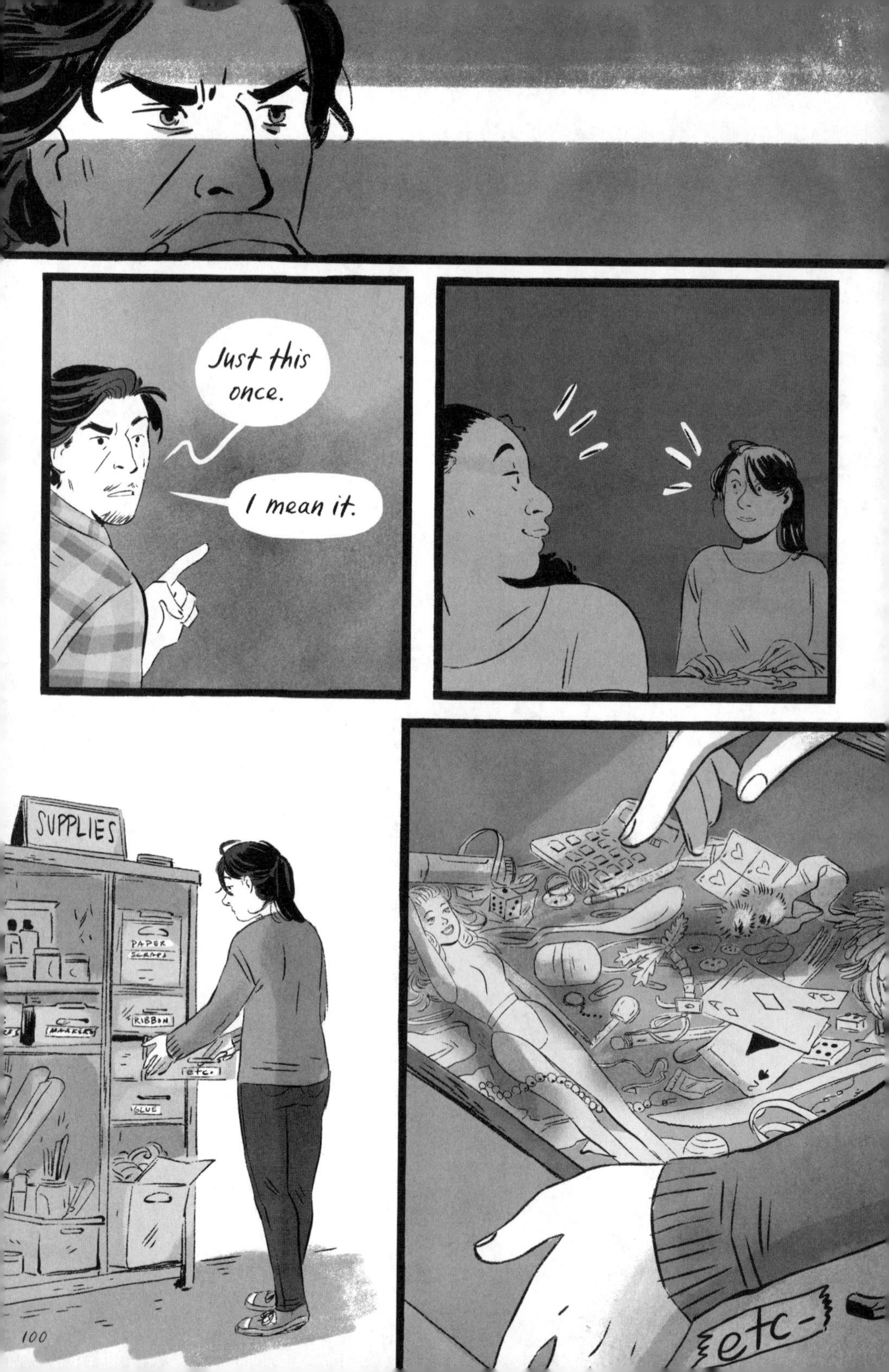
Just this once.
I mean it.
SUPPLIES
PAPER SCRAPS
MARKERS
RIBBON
etc.
GLUE
etc-

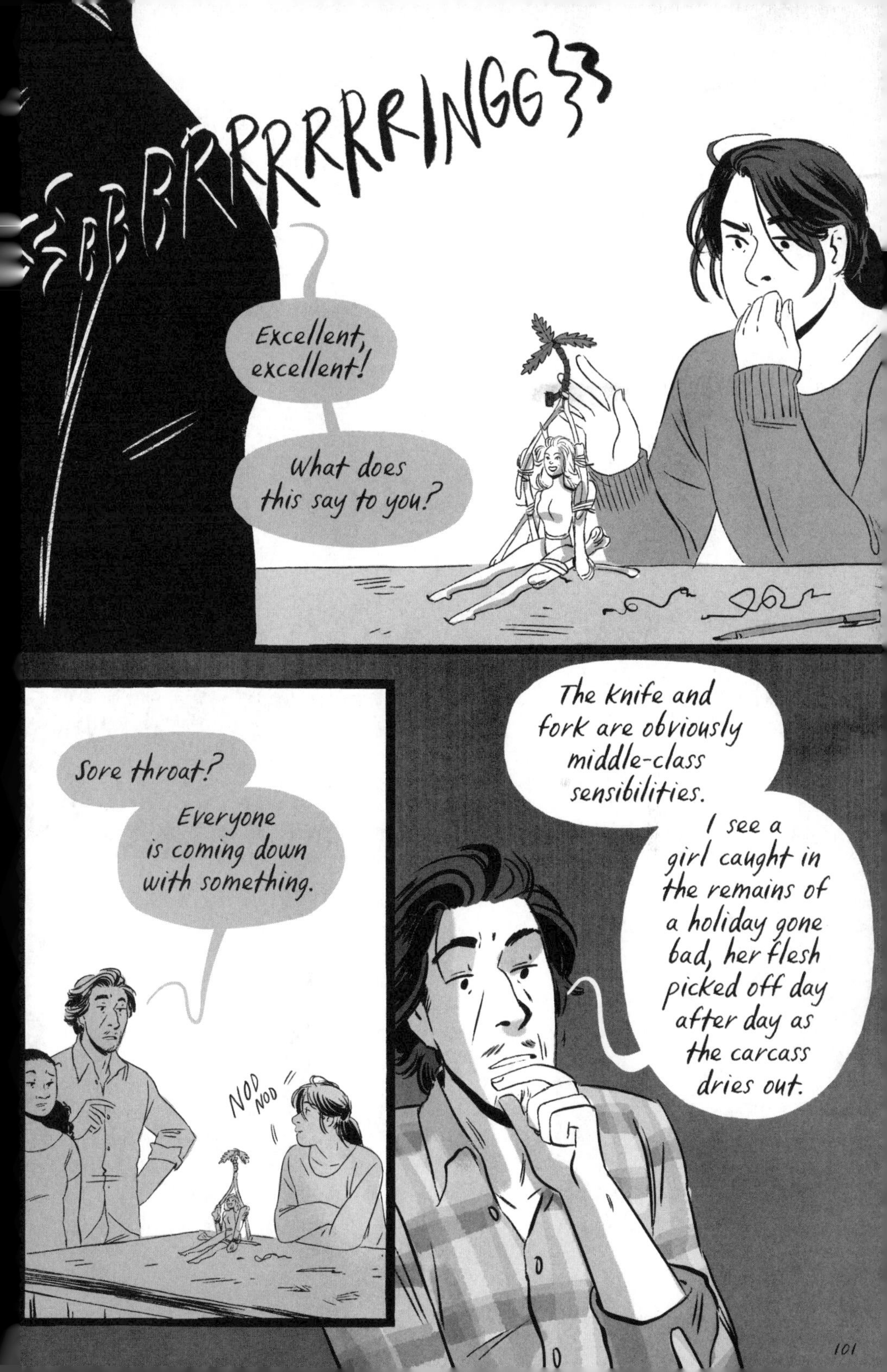
BBRRRRRRRINGG
Excellent, excellent!
What does this say to you?
Sore throat?
Everyone is coming down with something.
NOD NOD
The knife and fork are obviously middle-class sensibilities.
I see a girl caught in the remains of a holiday gone bad, her flesh picked off day after day as the carcass dries out.

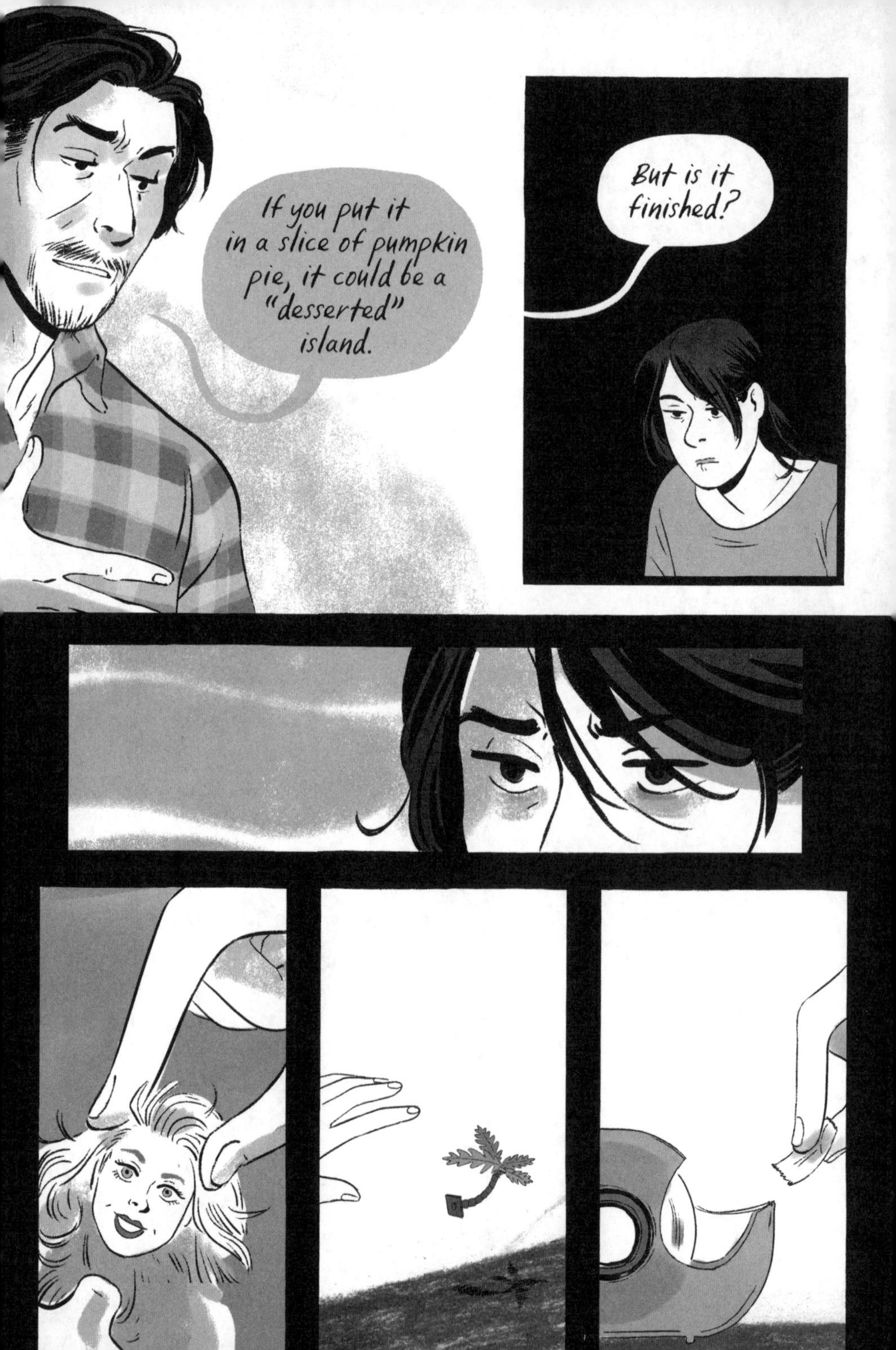
If you put it in a slice of pumpkin pie, it could be a "desserted" island.
But is it finished?

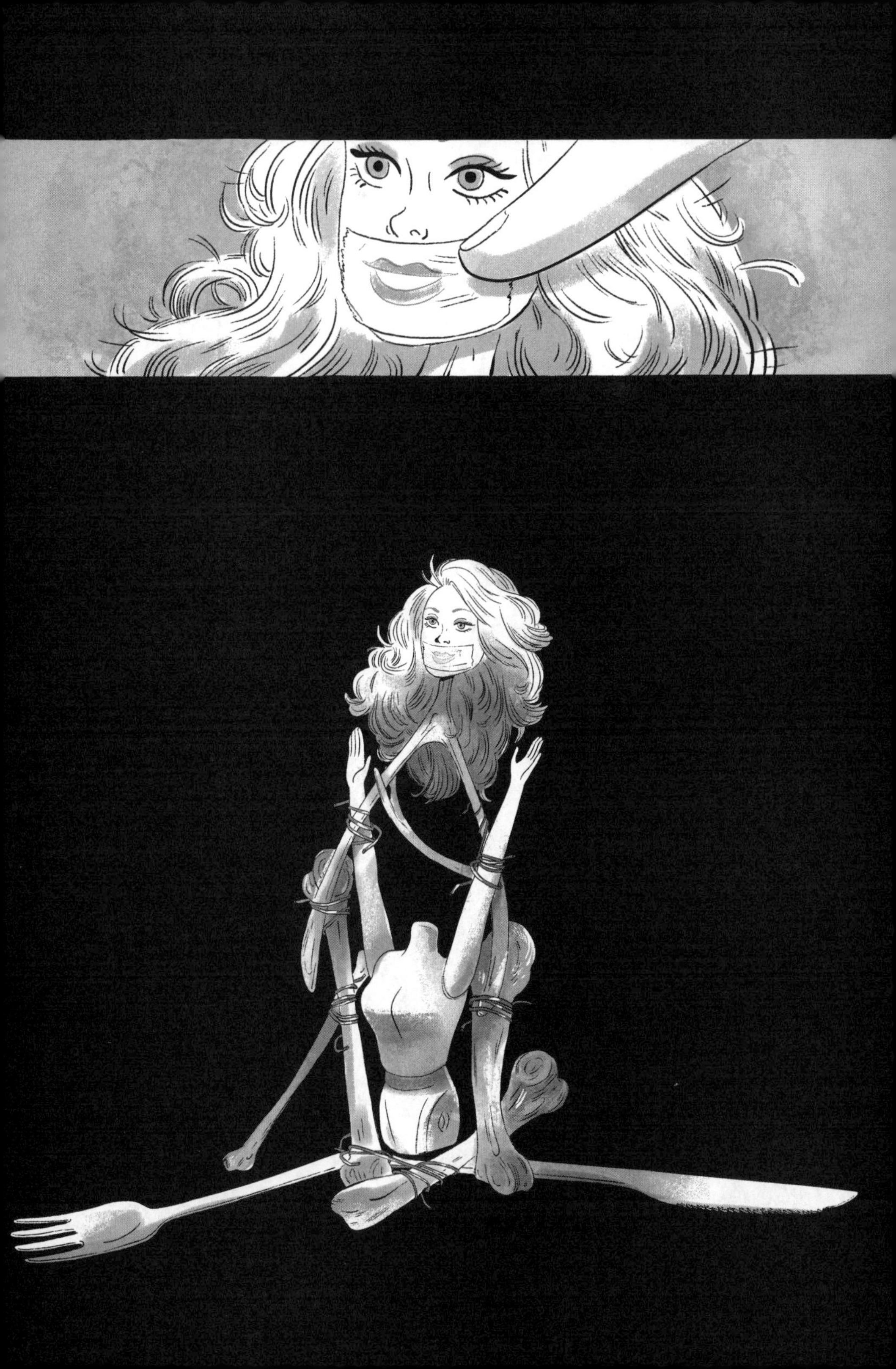

It's scary, in a weird way. Not clown-scary, um, how do I say this?
Like you don't want to look at it too long. Nice job, Mel.
This means pain, doesn't it?
I leave before he can say more.

My Spanish homework is to choose five verbs and conjugate them.

TO TRANSLATE: traducir (I traducate.)

TO FLUNK: fracasar (Yo am almost facrasaring.)

TO HIDE: esconder

TO ESCAPE: escapar

TO FORGET: olvidar

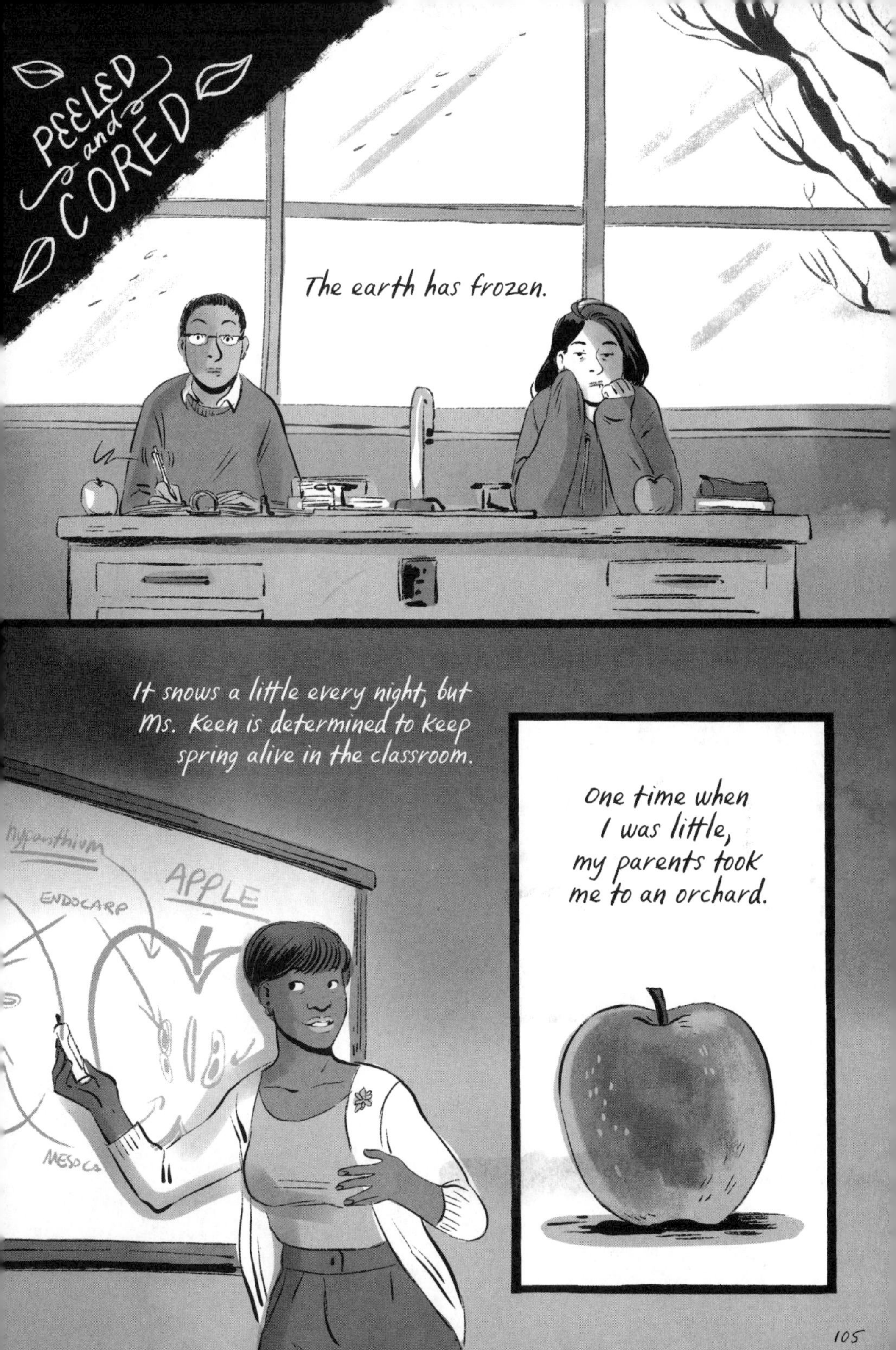
PEELED and CORED
The earth has frozen.
It snows a little every night, but Ms. Keen is determined to keep spring alive in the classroom.
hypanthium
APPLE
ENDOCARP
One time when I was little, my parents took me to an orchard.

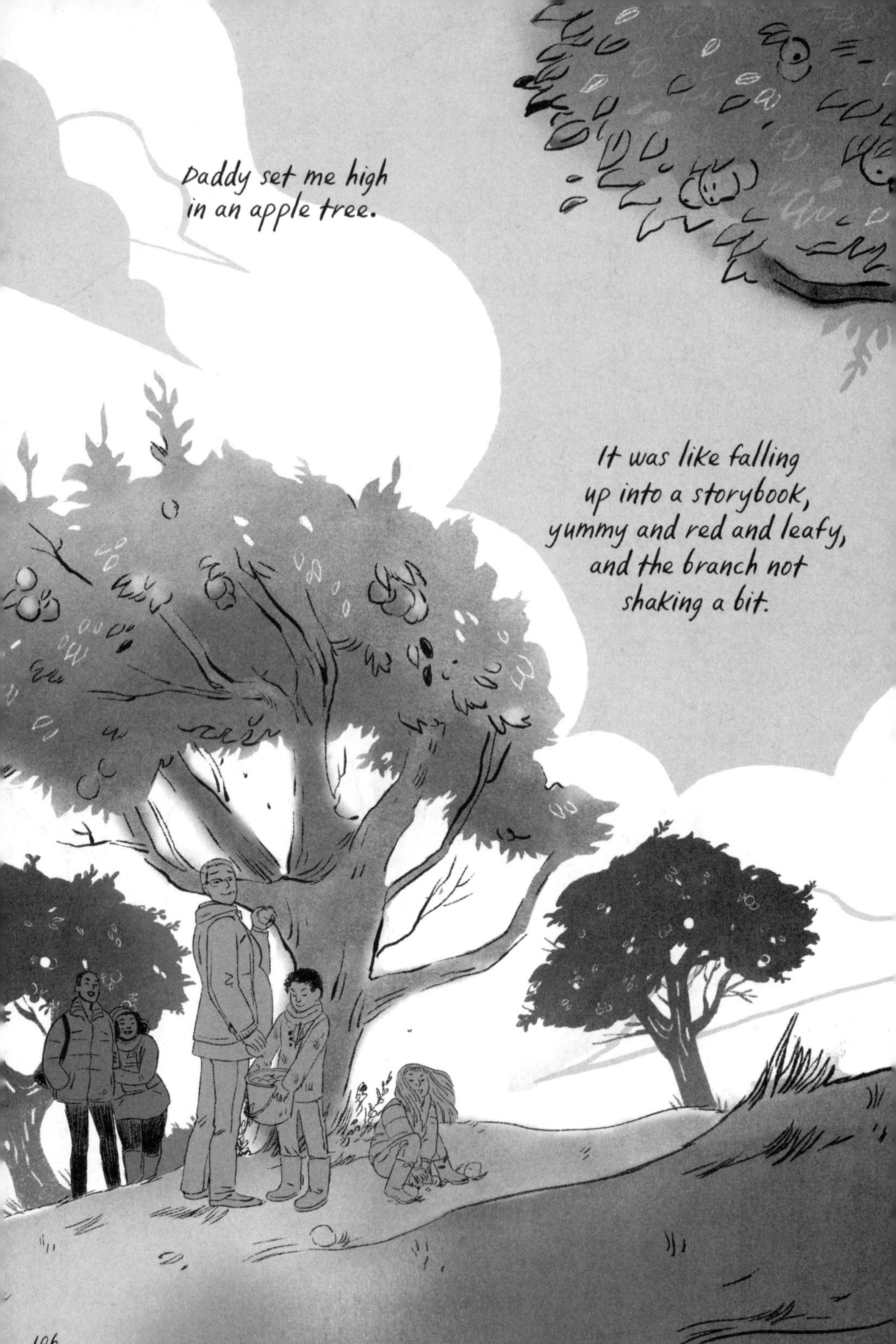
Daddy set me high in an apple tree.
It was like falling up into a storybook, yummy and red and leafy, and the branch not shaking a bit.

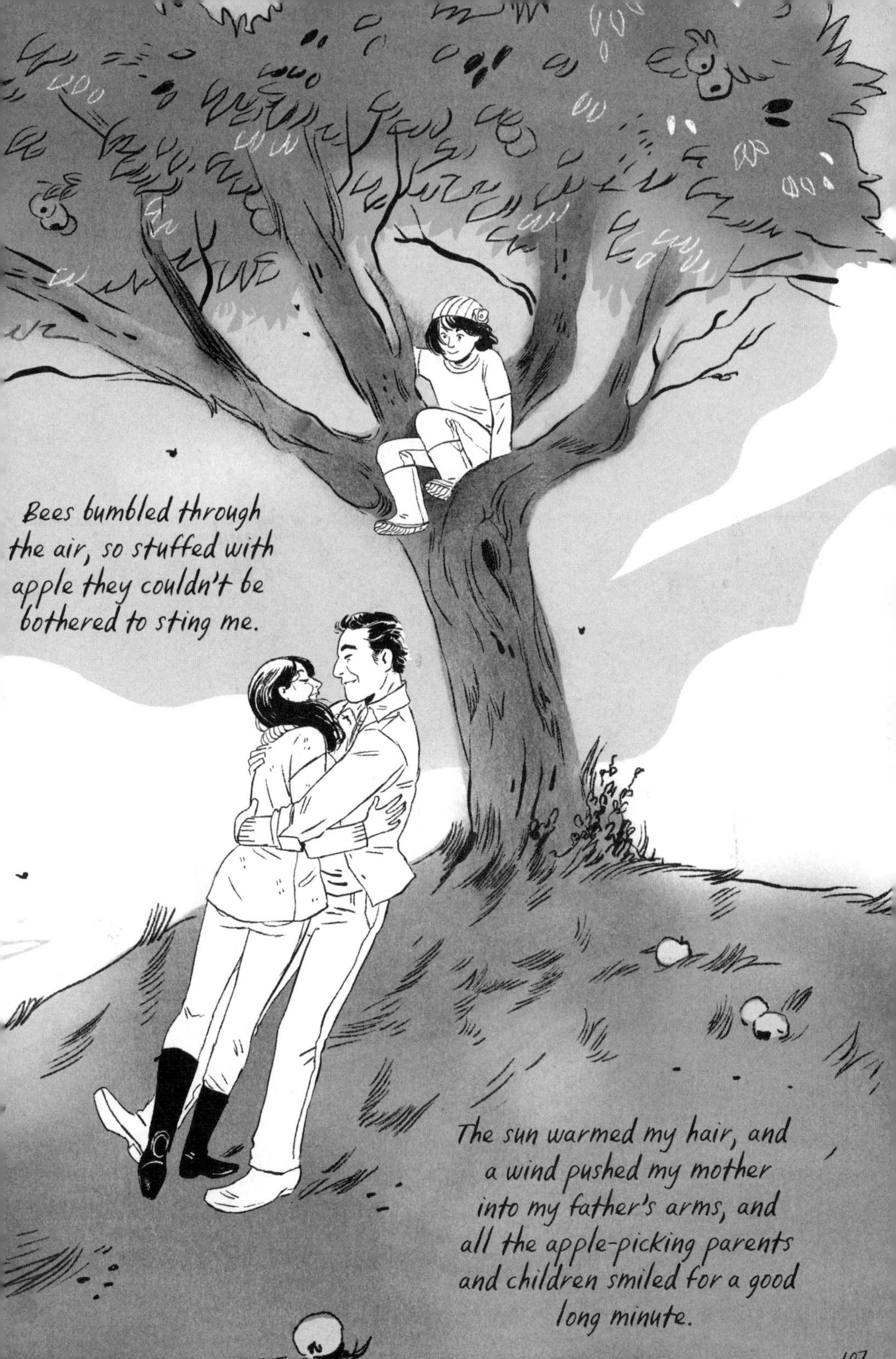
Bees bumbled through the air, so stuffed with apple they couldn't be bothered to sting me.
The sun warmed my hair, and a wind pushed my mother into my father's arms, and all the apple-picking parents and children smiled for a good long minute.

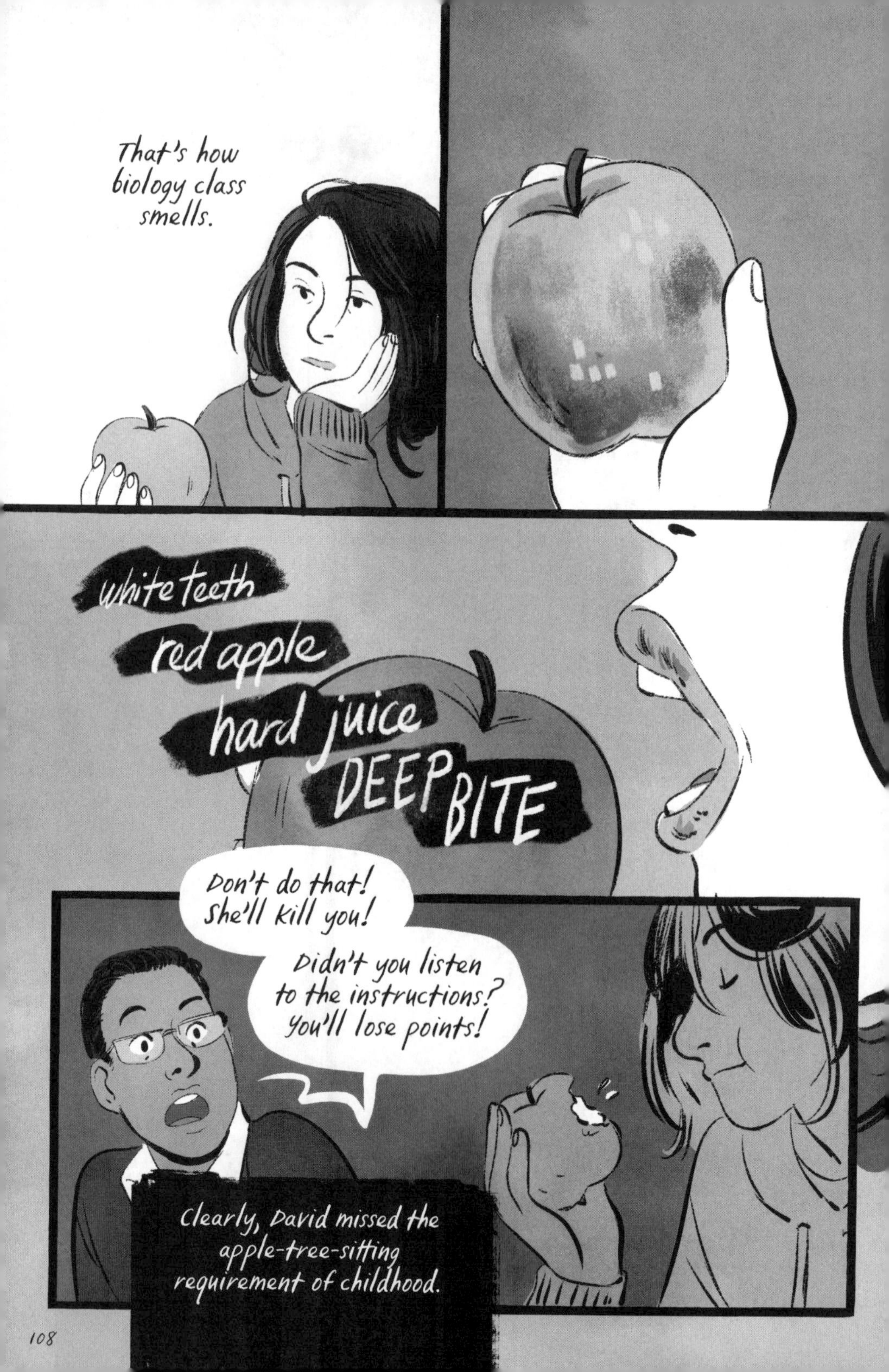
That's how biology class smells.
white teeth
red apple
hard juice
DEEP BITE
Don't do that! She'll kill you!
Didn't you listen to the instructions? You'll lose points!
Clearly, David missed the apple-tree-sitting requirement of childhood.

An apple tree growing
from an apple seed
growing in an apple.

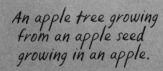

Biology is so cool.

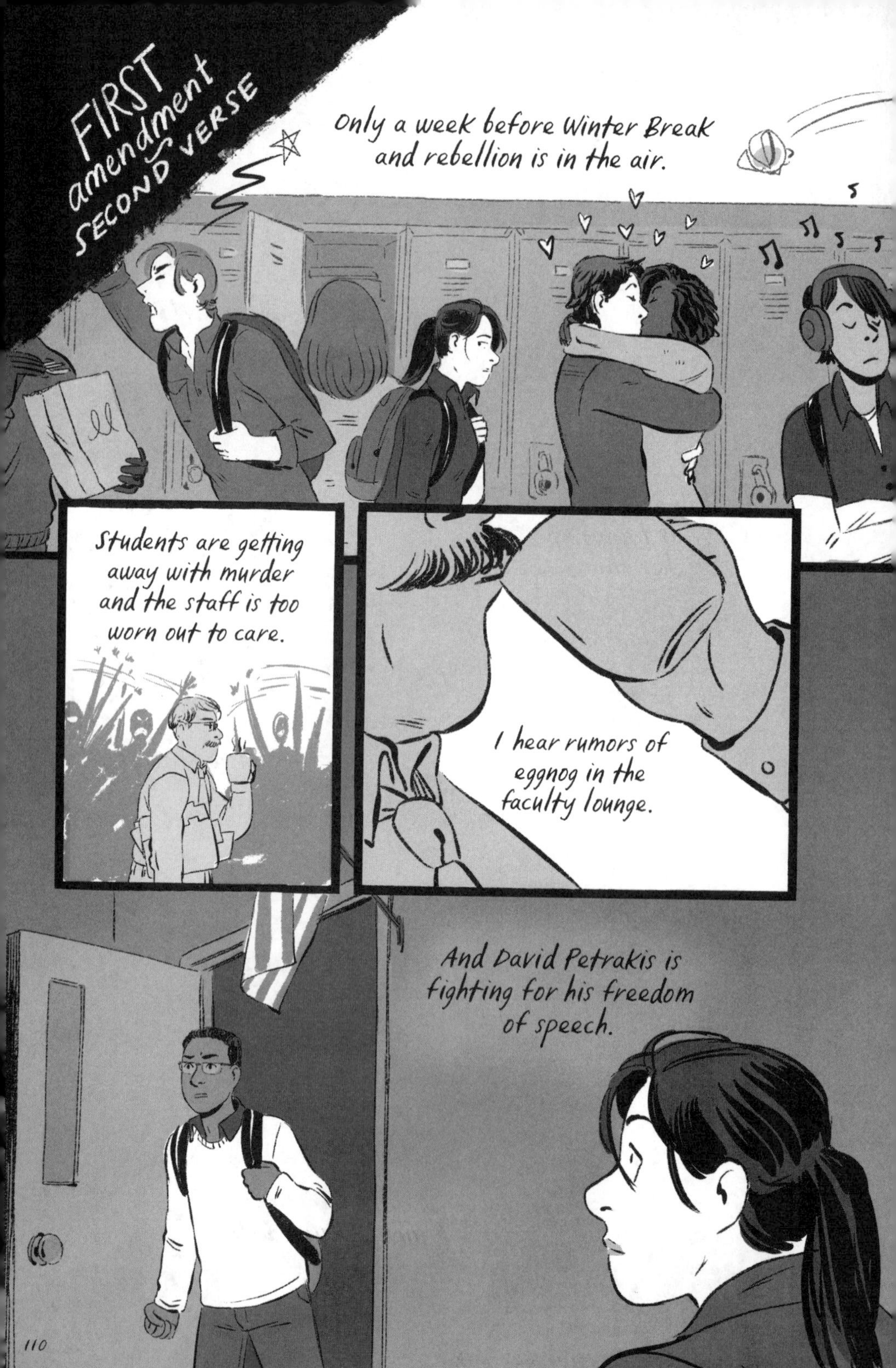
FIRST amendment SECOND VERSE
Only a week before Winter Break and rebellion is in the air.
Students are getting away with murder and the staff is too worn out to care.
I hear rumors of eggnog in the faculty lounge.
And David Petrakis is fighting for his freedom of speech.

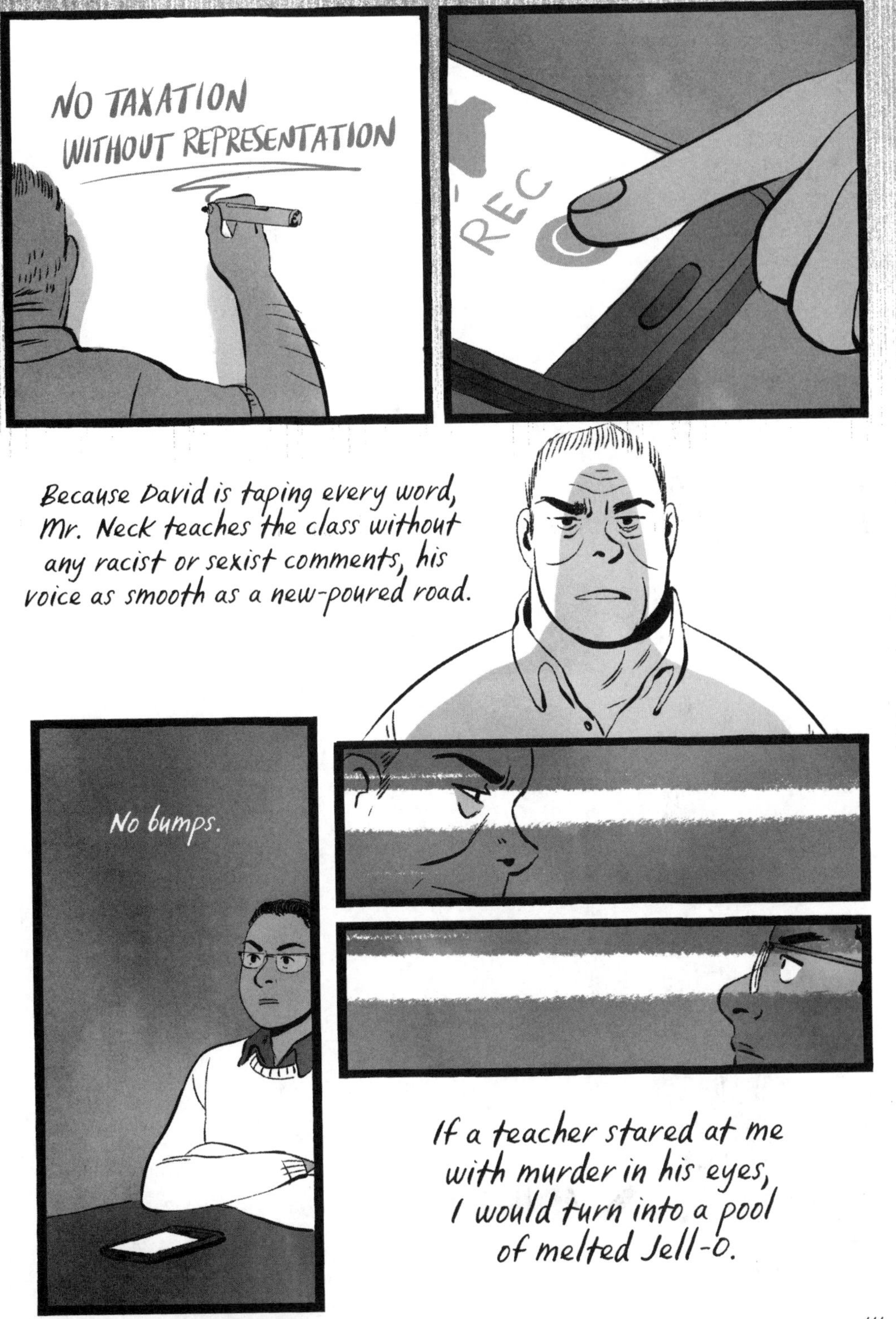
NO TAXATION WITHOUT REPRESENTATION
REC
Because David is taping every word, Mr. Neck teaches the class without any racist or sexist comments, his voice as smooth as a new-poured road.
No bumps.
If a teacher stared at me with murder in his eyes, I would turn into a pool of melted Jell-O.

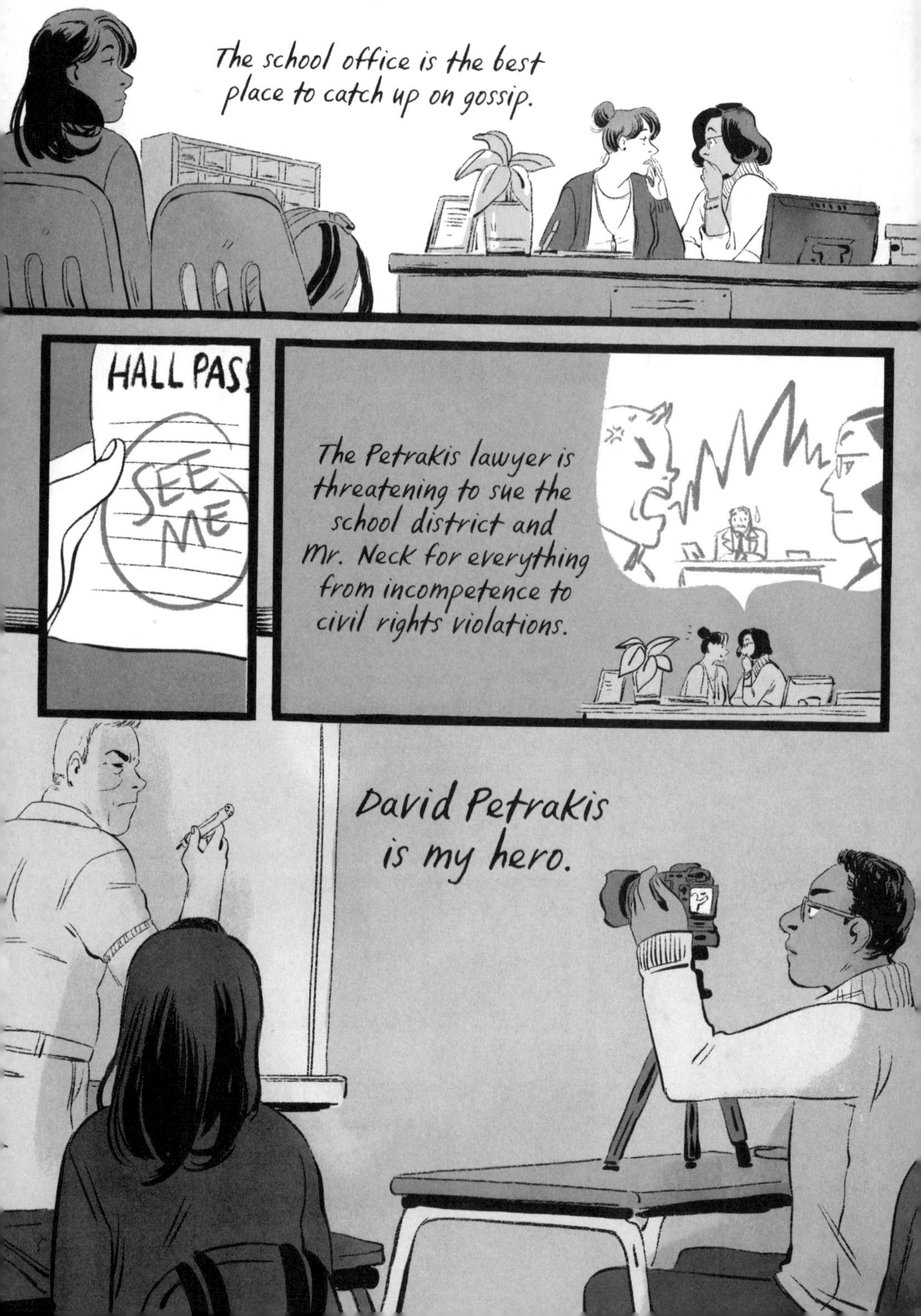
The school office is the best place to catch up on gossip.
HALL PASS
SEE ME
The Petrakis lawyer is threatening to sue the school district and Mr. Neck for everything from incompetence to civil rights violations.
David Petrakis is my hero.

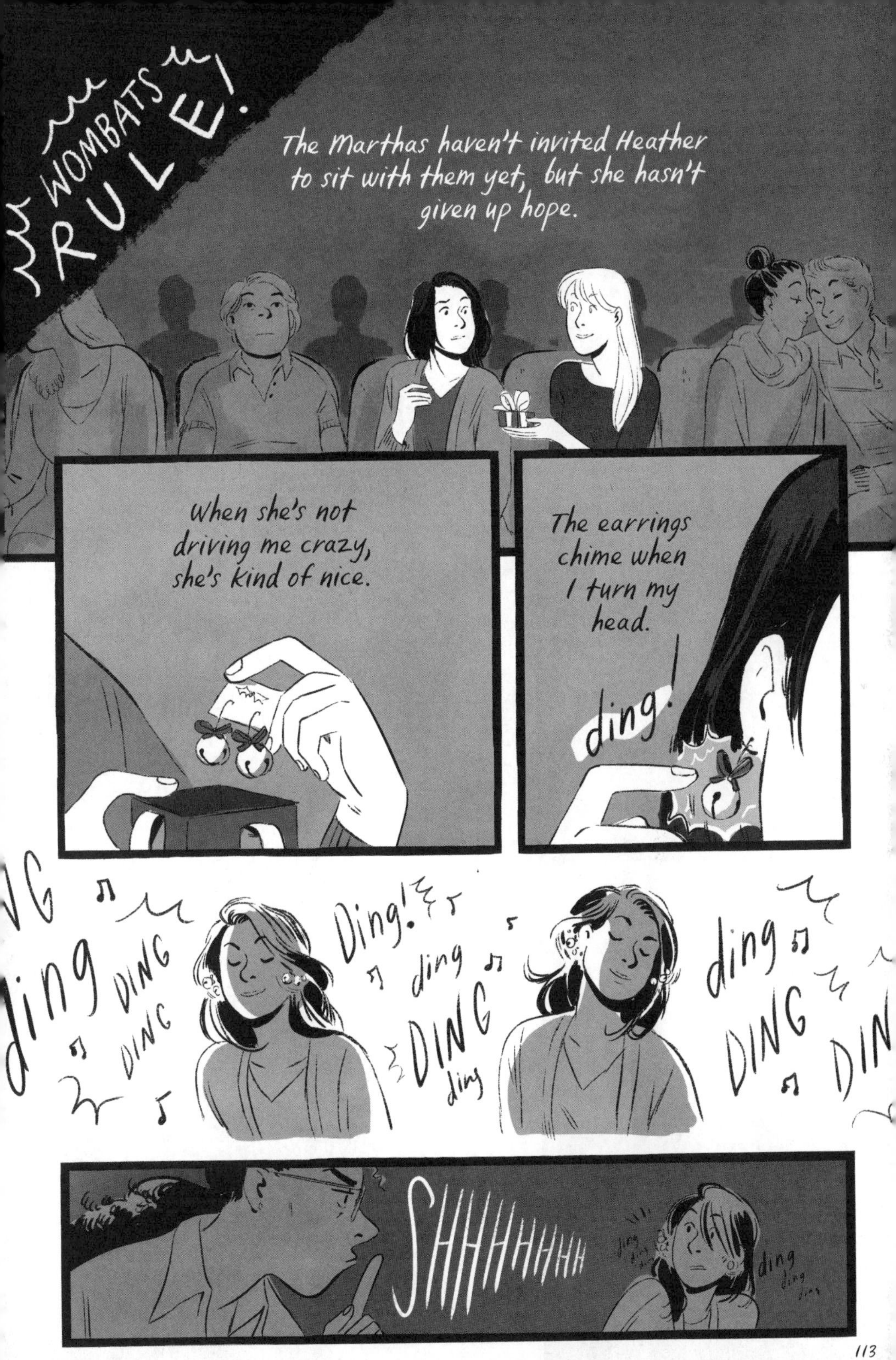
WOMBATS RULE!
The Marthas haven't invited Heather to sit with them yet, but she hasn't given up hope.
When she's not driving me crazy, she's kind of nice.
The earrings chime when I turn my head.
ding!
ding DING DING
Ding! ding DING ding
ding DING DIN
SHHHHHHH
ding ding ding
ding ding ding

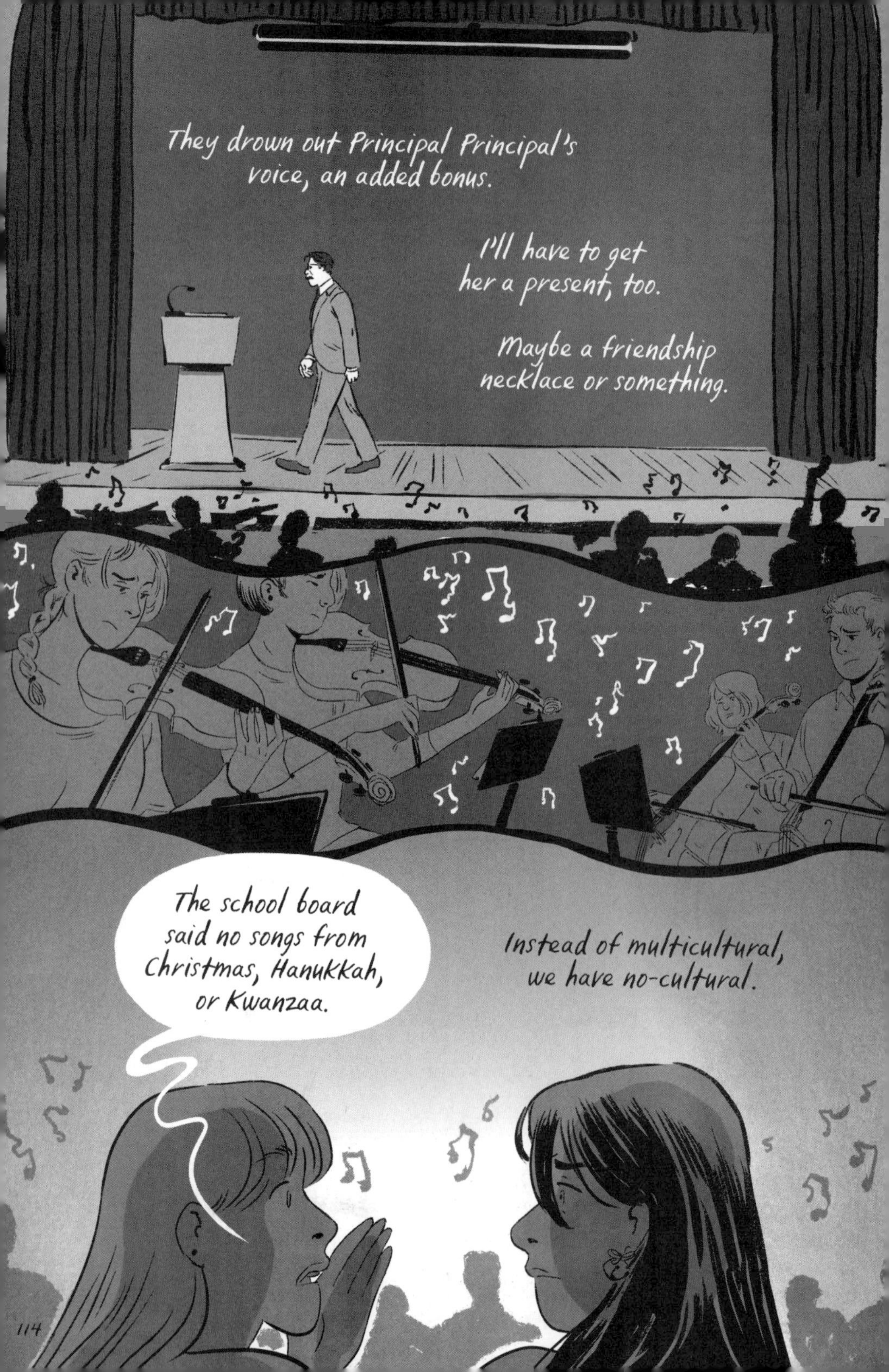
They drown out Principal Principal's voice, an added bonus.
I'll have to get her a present, too.
Maybe a friendship necklace or something.
The school board said no songs from Christmas, Hanukkah, or Kwanzaa.
Instead of multicultural, we have no-cultural.

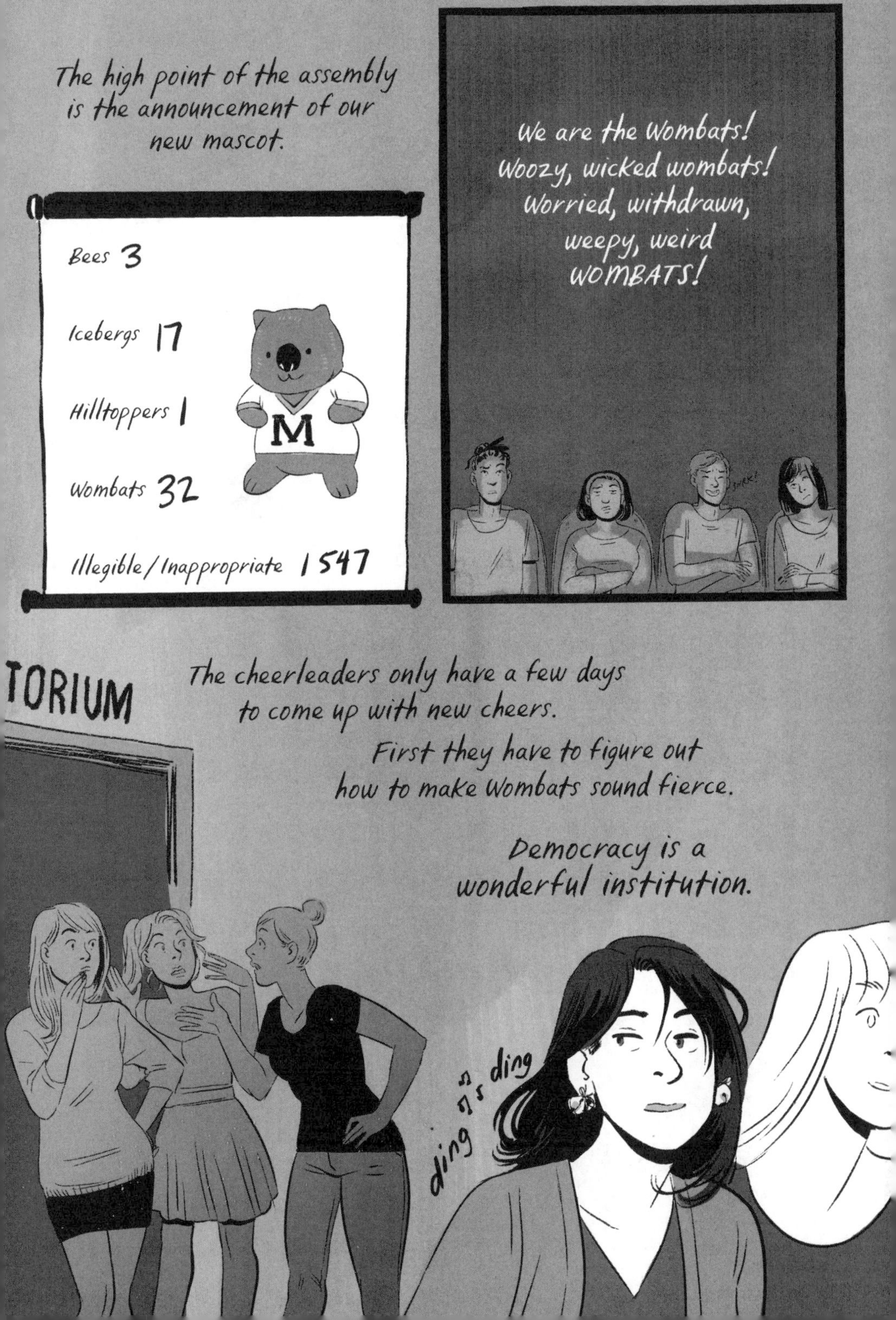

The high point of the assembly is the announcement of our new mascot.
Bees 3
Icebergs 17
Hilltoppers 1
Wombats 32
Illegible/Inappropriate 1547
M
We are the Wombats! Woozy, wicked wombats! Worried, withdrawn, weepy, weird WOMBATS!
TORIUM
The cheerleaders only have a few days to come up with new cheers.
First they have to figure out how to make Wombats sound fierce.
Democracy is a wonderful institution.
ding ding

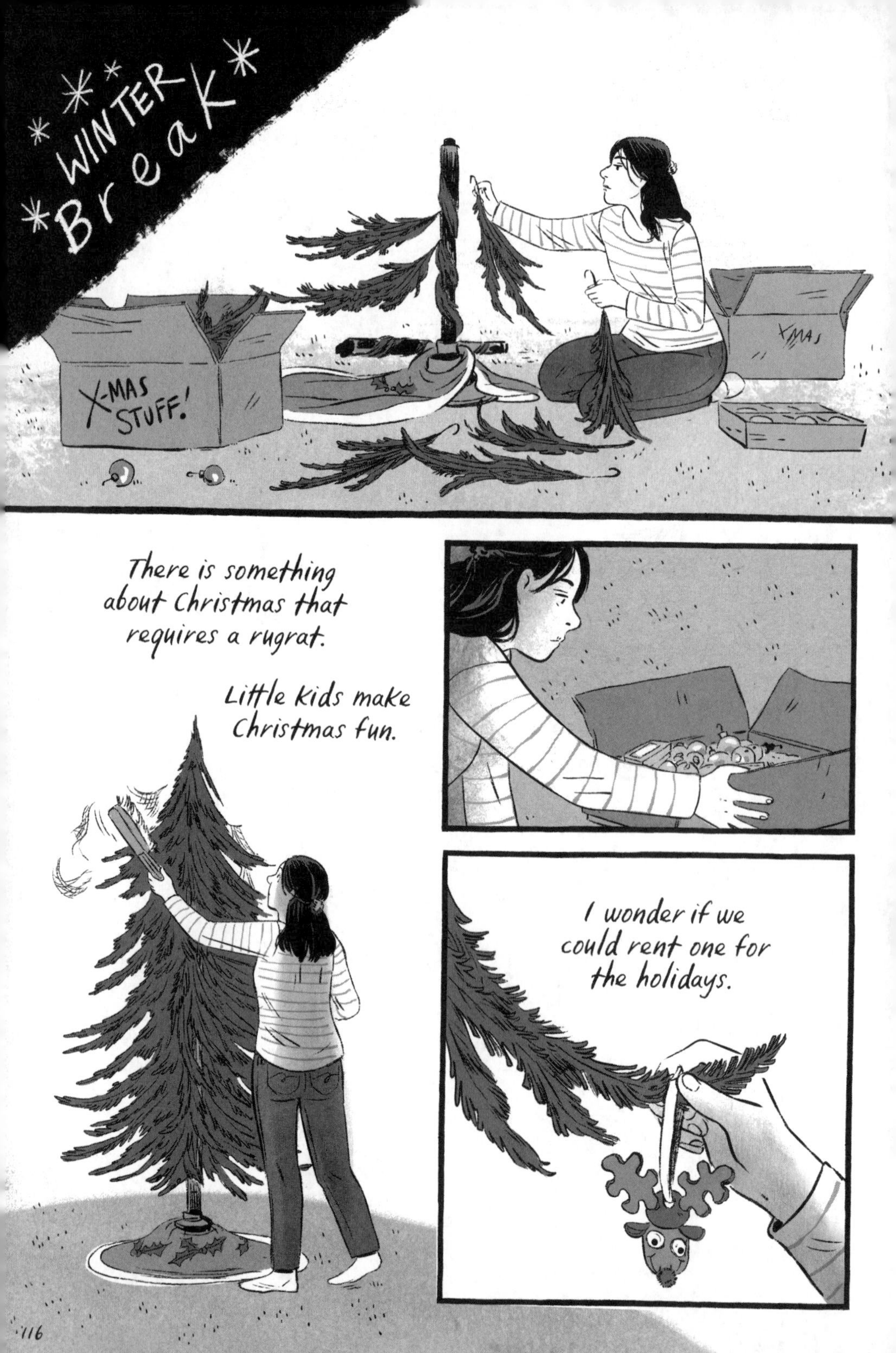

WINTER Break
X-MAS STUFF!
X-MAS
There is something about Christmas that requires a rugrat.
Little kids make Christmas fun.
I wonder if we could rent one for the holidays.

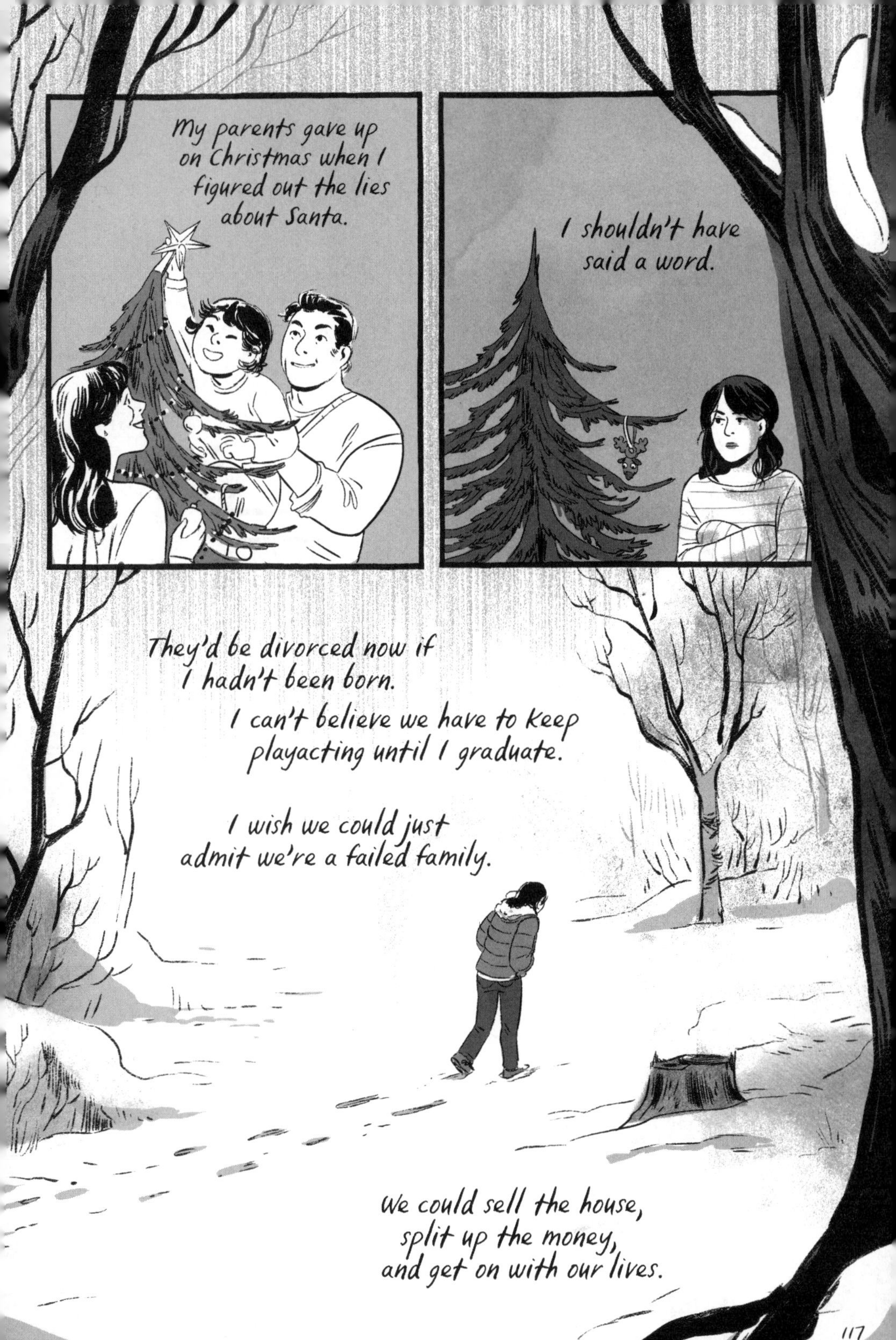
My parents gave up on Christmas when I figured out the lies about Santa.
I shouldn't have said a word.
They'd be divorced now if I hadn't been born.
I can't believe we have to keep playacting until I graduate.
I wish we could just admit we're a failed family.
We could sell the house, split up the money, and get on with our lives.

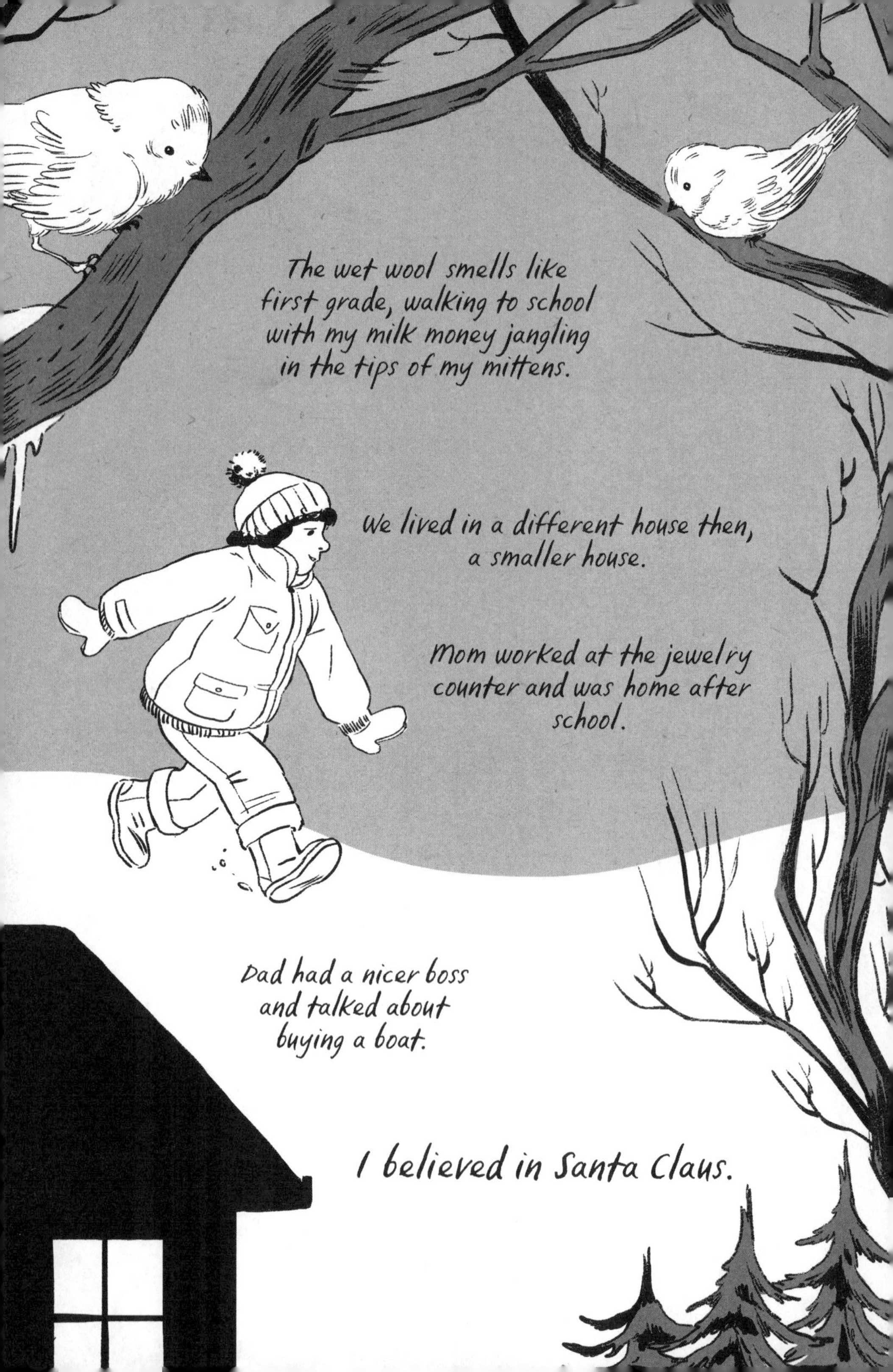
The wet wool smells like first grade, walking to school with my milk money jangling in the tips of my mittens.
We lived in a different house then, a smaller house.
Mom worked at the jewelry counter and was home after school.
Dad had a nicer boss and talked about buying a boat.
I believed in Santa Claus.

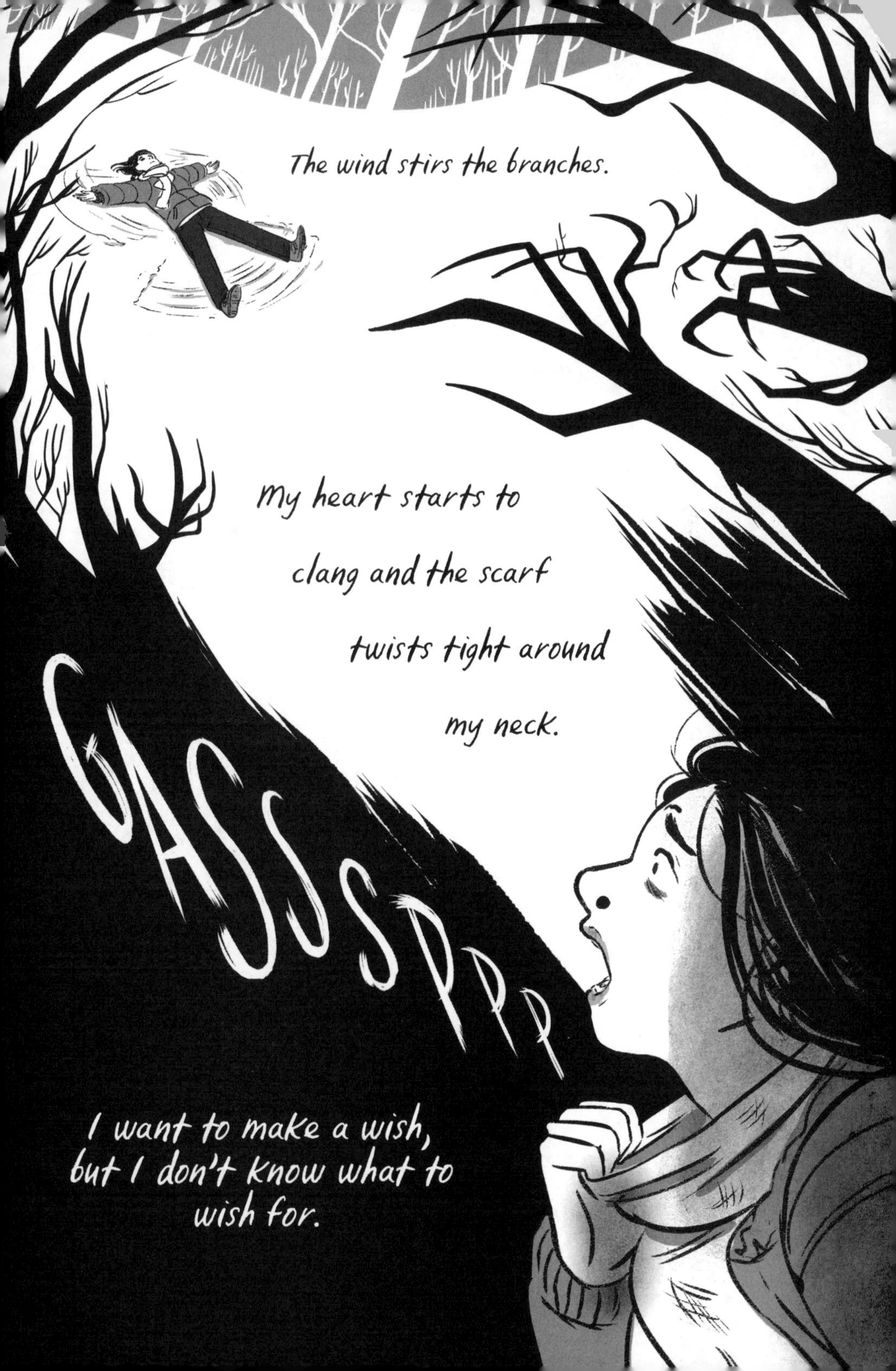
The wind stirs the branches.
My heart starts to clang and the scarf twists tight around my neck.
GASSSPPP
I want to make a wish, but I don't know what to wish for.

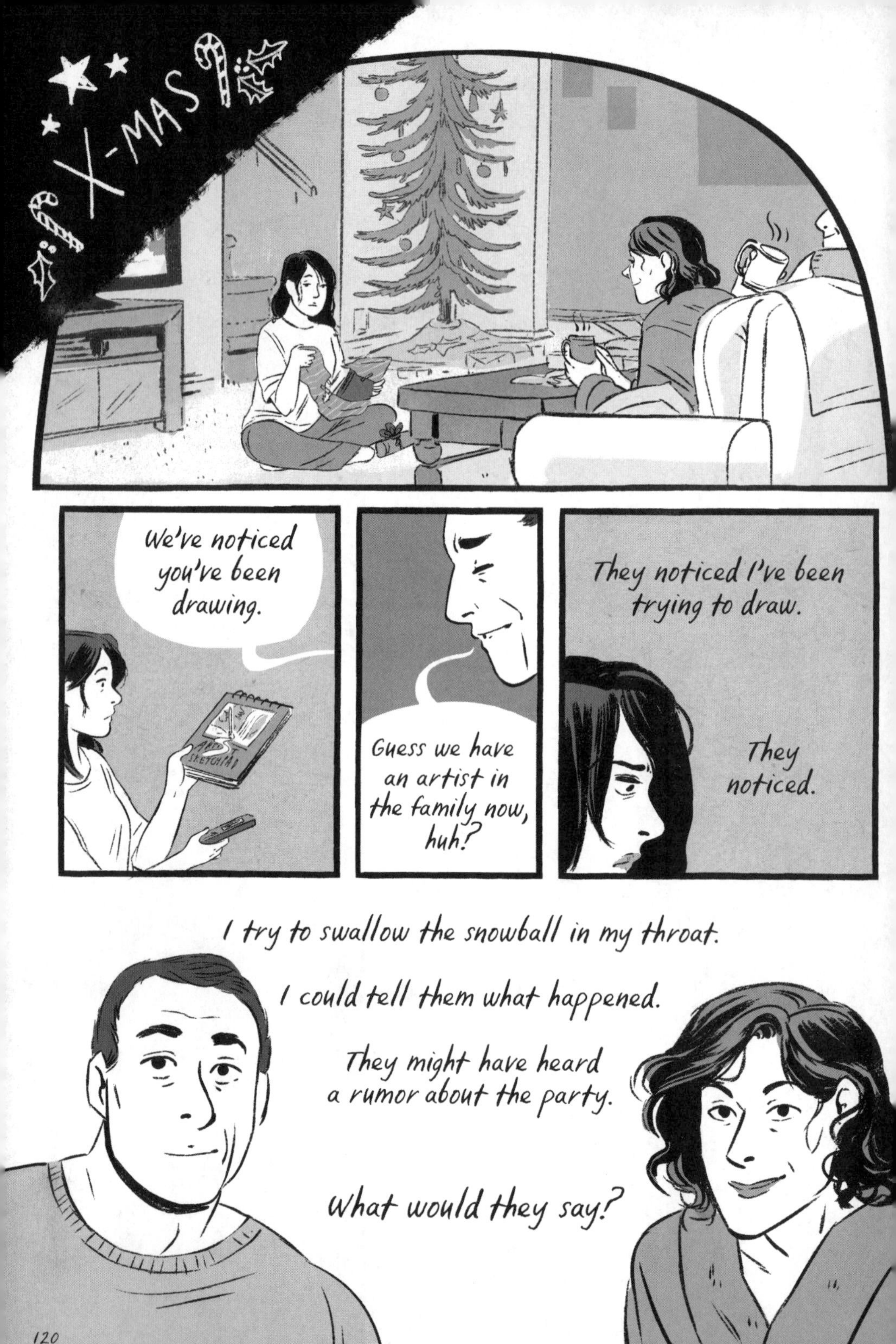
X-MAS
We've noticed you've been drawing.
ARTIST SKETCHPAD
Guess we have an artist in the family now, huh?
They noticed I've been trying to draw.
They noticed.
I try to swallow the snowball in my throat.
I could tell them what happened.
They might have heard a rumor about the party.
What would they say?

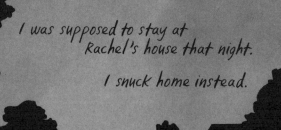

I was supposed to stay at
Rachel's house that night.

I snuck home instead.

Mom and Dad
were gone.
Both cars, too.

I showered until the hot water
was gone, then I crawled into bed
and did not sleep.

Mom pulled in around 2 a.m.

Dad came home at dawn.

They had not been
together.

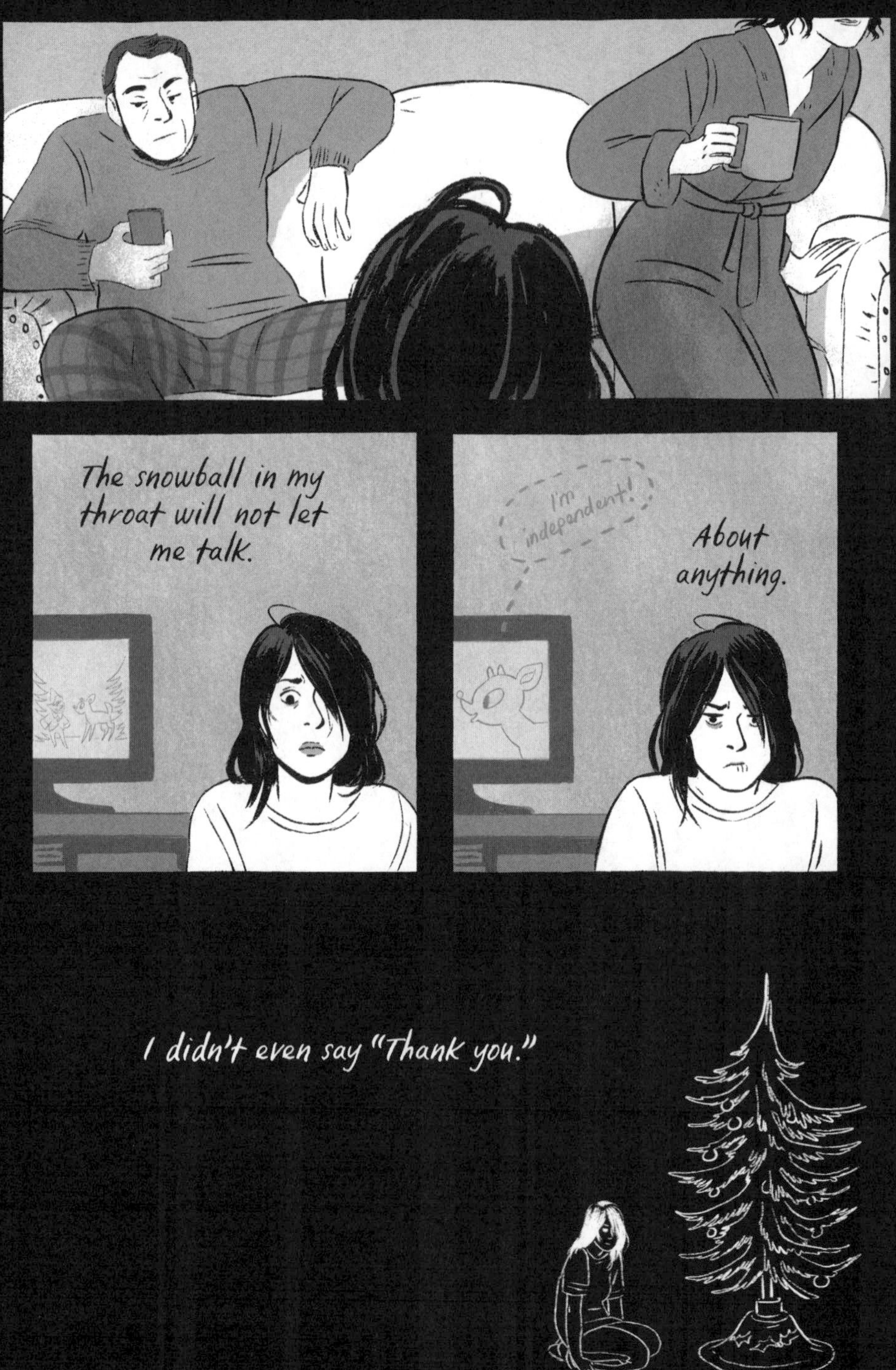
The snowball in my throat will not let me talk.
I'm independent!
About anything.
I didn't even say "Thank you."

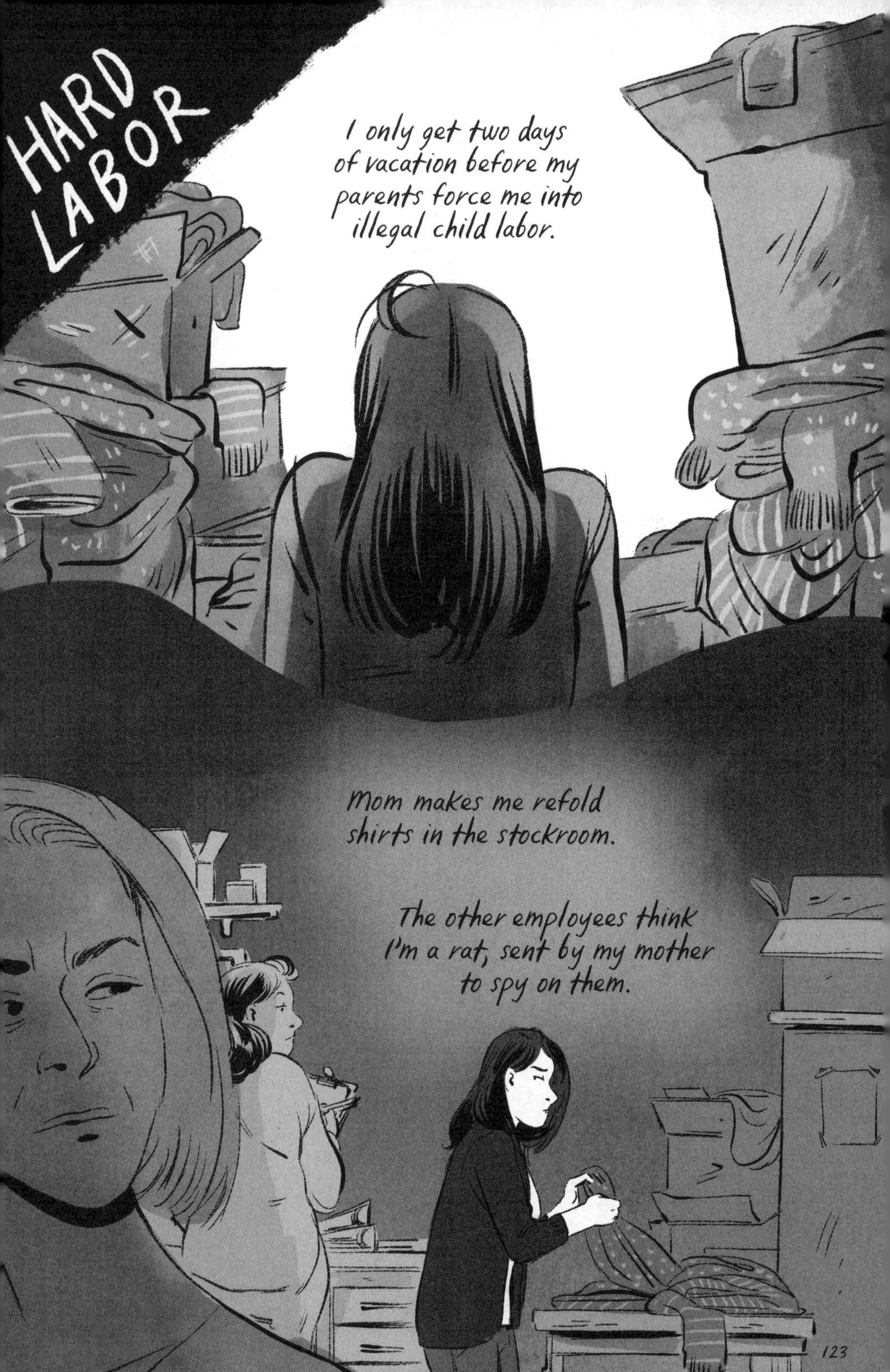
HARD LABOR
I only get two days of vacation before my parents force me into illegal child labor.
Mom makes me refold shirts in the stockroom.
The other employees think I'm a rat, sent by my mother to spy on them.

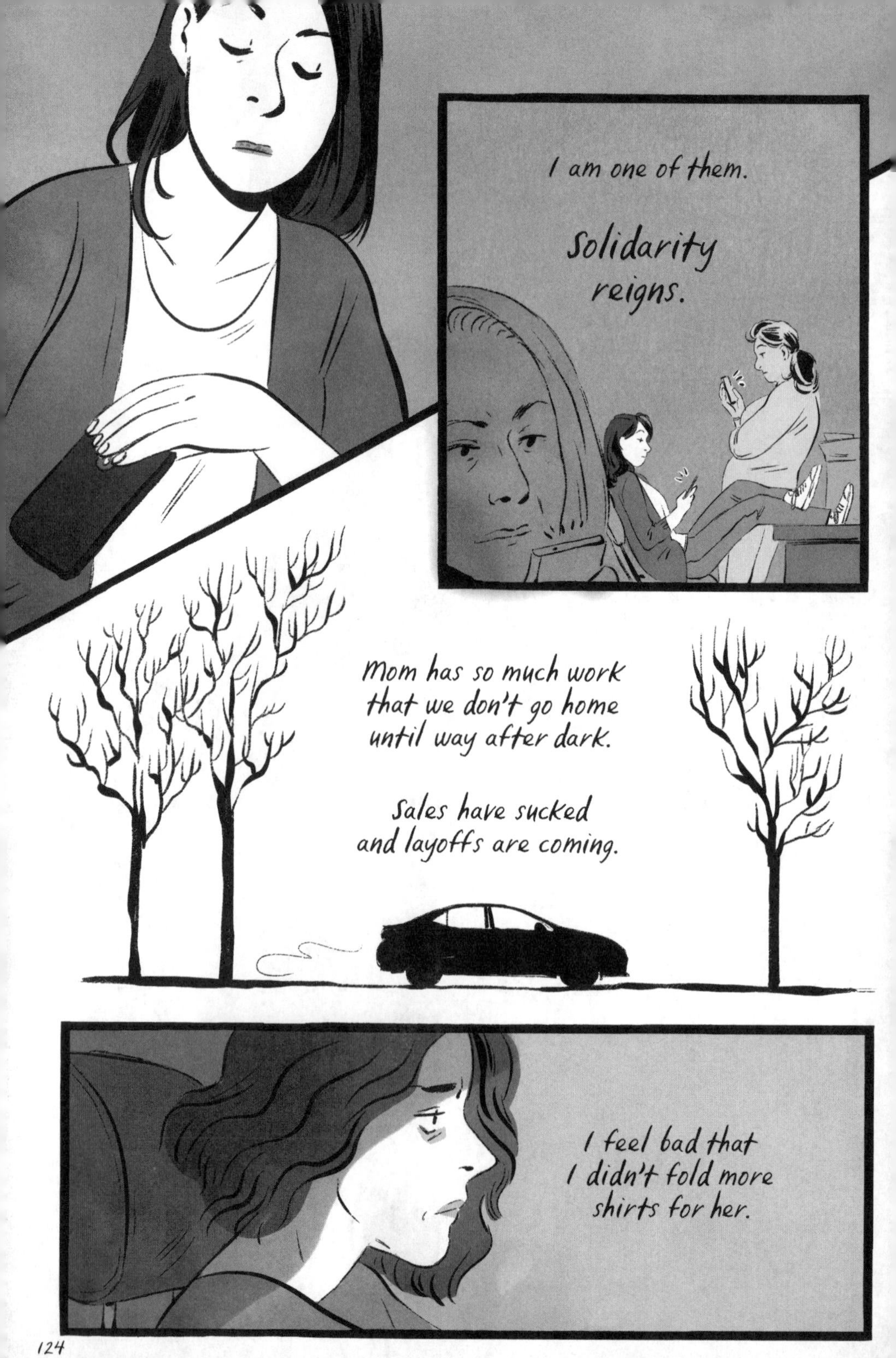
I am one of them.
Solidarity reigns.
Mom has so much work that we don't go home until way after dark.
Sales have sucked and layoffs are coming.
I feel bad that I didn't fold more shirts for her.

The next day I have to go to work with my father.

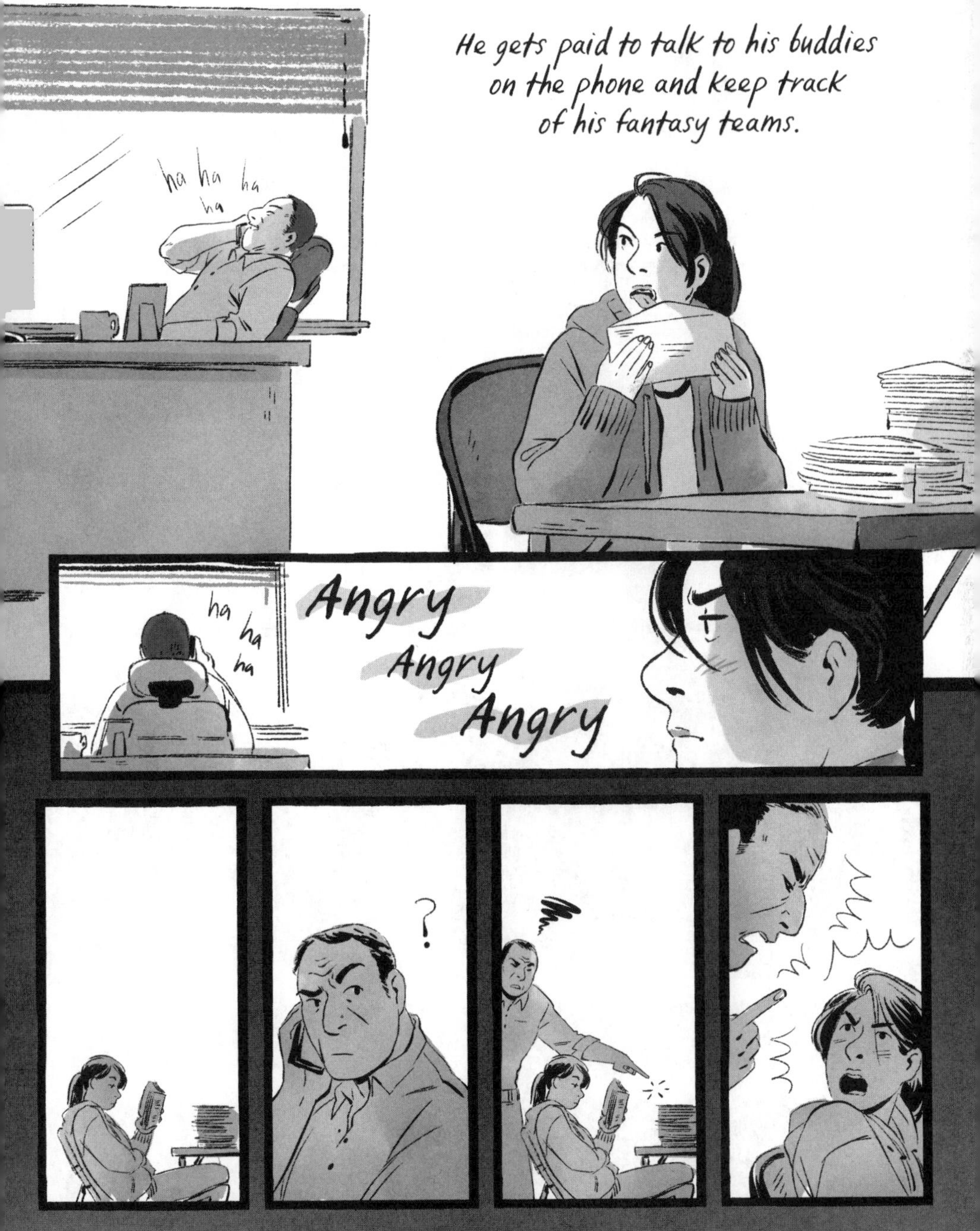
He gets paid to talk to his buddies on the phone and keep track of his fantasy teams.
ha ha ha ha
ha ha ha
Angry
Angry
Angry
?

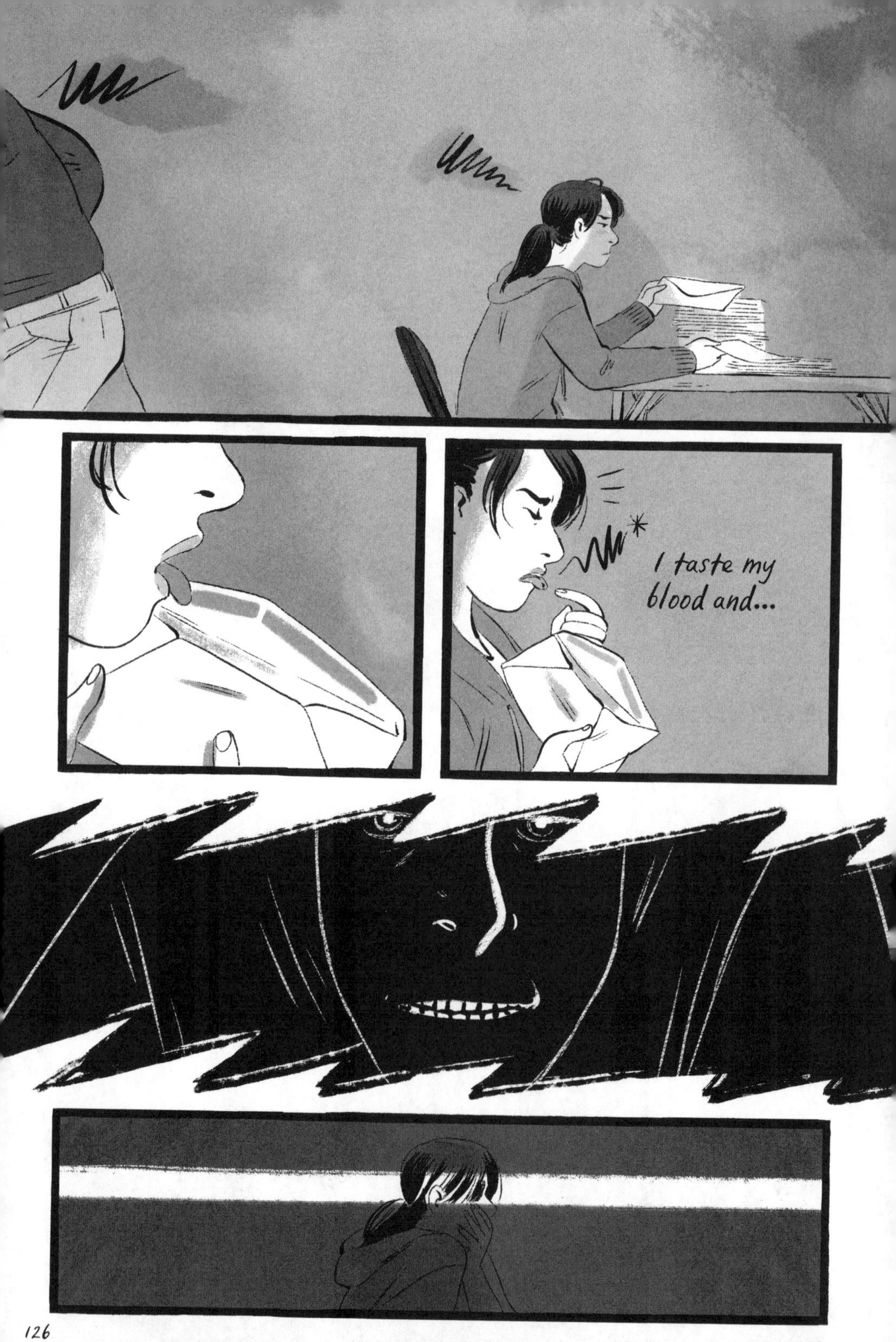
I taste my
blood and...

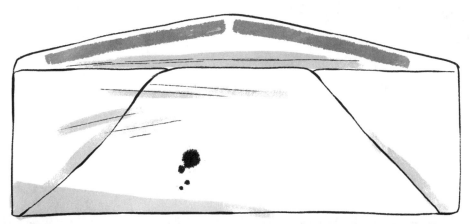

It can't hurt that much, can it?

I am actually grateful to go back to school.

FOUL

Let's start with some foul shots.

Now that there is two feet of snow on the ground, the fizz-ed teachers let us have class inside.

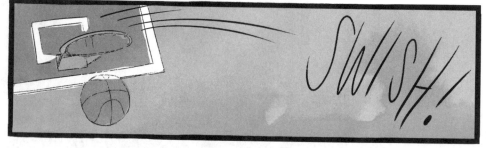

SWISH!

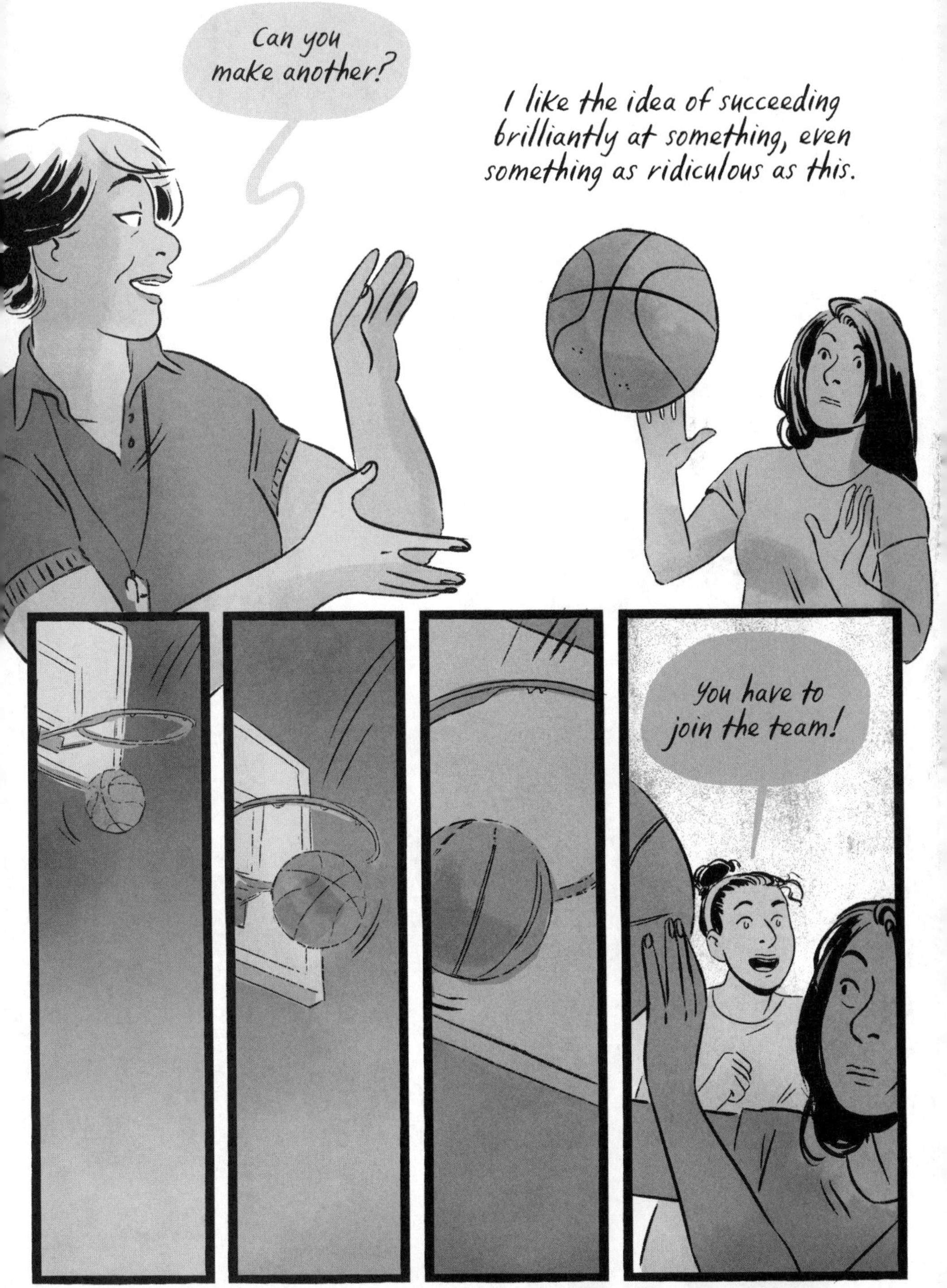
Can you make another?
I like the idea of succeeding brilliantly at something, even something as ridiculous as this.
You have to join the team!

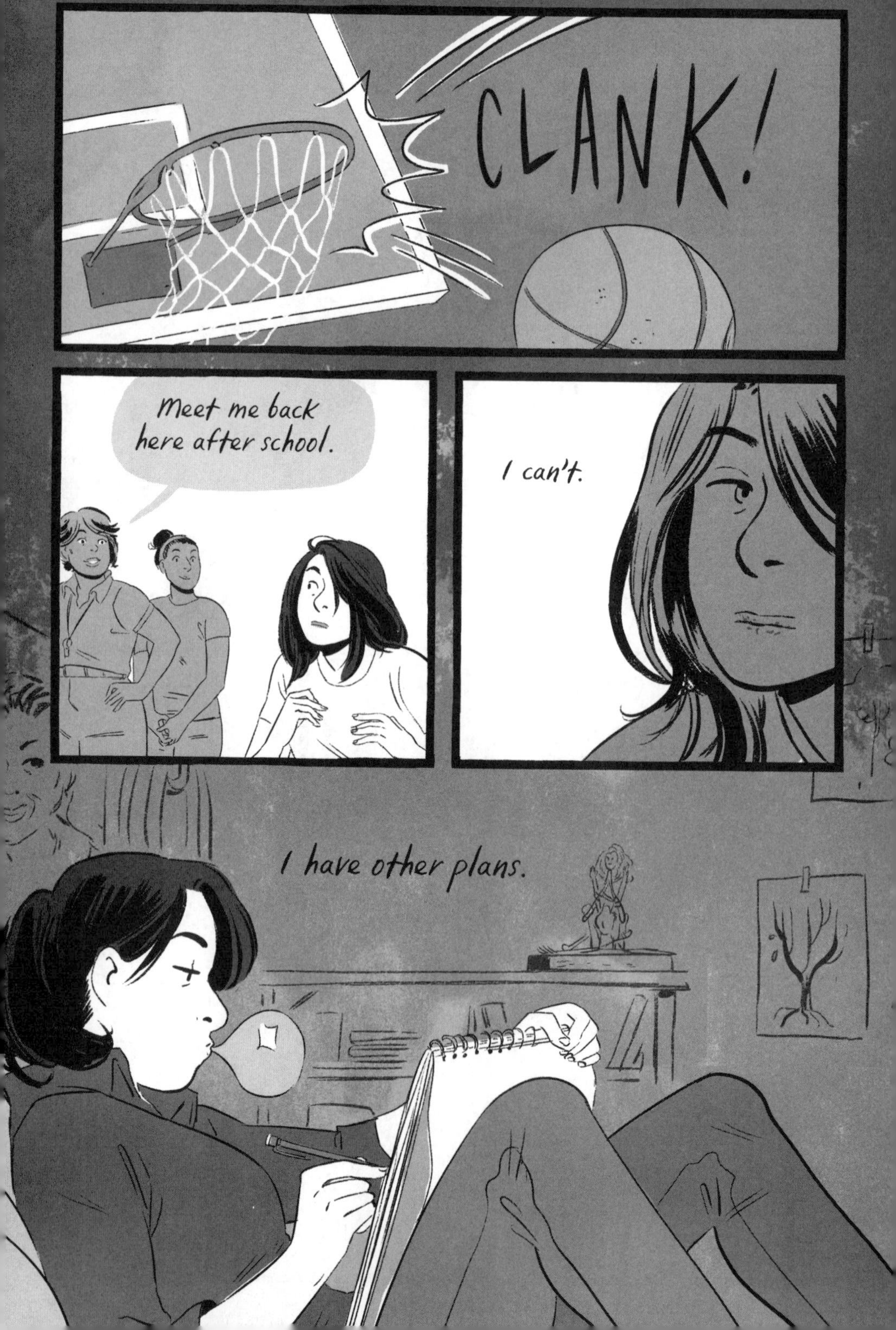
CLANK!
Meet me back here after school.
I can't.
I have other plans.

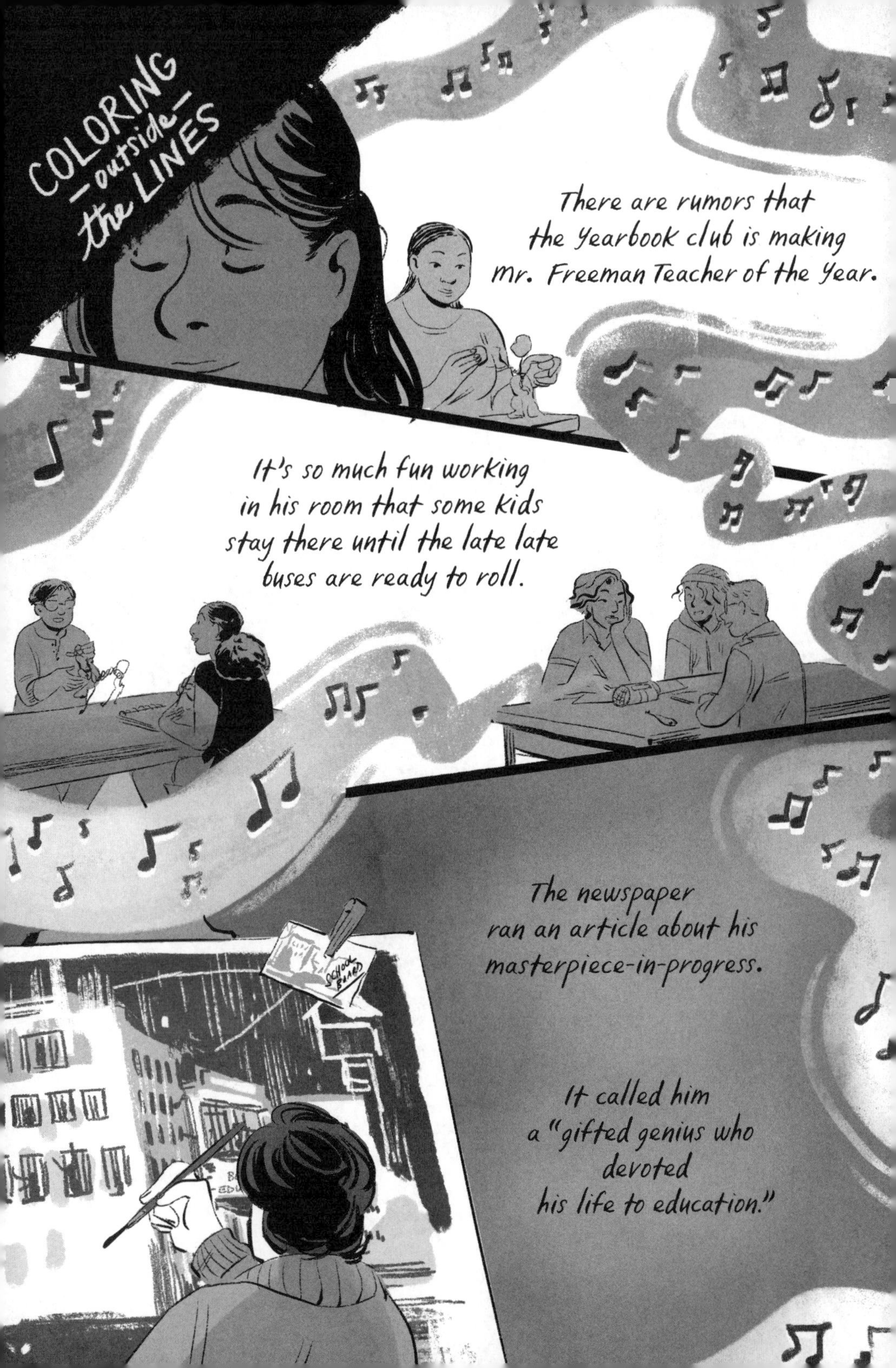
COLORING
—outside—
the LINES
There are rumors that the Yearbook club is making mr. Freeman Teacher of the Year.
It's so much fun working in his room that some kids stay there until the late late buses are ready to roll.
SCHOOL BOARD
The newspaper ran an article about his masterpiece-in-progress.
It called him a "gifted genius who devoted his life to education."

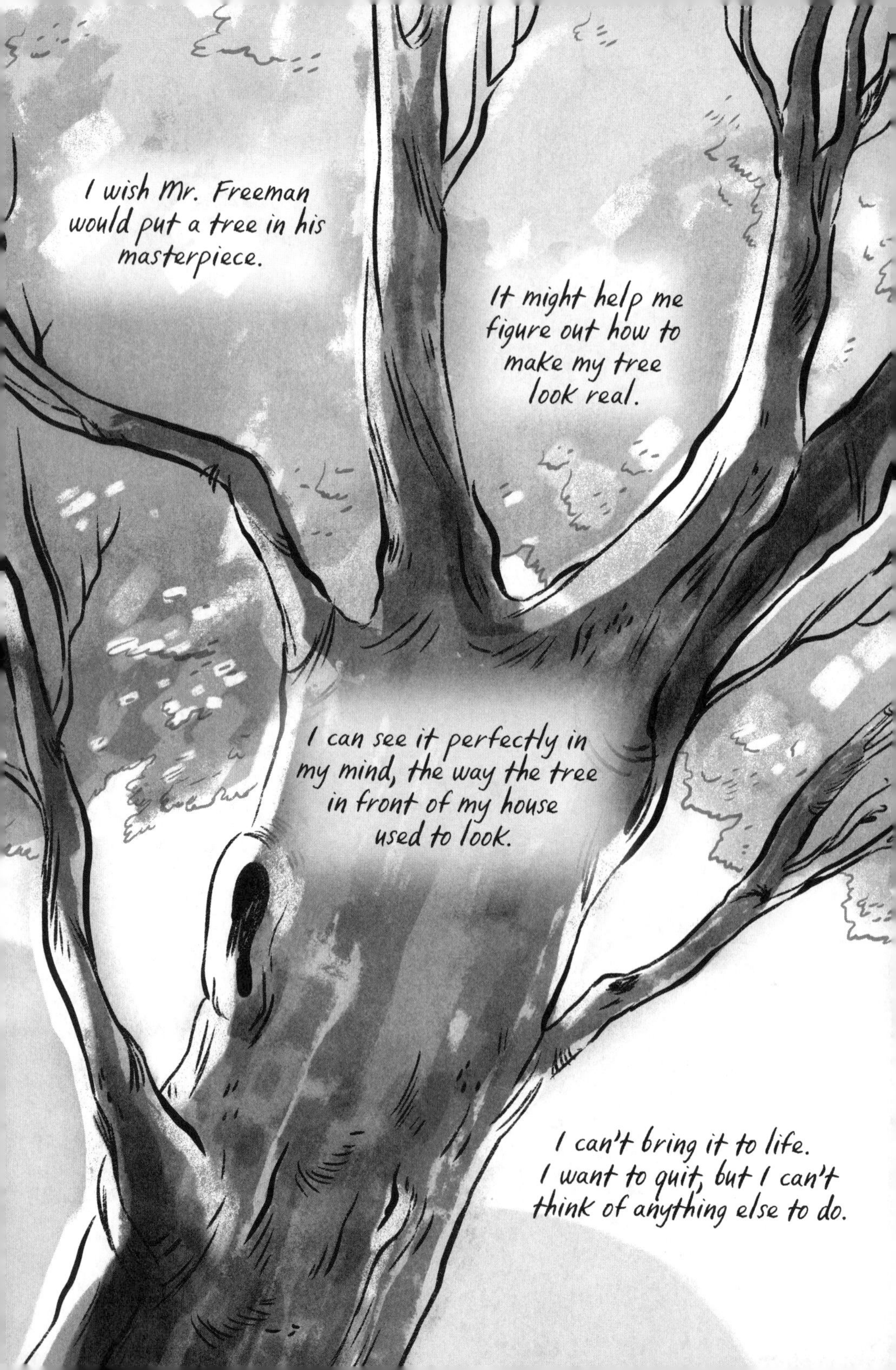
I wish Mr. Freeman would put a tree in his masterpiece.
It might help me figure out how to make my tree look real.
I can see it perfectly in my mind, the way the tree in front of my house used to look.
I can't bring it to life. I want to quit, but I can't think of anything else to do.

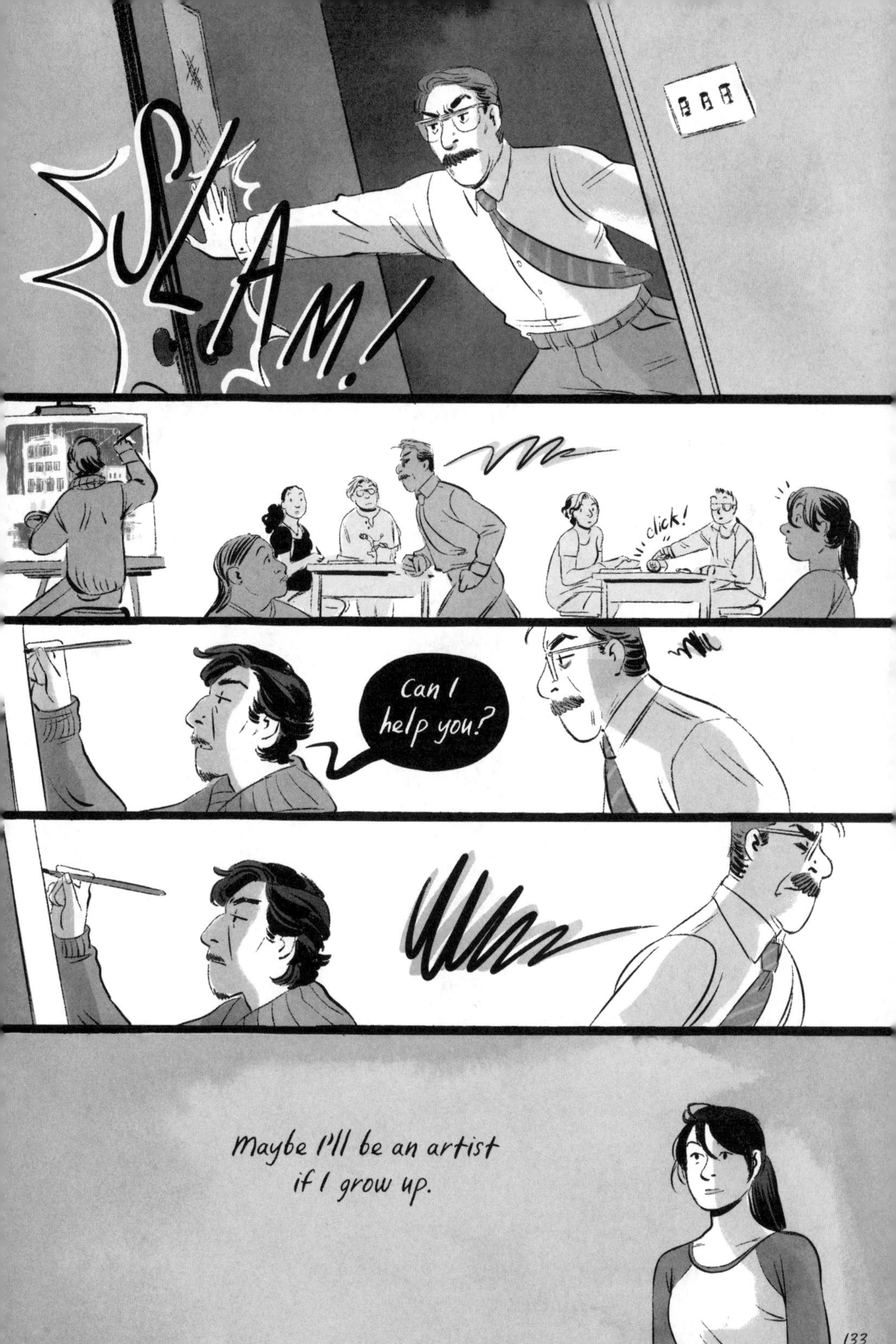
SLAM!
click!
Can I help you?
Maybe I'll be an artist if I grow up.

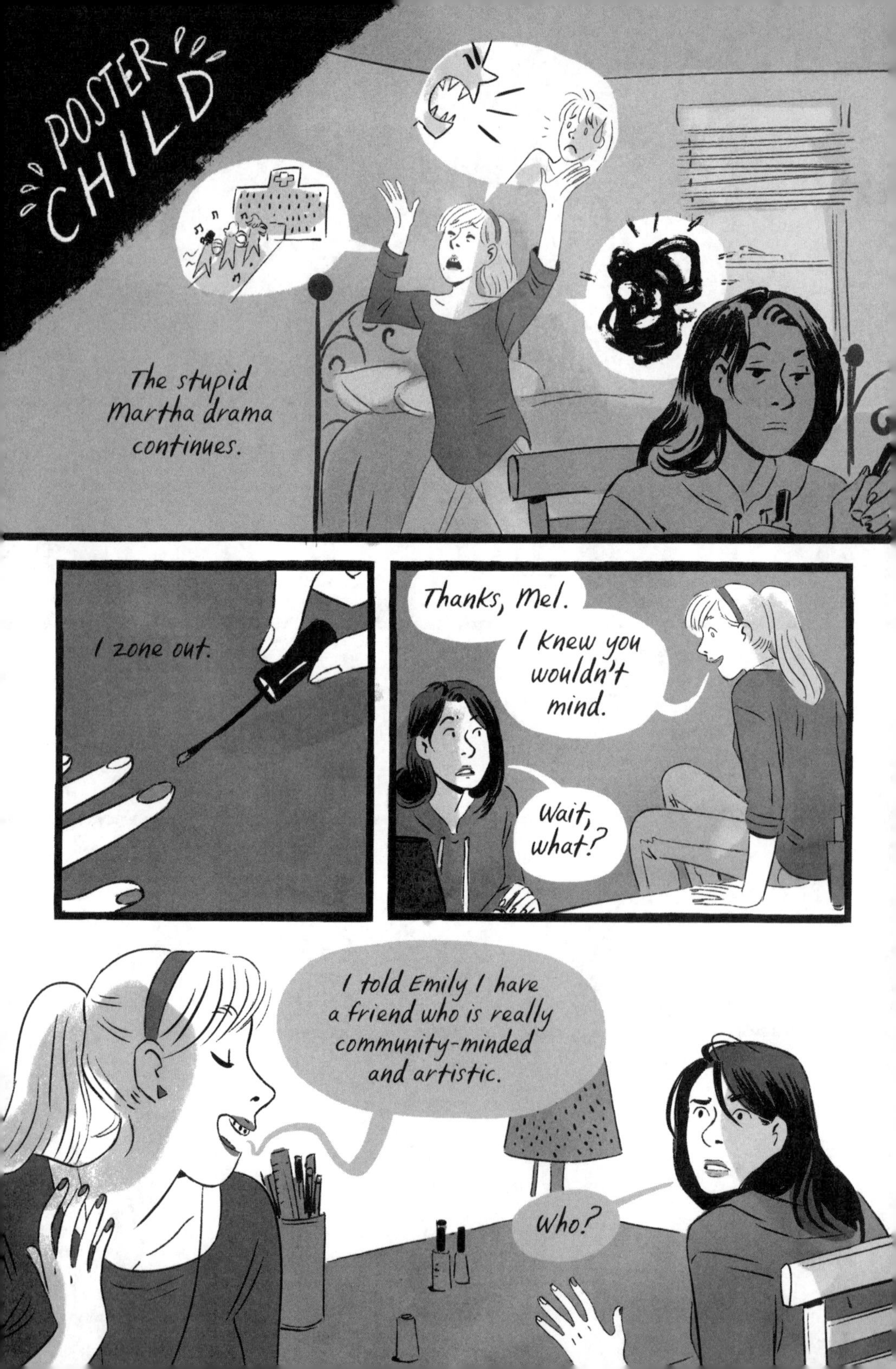
POSTER CHILD
The stupid Martha drama continues.
I zone out.
Thanks, Mel.
I knew you wouldn't mind.
Wait, what?
I told Emily I have a friend who is really community-minded and artistic.
Who?

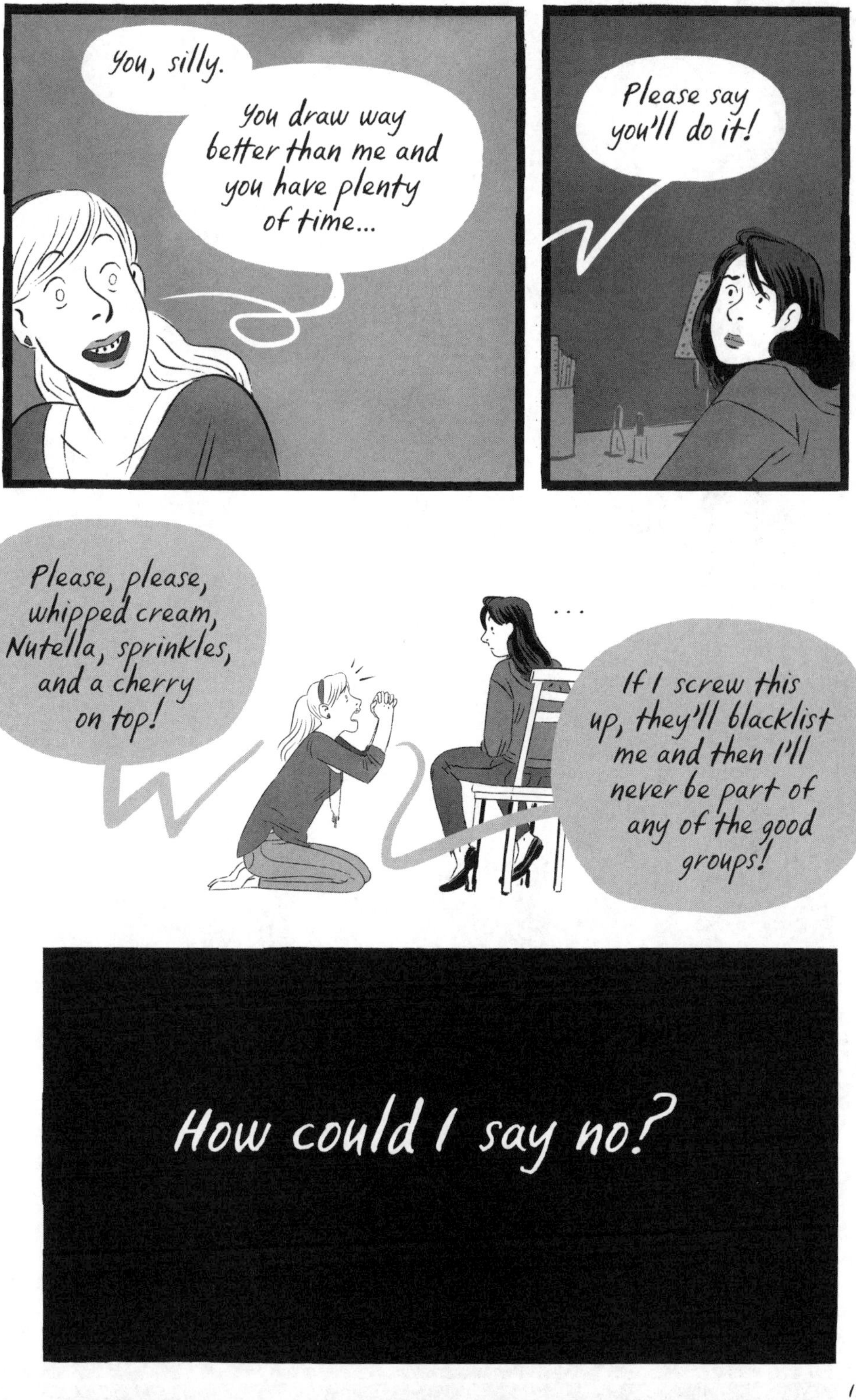
You, silly.
You draw way better than me and you have plenty of time...
Please say you'll do it!
Please, please, whipped cream, Nutella, sprinkles, and a cherry on top!
...
If I screw this up, they'll blacklist me and then I'll never be part of any of the good groups!
How could I say no?

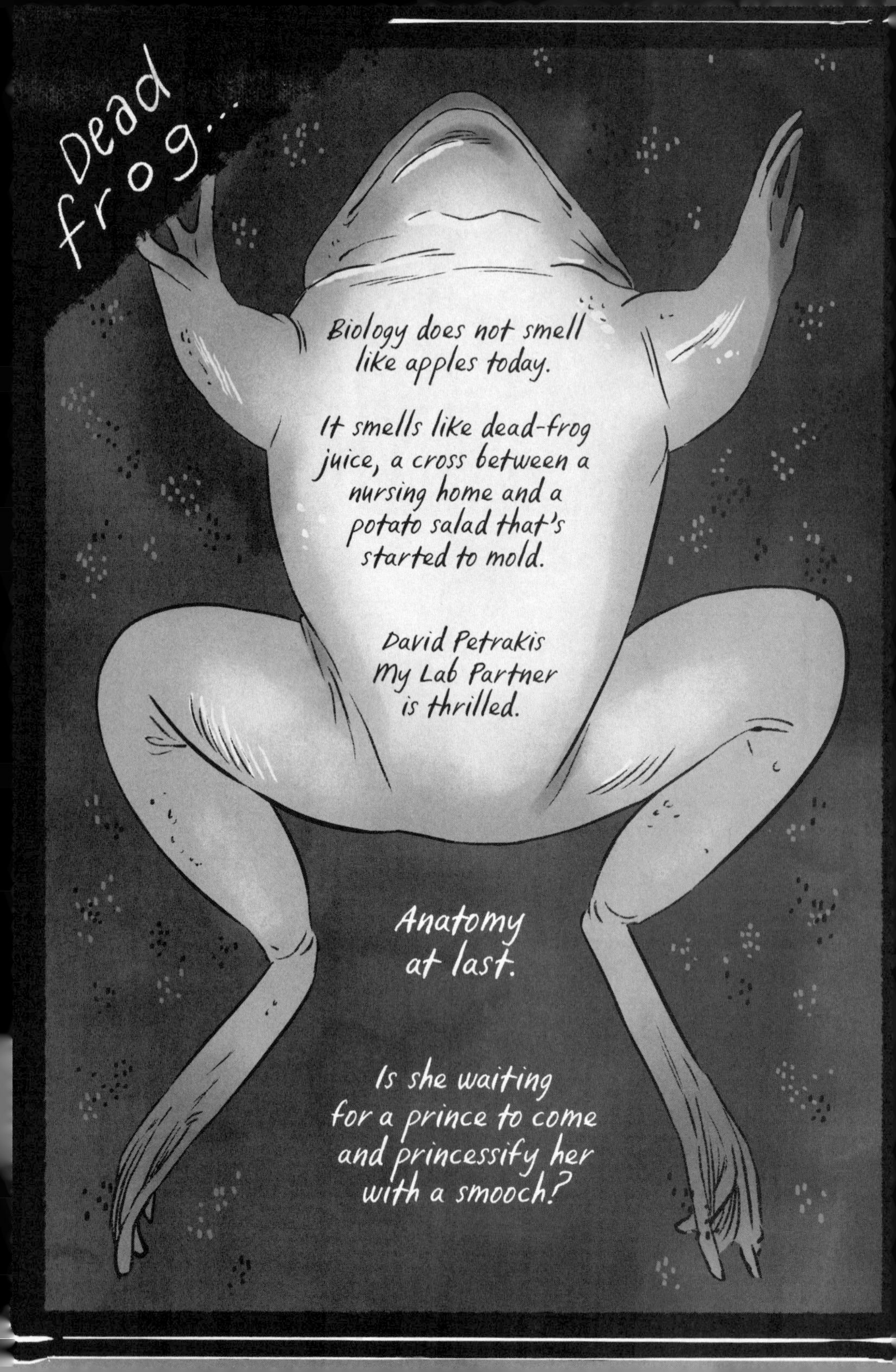

Dead frog...
Biology does not smell like apples today.
It smells like dead-frog juice, a cross between a nursing home and a potato salad that's started to mold.
David Petrakis My Lab Partner is thrilled.
Anatomy at last.
Is she waiting for a prince to come and princessify her with a smooch?

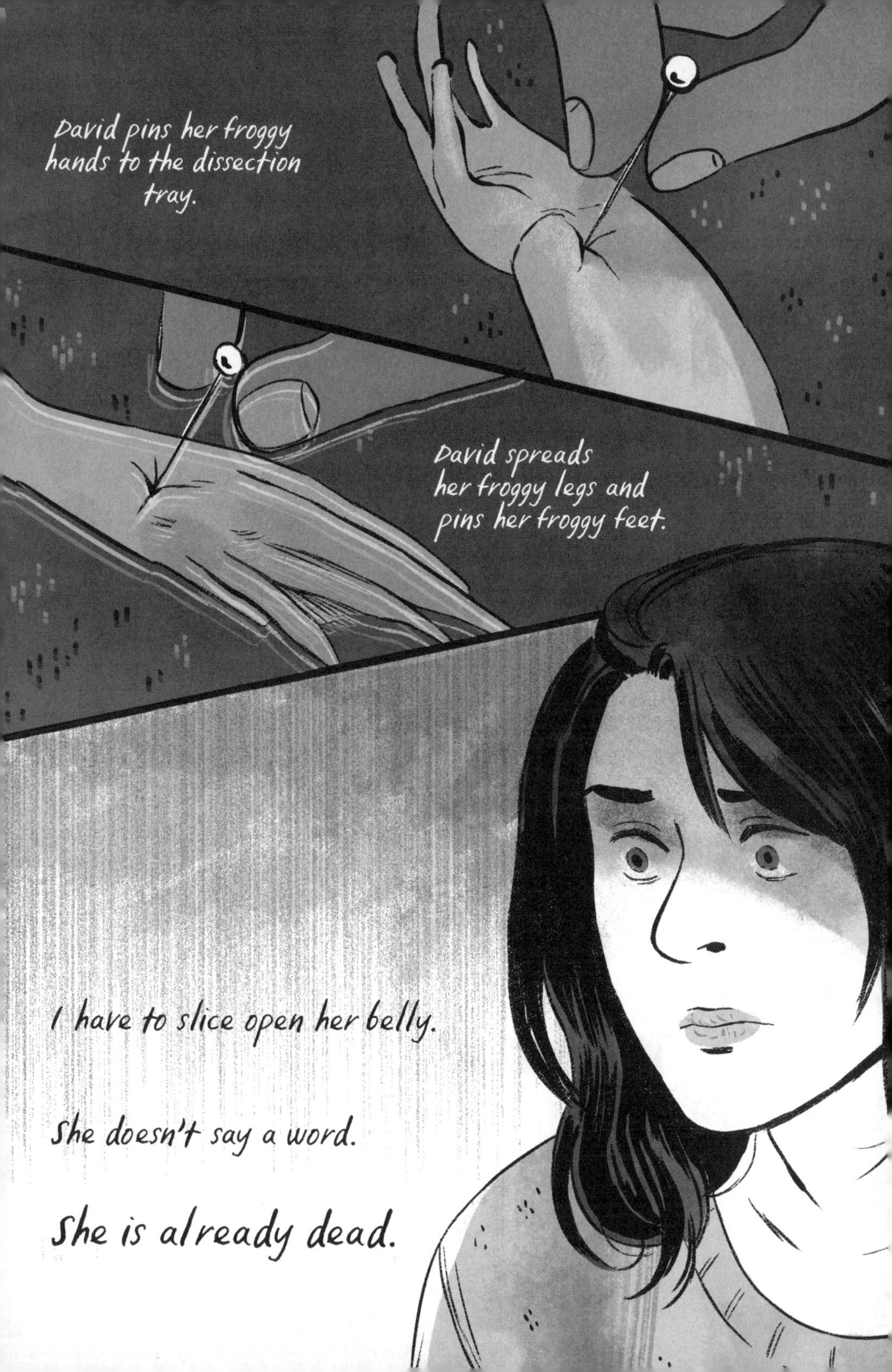
David pins her froggy hands to the dissection tray.
David spreads her froggy legs and pins her froggy feet.
I have to slice open her belly.
She doesn't say a word.
She is already dead.

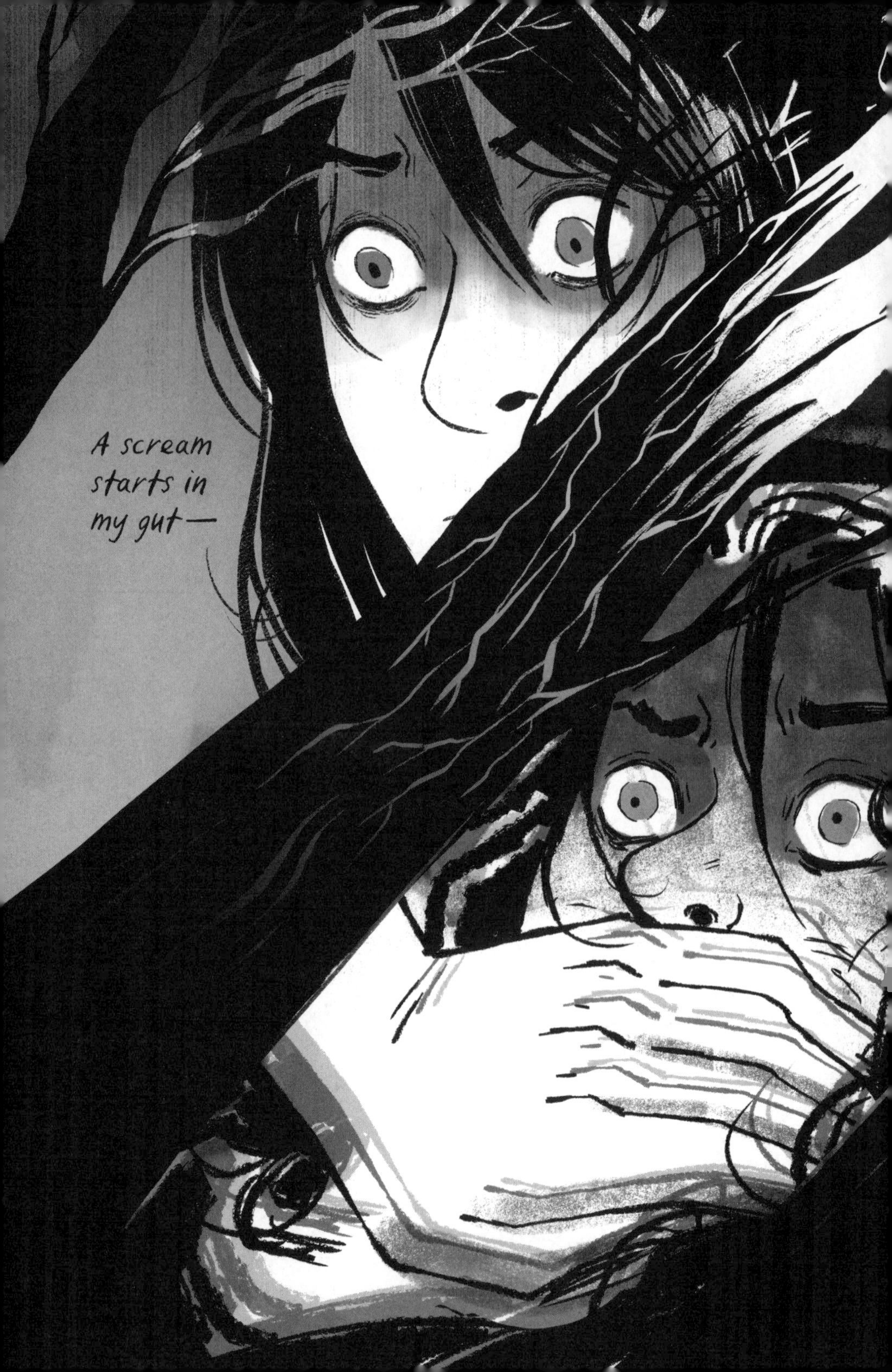
A scream starts in my gut—

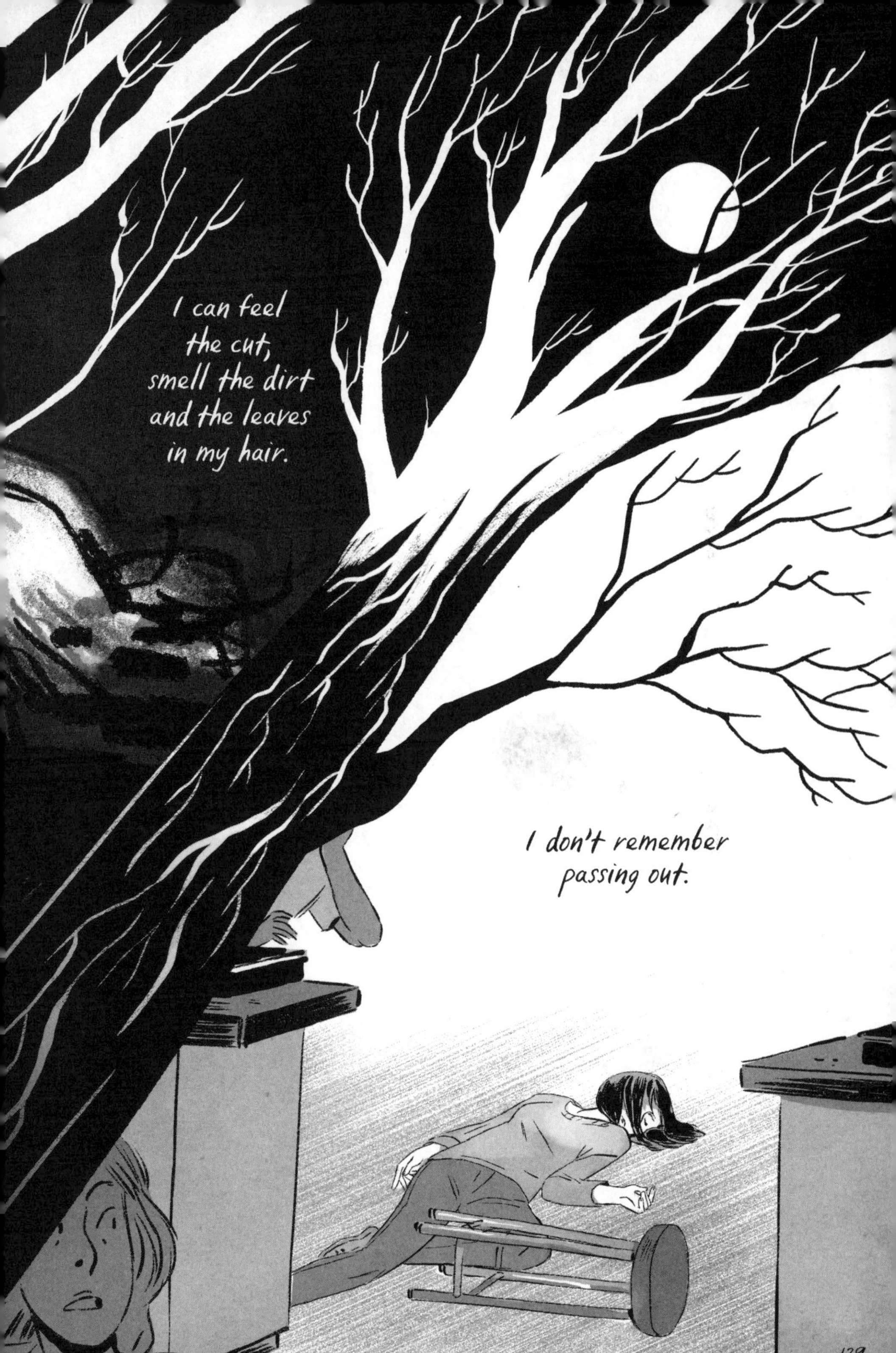
I can feel the cut, smell the dirt and the leaves in my hair.
I don't remember passing out.

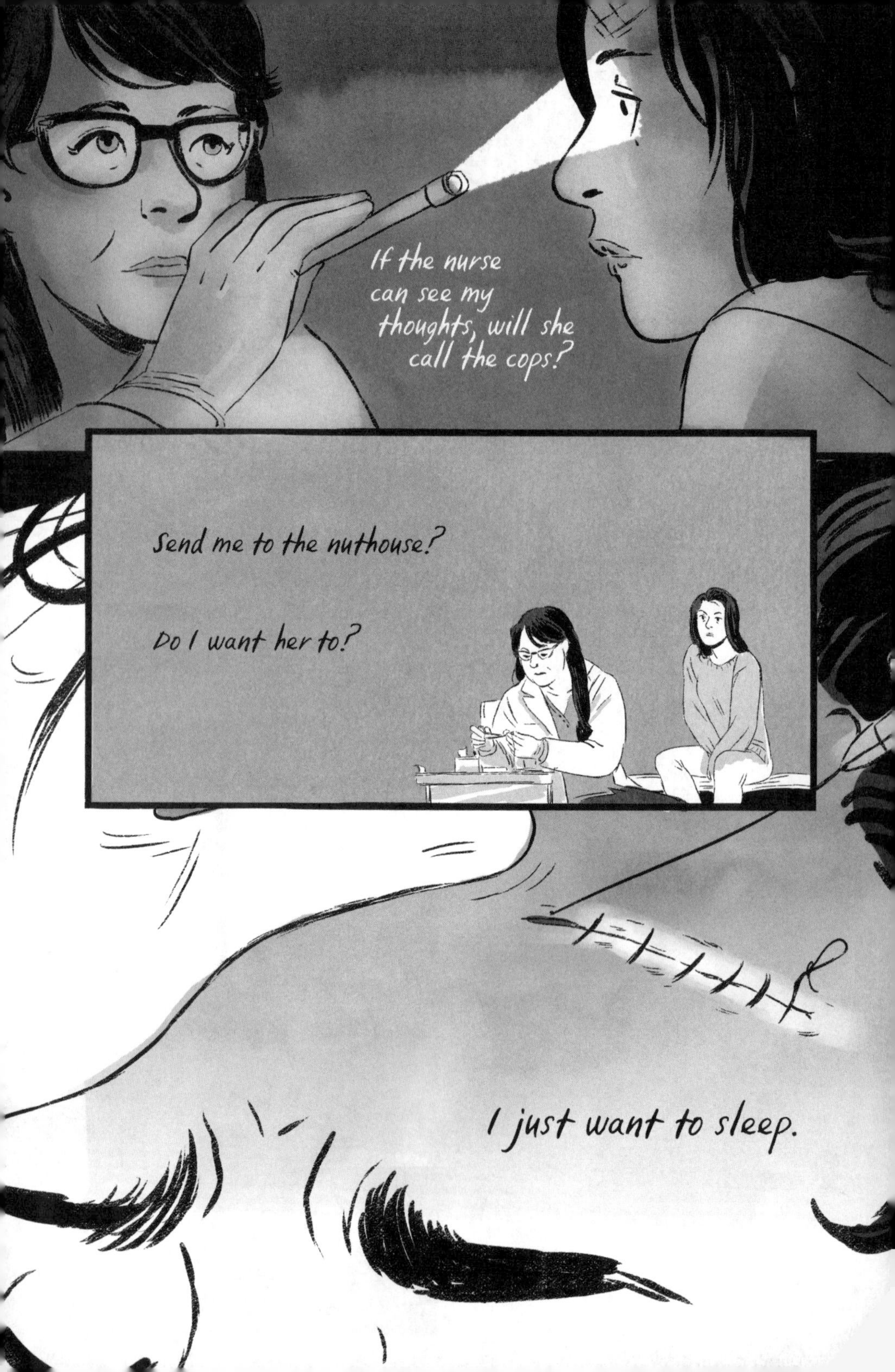
If the nurse can see my thoughts, will she call the cops?
Send me to the nuthouse?
Do I want her to?
I just want to sleep.

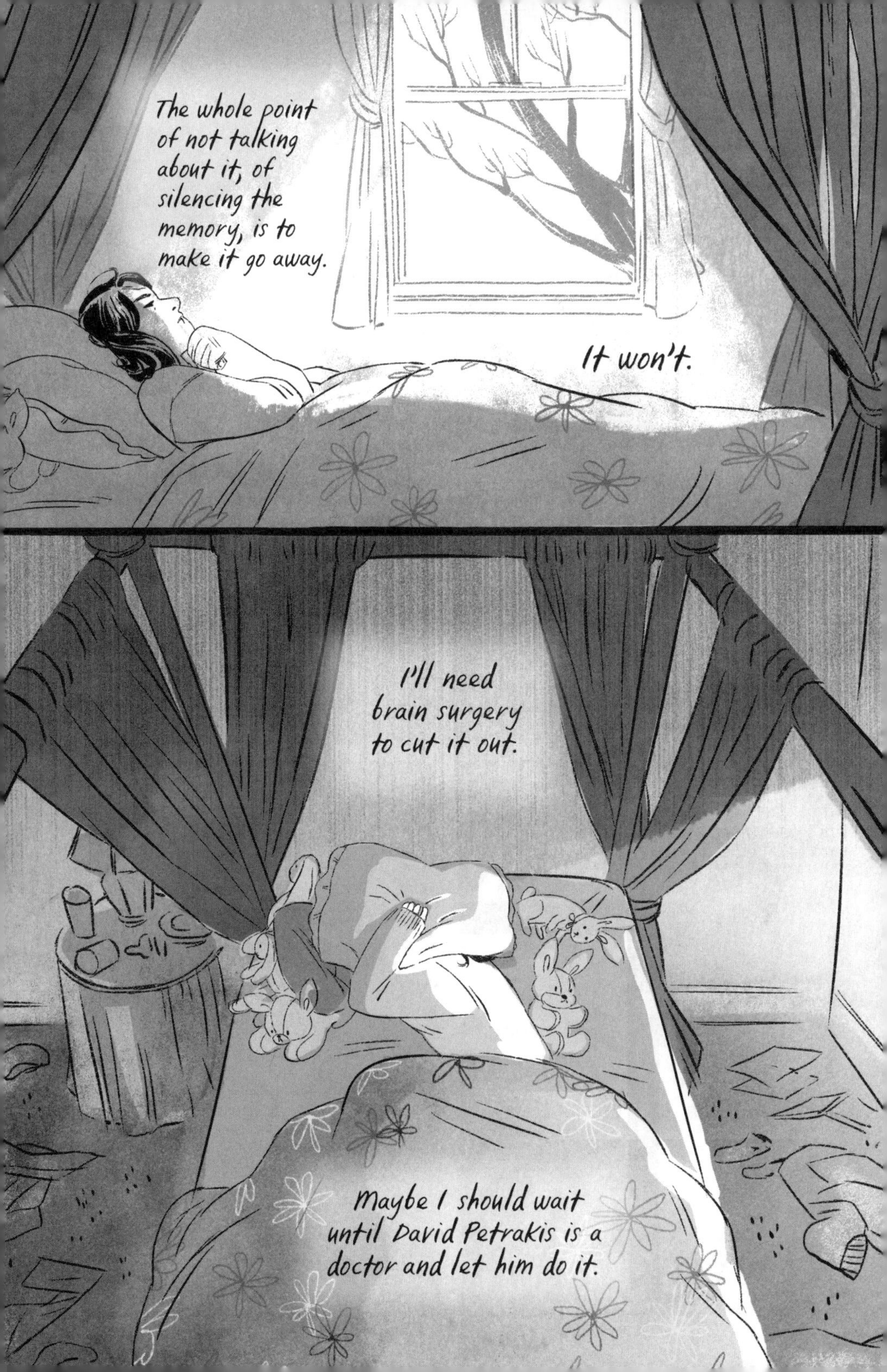
The whole point of not talking about it, of silencing the memory, is to make it go away.
It won't.
I'll need brain surgery to cut it out.
Maybe I should wait until David Petrakis is a doctor and let him do it.

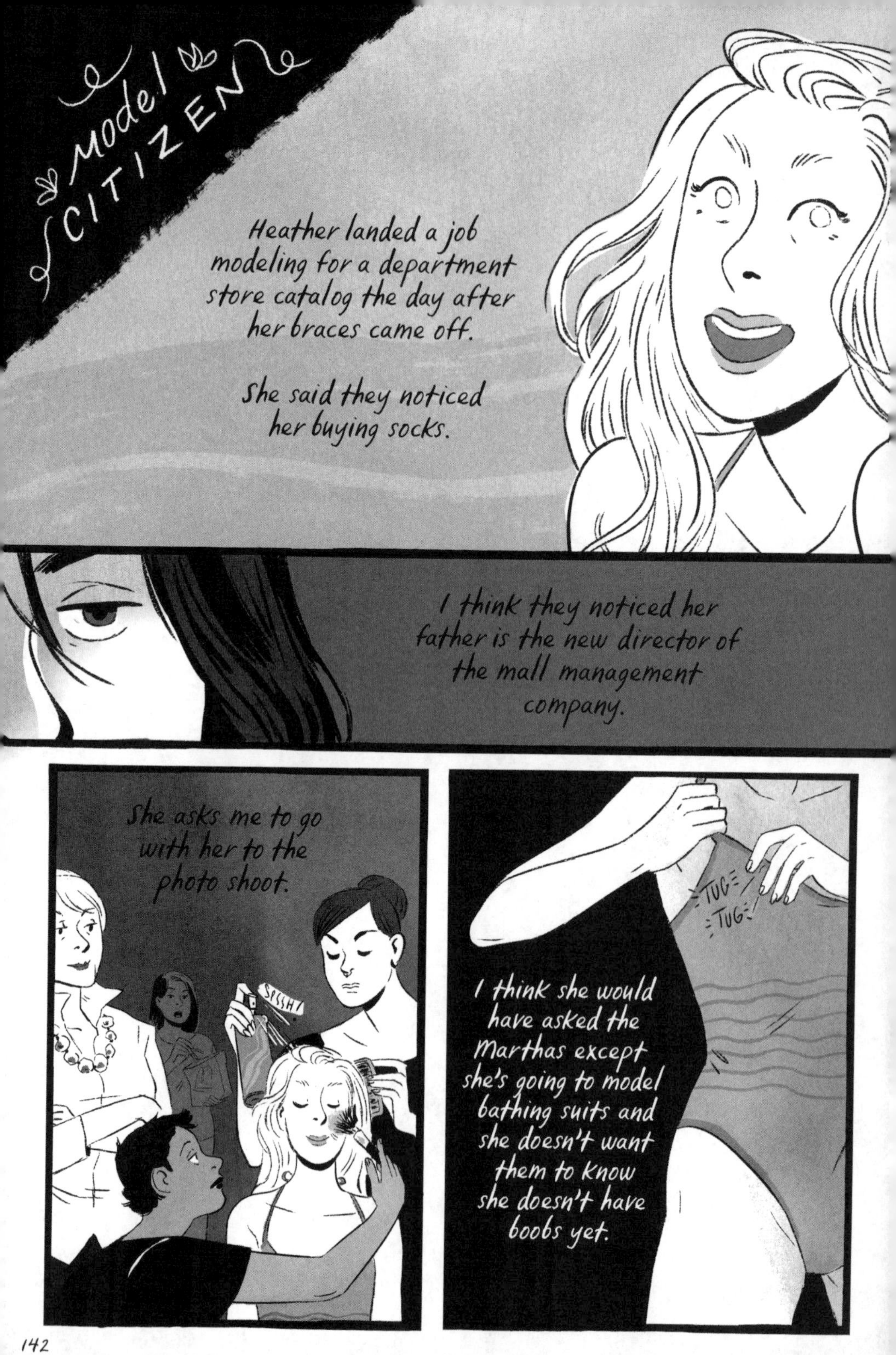
Model CITIZEN
Heather landed a job modeling for a department store catalog the day after her braces came off.
She said they noticed her buying socks.
I think they noticed her father is the new director of the mall management company.
She asks me to go with her to the photo shoot.
SPSSH!
TUG
TUG!
I think she would have asked the Marthas except she's going to model bathing suits and she doesn't want them to know she doesn't have boobs yet.

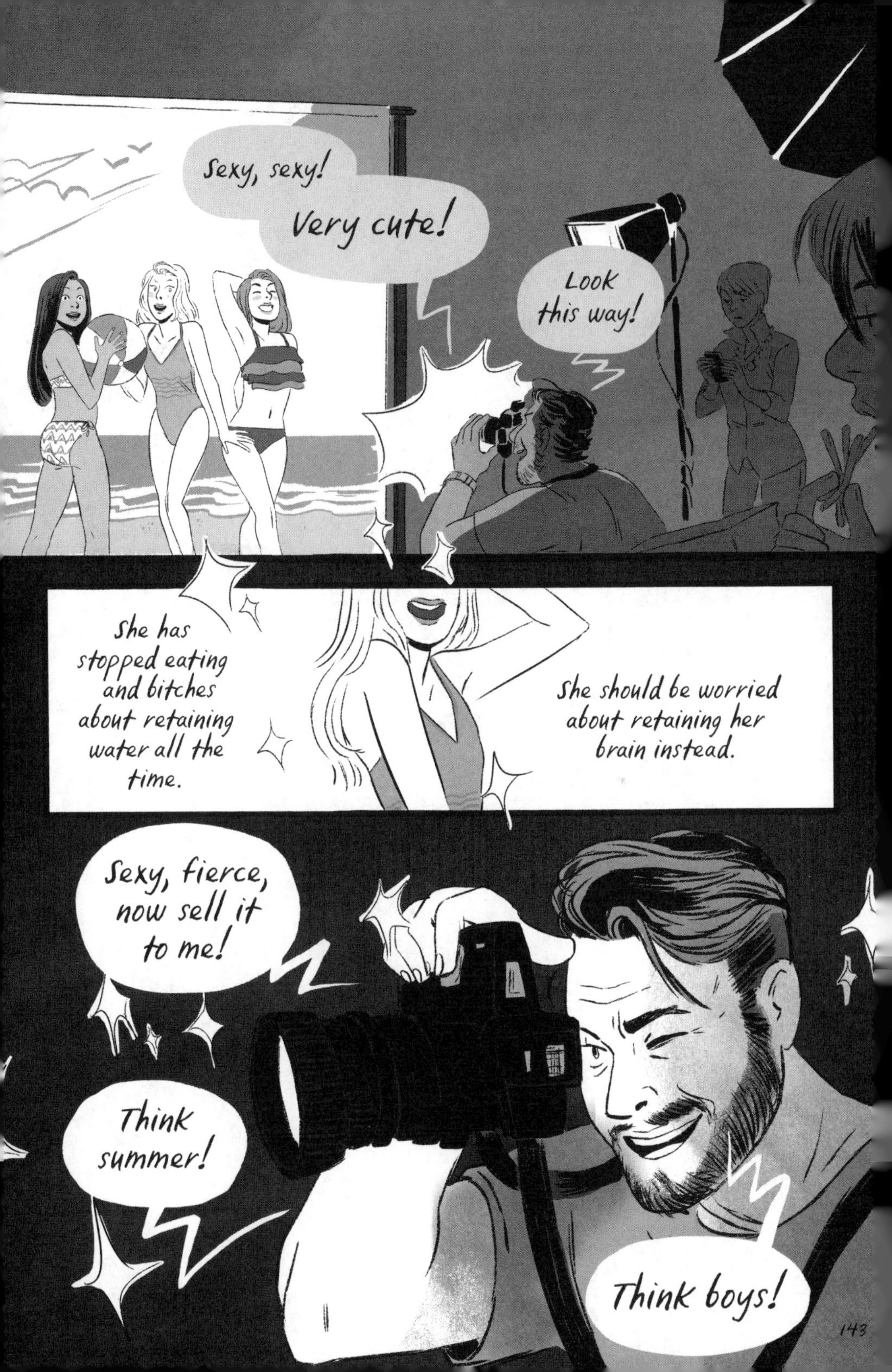
Sexy, sexy!
Very cute!
Look this way!
She has stopped eating and bitches about retaining water all the time.
She should be worried about retaining her brain instead.
Sexy, fierce, now sell it to me!
Think summer!
Think boys!

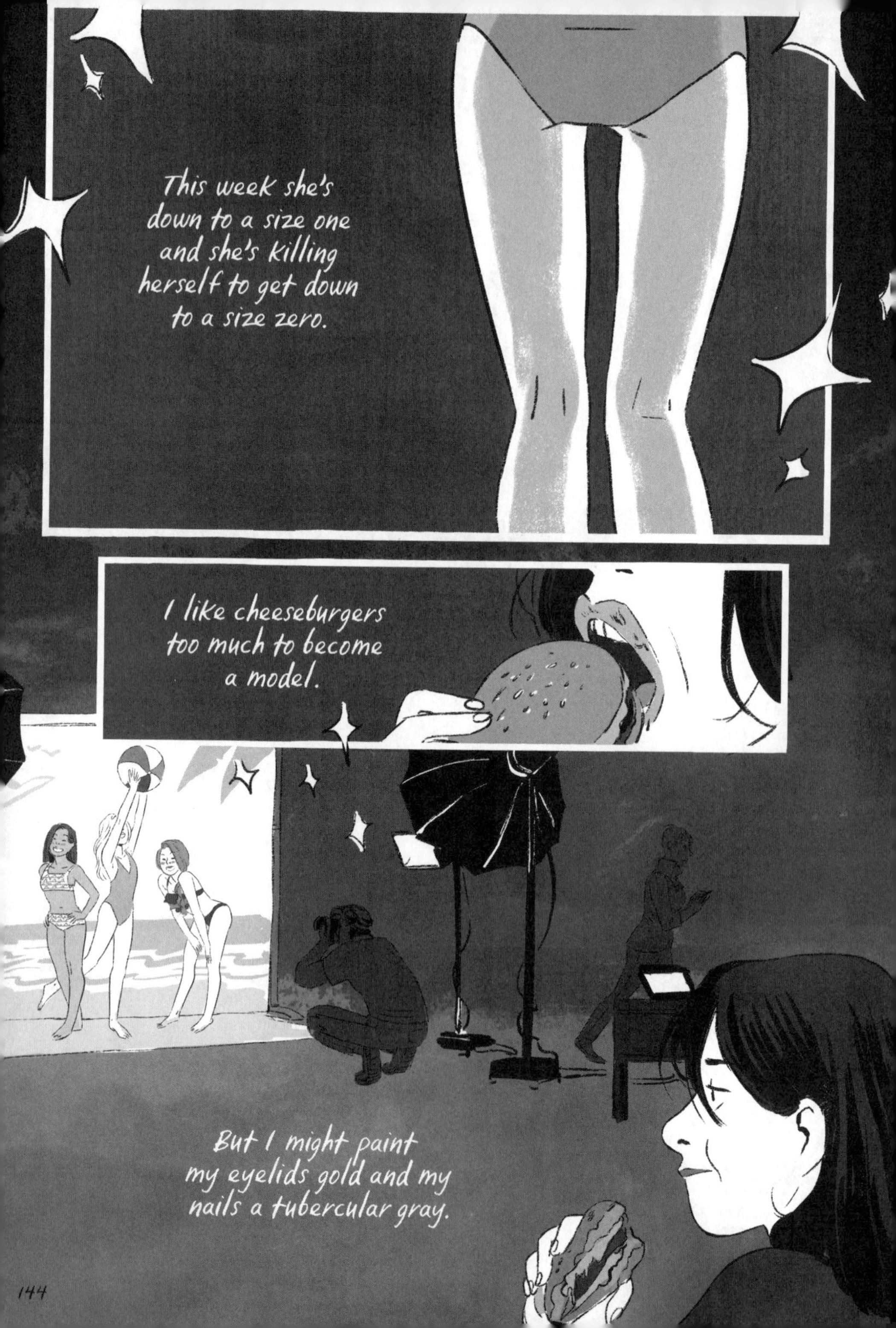
This week she's down to a size one and she's killing herself to get down to a size zero.
I like cheeseburgers too much to become a model.
But I might paint my eyelids gold and my nails a tubercular gray.

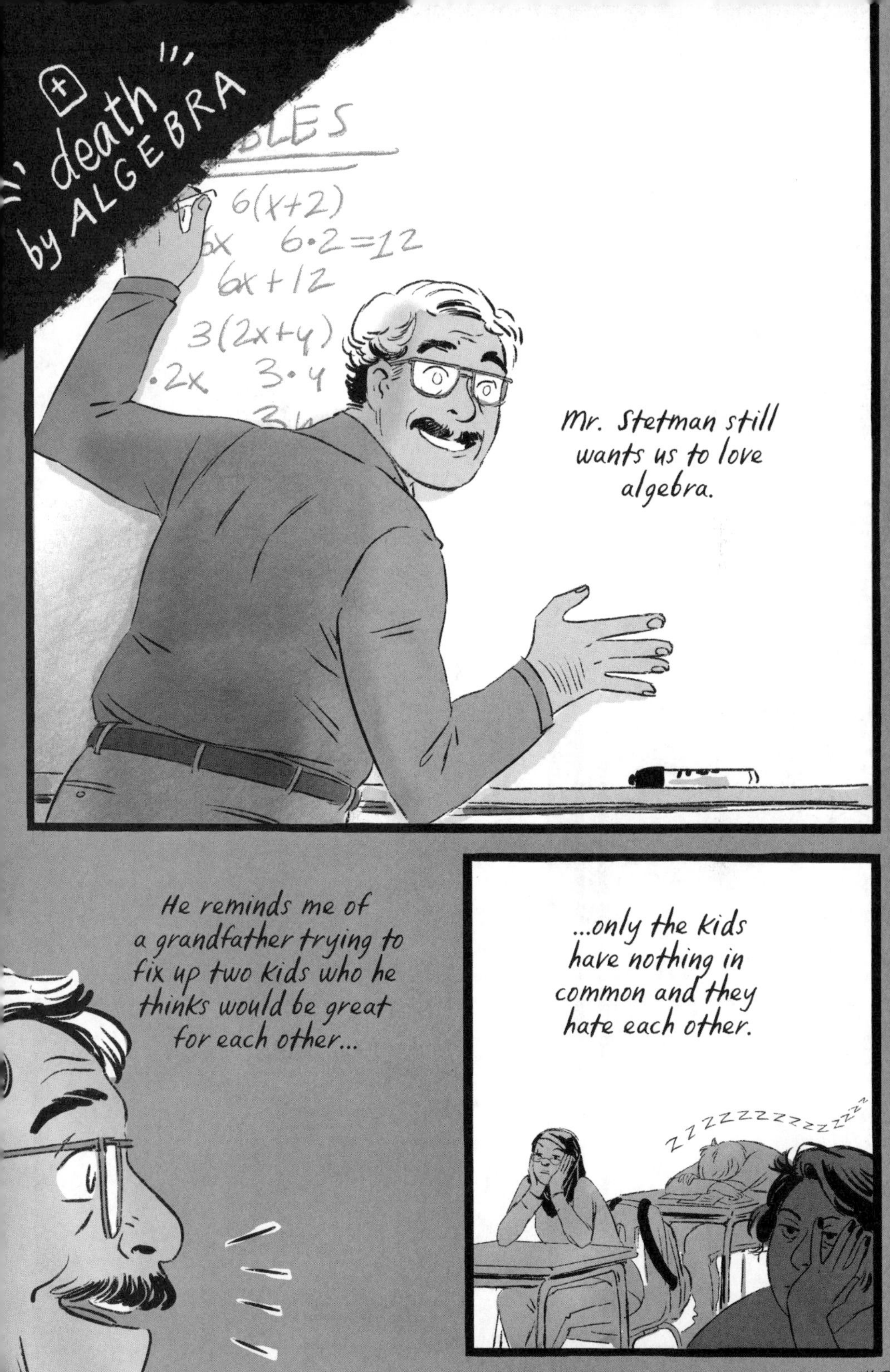
death by ALGEBRA
6(x+2)
6•2=12
6x+12
3(2x+y)
3•y
Mr. Stetman still wants us to love algebra.
He reminds me of a grandfather trying to fix up two kids who he thinks would be great for each other...
...only the kids have nothing in common and they hate each other.
ZZZZZZZZZZZZZZZ

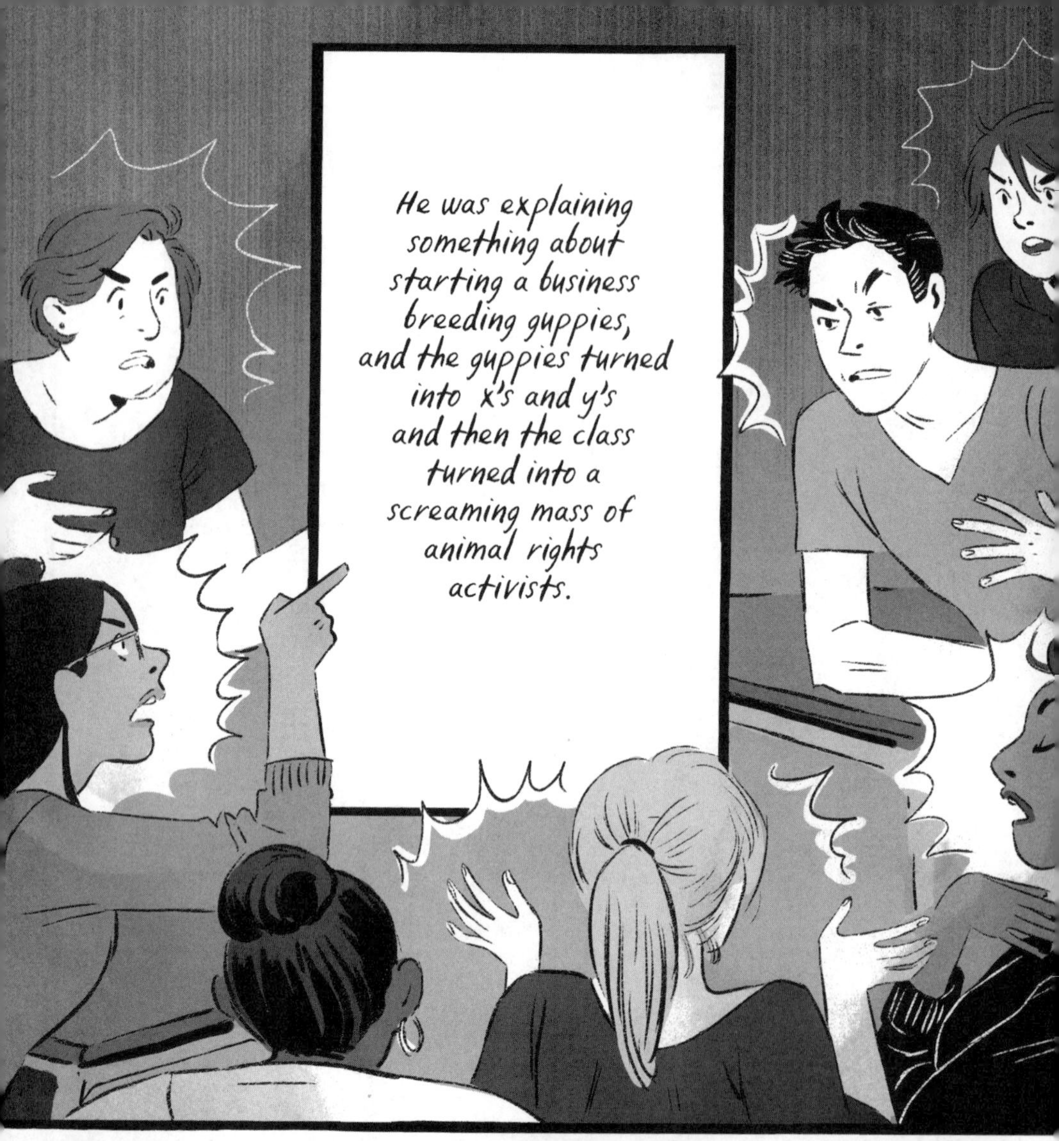
He was explaining something about starting a business breeding guppies, and the guppies turned into x's and y's and then the class turned into a screaming mass of animal rights activists.

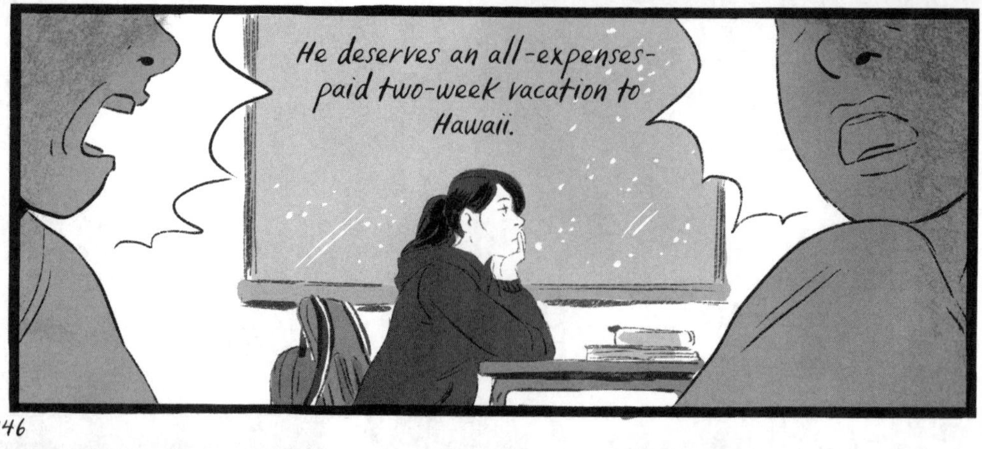
He deserves an all-expenses-paid two-week vacation to Hawaii.

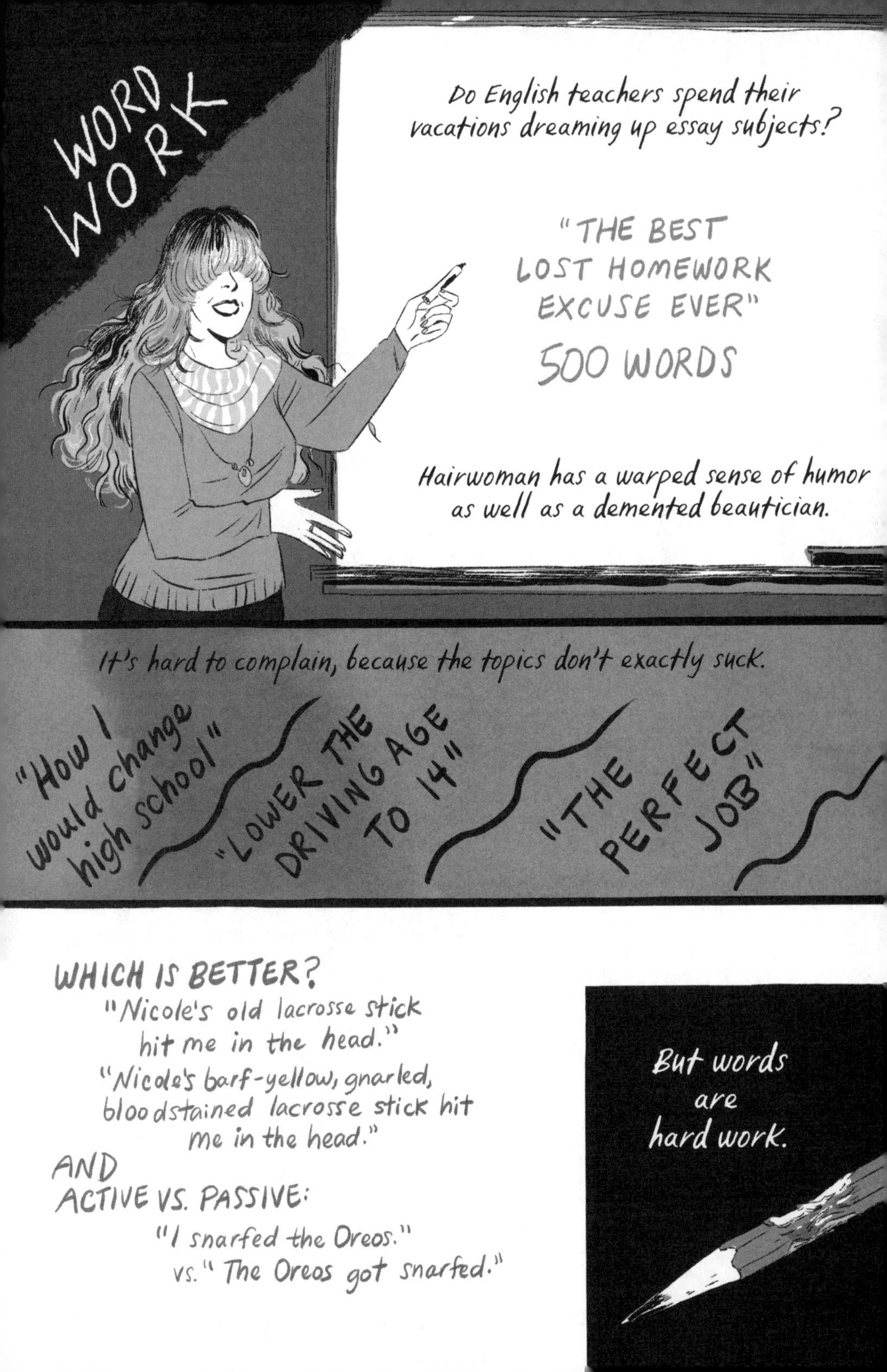
WORD WORK
Do English teachers spend their vacations dreaming up essay subjects?
"THE BEST LOST HOMEWORK EXCUSE EVER"
500 WORDS
Hairwoman has a warped sense of humor as well as a demented beautician.
It's hard to complain, because the topics don't exactly suck.
"How I would change high school"
"LOWER THE DRIVING AGE TO 14"
"THE PERFECT JOB"
WHICH IS BETTER?
"Nicole's old lacrosse stick hit me in the head."
"Nicole's barf-yellow, gnarled, bloodstained lacrosse stick hit me in the head."
AND
ACTIVE VS. PASSIVE:
"I snarfed the Oreos."
vs. "The Oreos got snarfed."
But words are hard work.

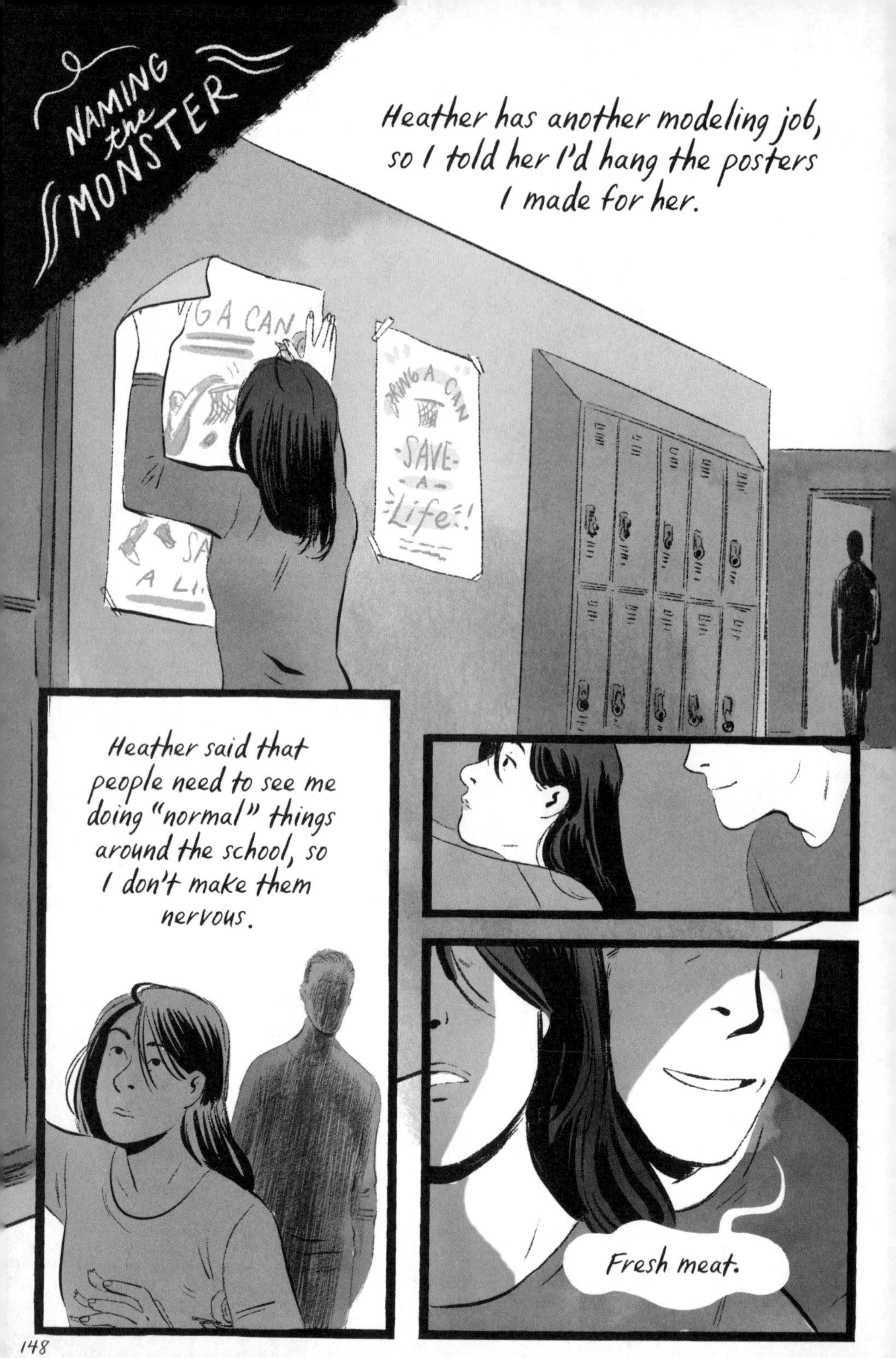
NAMING the MONSTER
Heather has another modeling job, so I told her I'd hang the posters I made for her.
G A CAN
BRING A CAN
SAVE
A
Life!
Heather said that people need to see me doing "normal" things around the school, so I don't make them nervous.
Fresh meat.

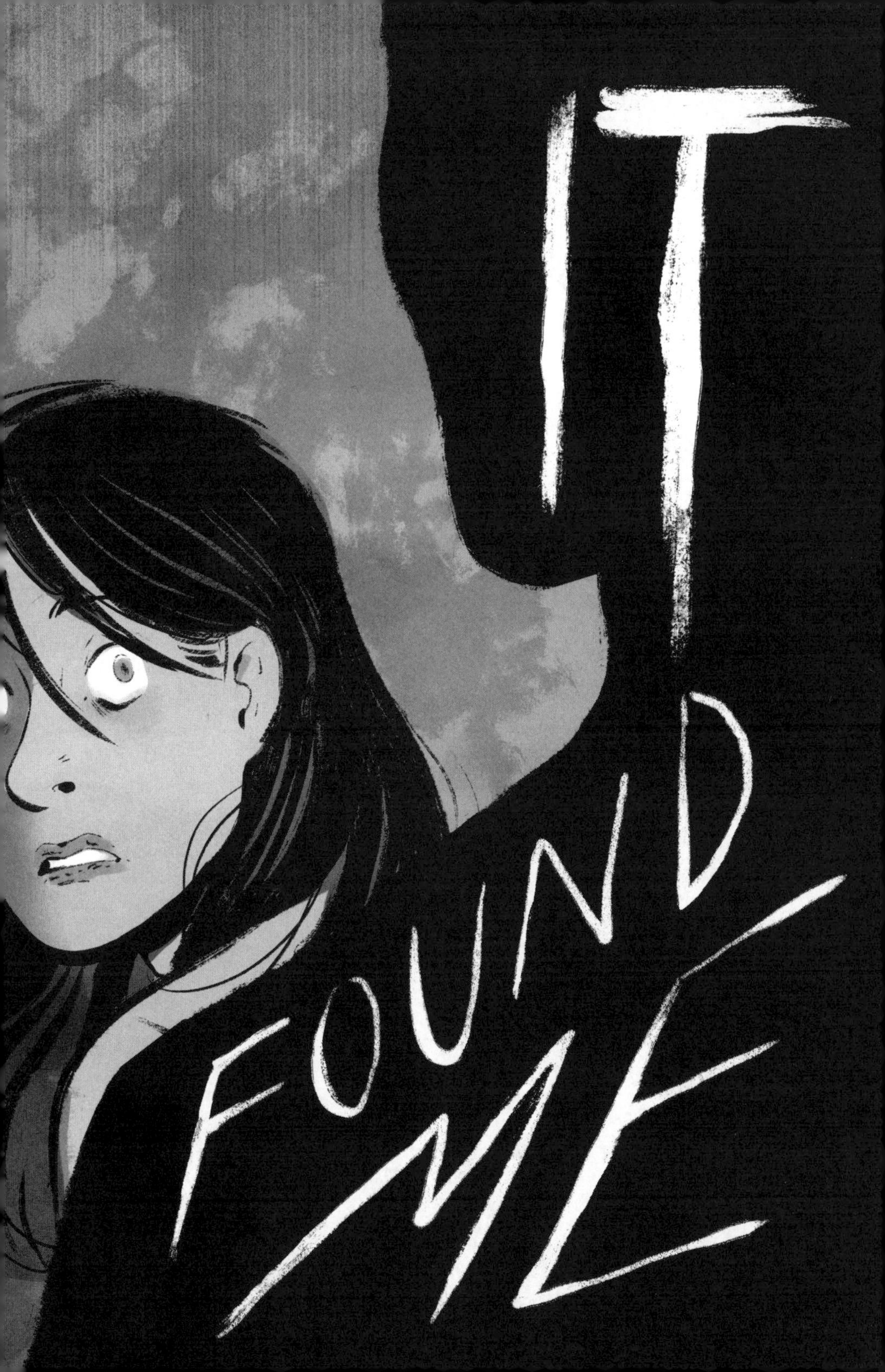
IT FOUND ME

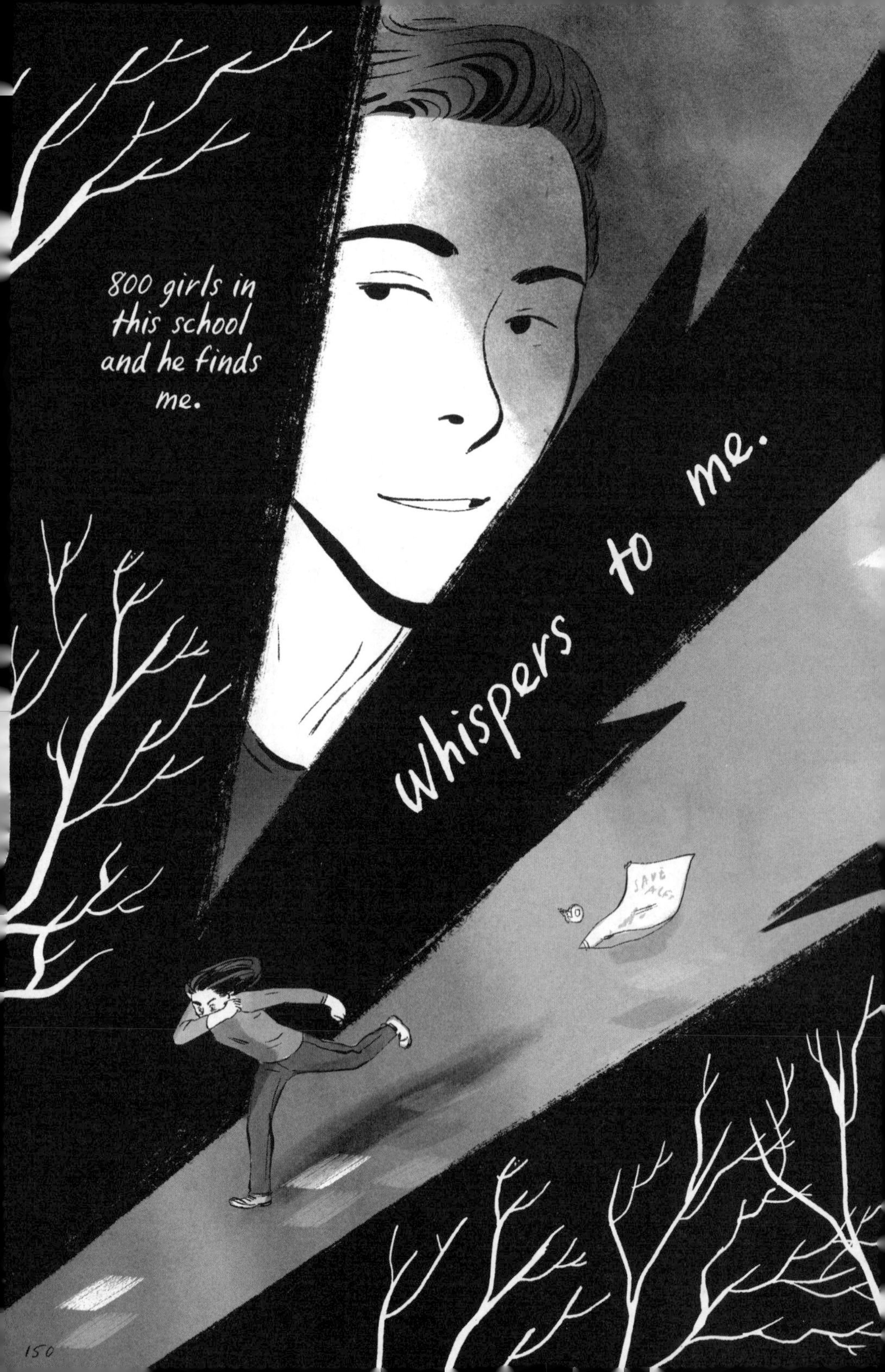
800 girls in this school and he finds me.
whispers to me.

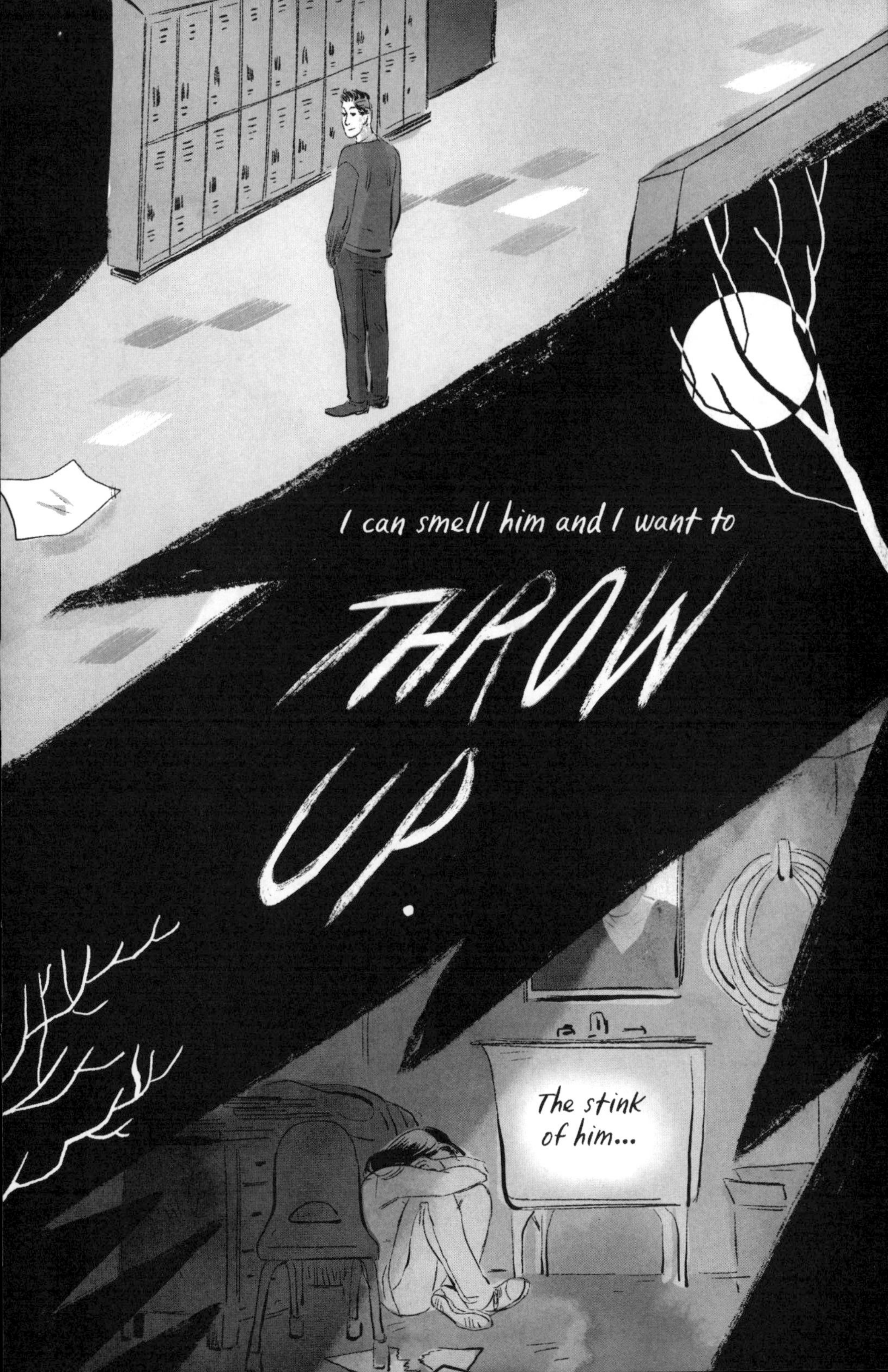
I can smell him and I want to
THROW UP.
The stink of him...

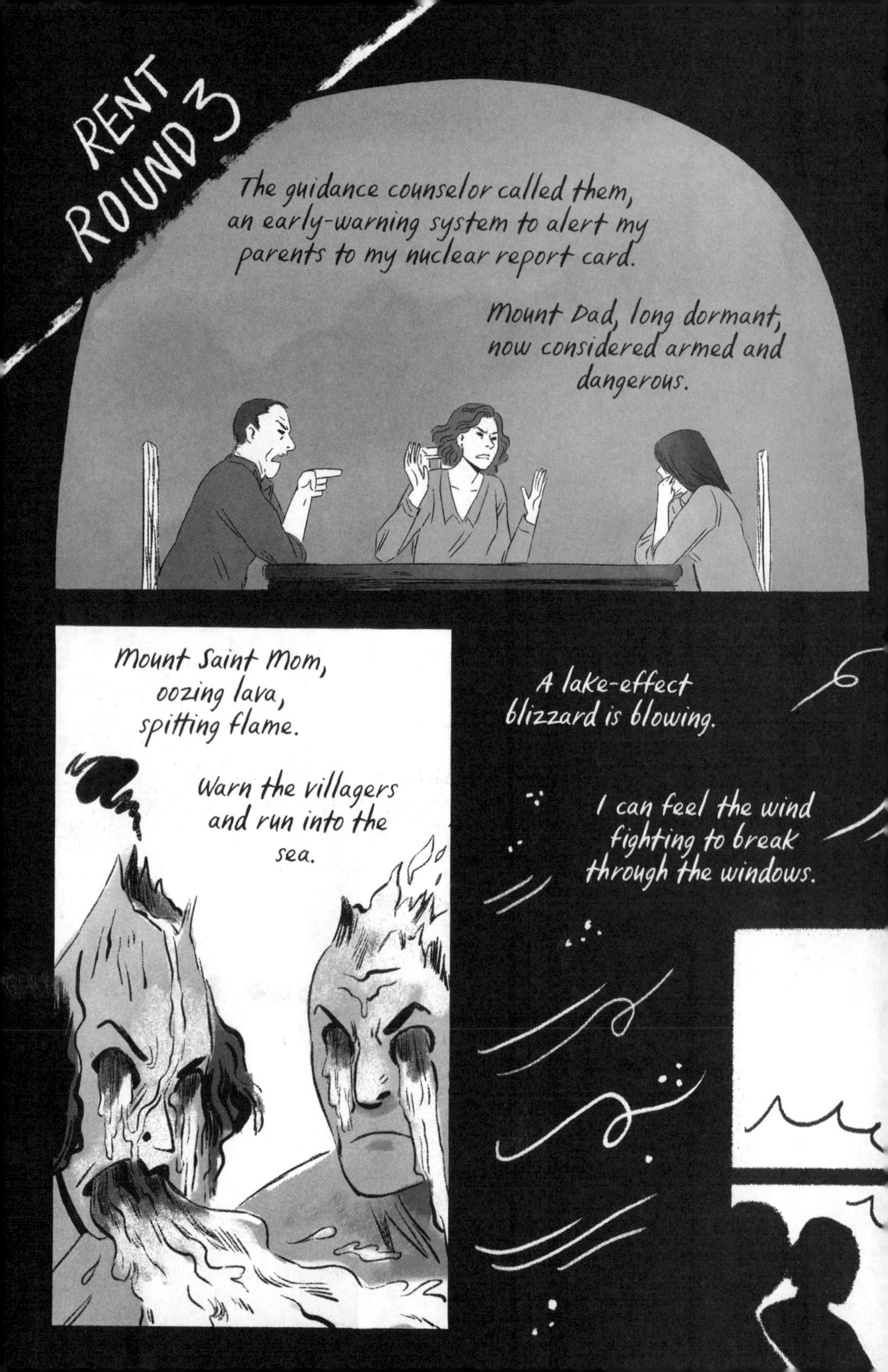
RENT ROUND 3
The guidance counselor called them, an early-warning system to alert my parents to my nuclear report card.
Mount Dad, long dormant, now considered armed and dangerous.
Mount Saint Mom, oozing lava, spitting flame.
Warn the villagers and run into the sea.
A lake-effect blizzard is blowing.
I can feel the wind fighting to break through the windows.

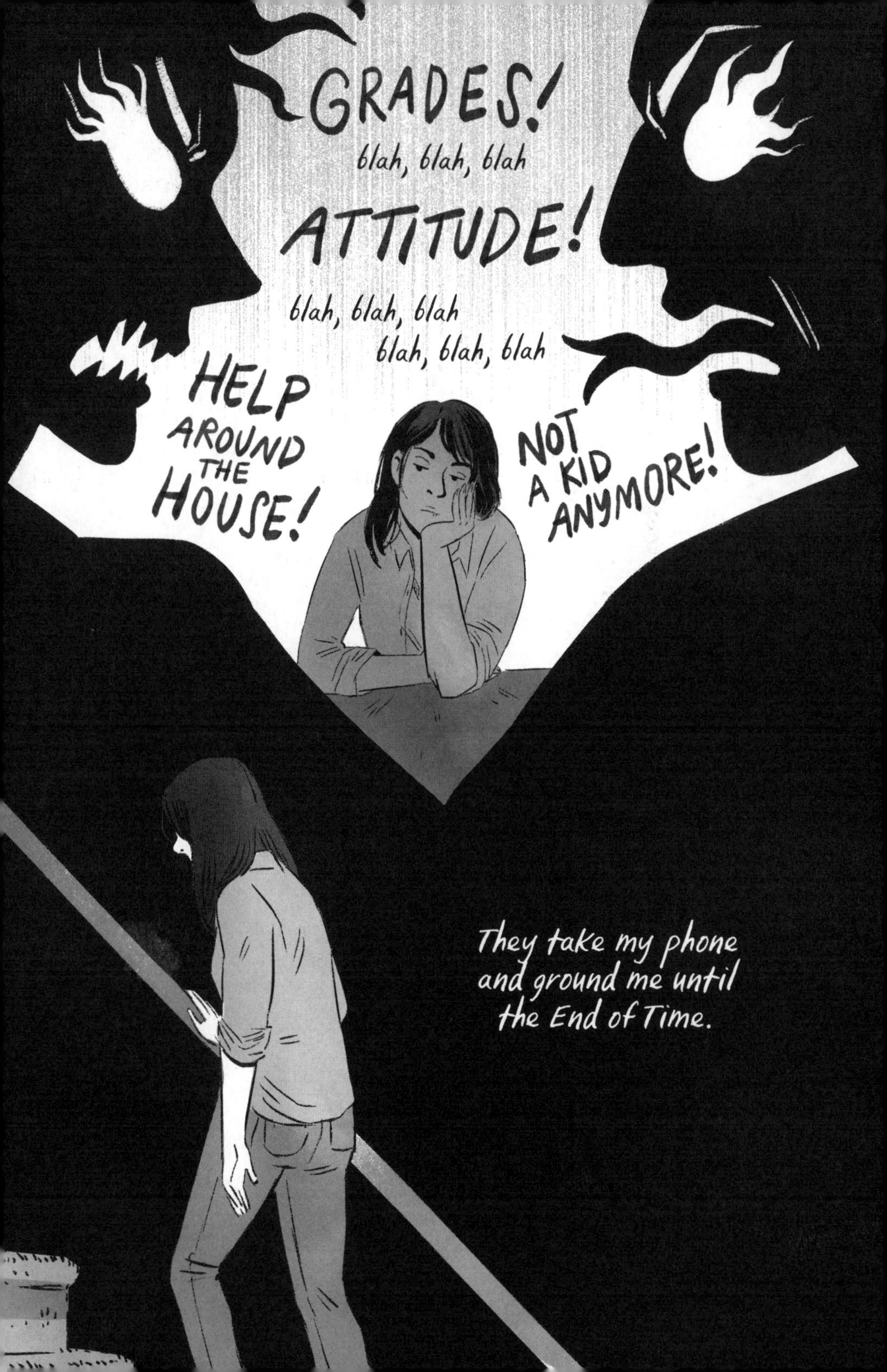
GRADES!
blah, blah, blah
ATTITUDE!
blah, blah, blah
blah, blah, blah
HELP AROUND THE HOUSE!
NOT A KID ANYMORE!
They take my phone and ground me until the End of Time.

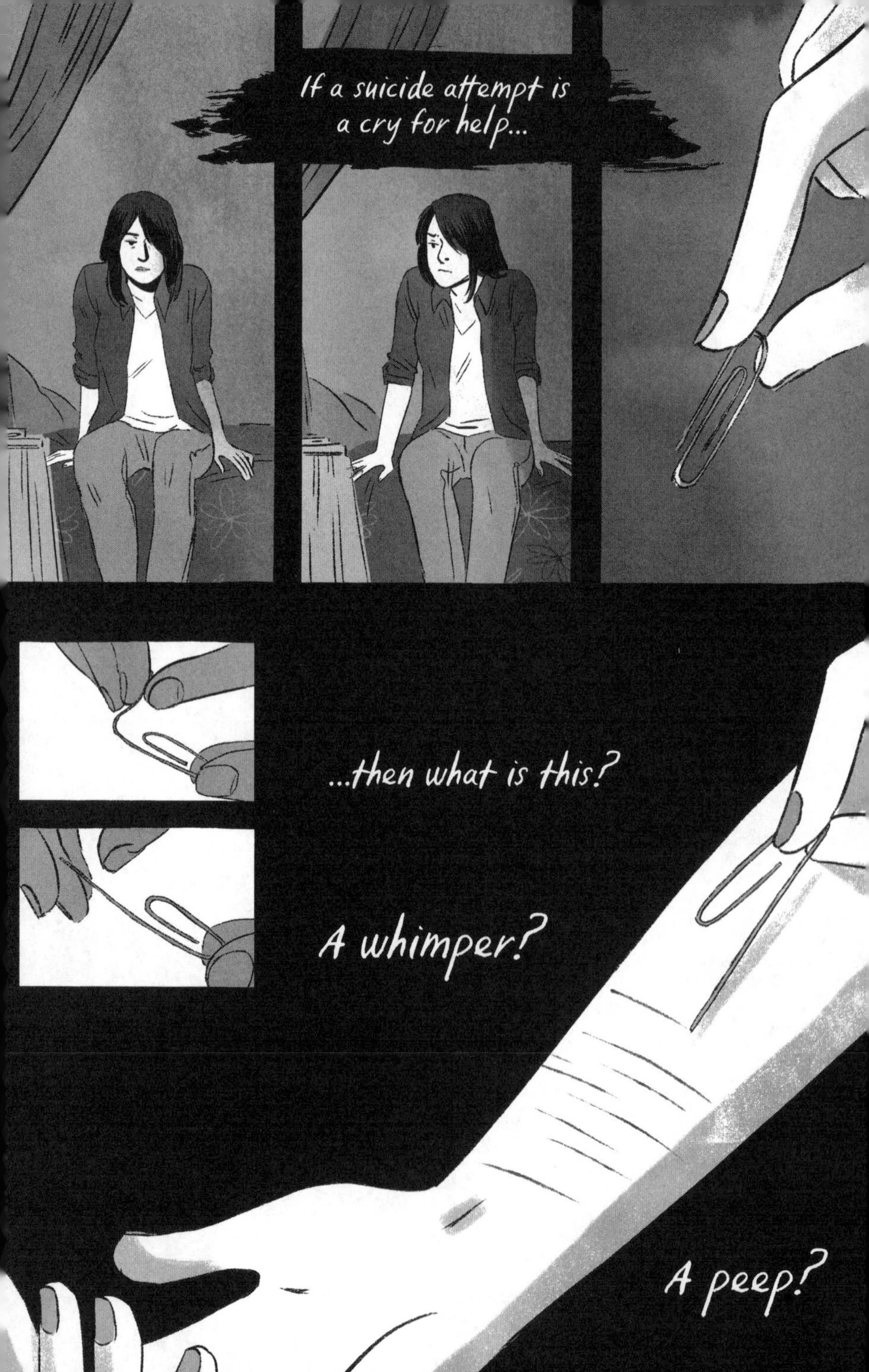
If a suicide attempt is a cry for help...
...then what is this?
A whimper?
A peep?

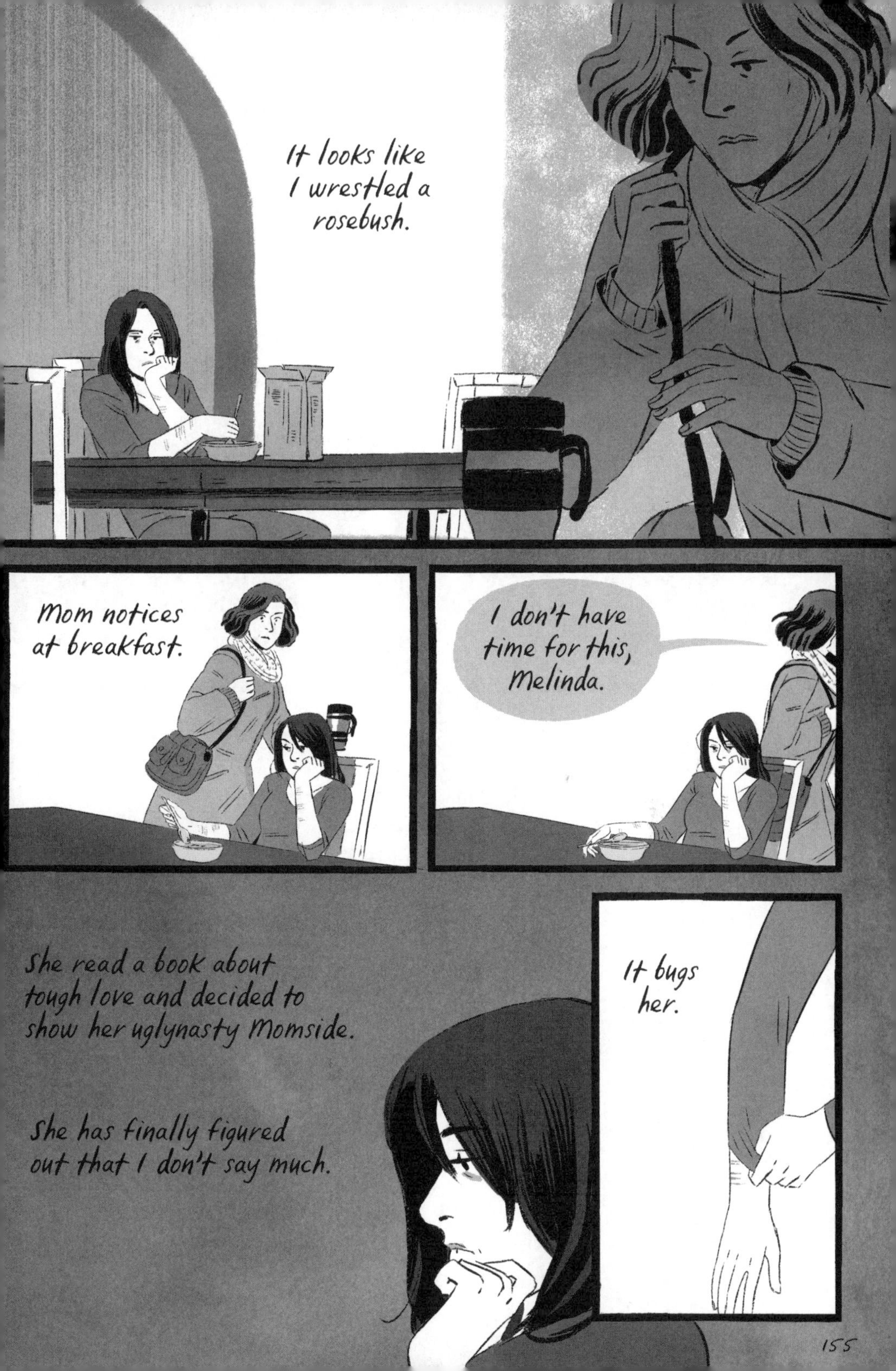
It looks like I wrestled a rosebush.
Mom notices at breakfast.
I don't have time for this, Melinda.
She read a book about tough love and decided to show her uglynasty Momside.
She has finally figured out that I don't say much.
It bugs her.

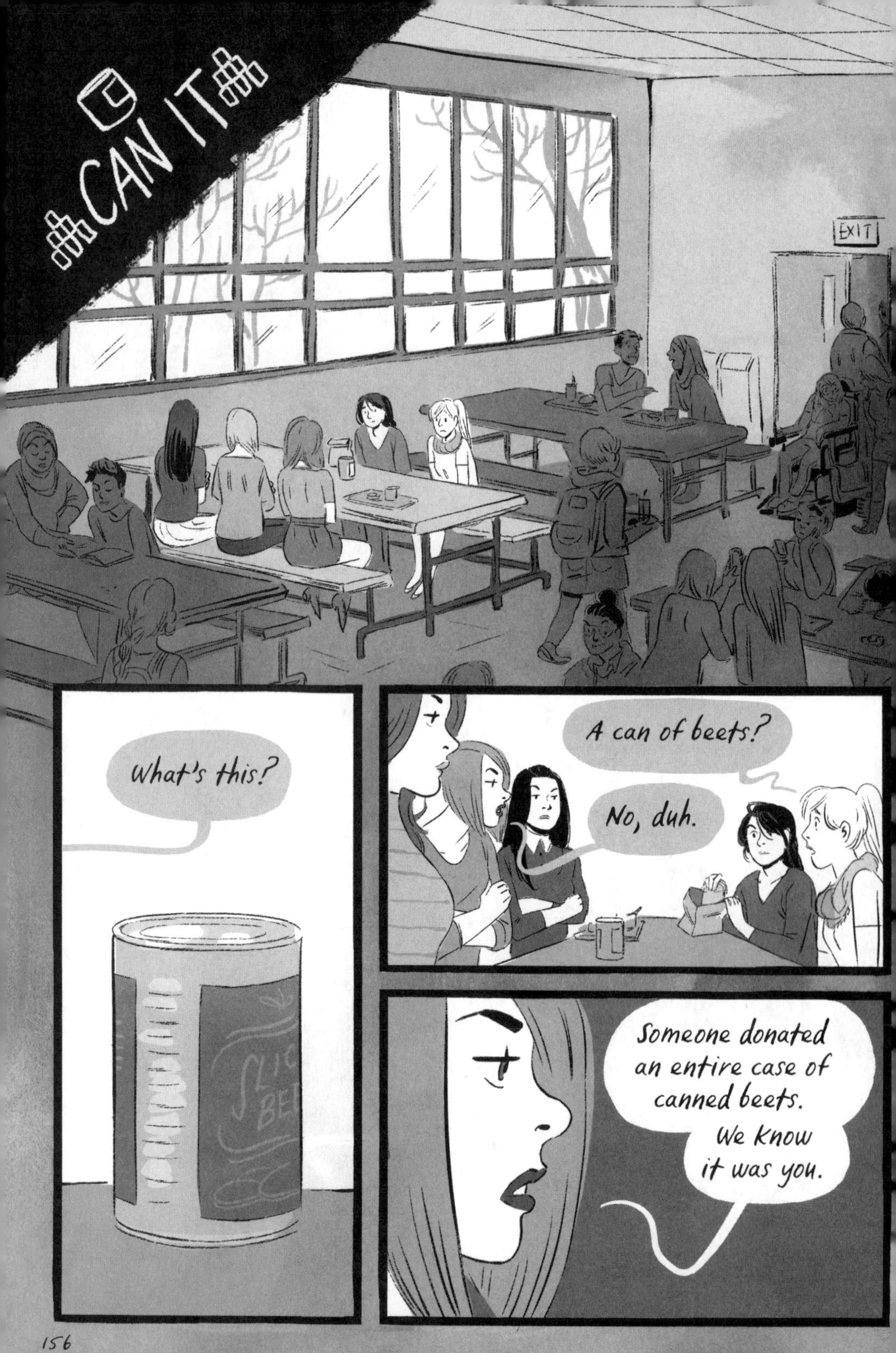
CAN IT
EXIT
What's this?
A can of beets?
No, duh.
Someone donated an entire case of canned beets.
We know it was you.

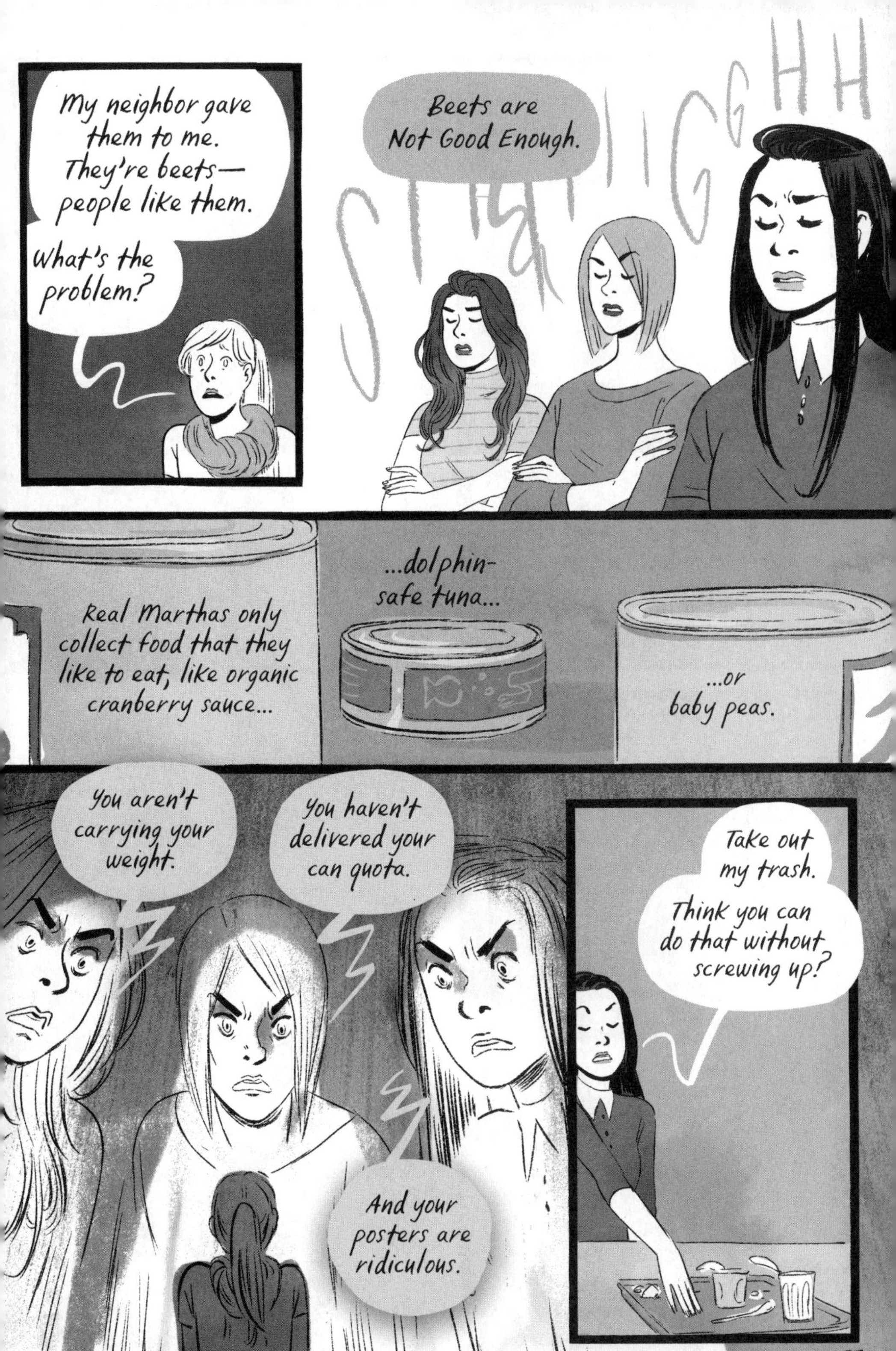
My neighbor gave them to me. They're beets— people like them.
What's the problem?
Beets are Not Good Enough.
Real Marthas only collect food that they like to eat, like organic cranberry sauce...
...dolphin-safe tuna...
...or baby peas.
You aren't carrying your weight.
You haven't delivered your can quota.
And your posters are ridiculous.
Take out my trash.
Think you can do that without screwing up?

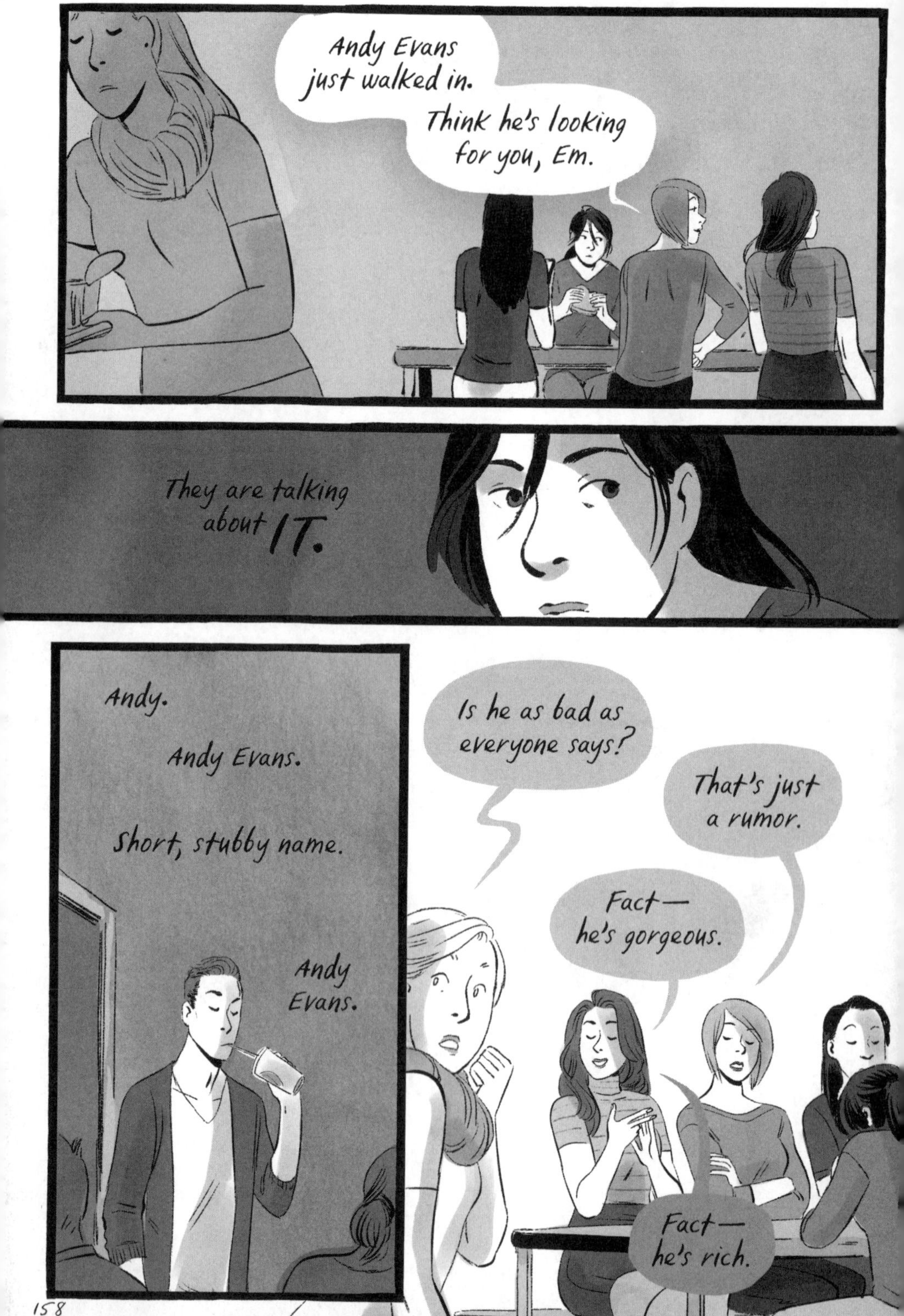
Andy Evans just walked in.
Think he's looking for you, Em.
They are talking about IT.
Andy.
Andy Evans.
Short, stubby name.
Andy Evans.
Is he as bad as everyone says?
That's just a rumor.
Fact— he's gorgeous.
Fact— he's rich.

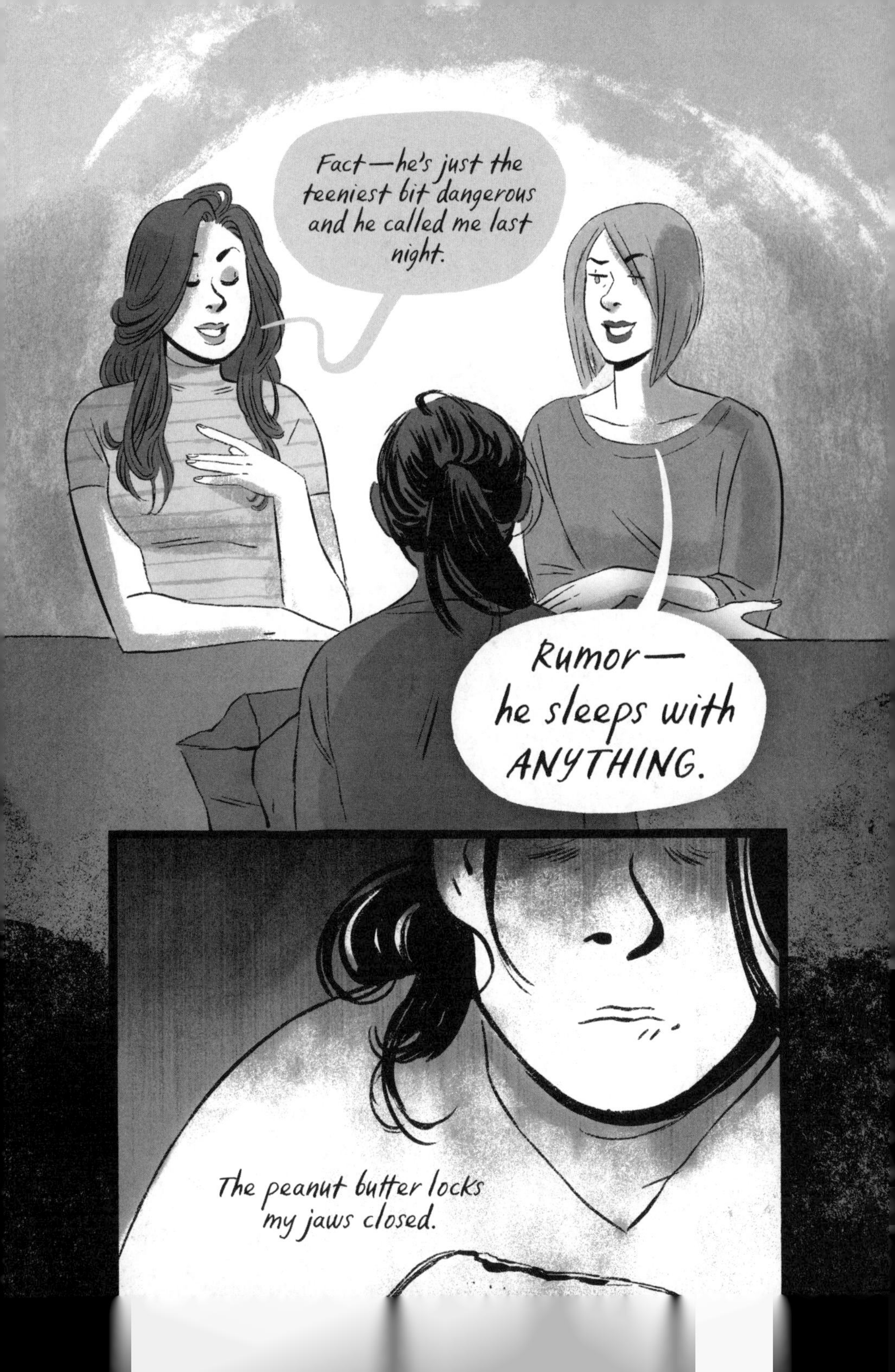
Fact—he's just the teeniest bit dangerous and he called me last night.
Rumor—he sleeps with ANYTHING.
The peanut butter locks my jaws closed.

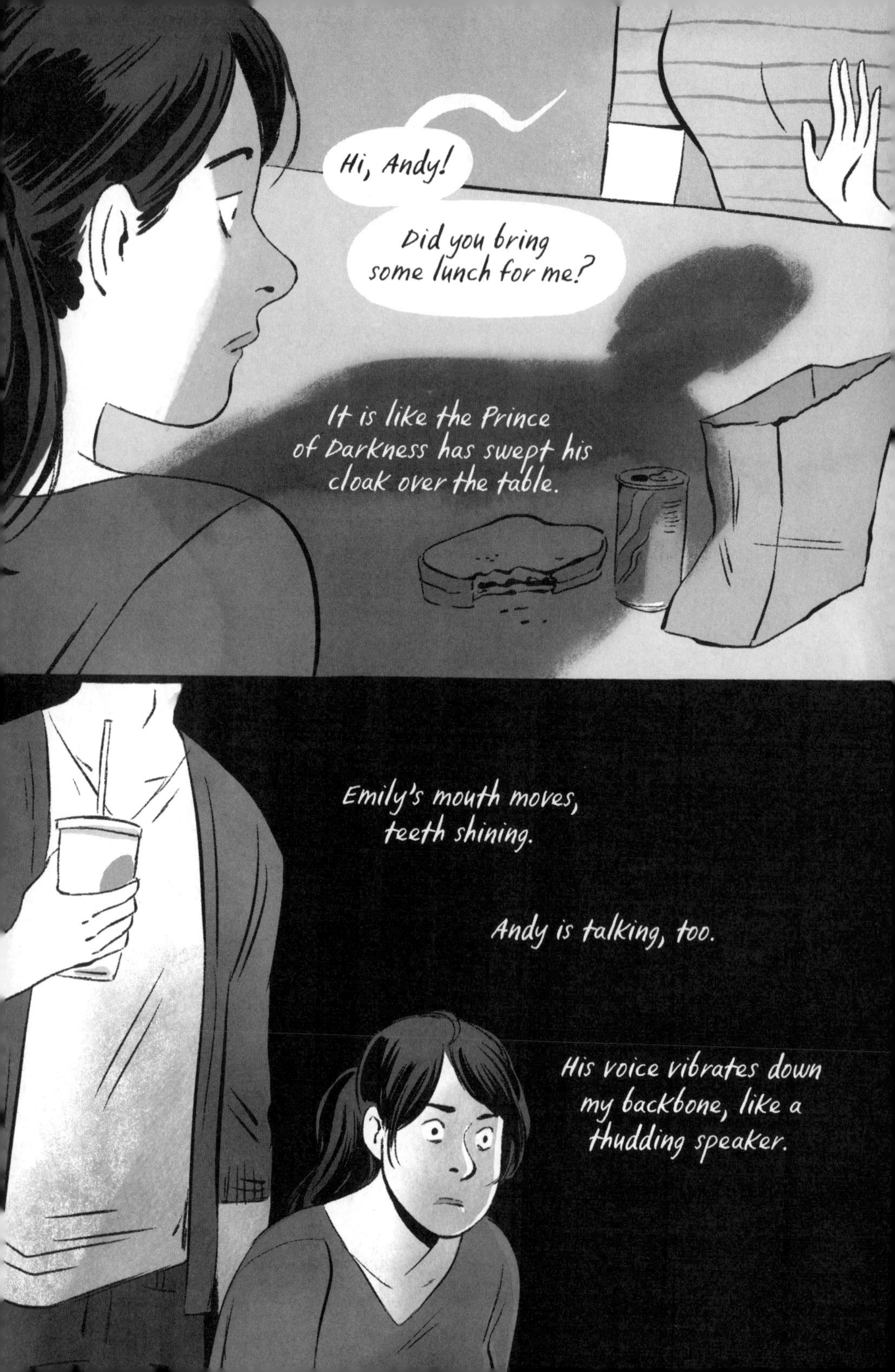
Hi, Andy!
Did you bring some lunch for me?
It is like the Prince of Darkness has swept his cloak over the table.
Emily's mouth moves, teeth shining.
Andy is talking, too.
His voice vibrates down my backbone, like a thudding speaker.

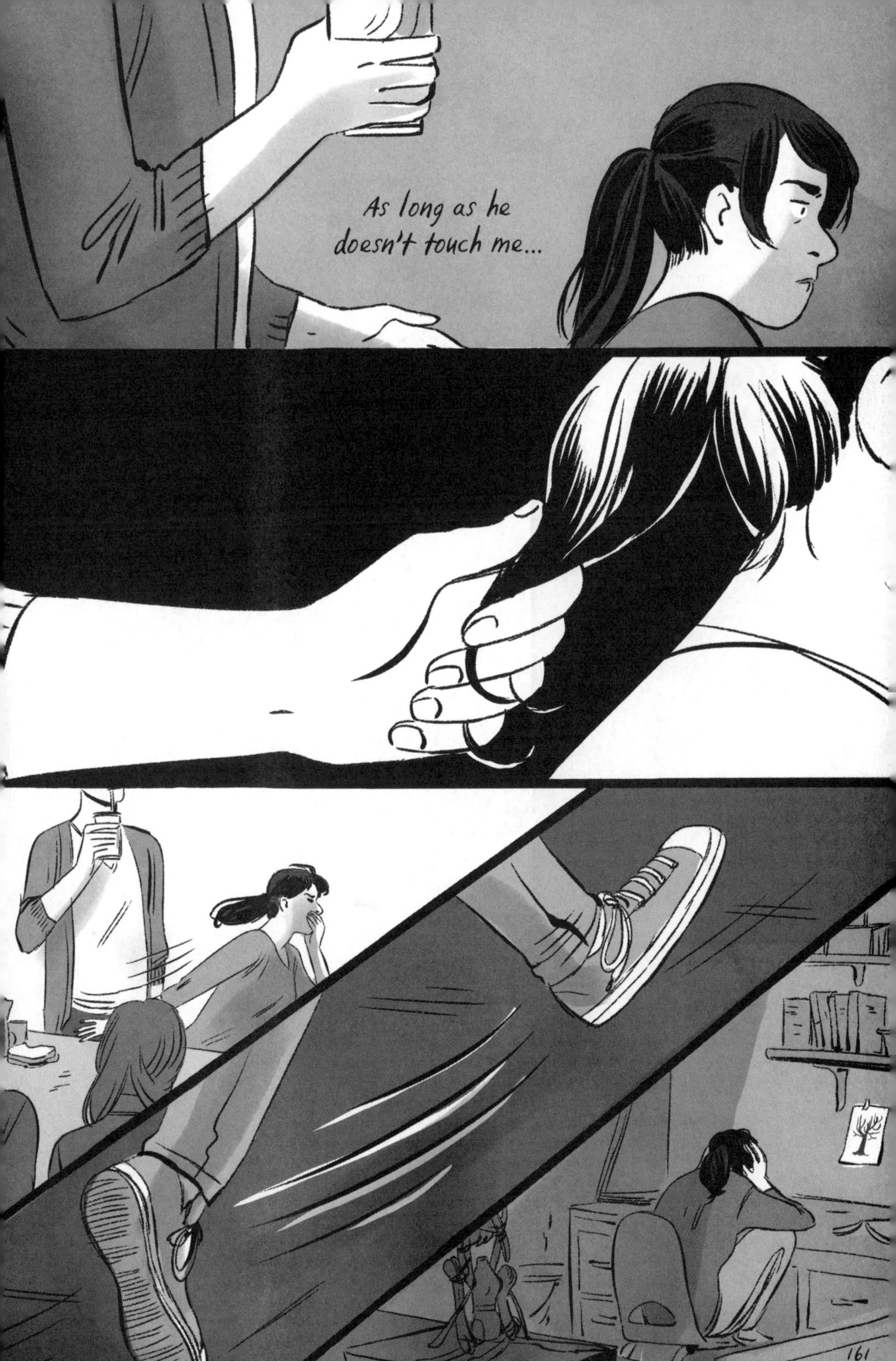
As long as he doesn't touch me...

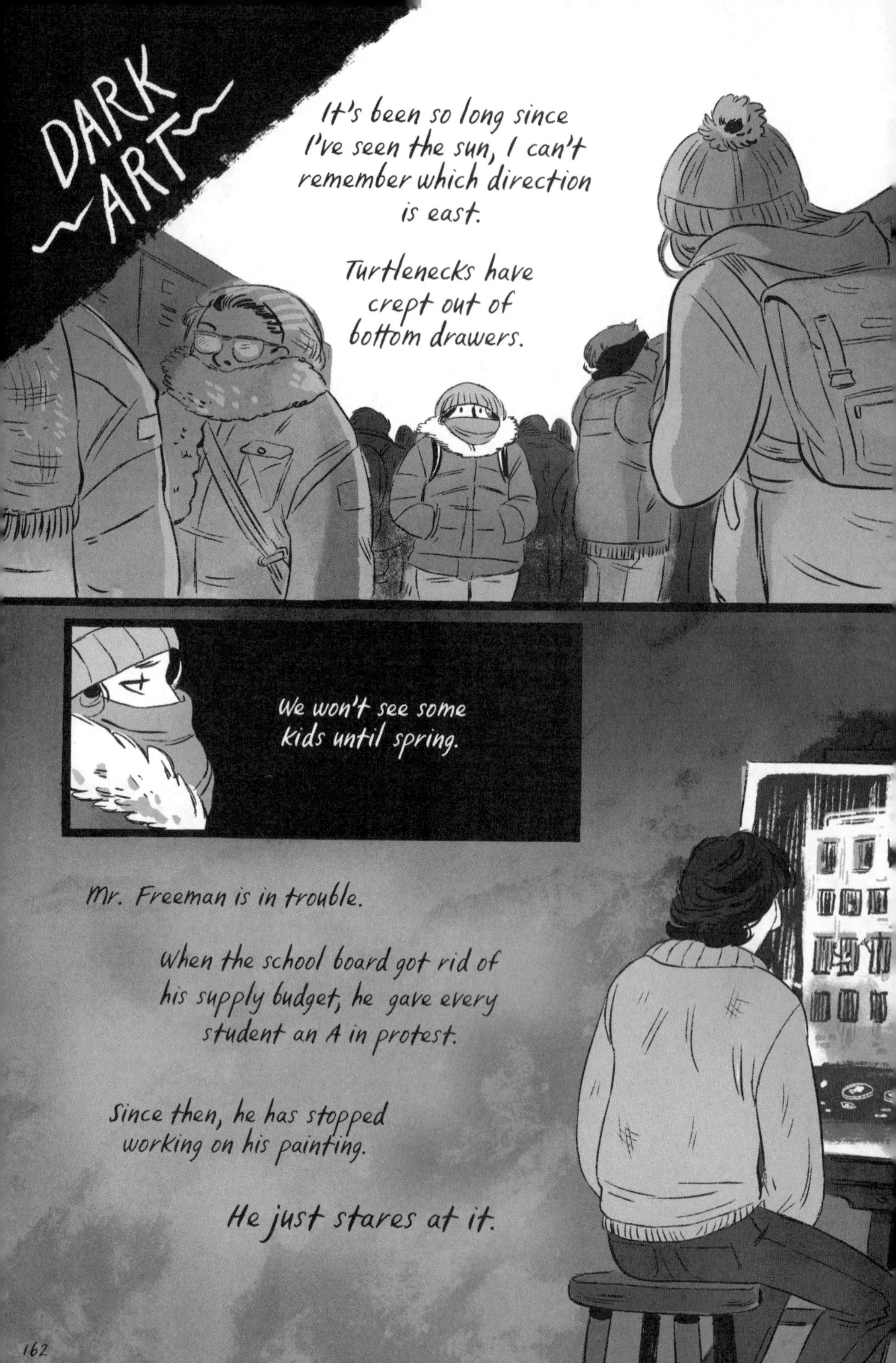
DARK ~ART~
It's been so long since I've seen the sun, I can't remember which direction is east.
Turtlenecks have crept out of bottom drawers.
We won't see some kids until spring.
Mr. Freeman is in trouble.
When the school board got rid of his supply budget, he gave every student an A in protest.
Since then, he has stopped working on his painting.
He just stares at it.

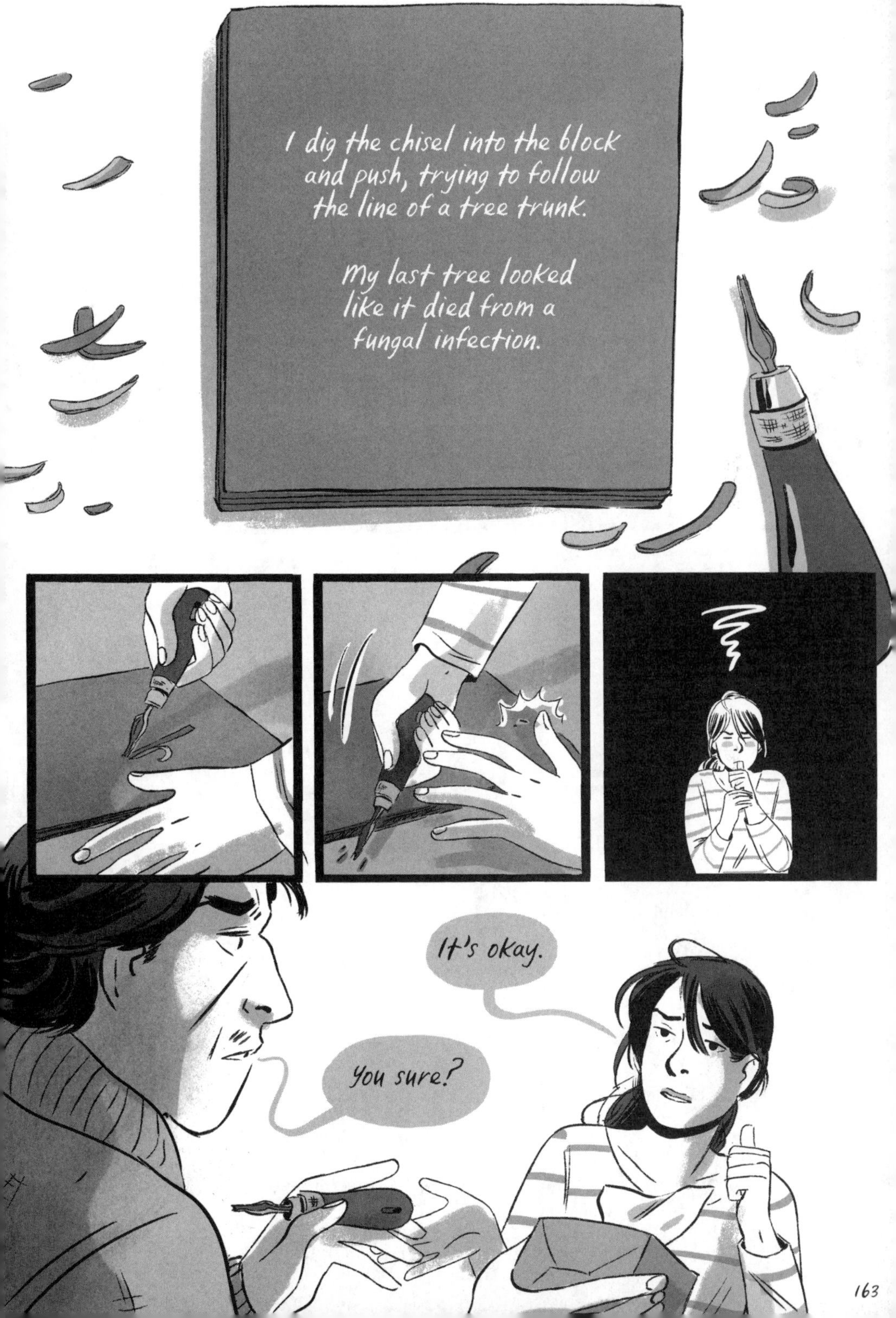
I dig the chisel into the block and push, trying to follow the line of a tree trunk.
My last tree looked like it died from a fungal infection.
It's okay.
You sure?

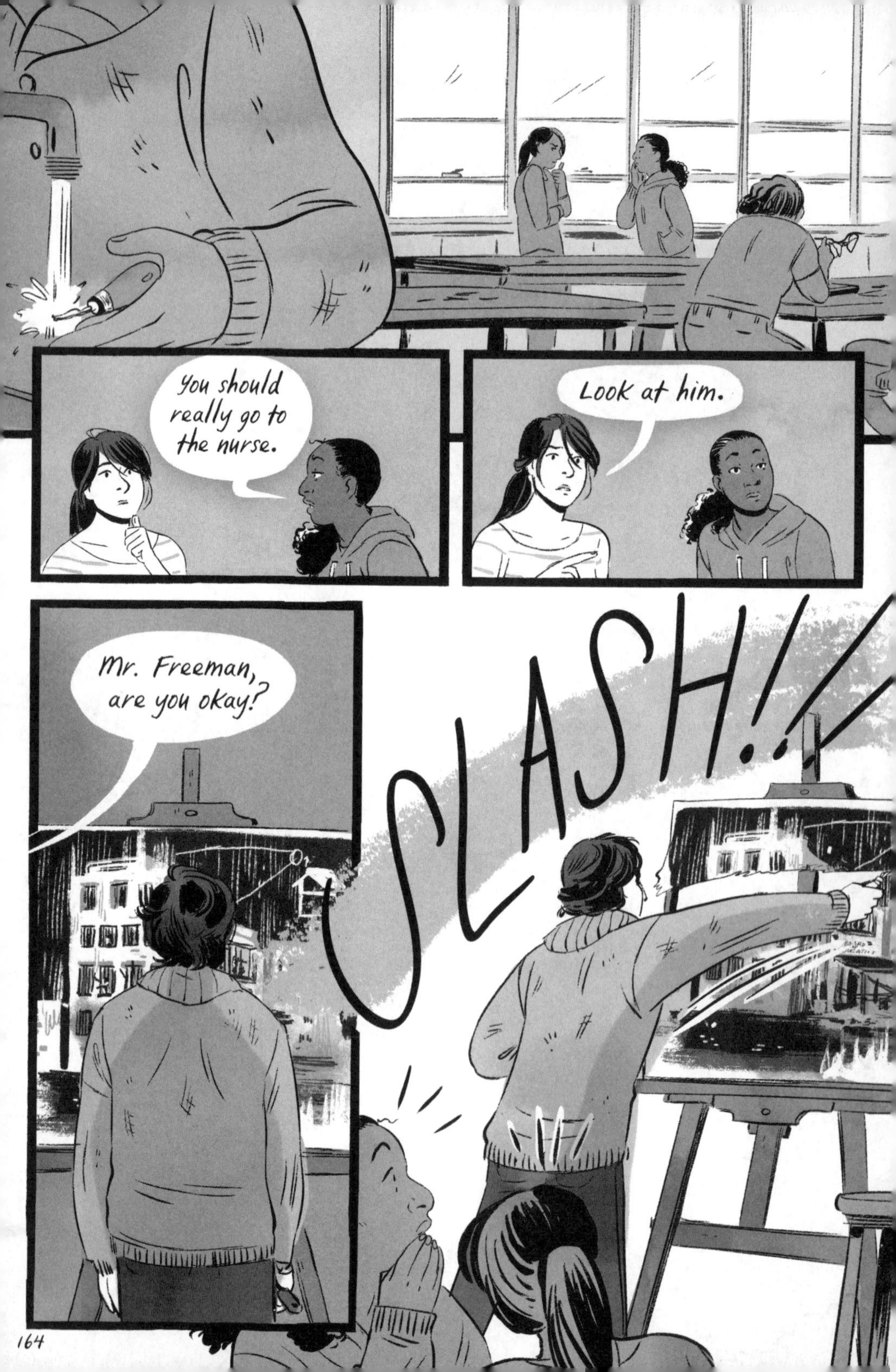
You should really go to the nurse.
Look at him.
Mr. Freeman, are you okay?
SLASH!!

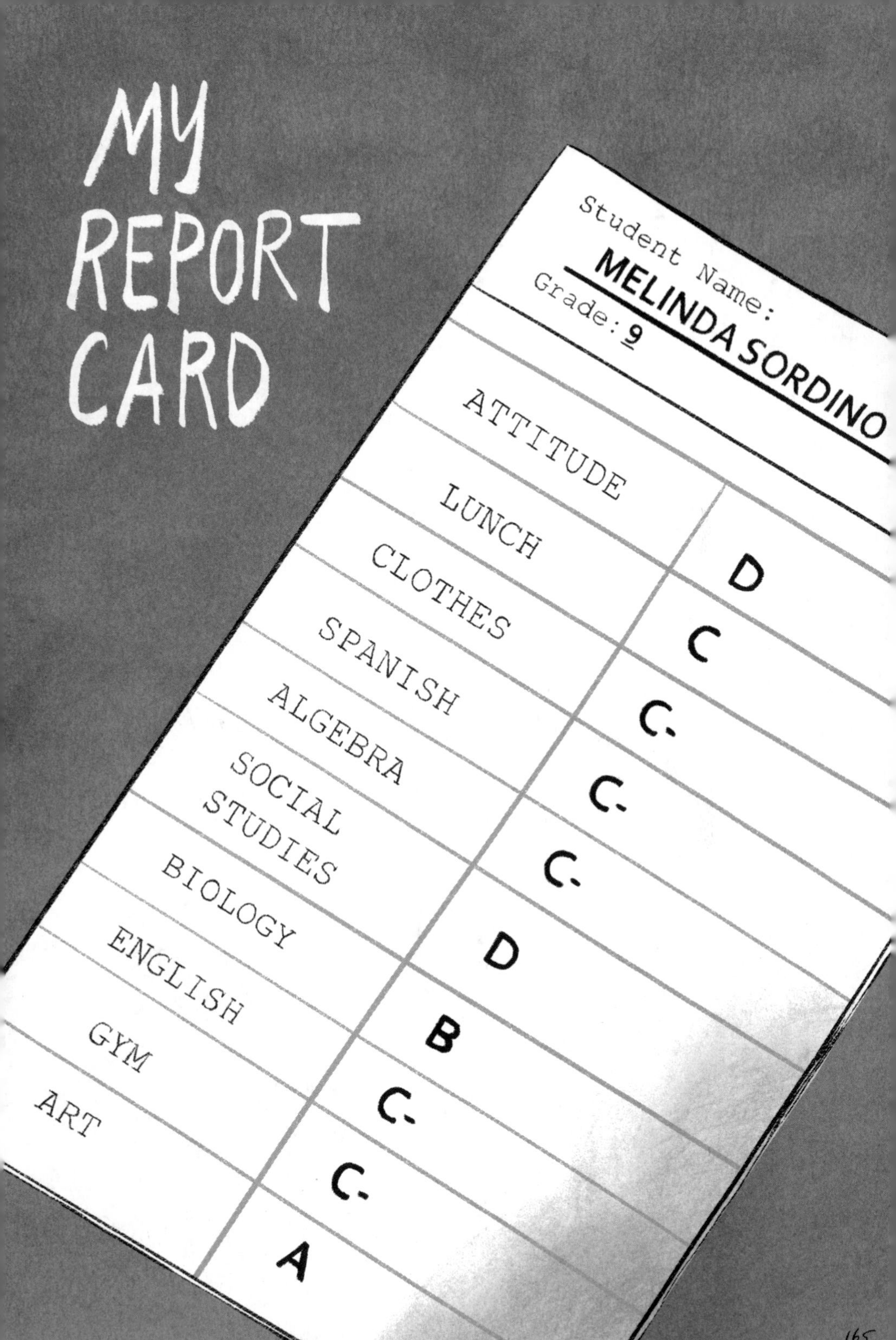
MY REPORT CARD
Student Name:
MELINDA SORDINO
Grade: 9
ATTITUDE D
LUNCH C
CLOTHES C-
SPANISH C-
ALGEBRA C-
SOCIAL STUDIES D
BIOLOGY B
ENGLISH C-
GYM C-
ART A

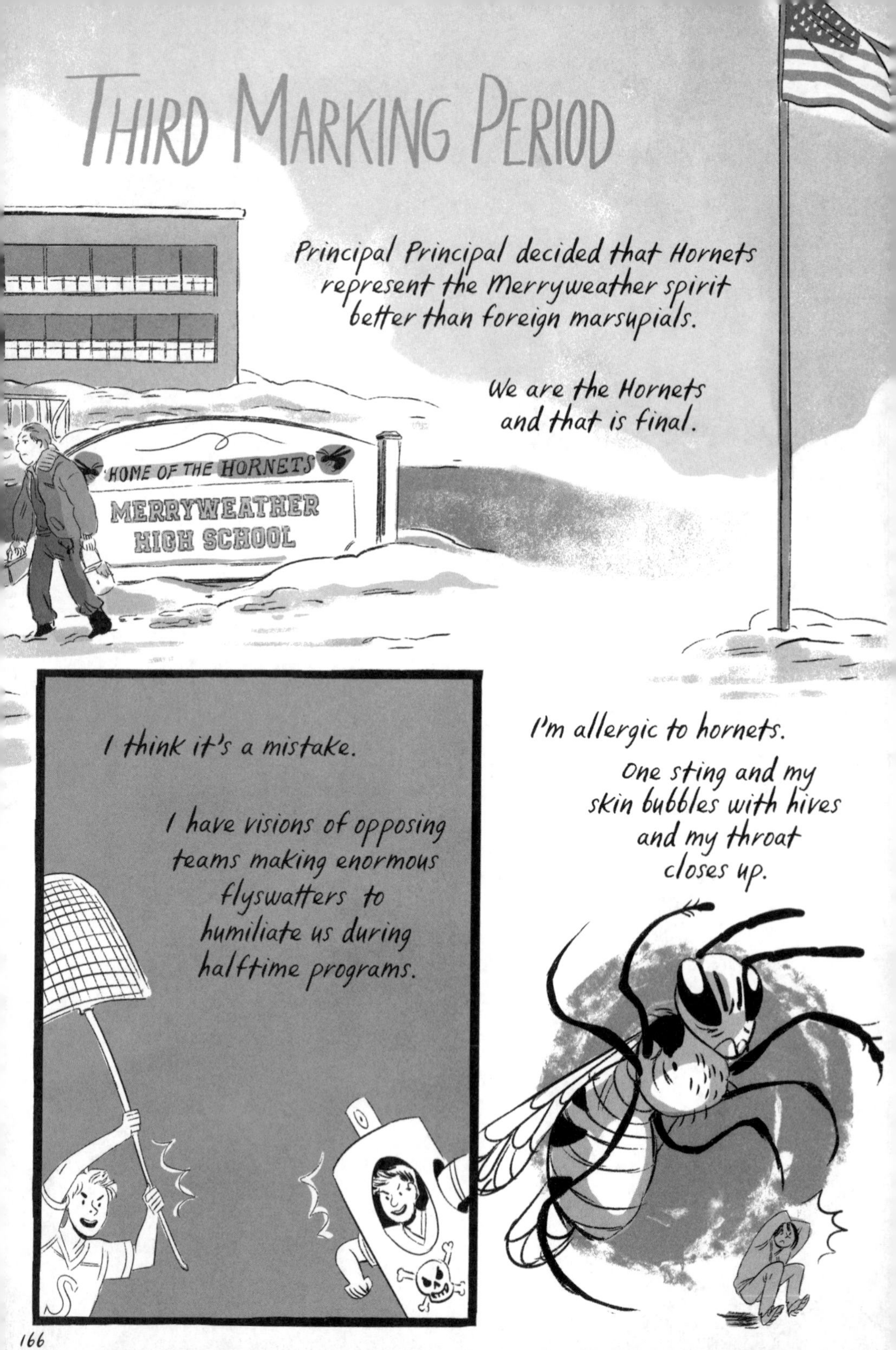
THIRD MARKING PERIOD
Principal Principal decided that Hornets represent the Merryweather spirit better than foreign marsupials.
We are the Hornets and that is final.
HOME OF THE HORNETS
MERRYWEATHER HIGH SCHOOL
I think it's a mistake.
I have visions of opposing teams making enormous flyswatters to humiliate us during halftime programs.
I'm allergic to hornets.
One sting and my skin bubbles with hives and my throat closes up.

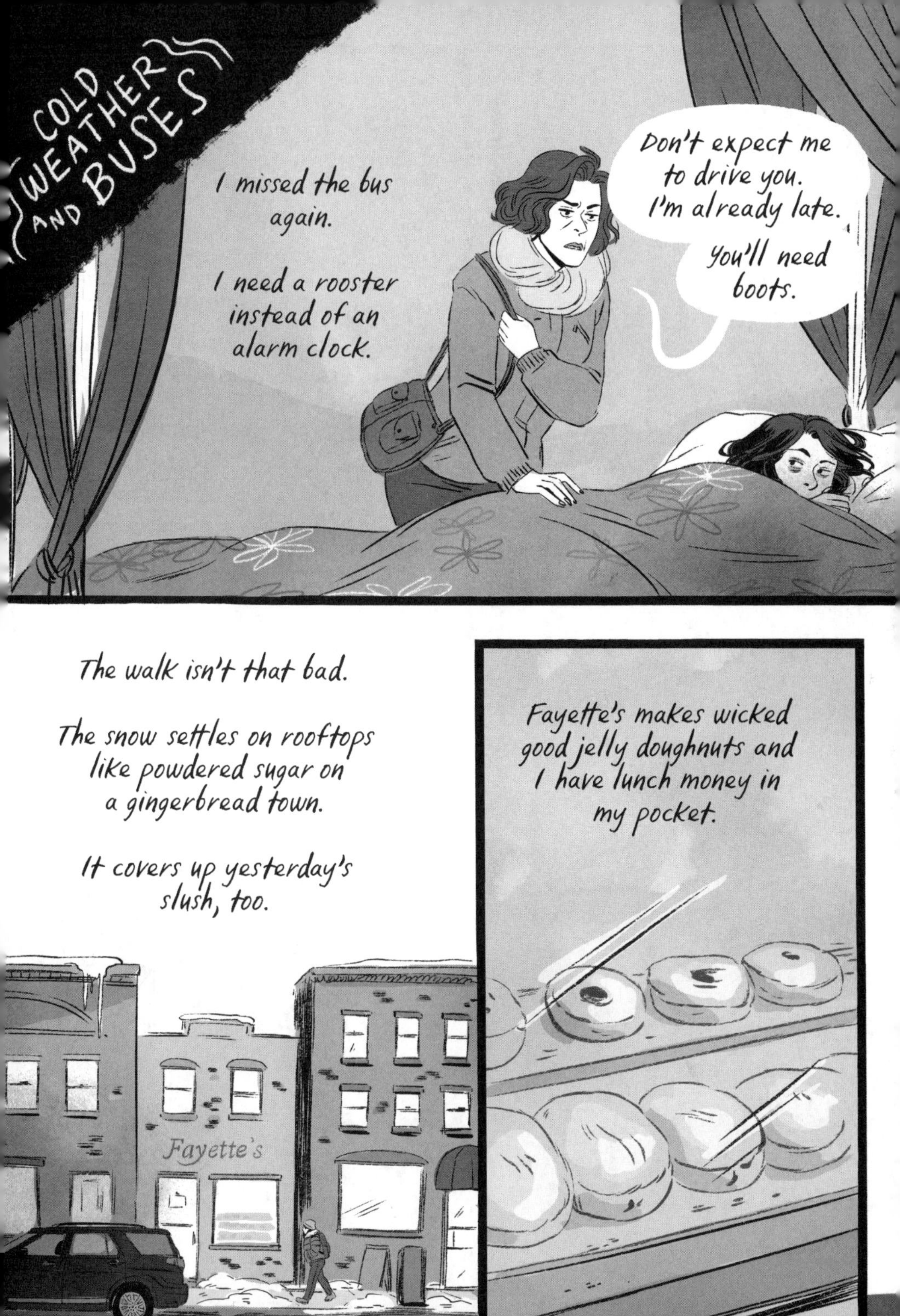
COLD WEATHER AND BUSES
I missed the bus again.
I need a rooster instead of an alarm clock.
Don't expect me to drive you. I'm already late.
You'll need boots.
The walk isn't that bad.
The snow settles on rooftops like powdered sugar on a gingerbread town.
It covers up yesterday's slush, too.
Fayette's
Fayette's makes wicked good jelly doughnuts and I have lunch money in my pocket.

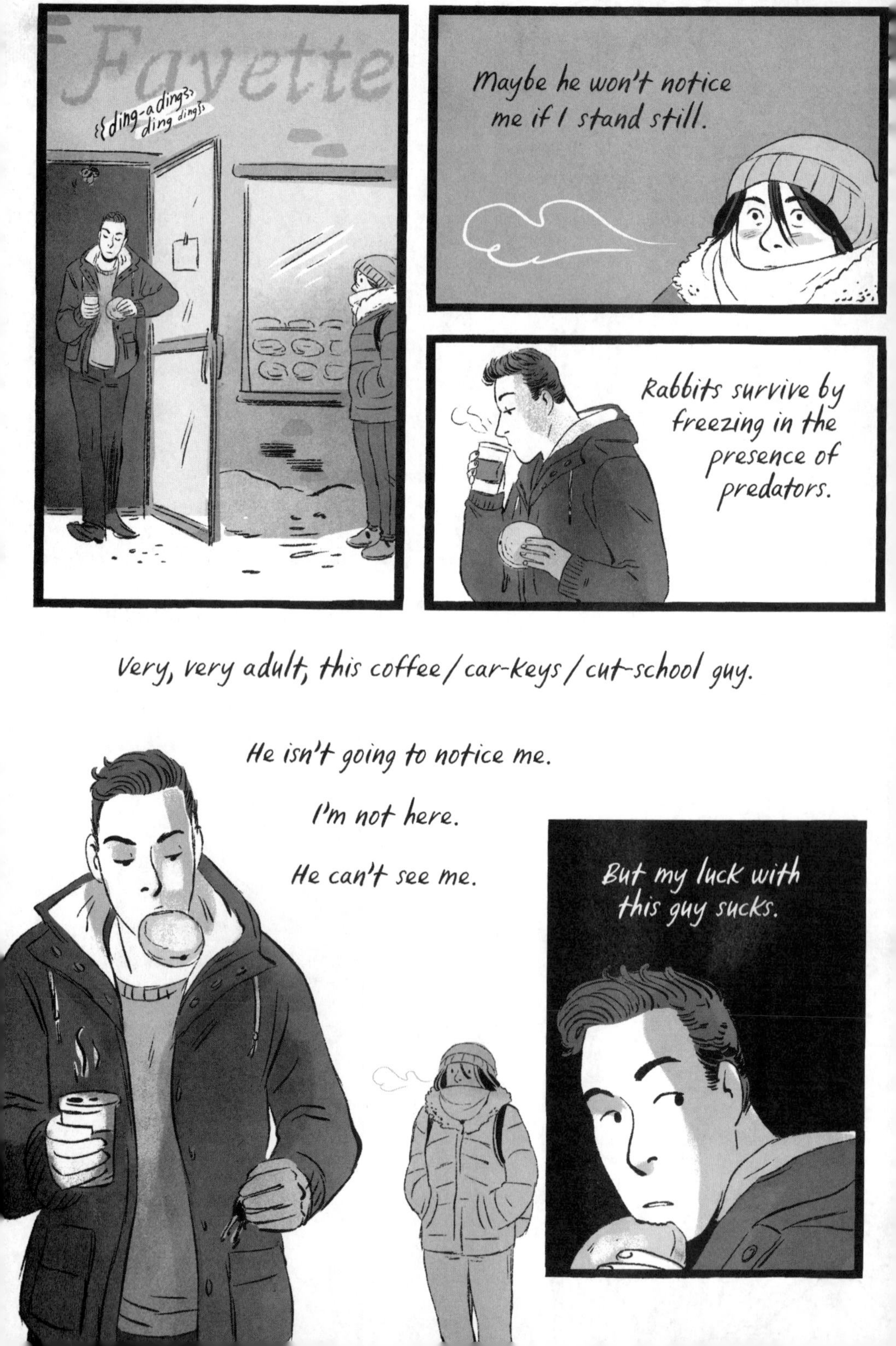
Fayette
ding-a-ding ding ding
Maybe he won't notice me if I stand still.
Rabbits survive by freezing in the presence of predators.
Very, very adult, this coffee / car-keys / cut-school guy.
He isn't going to notice me.
I'm not here.
He can't see me.
But my luck with this guy sucks.

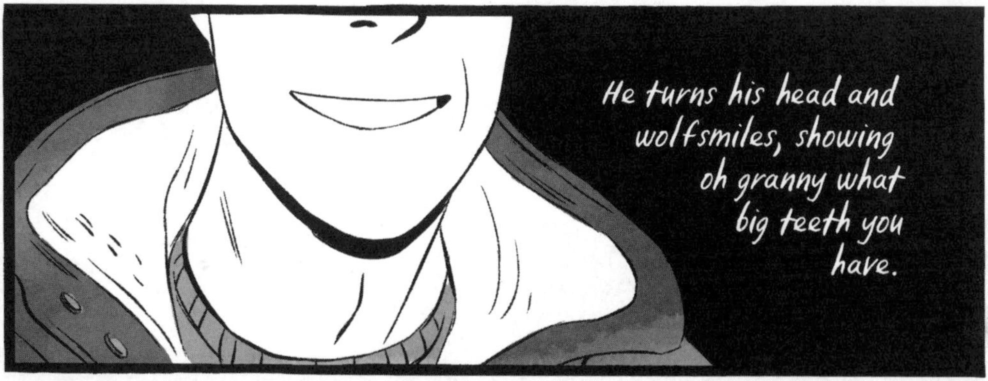
He turns his head and wolfsmiles, showing oh granny what big teeth you have.

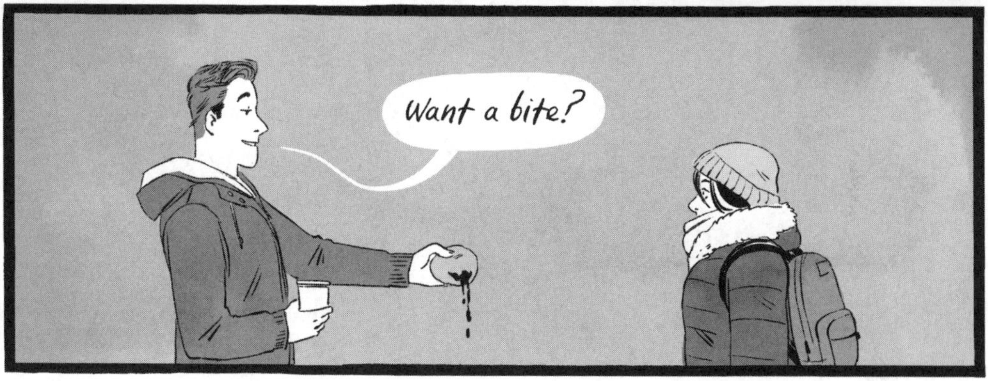
Want a bite?

Bunny Rabbit bolts, leaving fast tracks in the snow.

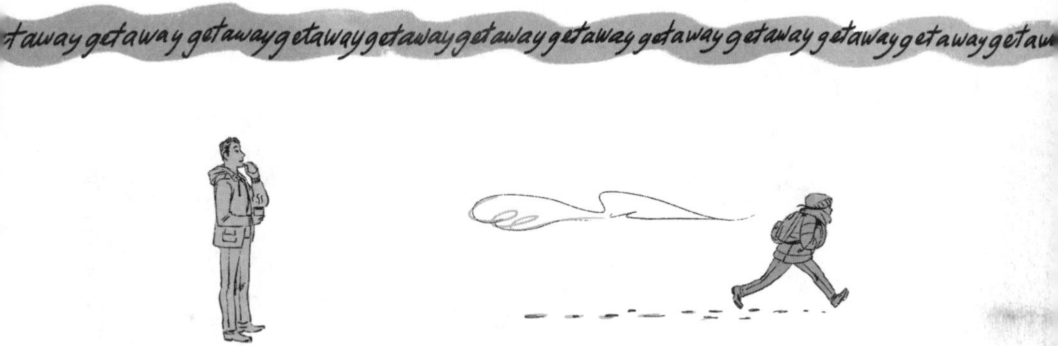
getaway getaway getaway getaway getaway getaway getaway getaway getaway getaway getaway

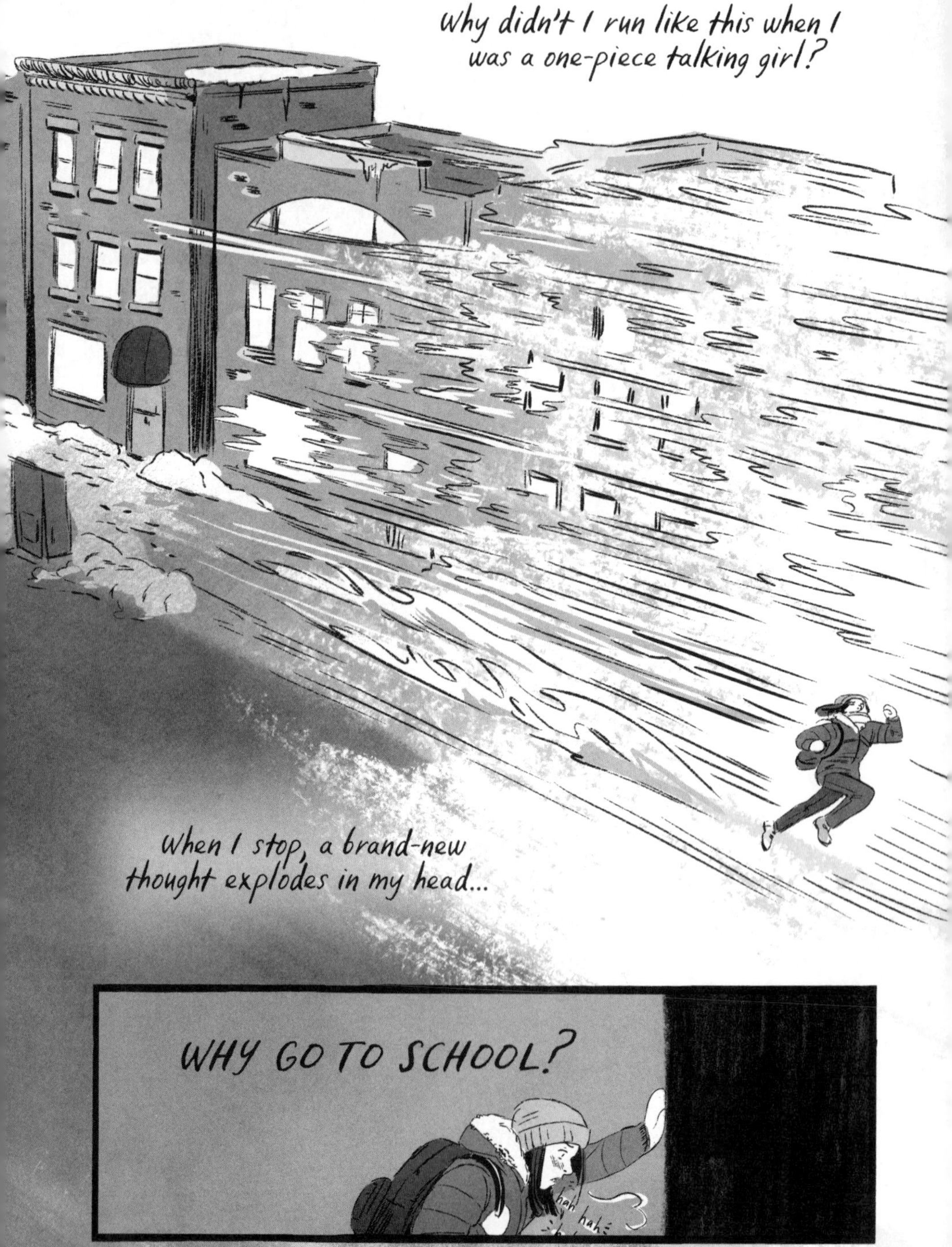
Why didn't I run like this when I
was a one-piece talking girl?
When I stop, a brand-new
thought explodes in my head...
WHY GO TO SCHOOL?
hah hah

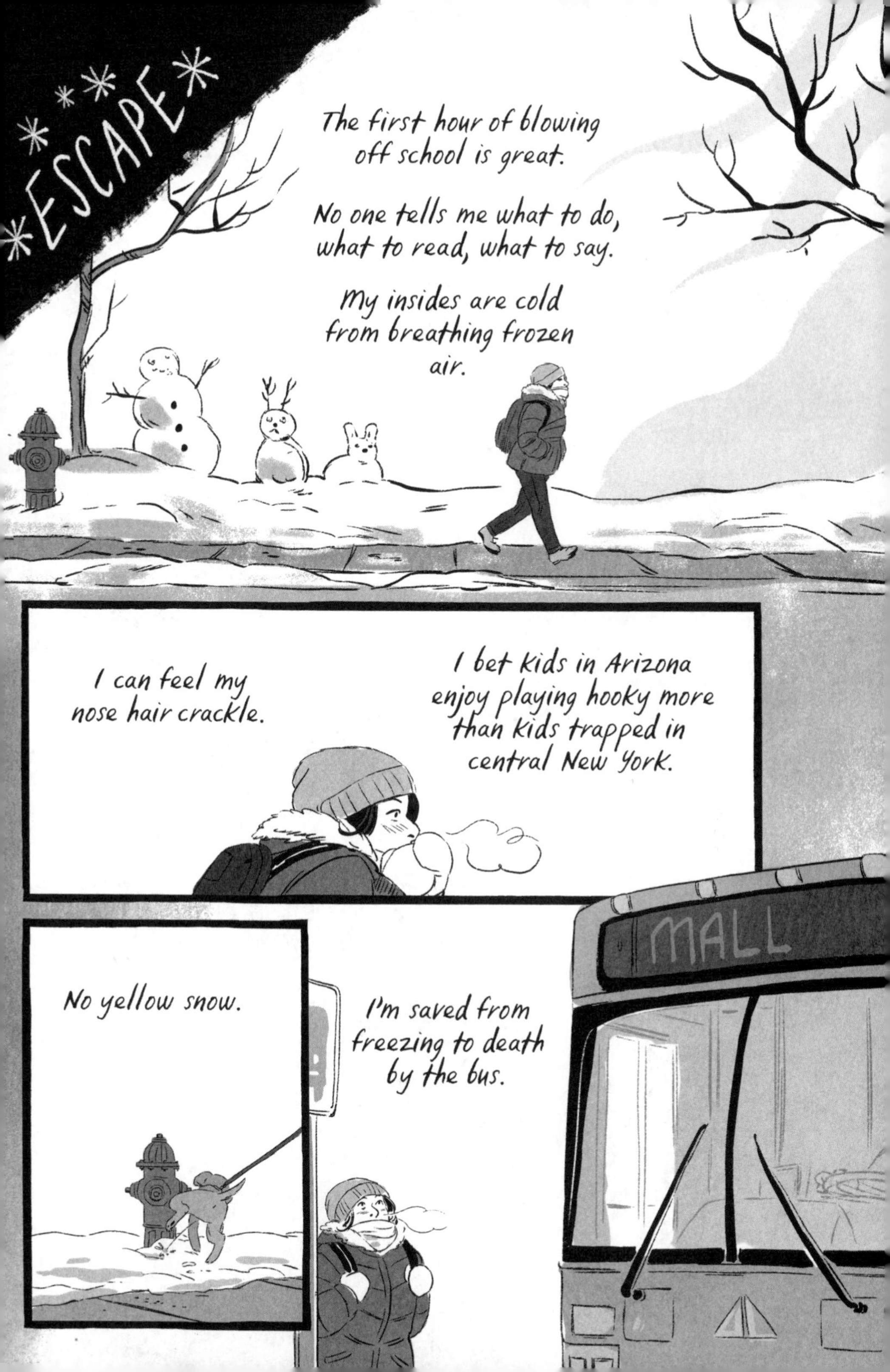
ESCAPE
The first hour of blowing off school is great.
No one tells me what to do, what to read, what to say.
My insides are cold from breathing frozen air.
I can feel my nose hair crackle.
I bet kids in Arizona enjoy playing hooky more than kids trapped in central New York.
No yellow snow.
I'm saved from freezing to death by the bus.
MALL

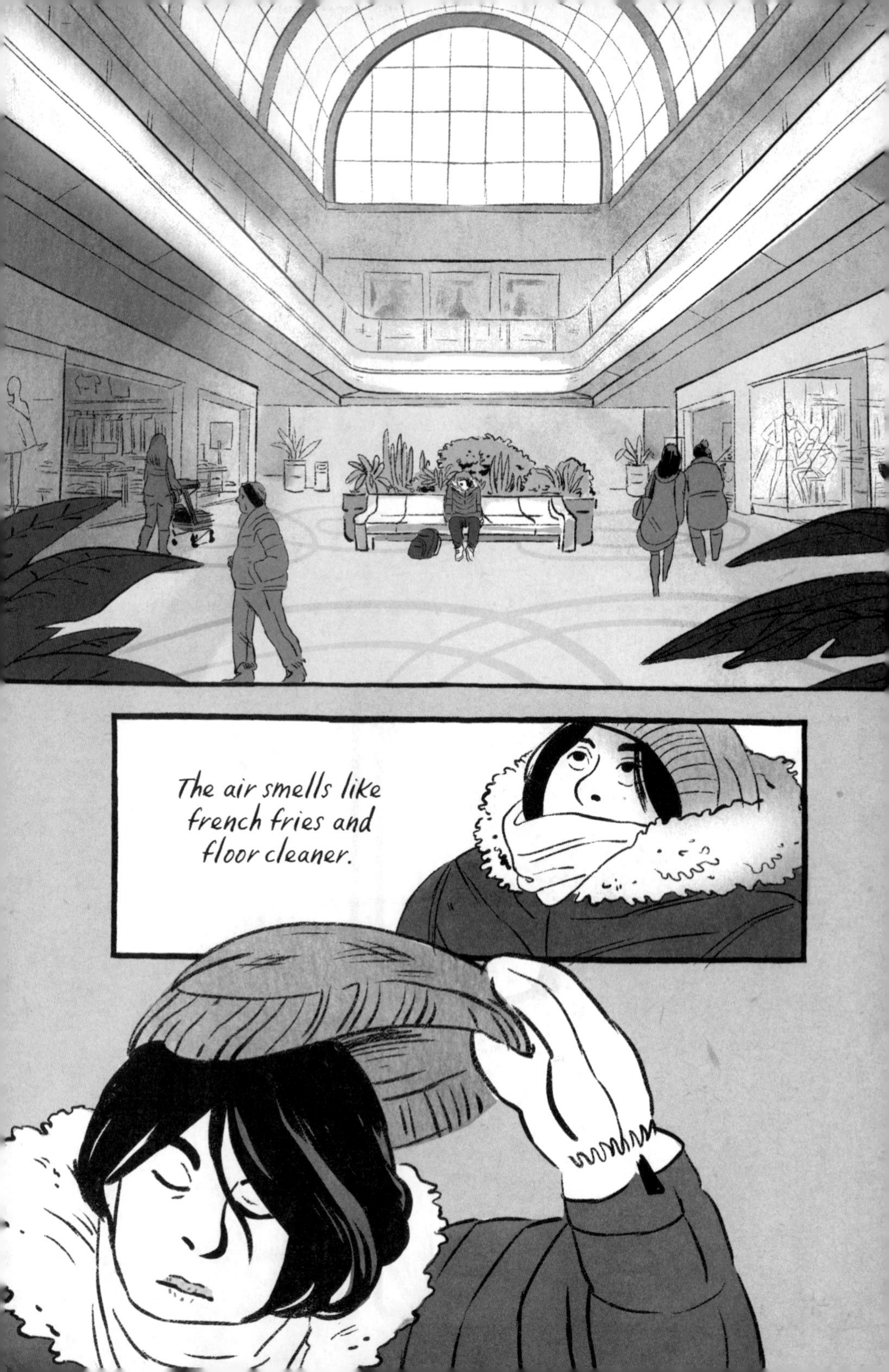
The air smells like french fries and floor cleaner.

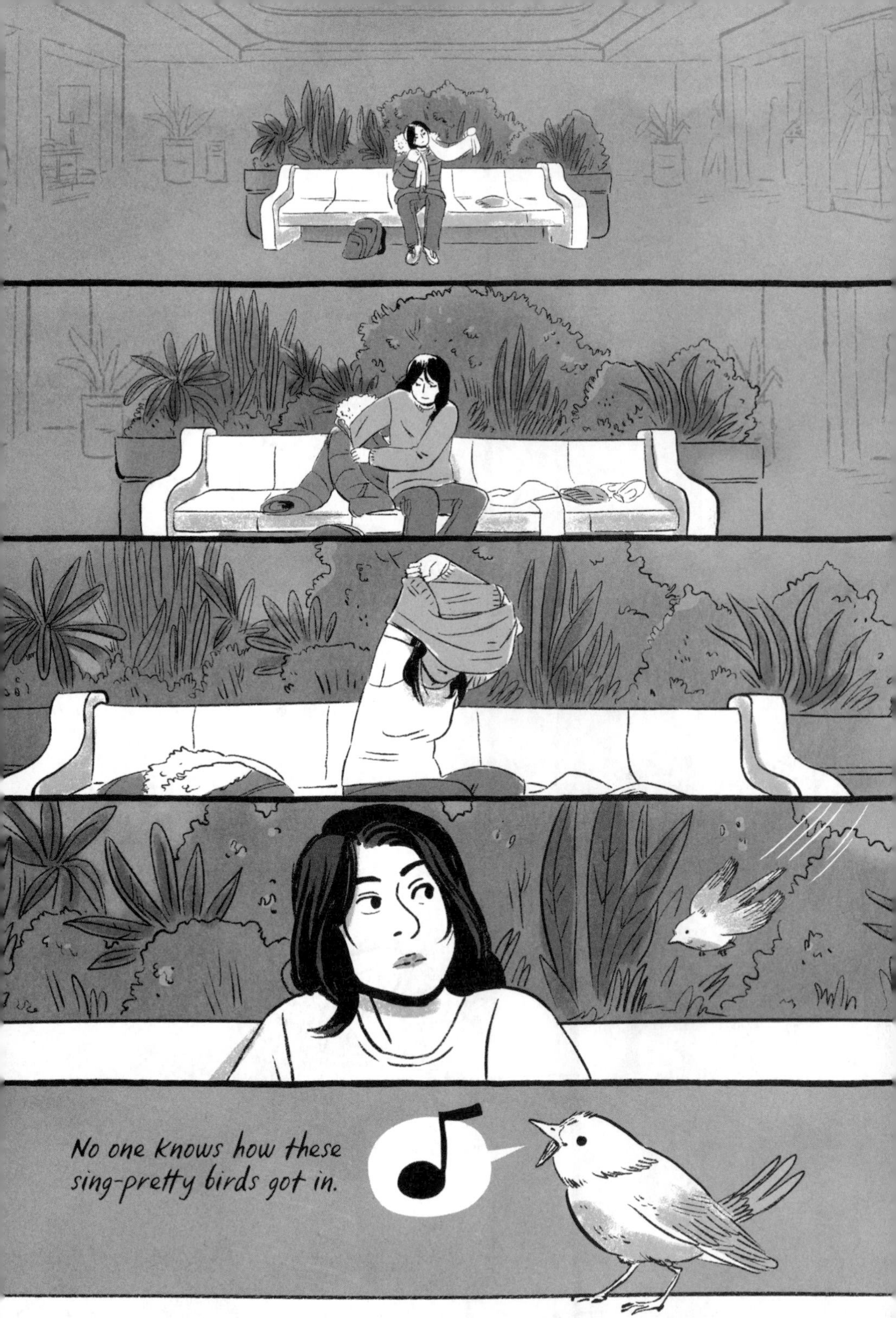
No one knows how these sing-pretty birds got in.
♪

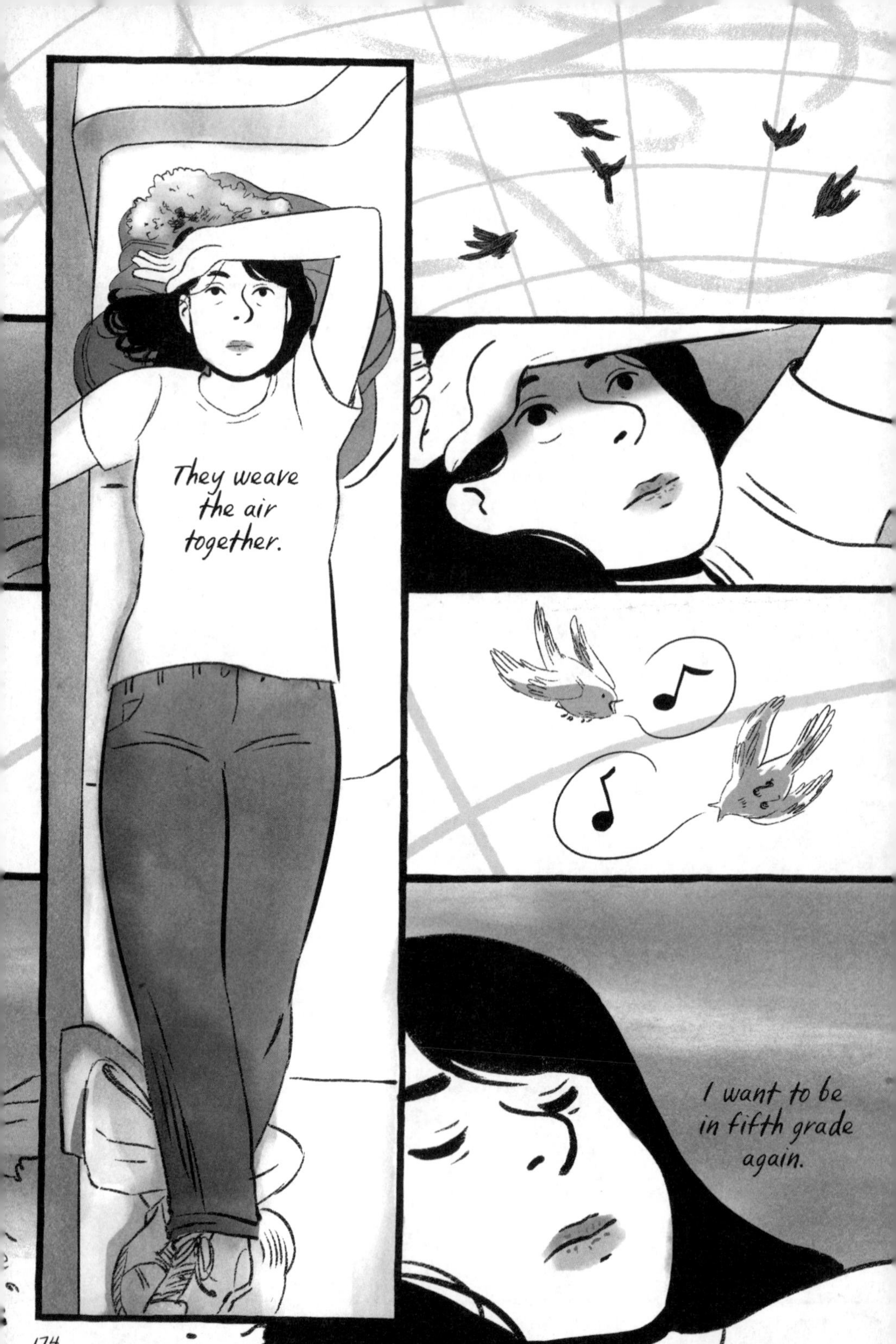
They weave the air together.
I want to be in fifth grade again.

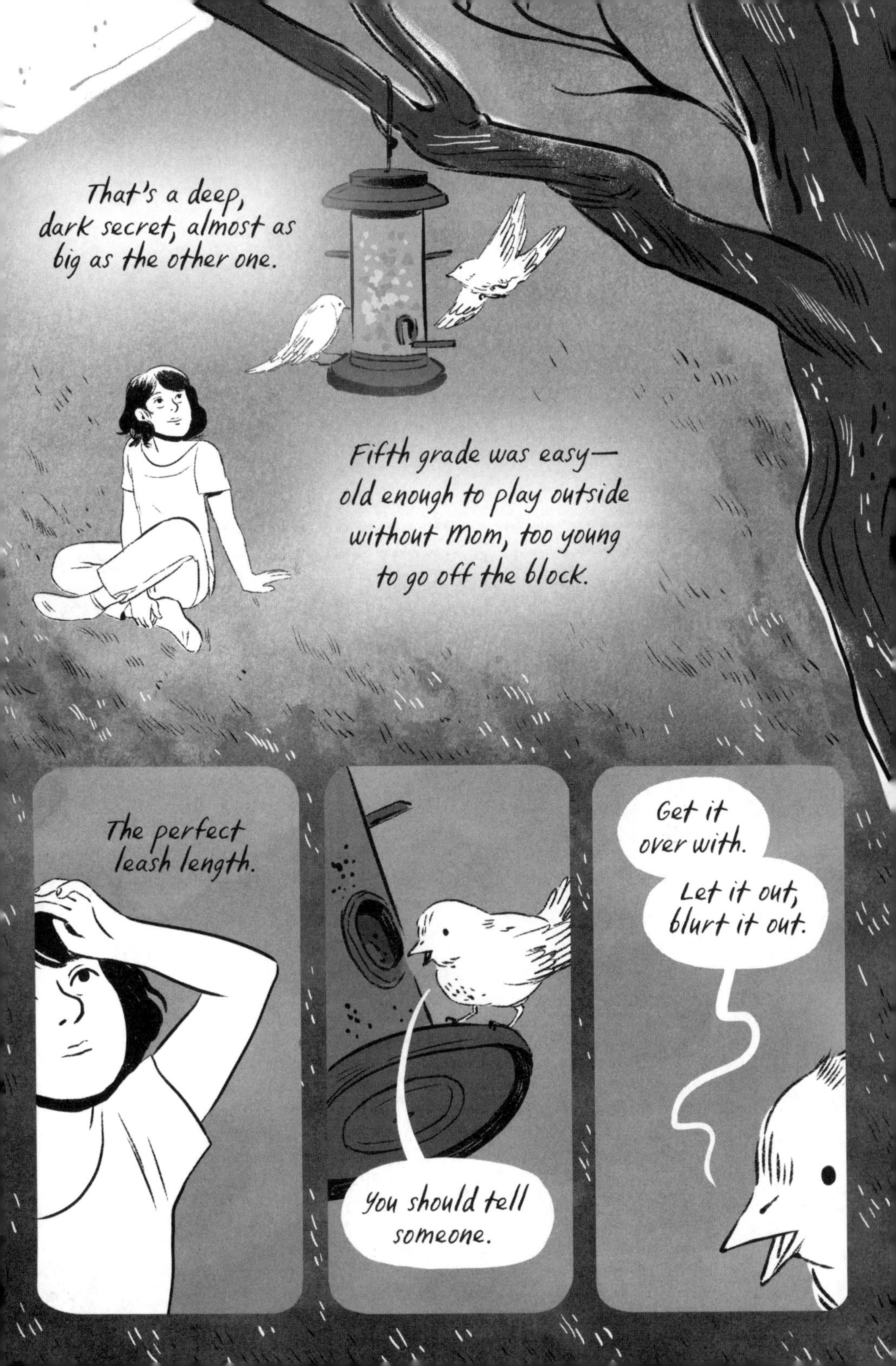
That's a deep, dark secret, almost as big as the other one.
Fifth grade was easy—old enough to play outside without Mom, too young to go off the block.
The perfect leash length.
You should tell someone.
Get it over with.
Let it out, blurt it out.

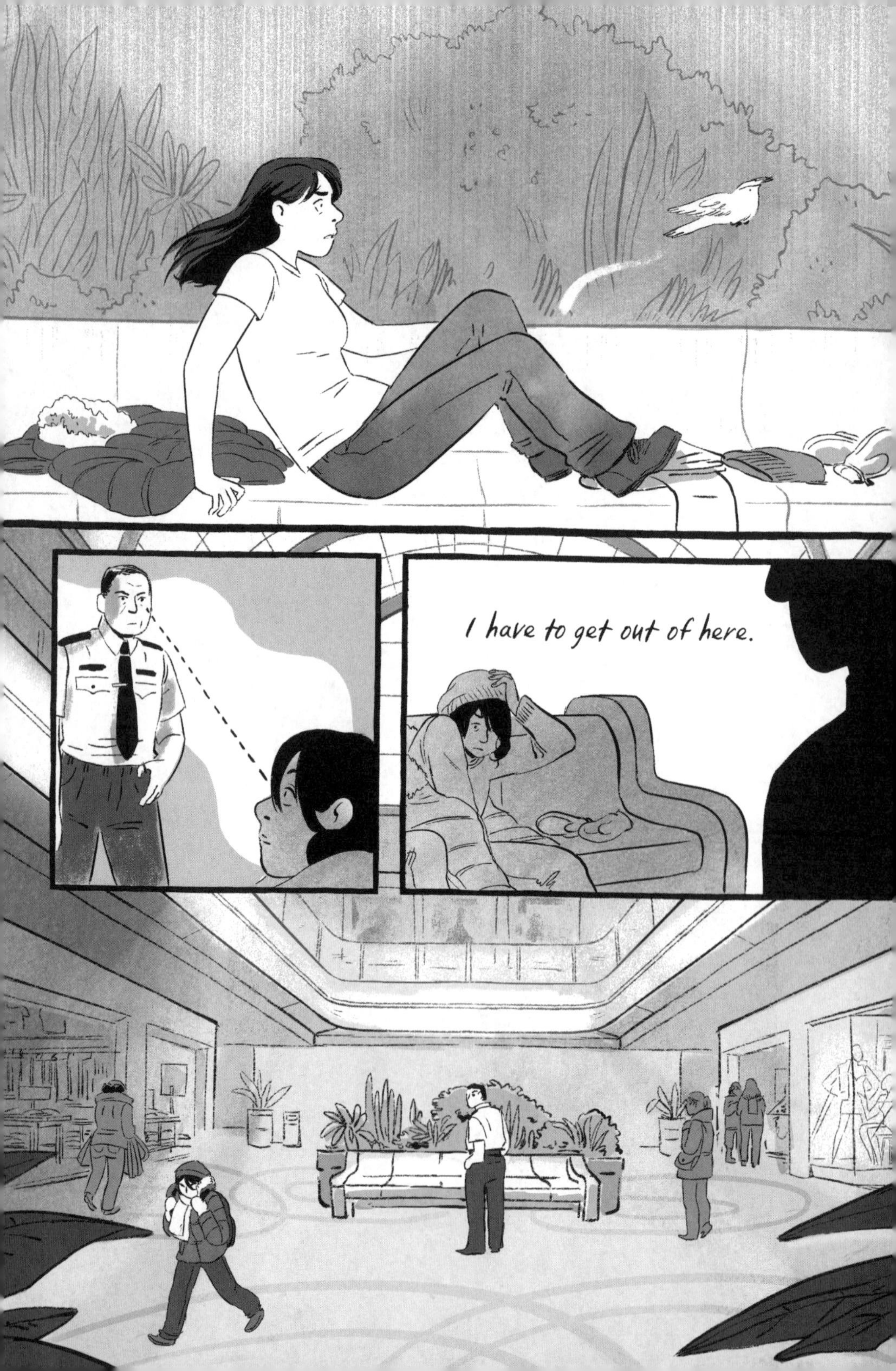
I have to get out of here.

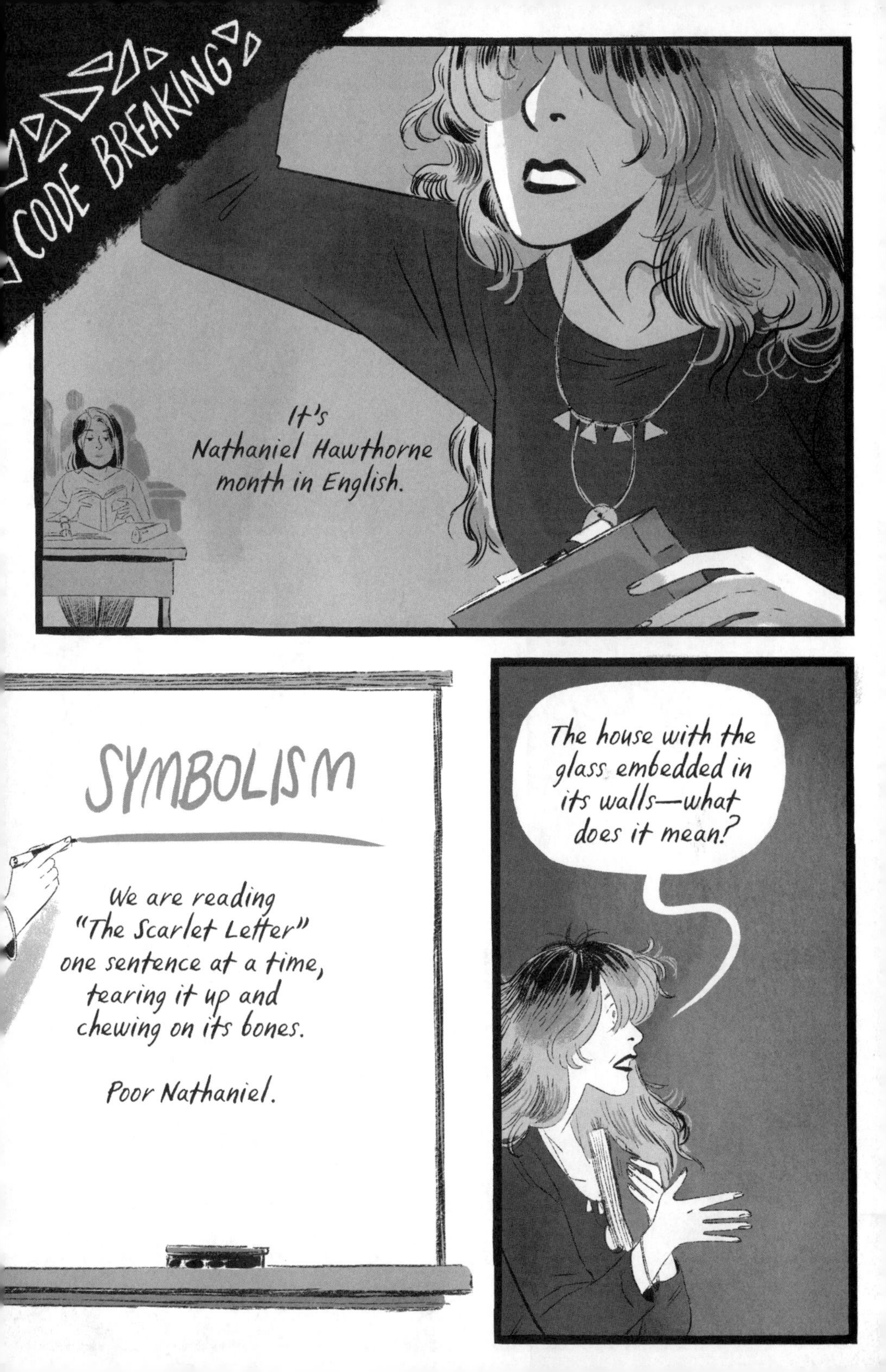
CODE BREAKING
It's Nathaniel Hawthorne month in English.
SYMBOLISM
We are reading "The Scarlet Letter" one sentence at a time, tearing it up and chewing on its bones.
Poor Nathaniel.
The house with the glass embedded in its walls—what does it mean?

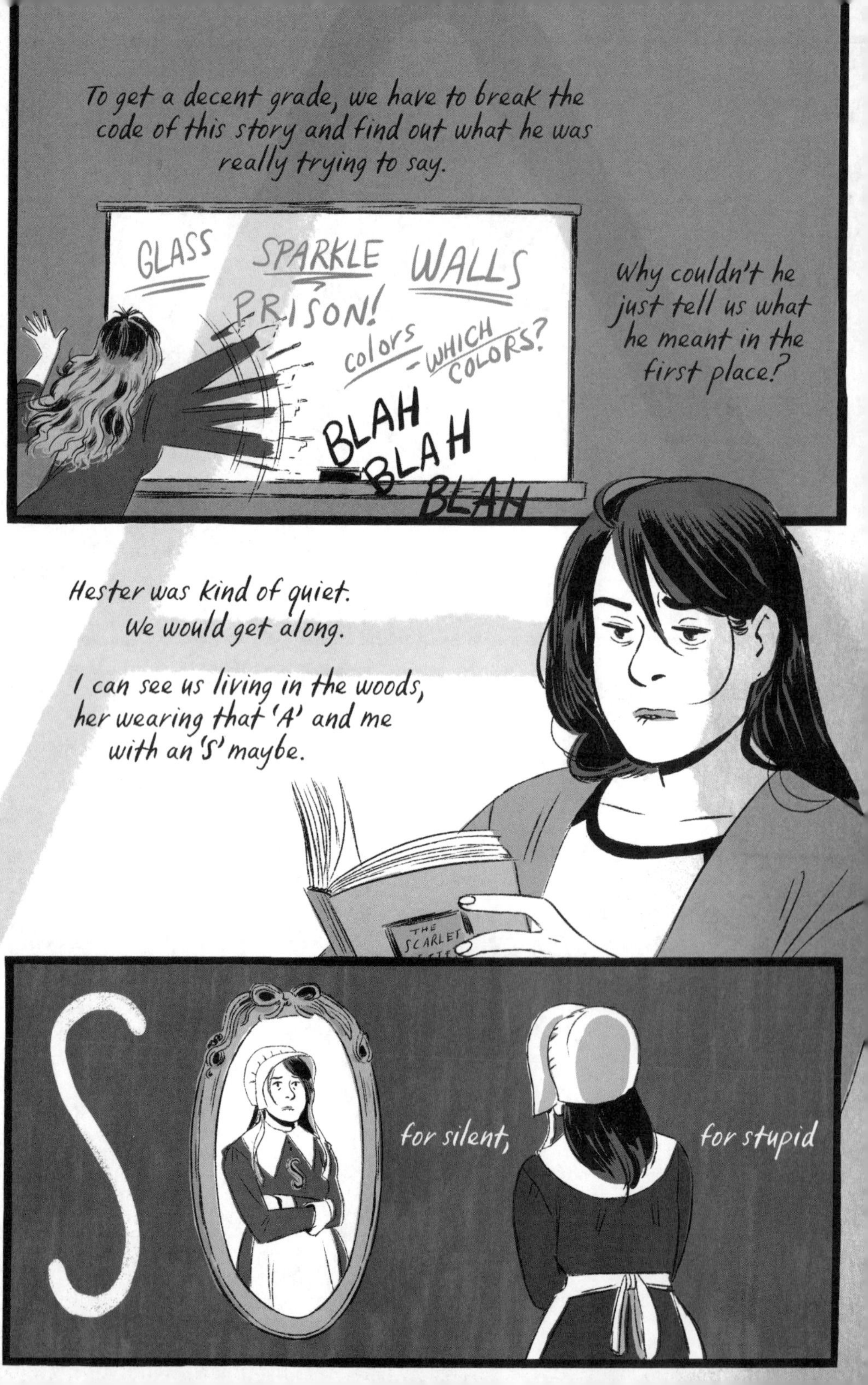
To get a decent grade, we have to break the code of this story and find out what he was really trying to say.
GLASS
SPARKLE
WALLS
PRISON!
colors
-WHICH COLORS?
BLAH
BLAH
BLAH
Why couldn't he just tell us what he meant in the first place?
Hester was kind of quiet.
We would get along.
I can see us living in the woods, her wearing that 'A' and me with an 'S' maybe.
THE SCARLET
S
for silent,
for stupid

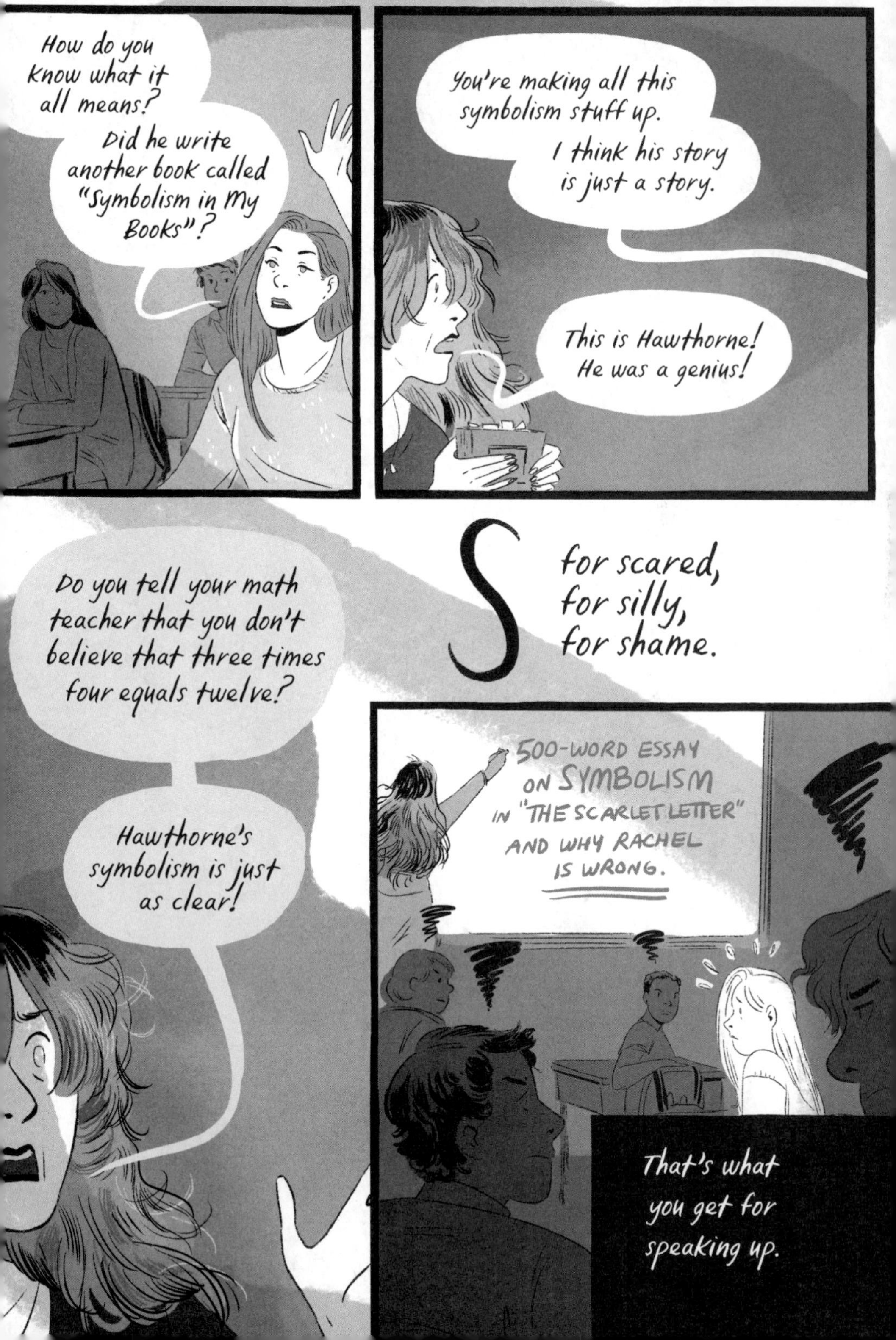
How do you know what it all means?
Did he write another book called "Symbolism in My Books"?
You're making all this symbolism stuff up.
I think his story is just a story.
This is Hawthorne! He was a genius!
Do you tell your math teacher that you don't believe that three times four equals twelve?
Hawthorne's symbolism is just as clear!
S for scared, for silly, for shame.
500-WORD ESSAY ON SYMBOLISM IN "THE SCARLET LETTER" AND WHY RACHEL IS WRONG.
That's what you get for speaking up.

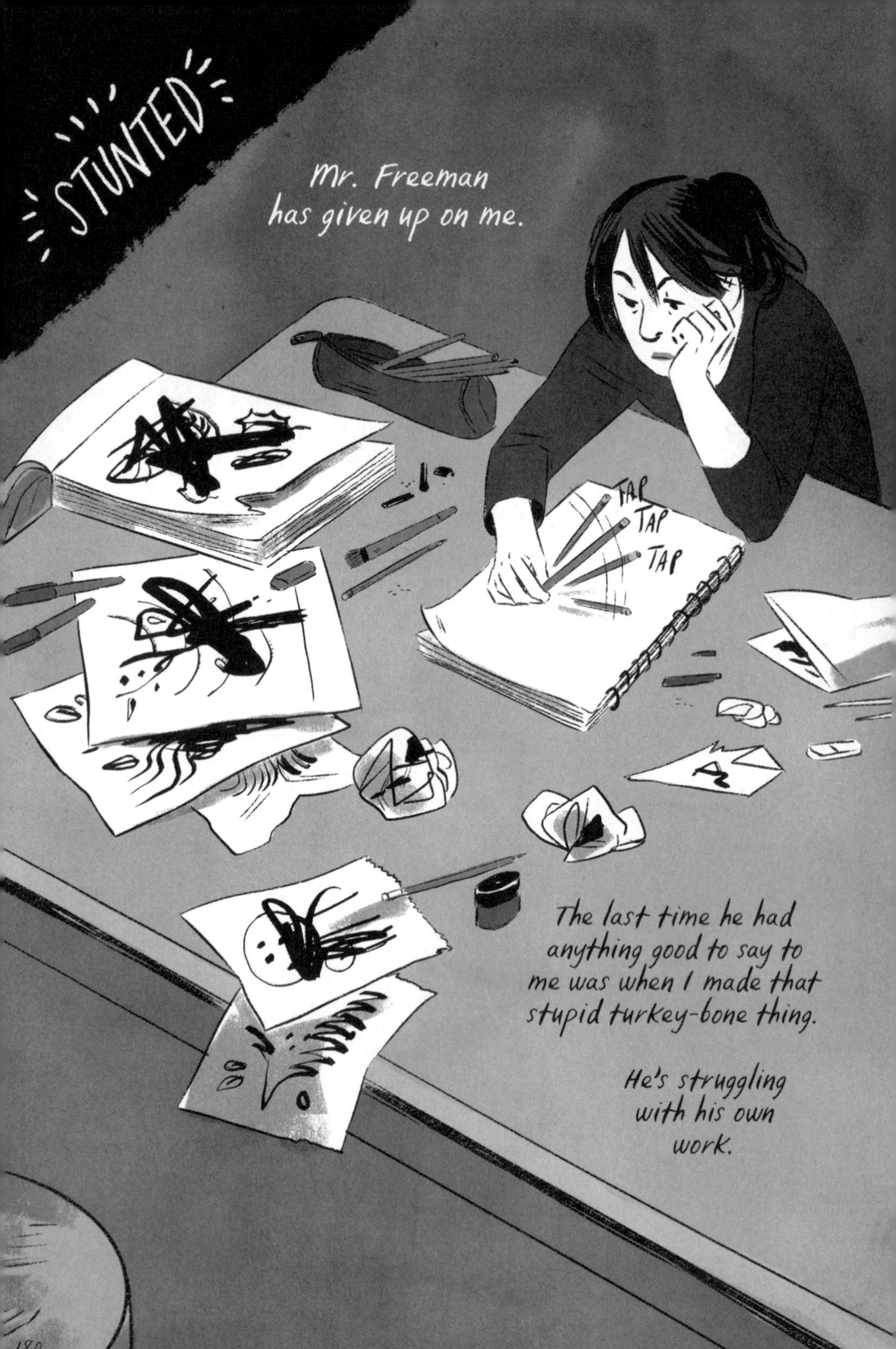
STUNTED
Mr. Freeman has given up on me.
TAP
TAP
TAP
The last time he had anything good to say to me was when I made that stupid turkey-bone thing.
He's struggling with his own work.

A kid asked him what his painting was.

"It's Venice at night,
        an accountant's soul,
                the blood of imbeciles.

                Smoker's lung.

                Tenure.

The inside of a lock,
        the taste of iron.

                        Despair.

A city with the streetlights
                shot out,

                        the heart of
a school board director."

Some teachers whisper he's having a breakdown.

I think he's the sanest person I know.

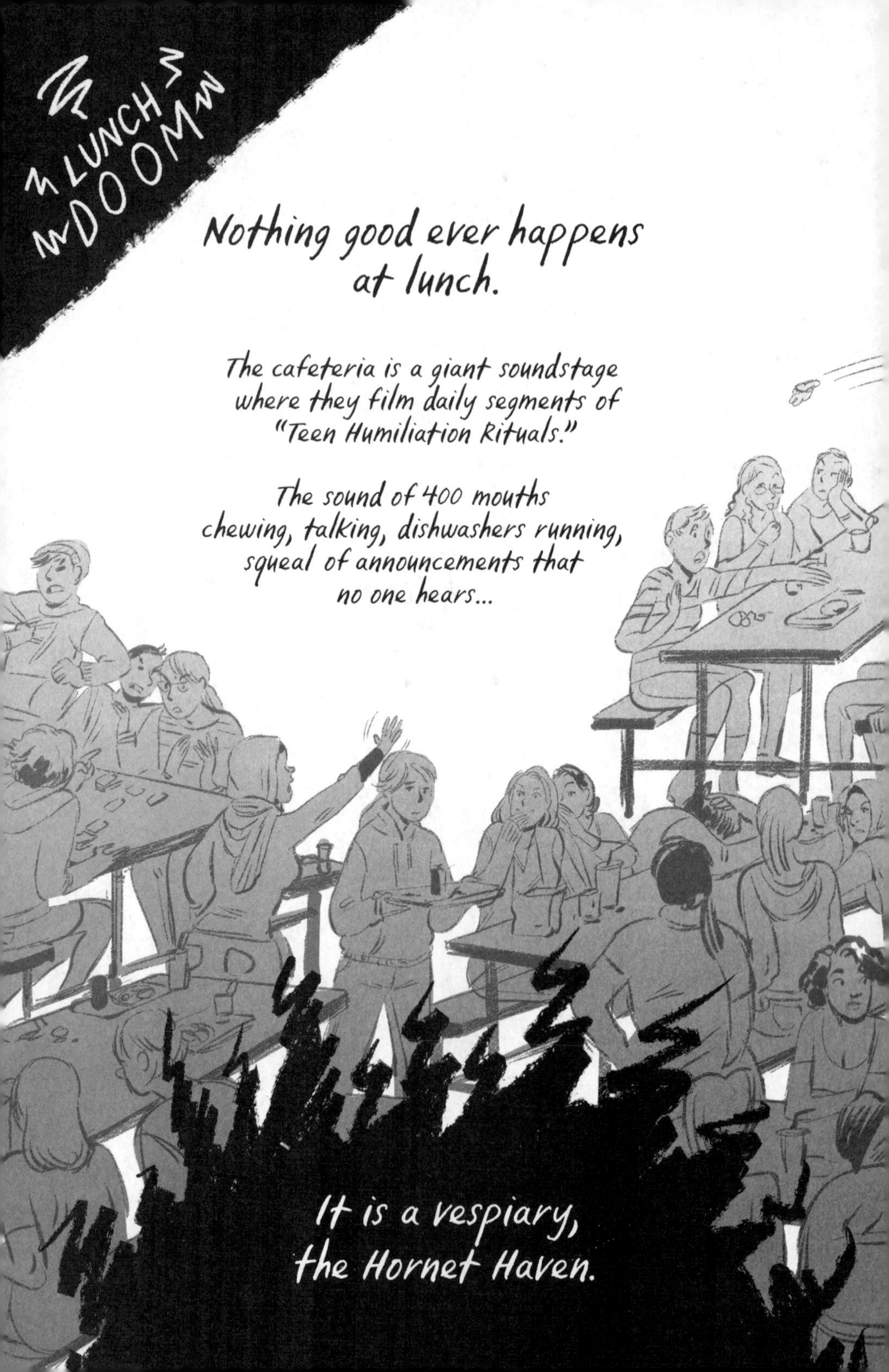
LUNCH DOOM
Nothing good ever happens at lunch.
The cafeteria is a giant soundstage where they film daily segments of "Teen Humiliation Rituals."
The sound of 400 mouths chewing, talking, dishwashers running, squeal of announcements that no one hears...
It is a vespiary, the Hornet Haven.

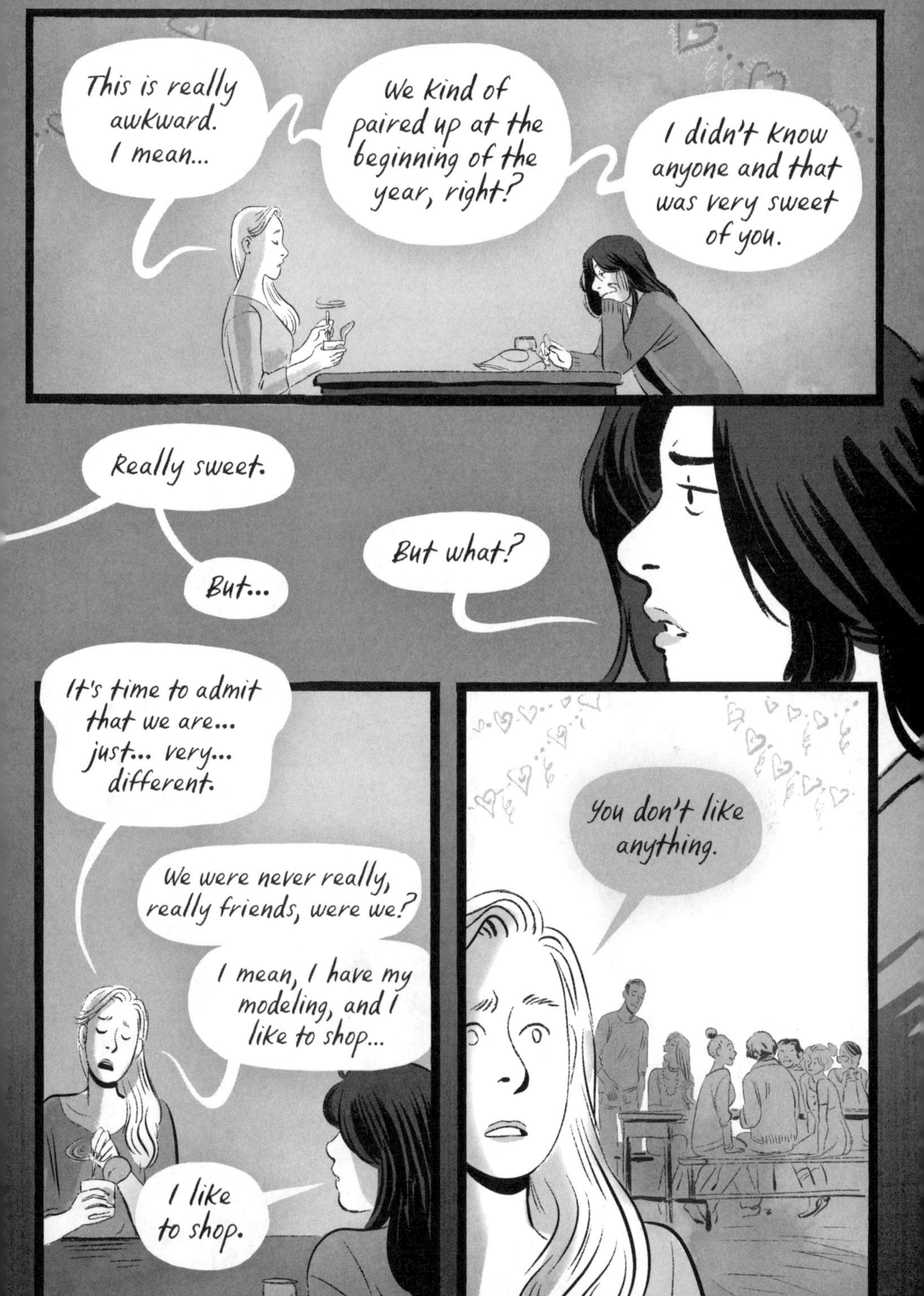
This is really awkward. I mean...
We kind of paired up at the beginning of the year, right?
I didn't know anyone and that was very sweet of you.
Really sweet.
But...
But what?
It's time to admit that we are... just... very... different.
We were never really, really friends, were we?
I mean, I have my modeling, and I like to shop...
I like to shop.
You don't like anything.

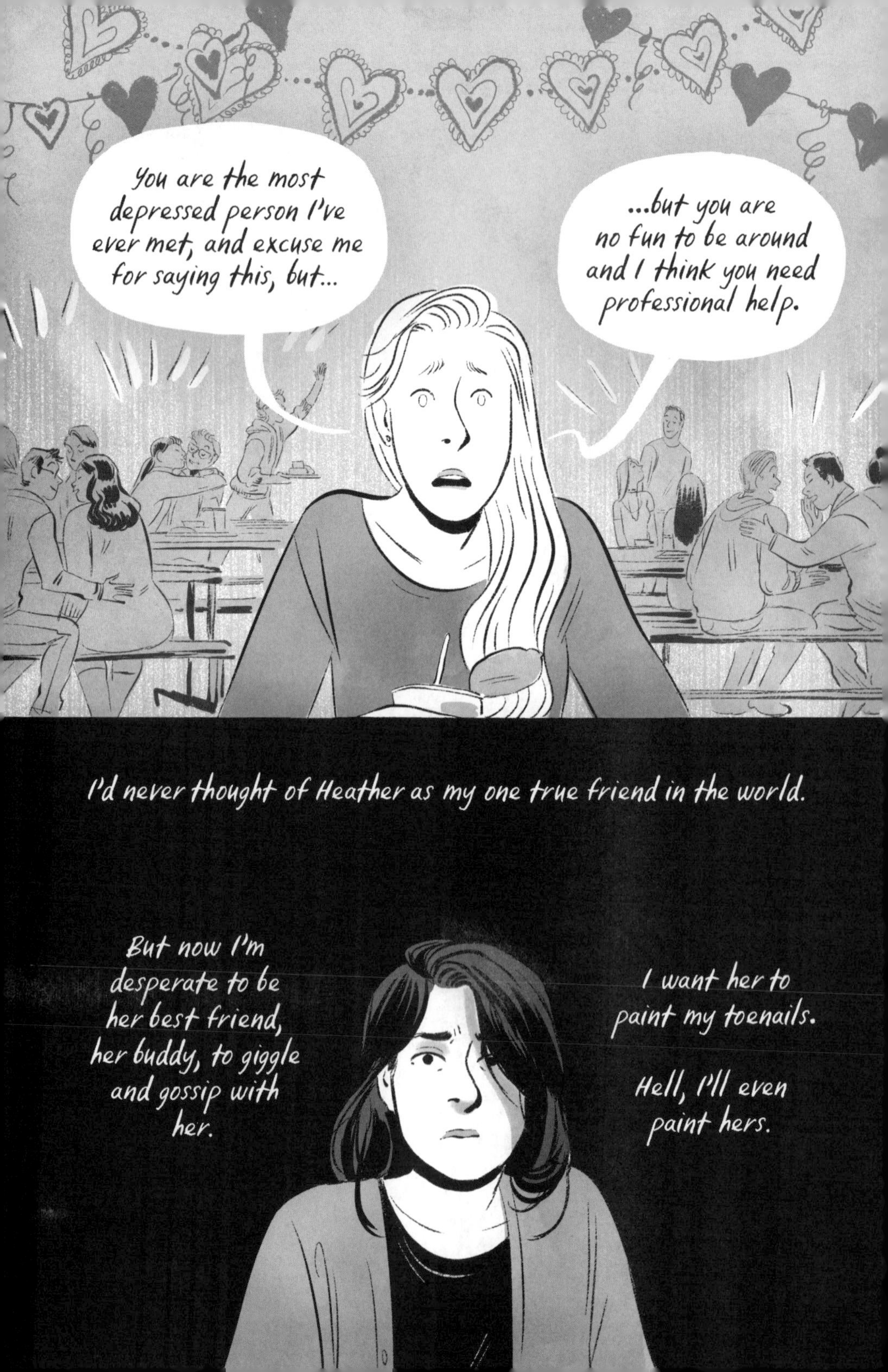
You are the most depressed person I've ever met, and excuse me for saying this, but...
...but you are no fun to be around and I think you need professional help.
I'd never thought of Heather as my one true friend in the world.
But now I'm desperate to be her best friend, her buddy, to giggle and gossip with her.
I want her to paint my toenails.
Hell, I'll even paint hers.

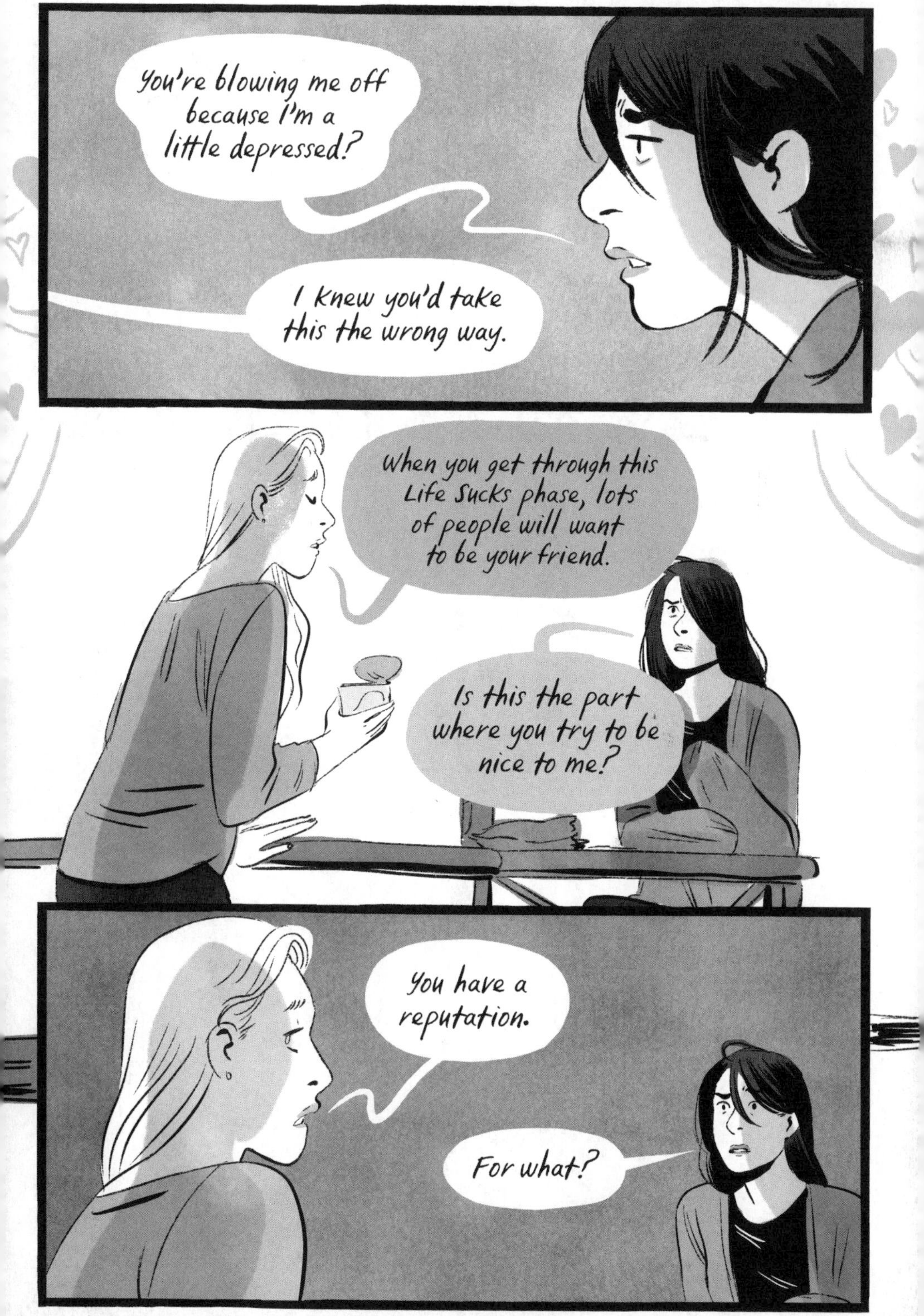
You're blowing me off because I'm a little depressed?
I knew you'd take this the wrong way.
When you get through this Life Sucks phase, lots of people will want to be your friend.
Is this the part where you try to be nice to me?
You have a reputation.
For what?

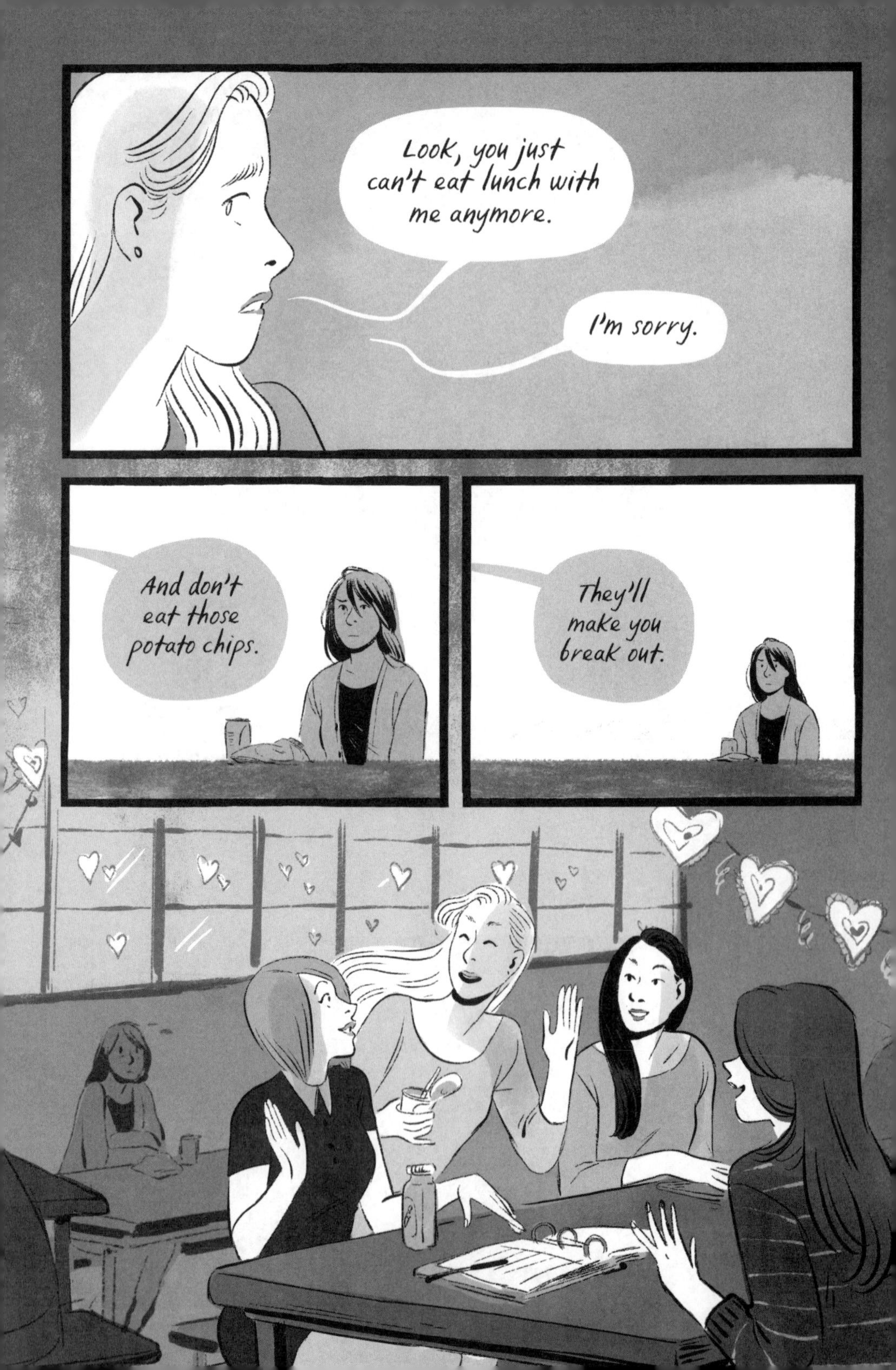
Look, you just can't eat lunch with me anymore.
I'm sorry.
And don't eat those potato chips.
They'll make you break out.

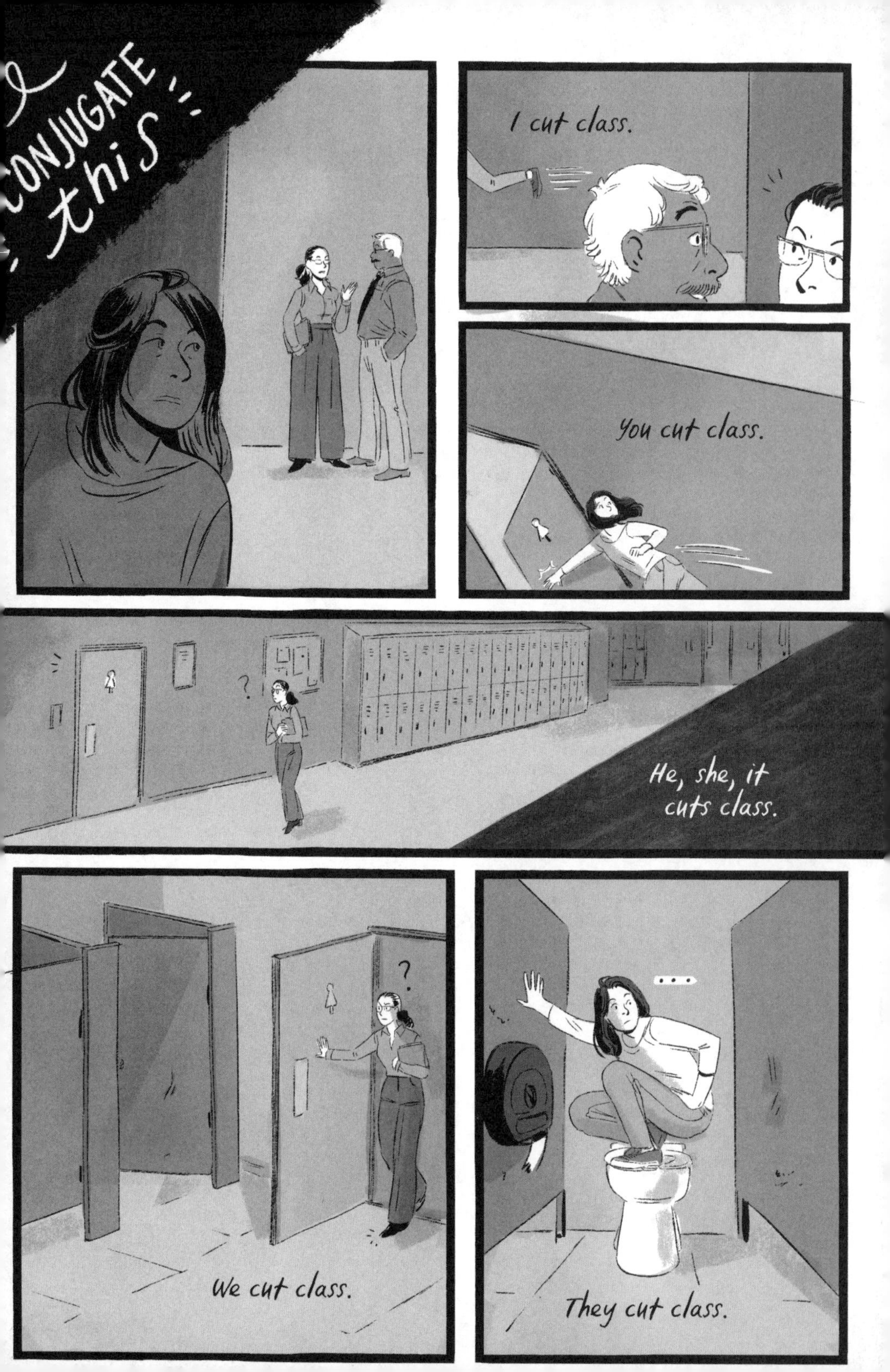
CONJUGATE this
I cut class.
You cut class.
He, she, it cuts class.
?
We cut class.
?
They cut class.
...

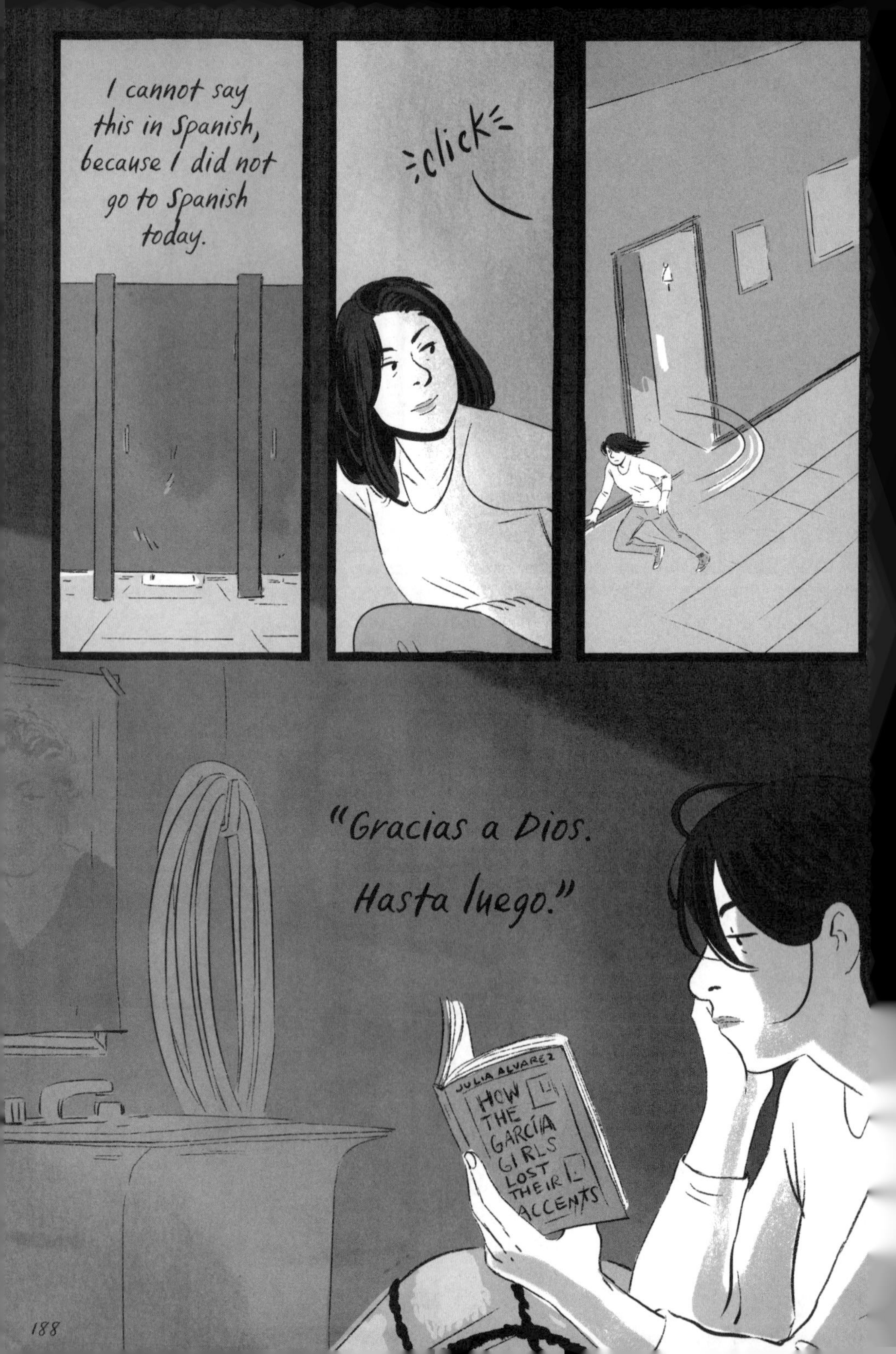
I cannot say this in Spanish, because I did not go to Spanish today.
click
"Gracias a Dios. Hasta luego."
JULIA ALVAREZ
HOW THE GARCÍA GIRLS LOST THEIR ACCENTS

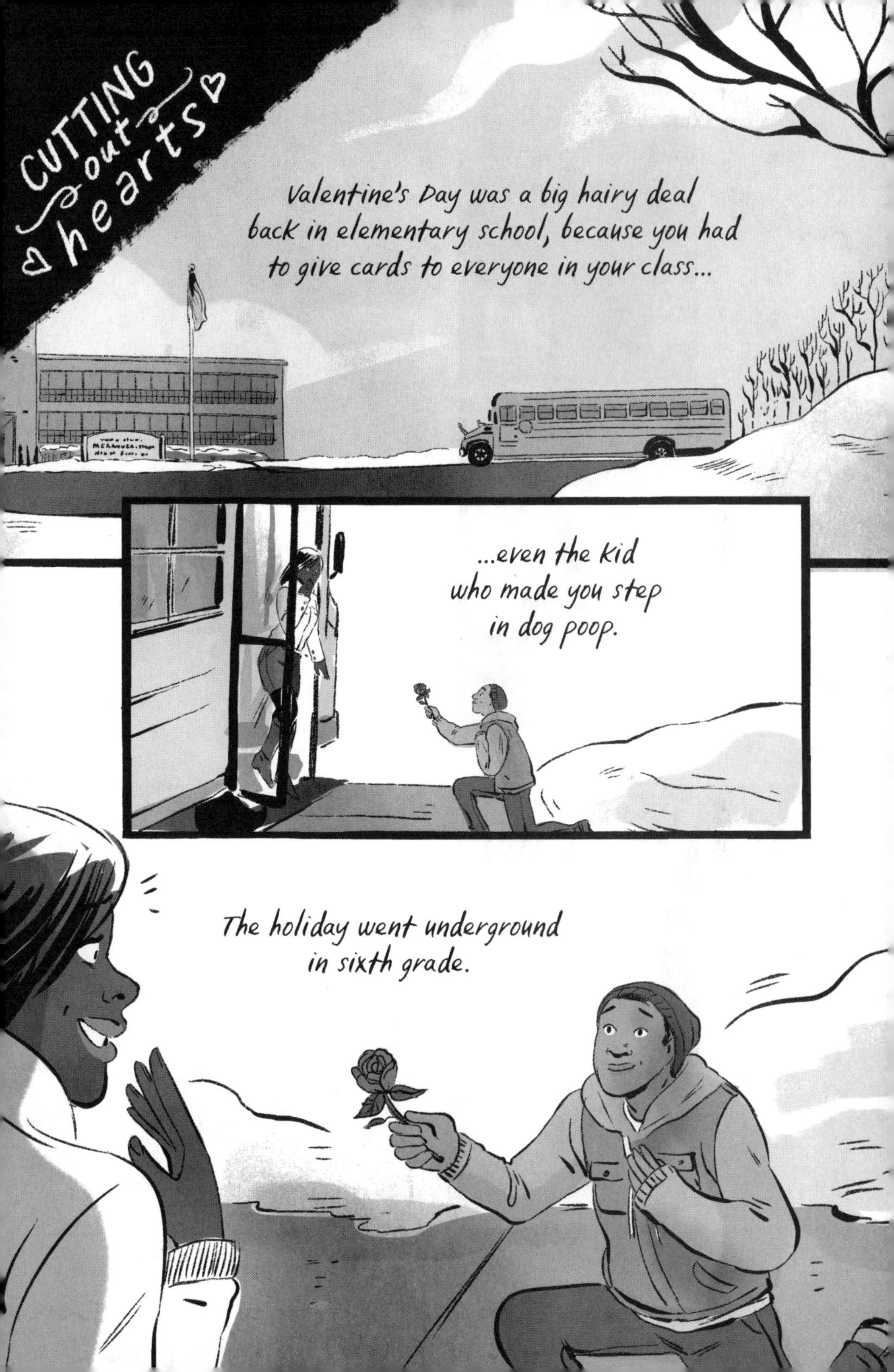
CUTTING out hearts
Valentine's Day was a big hairy deal back in elementary school, because you had to give cards to everyone in your class...
...even the kid who made you step in dog poop.
The holiday went underground in sixth grade.

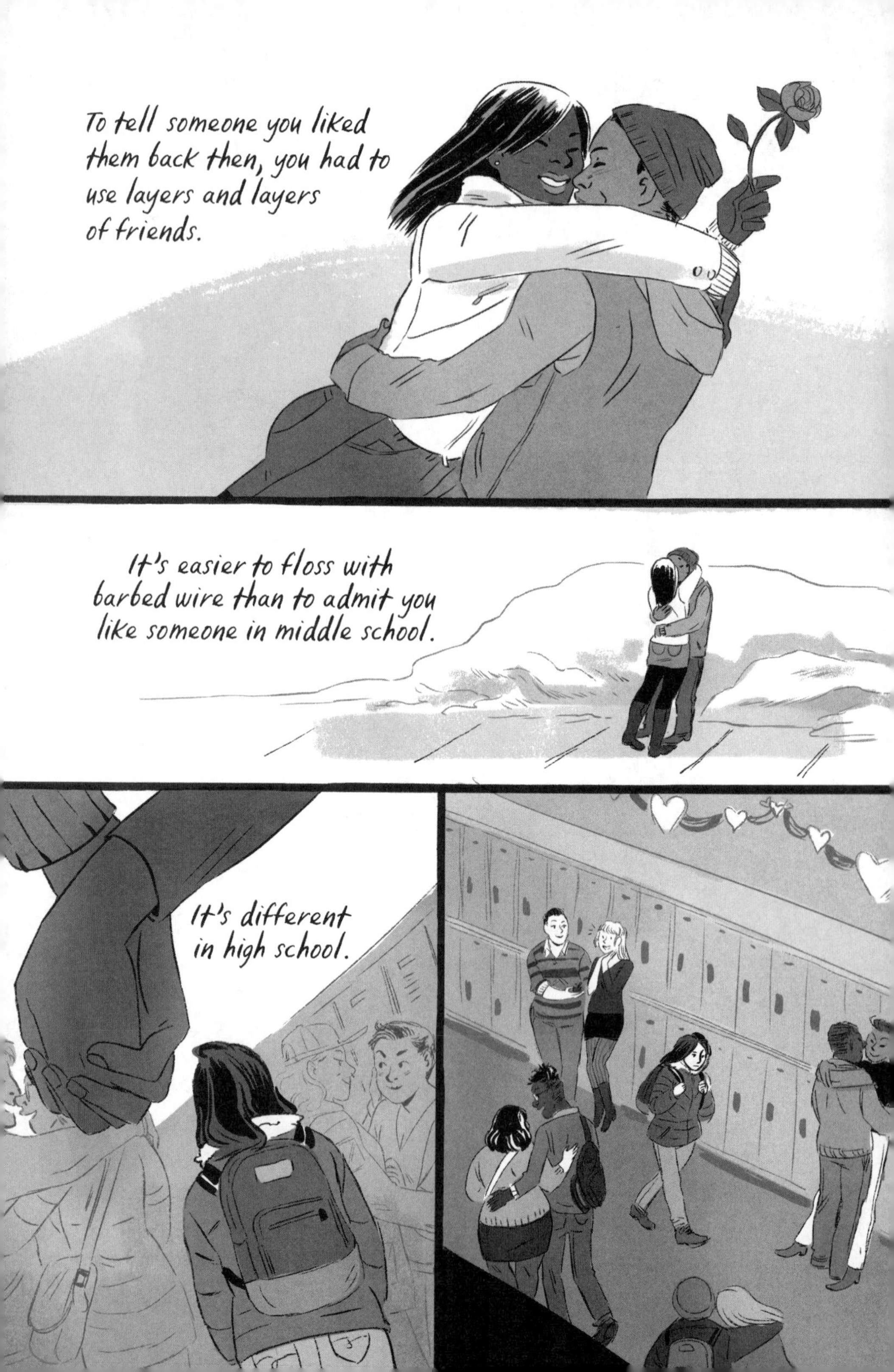
To tell someone you liked them back then, you had to use layers and layers of friends.
It's easier to floss with barbed wire than to admit you like someone in middle school.
It's different in high school.

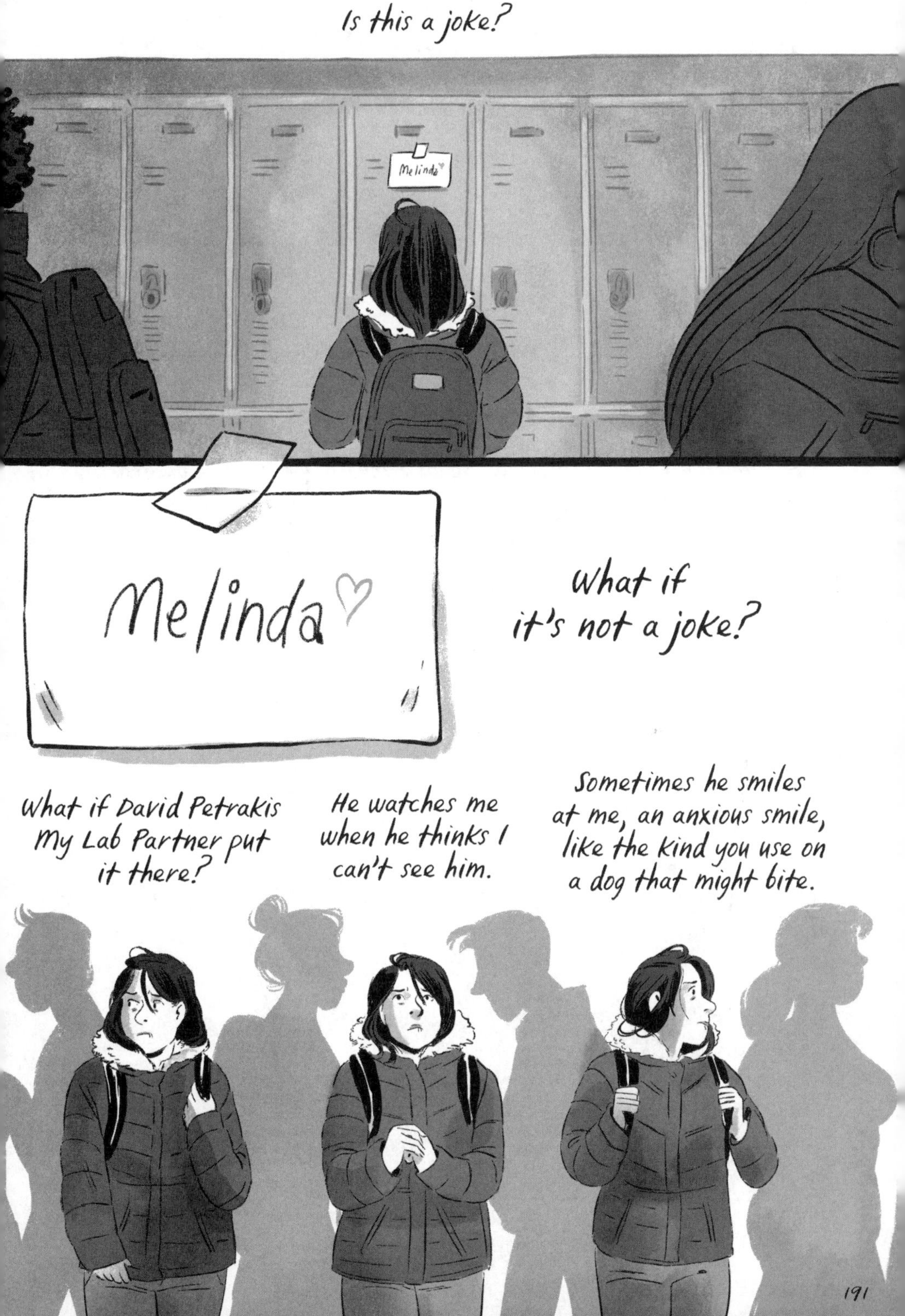
Is this a joke?
Melinda
Melinda
What if it's not a joke?
What if David Petrakis My Lab Partner put it there?
He watches me when he thinks I can't see him.
Sometimes he smiles at me, an anxious smile, like the kind you use on a dog that might bite.

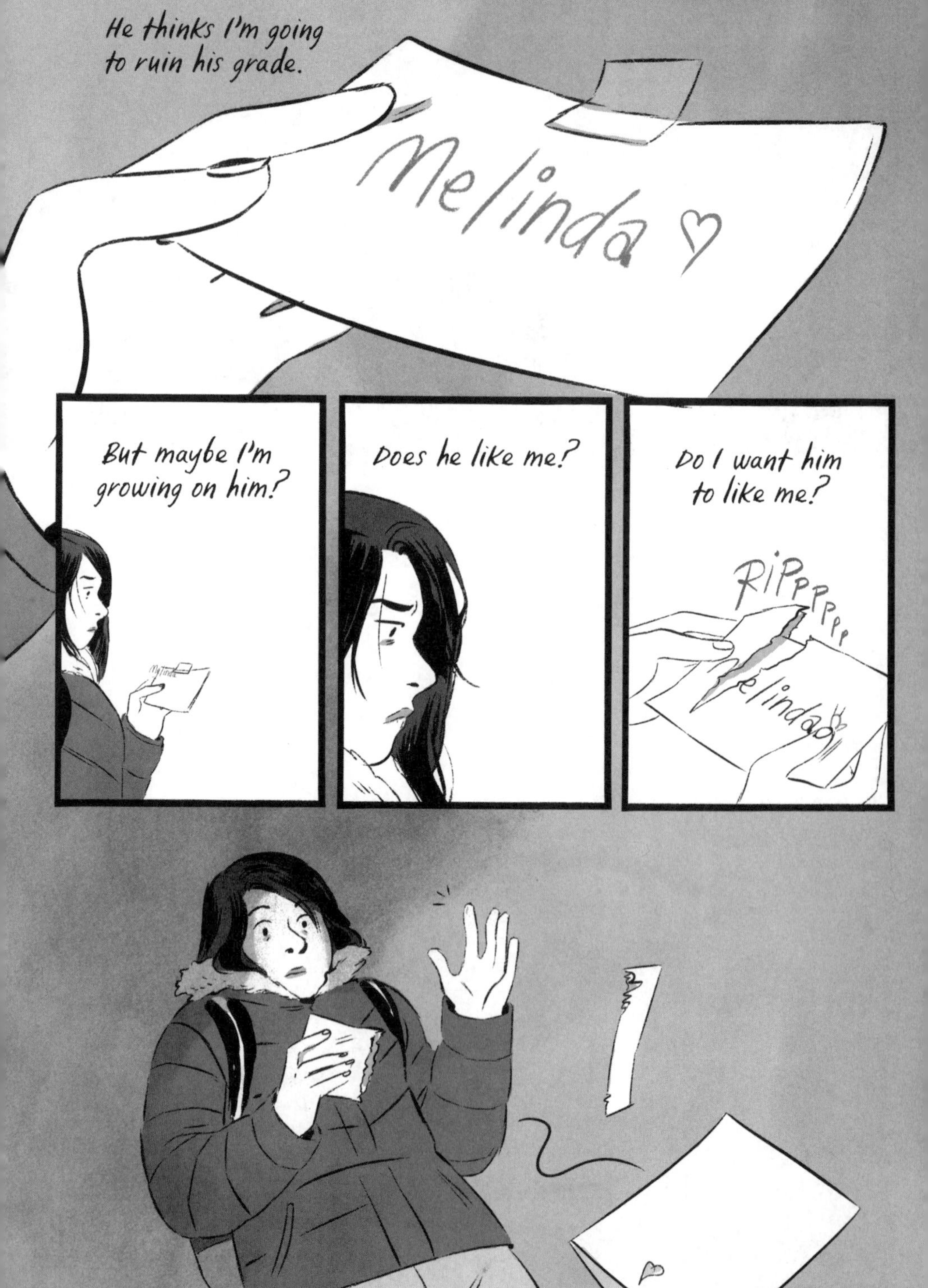
He thinks I'm going to ruin his grade.
Melinda ♡
But maybe I'm growing on him?
Does he like me?
Do I want him to like me?
RIPPPPPPP

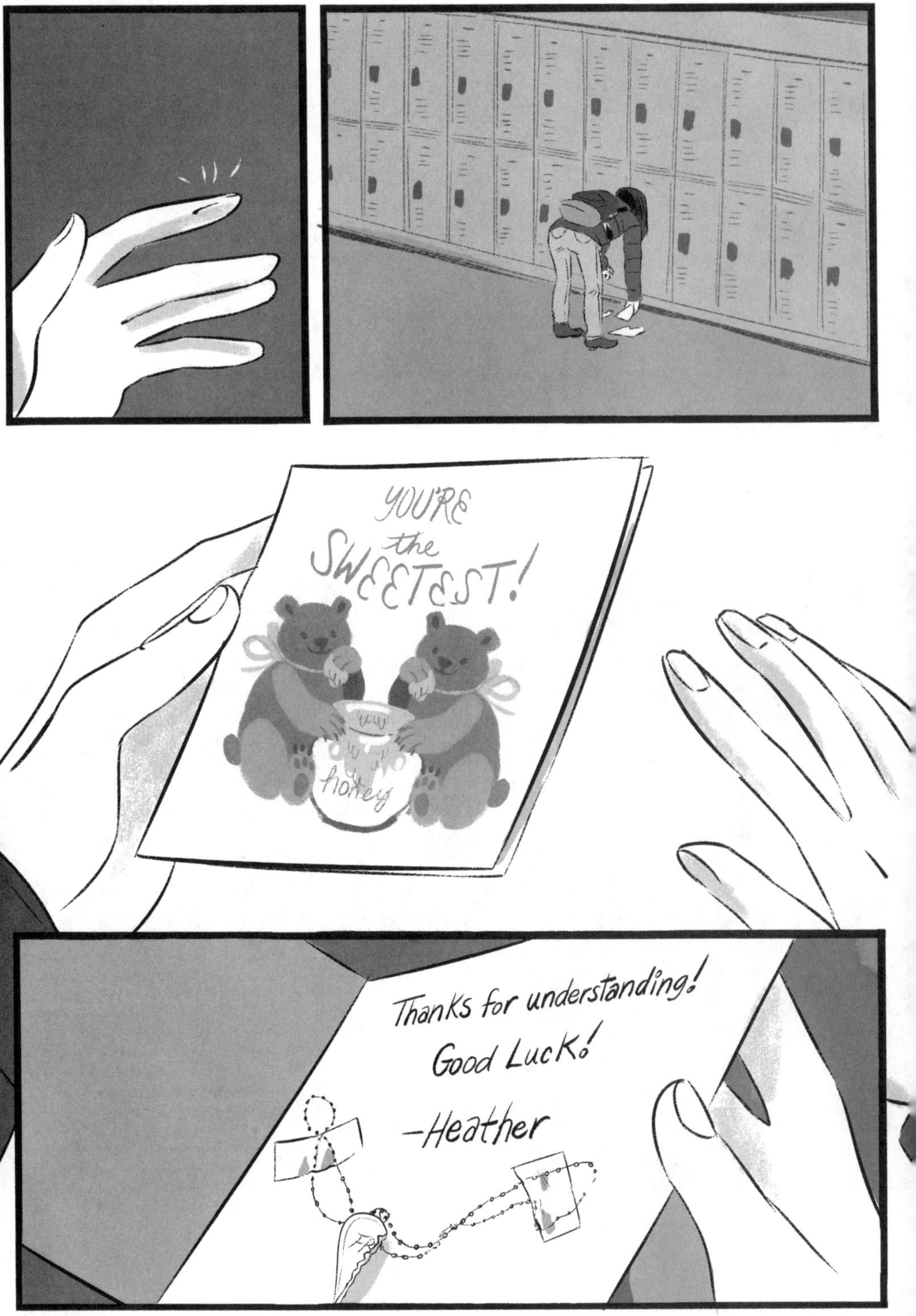
YOU'RE the SWEETEST!
honey
Thanks for understanding!
Good Luck!
-Heather

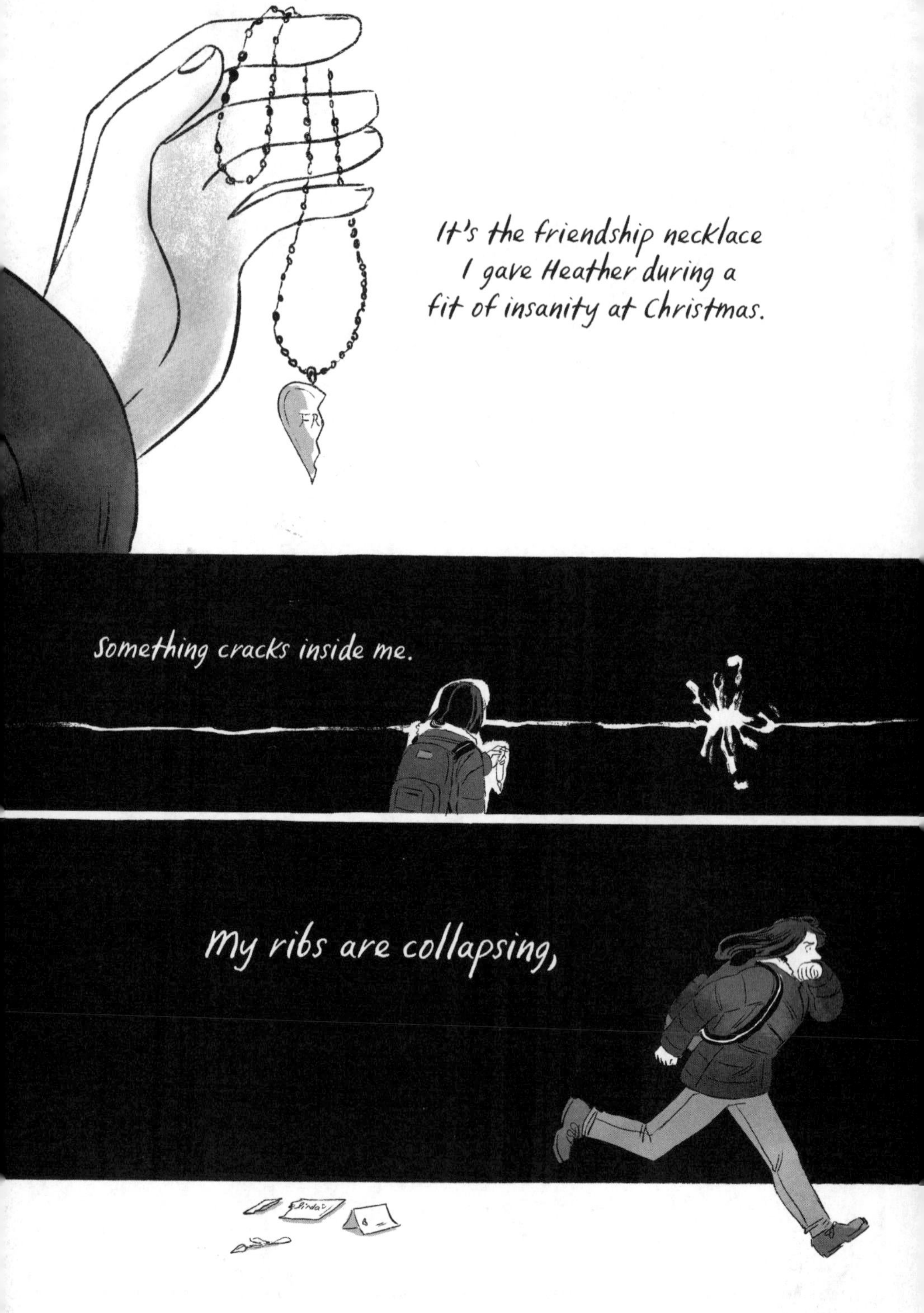
It's the friendship necklace
I gave Heather during a
fit of insanity at Christmas.
FR
Something cracks inside me.
My ribs are collapsing,

PIERCING MY LUNGS.

Stupid holiday unveiled every knife that is stuck inside me, every cut that keeps bleeding.

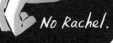

No Rachel.

No Heather.

Not even a silly, geeky boy likes the inside girl I think I am.

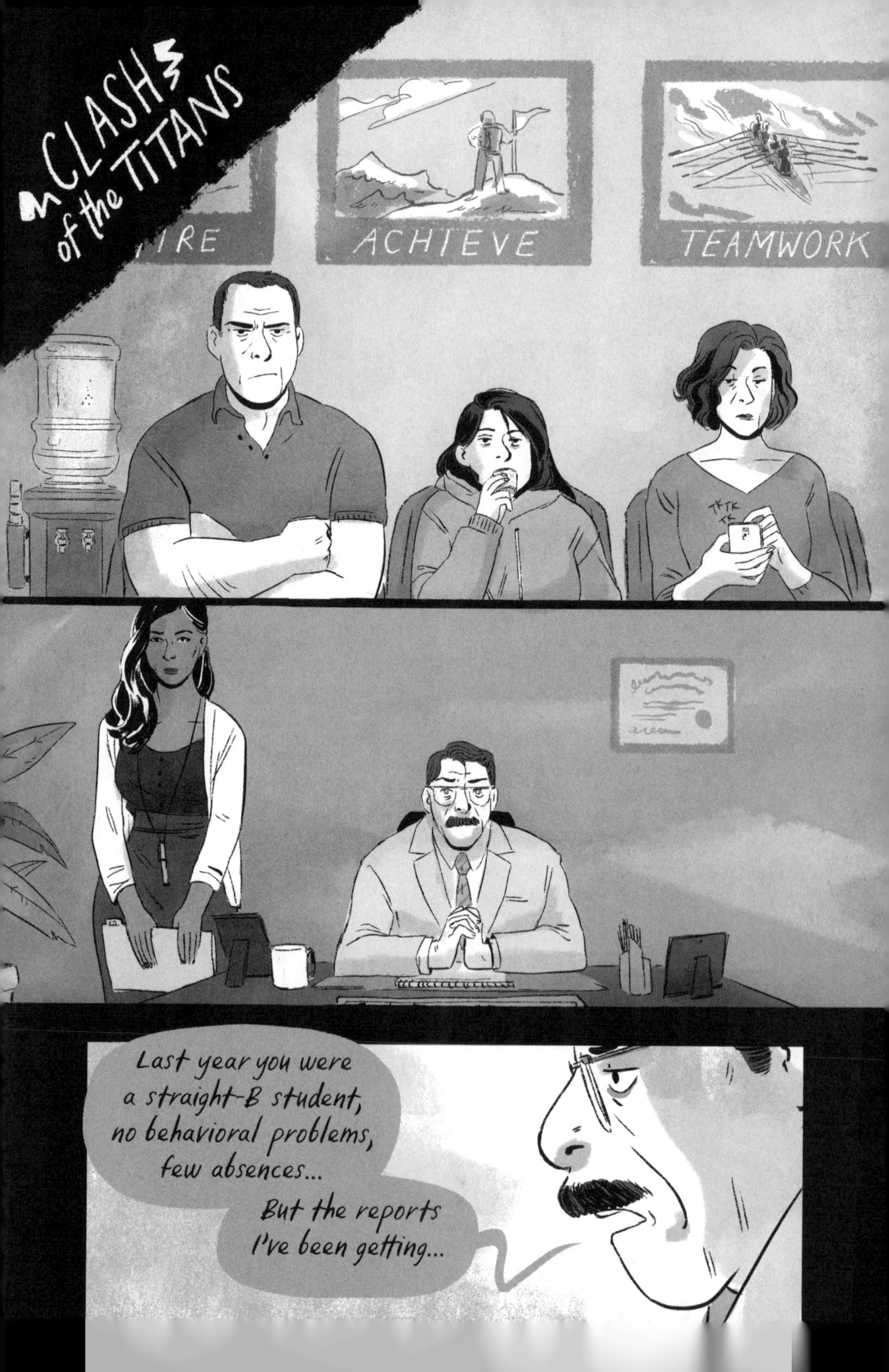
CLASH of the TITANS
...IRE
ACHIEVE
TEAMWORK
TKTK TK
Last year you were a straight-B student, no behavioral problems, few absences...
But the reports I've been getting...

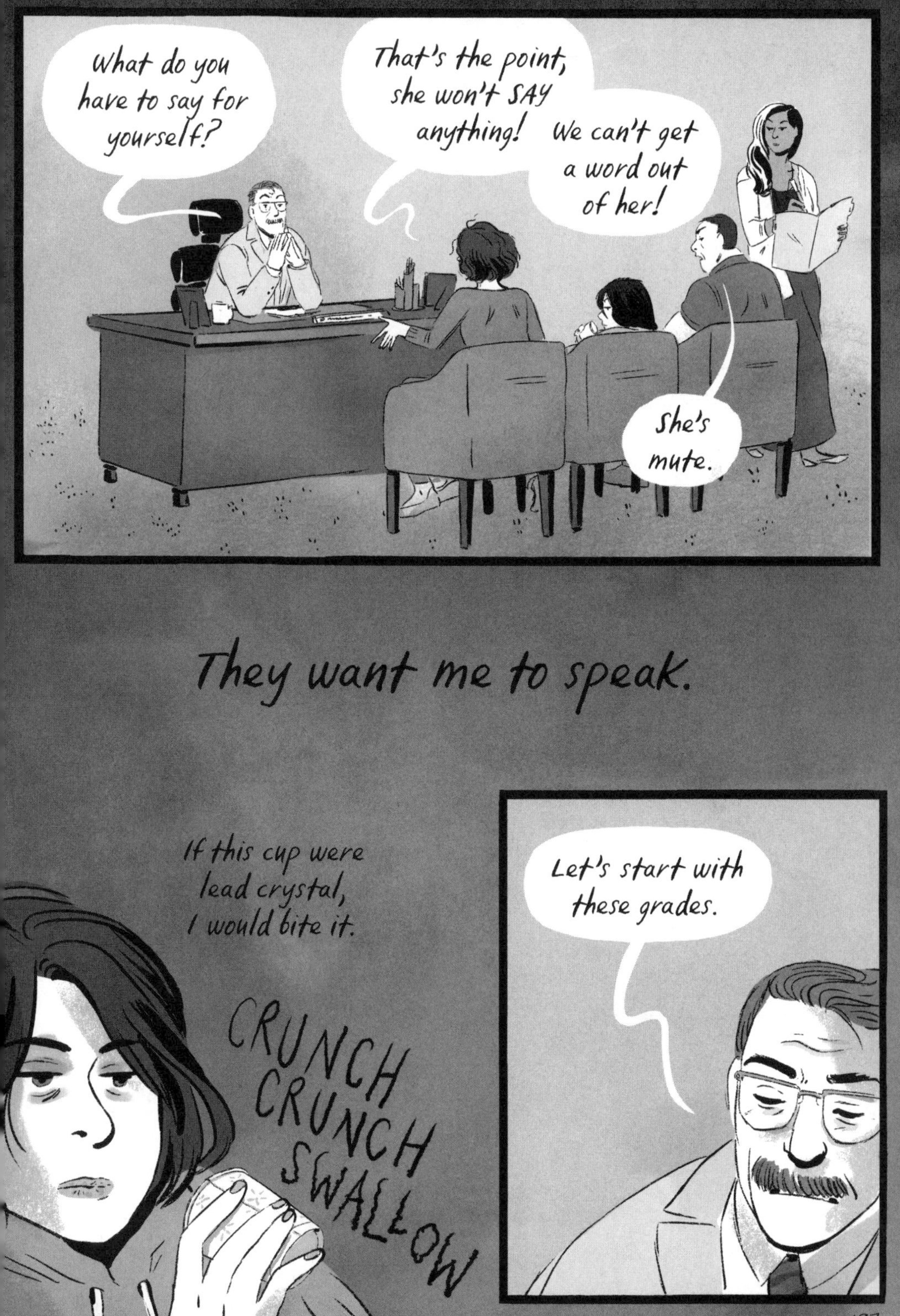

What do you have to say for yourself?
That's the point, she won't SAY anything!
We can't get a word out of her!
She's mute.
They want me to speak.
If this cup were lead crystal, I would bite it.
CRUNCH CRUNCH SWALLOW
Let's start with these grades.

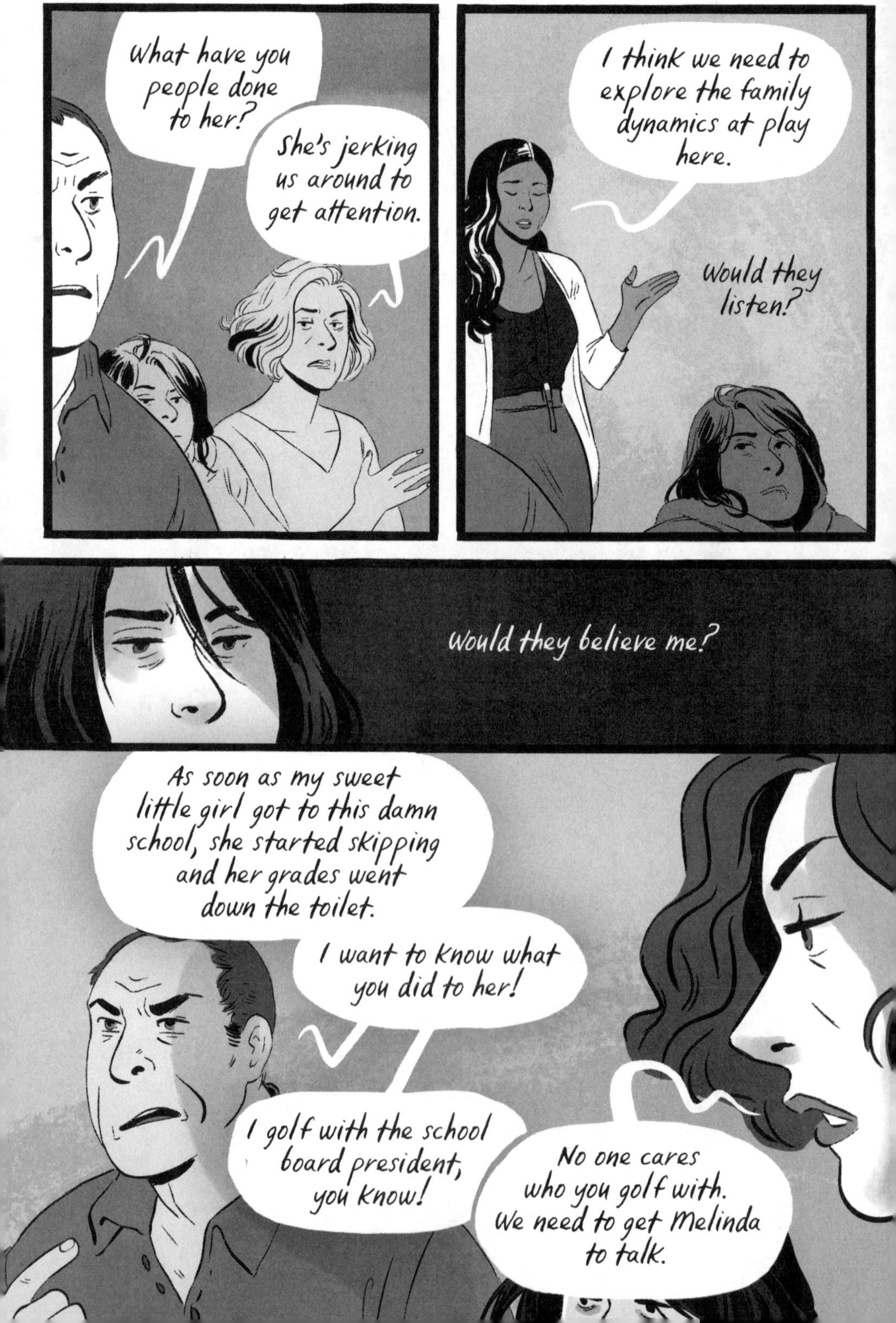

What have you people done to her?
She's jerking us around to get attention.
I think we need to explore the family dynamics at play here.
Would they listen?
Would they believe me?
As soon as my sweet little girl got to this damn school, she started skipping and her grades went down the toilet.
I want to know what you did to her!
I golf with the school board president, you know!
No one cares who you golf with. We need to get Melinda to talk.

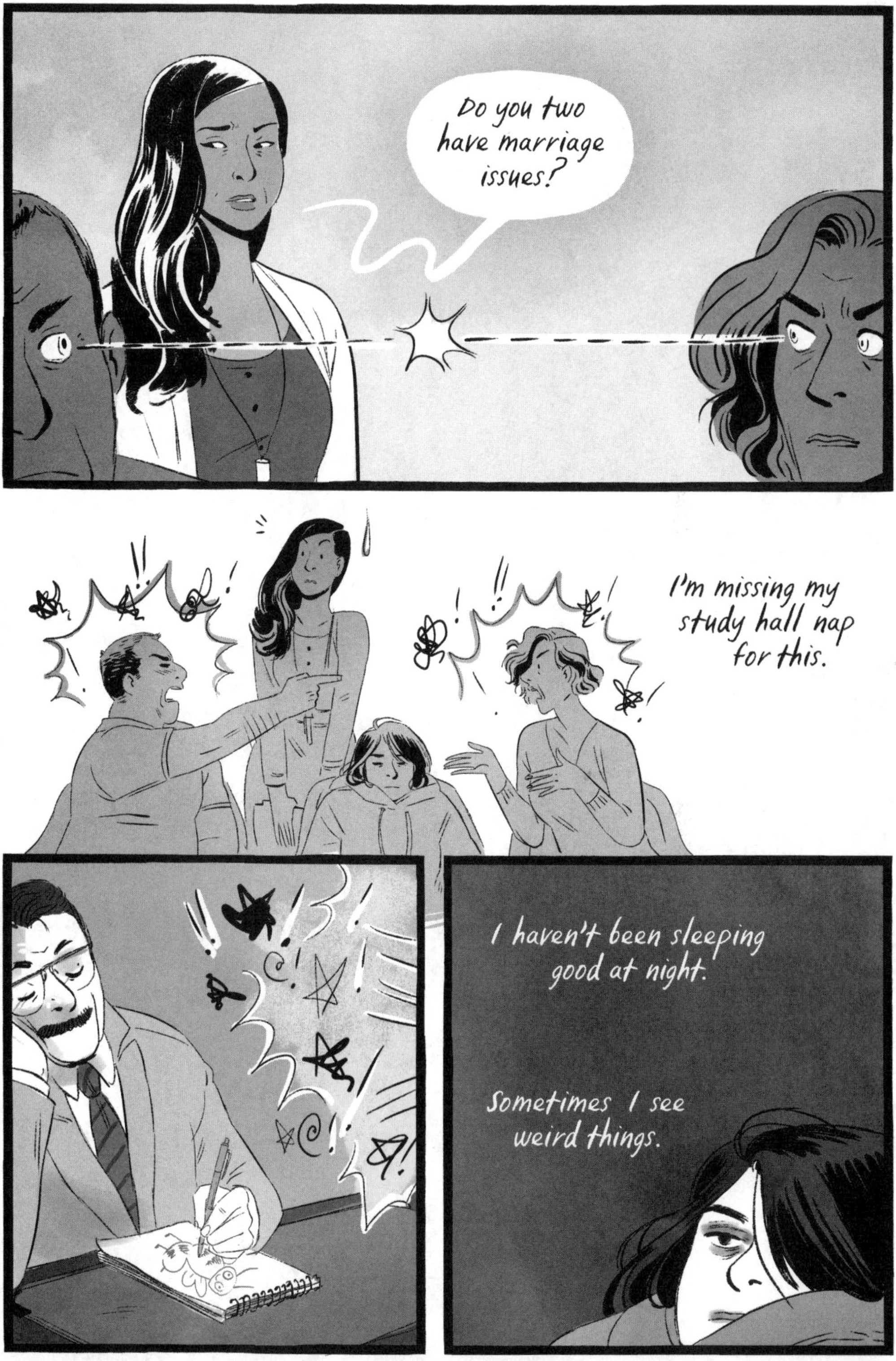
Do you two have marriage issues?
I'm missing my study hall nap for this.
I haven't been sleeping good at night.
Sometimes I see weird things.

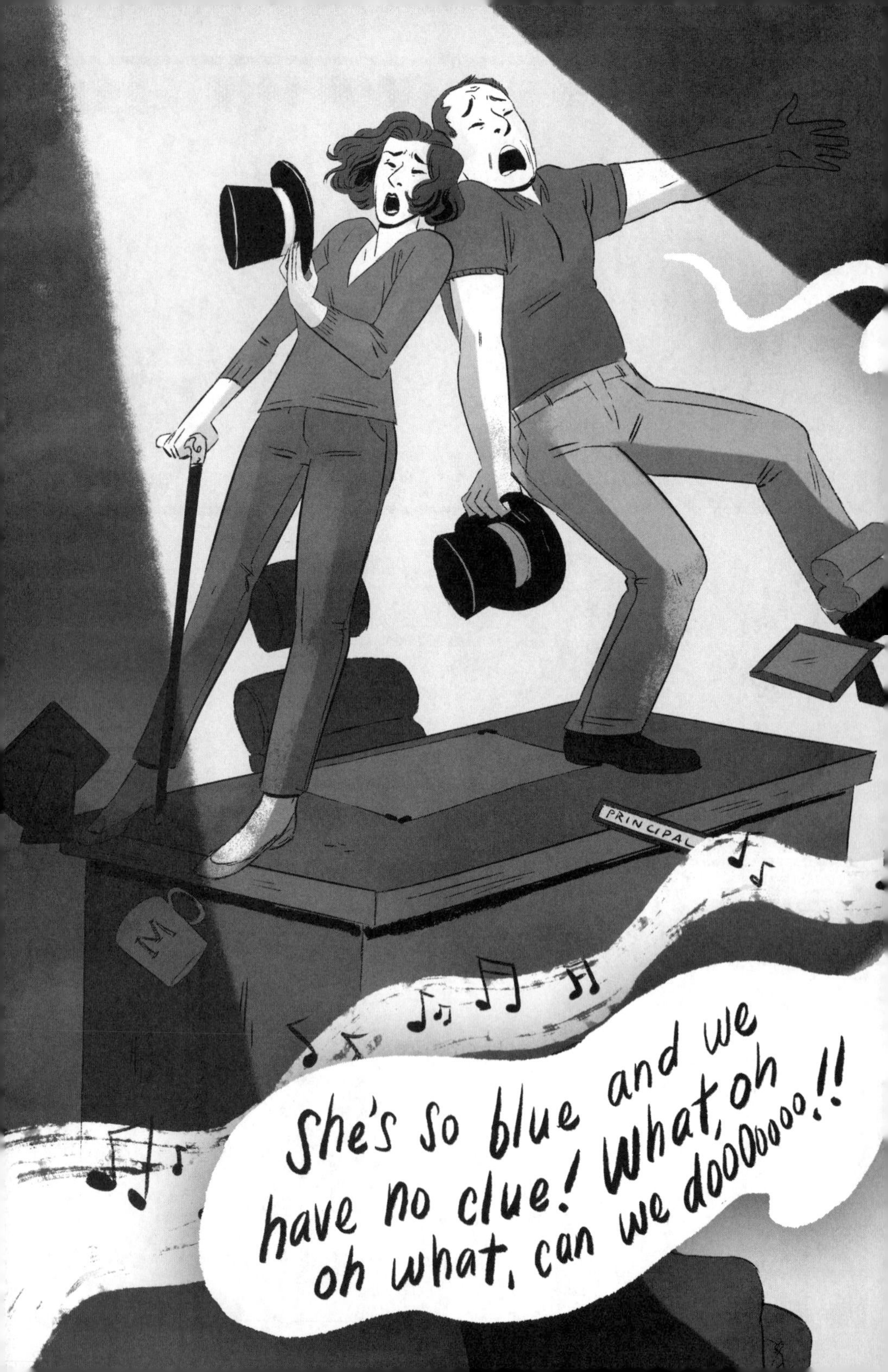
PRINCIPAL
M
She's so blue and we have no clue! What, oh oh what, can we doOOoooo!!

What can we do!
What can we doooooooo!
She's so blue! We're just two!
Hahaha...

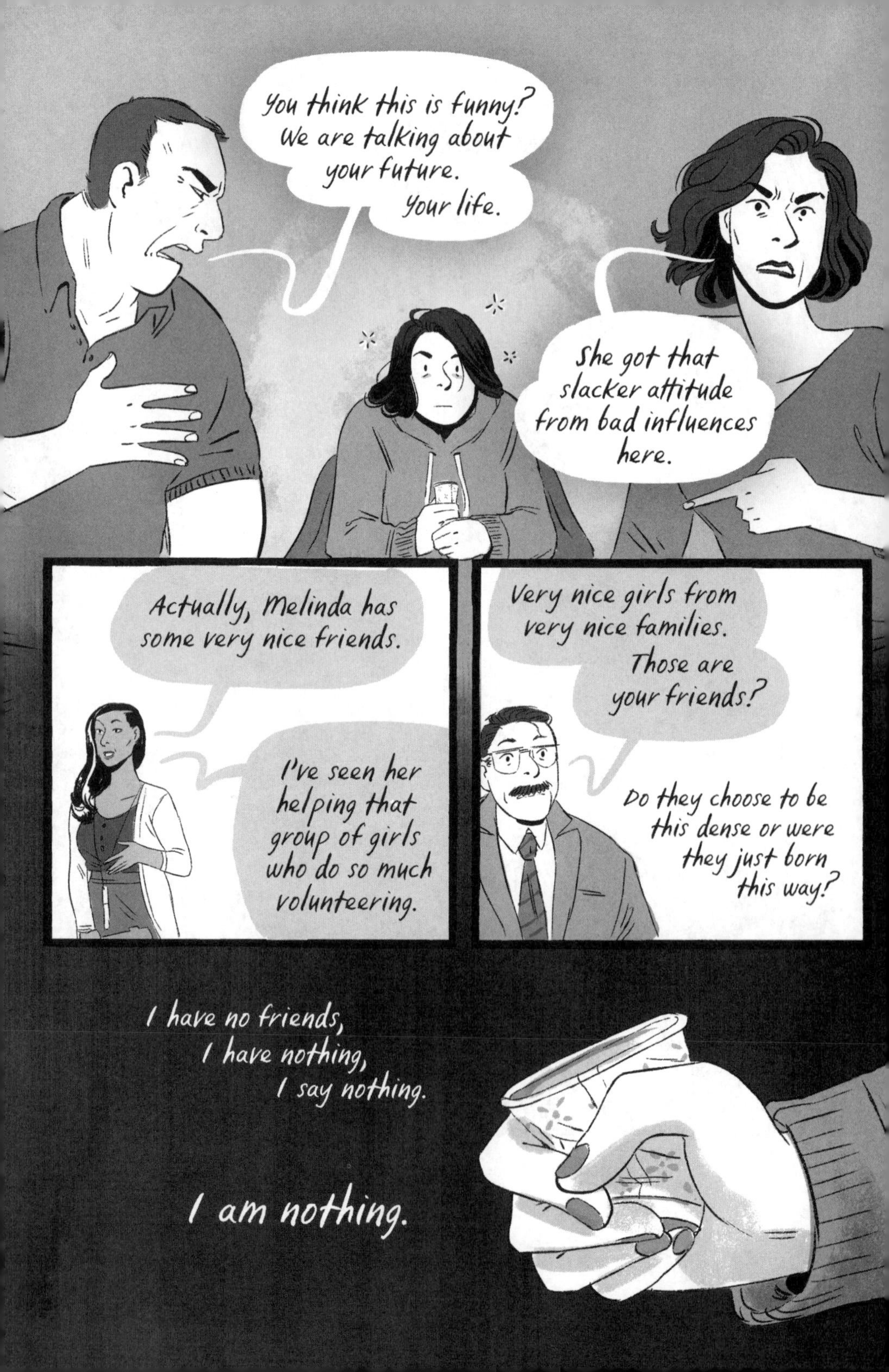
You think this is funny? We are talking about your future.
Your life.
She got that slacker attitude from bad influences here.
Actually, Melinda has some very nice friends.
I've seen her helping that group of girls who do so much volunteering.
Very nice girls from very nice families.
Those are your friends?
Do they choose to be this dense or were they just born this way?
I have no friends,
I have nothing,
I say nothing.
I am nothing.

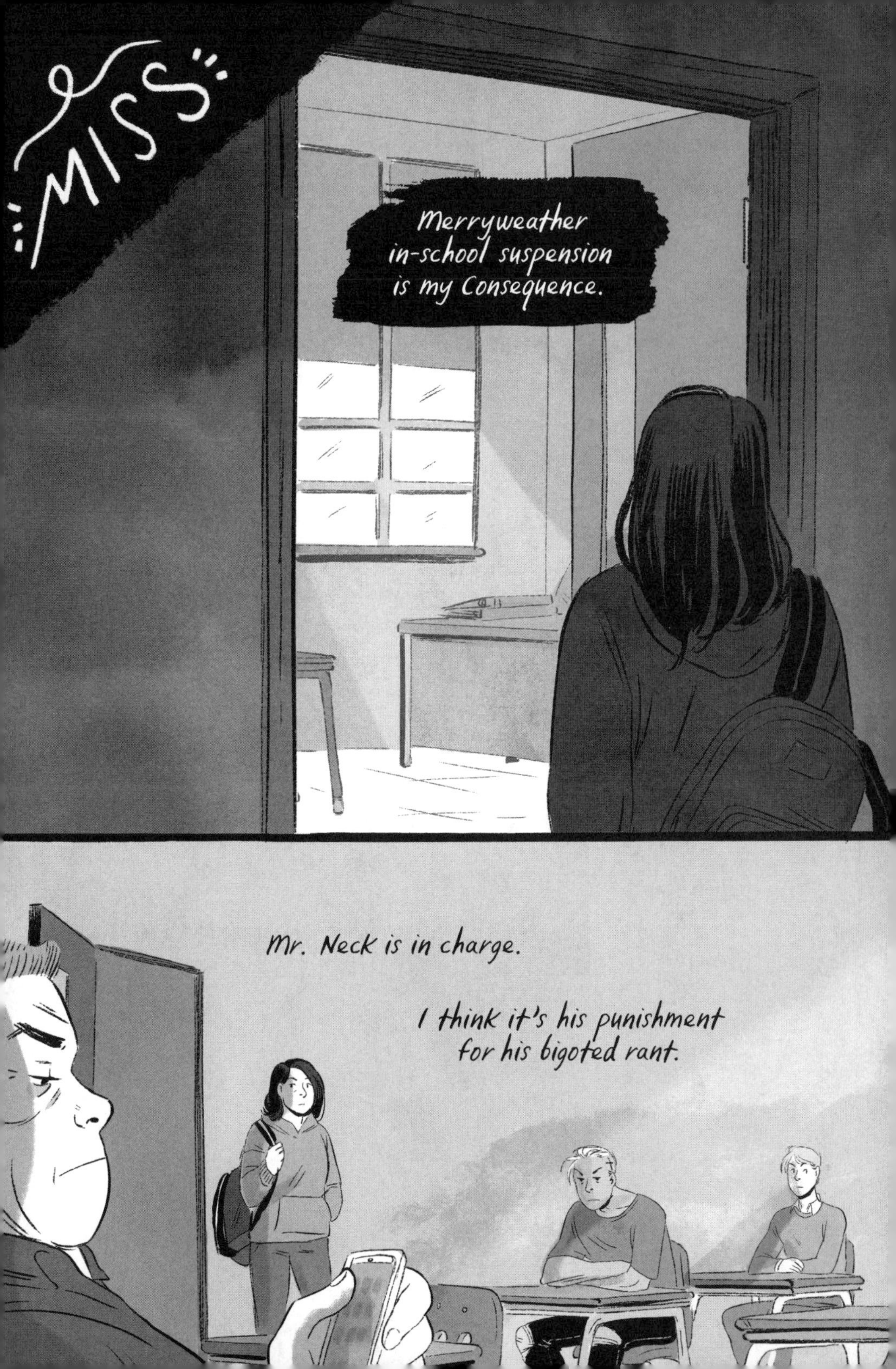
MISS
Merryweather in-school suspension is my Consequence.
Mr. Neck is in charge.
I think it's his punishment for his bigoted rant.

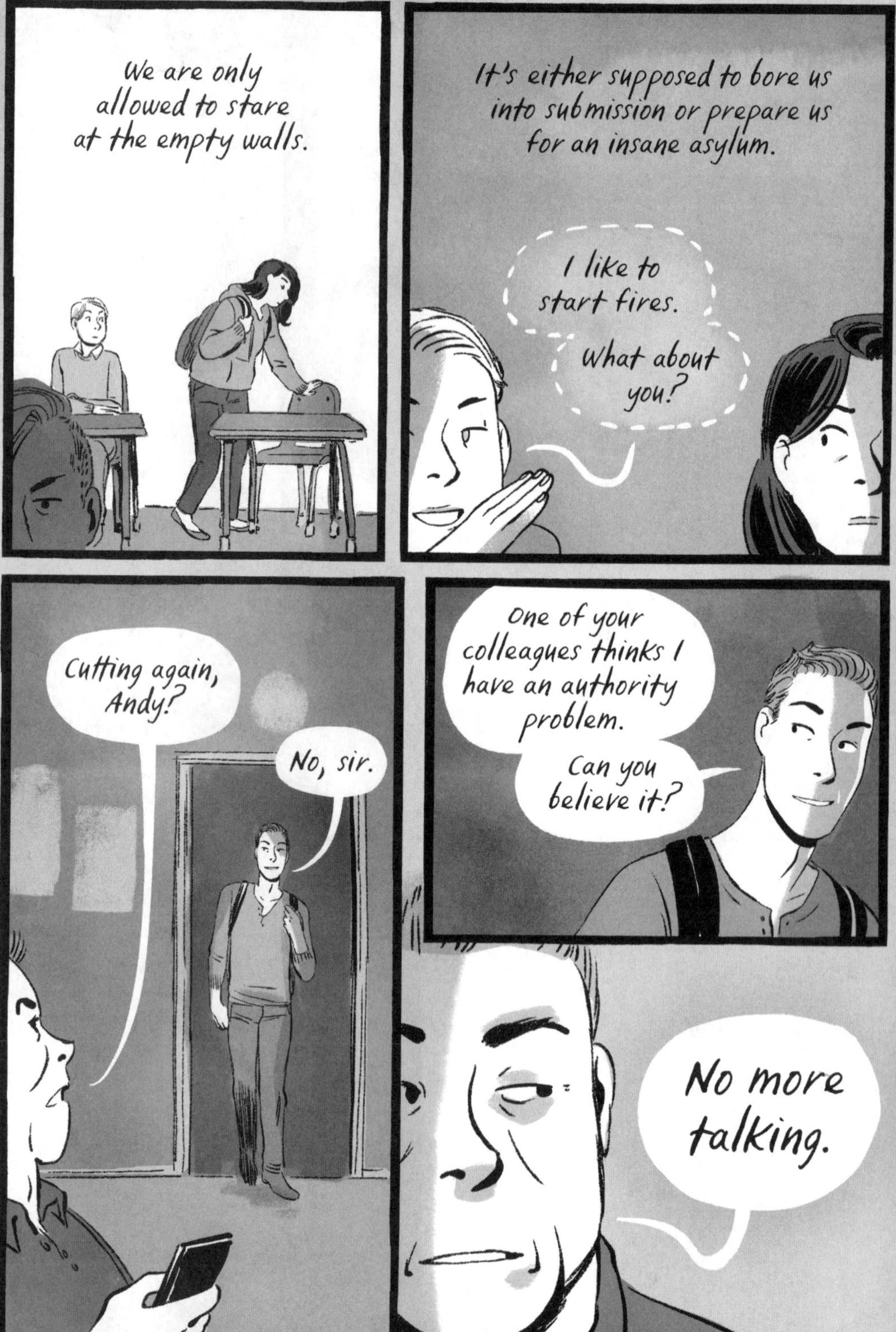
We are only allowed to stare at the empty walls.
It's either supposed to bore us into submission or prepare us for an insane asylum.
I like to start fires.
What about you?
Cutting again, Andy?
No, sir.
One of your colleagues thinks I have an authority problem.
Can you believe it?
No more talking.

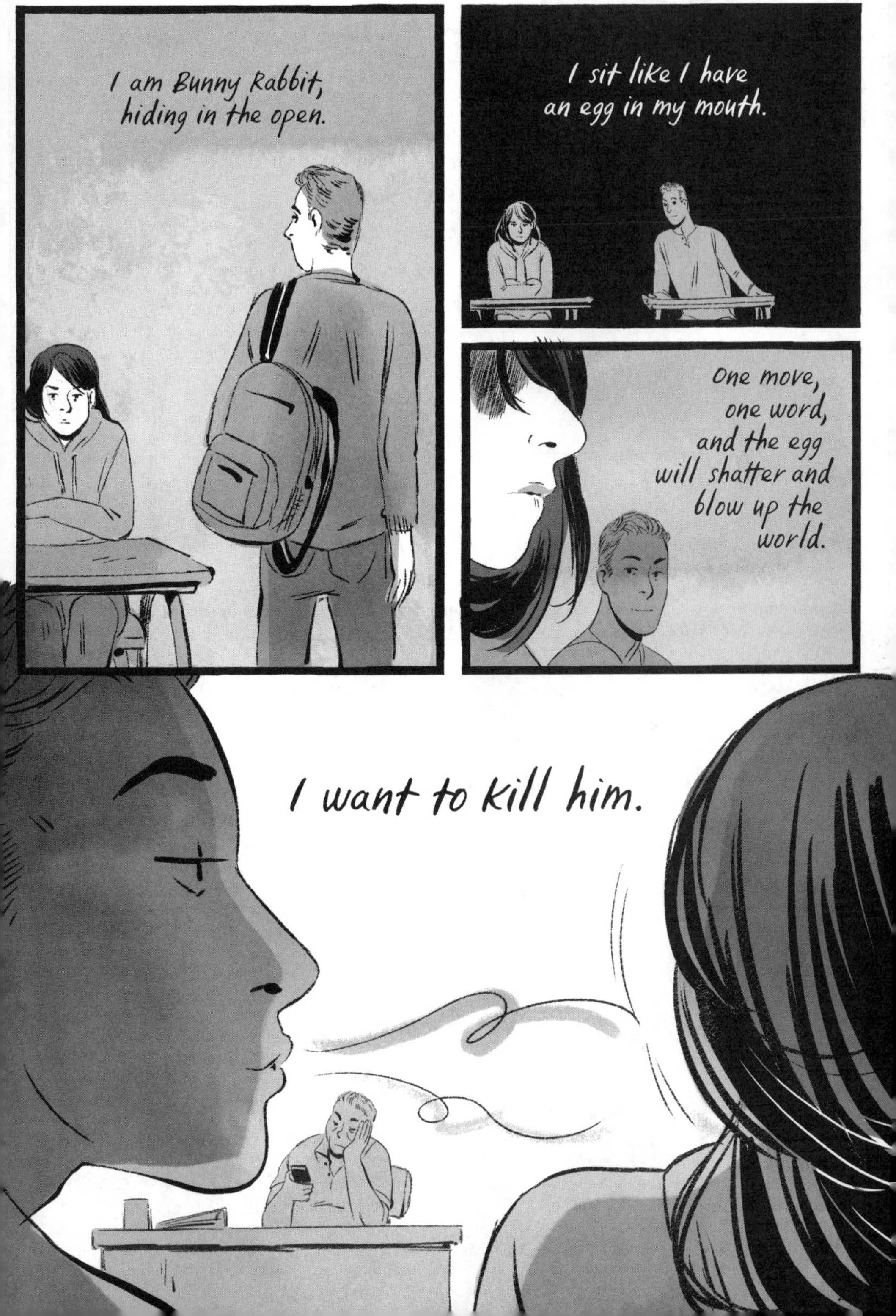
I am Bunny Rabbit, hiding in the open.
I sit like I have an egg in my mouth.
One move, one word, and the egg will shatter and blow up the world.
I want to kill him.

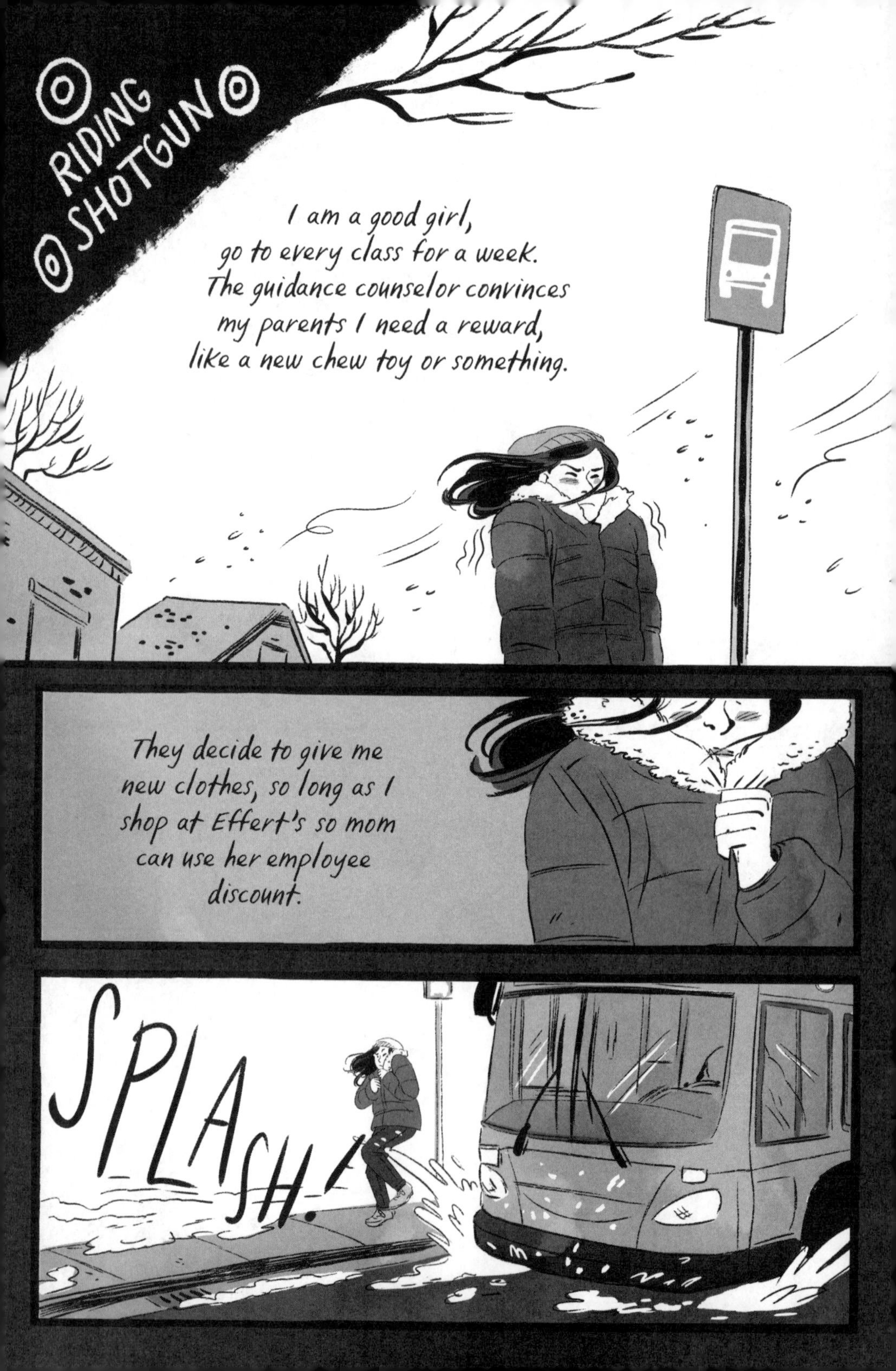
RIDING SHOTGUN
I am a good girl, go to every class for a week. The guidance counselor convinces my parents I need a reward, like a new chew toy or something.
They decide to give me new clothes, so long as I shop at Effert's so mom can use her employee discount.
SPLASH!

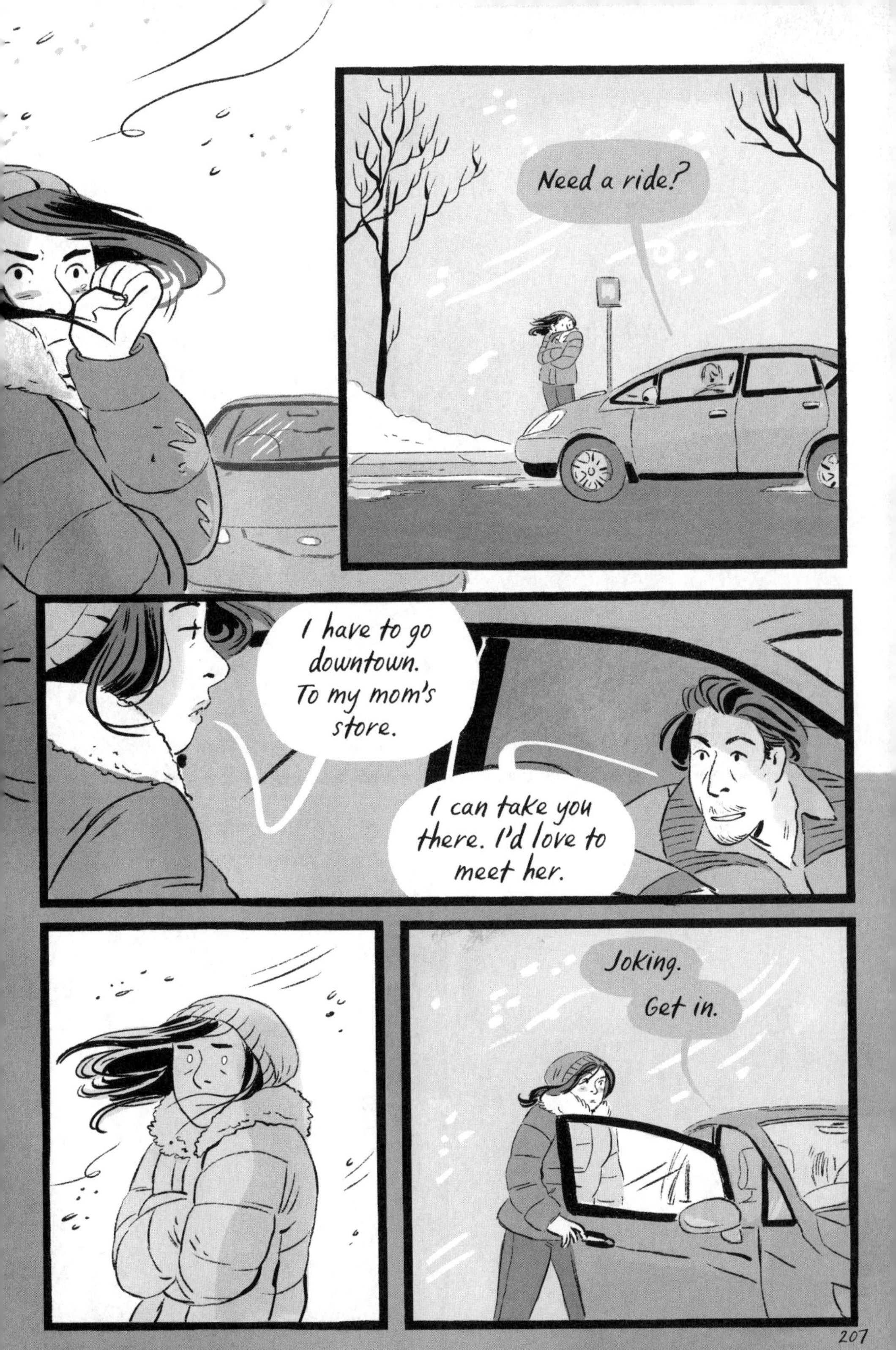
Need a ride?
I have to go downtown. To my mom's store.
I can take you there. I'd love to meet her.
Joking.
Get in.

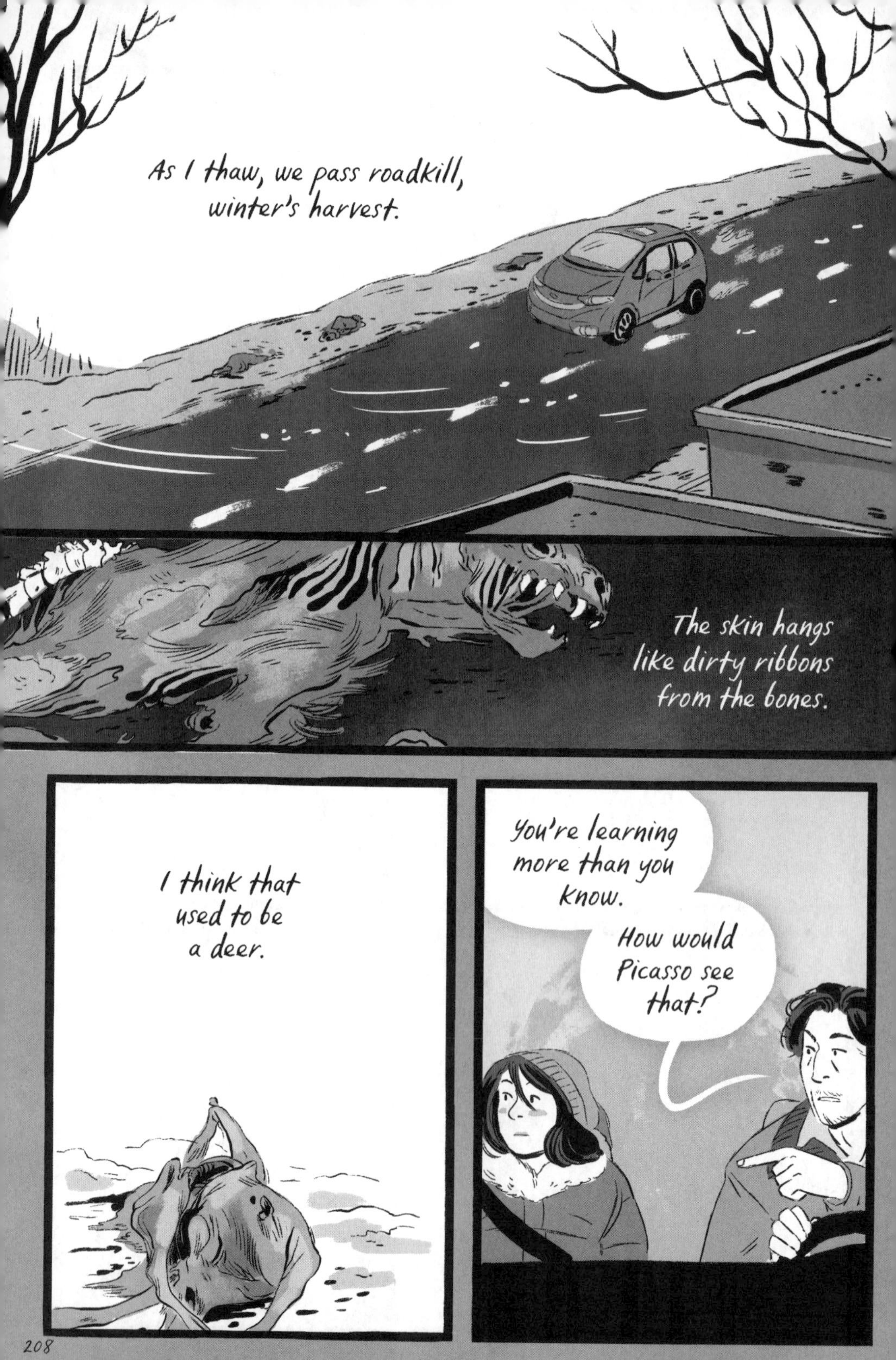
As I thaw, we pass roadkill,
winter's harvest.
The skin hangs
like dirty ribbons
from the bones.
I think that
used to be
a deer.
You're learning
more than you
know.
How would
Picasso see
that?

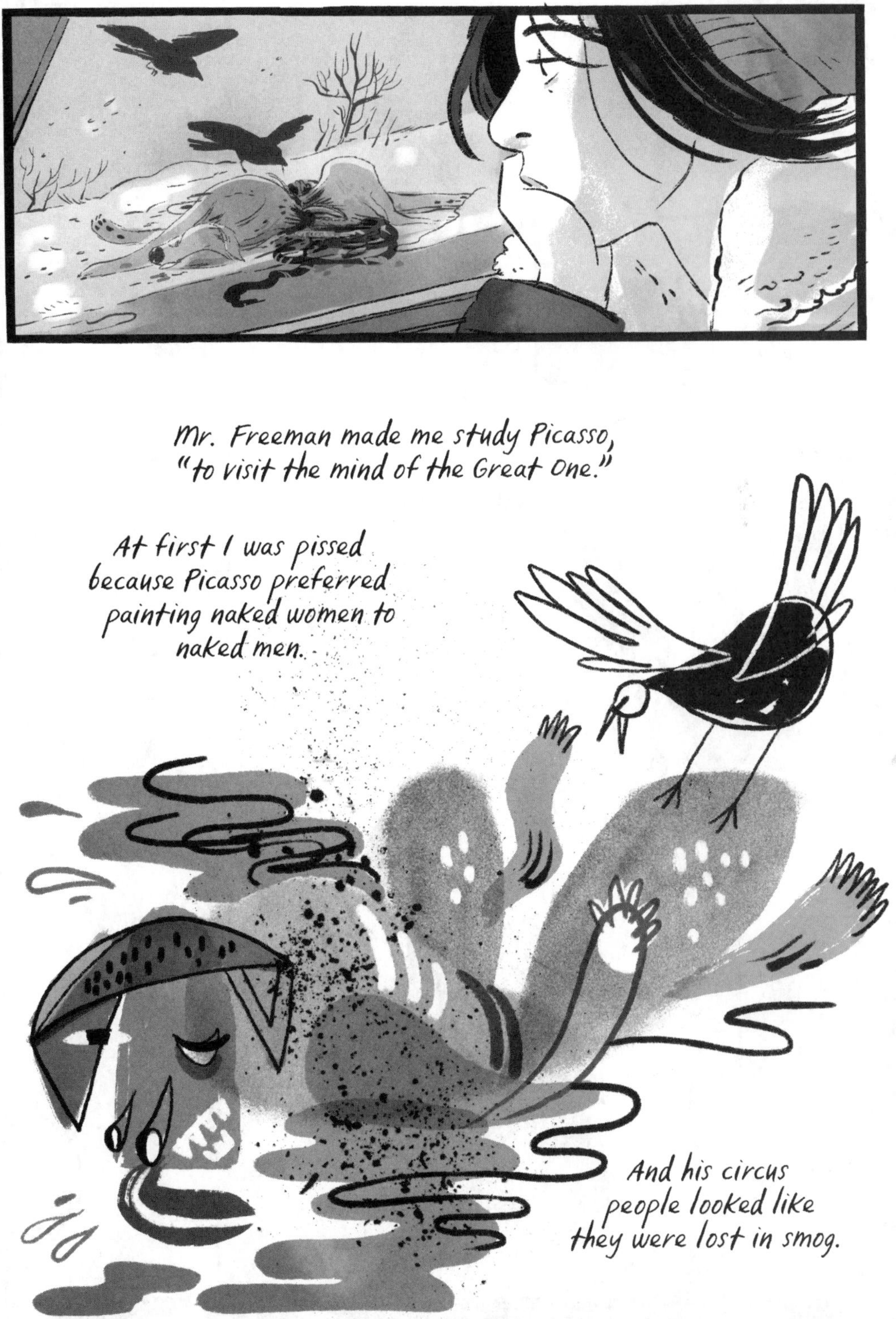
Mr. Freeman made me study Picasso, "to visit the mind of the Great One."
At first I was pissed because Picasso preferred painting naked women to naked men.
And his circus people looked like they were lost in smog.

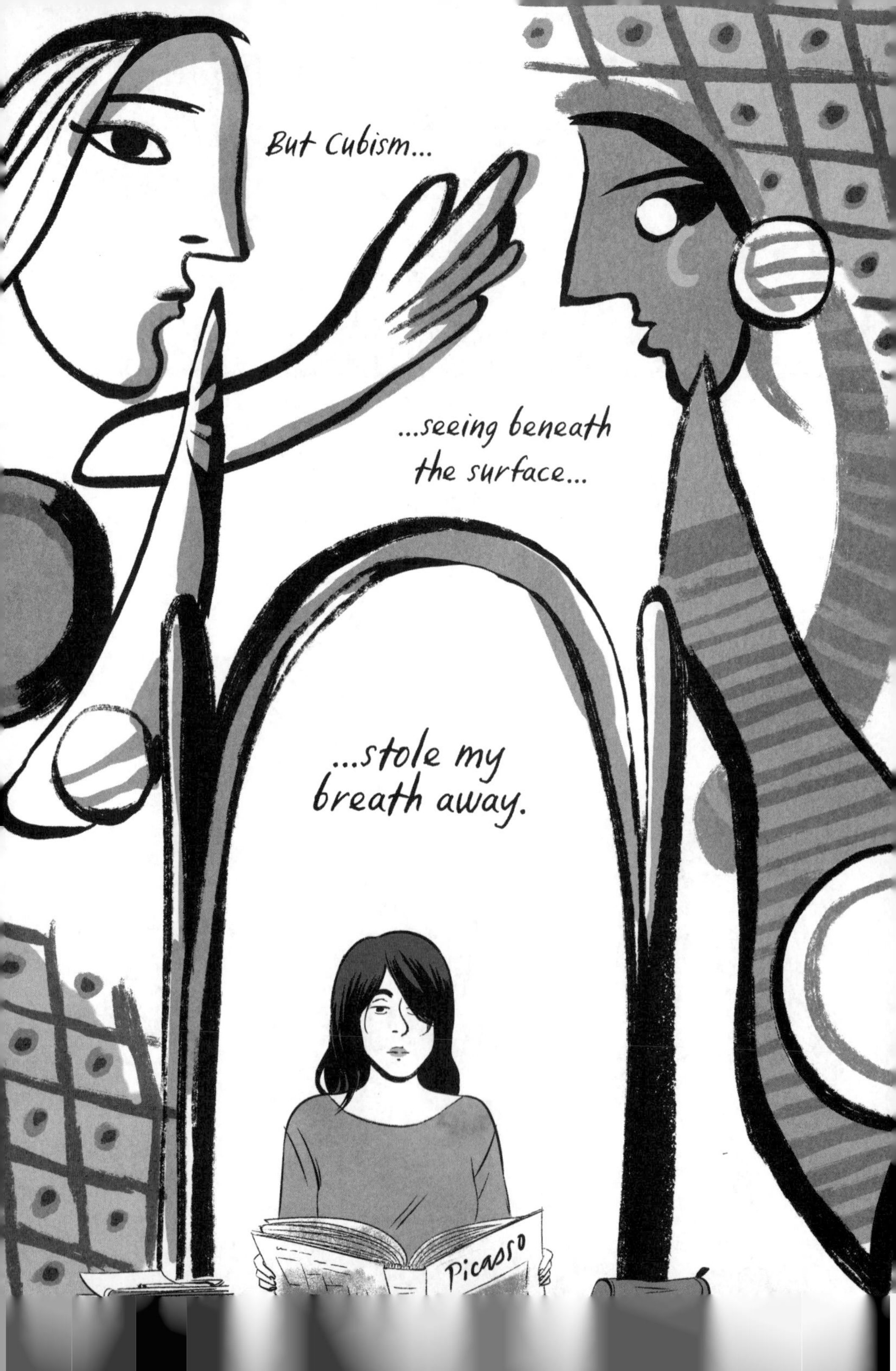
But Cubism...
...seeing beneath the surface...
...stole my breath away.
Picasso

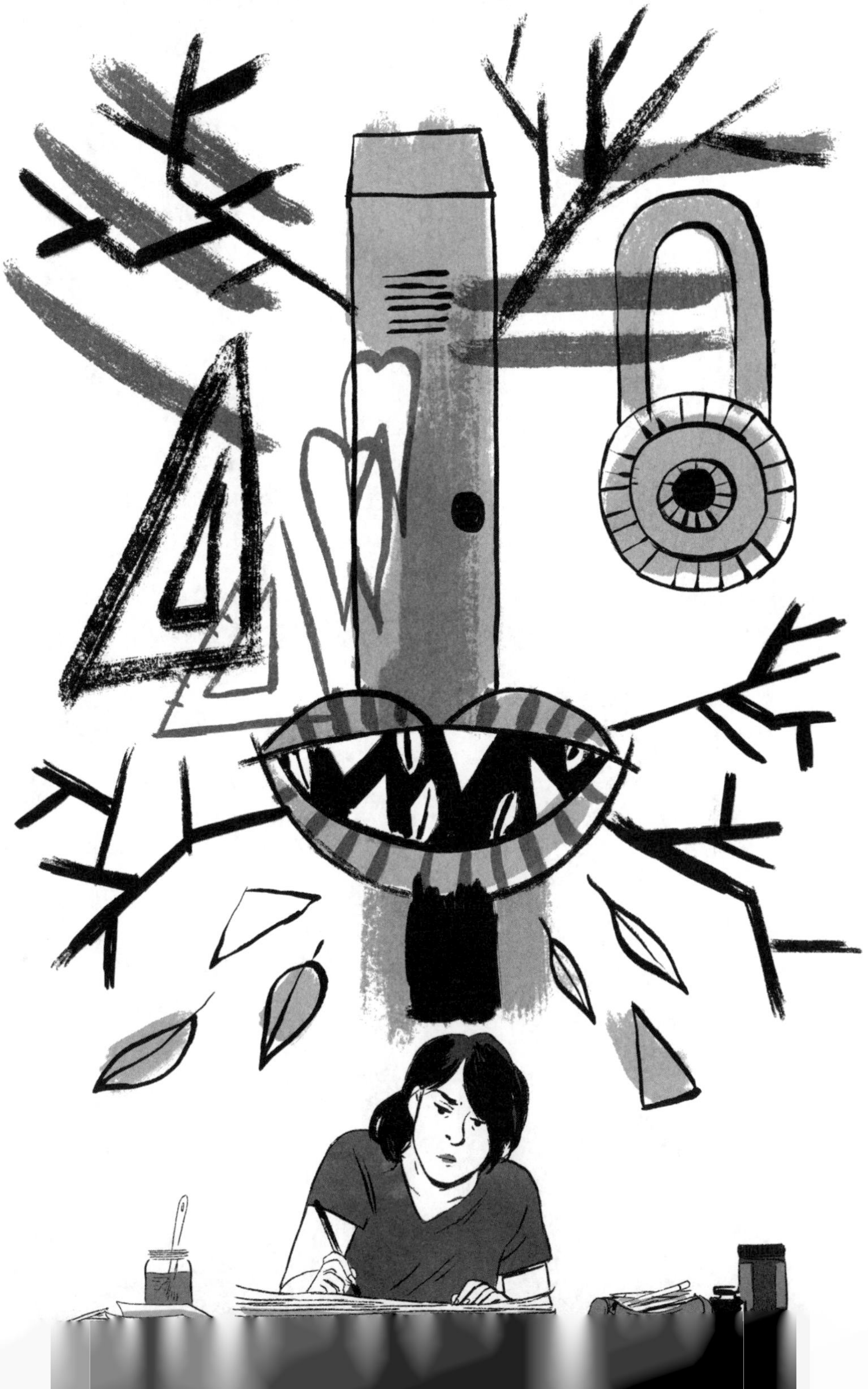

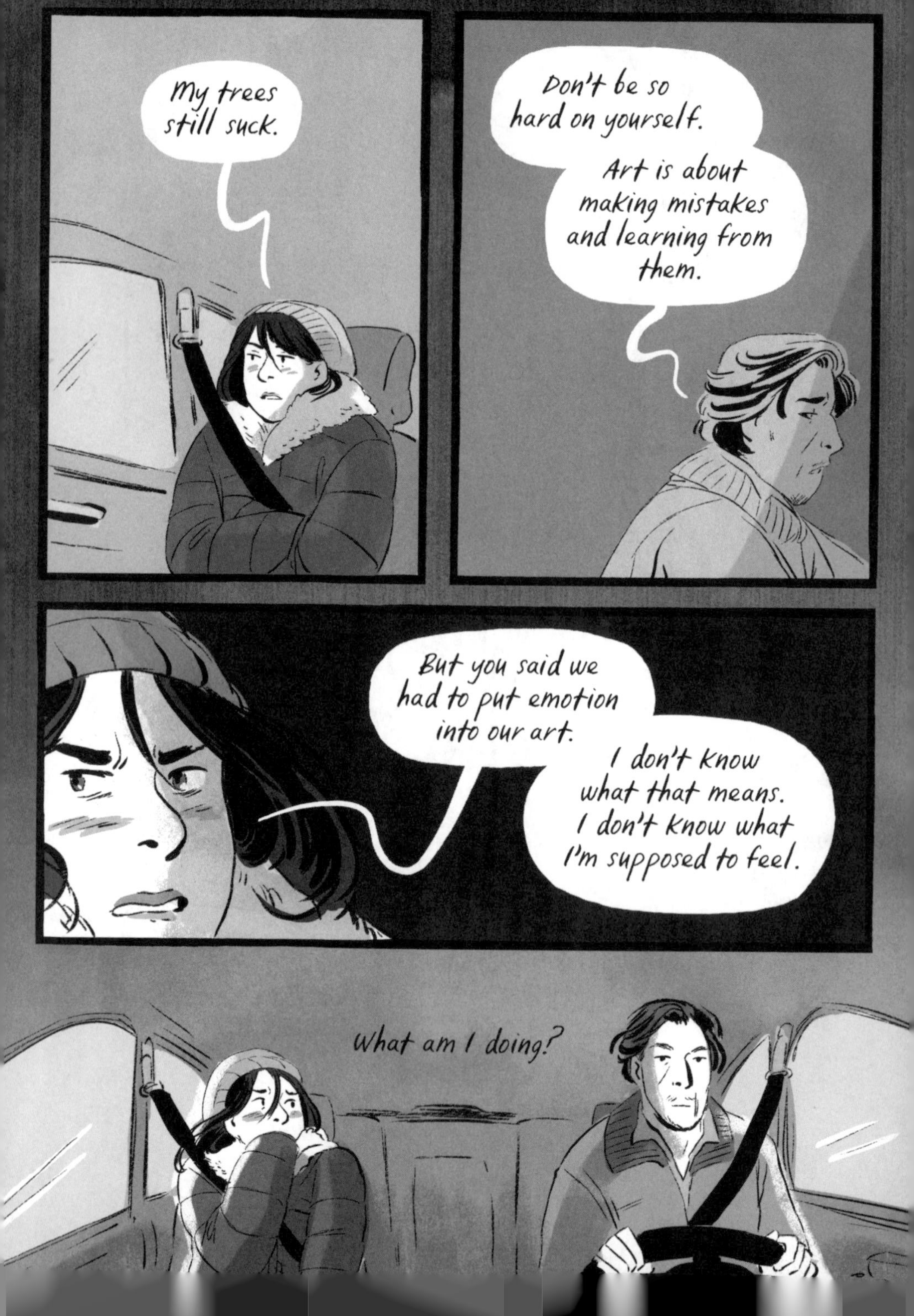
My trees still suck.
Don't be so hard on yourself.
Art is about making mistakes and learning from them.
But you said we had to put emotion into our art.
I don't know what that means. I don't know what I'm supposed to feel.
What am I doing?

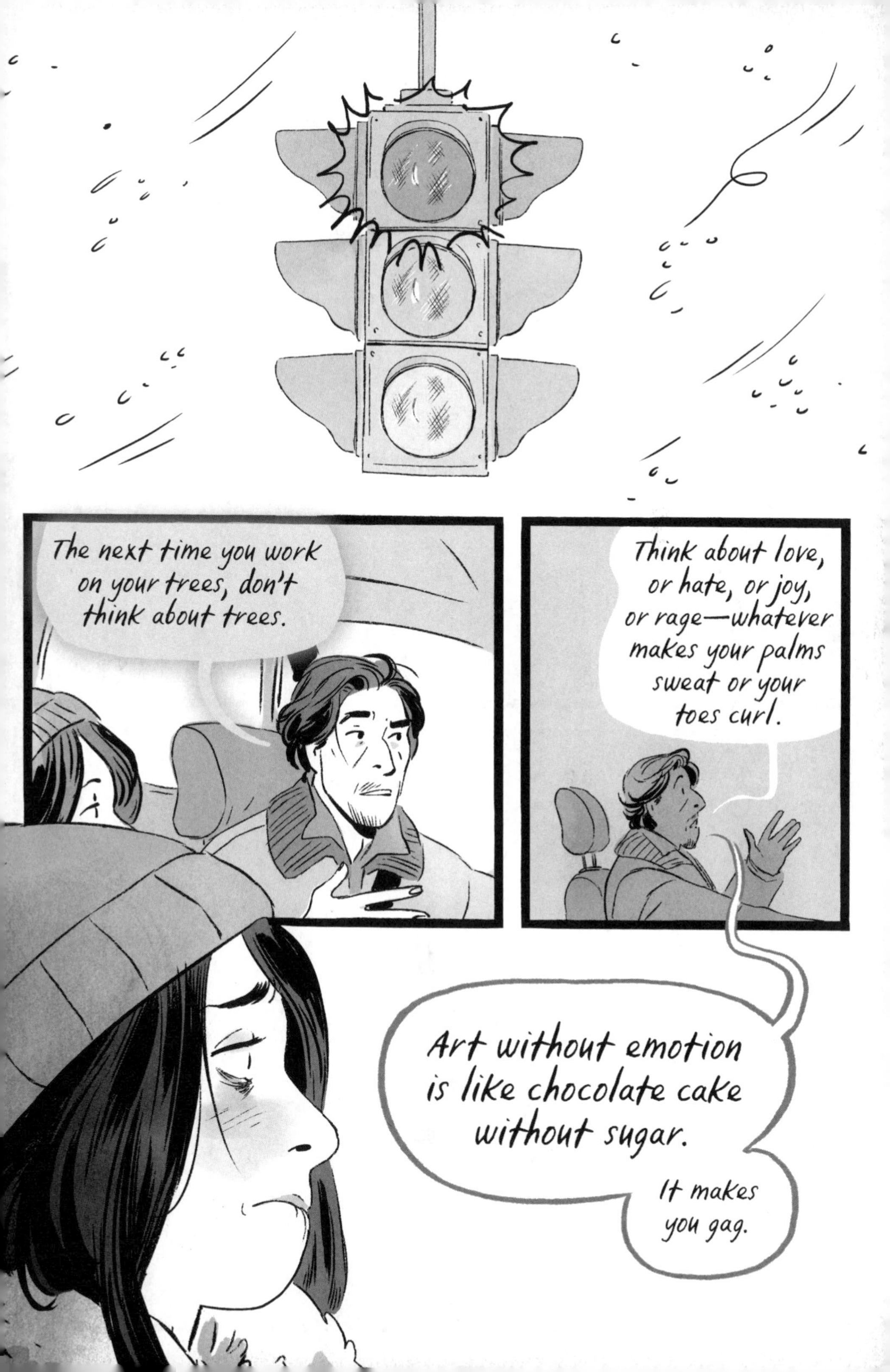
The next time you work on your trees, don't think about trees.
Think about love, or hate, or joy, or rage—whatever makes your palms sweat or your toes curl.
Art without emotion is like chocolate cake without sugar.
It makes you gag.

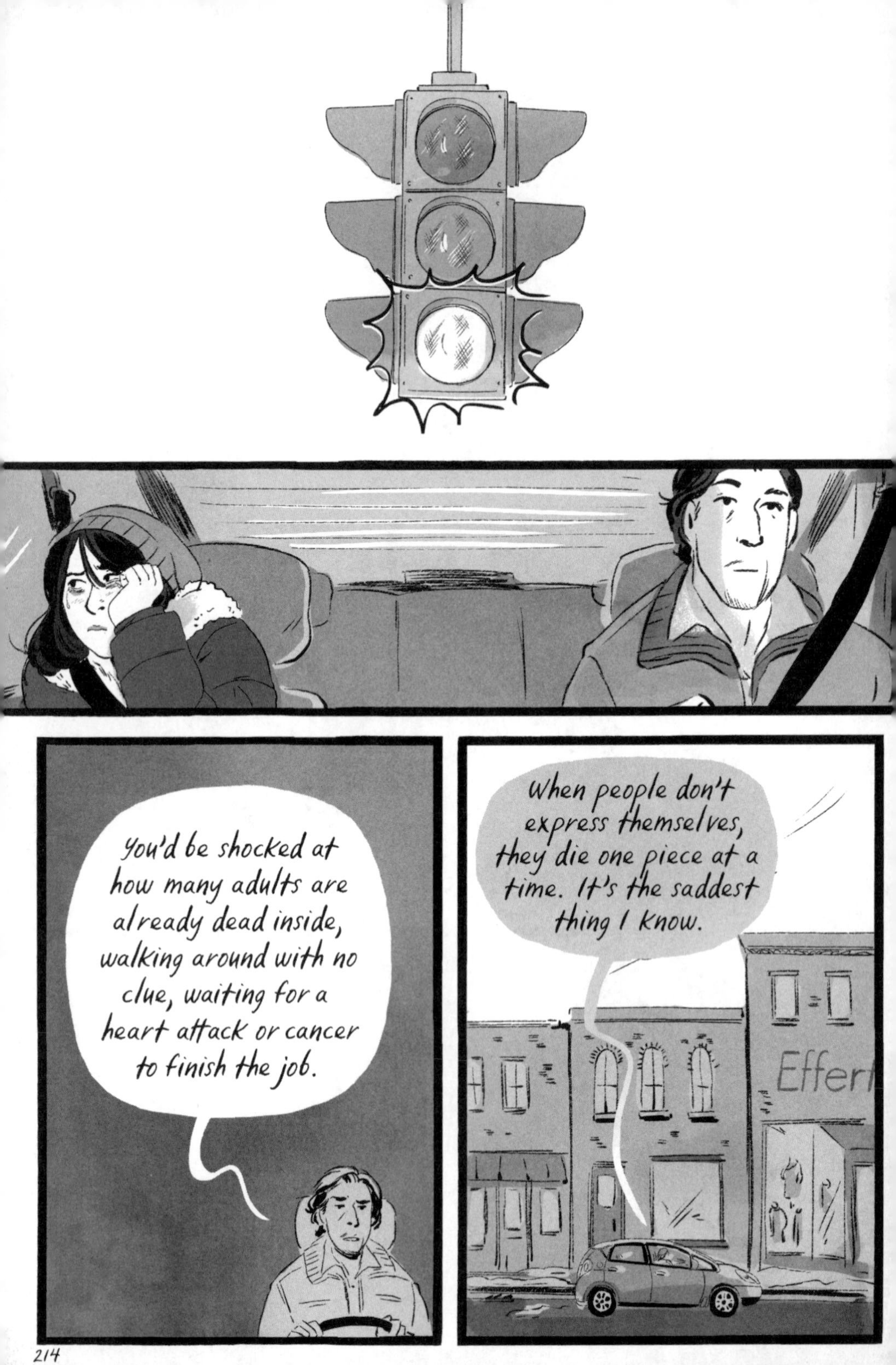
You'd be shocked at how many adults are already dead inside, walking around with no clue, waiting for a heart attack or cancer to finish the job.
When people don't express themselves, they die one piece at a time. It's the saddest thing I know.
Effer

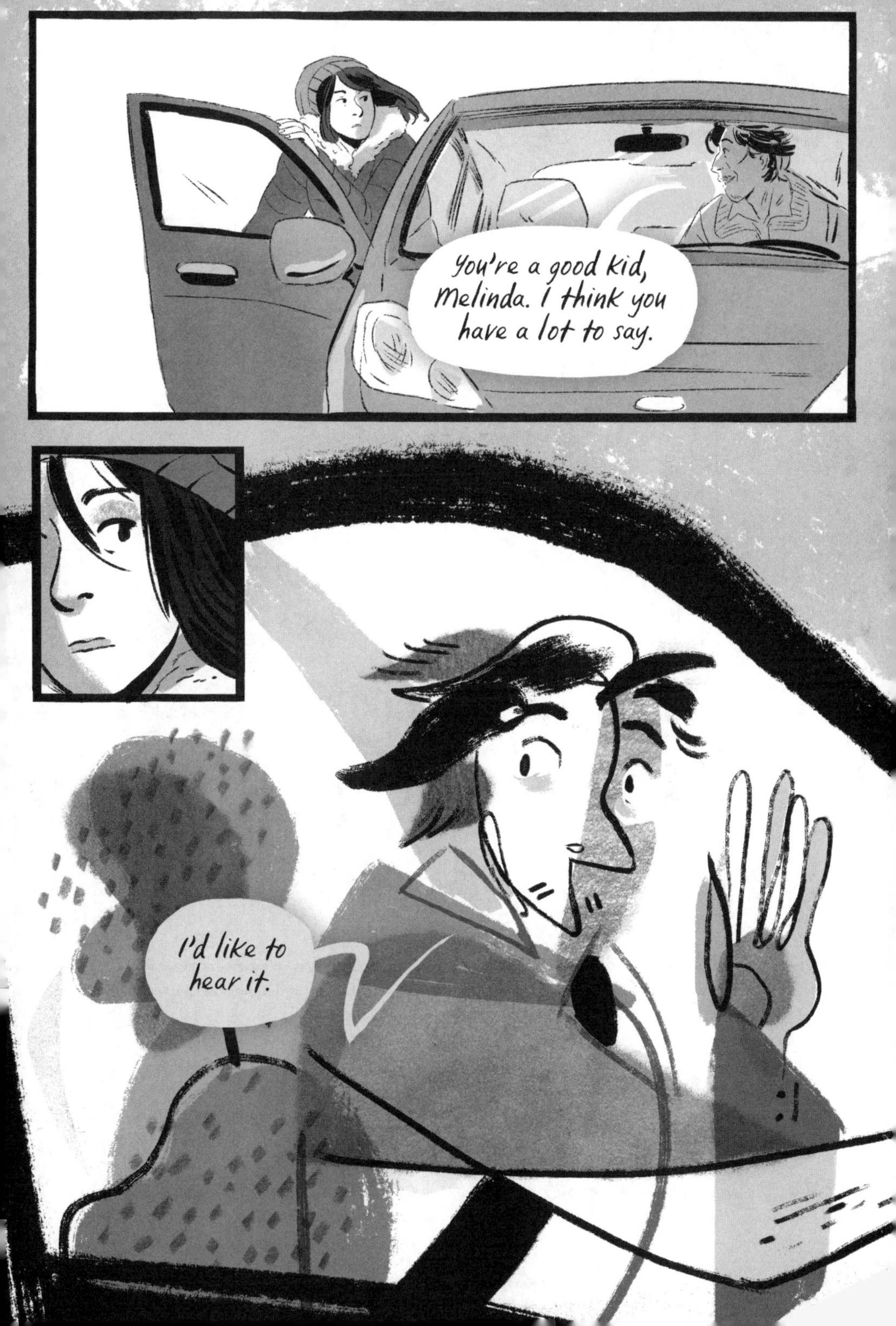
You're a good kid, Melinda. I think you have a lot to say.
I'd like to hear it.

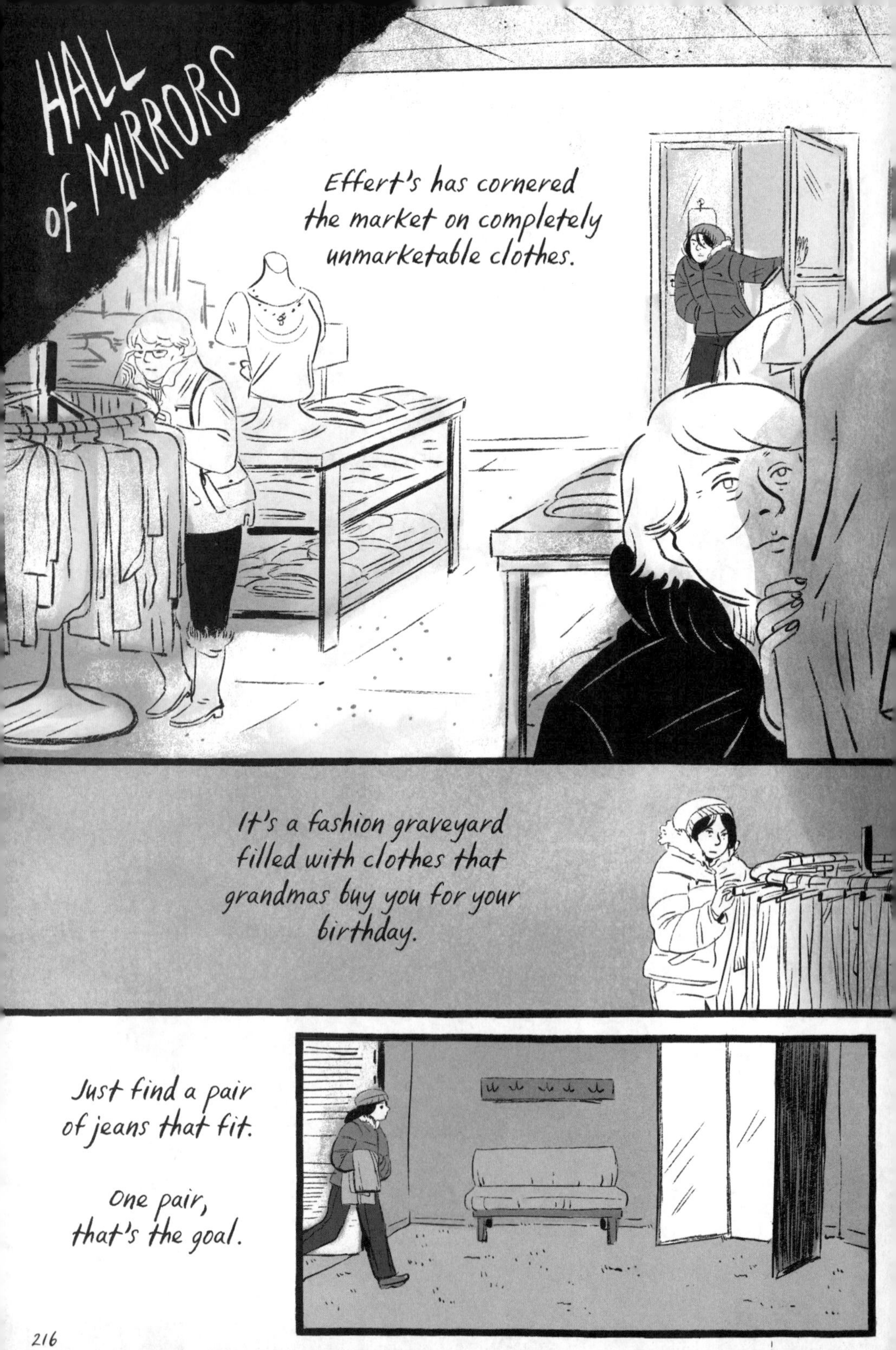
HALL of MIRRORS
Effert's has cornered the market on completely unmarketable clothes.
It's a fashion graveyard filled with clothes that grandmas buy you for your birthday.
Just find a pair of jeans that fit.
One pair, that's the goal.

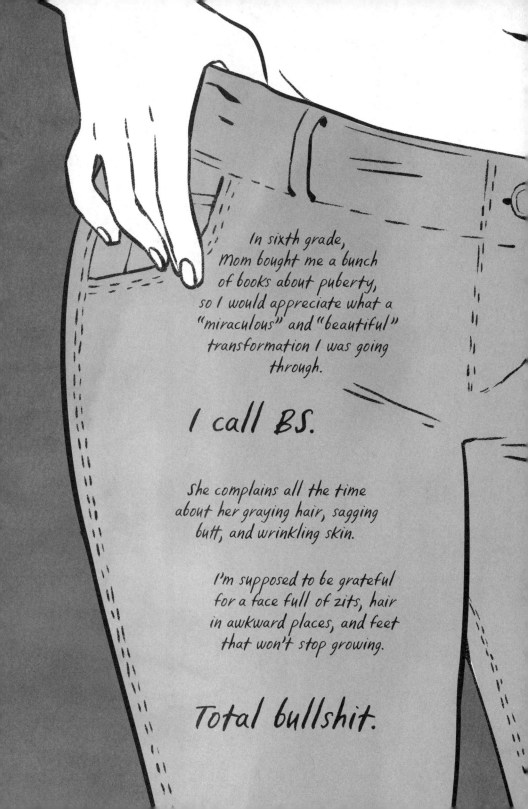

In sixth grade, Mom bought me a bunch of books about puberty, so I would appreciate what a "miraculous" and "beautiful" transformation I was going through.

I call BS.

She complains all the time about her graying hair, sagging butt, and wrinkling skin.

I'm supposed to be grateful for a face full of zits, hair in awkward places, and feet that won't stop growing.

Total bullshit.

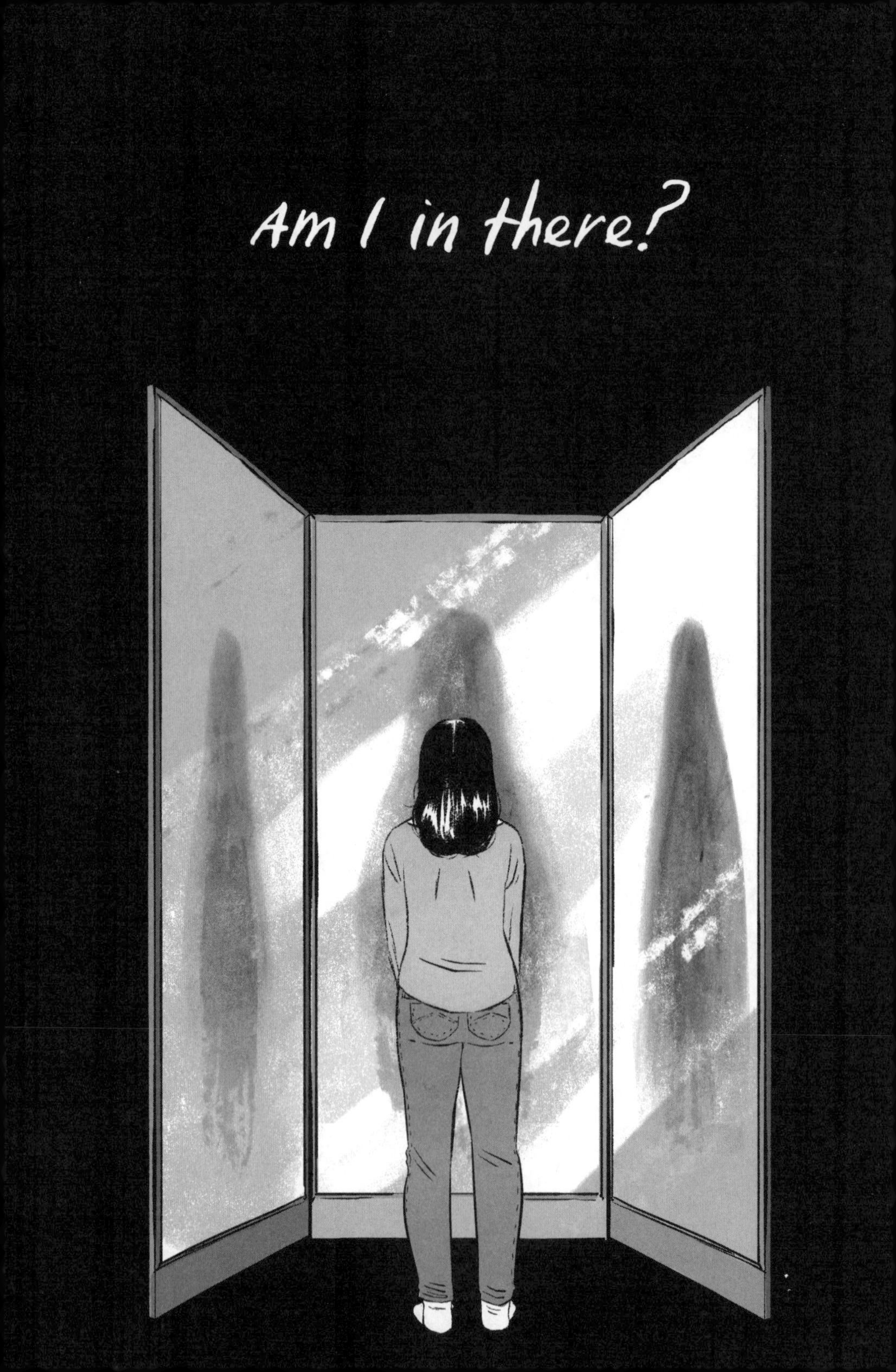
Am I in there?

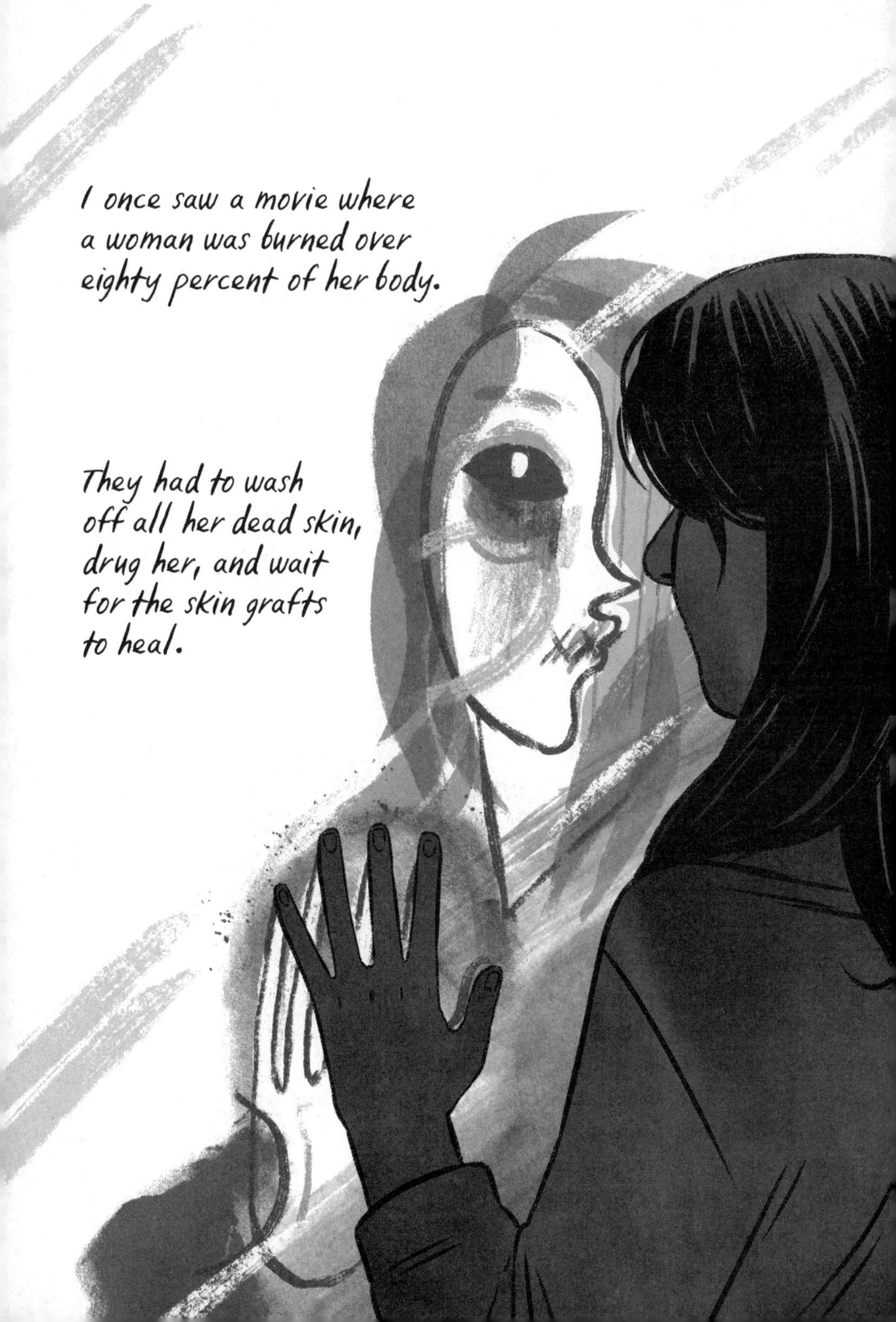
I once saw a movie where a woman was burned over eighty percent of her body.
They had to wash off all her dead skin, drug her, and wait for the skin grafts to heal.

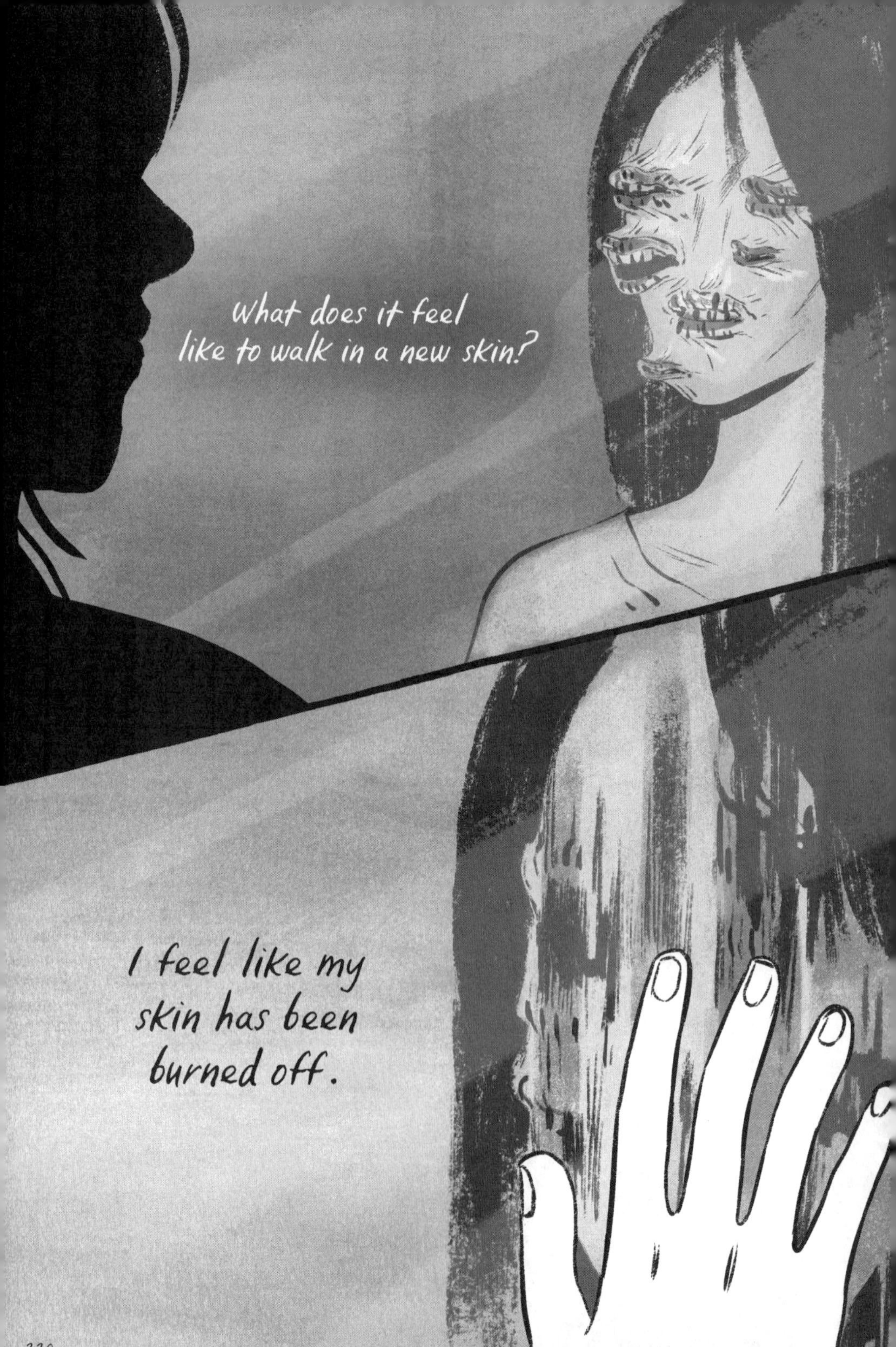
What does it feel like to walk in a new skin?
I feel like my skin has been burned off.

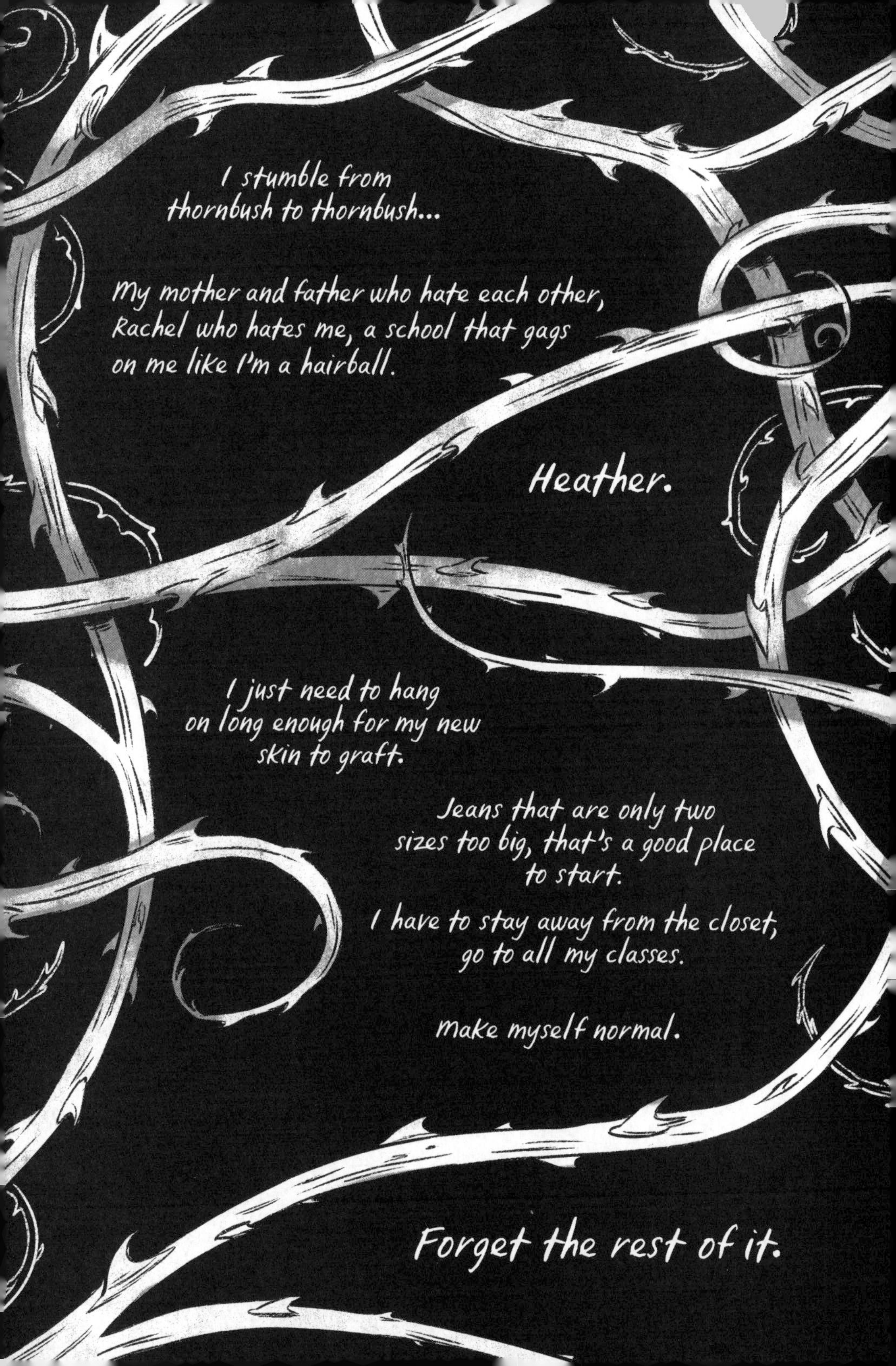
I stumble from thornbush to thornbush...
My mother and father who hate each other, Rachel who hates me, a school that gags on me like I'm a hairball.
Heather.
I just need to hang on long enough for my new skin to graft.
Jeans that are only two sizes too big, that's a good place to start.
I have to stay away from the closet, go to all my classes.
Make myself normal.
Forget the rest of it.

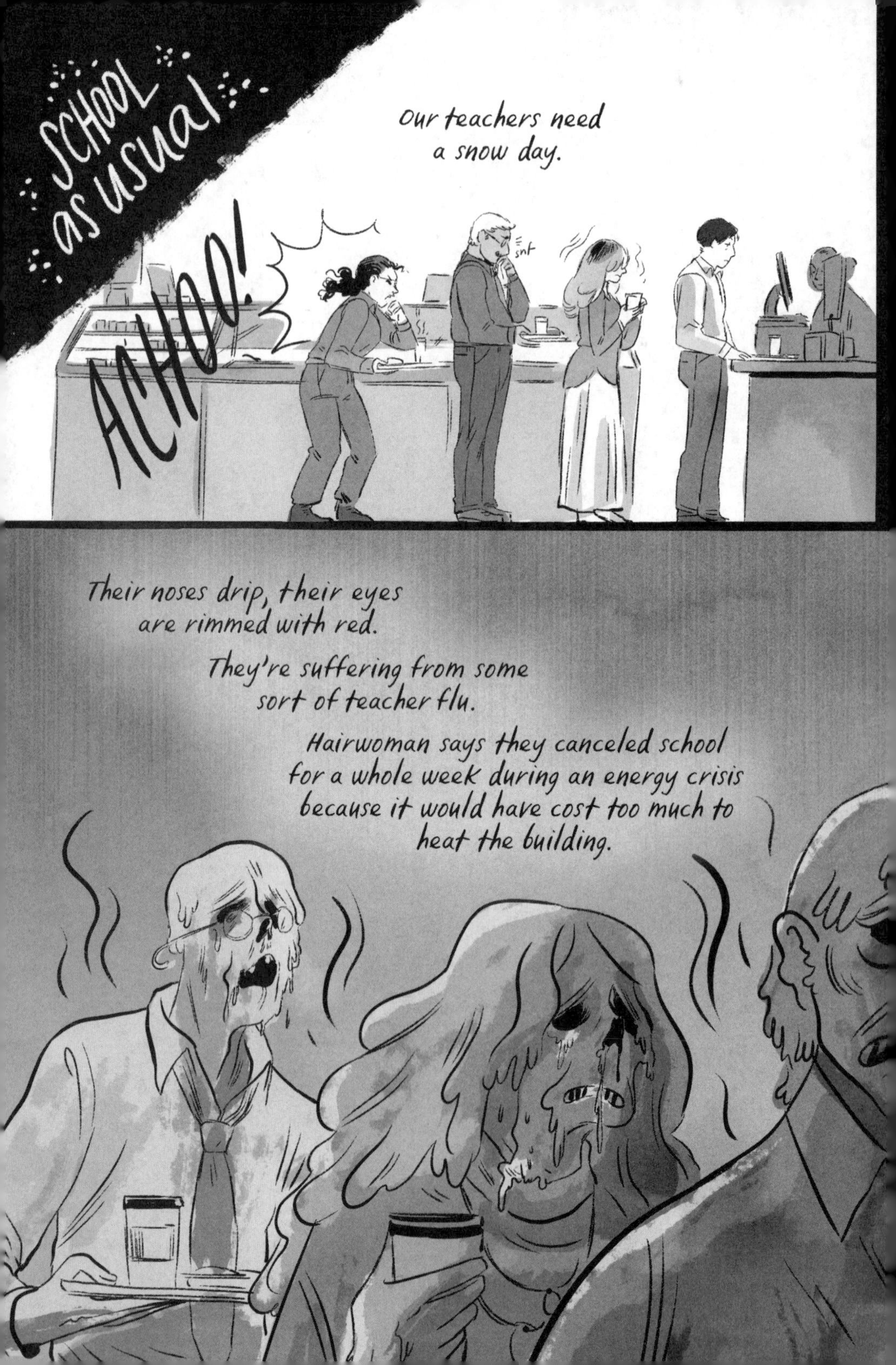
SCHOOL as usual!
Our teachers need
a snow day.
ACHOO!
snf
Their noses drip, their eyes
are rimmed with red.
They're suffering from some
sort of teacher flu.
Hairwoman says they canceled school
for a whole week during an energy crisis
because it would have cost too much to
heat the building.

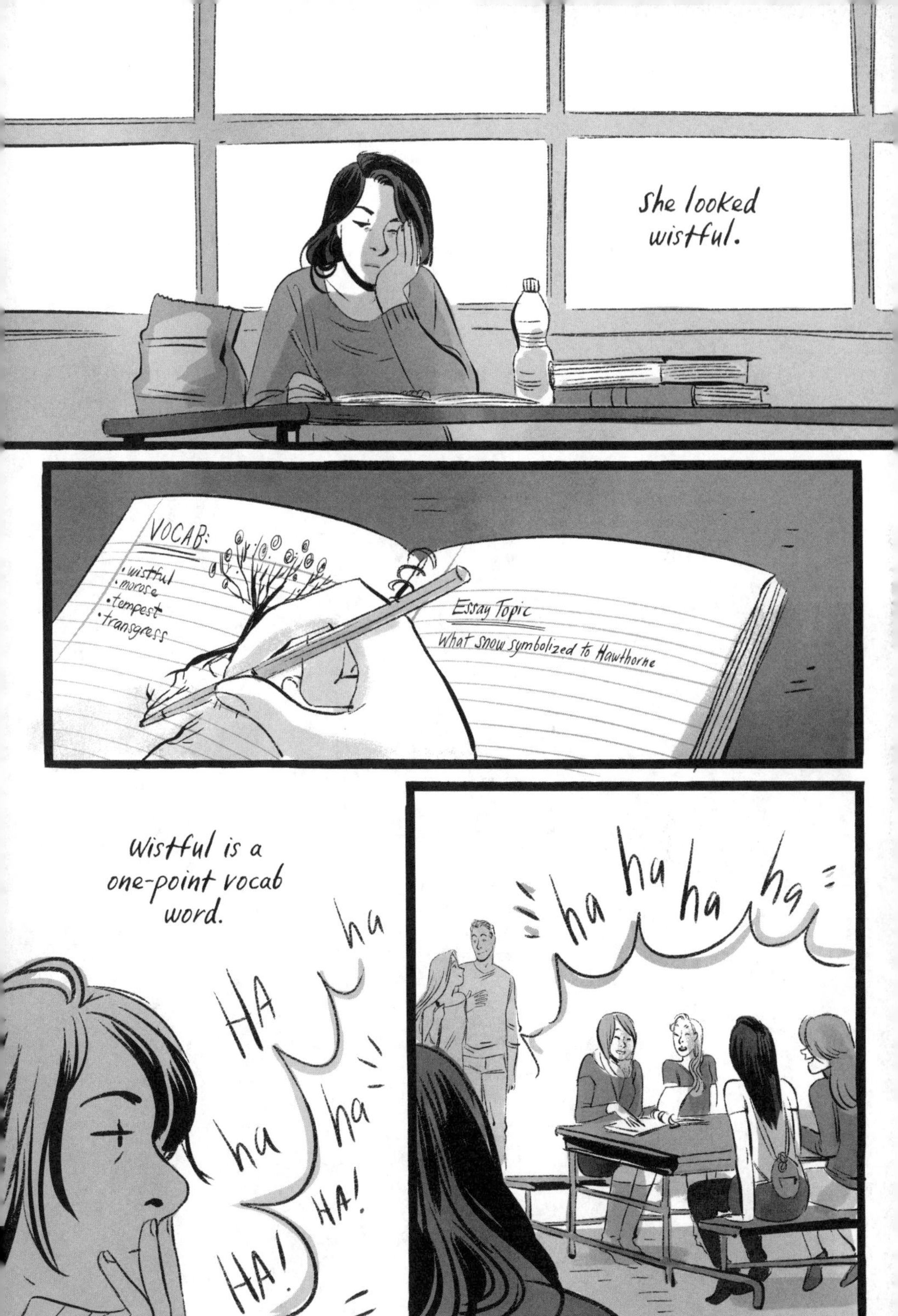

She looked wistful.
VOCAB:
• wistful
• morose
• tempest
• transgress
Essay Topic
What snow symbolized to Hawthorne
Wistful is a one-point vocab word.
HA ha ha ha HA! HA!
ha ha ha ha

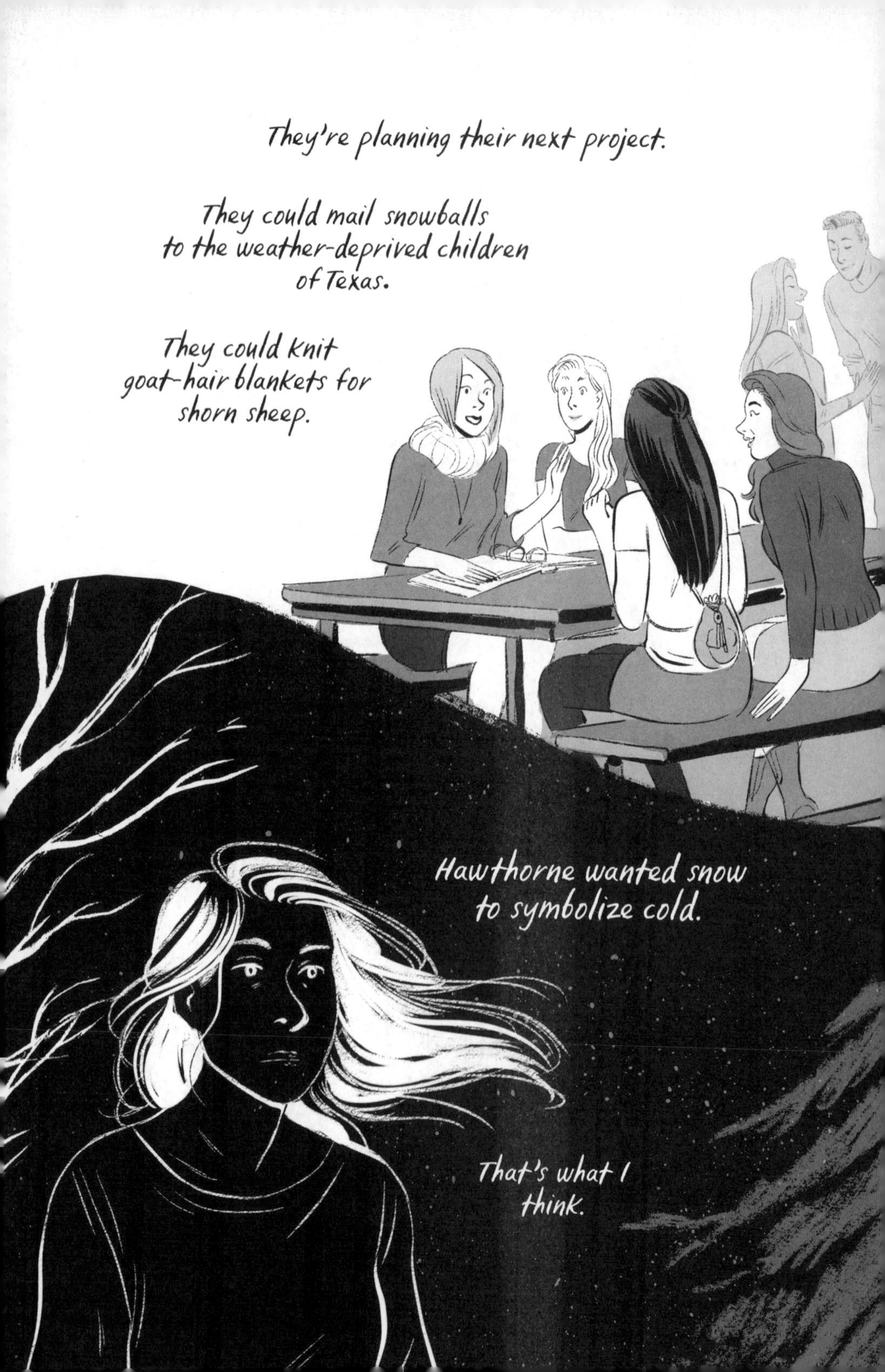
They're planning their next project.
They could mail snowballs to the weather-deprived children of Texas.
They could knit goat-hair blankets for shorn sheep.
Hawthorne wanted snow to symbolize cold.
That's what I think.

Cold and silence.

There is nothing quieter than snow.

The sky screams to deliver it,
a hundred banshees flying on
the edge of the blizzard.

But once snow covers the ground,
it hushes as still as my heart.

Essay Topic

What snow symbolized

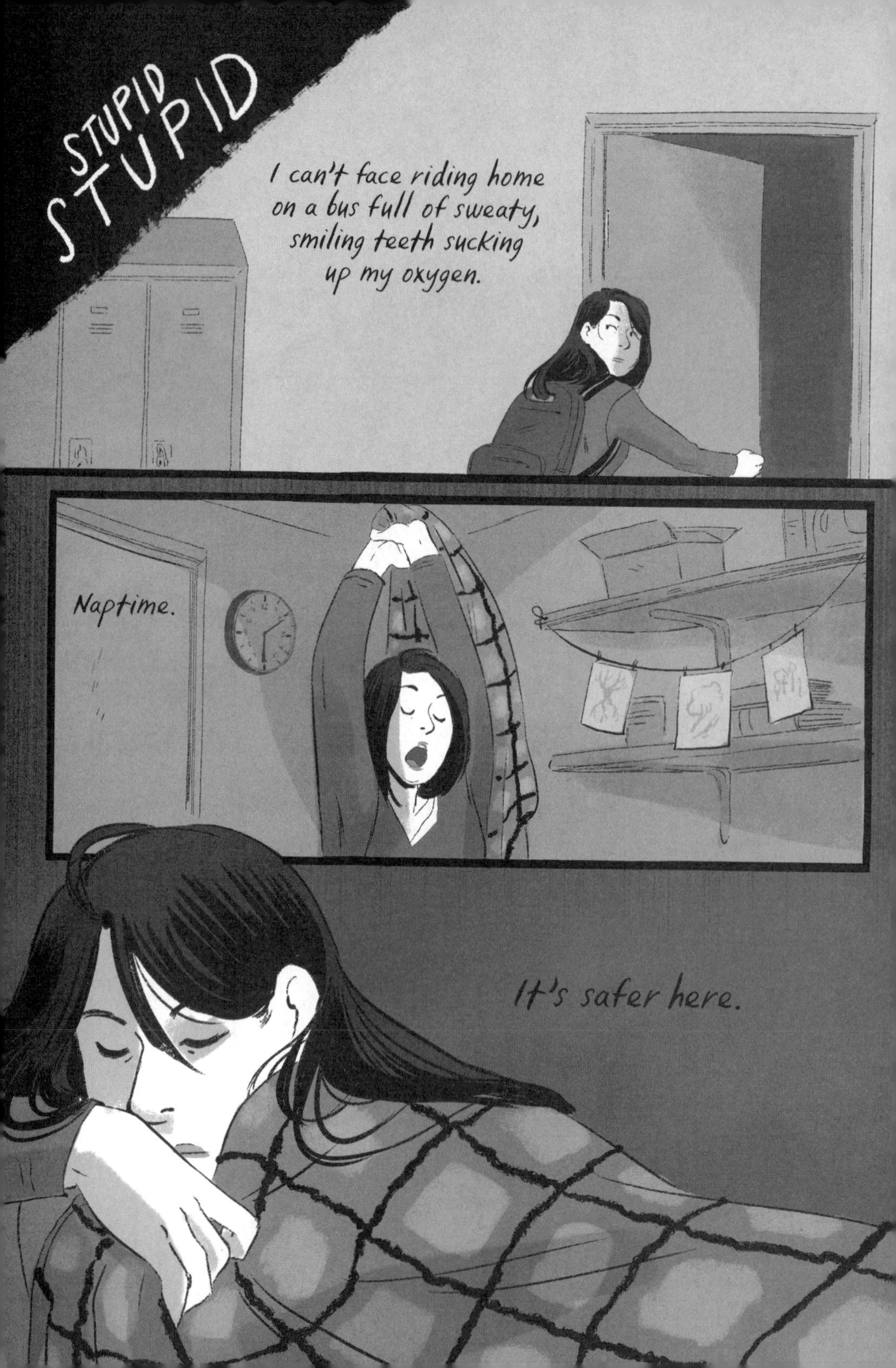
STUPID STUPID
I can't face riding home on a bus full of sweaty, smiling teeth sucking up my oxygen.
Naptime.
It's safer here.

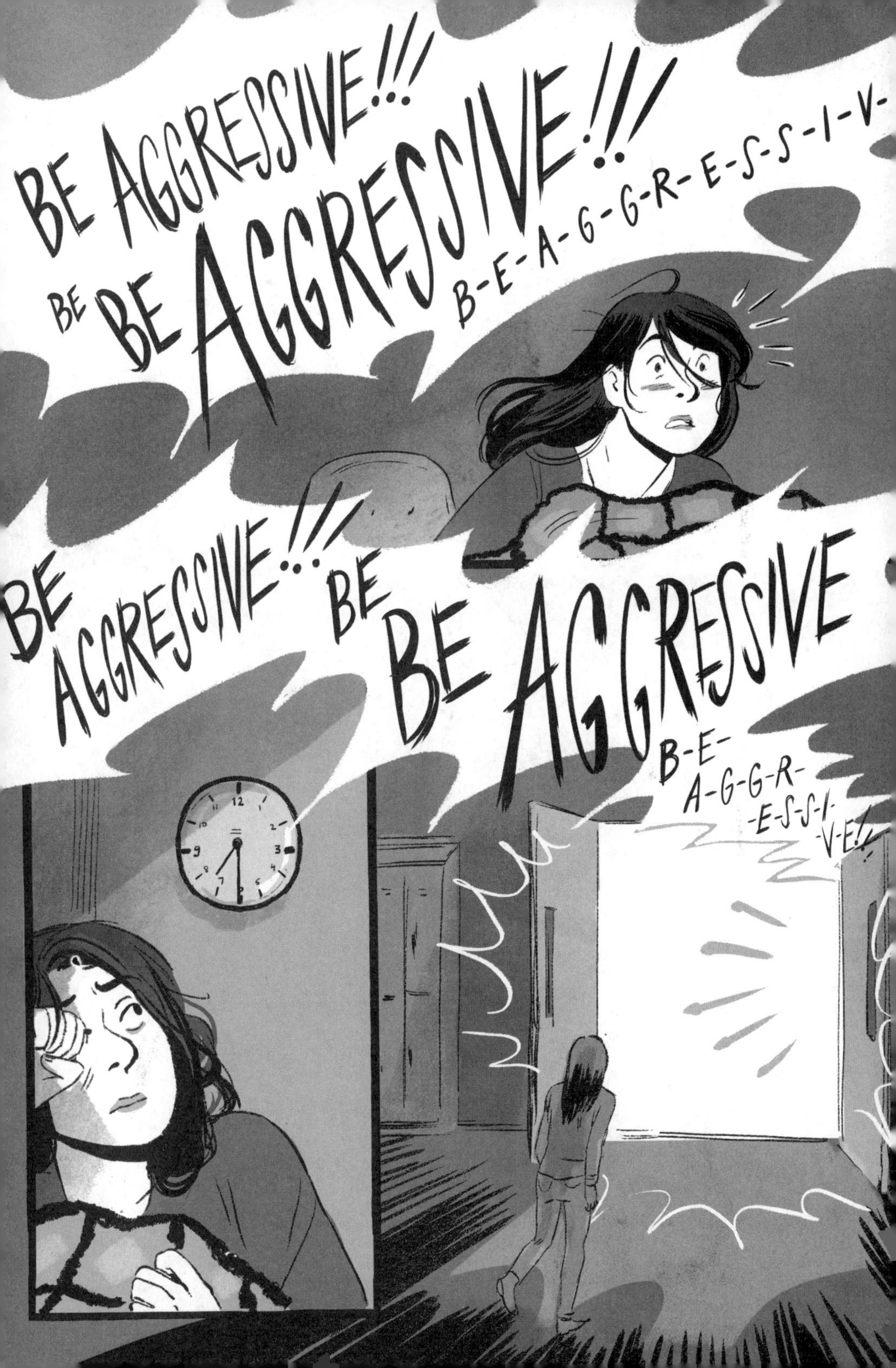
BE AGGRESSIVE!!!
BE BE AGGRESSIVE!!!
B-E-A-G-G-R-E-S-S-I-V-
BE AGGRESSIVE!!!
BE BE AGGRESSIVE
B-E-A-G-G-R-E-S-S-I-V-E!!

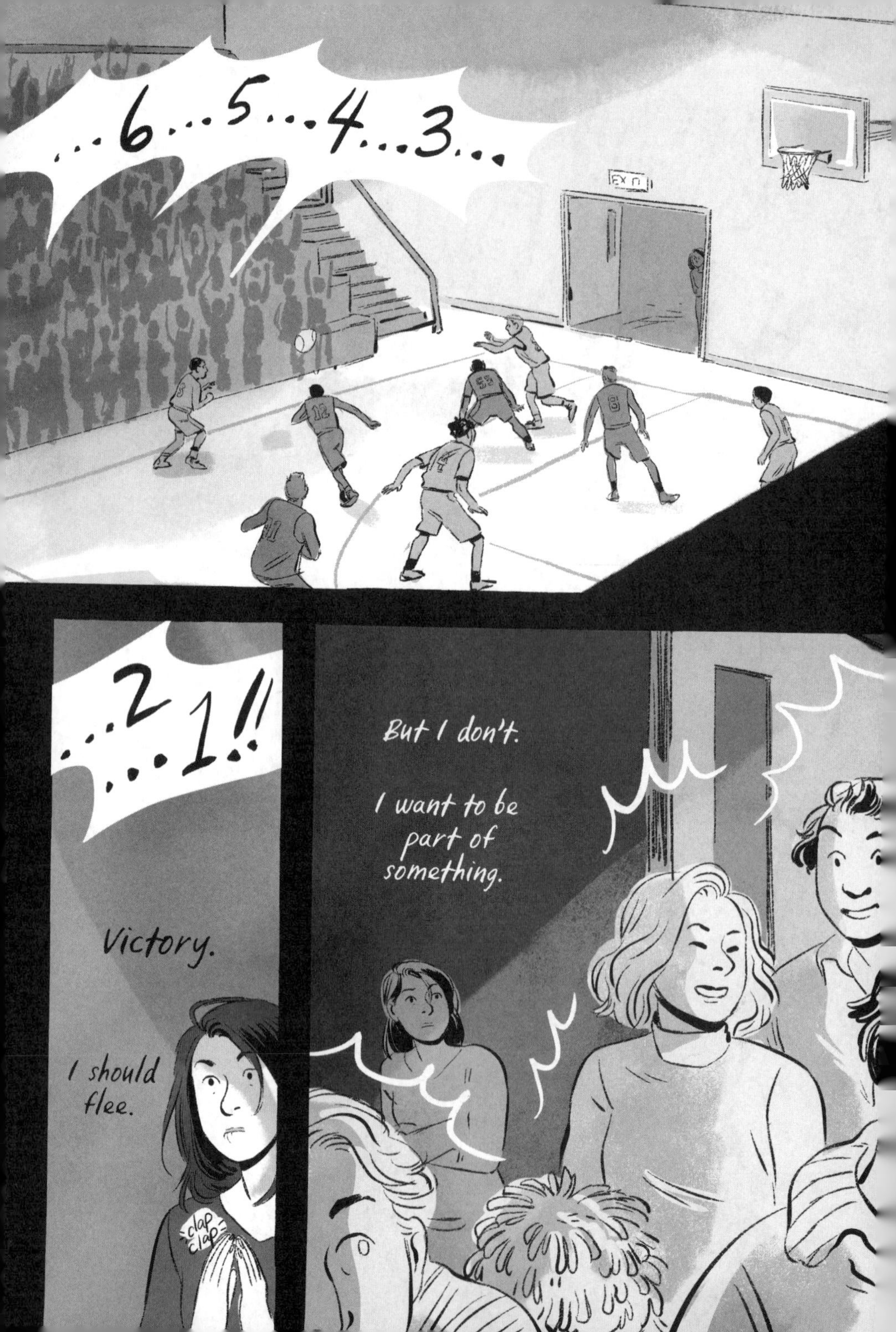
...6...5...4...3...
EXIT
...2
...1!!
Victory.
I should flee.
clap clap
But I don't.
I want to be part of something.

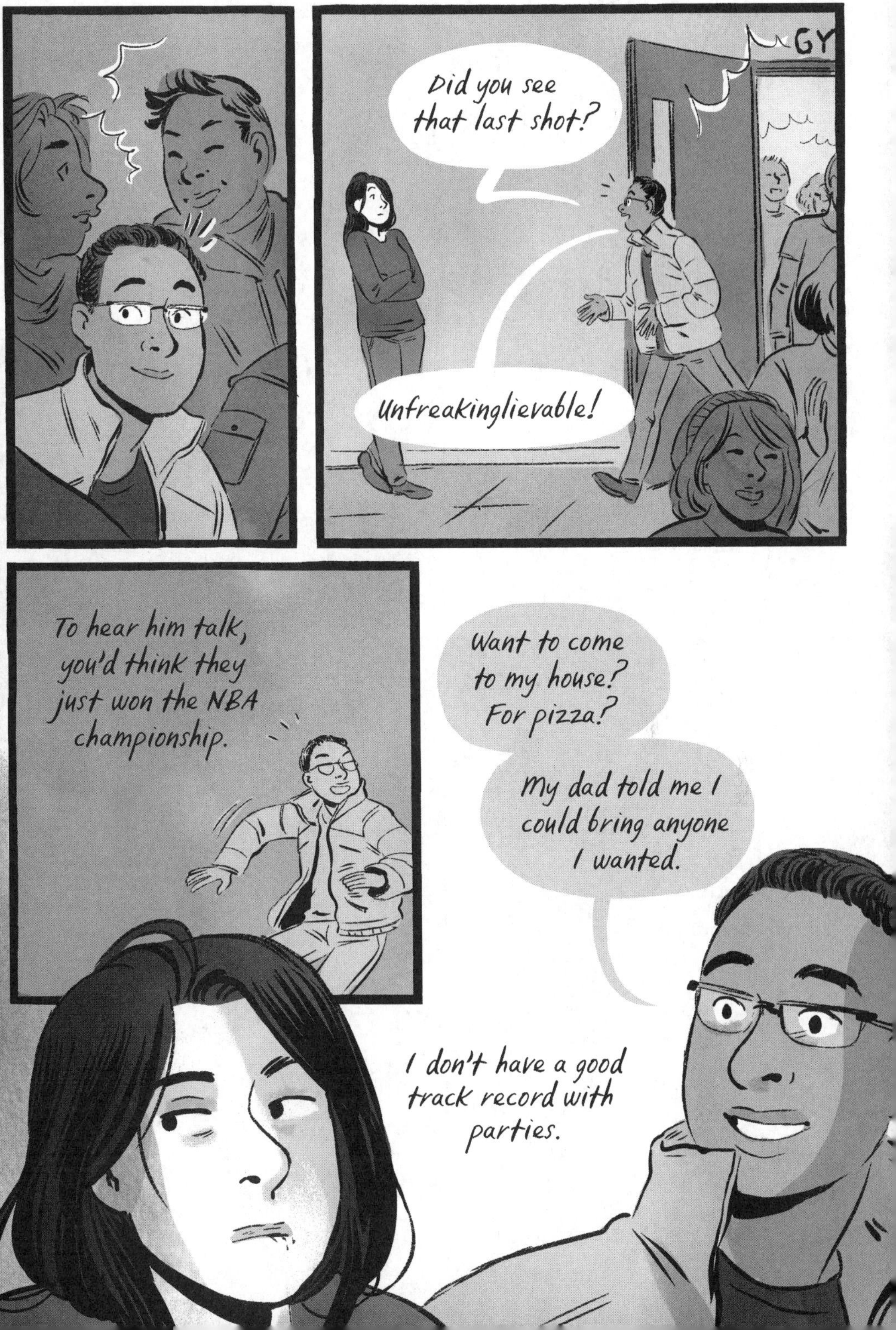
GY
Did you see that last shot?
Unfreakinglievable!
To hear him talk, you'd think they just won the NBA championship.
Want to come to my house? For pizza?
My dad told me I could bring anyone I wanted.
I don't have a good track record with parties.

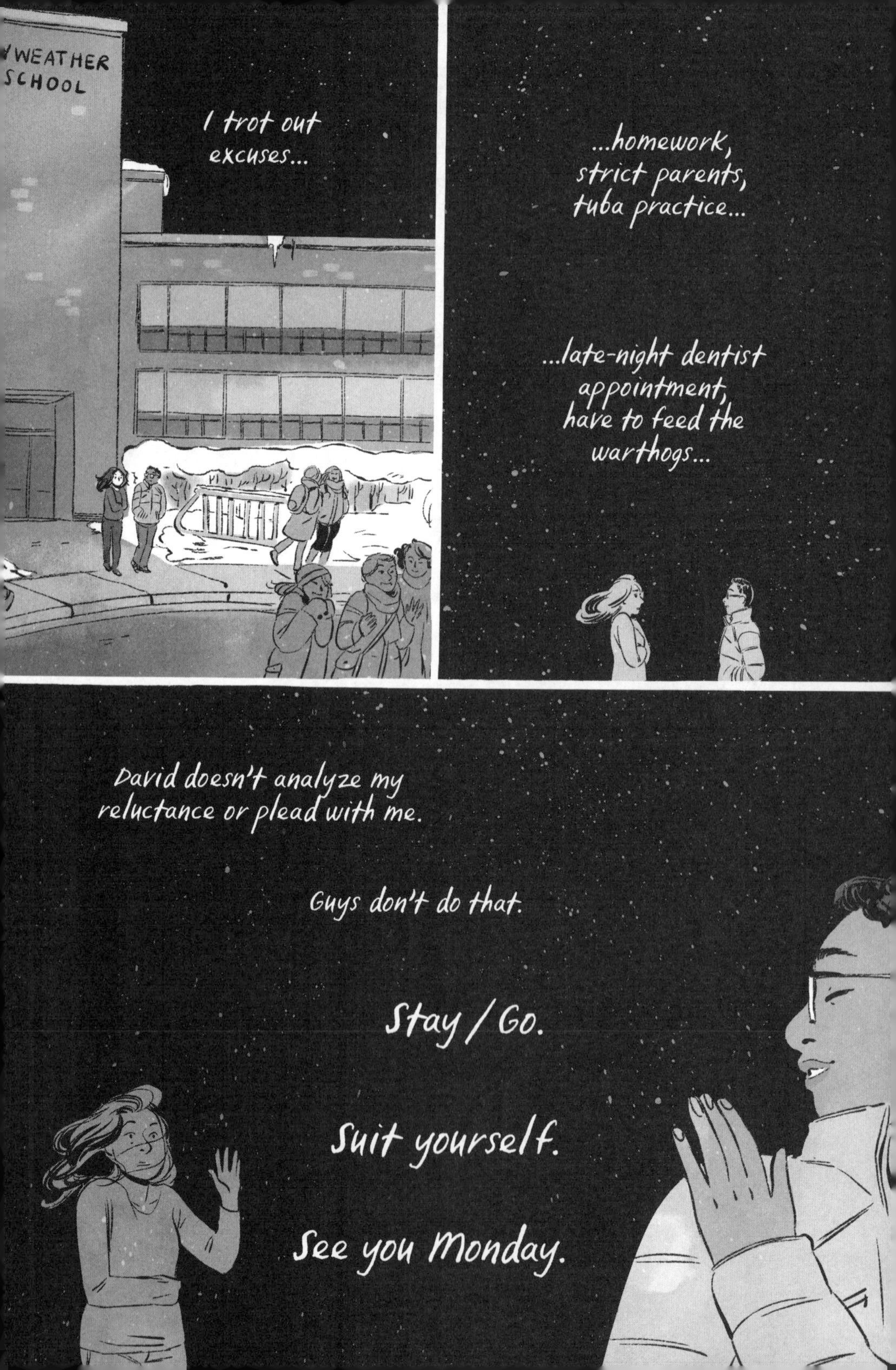

WEATHER SCHOOL
I trot out excuses...
...homework, strict parents, tuba practice...
...late-night dentist appointment, have to feed the warthogs...
David doesn't analyze my reluctance or plead with me.
Guys don't do that.
Stay / Go.
Suit yourself.
See you Monday.

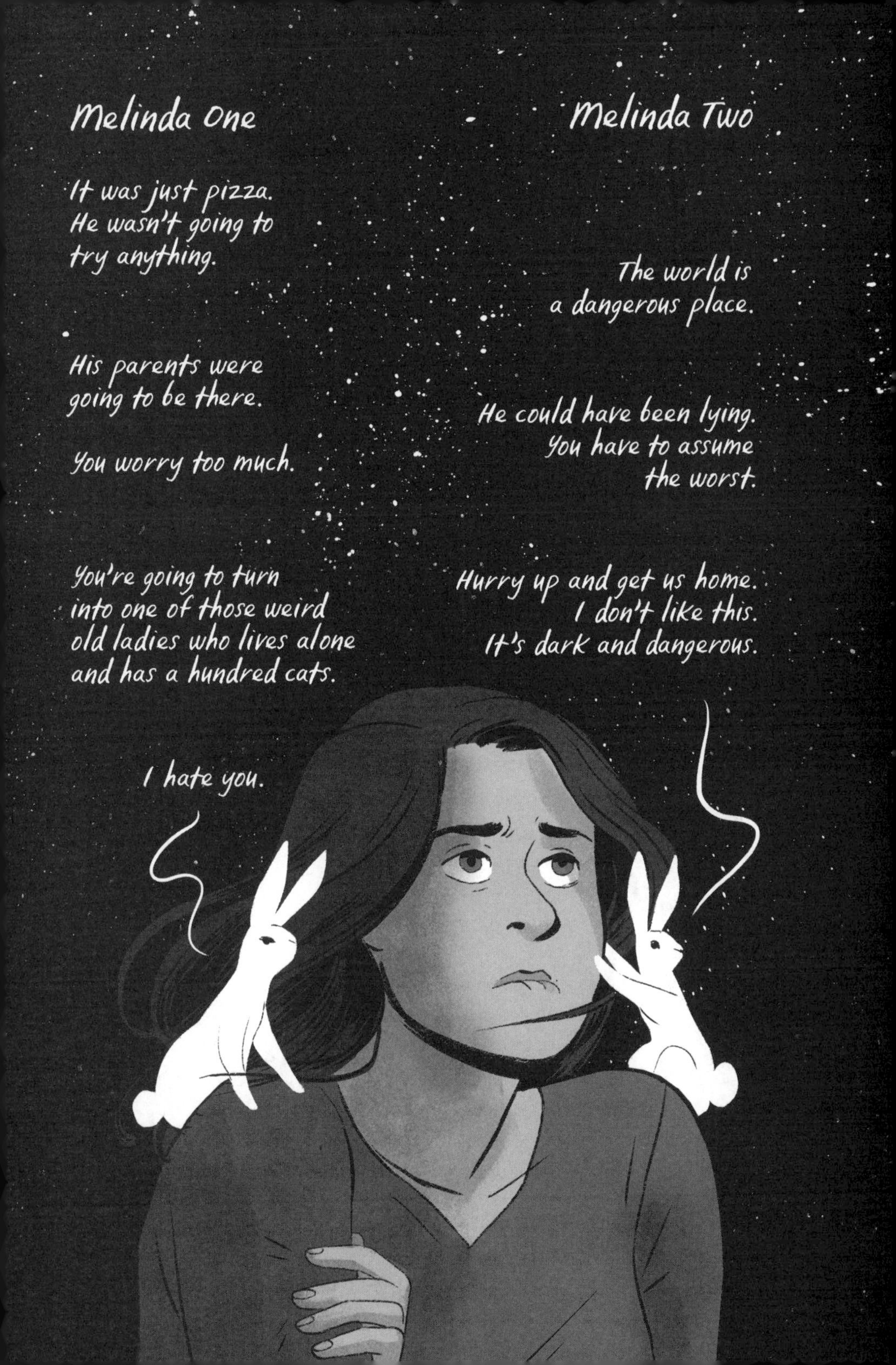
Melinda One
Melinda Two
It was just pizza. He wasn't going to try anything.
The world is a dangerous place.
His parents were going to be there.
He could have been lying. You have to assume the worst.
You worry too much.
You're going to turn into one of those weird old ladies who lives alone and has a hundred cats.
Hurry up and get us home. I don't like this. It's dark and dangerous.
I hate you.

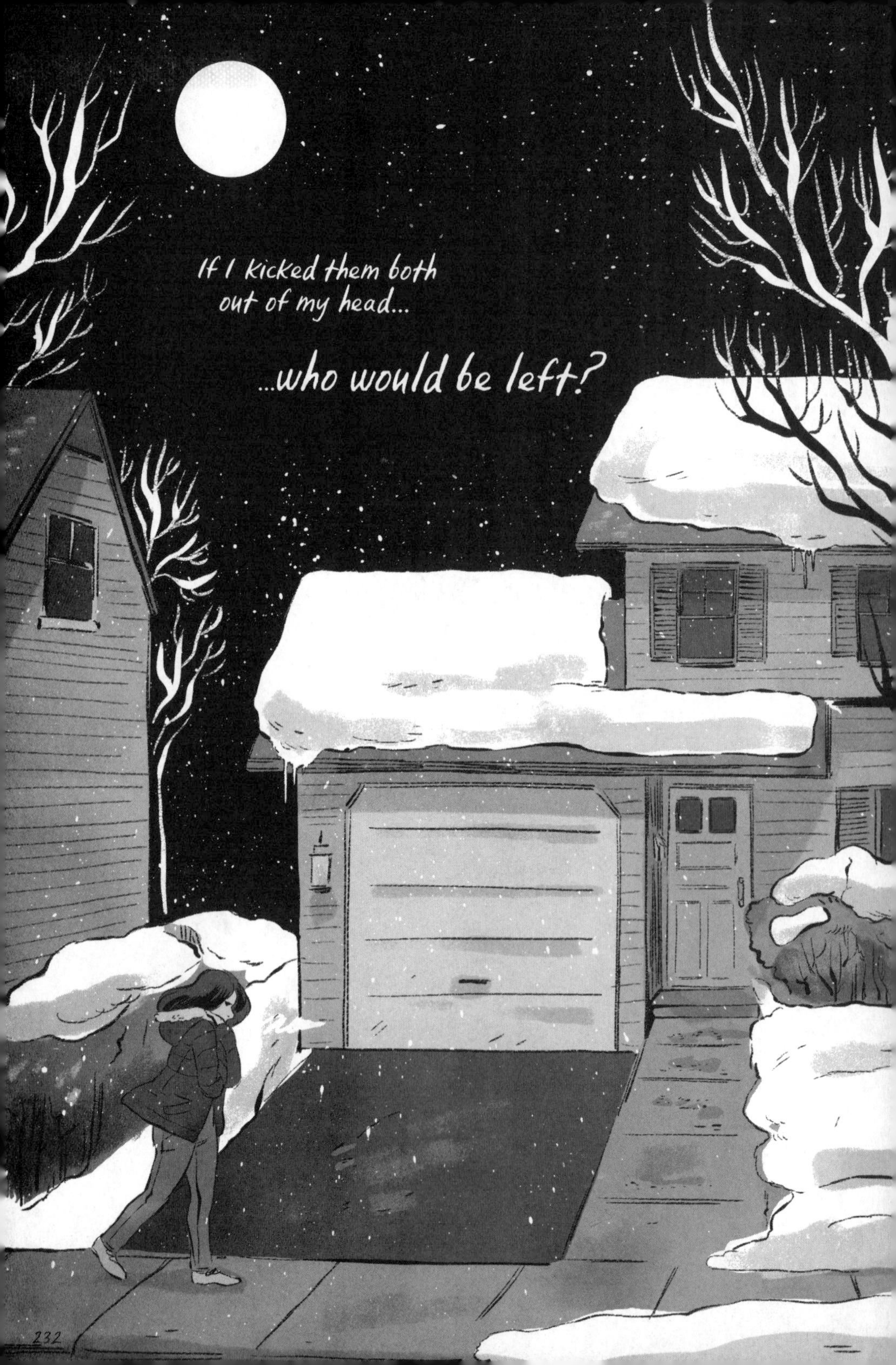
If I kicked them both out of my head...
...who would be left?

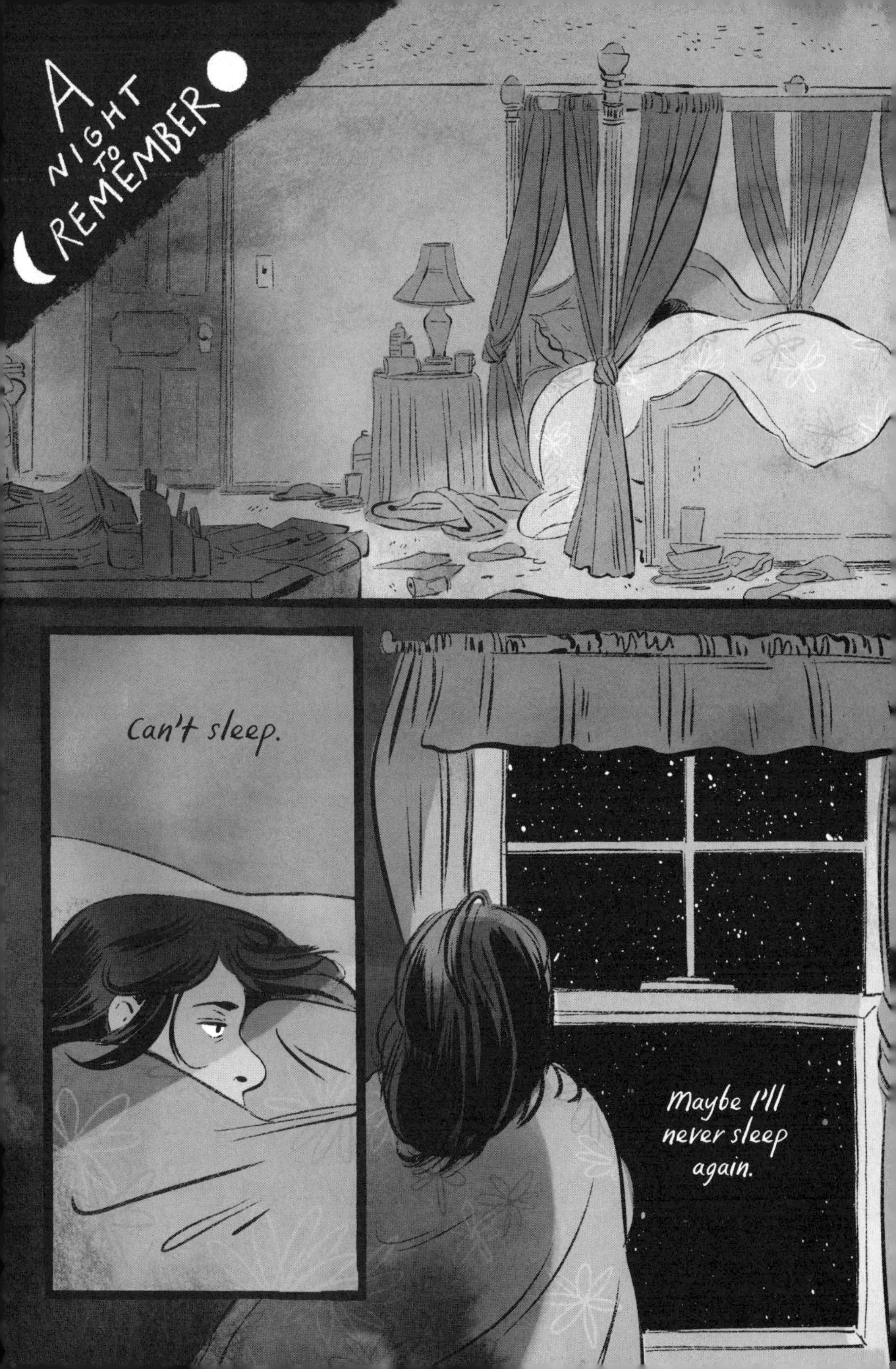
A NIGHT TO REMEMBER
Can't sleep.
Maybe I'll never sleep again.

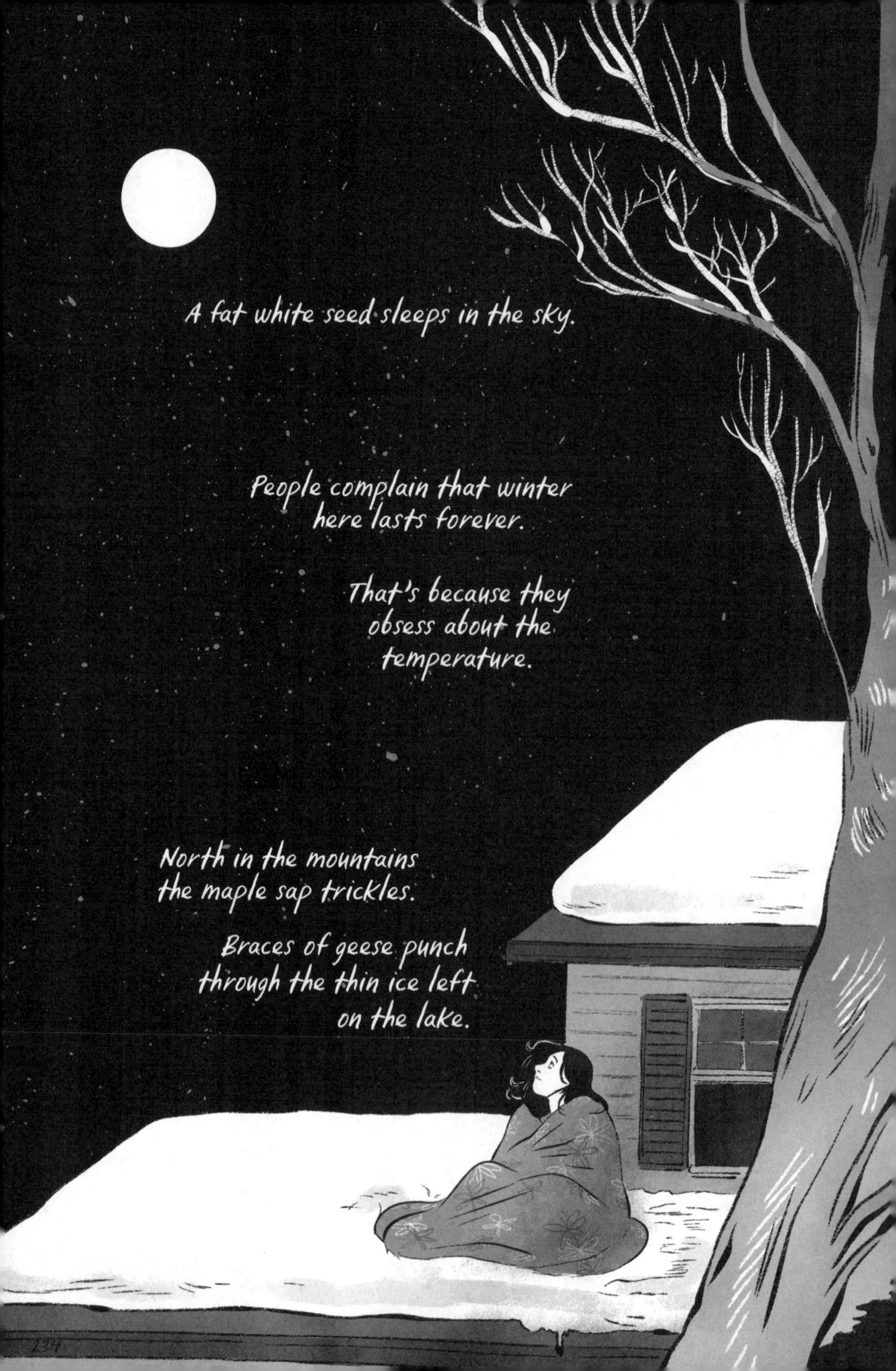
A fat white seed sleeps in the sky.
People complain that winter here lasts forever.
That's because they obsess about the temperature.
North in the mountains the maple sap trickles.
Braces of geese punch through the thin ice left on the lake.

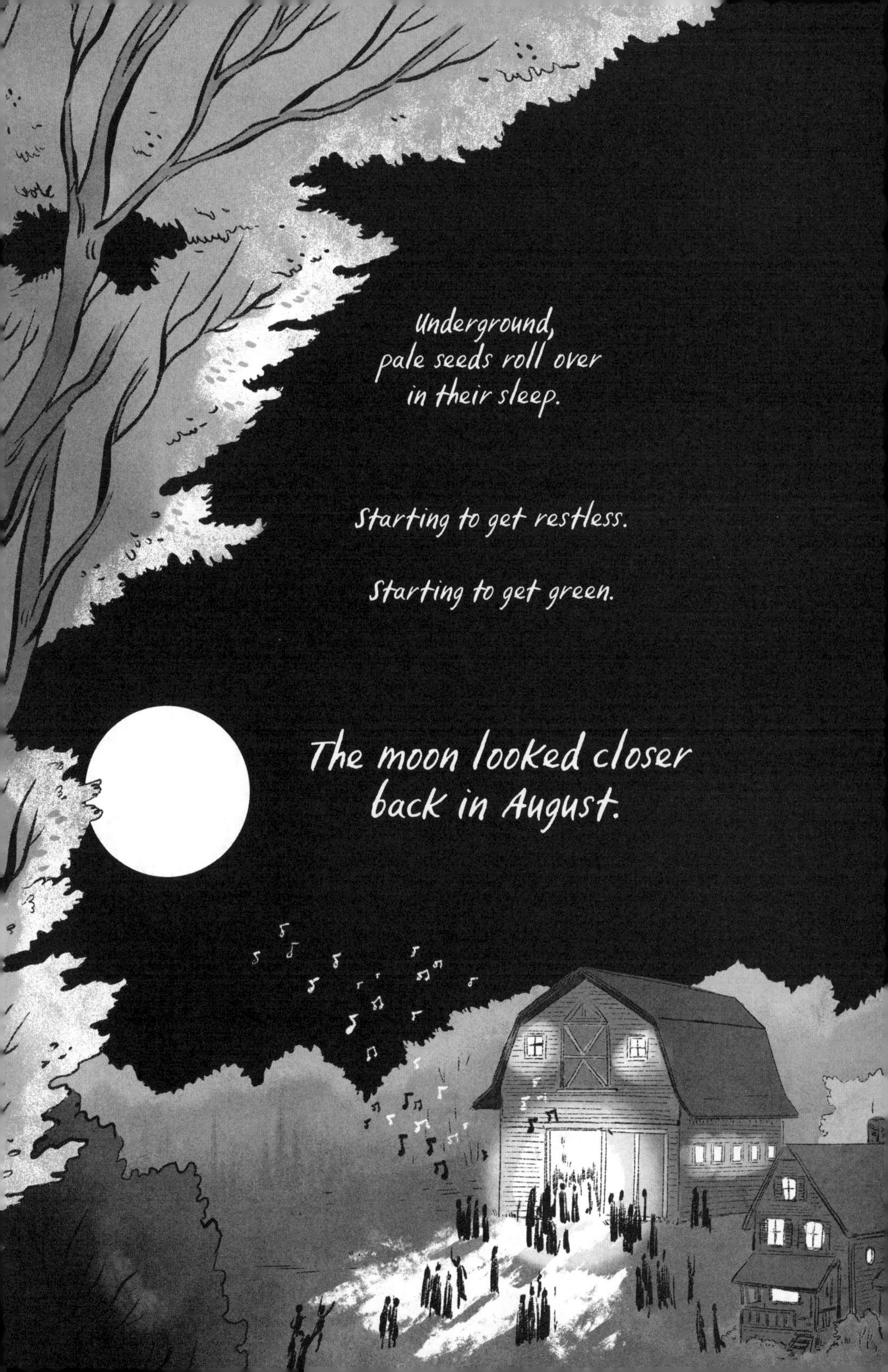
Underground,
pale seeds roll over
in their sleep.
Starting to get restless.
Starting to get green.
The moon looked closer
back in August.

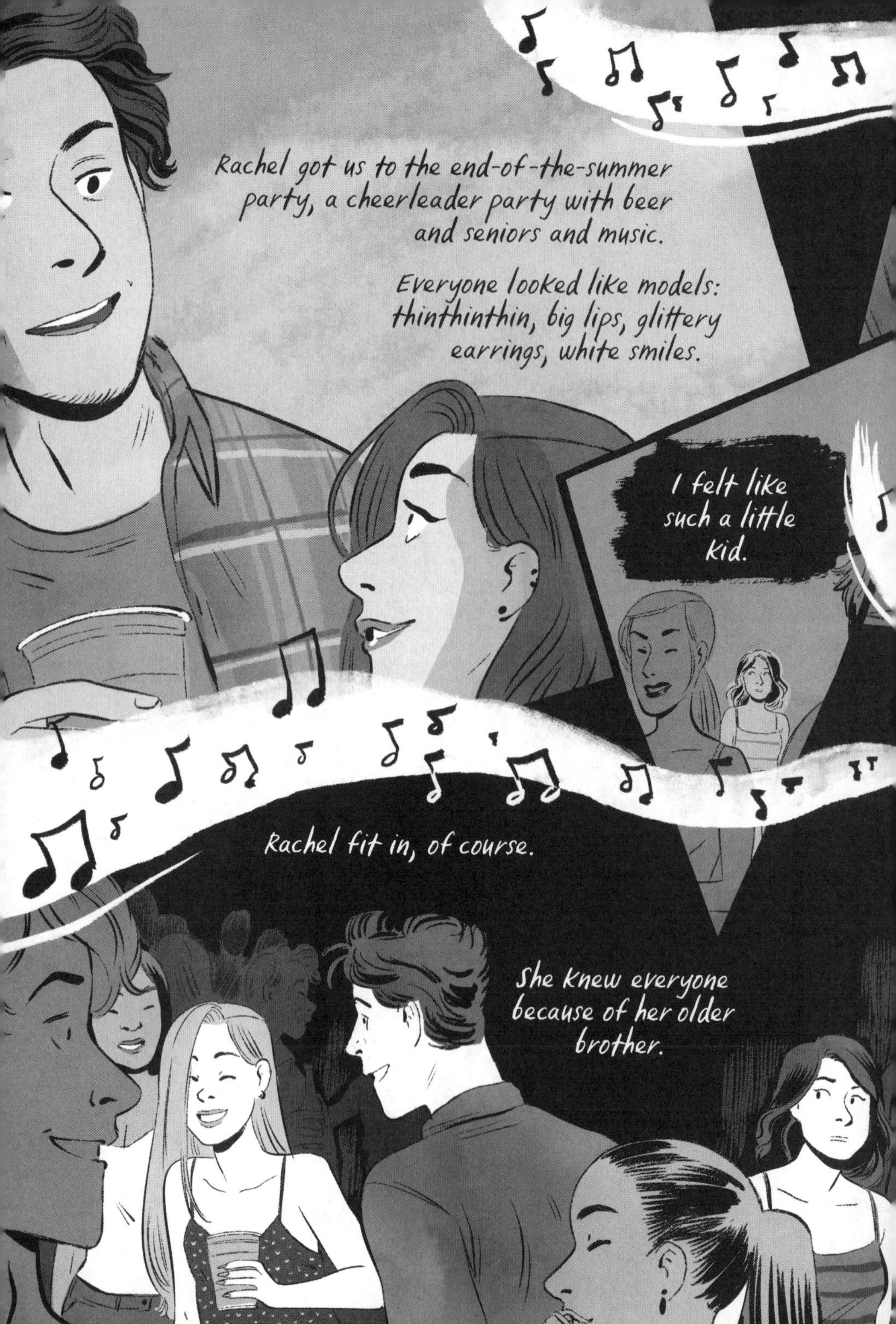
Rachel got us to the end-of-the-summer party, a cheerleader party with beer and seniors and music.
Everyone looked like models: thinthinthin, big lips, glittery earrings, white smiles.
I felt like such a little kid.
Rachel fit in, of course.
She knew everyone because of her older brother.

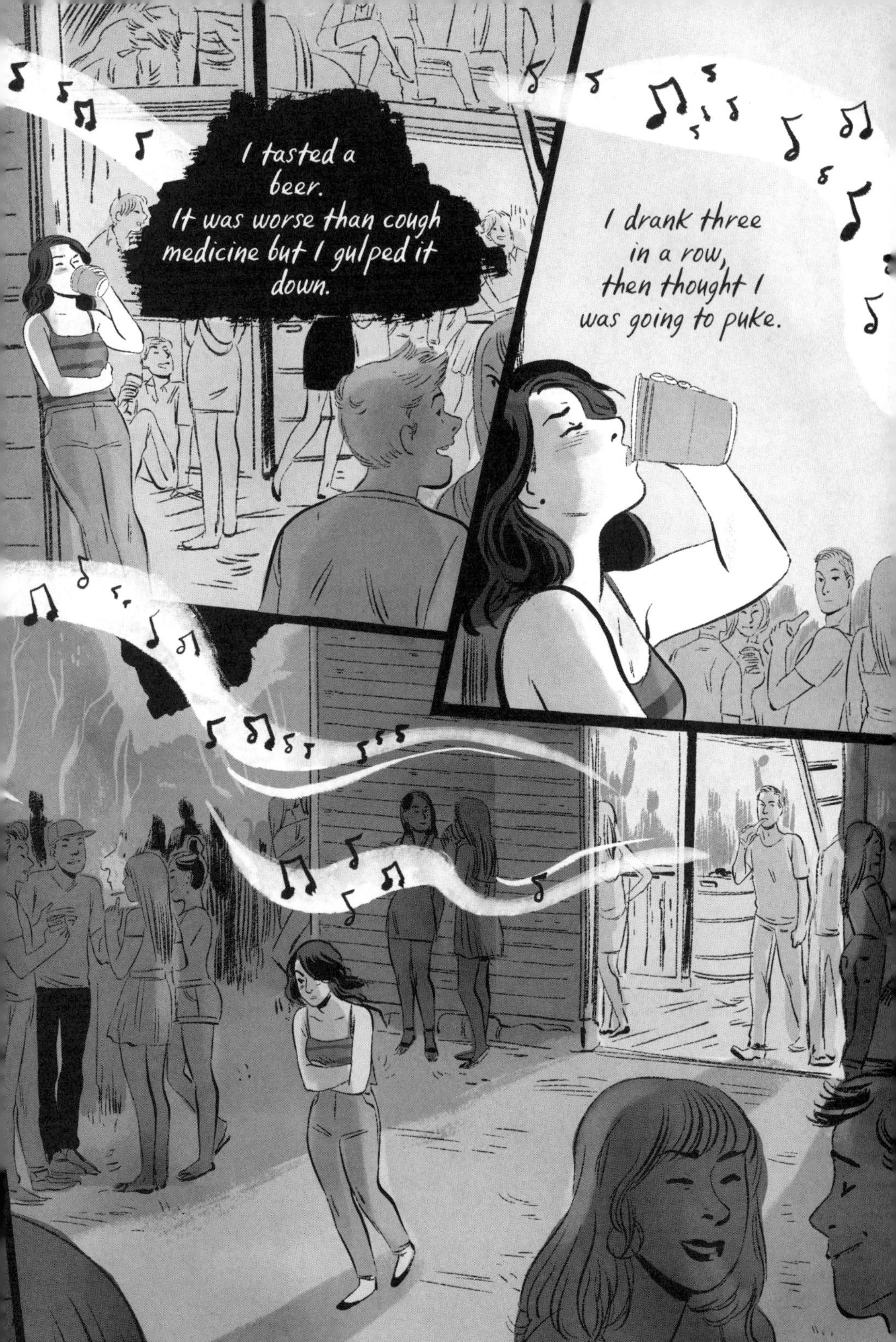
I tasted a beer. It was worse than cough medicine but I gulped it down.
I drank three in a row, then thought I was going to puke.

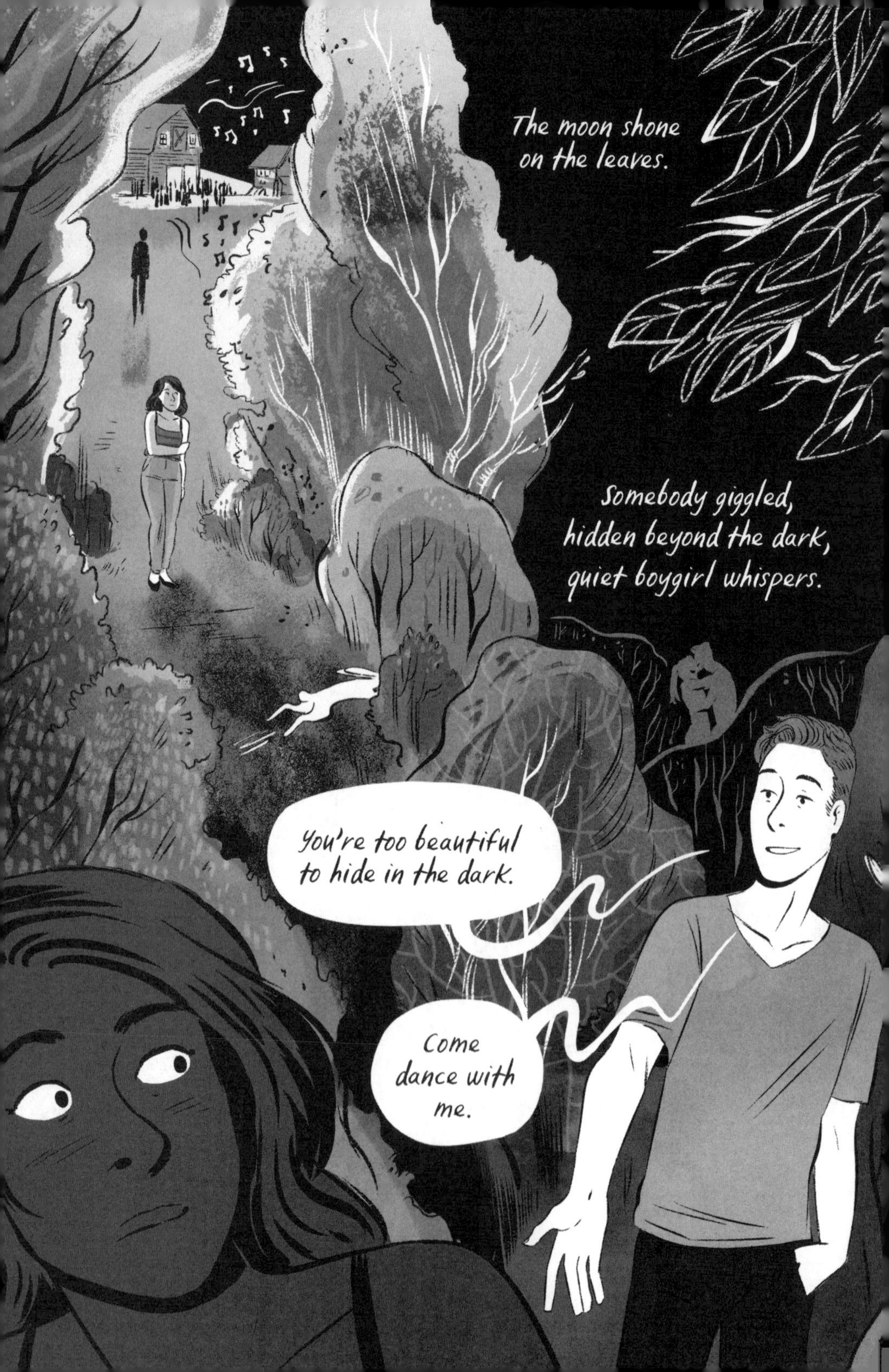
The moon shone on the leaves.
Somebody giggled, hidden beyond the dark, quiet boygirl whispers.
You're too beautiful to hide in the dark.
Come dance with me.

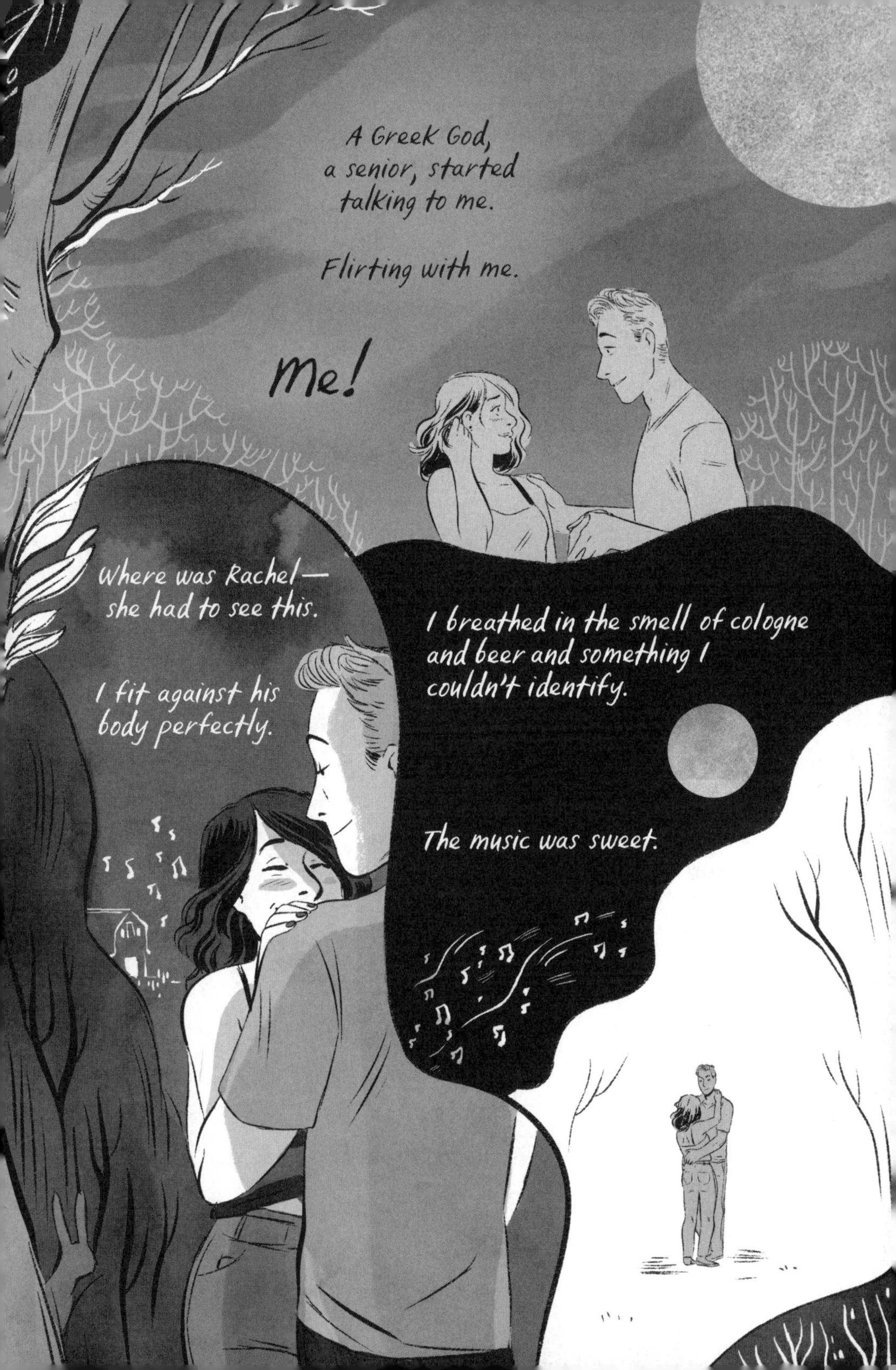
A Greek God,
a senior, started
talking to me.
Flirting with me.
me!
Where was Rachel—
she had to see this.
I fit against his
body perfectly.
I breathed in the smell of cologne
and beer and something I
couldn't identify.
The music was sweet.

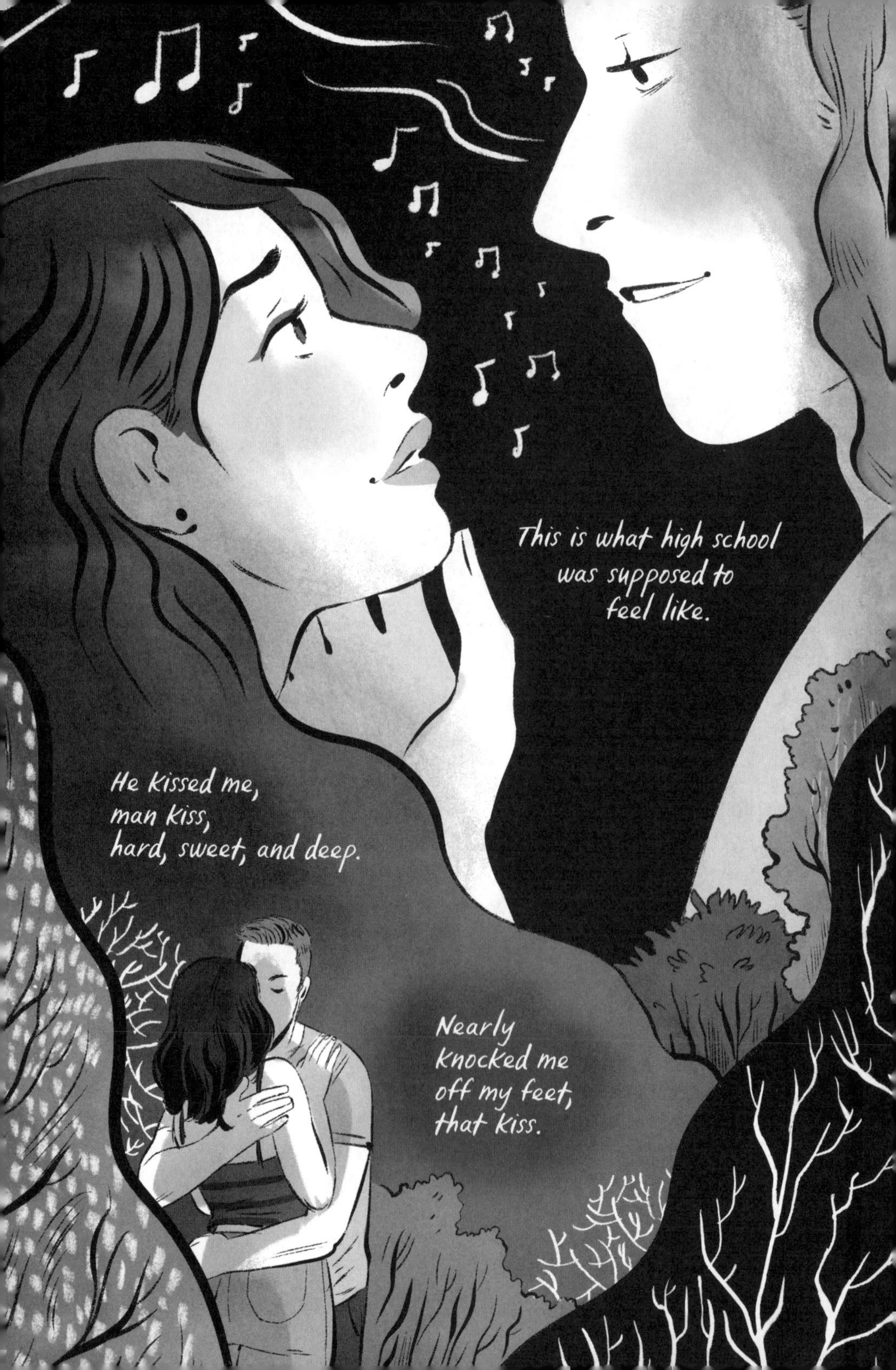
This is what high school was supposed to feel like.
He kissed me, man kiss, hard, sweet, and deep.
Nearly knocked me off my feet, that kiss.

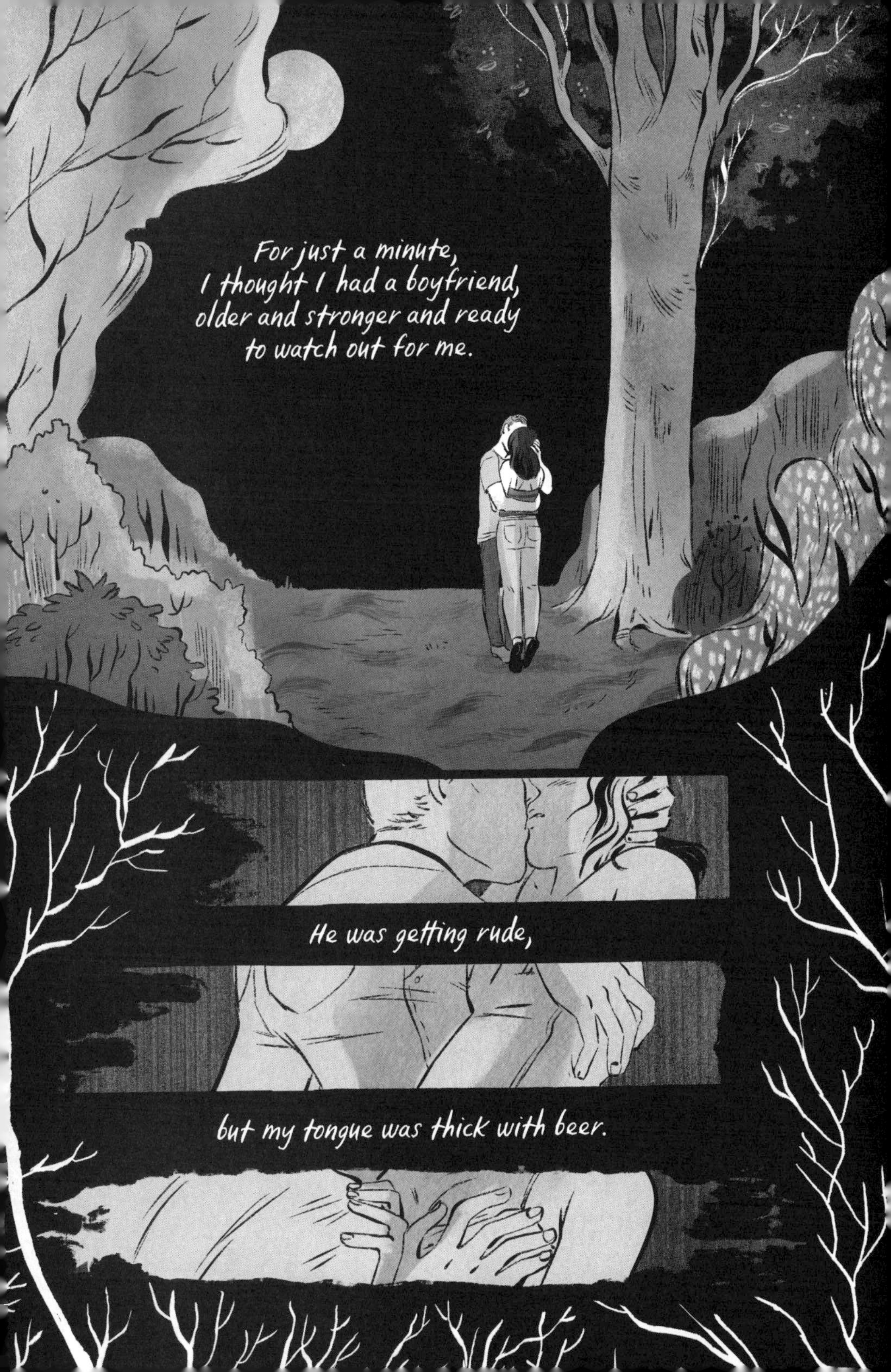
For just a minute, I thought I had a boyfriend, older and stronger and ready to watch out for me.
He was getting rude,
but my tongue was thick with beer.

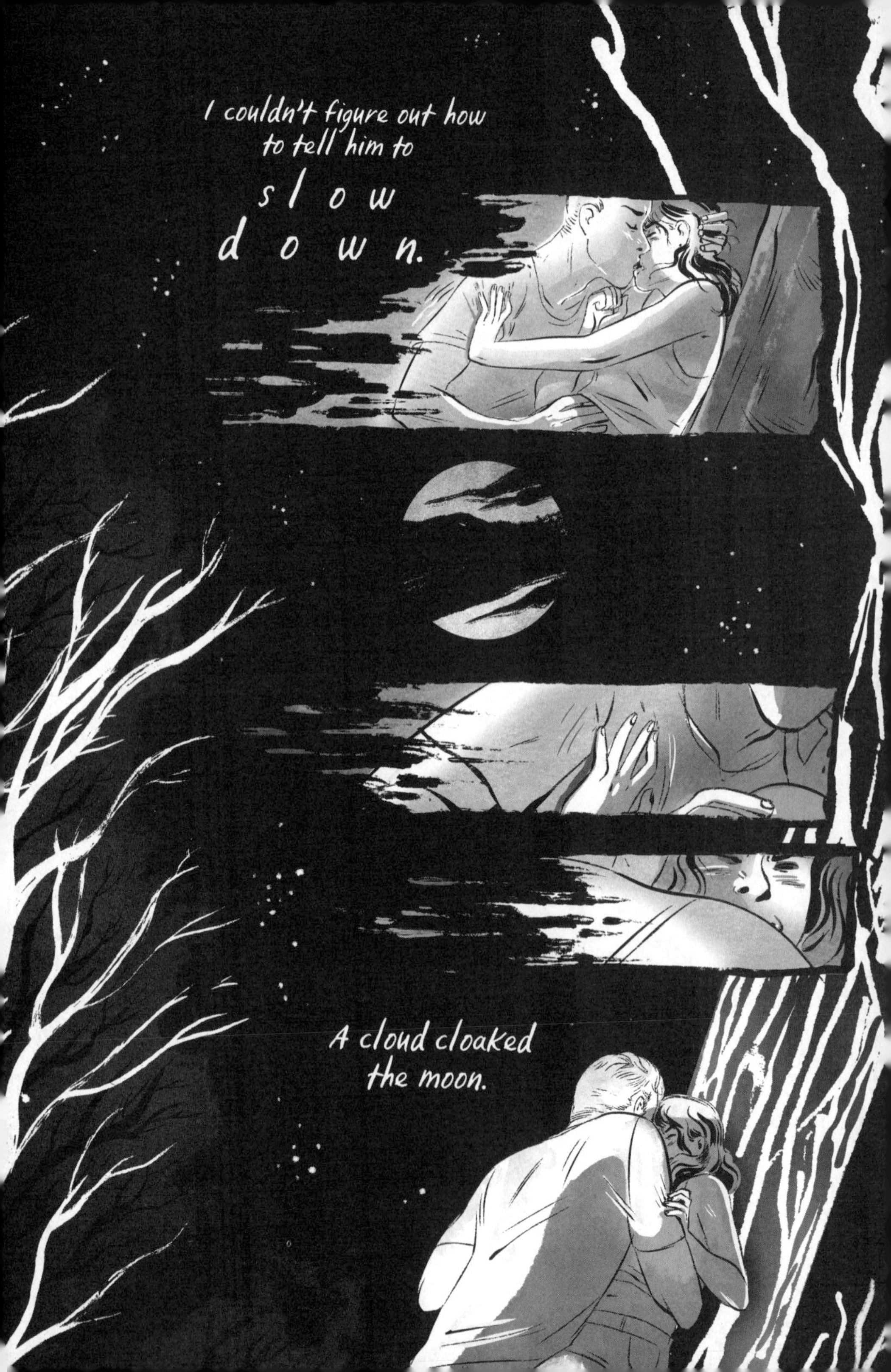
I couldn't figure out how to tell him to
s l o w
d o w n.
A cloud cloaked the moon.

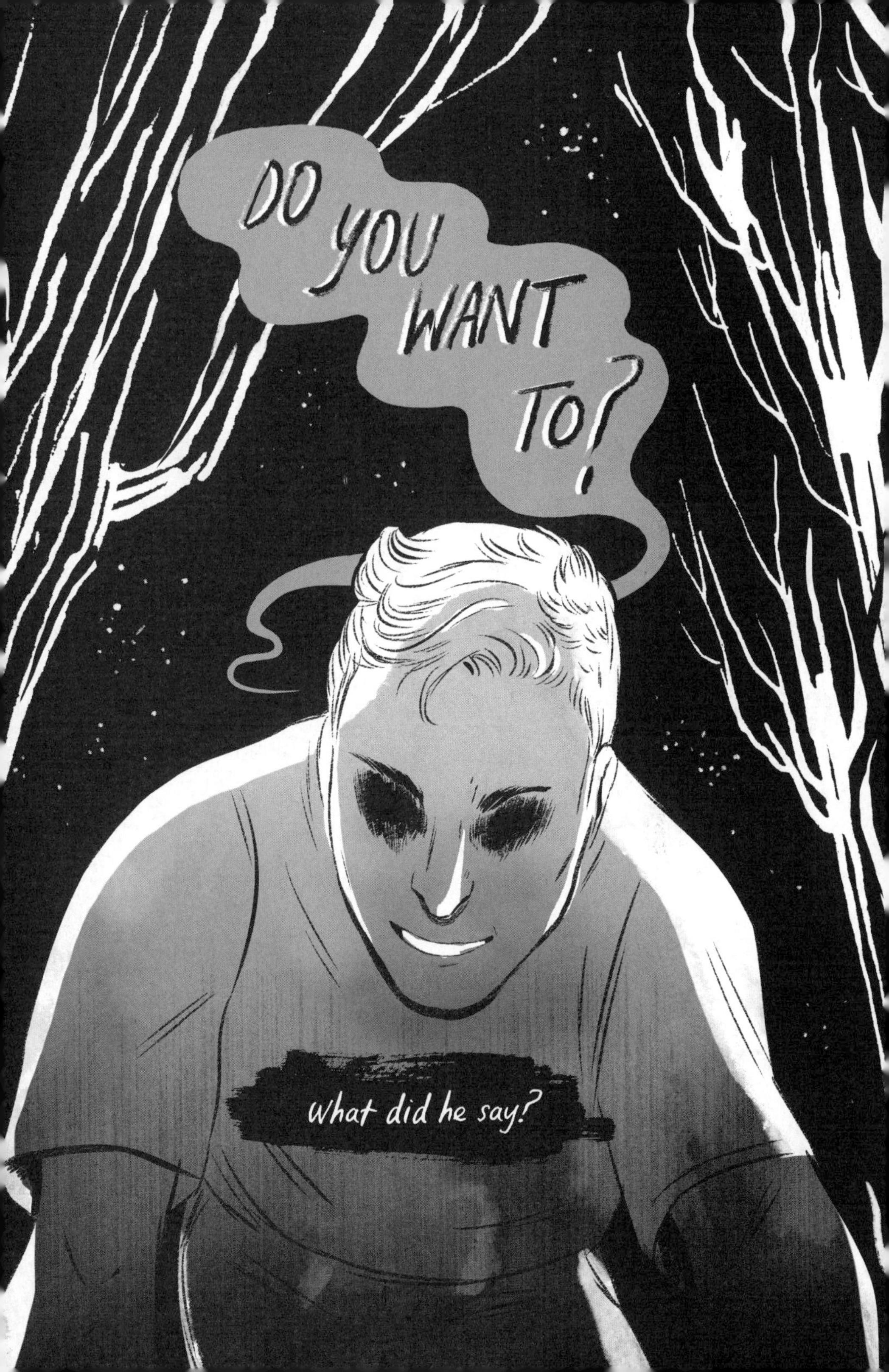
DO YOU WANT TO?
What did he say?

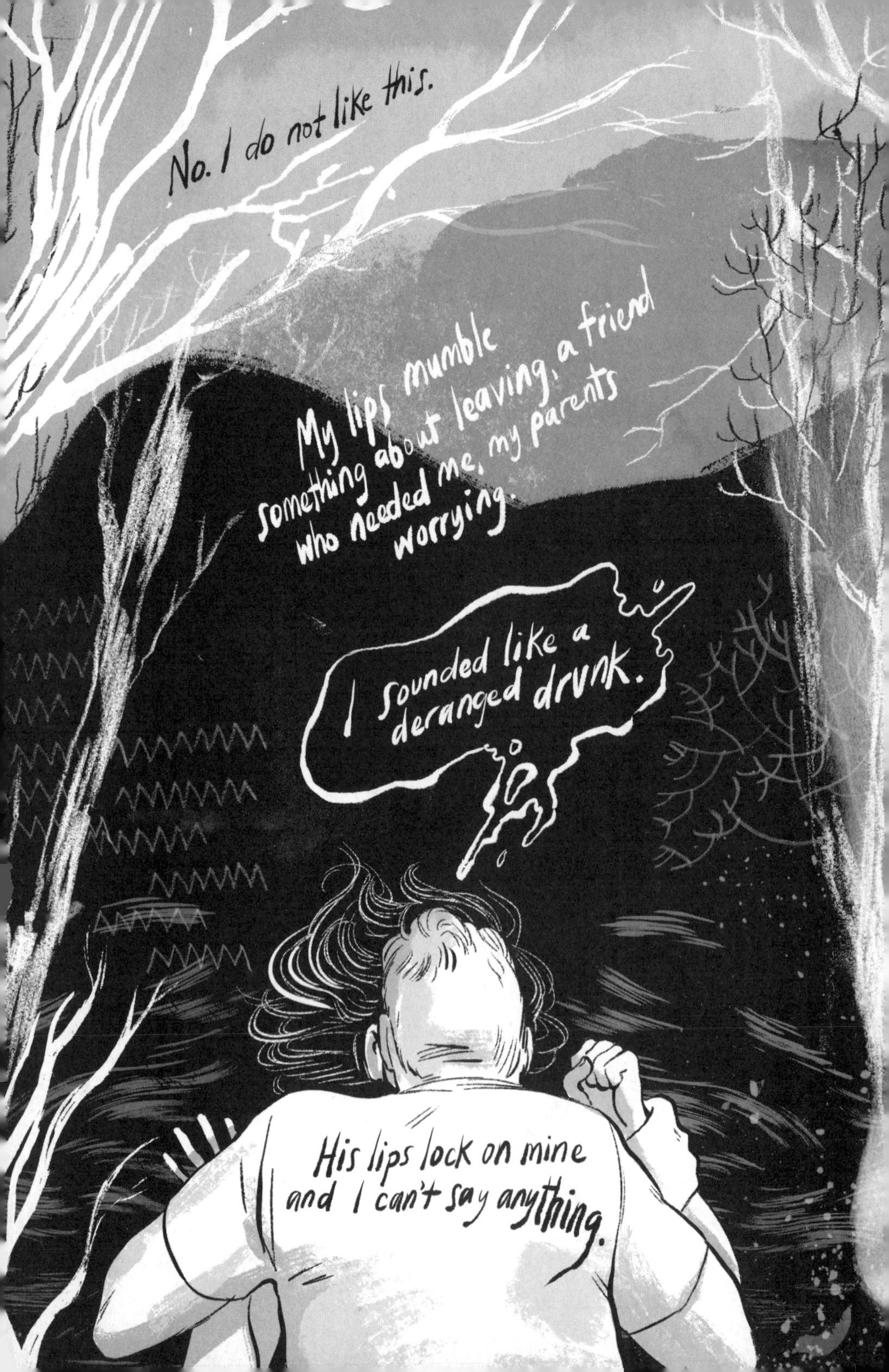
No. I do not like this.
My lips mumble something about leaving, a friend who needed me, my parents worrying.
I sounded like a deranged drunk.
His lips lock on mine and I can't say anything.

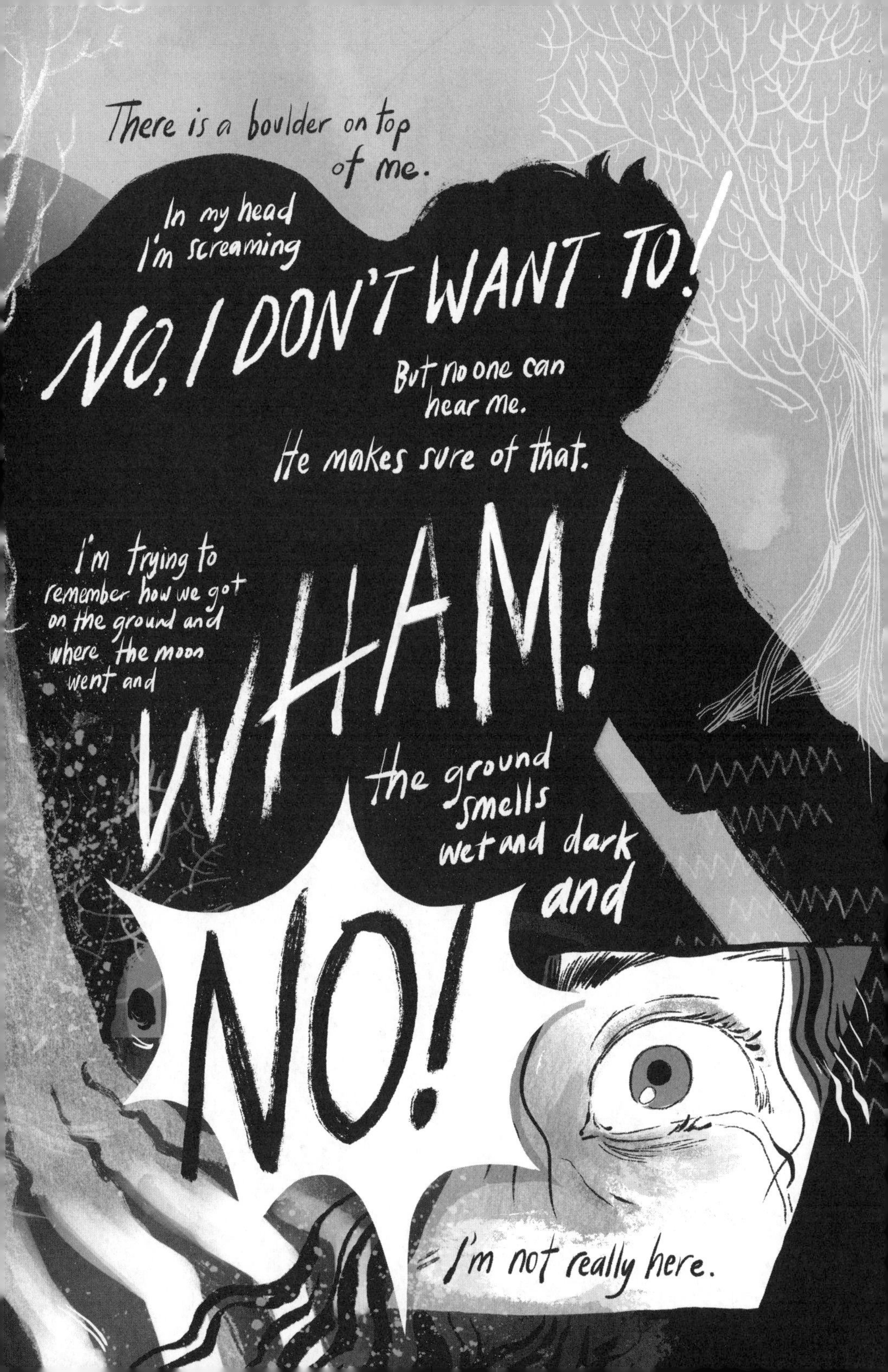
There is a boulder on top of me.
In my head I'm screaming
NO, I DON'T WANT TO!
But no one can hear me.
He makes sure of that.
I'm trying to remember how we got on the ground and where the moon went and
WHAM!
the ground smells wet and dark and
NO!
I'm not really here.

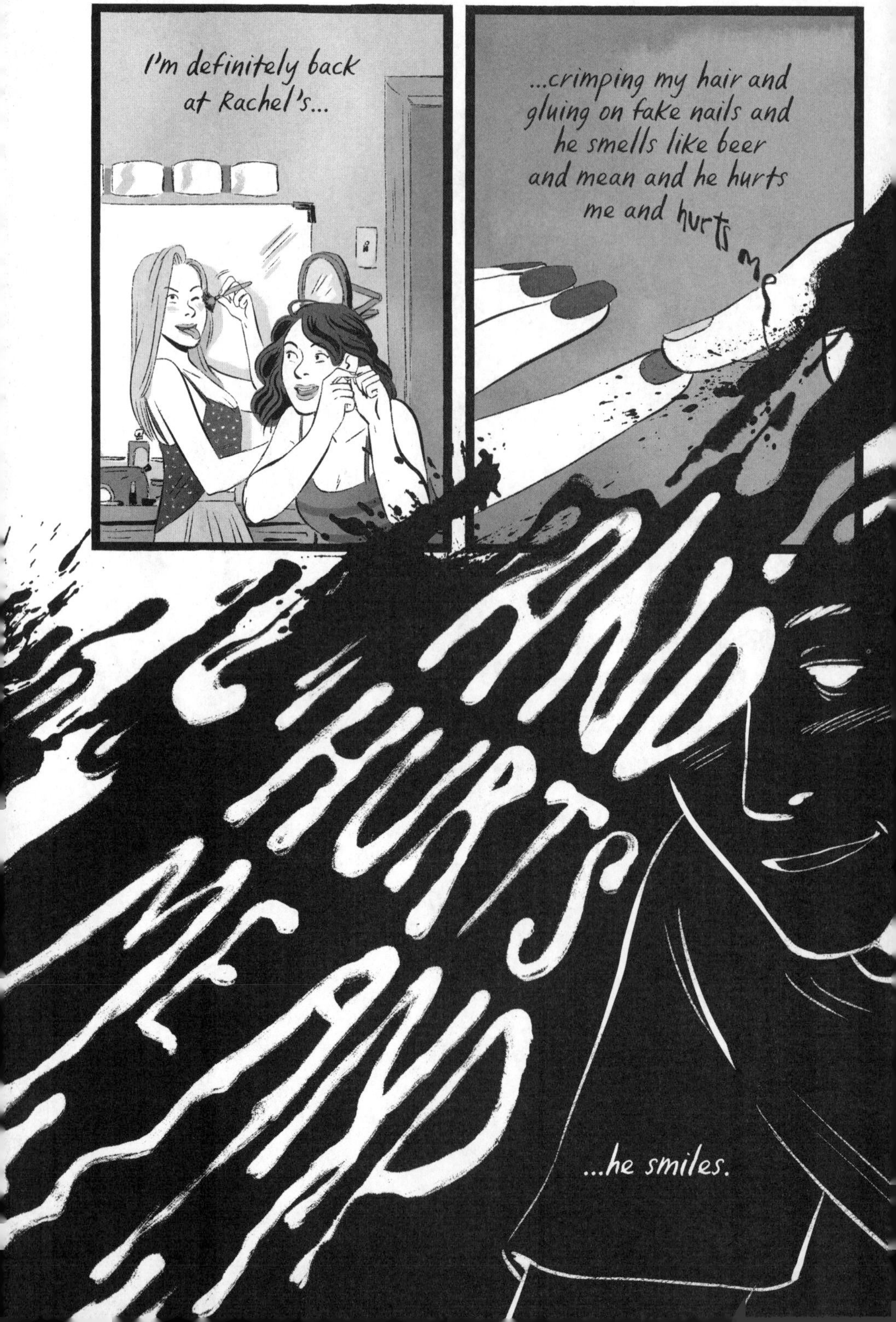
I'm definitely back at Rachel's...
...crimping my hair and gluing on fake nails and he smells like beer and mean and he hurts me and hurts me
AND HURTS ME AND
...he smiles.

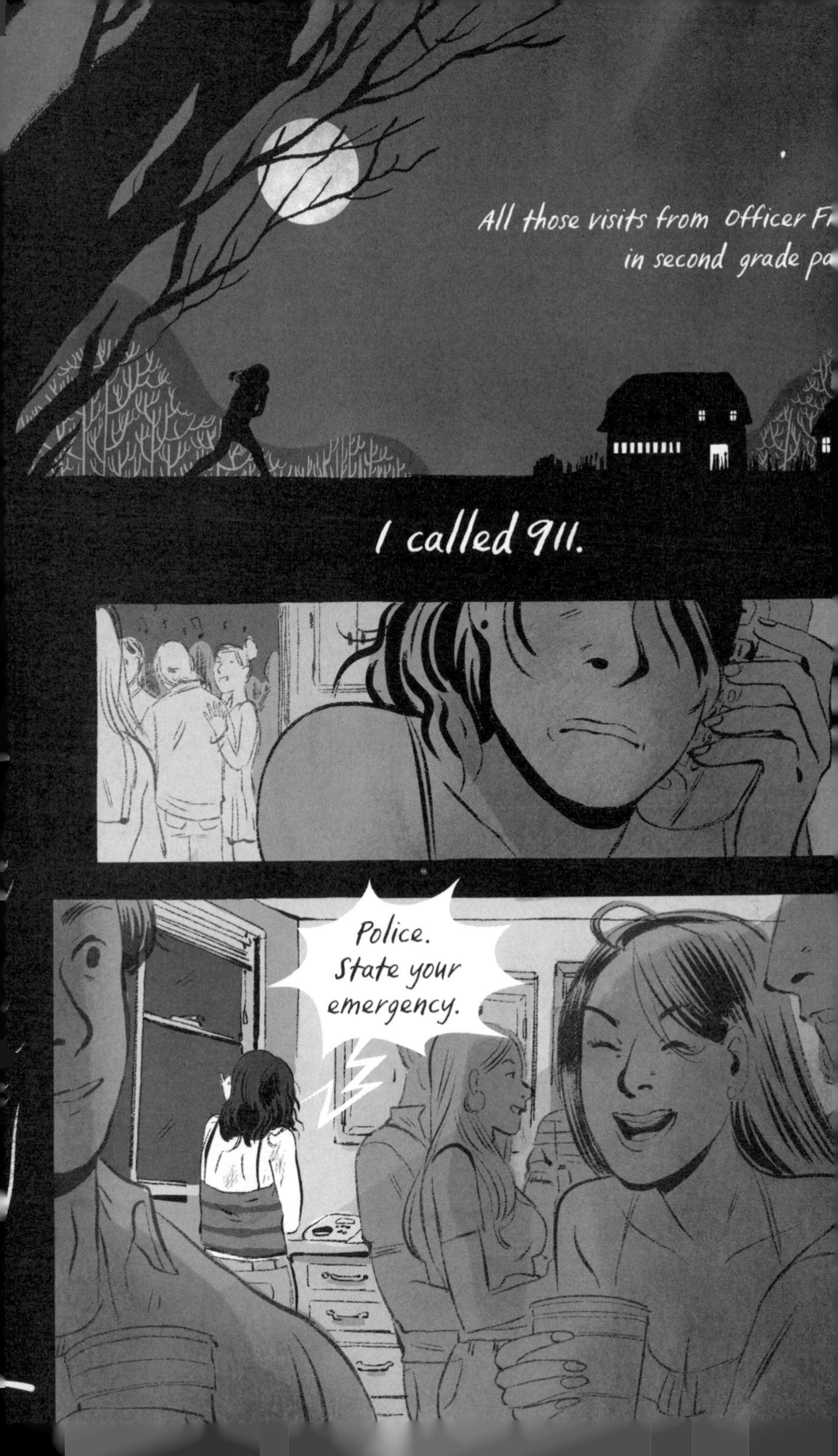
All those visits from Officer
in second grade
I called 911.
Police. State your emergency.

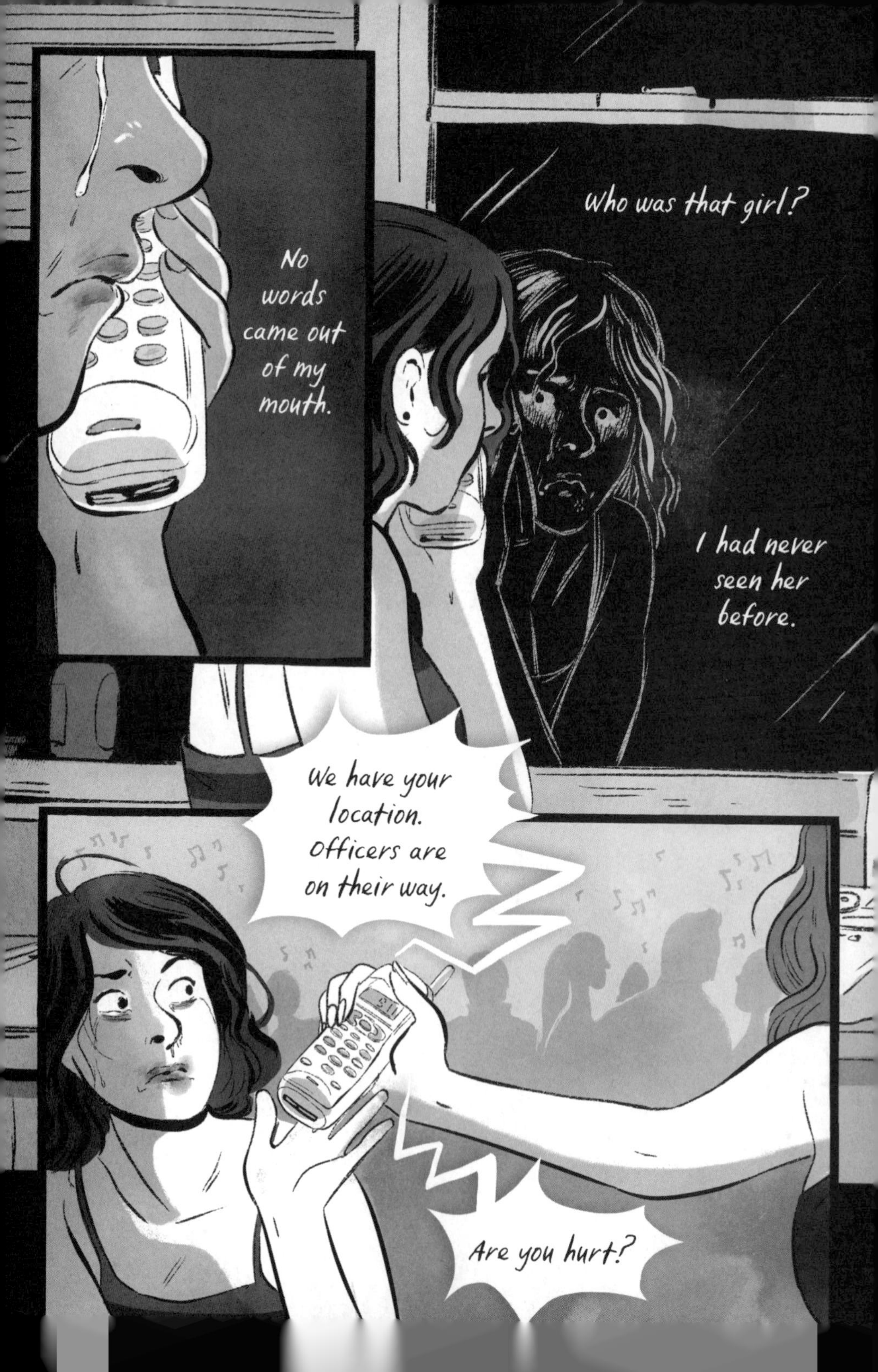
No words came out of my mouth.
Who was that girl?
I had never seen her before.
We have your location. Officers are on their way.
Are you hurt?

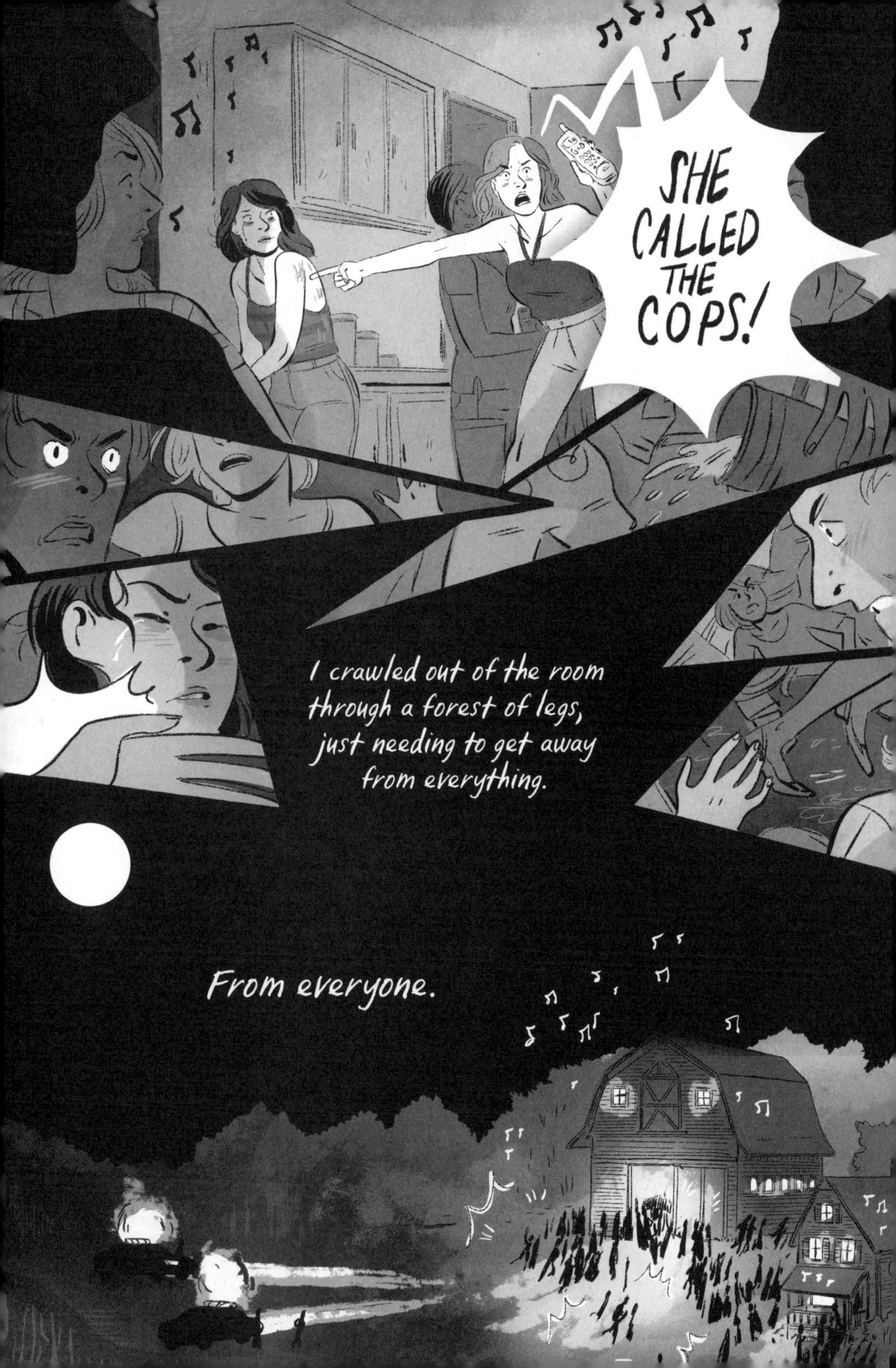
SHE CALLED THE COPS!
I crawled out of the room through a forest of legs, just needing to get away from everything.
From everyone.

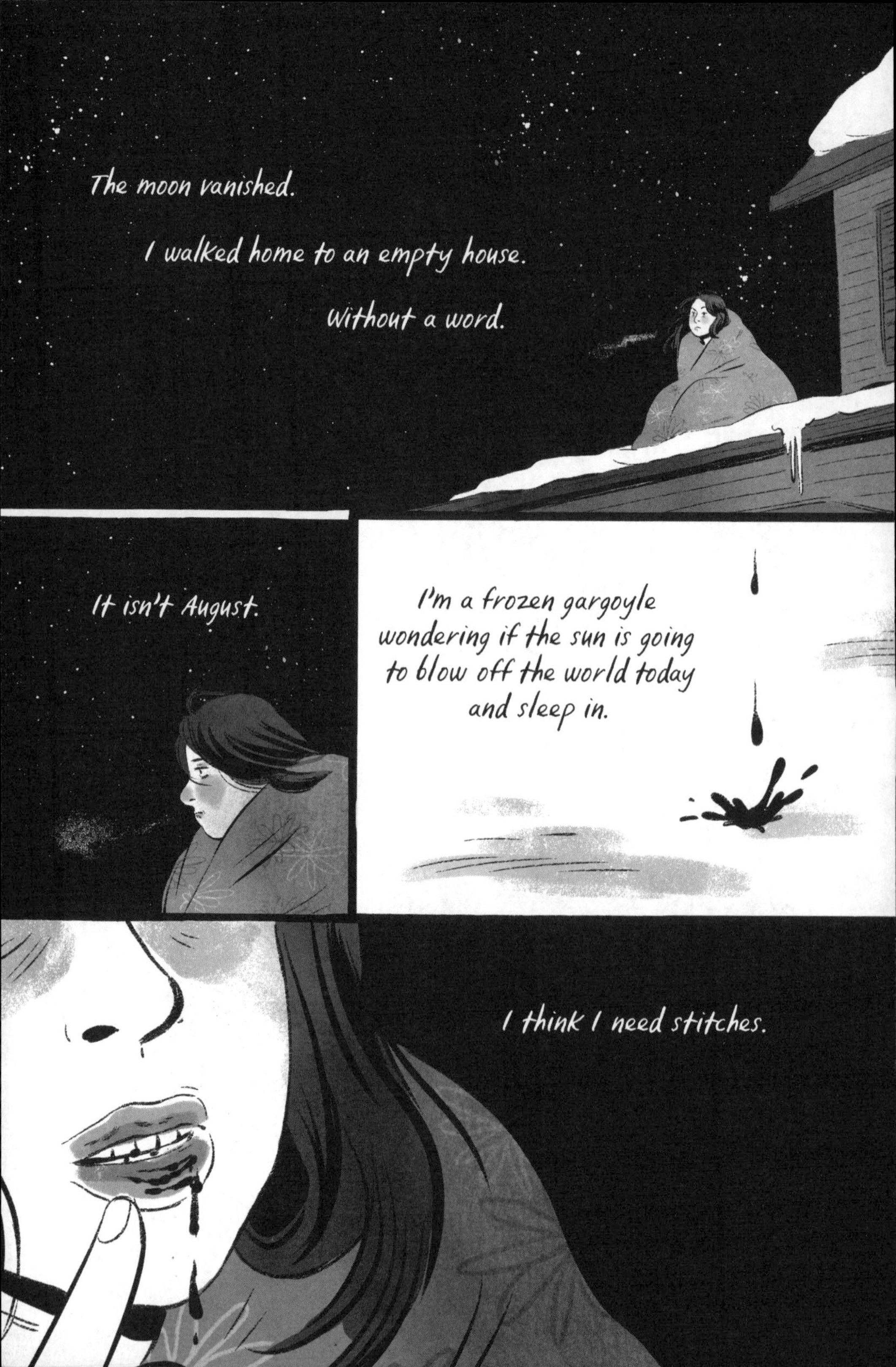
The moon vanished.
I walked home to an empty house.
Without a word.
It isn't August.
I'm a frozen gargoyle wondering if the sun is going to blow off the world today and sleep in.
I think I need stitches.

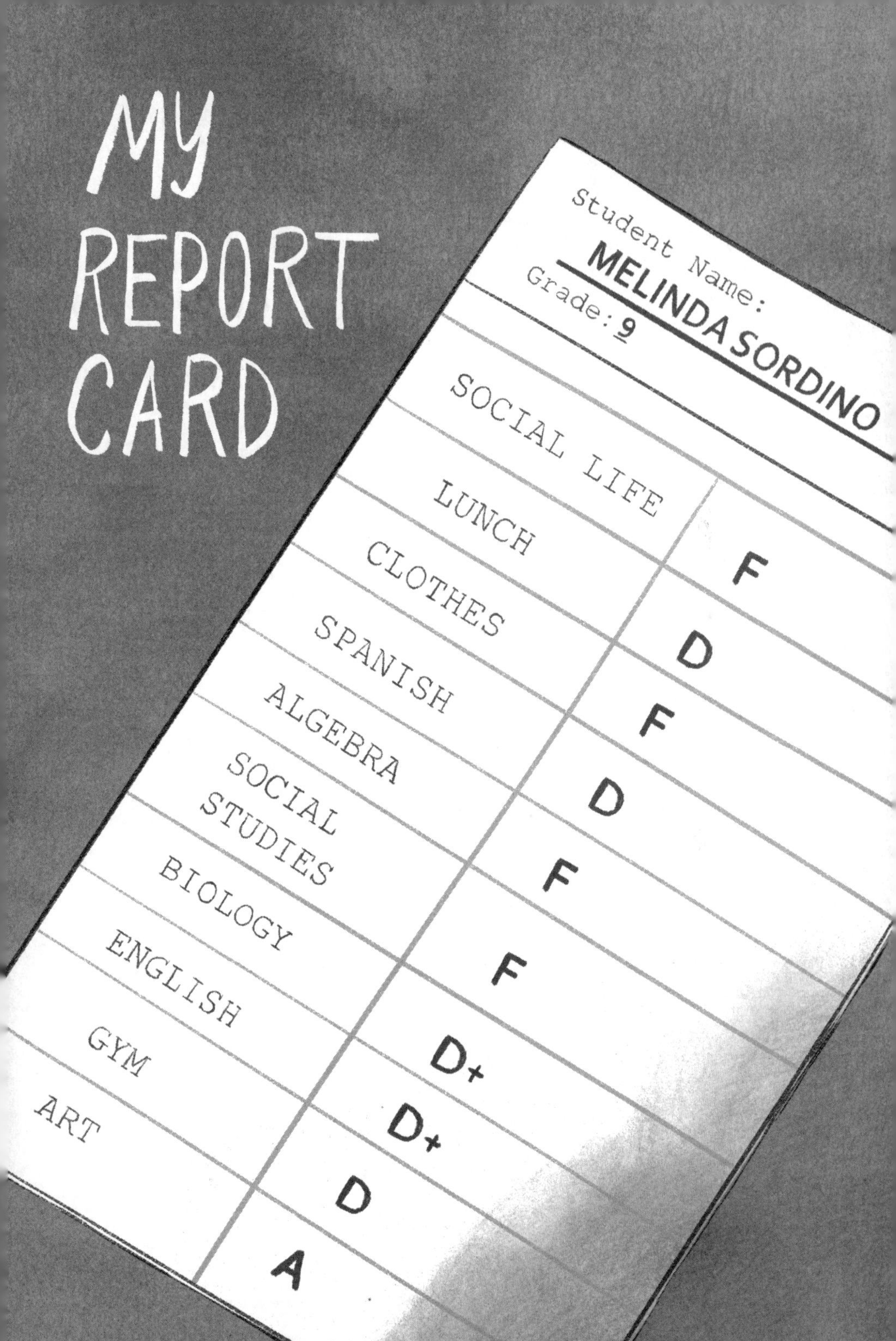
MY REPORT CARD
Student Name:
MELINDA SORDINO
Grade: 9
SOCIAL LIFE
F
LUNCH
D
CLOTHES
F
SPANISH
D
ALGEBRA
F
SOCIAL STUDIES
F
BIOLOGY
D+
ENGLISH
D+
GYM
D
ART
A

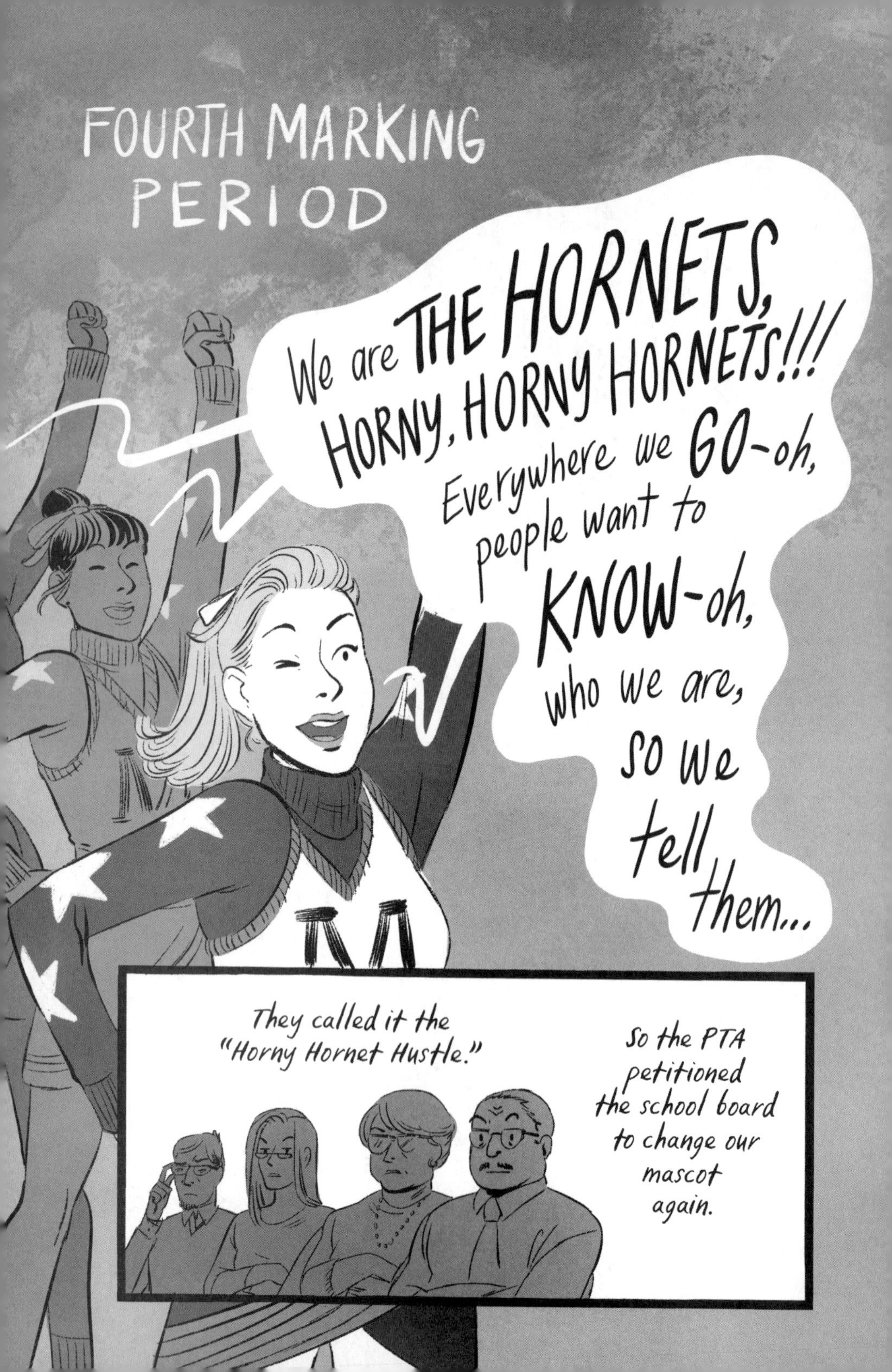
FOURTH MARKING PERIOD
We are THE HORNETS, HORNY, HORNY HORNETS!!! Everywhere we GO-oh, people want to KNOW-oh, who we are, so we tell them...
They called it the "Horny Hornet Hustle."
So the PTA petitioned the school board to change our mascot again.

The student council started a counter-petition,
describing the psychological harm we have all
suffered from this year's lack of identity.

We, the students of Merryweather High,
have become proud of our Hornet selves.
We are tenacious, stinging, clever.
We are a hive, a community of students.

Don't take away our Hornetdom.

We are Hornets.

Leslie
Will Brown
Caitlyn Carli

It won't be a real issue
until football season
starts up again.

Our baseball team
always stinks.

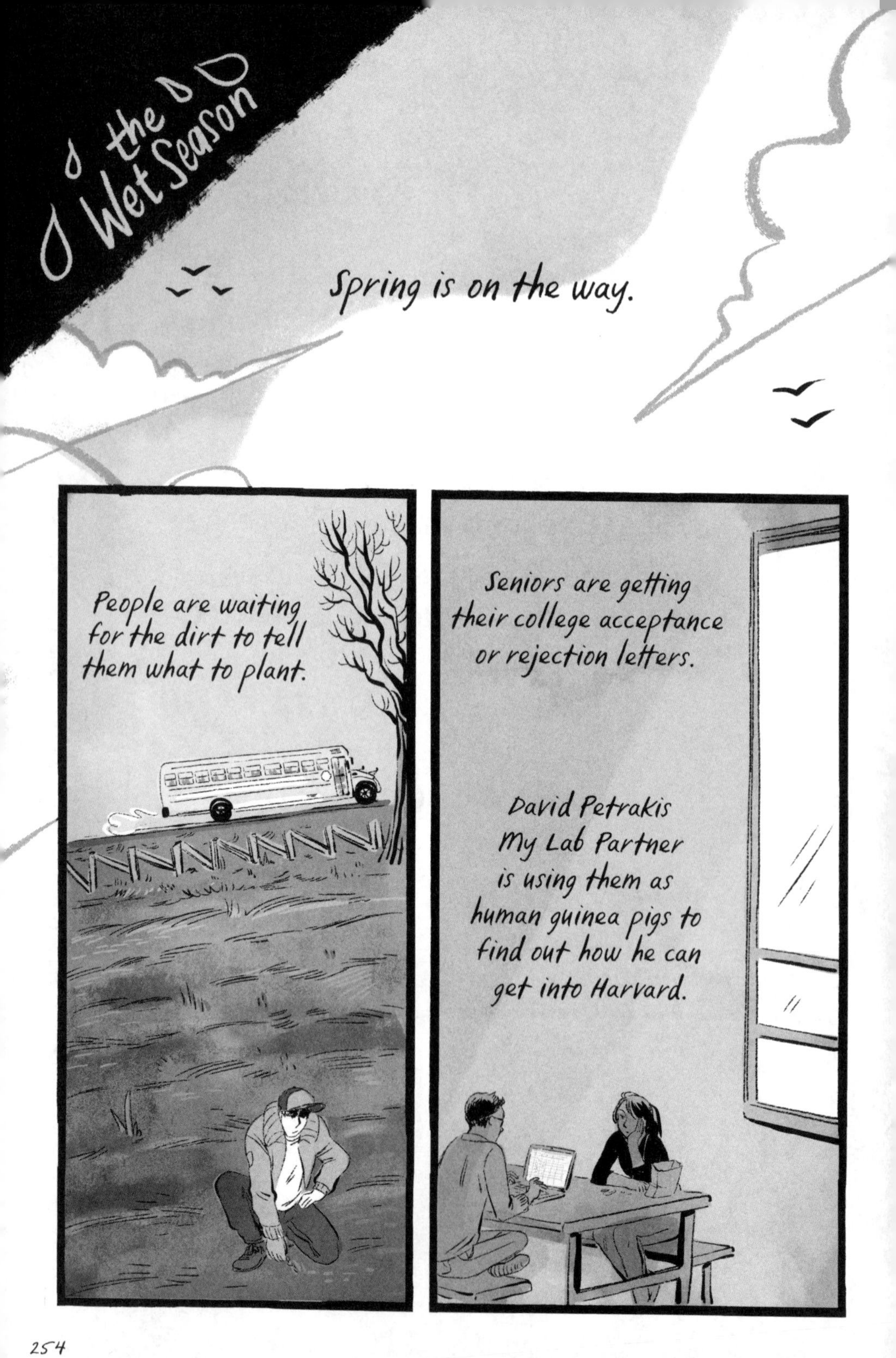
the Wet Season
Spring is on the way.
People are waiting for the dirt to tell them what to plant.
Seniors are getting their college acceptance or rejection letters.
David Petrakis My Lab Partner is using them as human guinea pigs to find out how he can get into Harvard.

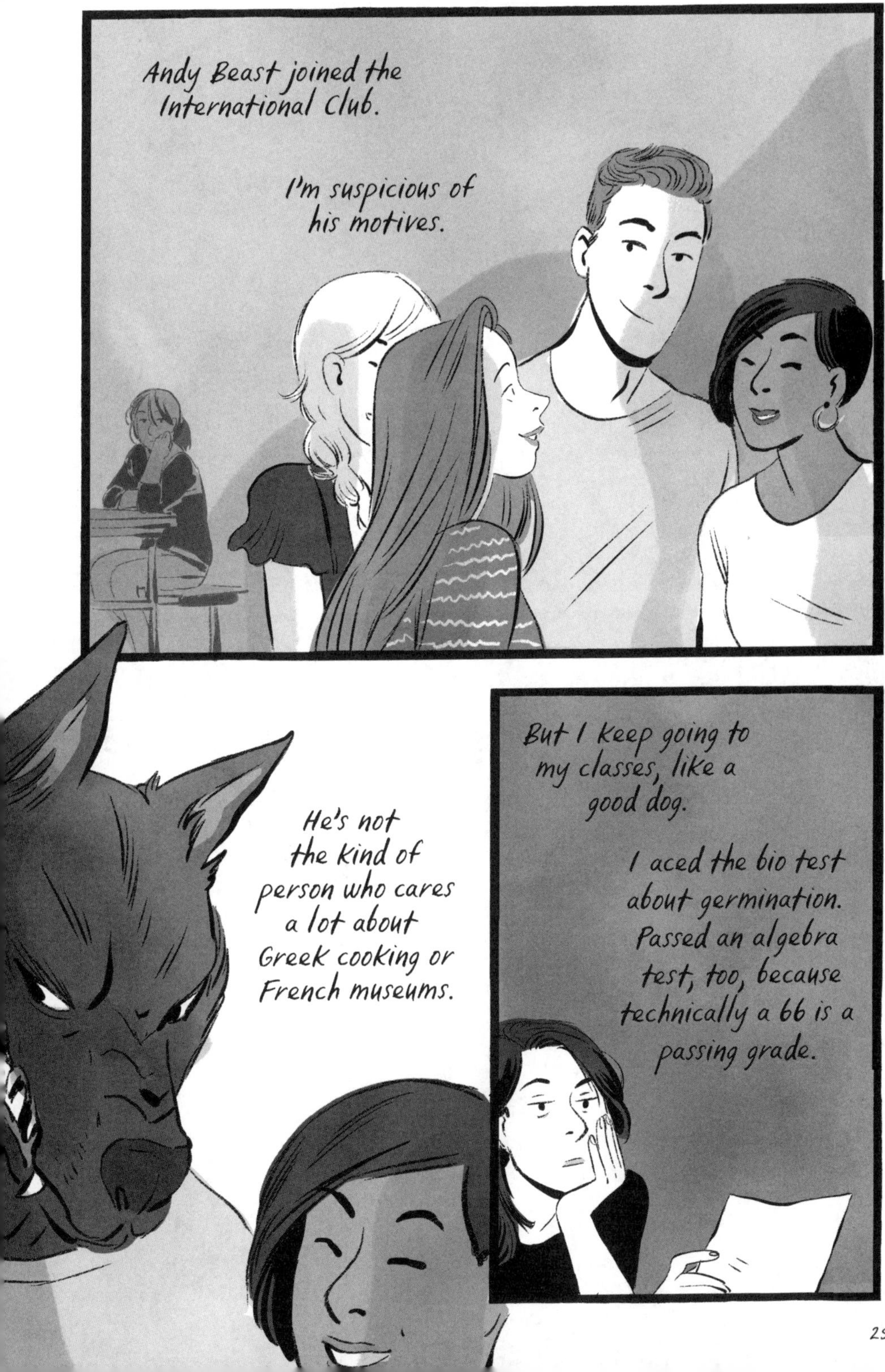
Andy Beast joined the International Club.
I'm suspicious of his motives.
He's not the kind of person who cares a lot about Greek cooking or French museums.
But I keep going to my classes, like a good dog.
I aced the bio test about germination. Passed an algebra test, too, because technically a 66 is a passing grade.

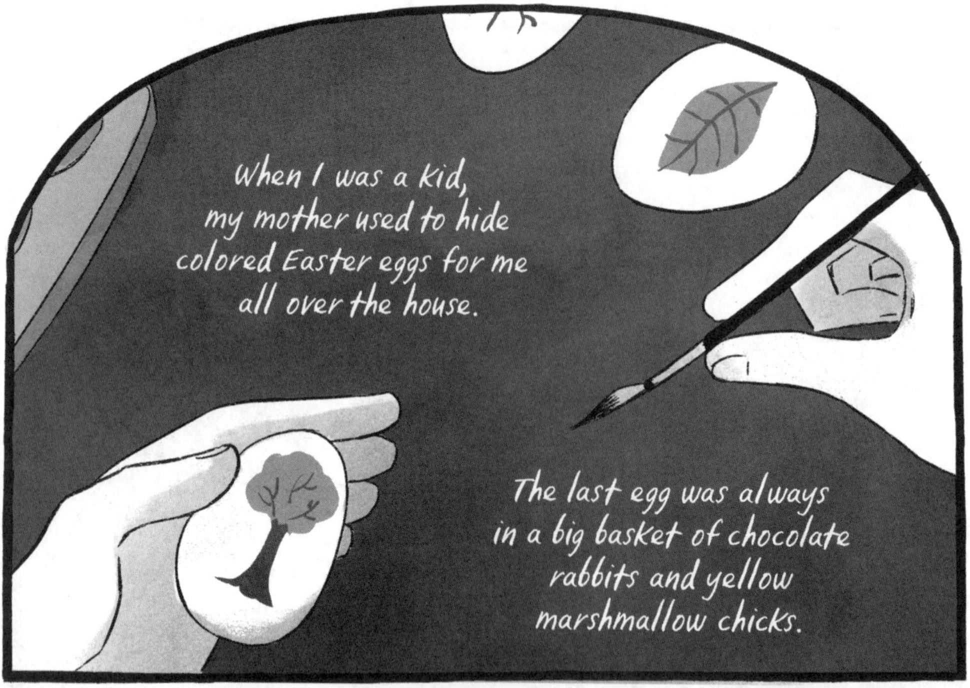
When I was a kid, my mother used to hide colored Easter eggs for me all over the house.
The last egg was always in a big basket of chocolate rabbits and yellow marshmallow chicks.
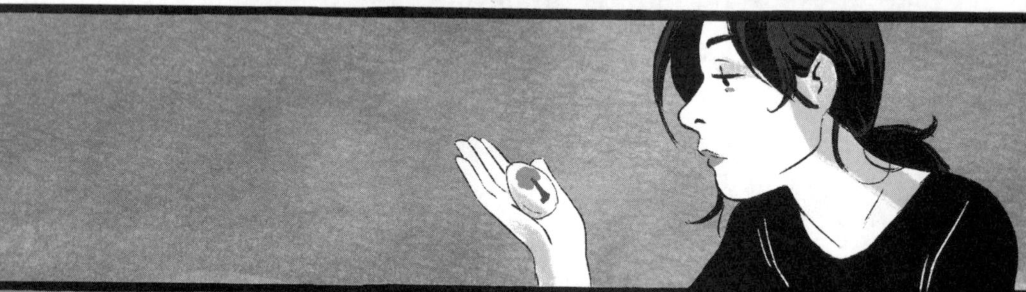
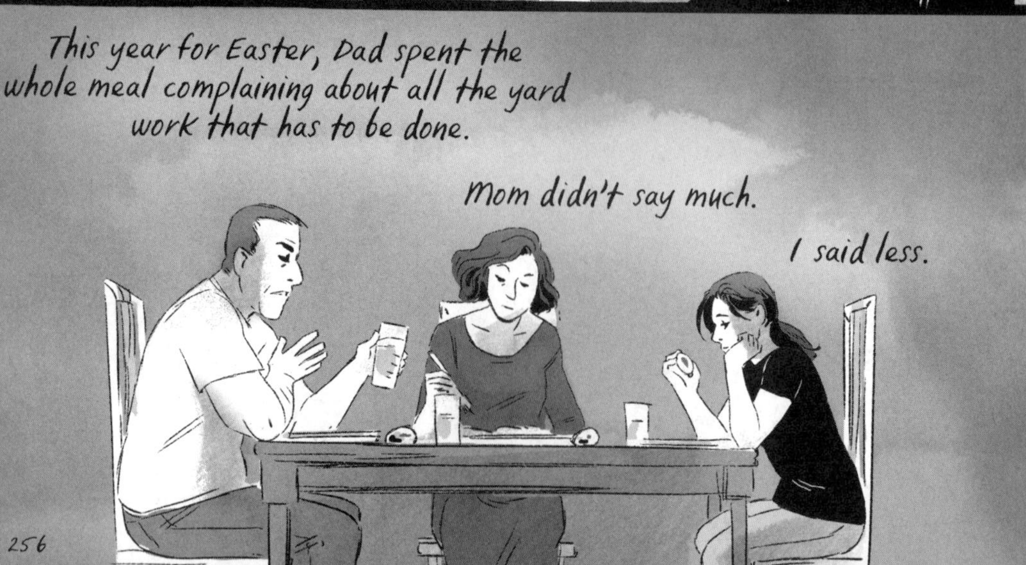
This year for Easter, Dad spent the whole meal complaining about all the yard work that has to be done.
Mom didn't say much.
I said less.

SPRING BREAK

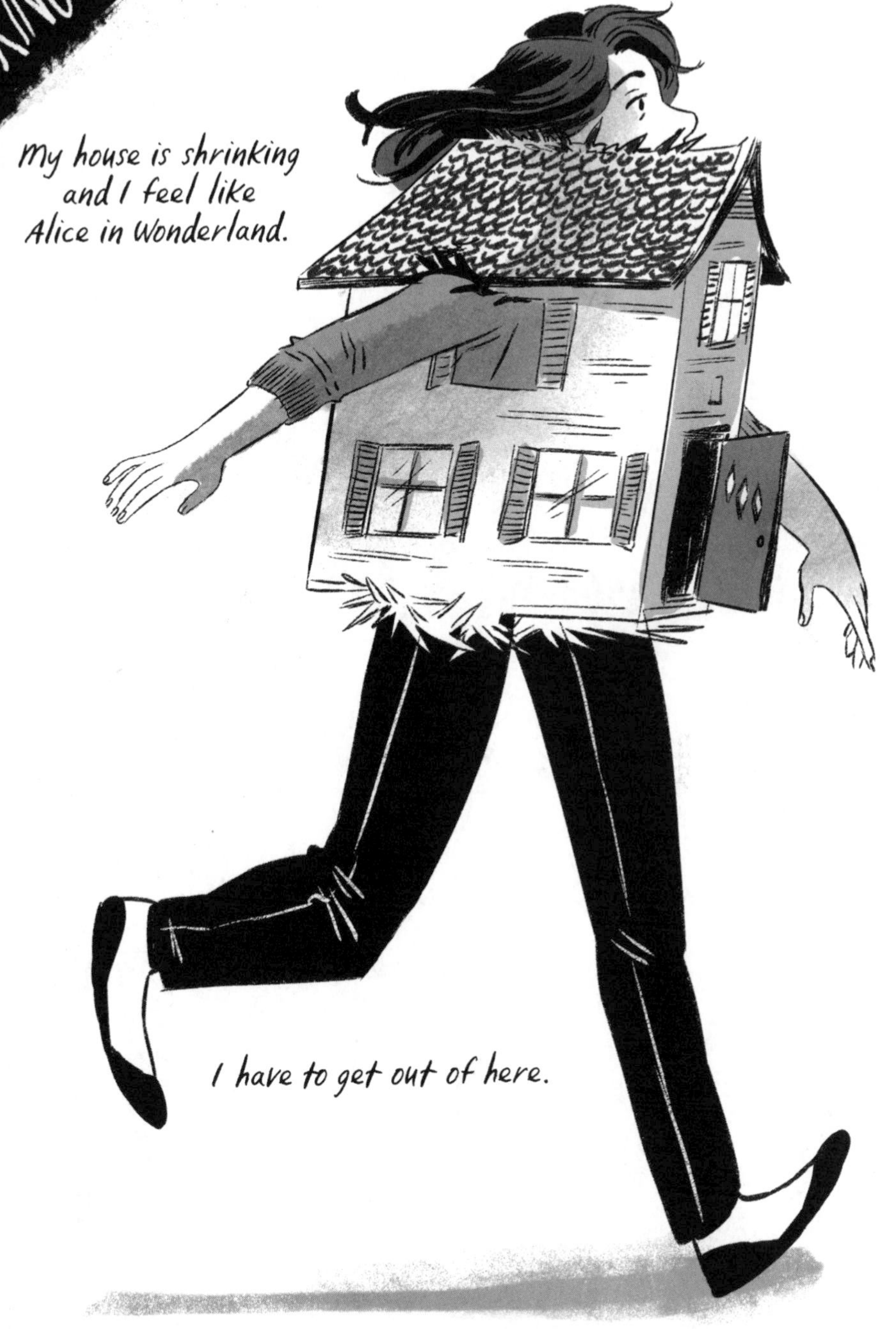
My house is shrinking and I feel like Alice in Wonderland.
I have to get out of here.

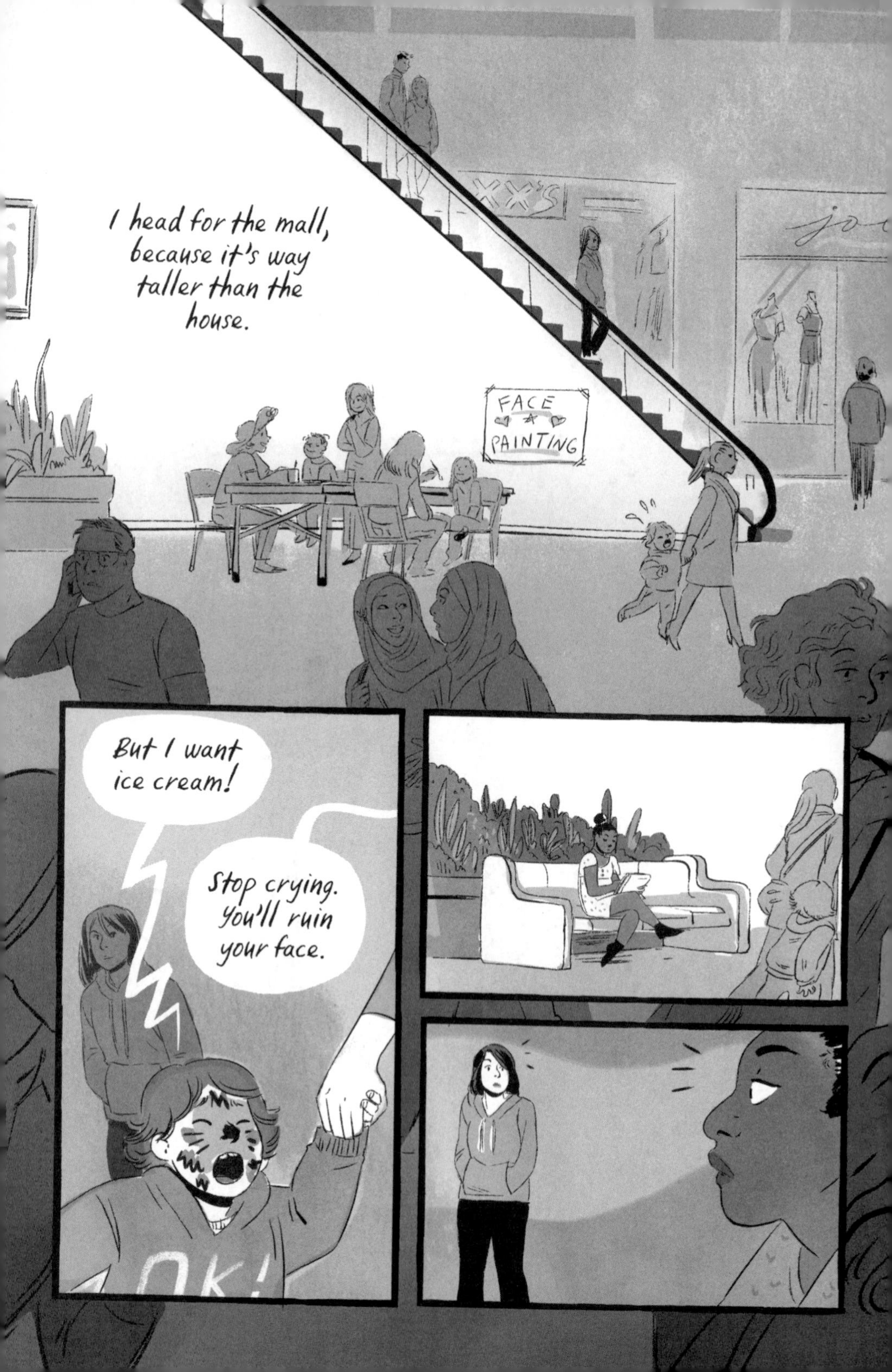
I head for the mall, because it's way taller than the house.
FACE PAINTING
But I want ice cream!
Stop crying. You'll ruin your face.
OK!

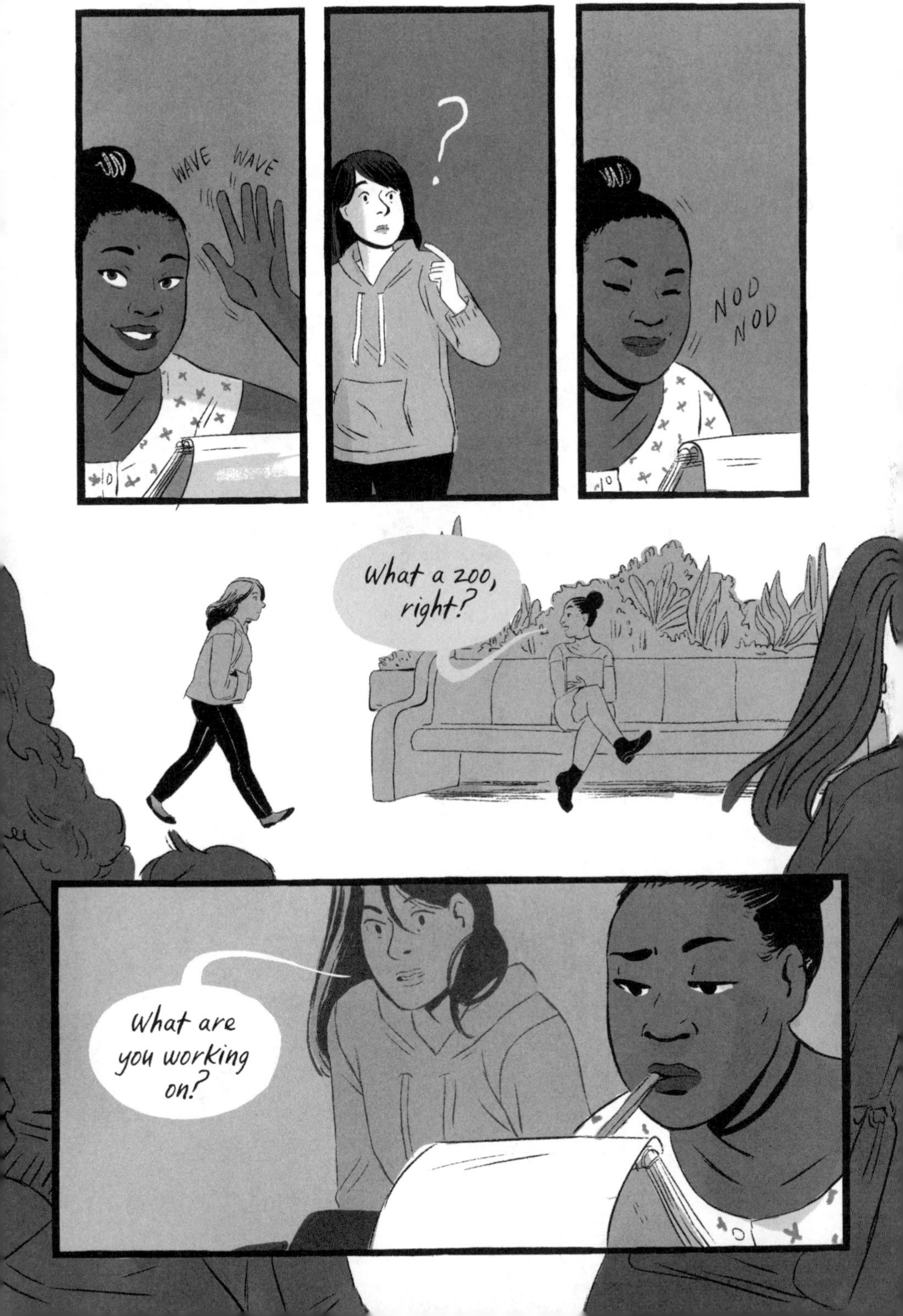
WAVE WAVE
?
NOD NOD
What a zoo, right?
What are you working on?

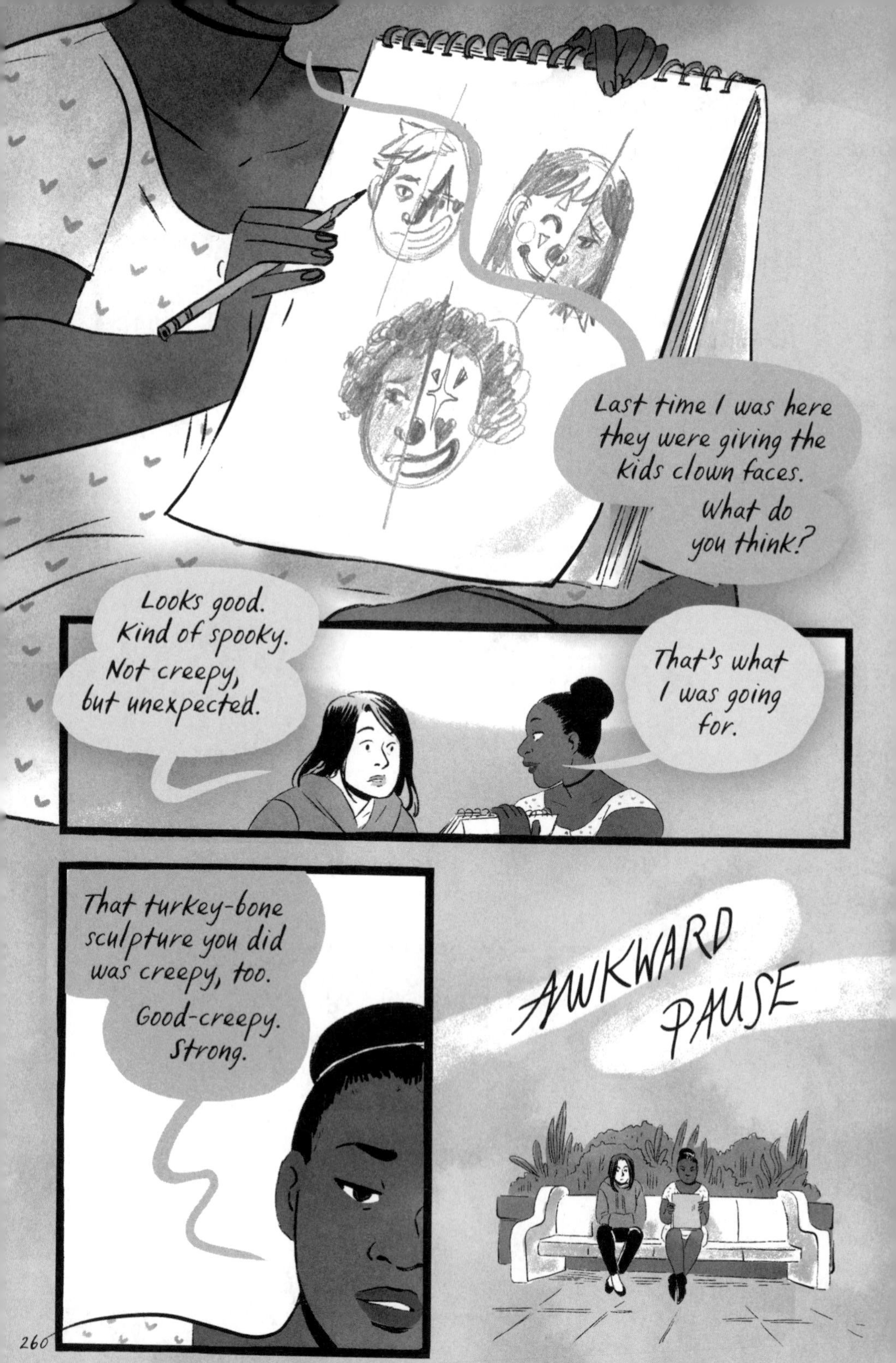
Last time I was here they were giving the kids clown faces.
What do you think?
Looks good. Kind of spooky.
Not creepy, but unexpected.
That's what I was going for.
That turkey-bone sculpture you did was creepy, too.
Good-creepy. Strong.
AWKWARD PAUSE

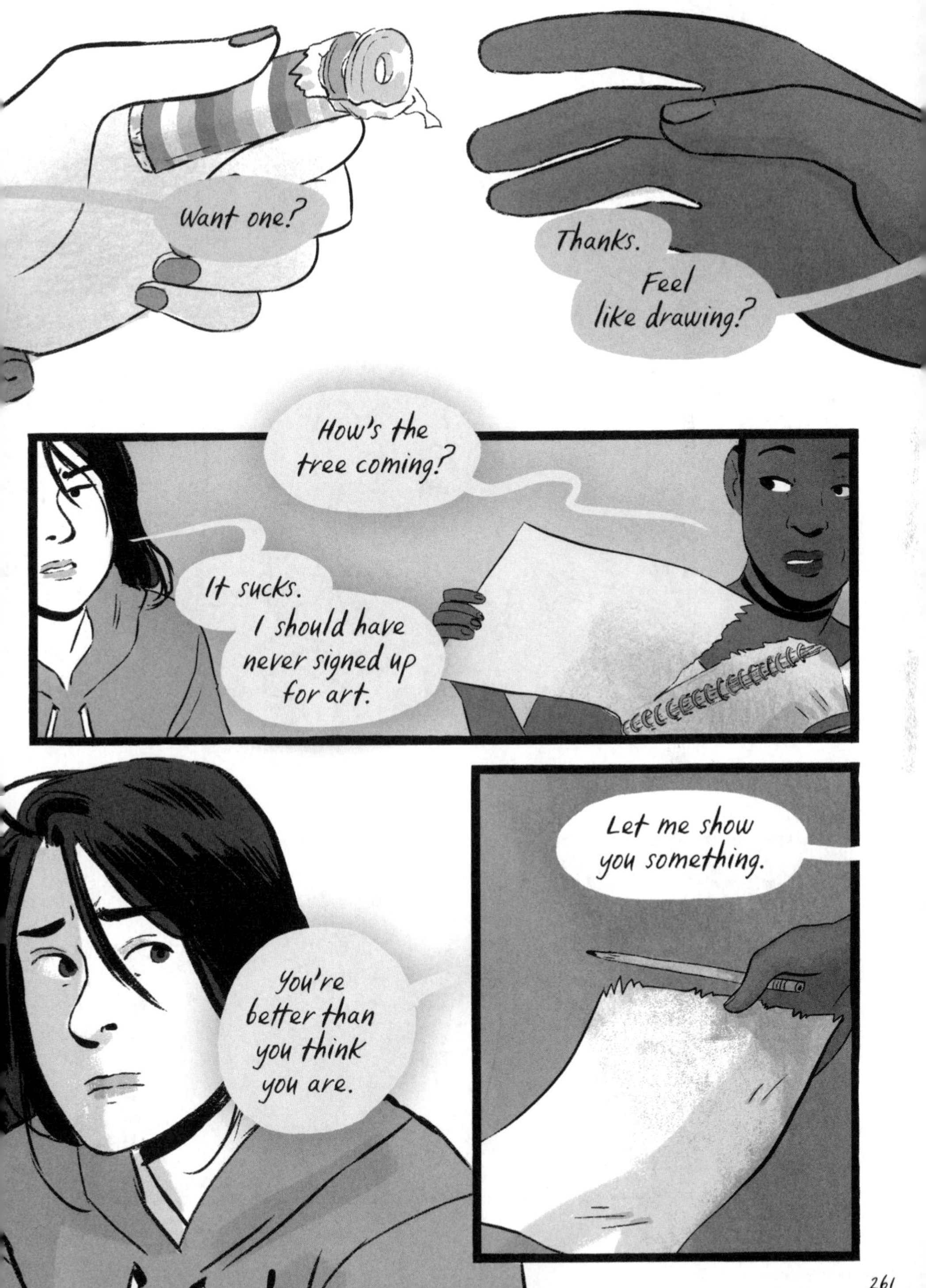
Want one?
Thanks.
Feel like drawing?
How's the tree coming?
It sucks.
I should have never signed up for art.
You're better than you think you are.
Let me show you something.

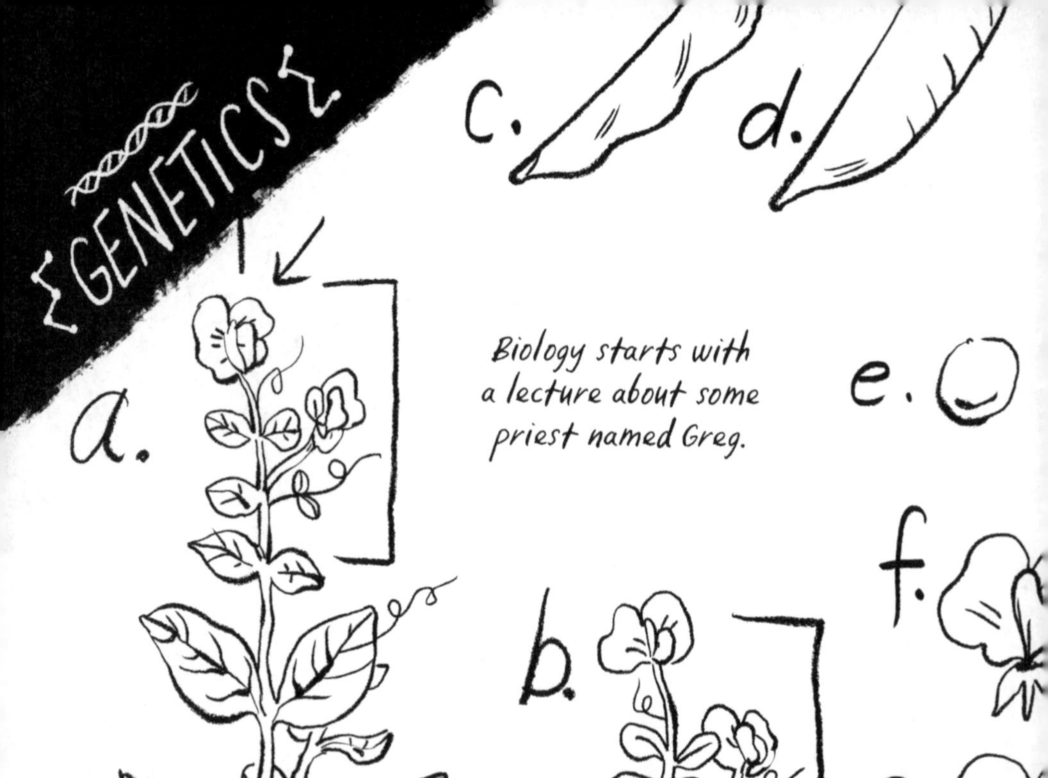
GENETICS
c.
d.
a.
Biology starts with a lecture about some priest named Greg.
e.
f.
b.
g.

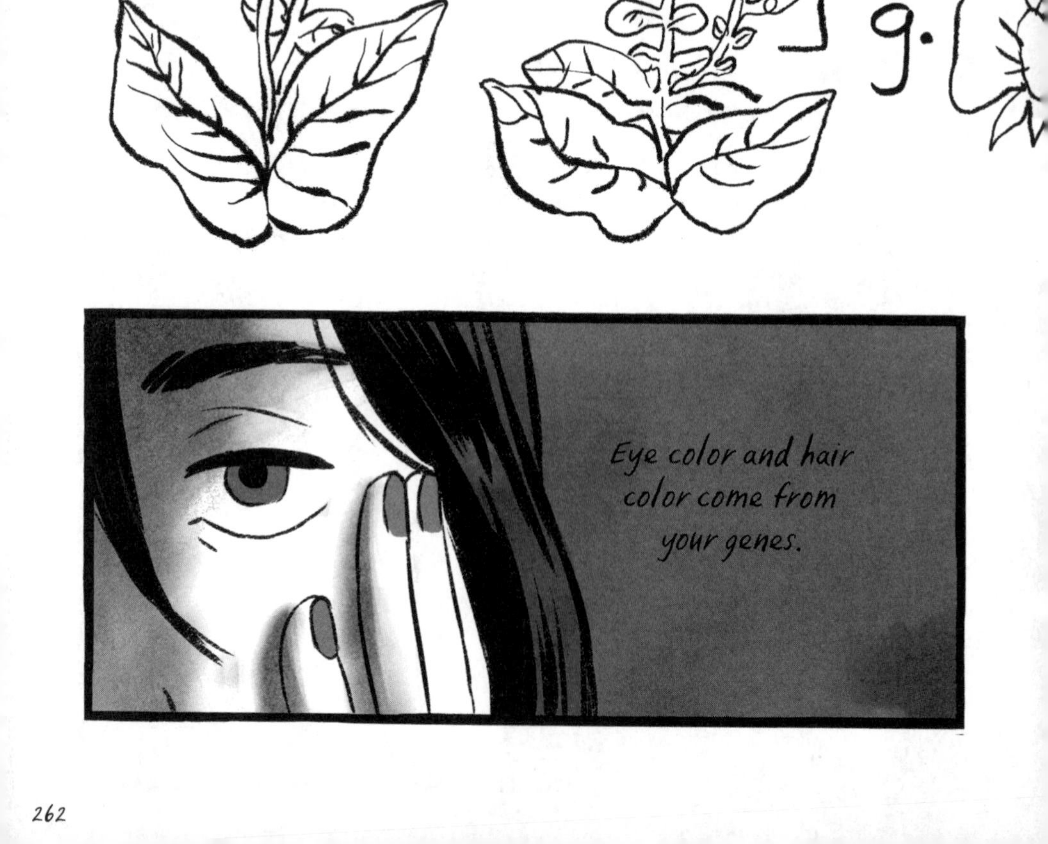
Eye color and hair color come from your genes.

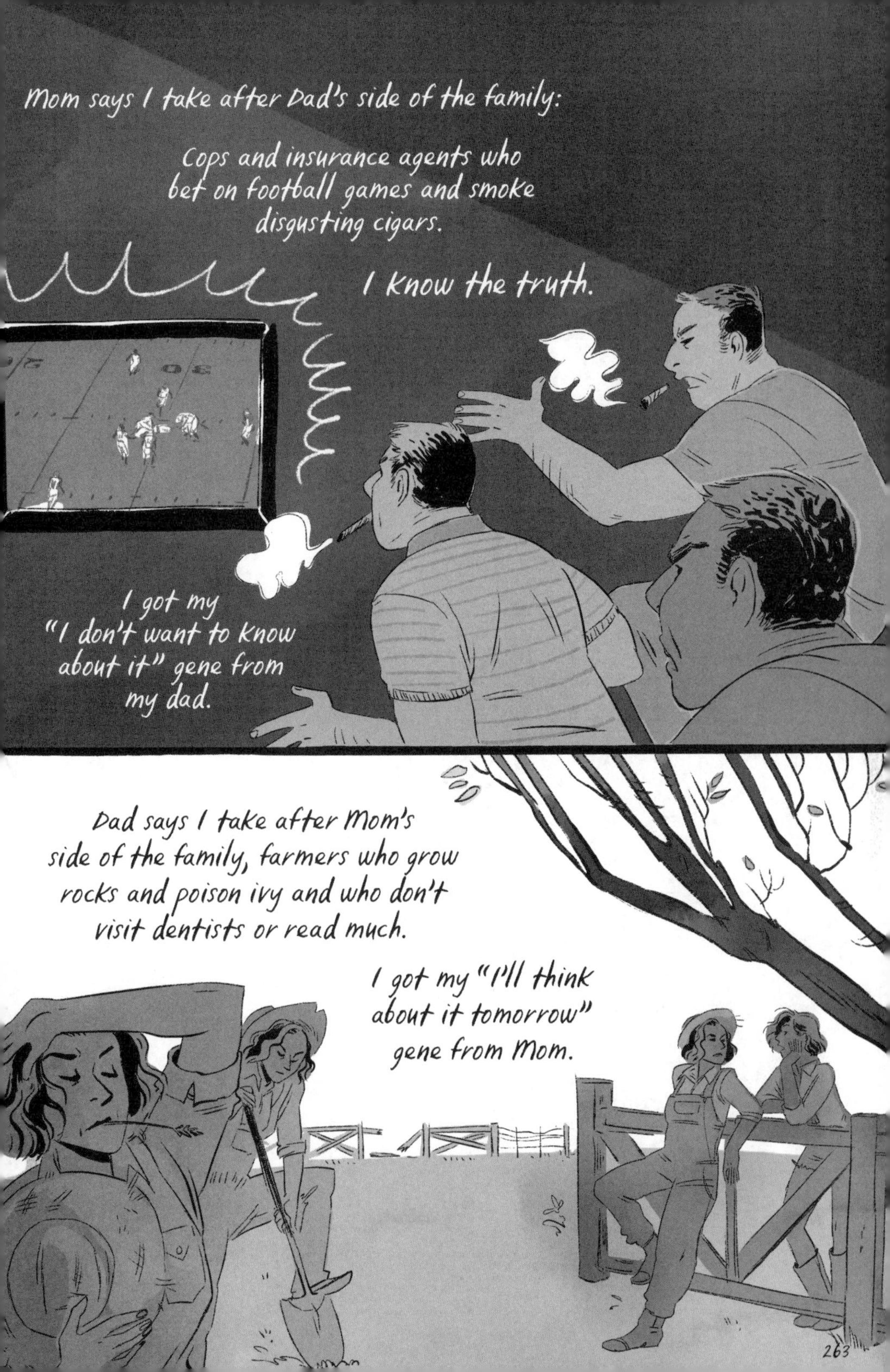
Mom says I take after Dad's side of the family:
Cops and insurance agents who bet on football games and smoke disgusting cigars.
I know the truth.
I got my "I don't want to know about it" gene from my dad.
Dad says I take after Mom's side of the family, farmers who grow rocks and poison ivy and who don't visit dentists or read much.
I got my "I'll think about it tomorrow" gene from Mom.

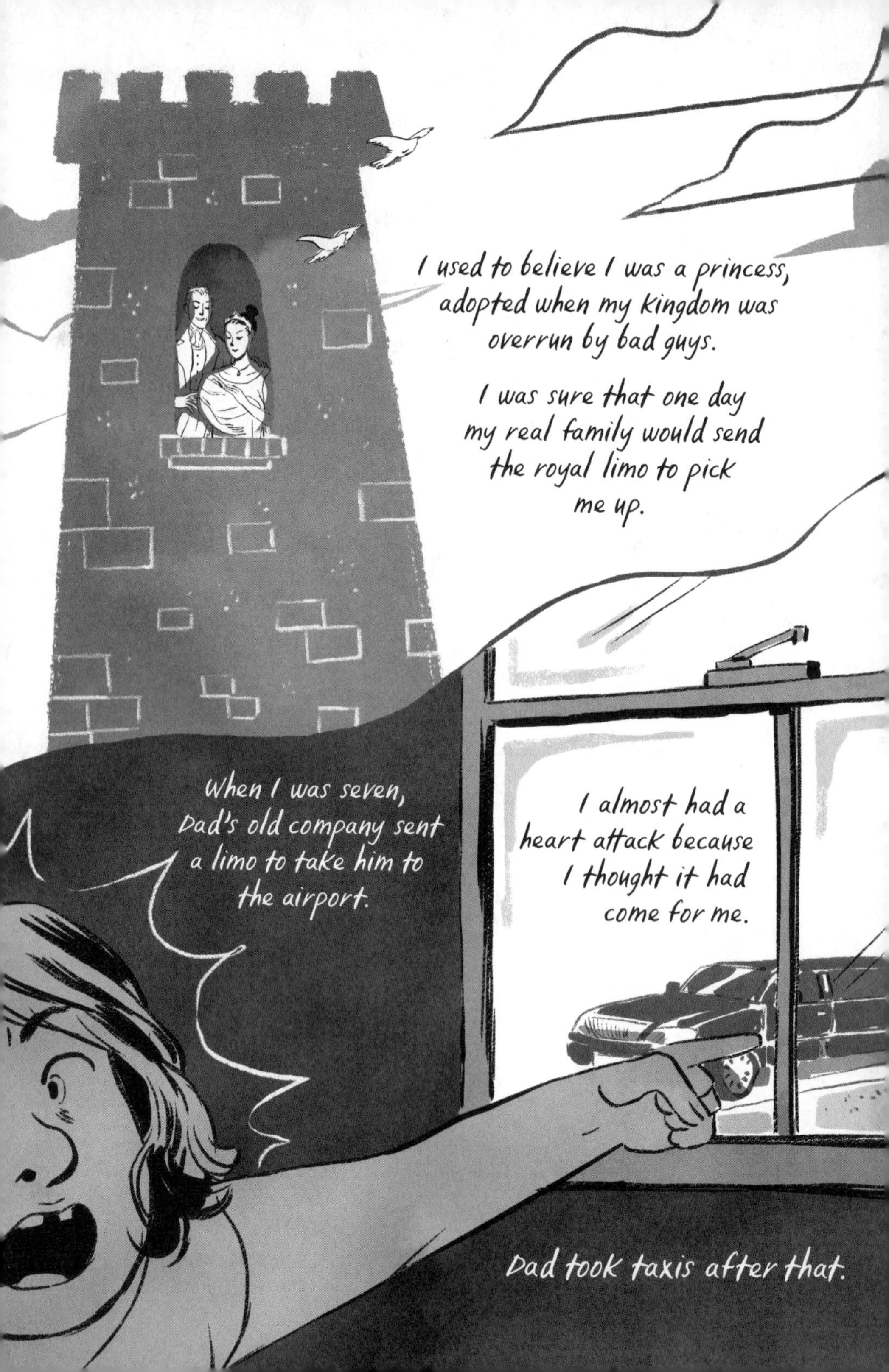
I used to believe I was a princess, adopted when my kingdom was overrun by bad guys.
I was sure that one day my real family would send the royal limo to pick me up.
When I was seven, Dad's old company sent a limo to take him to the airport.
I almost had a heart attack because I thought it had come for me.
Dad took taxis after that.

TEN MORE LIES THEY TELL YOU IN HIGH SCHOOL:

1. You will use algebra in your adult lives.

2. Driving to school is a privilege that can be taken away.

3. Students must stay on campus for lunch.

4. The new textbooks will arrive any day now.

5. Colleges care about more than your standardized test scores.

6. We are enforcing the dress code.

7. We will figure out how to turn off the heat soon.

8. Our bus drivers are highly trained professionals.

9. There is nothing wrong with summer school.

10. We want to hear what you have to say.

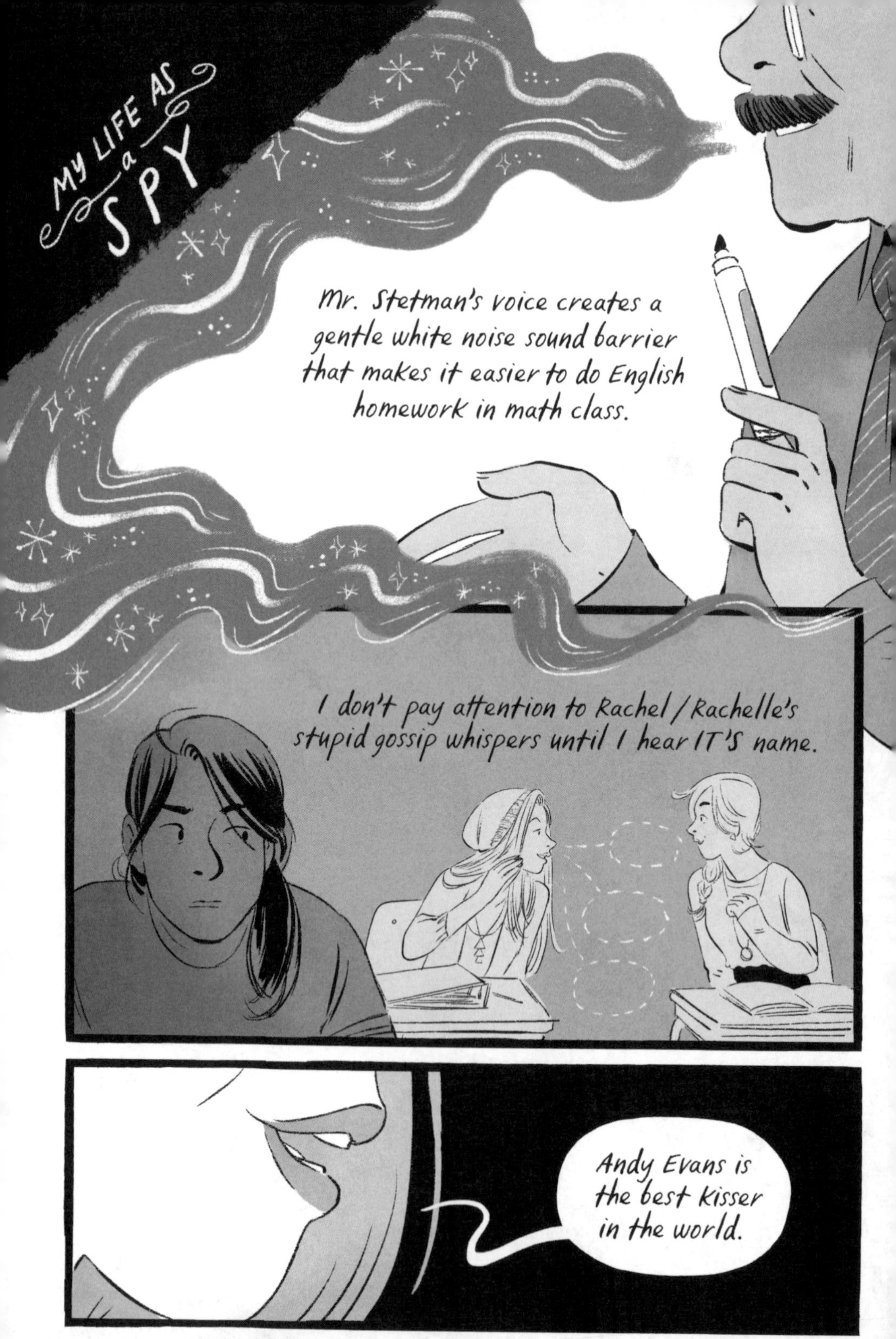
MY LIFE AS a SPY
Mr. Stetman's voice creates a gentle white noise sound barrier that makes it easier to do English homework in math class.
I don't pay attention to Rachel / Rachelle's stupid gossip whispers until I hear IT'S name.
Andy Evans is the best kisser in the world.

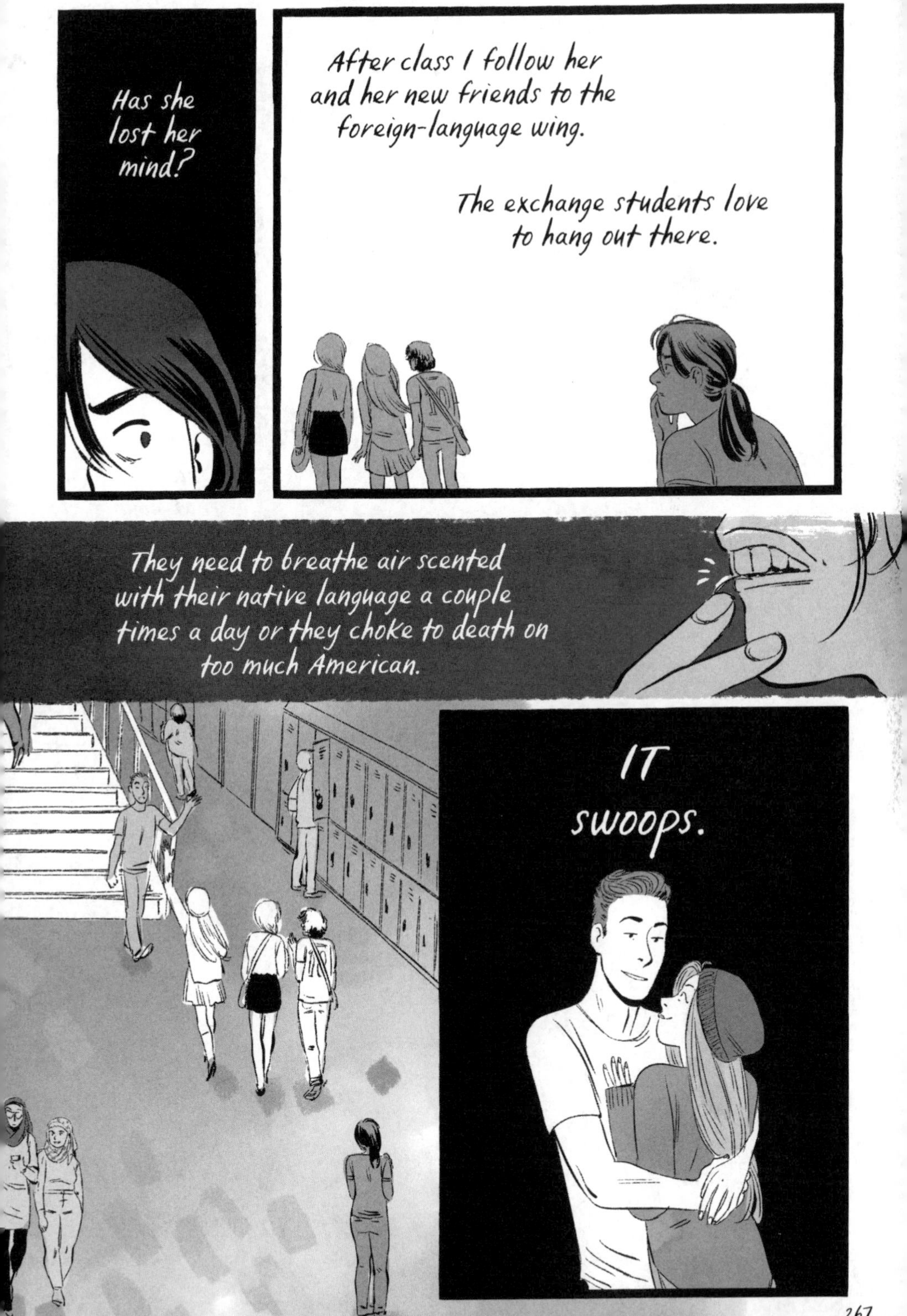
Has she lost her mind?
After class I follow her and her new friends to the foreign-language wing.
The exchange students love to hang out there.
They need to breathe the air scented with their native language a couple times a day or they choke to death on too much American.
IT swoops.

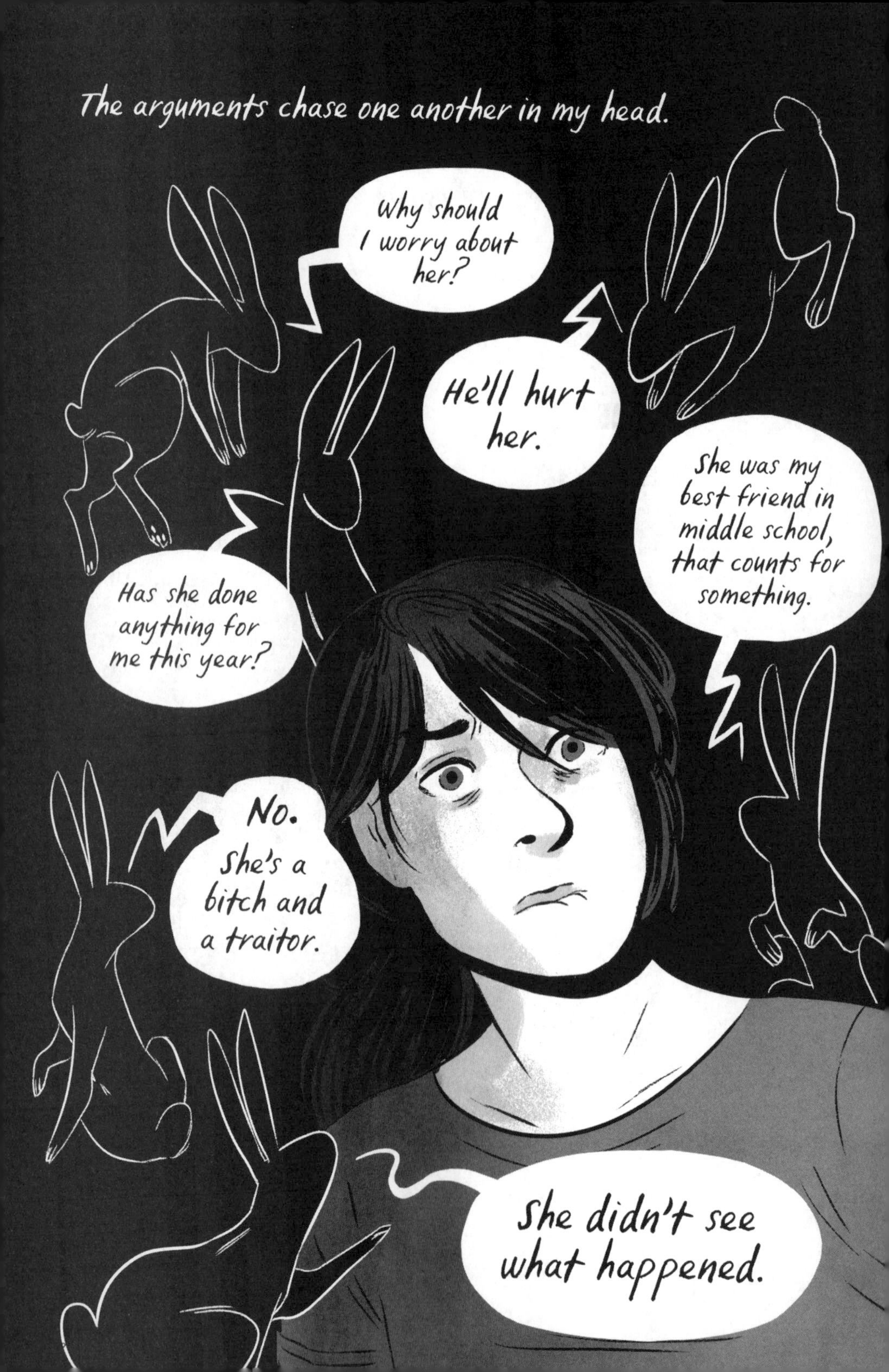
The arguments chase one another in my head.
Why should I worry about her?
He'll hurt her.
Has she done anything for me this year?
She was my best friend in middle school, that counts for something.
No. She's a bitch and a traitor.
She didn't see what happened.

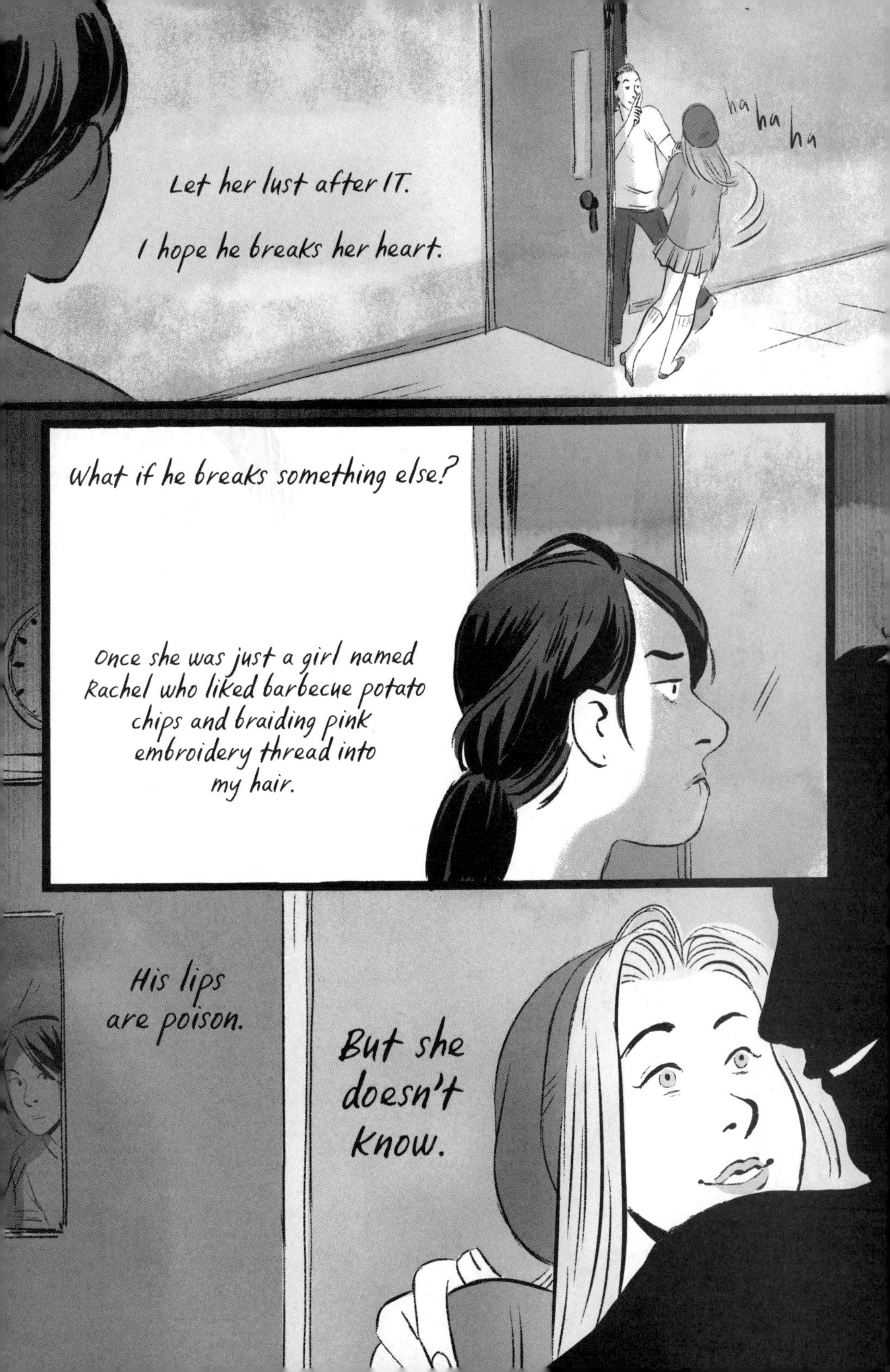
Let her lust after IT.
I hope he breaks her heart.
ha ha ha
What if he breaks something else?
Once she was just a girl named Rachel who liked barbecue potato chips and braiding pink embroidery thread into my hair.
His lips are poison.
But she doesn't know.

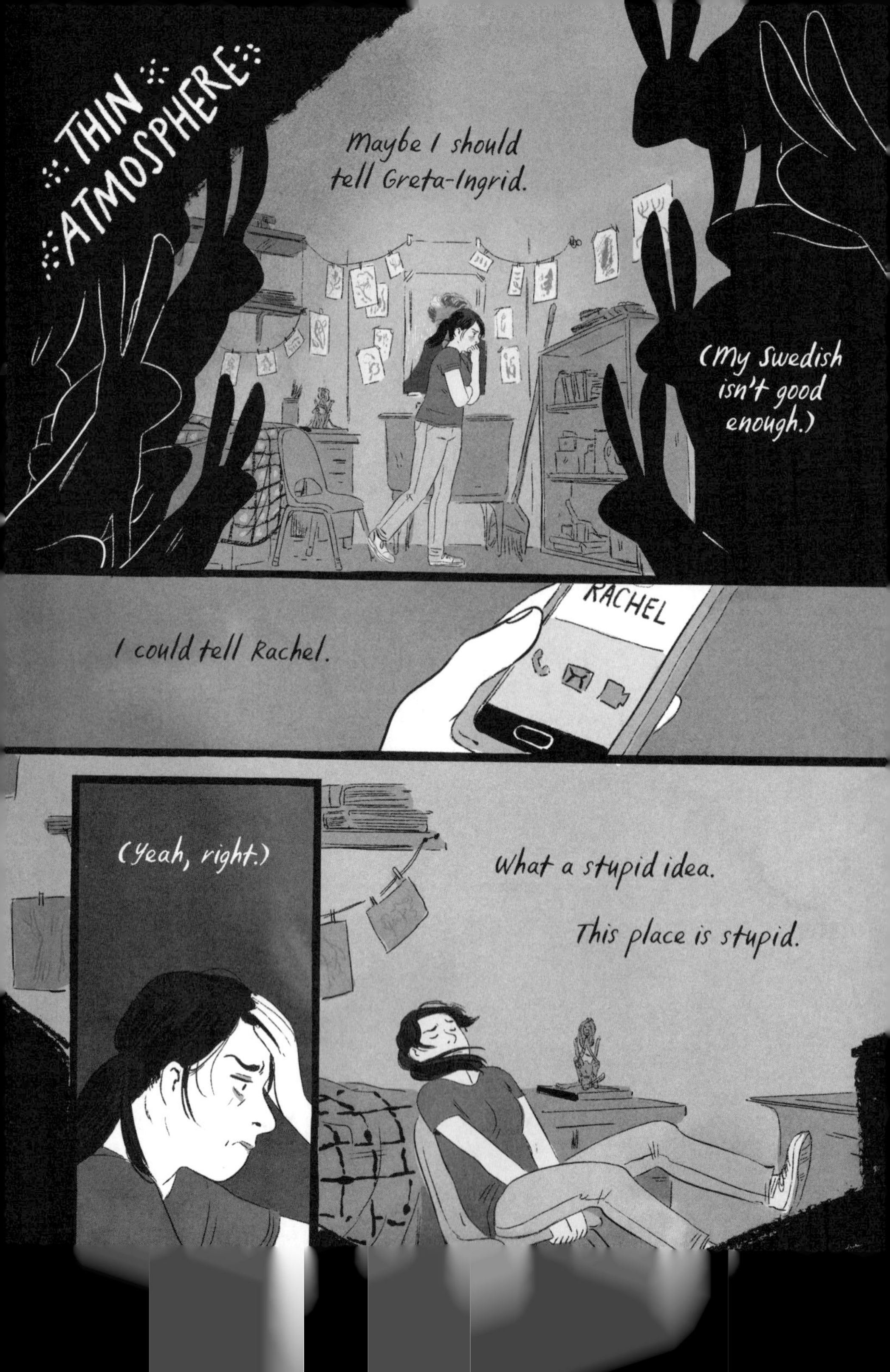
THIN ATMOSPHERE
Maybe I should tell Greta-Ingrid.
(My Swedish isn't good enough.)
RACHEL
I could tell Rachel.
(Yeah, right.)
What a stupid idea.
This place is stupid.

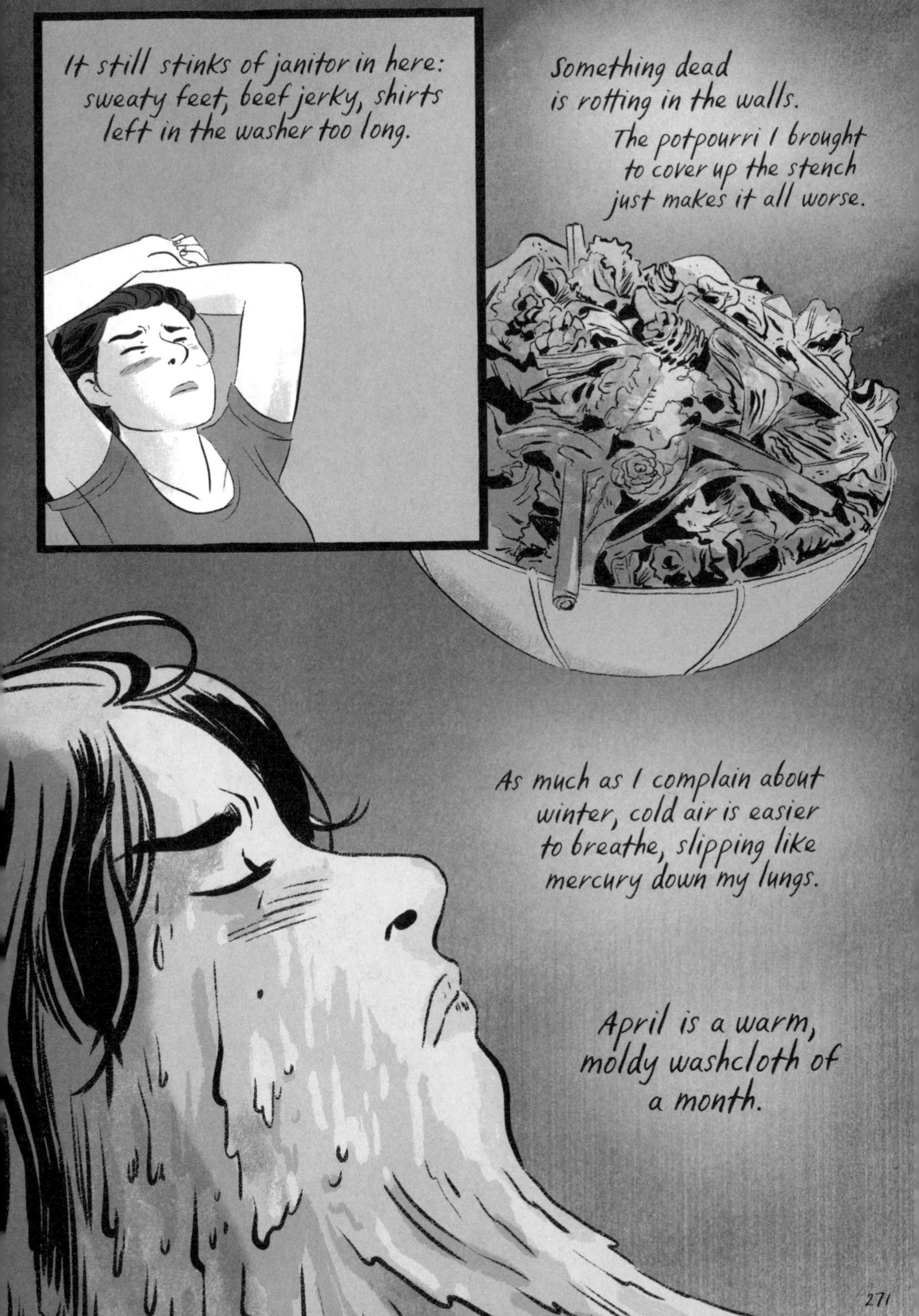
It still stinks of janitor in here: sweaty feet, beef jerky, shirts left in the washer too long.
Something dead is rotting in the walls.
The potpourri I brought to cover up the stench just makes it all worse.
As much as I complain about winter, cold air is easier to breathe, slipping like mercury down my lungs.
April is a warm, moldy washcloth of a month.

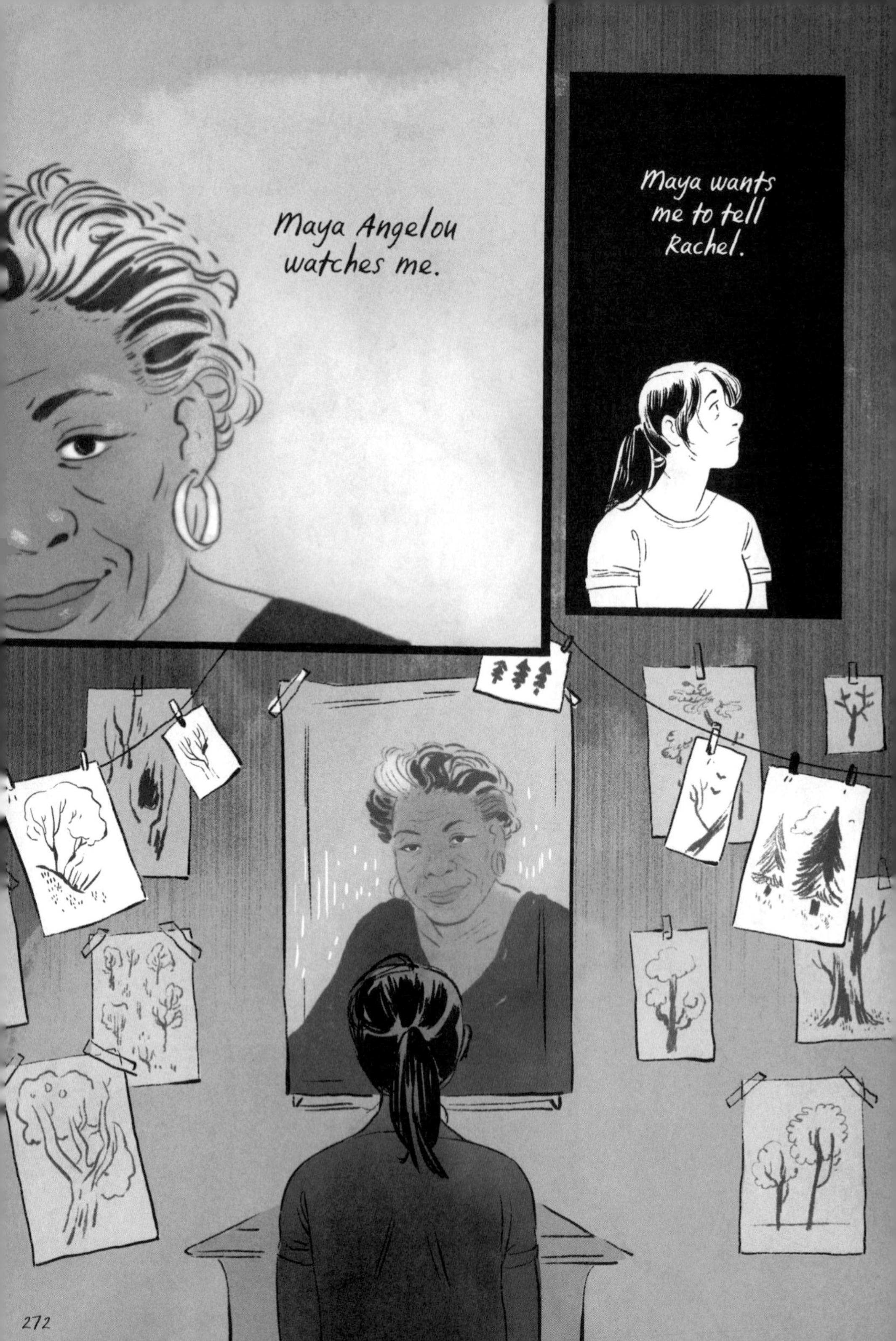
Maya Angelou watches me.
Maya wants me to tell Rachel.

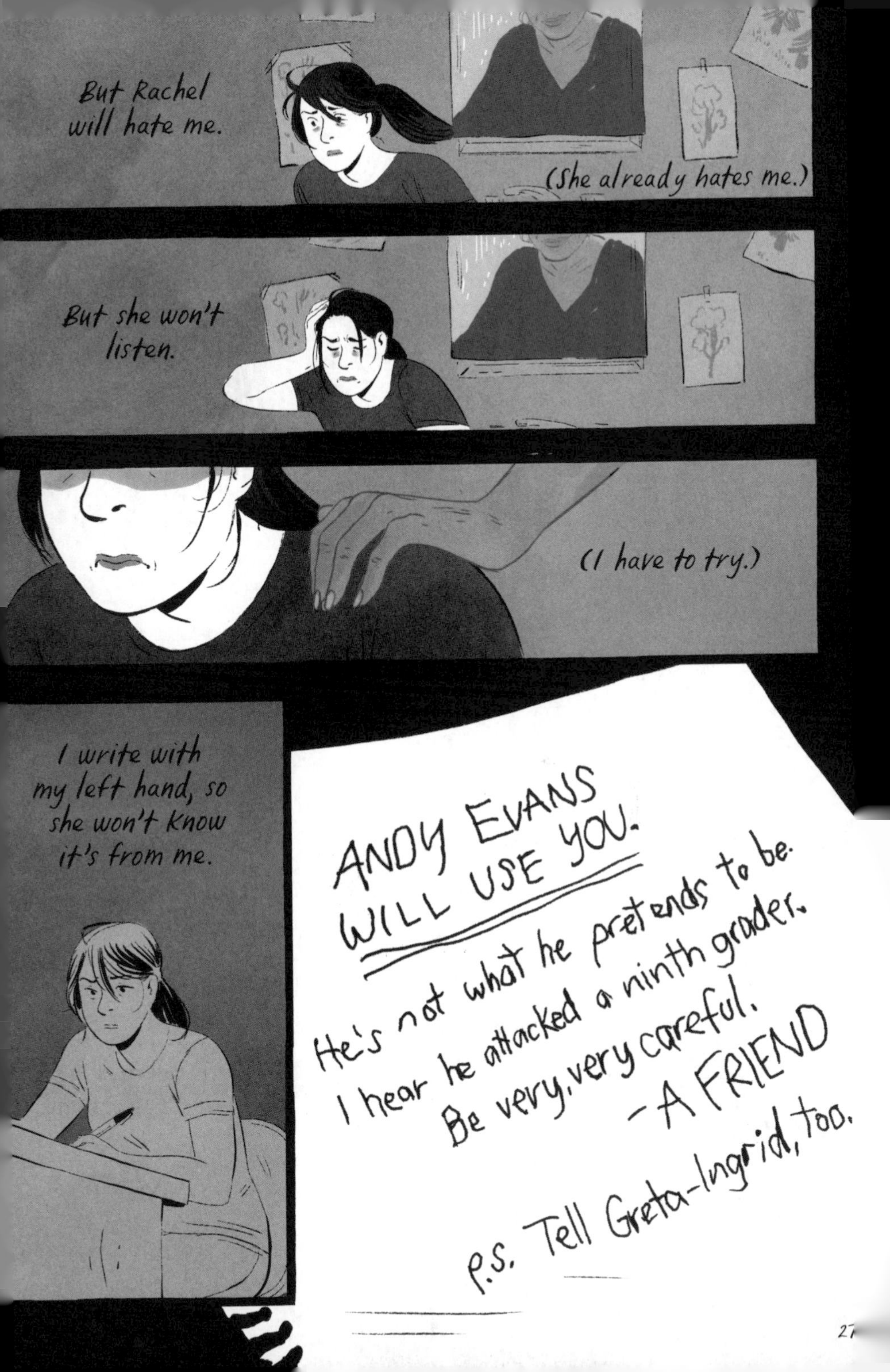

But Rachel will hate me.
(She already hates me.)
But she won't listen.
(I have to try.)
I write with my left hand, so she won't know it's from me.
ANDY EVANS WILL USE YOU.
He's not what he pretends to be.
I hear he attacked a ninth grader.
Be very, very careful.
-A FRIEND
P.S. Tell Greta-Ingrid, too.

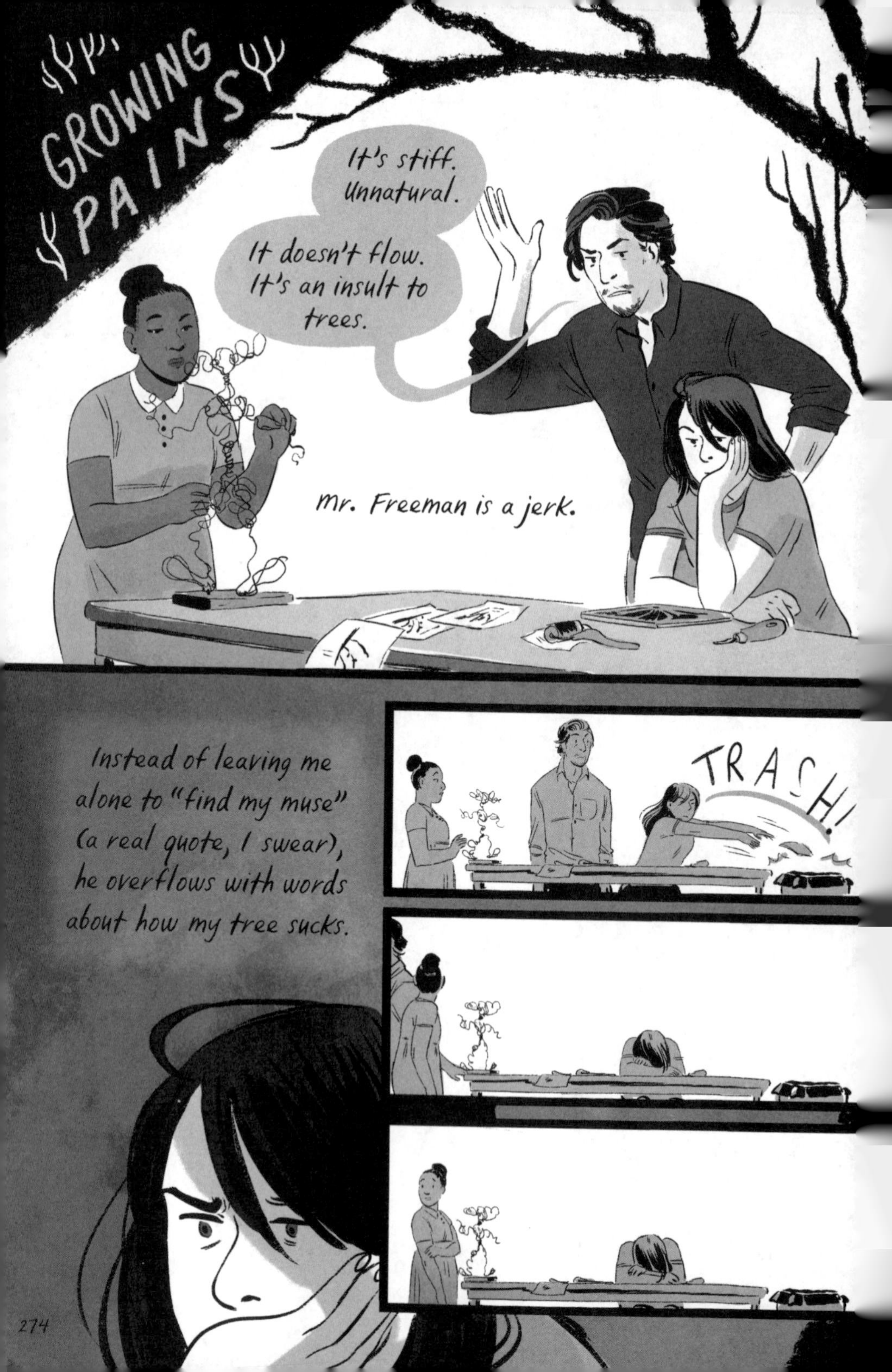
GROWING PAINS
It's stiff. Unnatural.
It doesn't flow. It's an insult to trees.
Mr. Freeman is a jerk.
Instead of leaving me alone to "find my muse" (a real quote, I swear), he overflows with words about how my tree sucks.
TRASH!

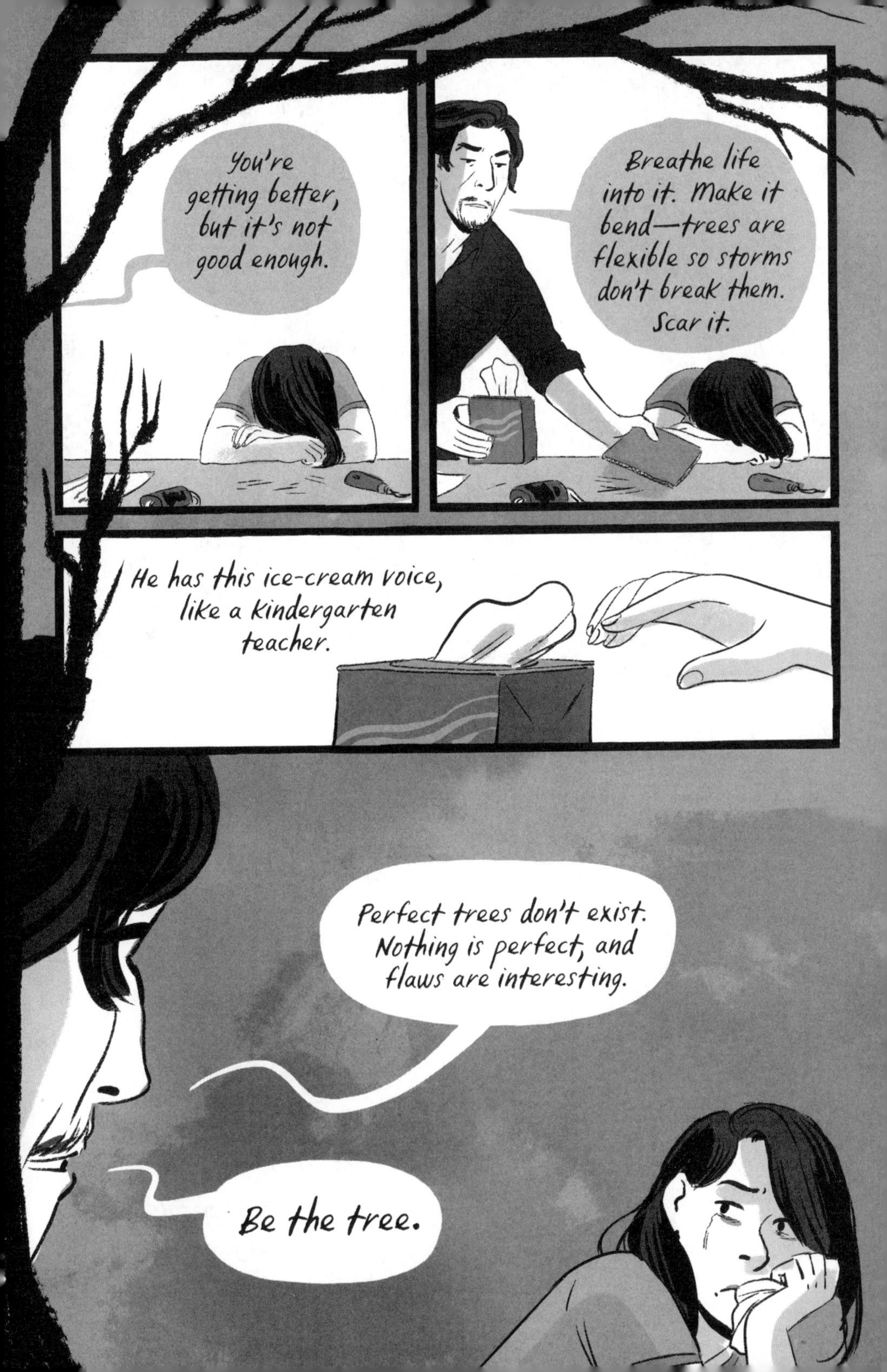
You're getting better, but it's not good enough.
Breathe life into it. Make it bend—trees are flexible so storms don't break them. Scar it.
He has this ice-cream voice, like a kindergarten teacher.
Perfect trees don't exist. Nothing is perfect, and flaws are interesting.
Be the tree.

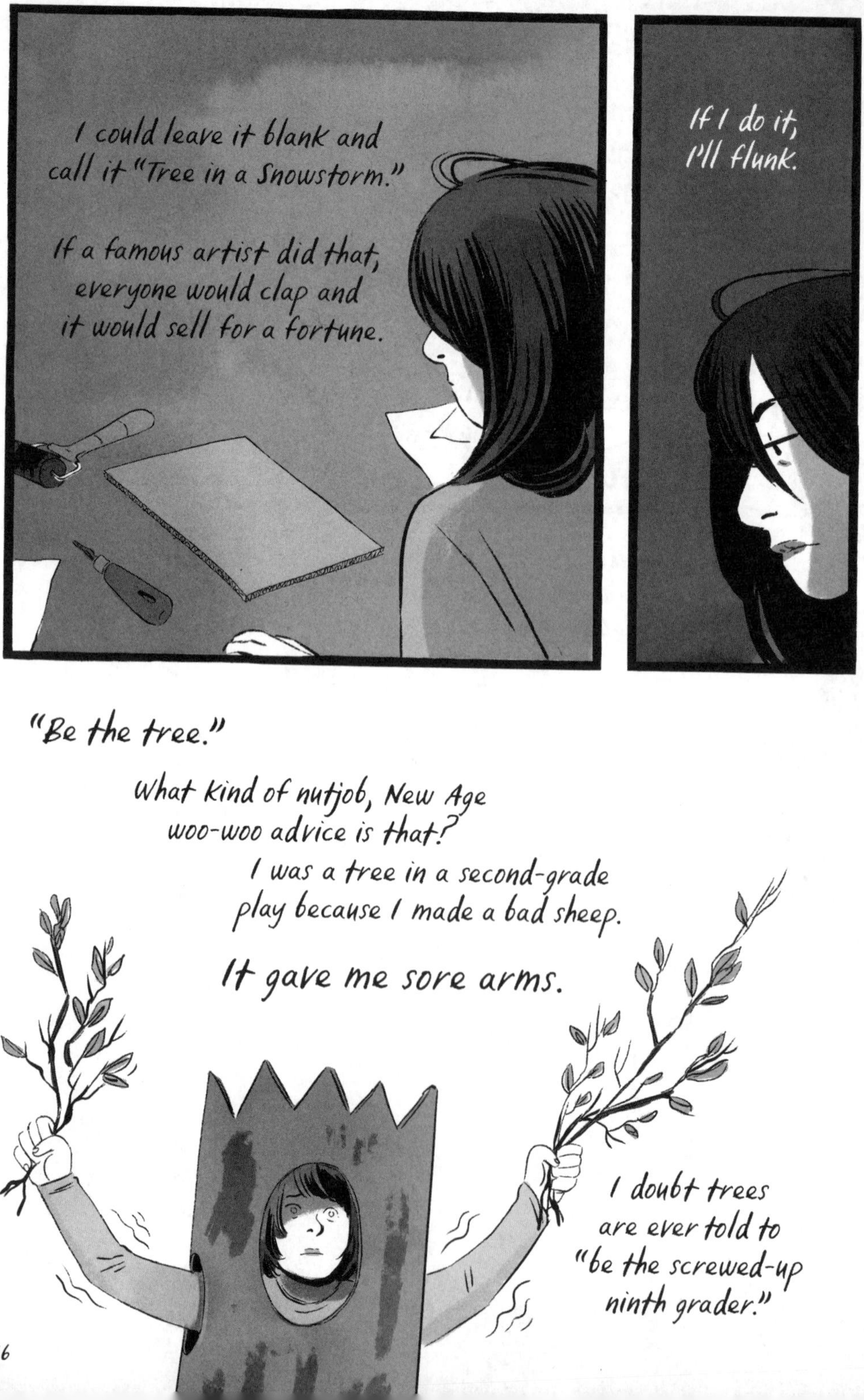
I could leave it blank and call it "Tree in a Snowstorm."
If a famous artist did that, everyone would clap and it would sell for a fortune.
If I do it, I'll flunk.
"Be the tree."
What kind of nutjob, New Age woo-woo advice is that?
I was a tree in a second-grade play because I made a bad sheep.
It gave me sore arms.
I doubt trees are ever told to "be the screwed-up ninth grader."

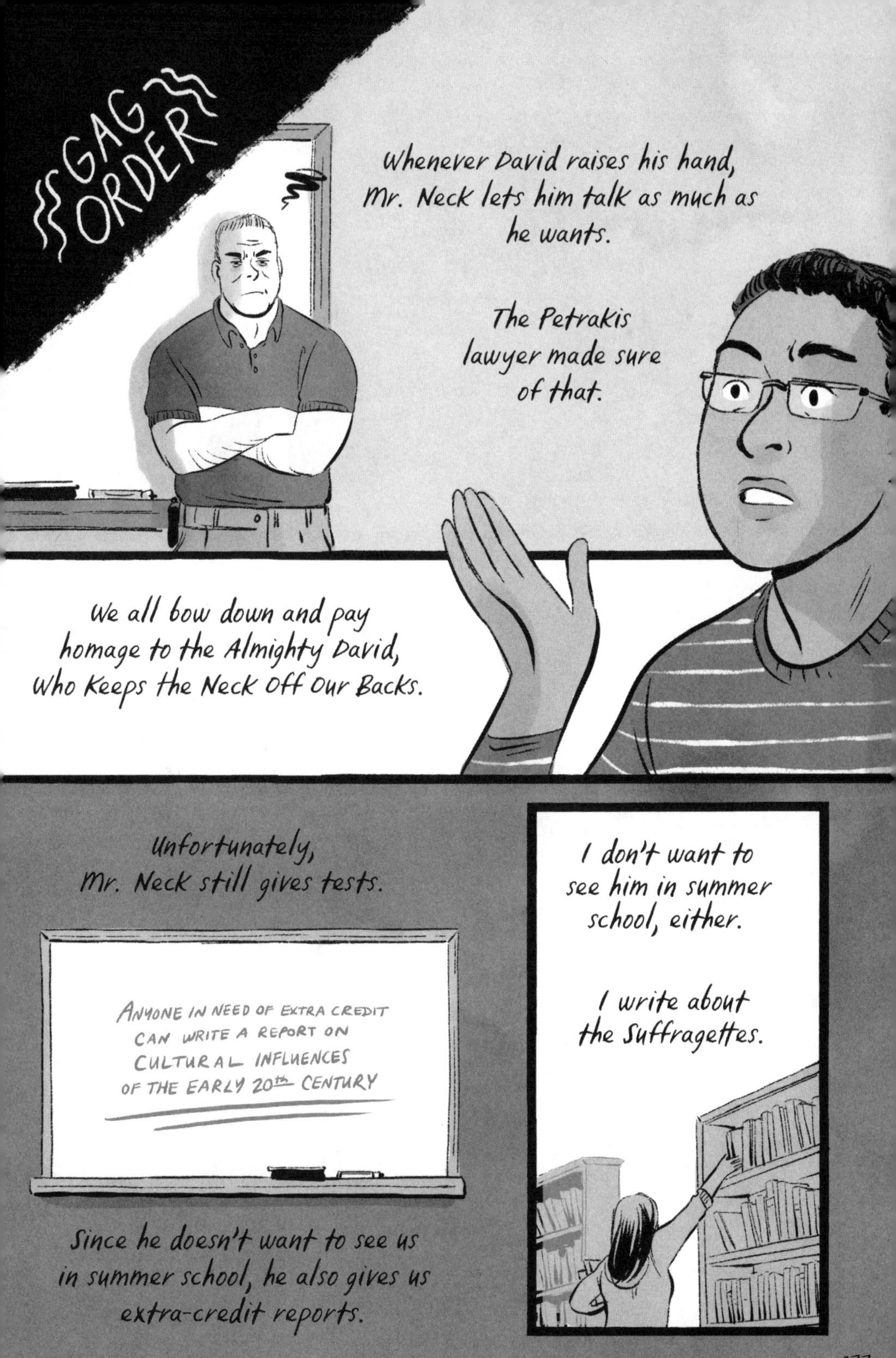
GAG ORDER
Whenever David raises his hand, Mr. Neck lets him talk as much as he wants.
The Petrakis lawyer made sure of that.
We all bow down and pay homage to the Almighty David, Who Keeps the Neck Off Our Backs.
Unfortunately, Mr. Neck still gives tests.
ANYONE IN NEED OF EXTRA CREDIT CAN WRITE A REPORT ON CULTURAL INFLUENCES OF THE EARLY 20th CENTURY
Since he doesn't want to see us in summer school, he also gives us extra-credit reports.
I don't want to see him in summer school, either.
I write about the Suffragettes.

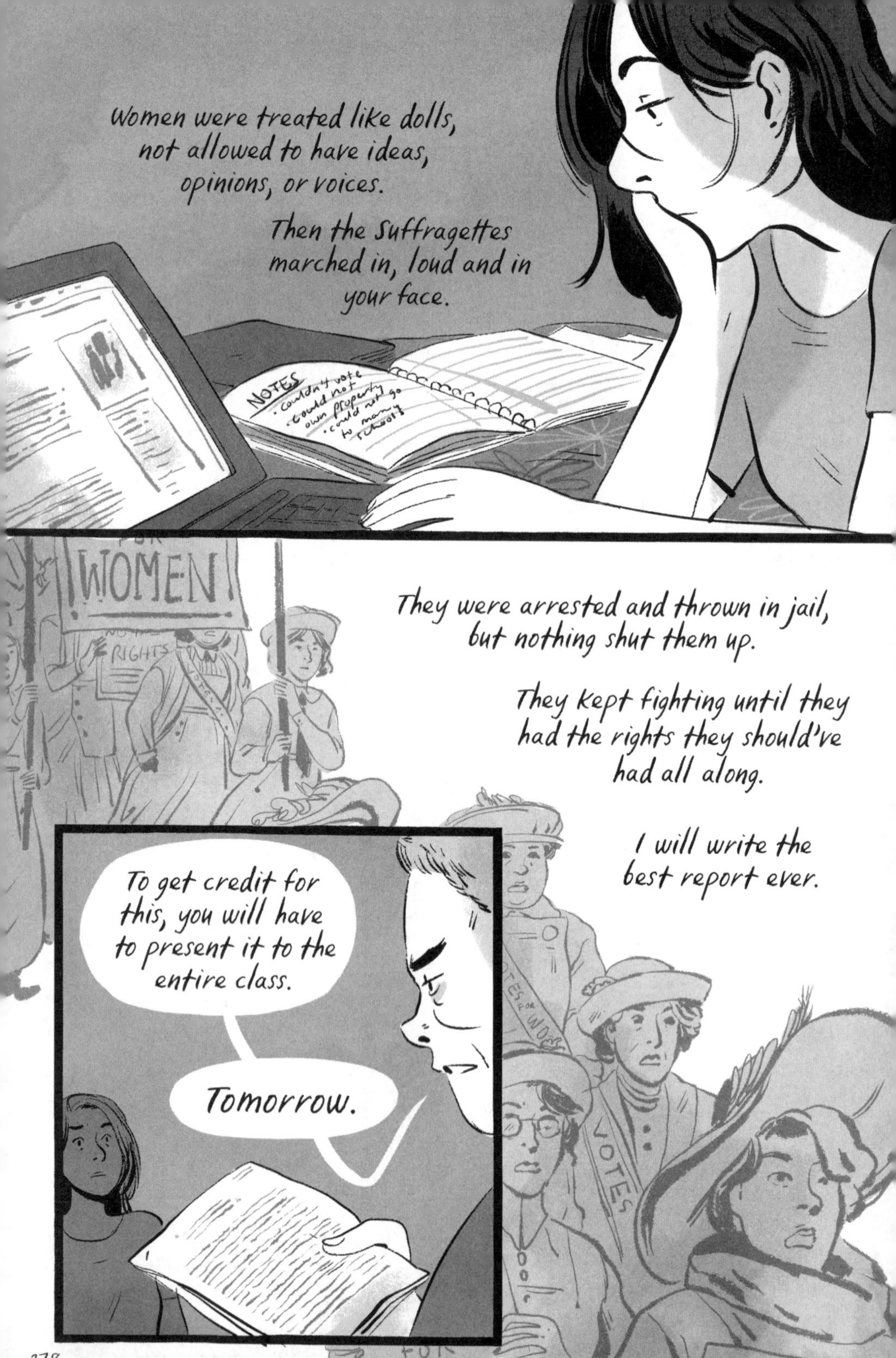

Women were treated like dolls, not allowed to have ideas, opinions, or voices.
Then the Suffragettes marched in, loud and in your face.
NOTES
• Couldn't vote
• Could not own property
• Could not go to many schools
WOMEN
RIGHTS
They were arrested and thrown in jail, but nothing shut them up.
They kept fighting until they had the rights they should've had all along.
I will write the best report ever.
To get credit for this, you will have to present it to the entire class.
Tomorrow.
VOTES

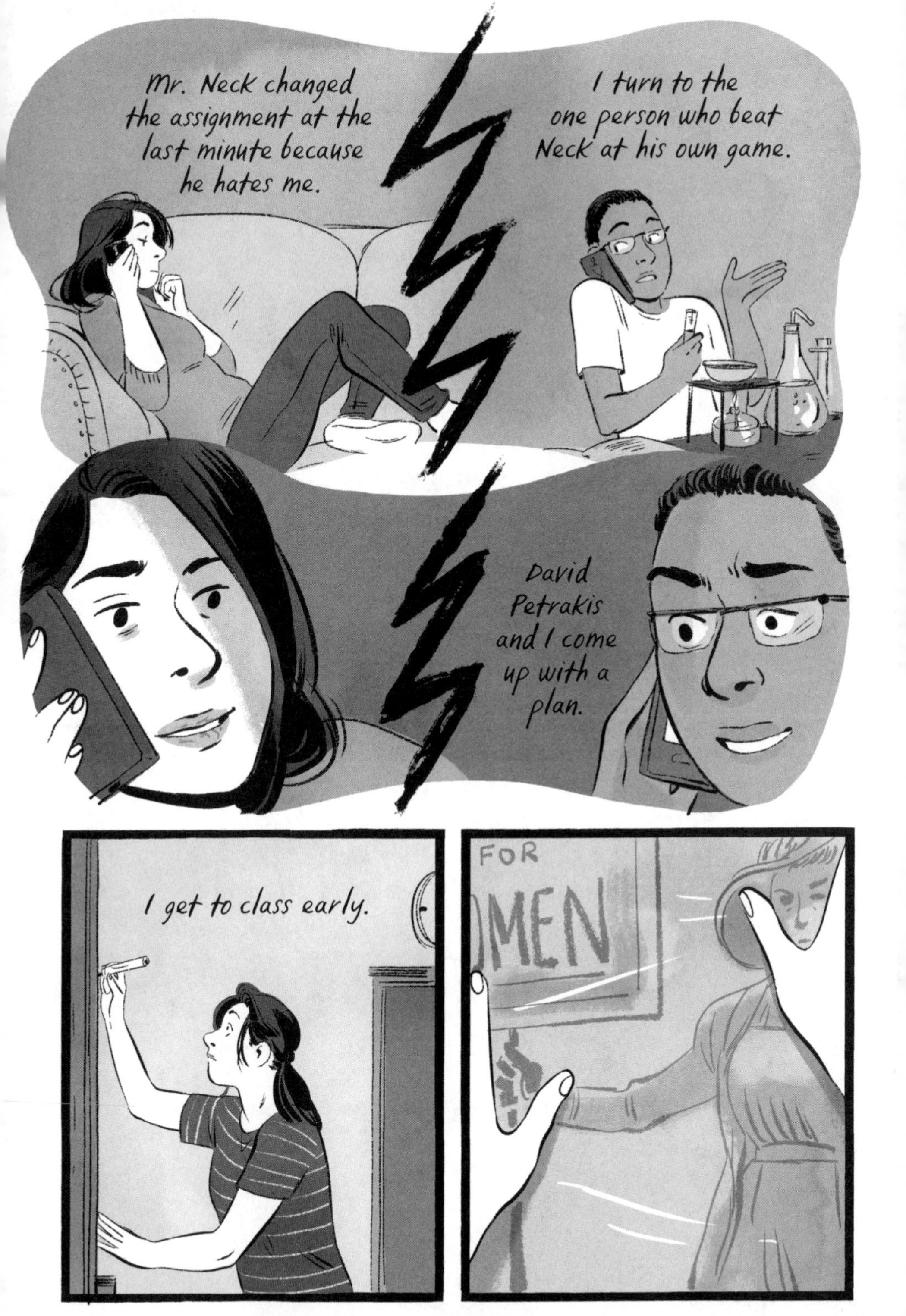
Mr. Neck changed the assignment at the last minute because he hates me.
I turn to the one person who beat Neck at his own game.
David Petrakis and I come up with a plan.
I get to class early.
FOR
MEN

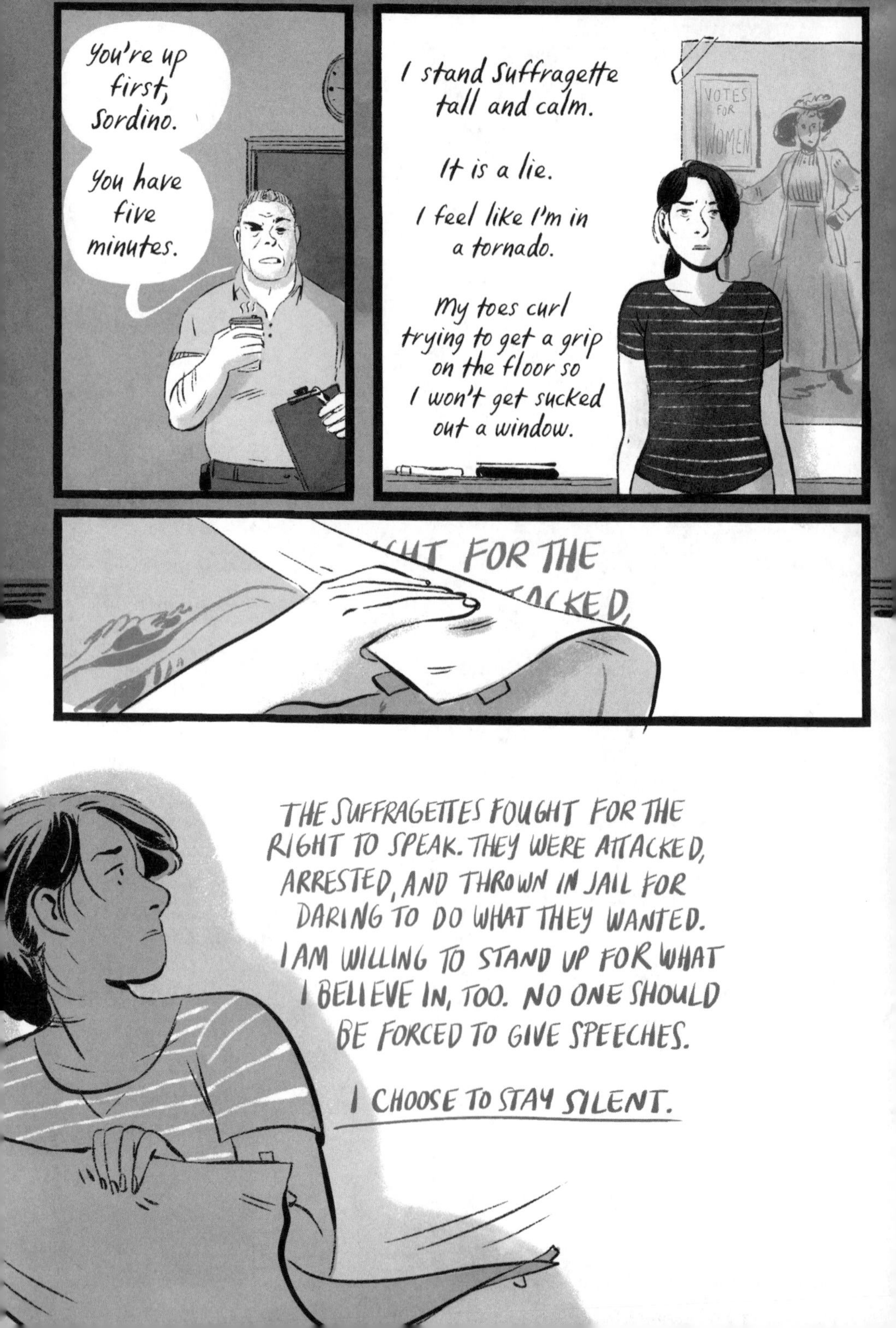
You're up first, Sordino.
You have five minutes.
I stand Suffragette tall and calm.
It is a lie.
I feel like I'm in a tornado.
My toes curl trying to get a grip on the floor so I won't get sucked out a window.
VOTES FOR WOMEN
THE SUFFRAGETTES FOUGHT FOR THE RIGHT TO SPEAK. THEY WERE ATTACKED, ARRESTED, AND THROWN IN JAIL FOR DARING TO DO WHAT THEY WANTED. I AM WILLING TO STAND UP FOR WHAT I BELIEVE IN, TOO. NO ONE SHOULD BE FORCED TO GIVE SPEECHES.
I CHOOSE TO STAY SILENT.

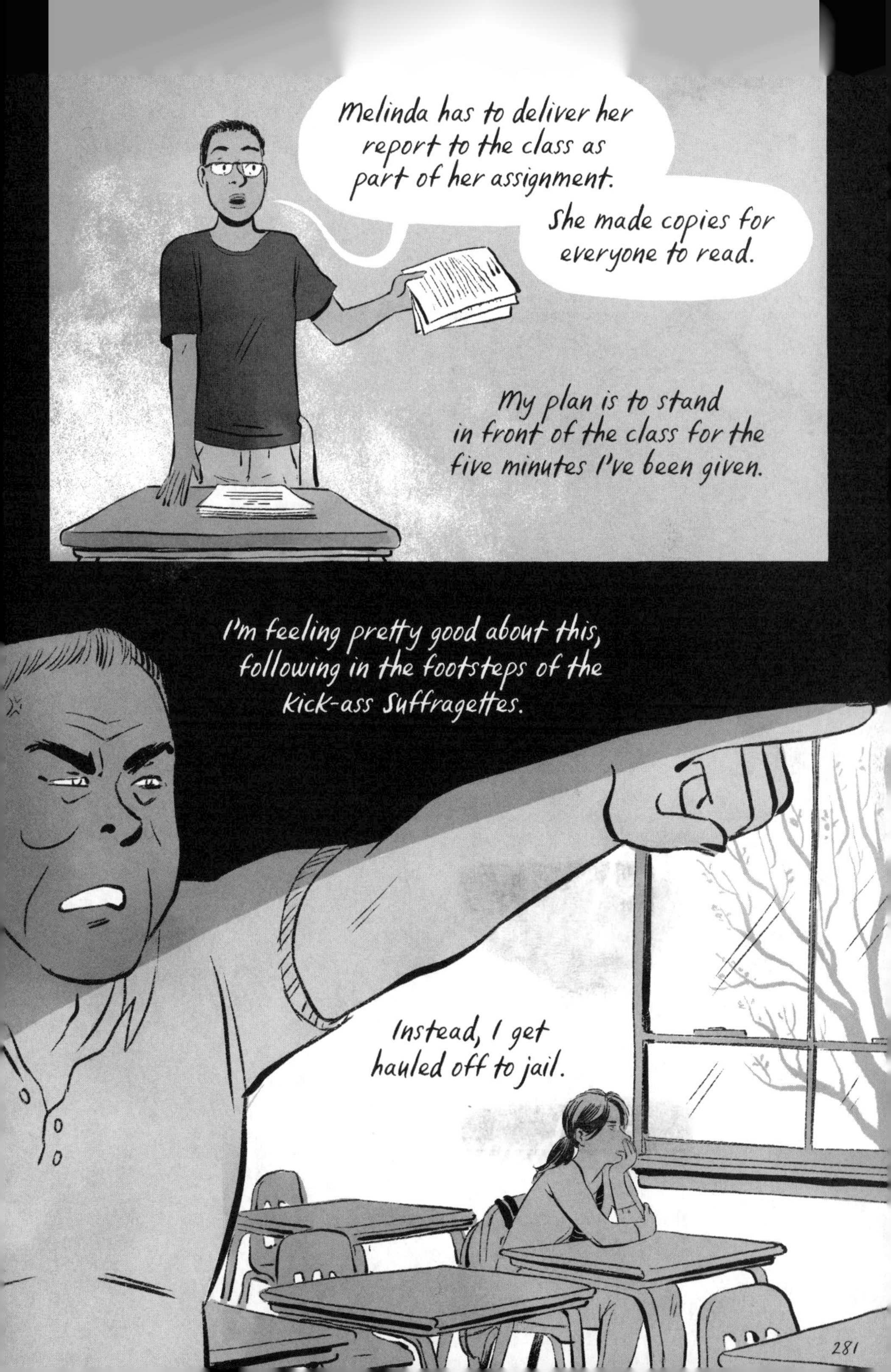
Melinda has to deliver her report to the class as part of her assignment.
She made copies for everyone to read.
My plan is to stand in front of the class for the five minutes I've been given.
I'm feeling pretty good about this, following in the footsteps of the kick-ass Suffragettes.
Instead, I get hauled off to jail.

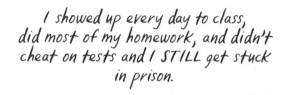

I showed up every day to class, did most of my homework, and didn't cheat on tests and I STILL get stuck in prison.

They can't punish me for not speaking.

It's not fair.

They don't even know me. They have no clue what's in my head.

FLASHES of LIGHTNING, CRYING CHILDREN CAUGHT IN A LANDSLIDE, PINNED BY WORRY, SQUIRMING UNDER the WEIGHT of DOUBT and GUILT.

FEAR.

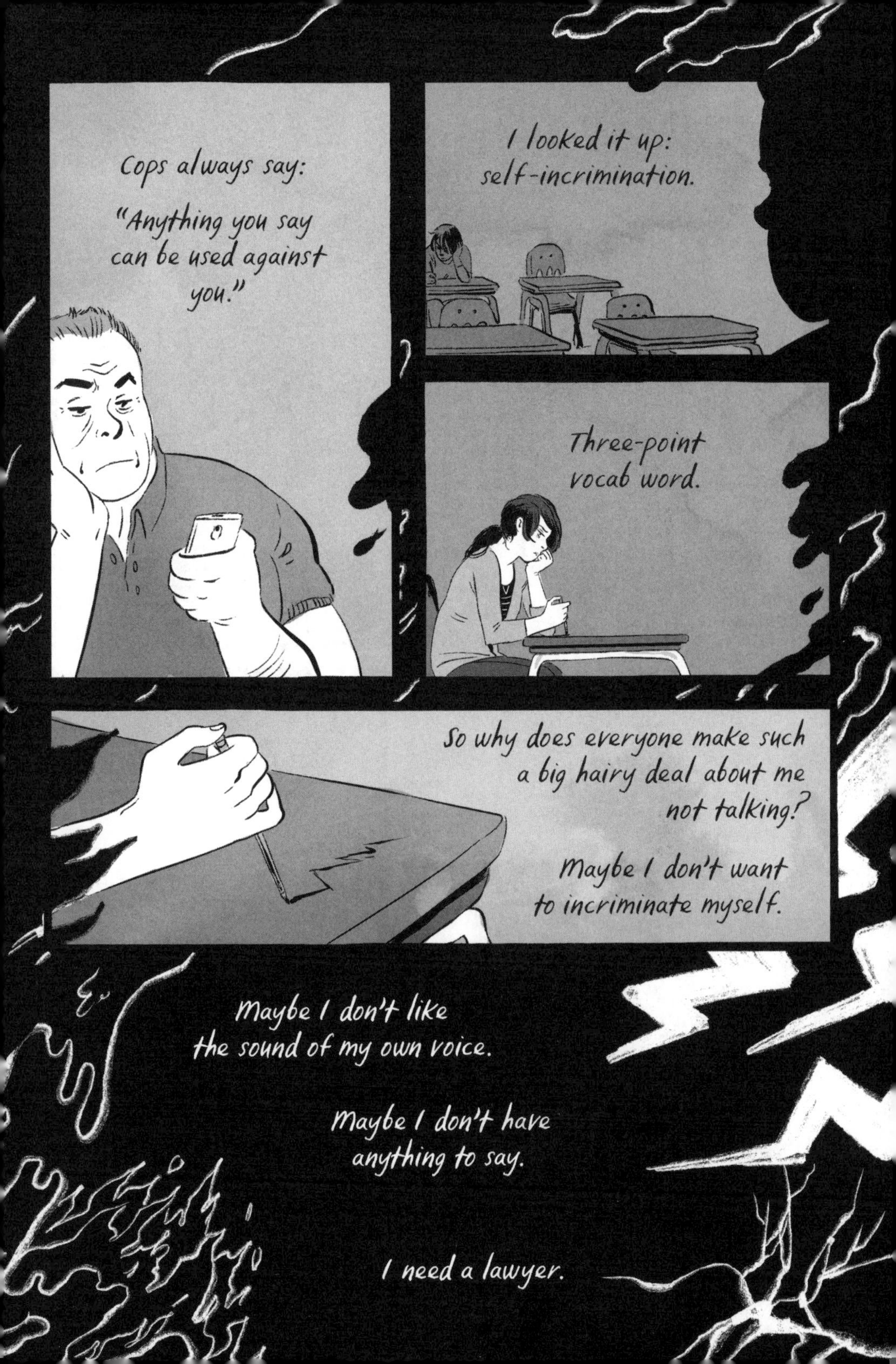
Cops always say:
"Anything you say can be used against you."
I looked it up: self-incrimination.
Three-point vocab word.
So why does everyone make such a big hairy deal about me not talking?
Maybe I don't want to incriminate myself.
Maybe I don't like the sound of my own voice.
Maybe I don't have anything to say.
I need a lawyer.

He gave me a D and a suspension.

He has a point.

Seriously?

Your presentation was about speaking up for the right to be silent.

If the Suffragettes stayed silent, women still wouldn't be able to vote.

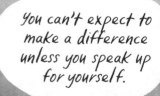

You can't expect to make a difference unless you speak up for yourself.

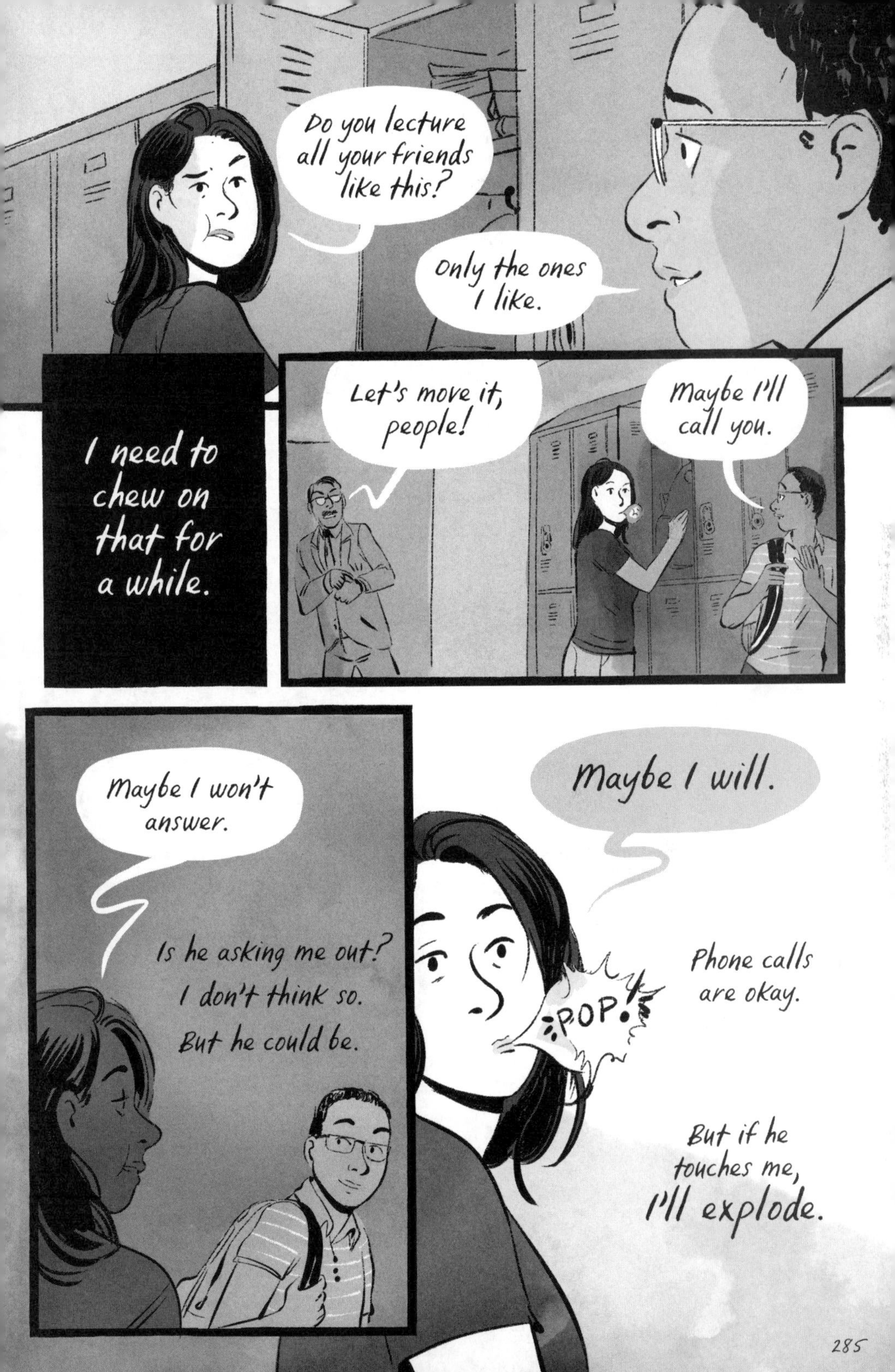
Do you lecture all your friends like this?
Only the ones I like.
I need to chew on that for a while.
Let's move it, people!
Maybe I'll call you.
Maybe I won't answer.
Maybe I will.
Is he asking me out? I don't think so. But he could be.
POP!
Phone calls are okay.
But if he touches me, I'll explode.

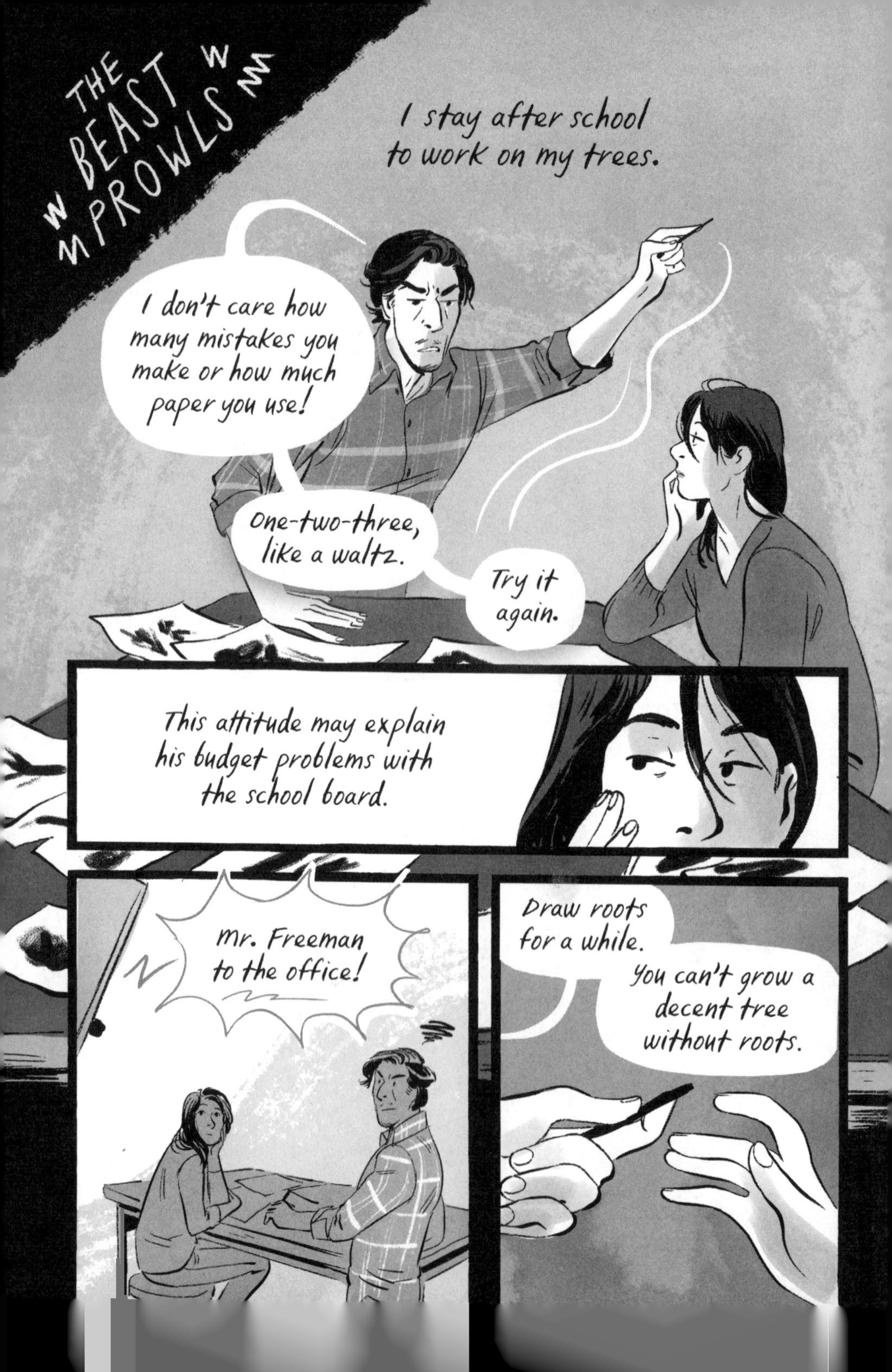
THE BEAST PROWLS
I stay after school to work on my trees.
I don't care how many mistakes you make or how much paper you use!
One-two-three, like a waltz.
Try it again.
This attitude may explain his budget problems with the school board.
Mr. Freeman to the office!
Draw roots for a while.
You can't grow a decent tree without roots.

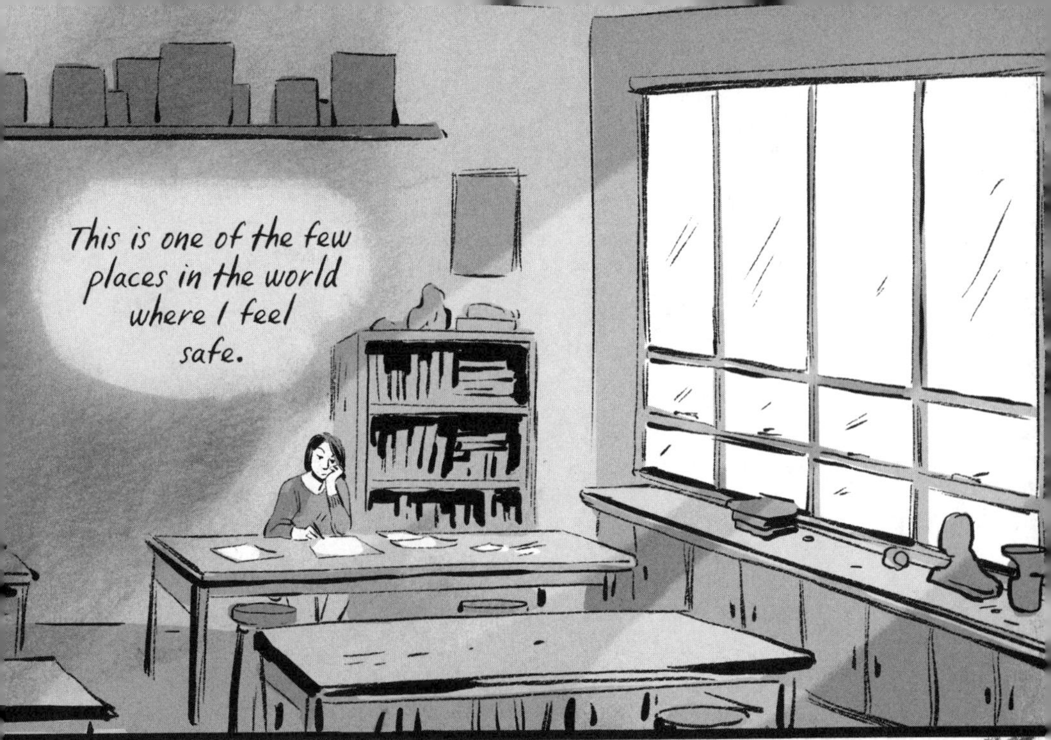
This is one of the few places in the world where I feel safe.

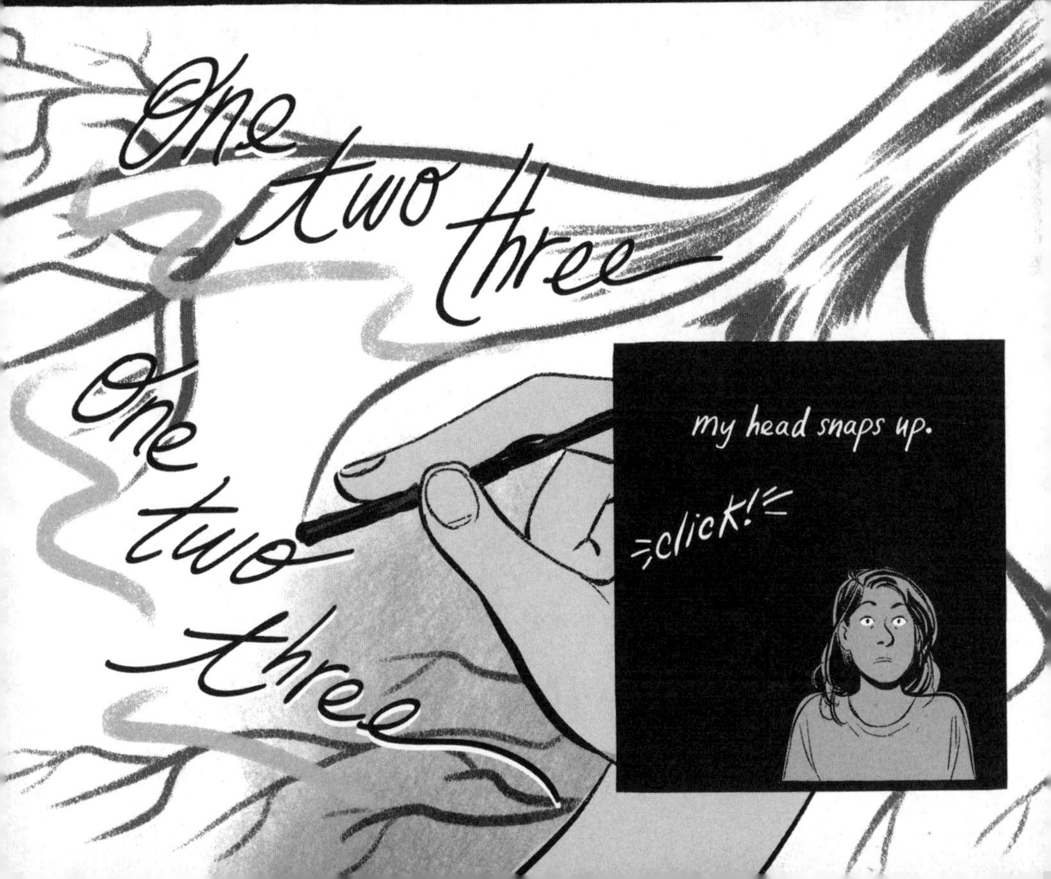
One two three
One two three
my head snaps up.
click!

You seen Rachelle?
Rachelle Bruin?
click
Andy Beast.
Little rabbit heart leaps out of my chest and scampers across the paper, leaving bloody footprints on the roots.
You know who she is?
I sit completely still.

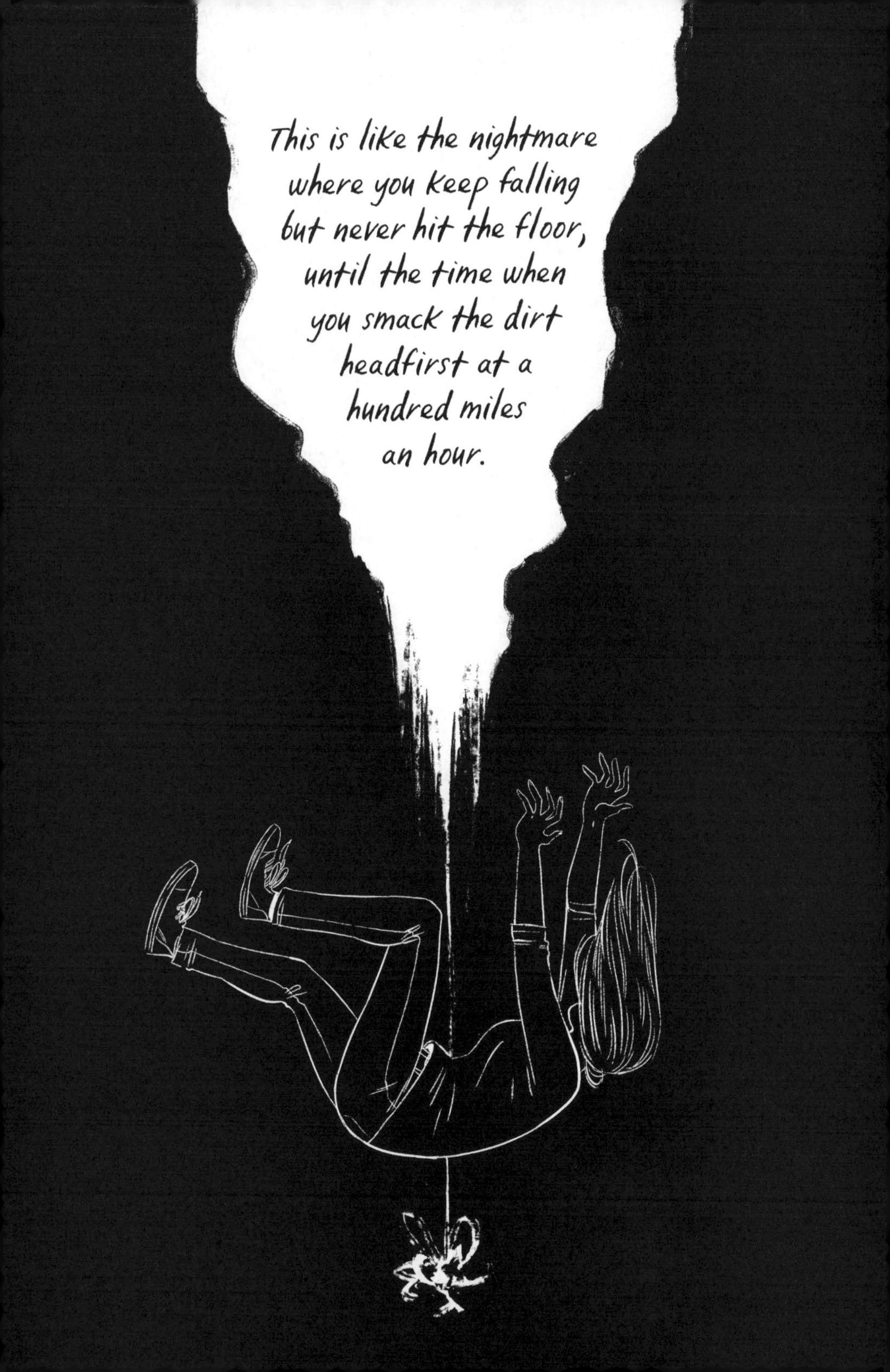
This is like the nightmare where you keep falling but never hit the floor, until the time when you smack the dirt headfirst at a hundred miles an hour.

Hello?
Anyone home?
Is he going to hurt me again?
Are you deaf?
He couldn't, not in school.
Could he?

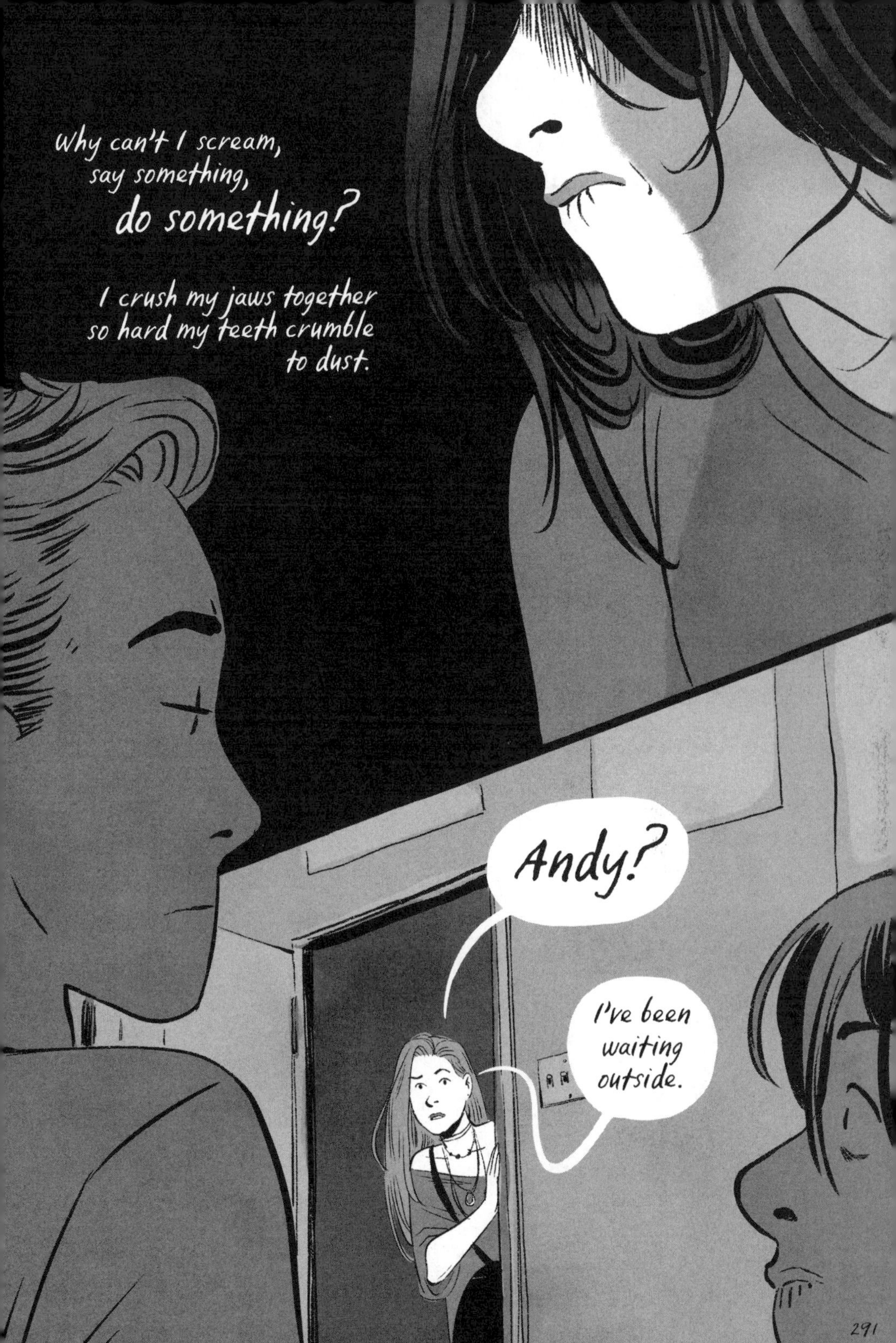
Why can't I scream,
say something,
do something?
I crush my jaws together
so hard my teeth crumble
to dust.
Andy?
I've been
waiting
outside.

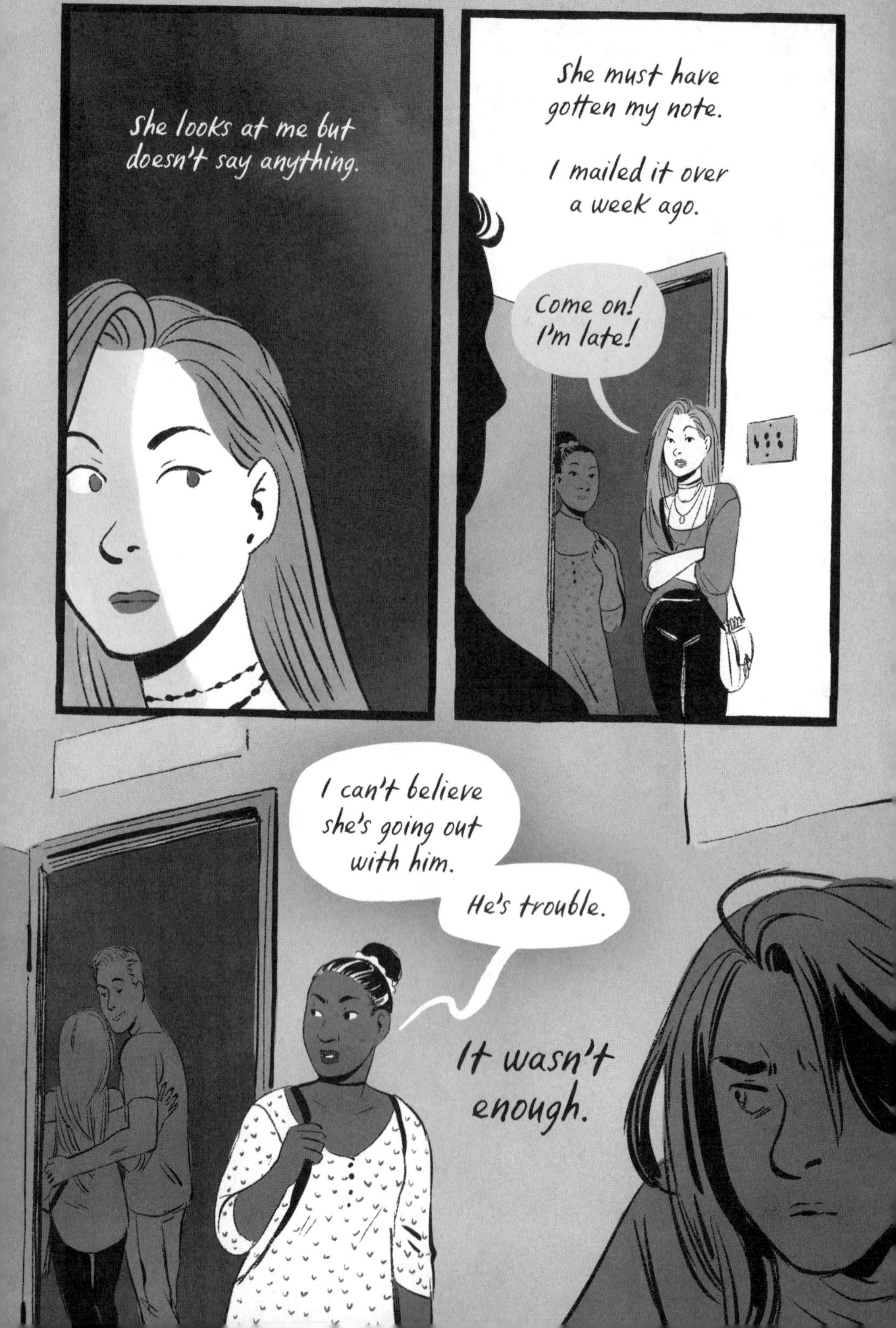

She looks at me but doesn't say anything.
She must have gotten my note.
I mailed it over a week ago.
Come on! I'm late!
I can't believe she's going out with him.
He's trouble.
It wasn't enough.

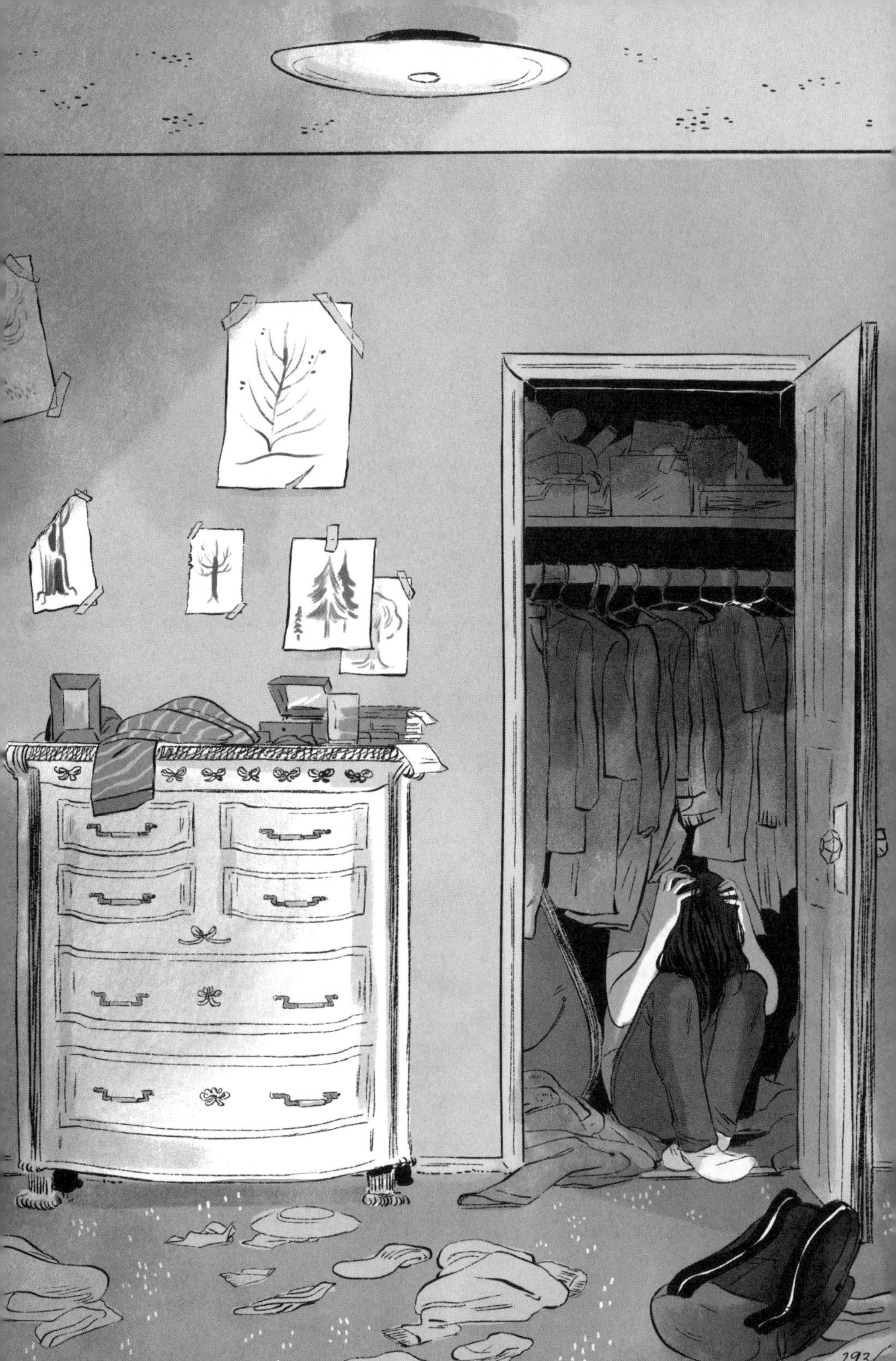

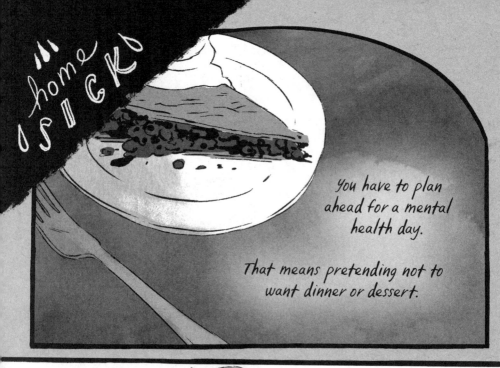

home SICK

You have to plan ahead for a mental health day.

That means pretending not to want dinner or dessert.

Coughing so much even Dad notices.

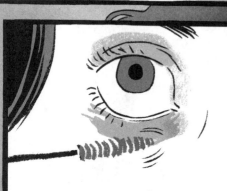

Turns out I have a fever.

Is it possible I'm really sick?

Makeup for dramatic effect.

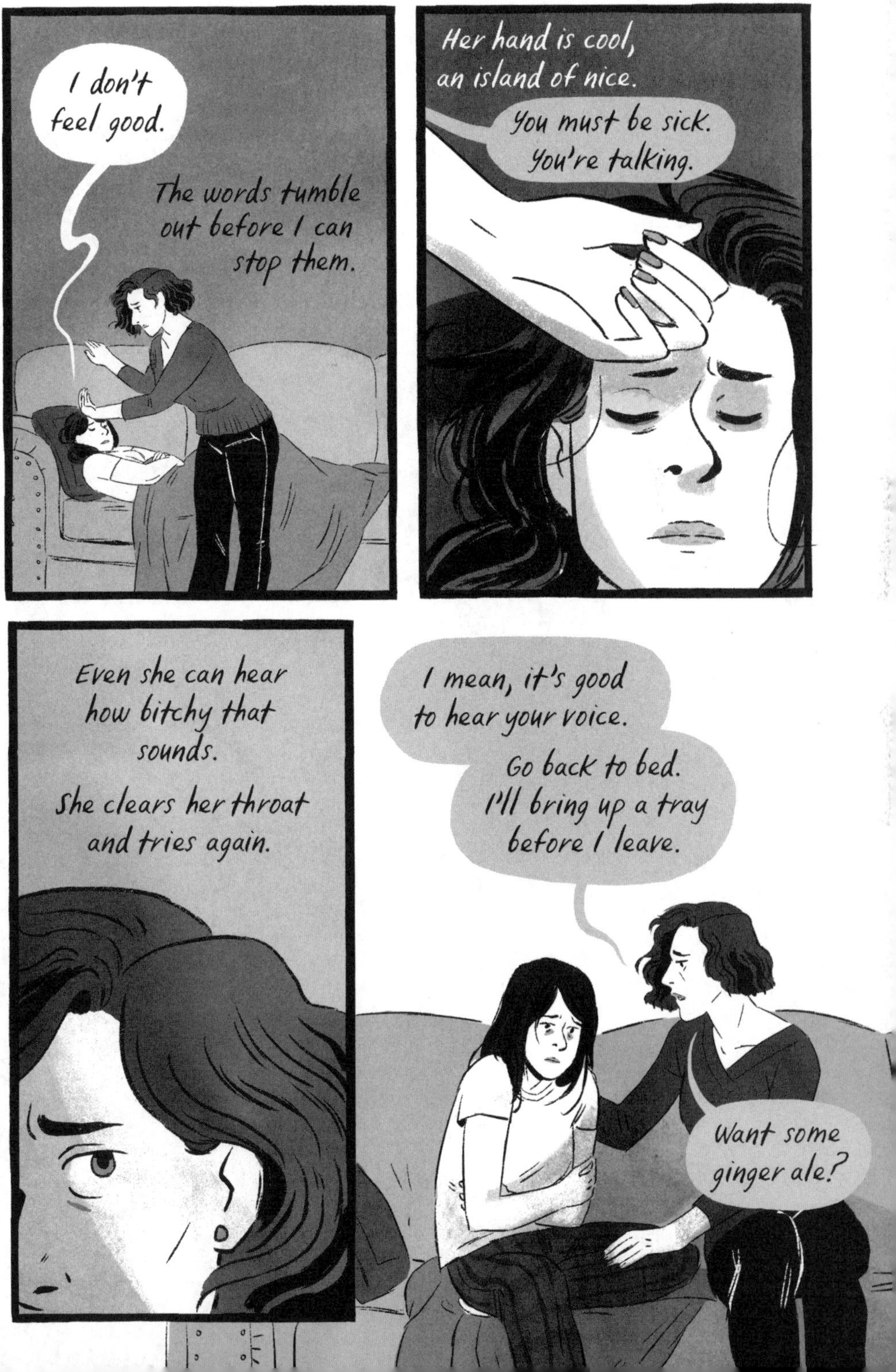
I don't feel good.
The words tumble out before I can stop them.
Her hand is cool, an island of nice.
You must be sick. You're talking.
Even she can hear how bitchy that sounds.
She clears her throat and tries again.
I mean, it's good to hear your voice.
Go back to bed. I'll bring up a tray before I leave.
Want some ginger ale?

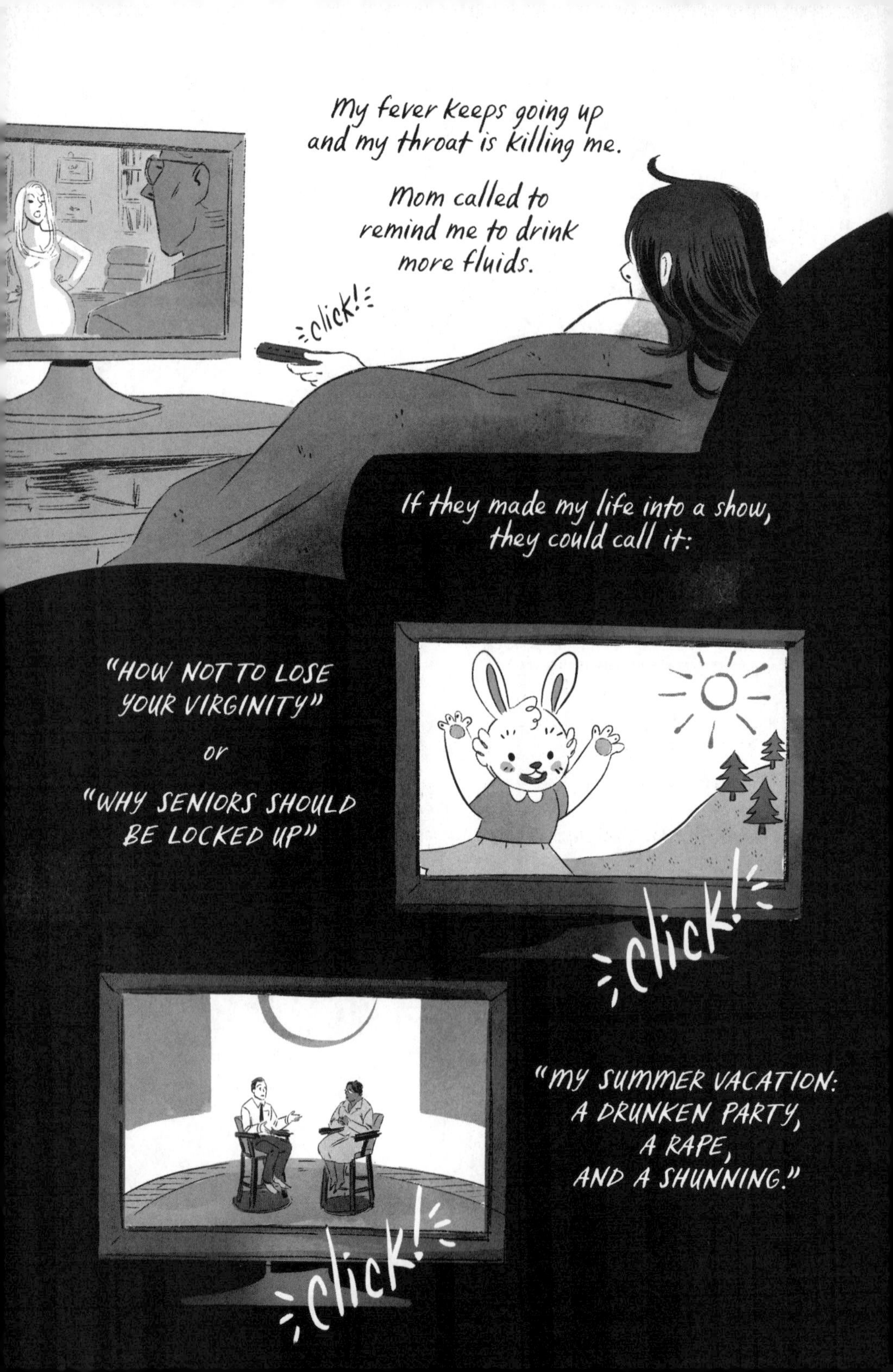
My fever keeps going up and my throat is killing me.
Mom called to remind me to drink more fluids.
click!
If they made my life into a show, they could call it:
"HOW NOT TO LOSE YOUR VIRGINITY"
or
"WHY SENIORS SHOULD BE LOCKED UP"
click!
"MY SUMMER VACATION: A DRUNKEN PARTY, A RAPE, AND A SHUNNING."
click!

My stomach bubbles with toxic waste.

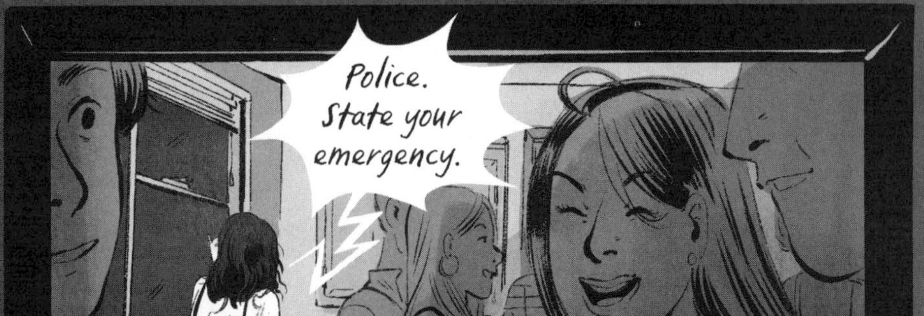
Police.
State your
emergency.
click!

Was I raped?

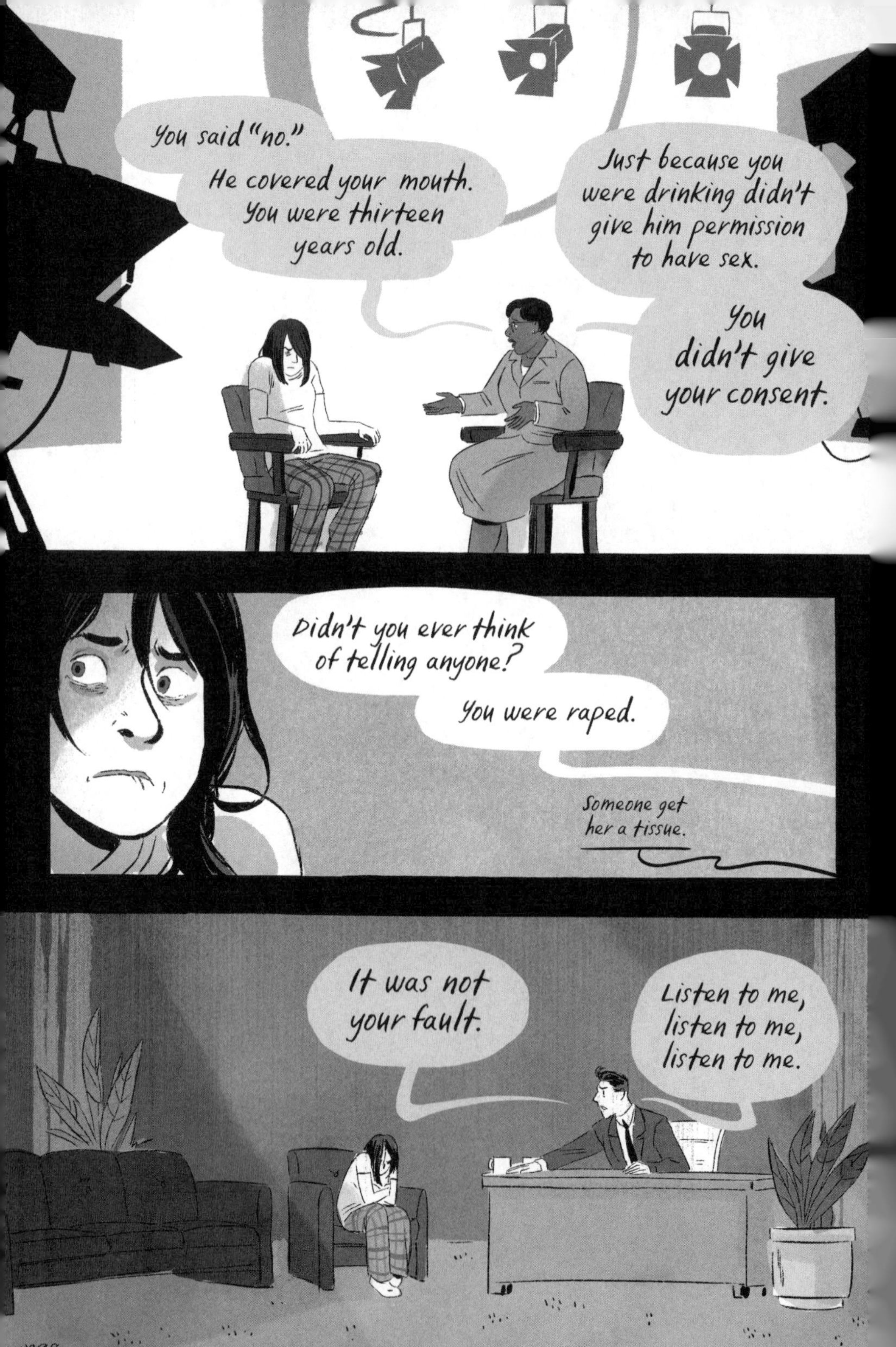

You said "no."
He covered your mouth. You were thirteen years old.
Just because you were drinking didn't give him permission to have sex.
You didn't give your consent.
Didn't you ever think of telling anyone?
You were raped.
Someone get her a tissue.
It was not your fault.
Listen to me, listen to me, listen to me.

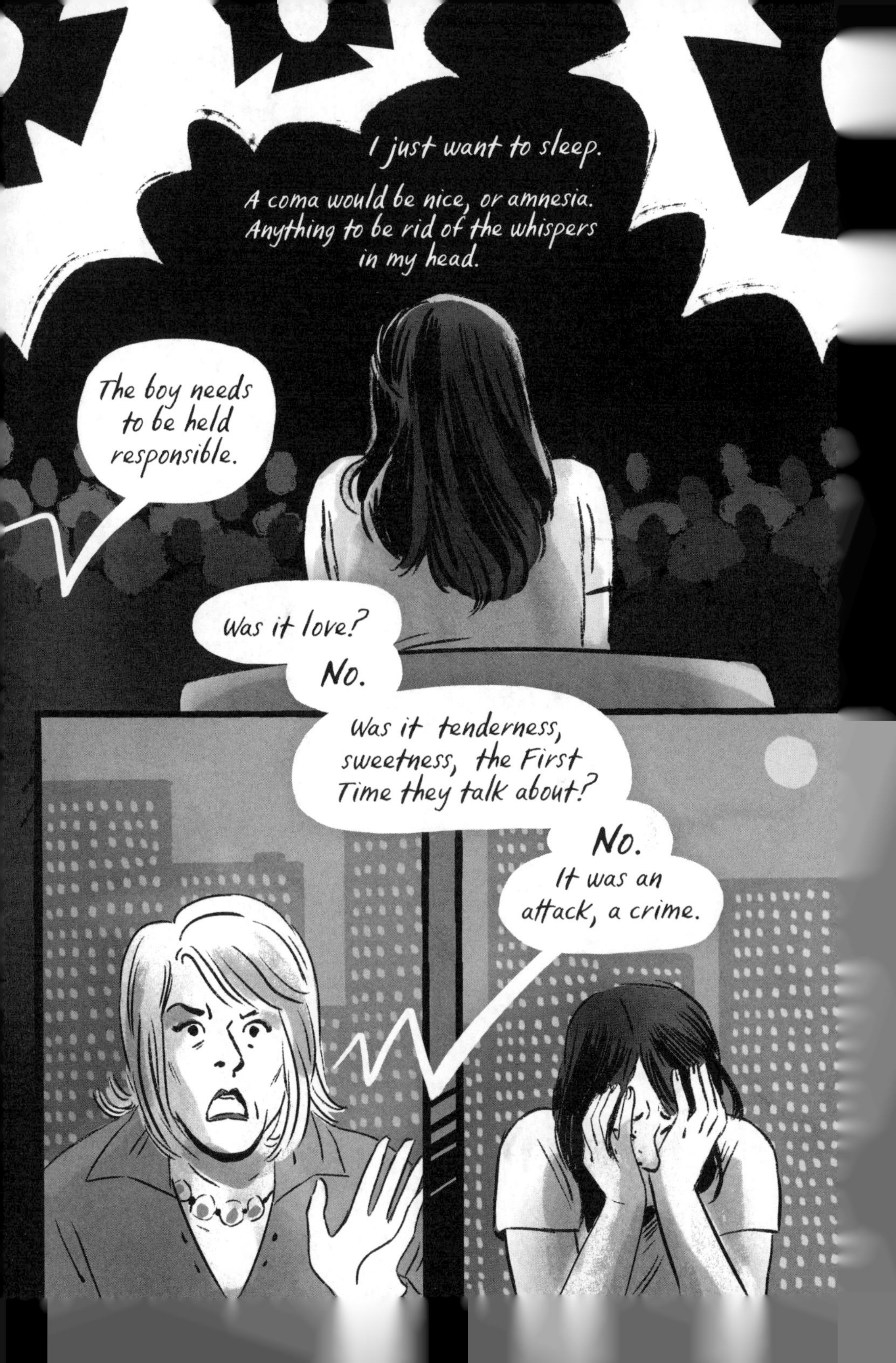
I just want to sleep.
A coma would be nice, or amnesia. Anything to be rid of the whispers in my head.
The boy needs to be held responsible.
Was it love?
No.
Was it tenderness, sweetness, the First Time they talk about?
No.
It was an attack, a crime.

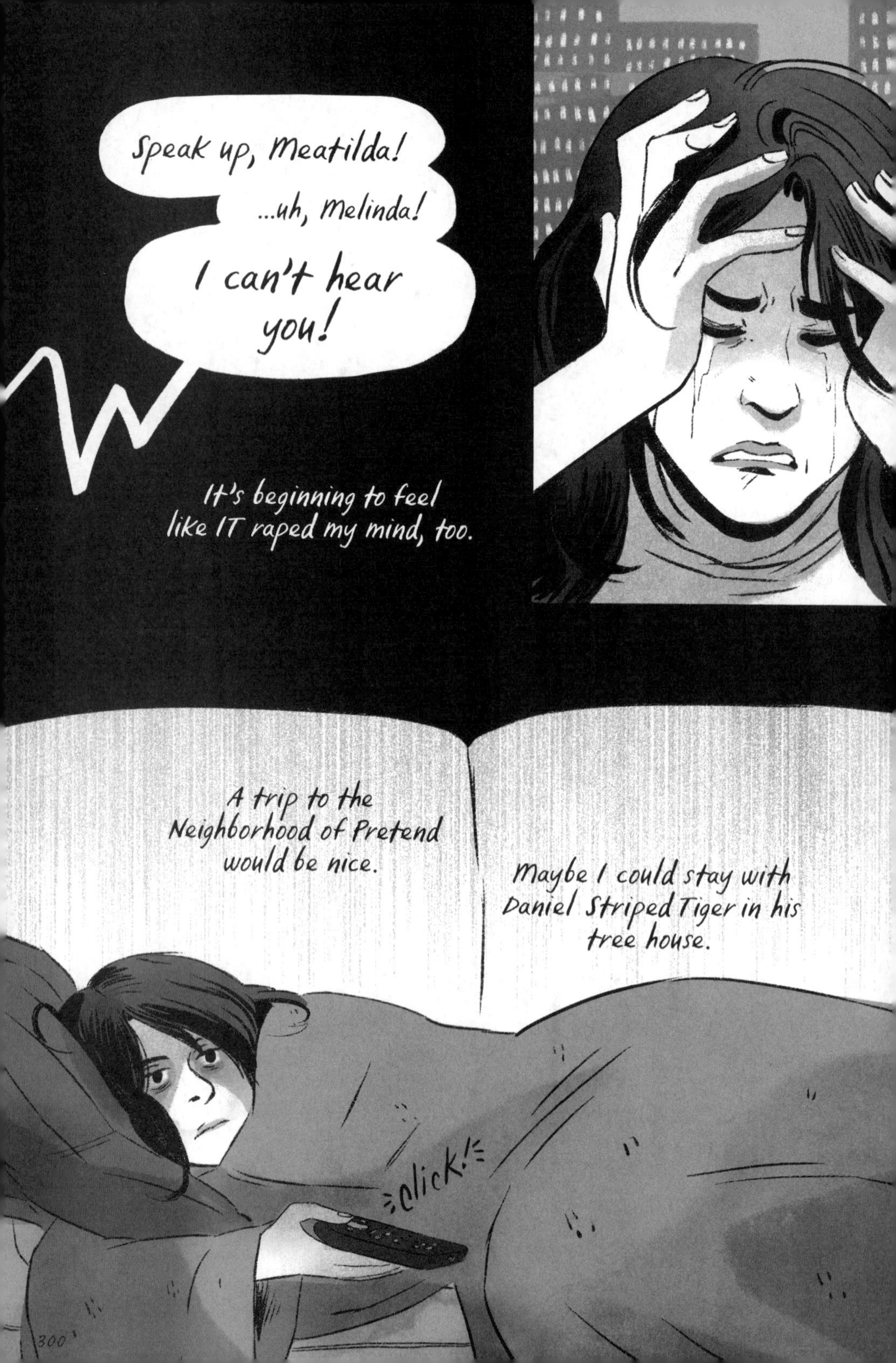
Speak up, Meatilda!
...uh, Melinda!
I can't hear you!
It's beginning to feel like IT raped my mind, too.
A trip to the Neighborhood of Pretend would be nice.
Maybe I could stay with Daniel Striped Tiger in his tree house.
click!

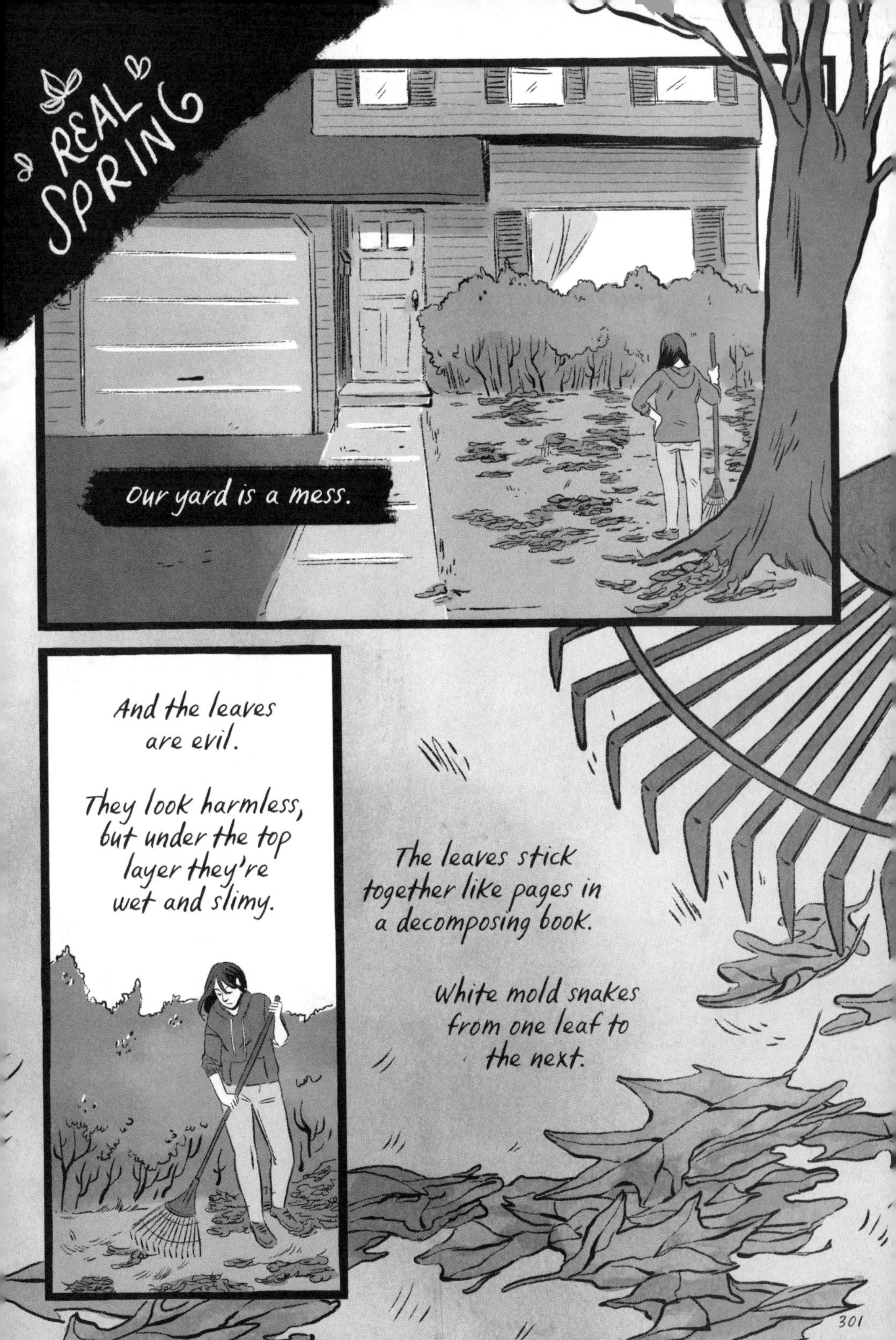
REAL SPRING
Our yard is a mess.
And the leaves are evil.
They look harmless, but under the top layer they're wet and slimy.
The leaves stick together like pages in a decomposing book.
White mold snakes from one leaf to the next.

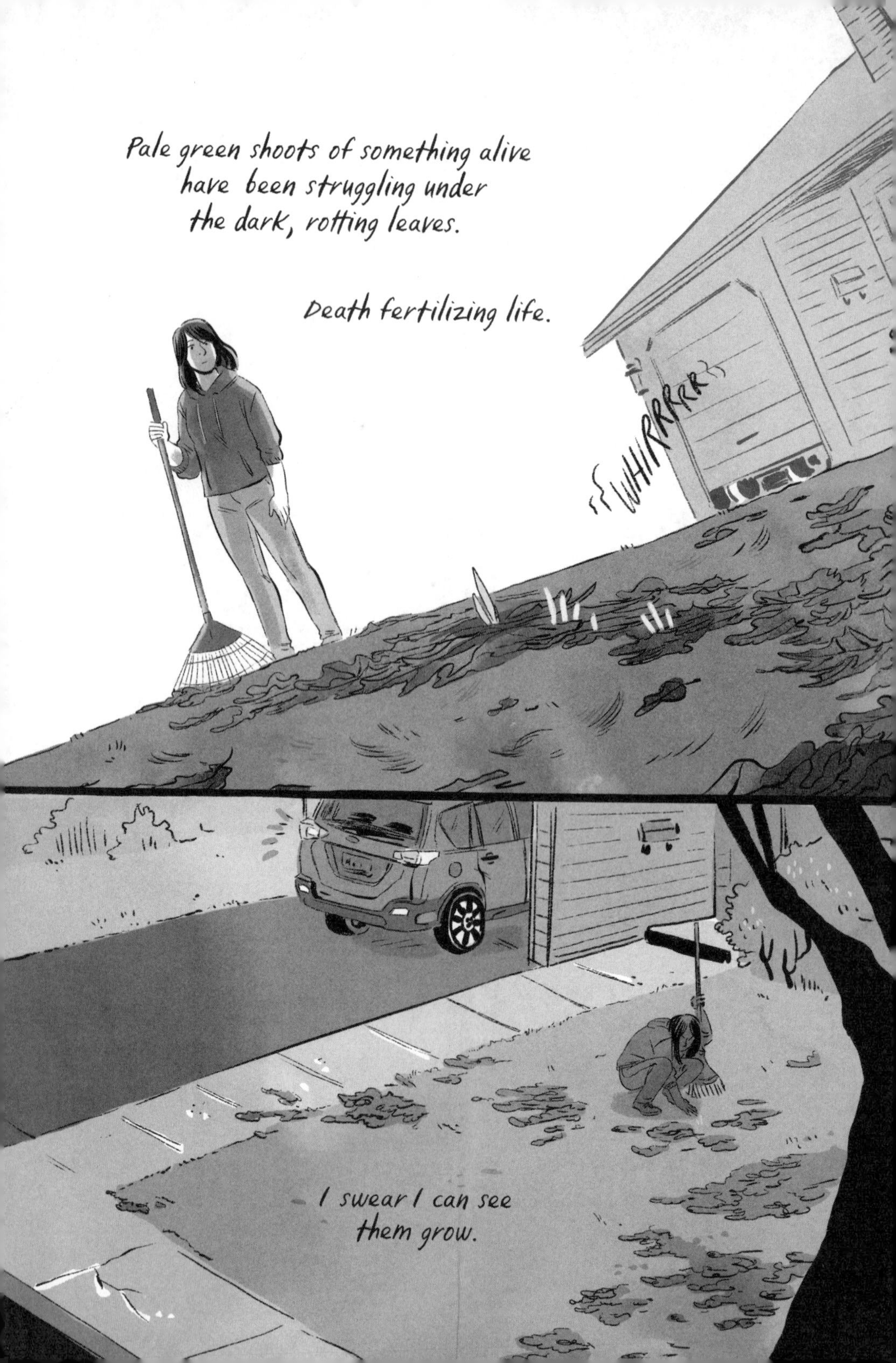
Pale green shoots of something alive have been struggling under the dark, rotting leaves.
Death fertilizing life.
WHIRRRRR
I swear I can see them grow.

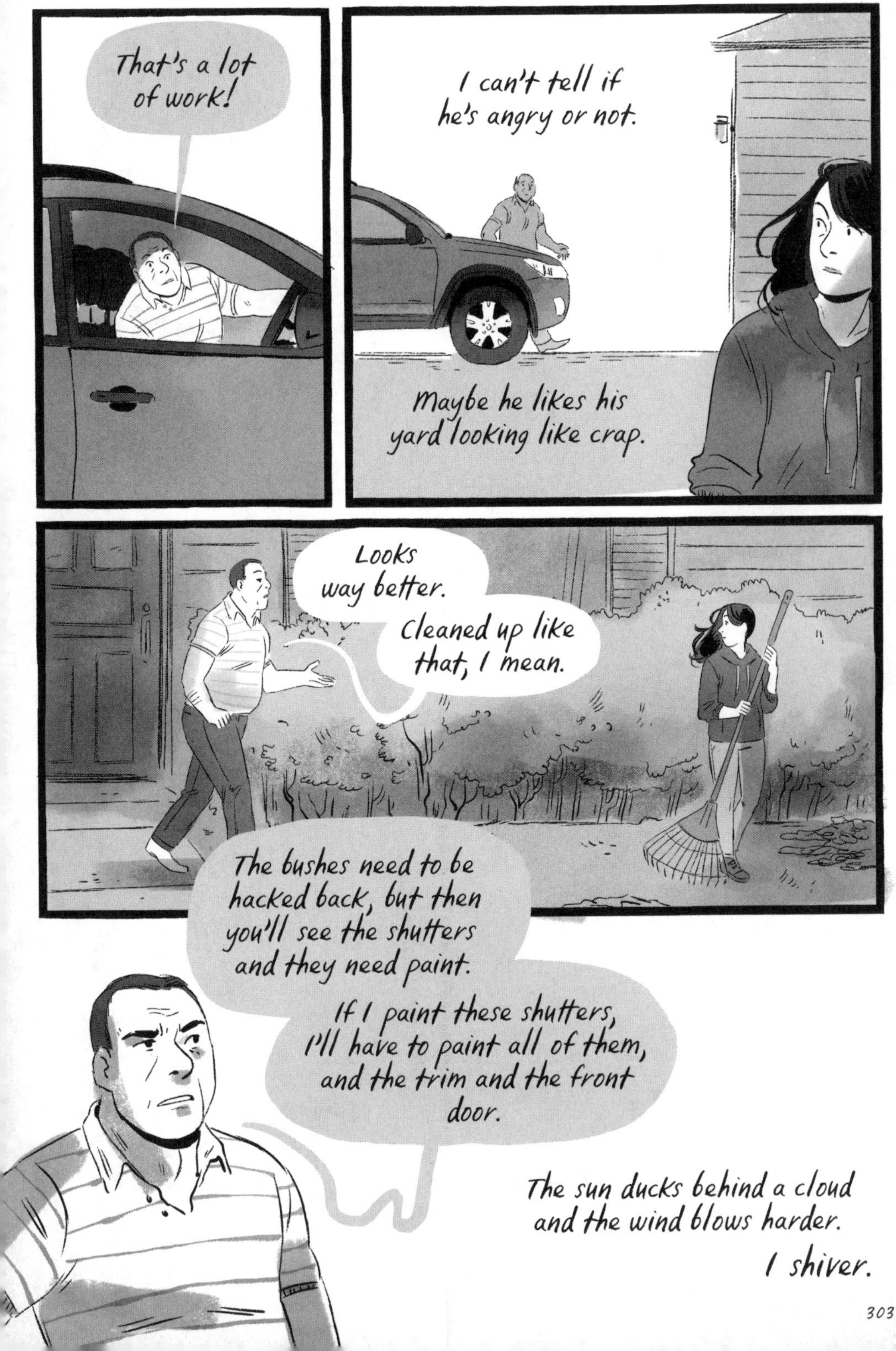
That's a lot of work!
I can't tell if he's angry or not.
Maybe he likes his yard looking like crap.
Looks way better.
Cleaned up like that, I mean.
The bushes need to be hacked back, but then you'll see the shutters and they need paint.
If I paint these shutters, I'll have to paint all of them, and the trim and the front door.
The sun ducks behind a cloud and the wind blows harder.
I shiver.

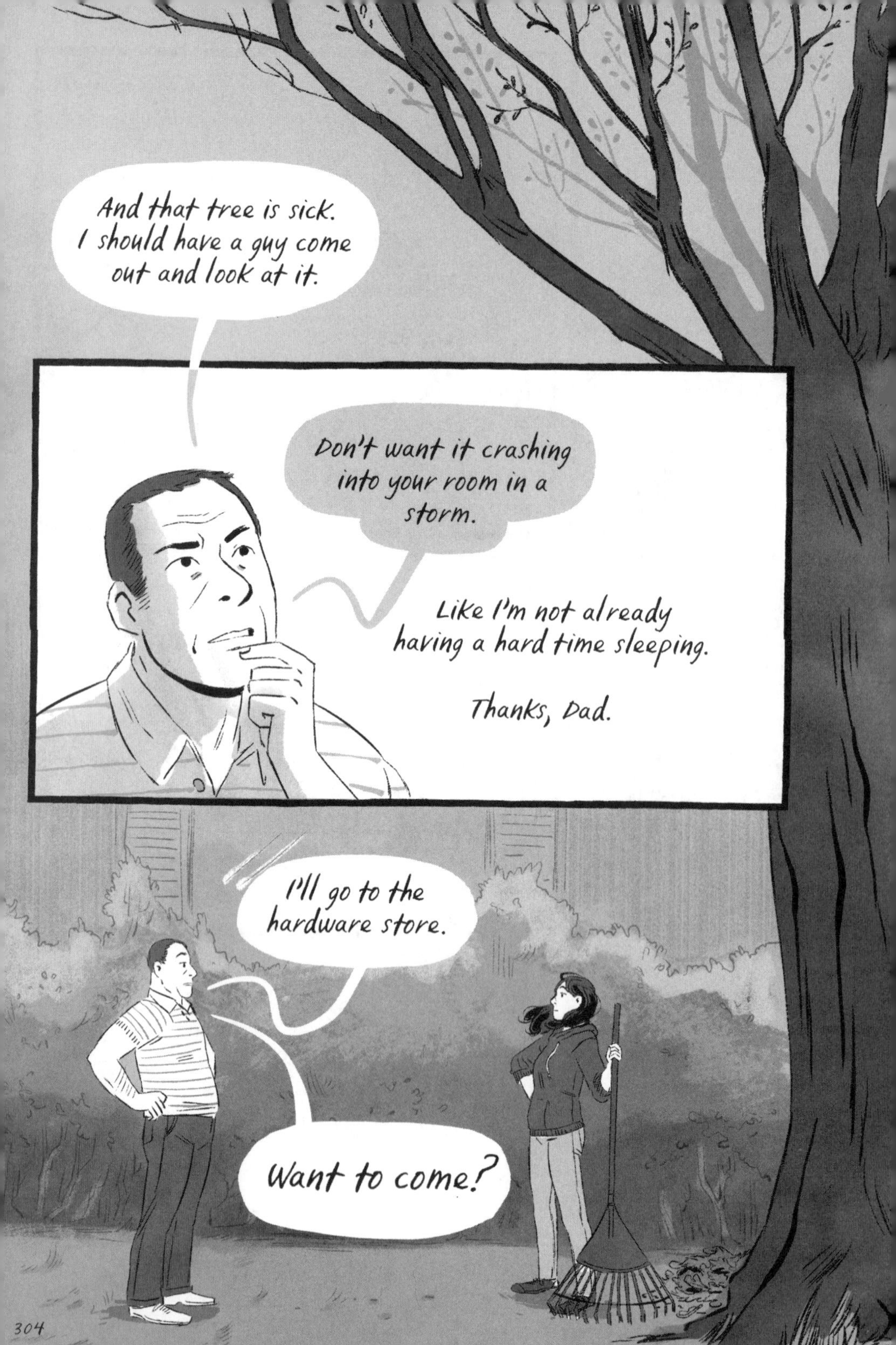
And that tree is sick. I should have a guy come out and look at it.
Don't want it crashing into your room in a storm.
Like I'm not already having a hard time sleeping.
Thanks, Dad.
I'll go to the hardware store.
Want to come?

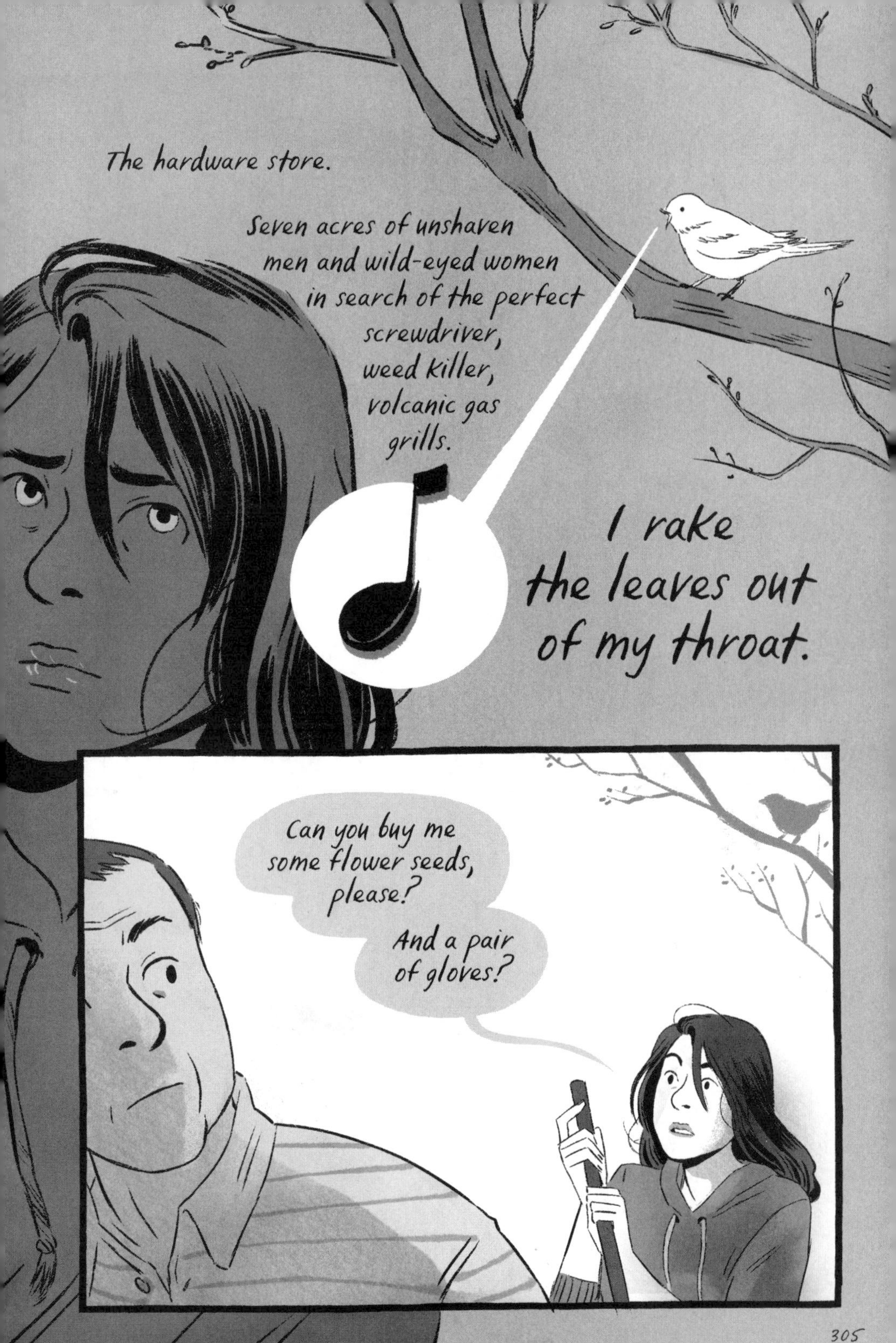
The hardware store.
Seven acres of unshaven men and wild-eyed women in search of the perfect screwdriver, weed killer, volcanic gas grills.
I rake the leaves out of my throat.
Can you buy me some flower seeds, please?
And a pair of gloves?

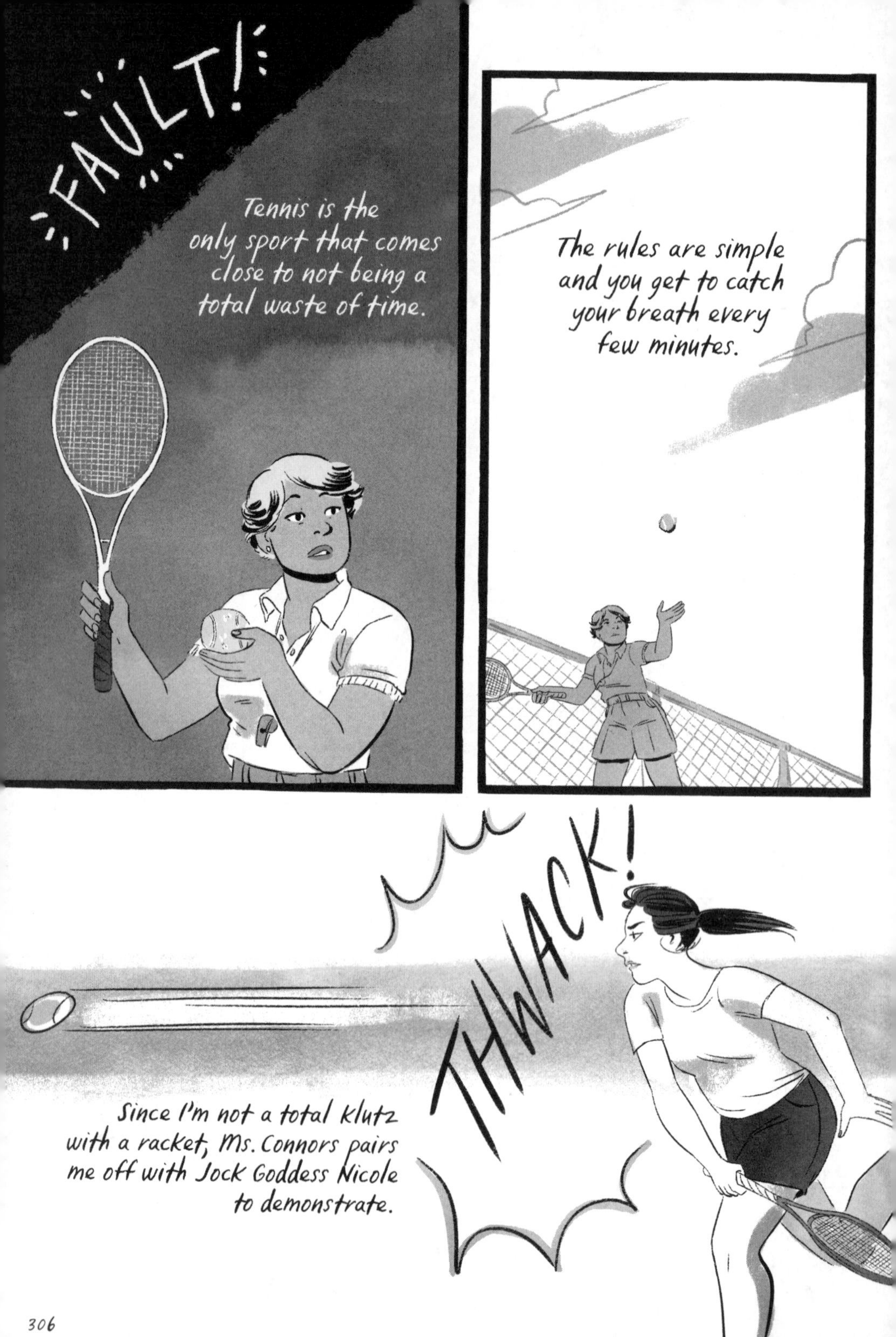
FAULT!
Tennis is the only sport that comes close to not being a total waste of time.
The rules are simple and you get to catch your breath every few minutes.
THWACK!
Since I'm not a total klutz with a racket, Ms. Connors pairs me off with Jock Goddess Nicole to demonstrate.

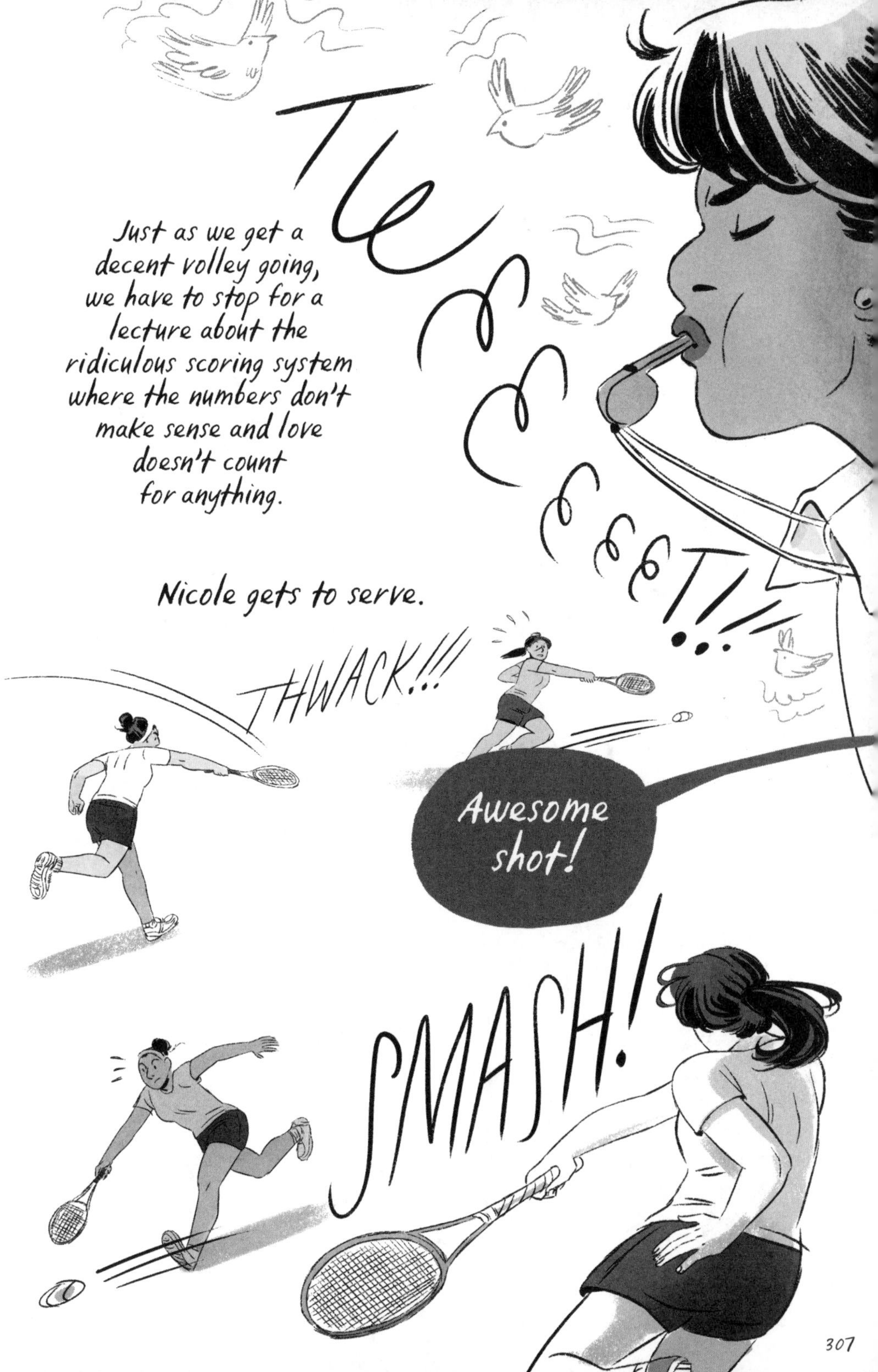
TWEEEEET!!!
Just as we get a decent volley going, we have to stop for a lecture about the ridiculous scoring system where the numbers don't make sense and love doesn't count for anything.
Nicole gets to serve.
THWACK!!!
Awesome shot!
SMASH!

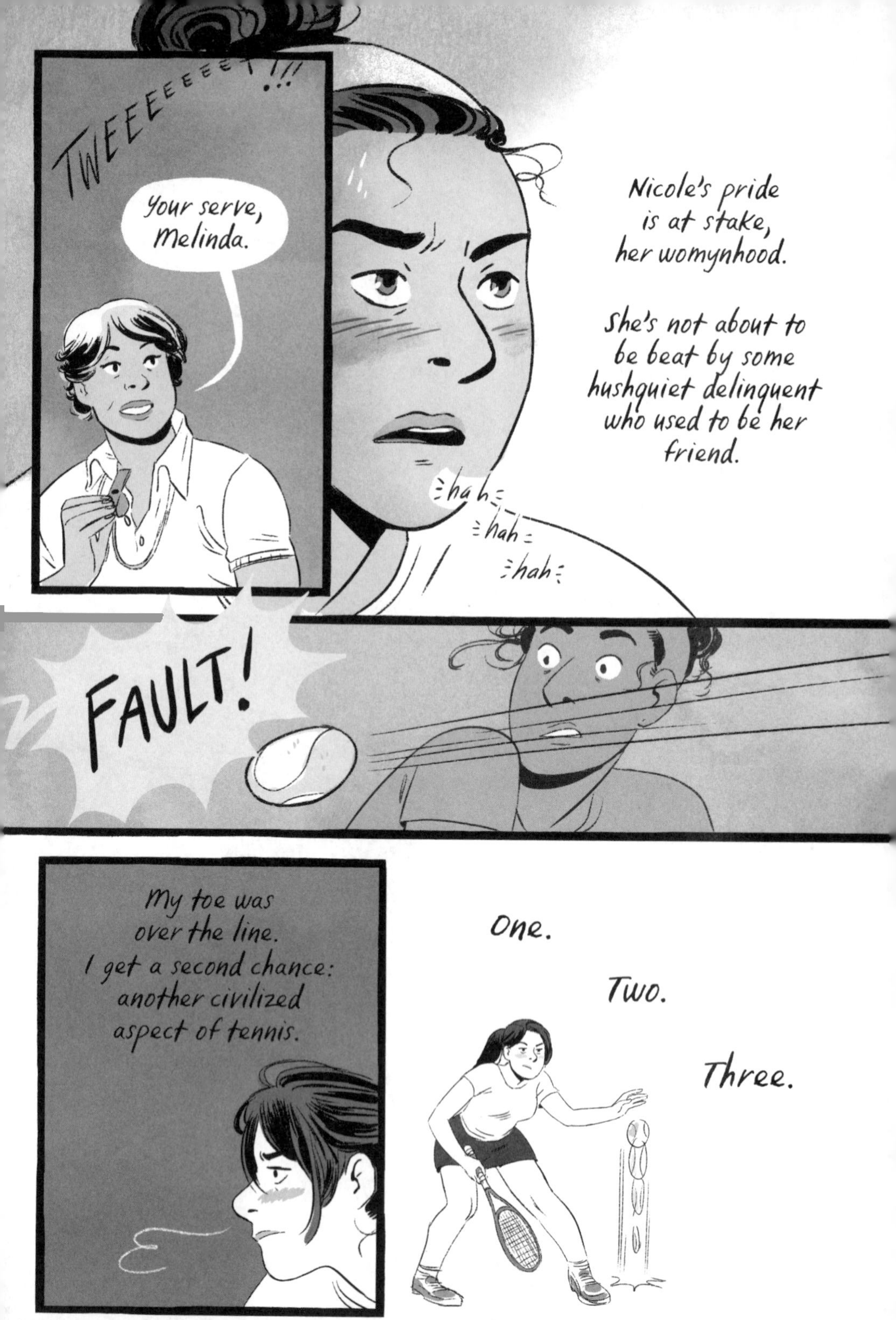
TWEEEEEEEET!!!
Your serve, Melinda.
Nicole's pride is at stake, her womynhood.
She's not about to be beat by some hushquiet delinquent who used to be her friend.
hah
hah
hah
FAULT!
My toe was over the line. I get a second chance: another civilized aspect of tennis.
One.
Two.
Three.

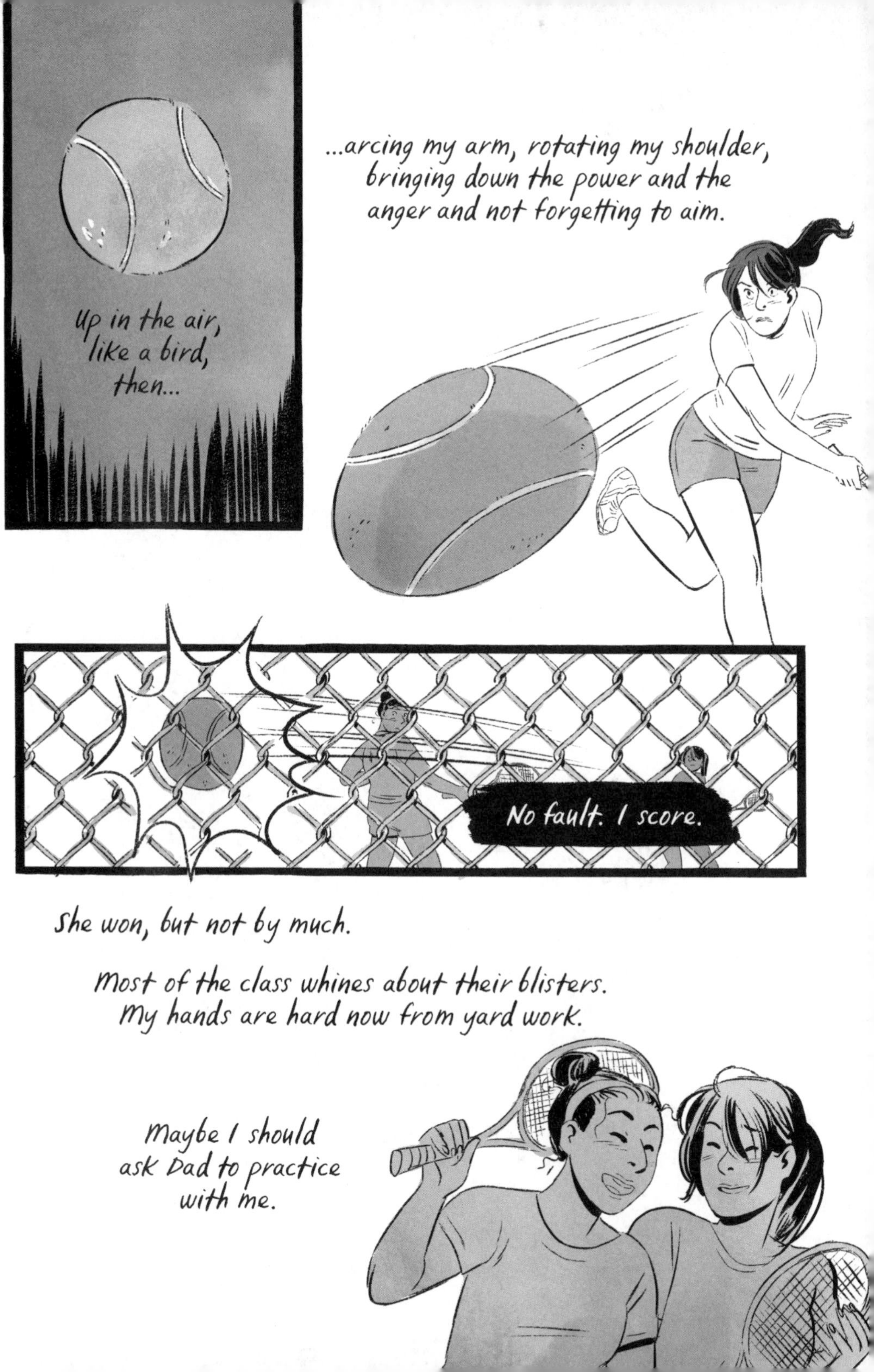

Up in the air,
like a bird,
then...
...arcing my arm, rotating my shoulder,
bringing down the power and the
anger and not forgetting to aim.
No fault. I score.
She won, but not by much.
Most of the class whines about their blisters.
My hands are hard now from yard work.
Maybe I should
ask Dad to practice
with me.

YEARBOOKS

The annual yearbook ritual is bizarre.

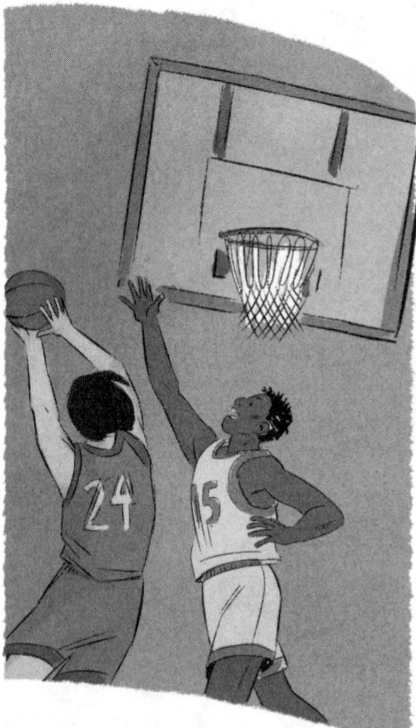
24
15

You hunt down every person who looks vaguely familiar and get them to write that you are best friends who will never forget each other.

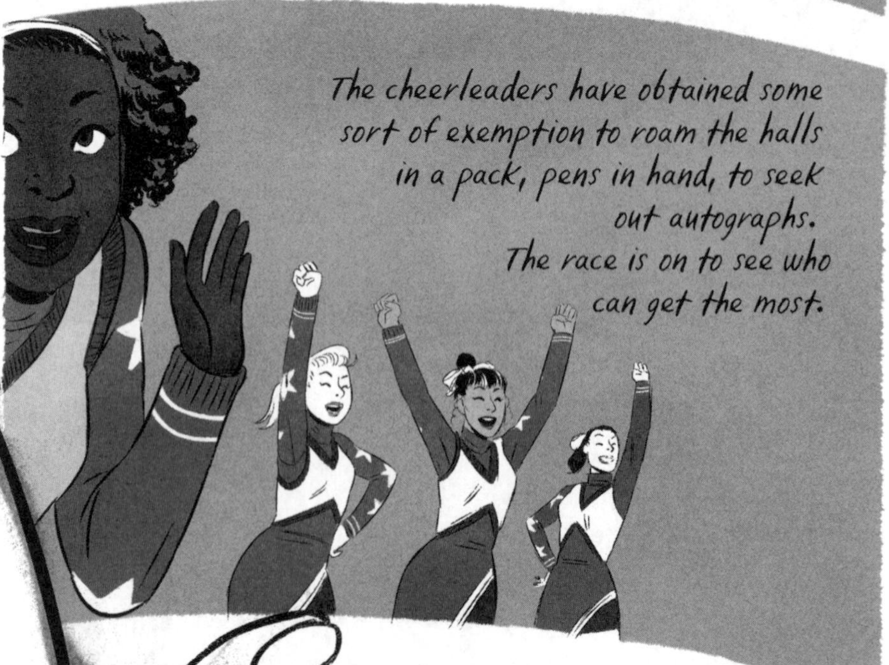
The cheerleaders have obtained some sort of exemption to roam the halls in a pack, pens in hand, to seek out autographs.
The race is on to see who can get the most.

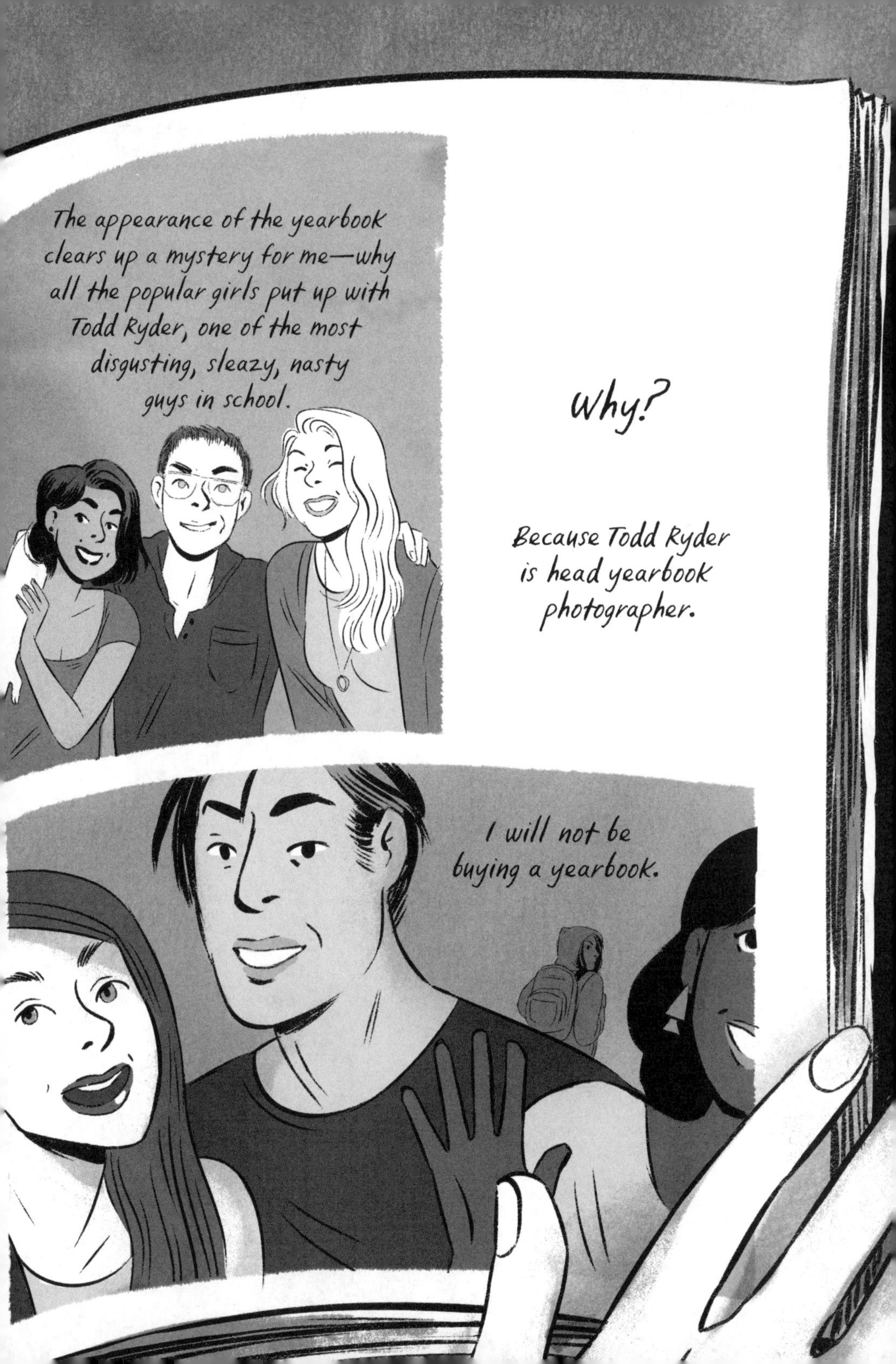
The appearance of the yearbook clears up a mystery for me—why all the popular girls put up with Todd Ryder, one of the most disgusting, sleazy, nasty guys in school.
Why?
Because Todd Ryder is head yearbook photographer.
I will not be buying a yearbook.

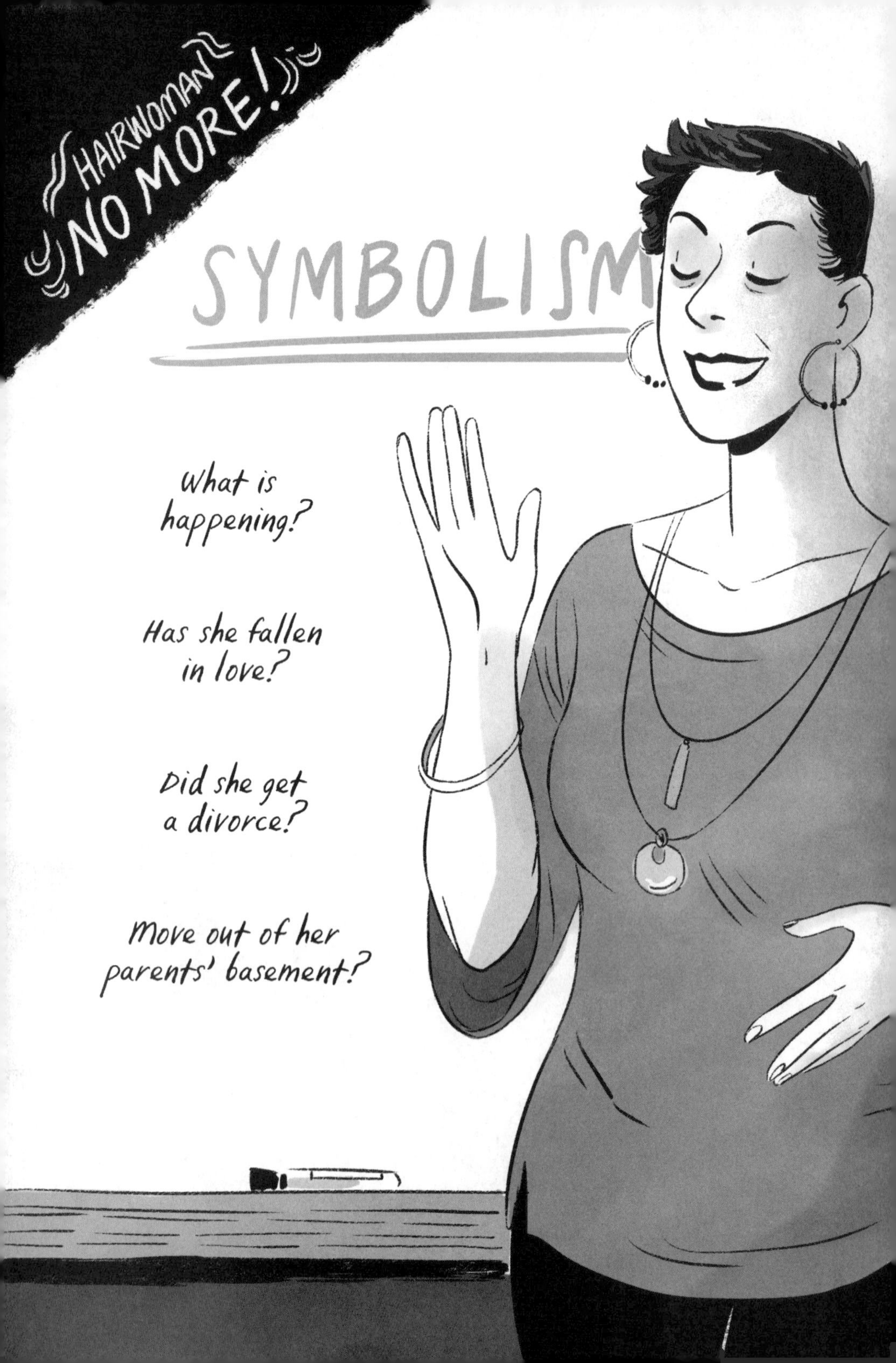
HAIRWOMAN NO MORE!
SYMBOLISM
What is happening?
Has she fallen in love?
Did she get a divorce?
Move out of her parents' basement?

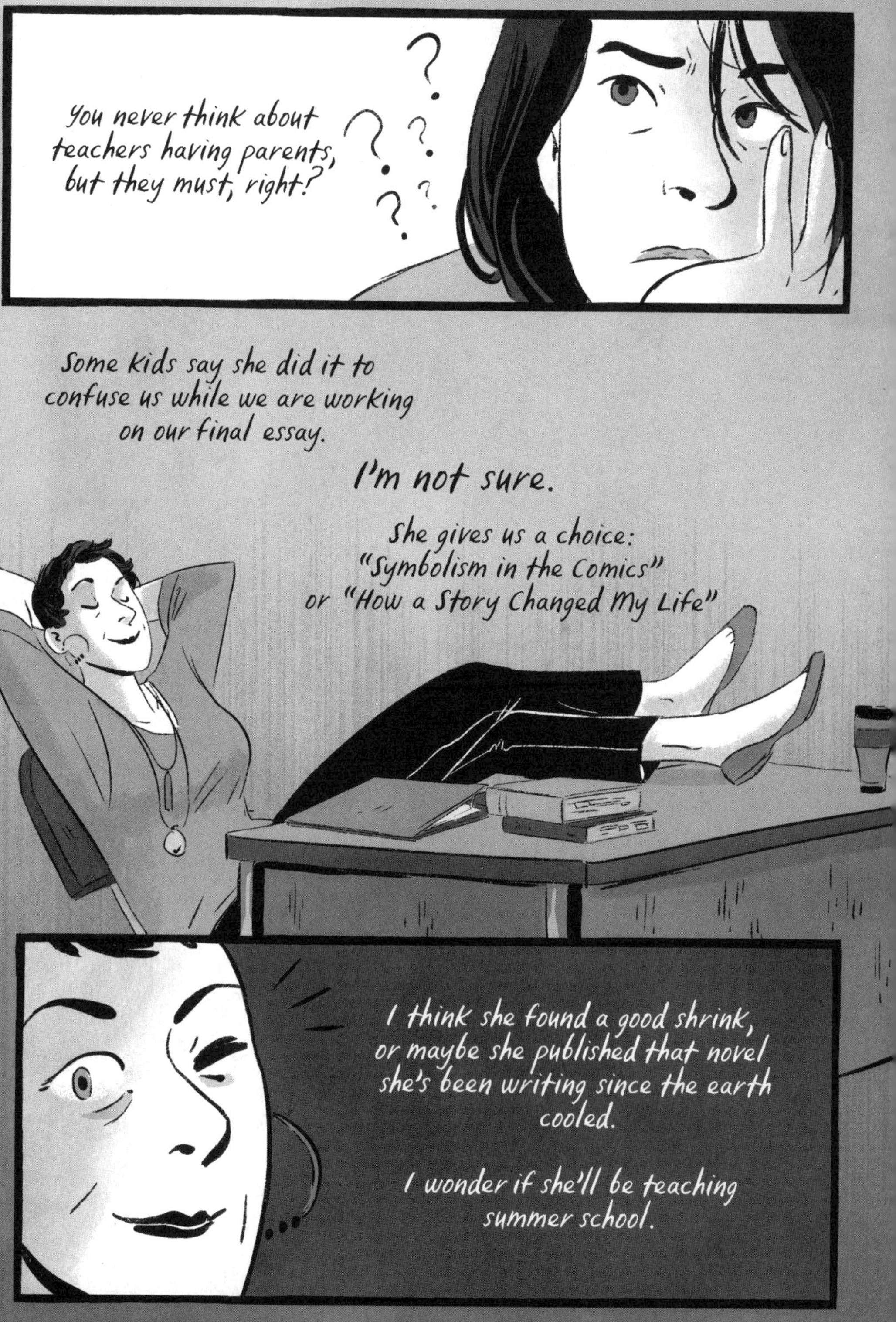
You never think about teachers having parents, but they must, right?
Some kids say she did it to confuse us while we are working on our final essay.
I'm not sure.
She gives us a choice: "Symbolism in the Comics" or "How a Story Changed My Life"
I think she found a good shrink, or maybe she published that novel she's been writing since the earth cooled.
I wonder if she'll be teaching summer school.

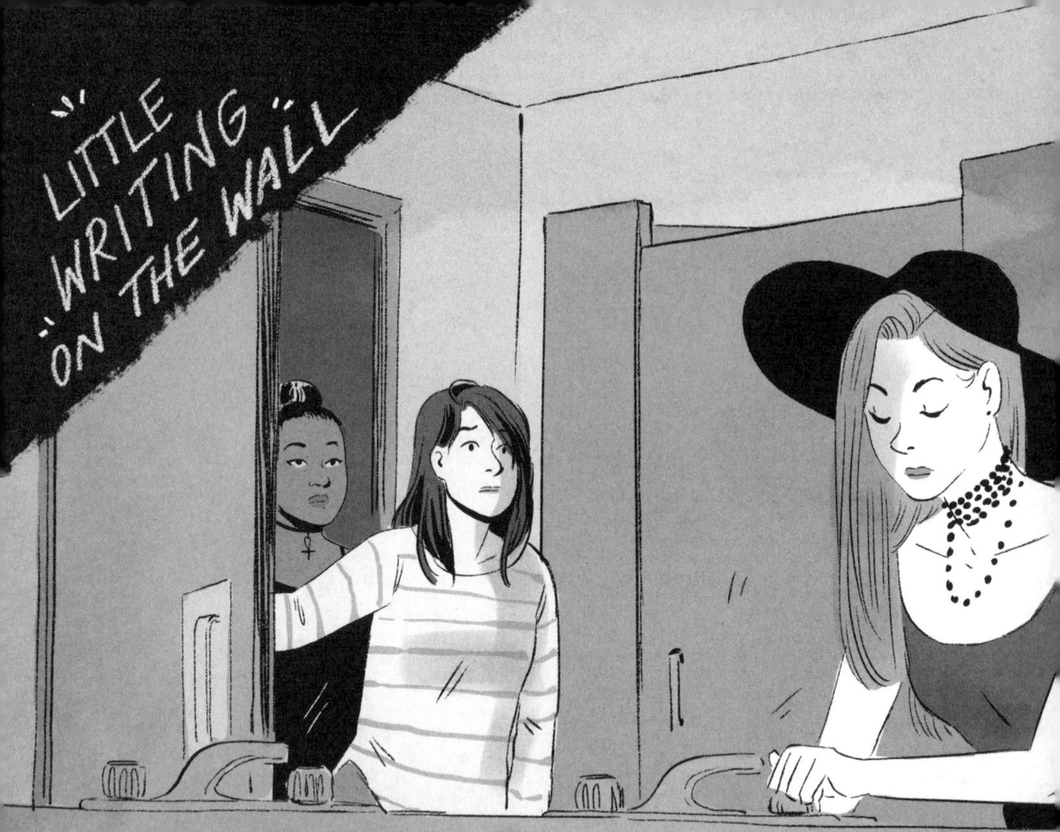
LITTLE WRITING ON THE WALL
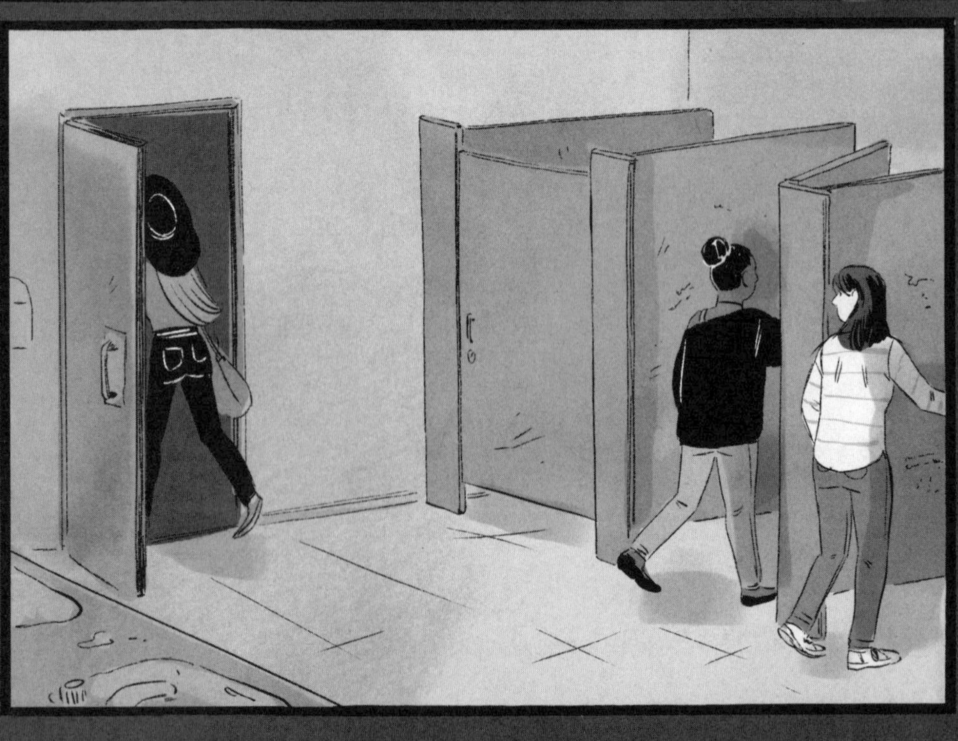

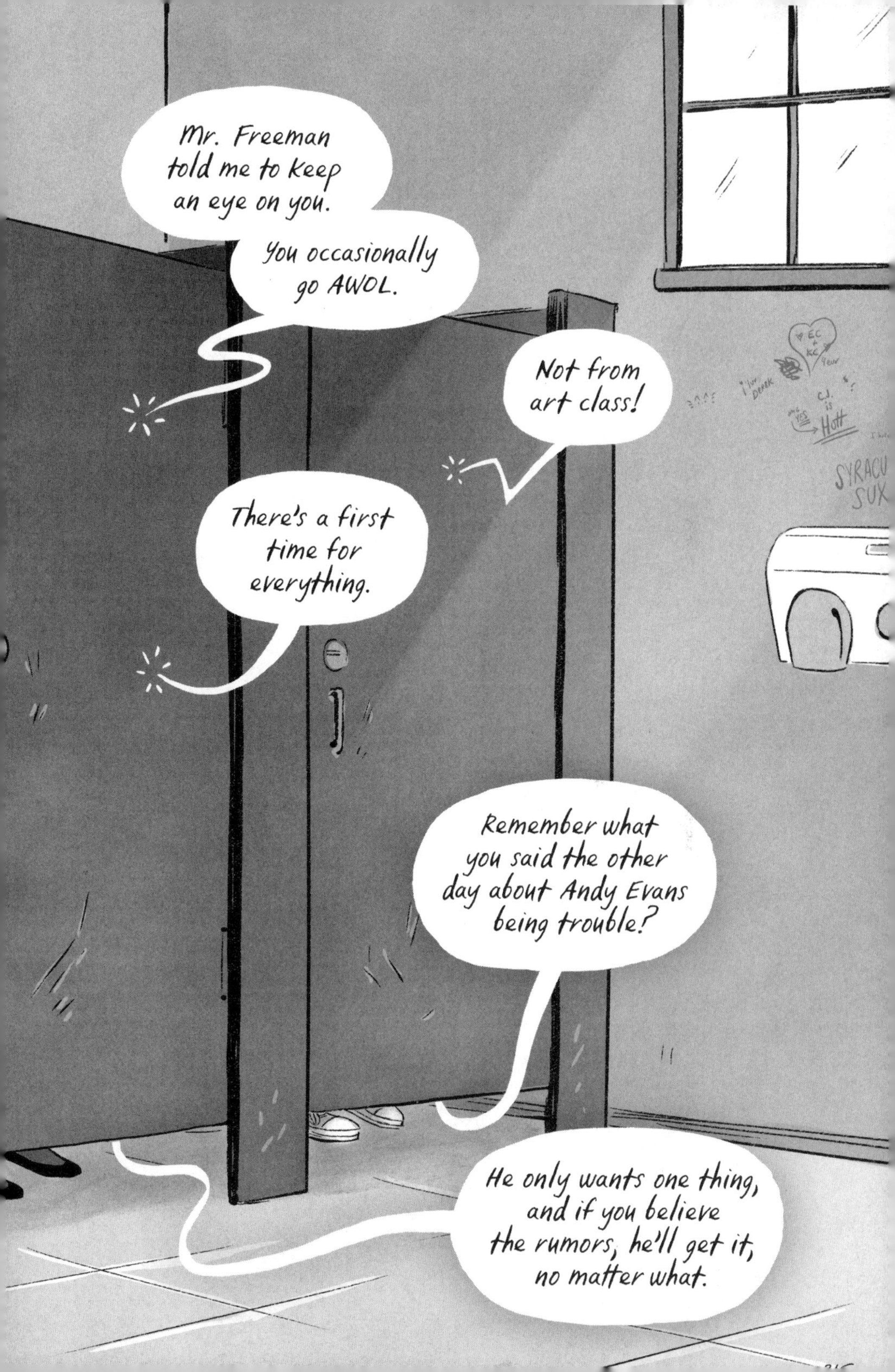
Mr. Freeman told me to keep an eye on you.
You occasionally go AWOL.
Not from art class!
There's a first time for everything.
Remember what you said the other day about Andy Evans being trouble?
He only wants one thing, and if you believe the rumors, he'll get it, no matter what.
C.J. is Hott
SYRACU SUX

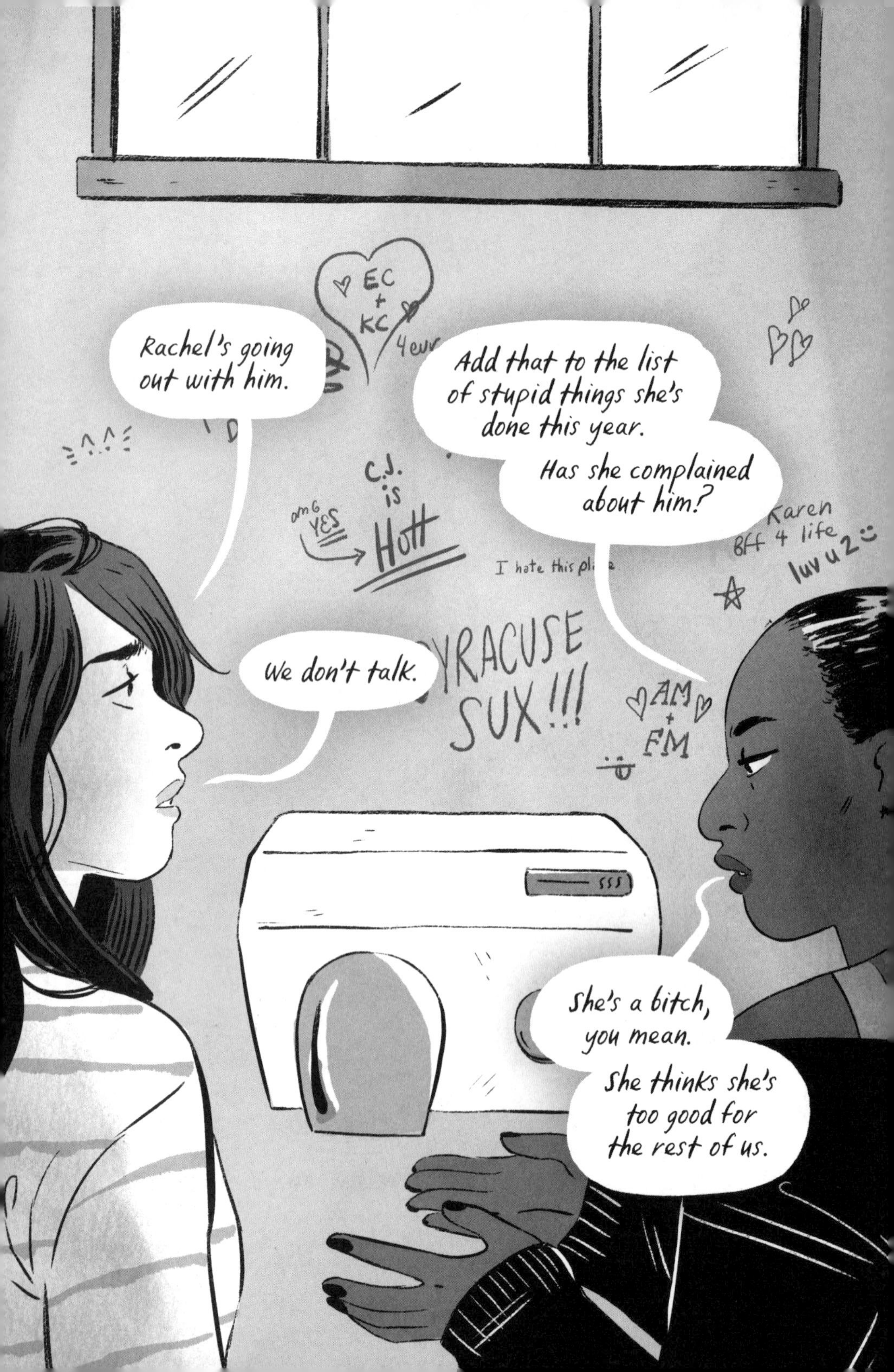
Rachel's going out with him.
Add that to the list of stupid things she's done this year.
Has she complained about him?
We don't talk.
She's a bitch, you mean.
She thinks she's too good for the rest of us.
EC + KC 4eur
C.J. is Hott
omG YES
I hate this pl
Karen BFF 4 life
luv u 2
SYRACUSE SUX!!!
AM + FM

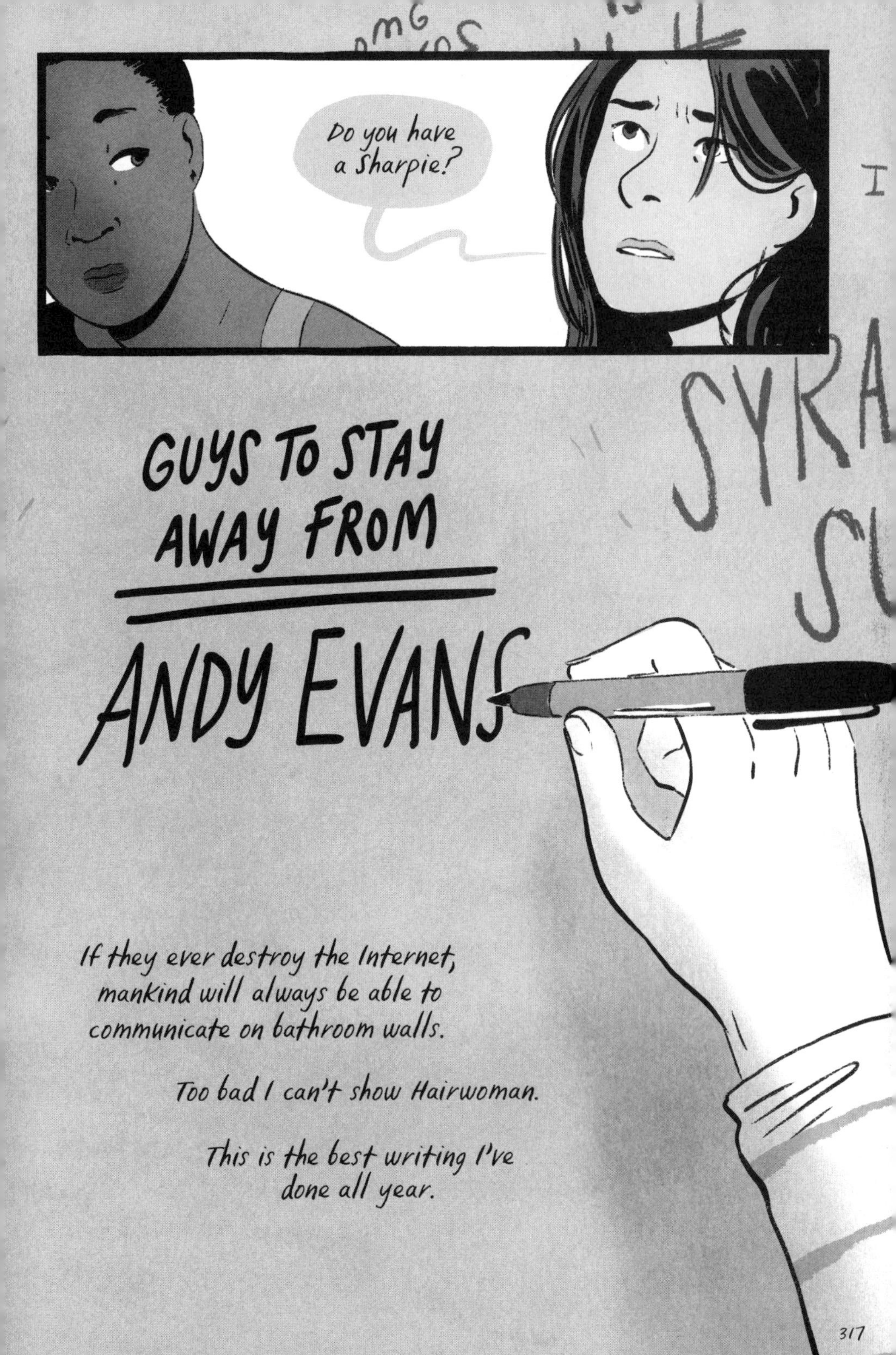
Do you have a Sharpie?
GUYS TO STAY AWAY FROM
ANDY EVANS
If they ever destroy the Internet, mankind will always be able to communicate on bathroom walls.
Too bad I can't show Hairwoman.
This is the best writing I've done all year.

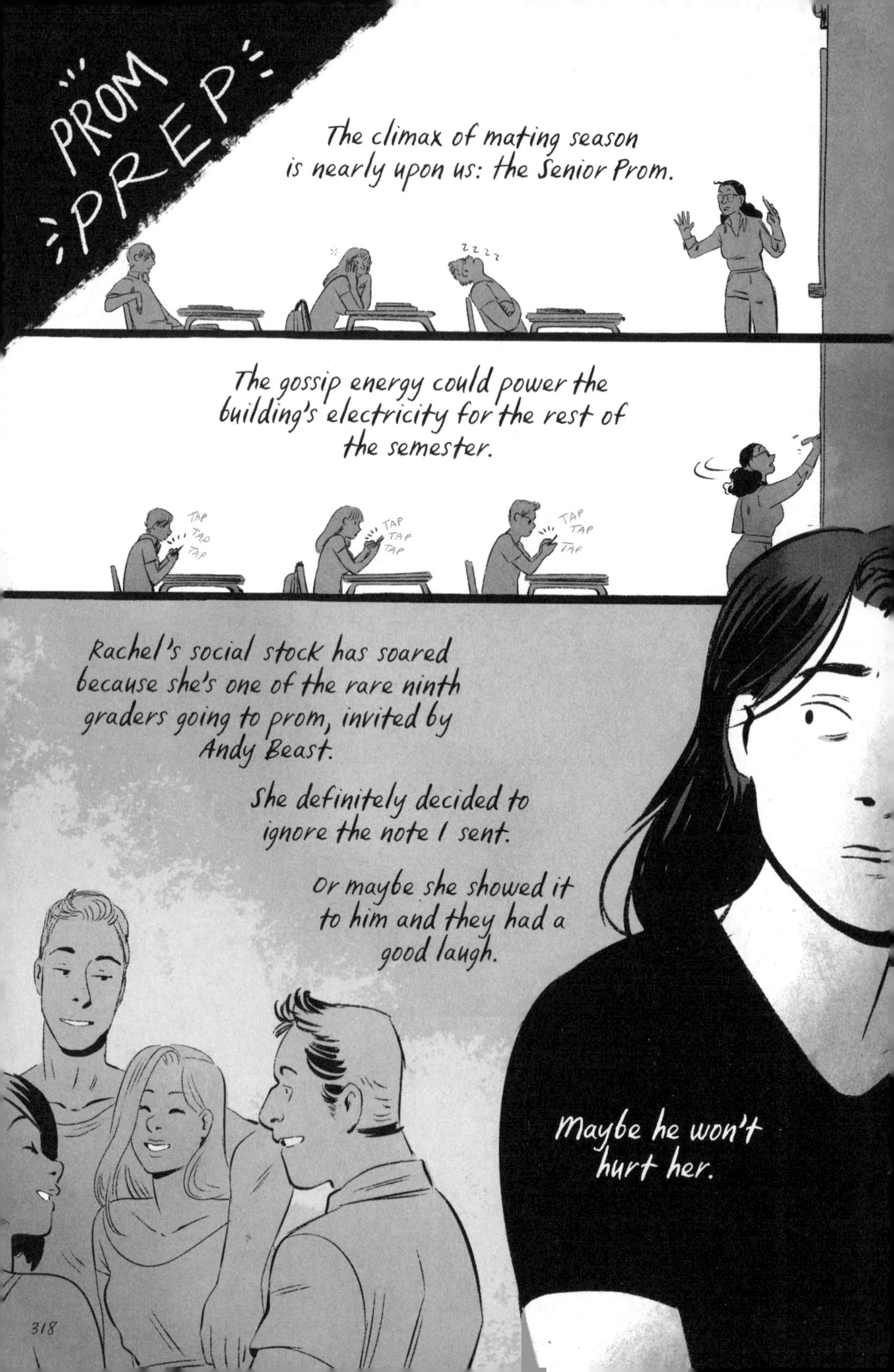
PROM PREP
The climax of mating season is nearly upon us: the Senior Prom.
ZZZZ
The gossip energy could power the building's electricity for the rest of the semester.
TAP TAP TAP
TAP TAP TAP
TAP TAP TAP
Rachel's social stock has soared because she's one of the rare ninth graders going to prom, invited by Andy Beast.
She definitely decided to ignore the note I sent.
Or maybe she showed it to him and they had a good laugh.
Maybe he won't hurt her.

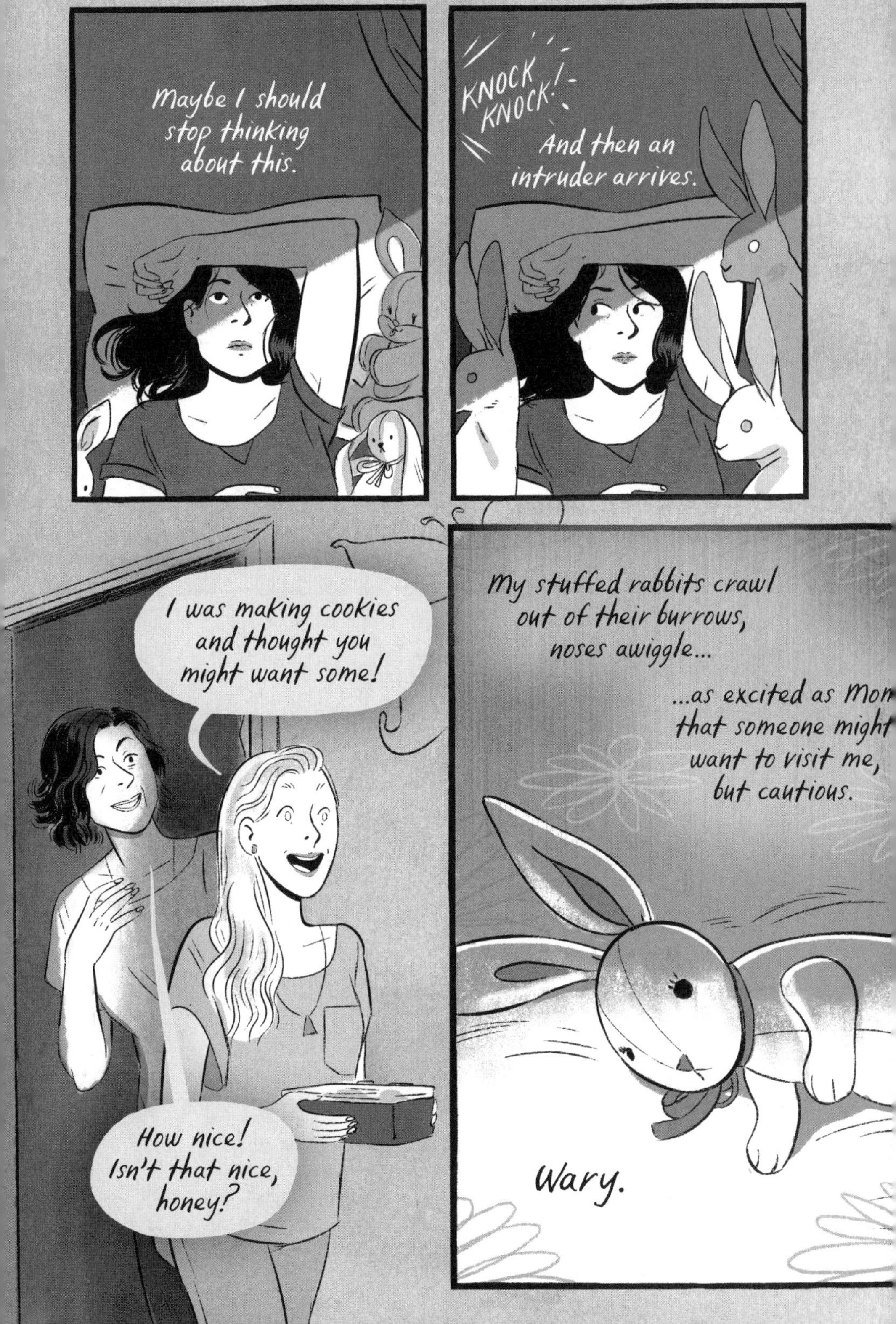
Maybe I should stop thinking about this.
KNOCK KNOCK!
And then an intruder arrives.
I was making cookies and thought you might want some!
How nice! Isn't that nice, honey?
My stuffed rabbits crawl out of their burrows, noses awiggle...
...as excited as Mom that someone might want to visit me, but cautious.
Wary.

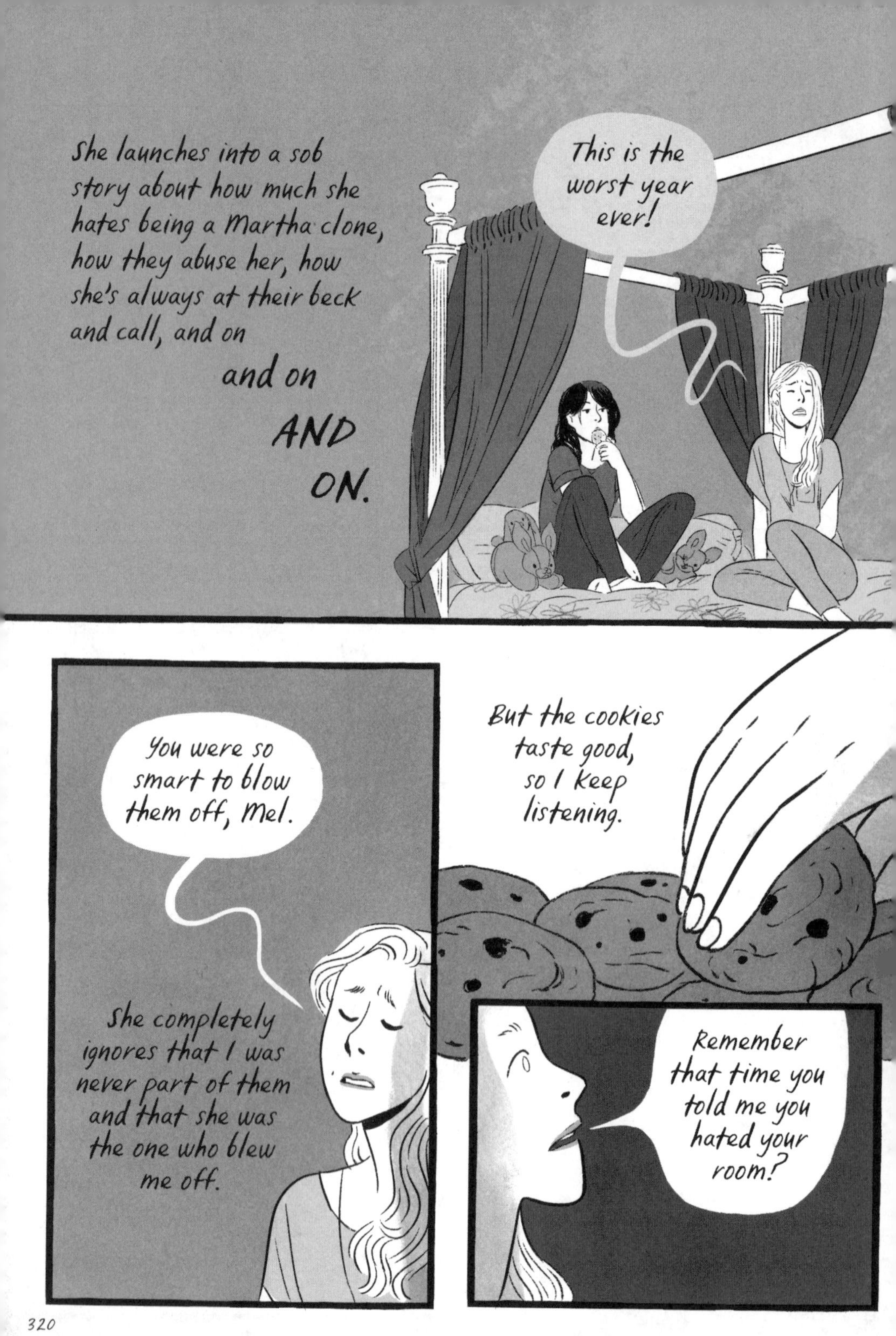

She launches into a sob story about how much she hates being a Martha clone, how they abuse her, how she's always at their beck and call, and on
and on
AND
ON.
This is the worst year ever!
You were so smart to blow them off, Mel.
She completely ignores that I was never part of them and that she was the one who blew me off.
But the cookies taste good, so I keep listening.
Remember that time you told me you hated your room?

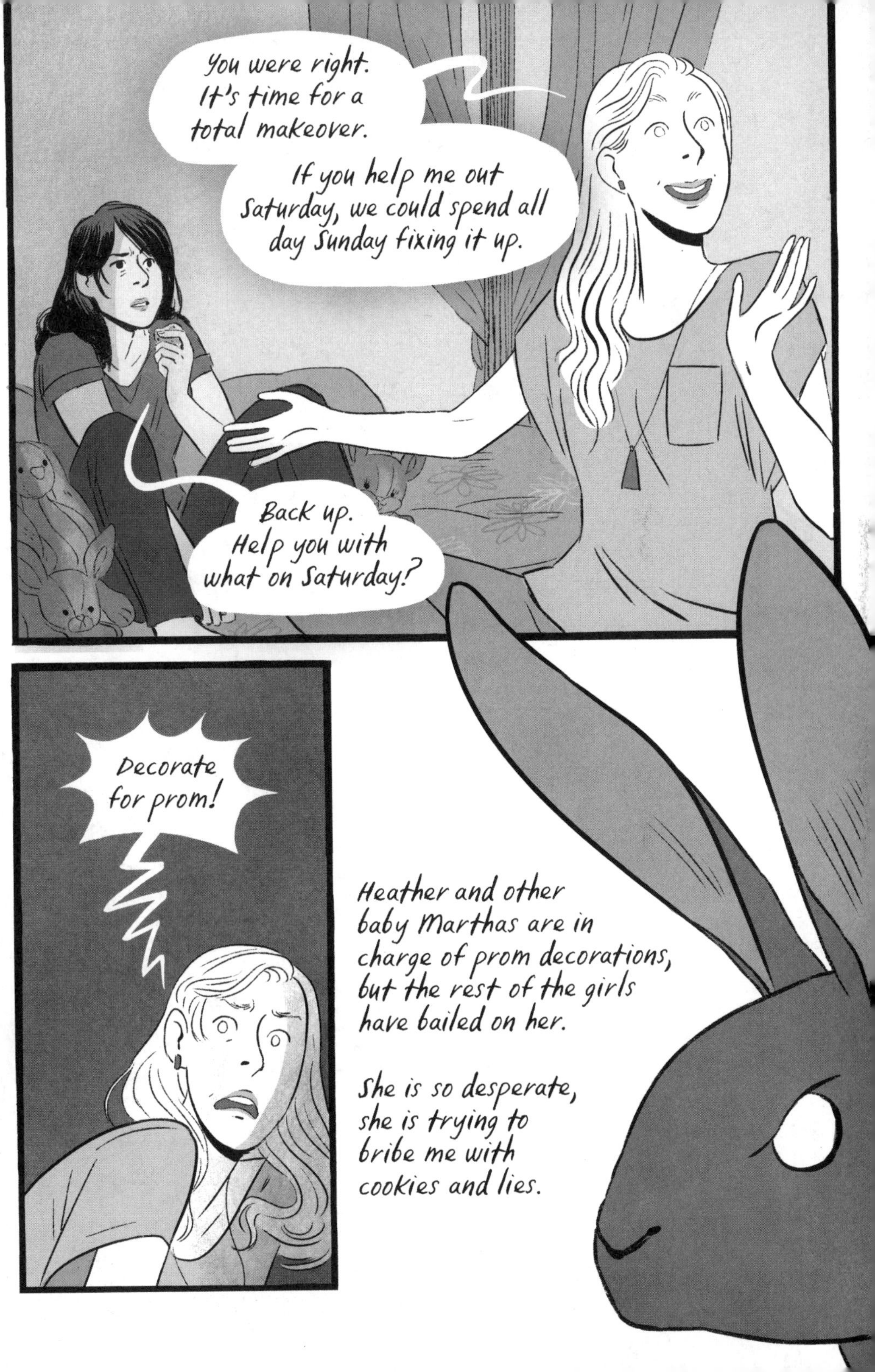
You were right. It's time for a total makeover.
If you help me out Saturday, we could spend all day Sunday fixing it up.
Back up. Help you with what on Saturday?
Decorate for prom!
Heather and other baby Marthas are in charge of prom decorations, but the rest of the girls have bailed on her.
She is so desperate, she is trying to bribe me with cookies and lies.

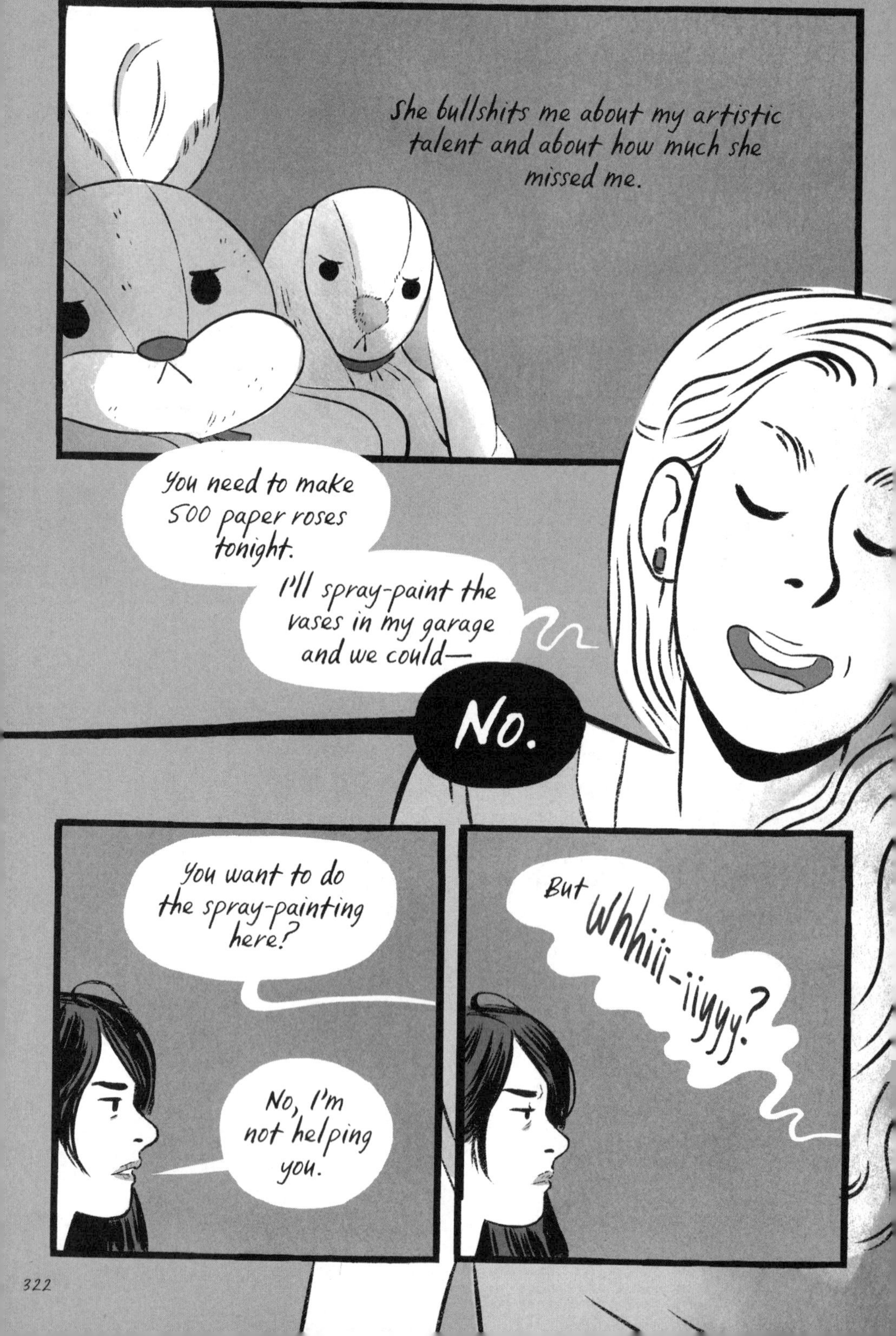
She bullshits me about my artistic talent and about how much she missed me.
You need to make 500 paper roses tonight.
I'll spray-paint the vases in my garage and we could—
No.
You want to do the spray-painting here?
No, I'm not helping you.
But Whhiii-iiyyy?

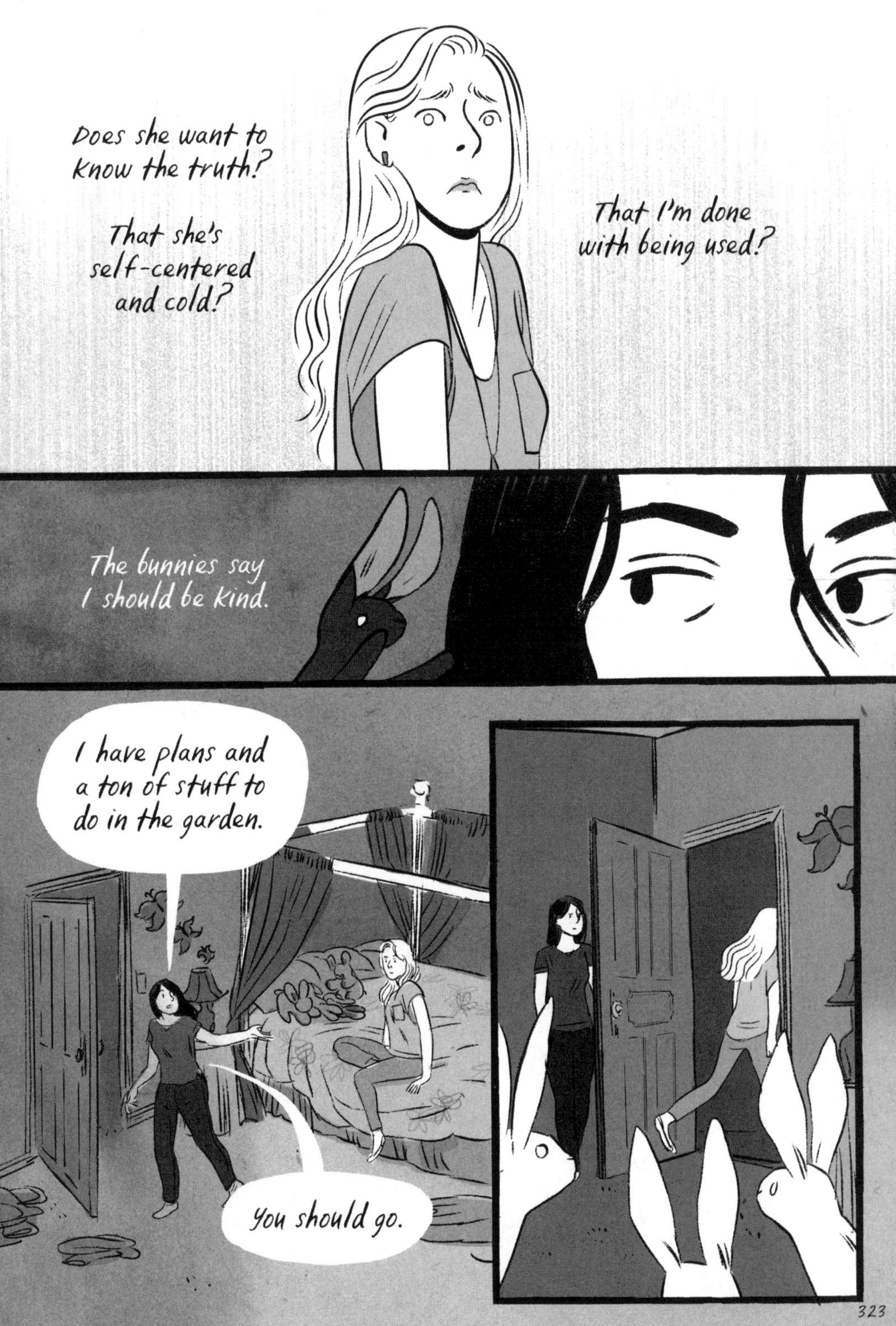
Does she want to know the truth?
That she's self-centered and cold?
That I'm done with being used?
The bunnies say I should be kind.
I have plans and a ton of stuff to do in the garden.
You should go.

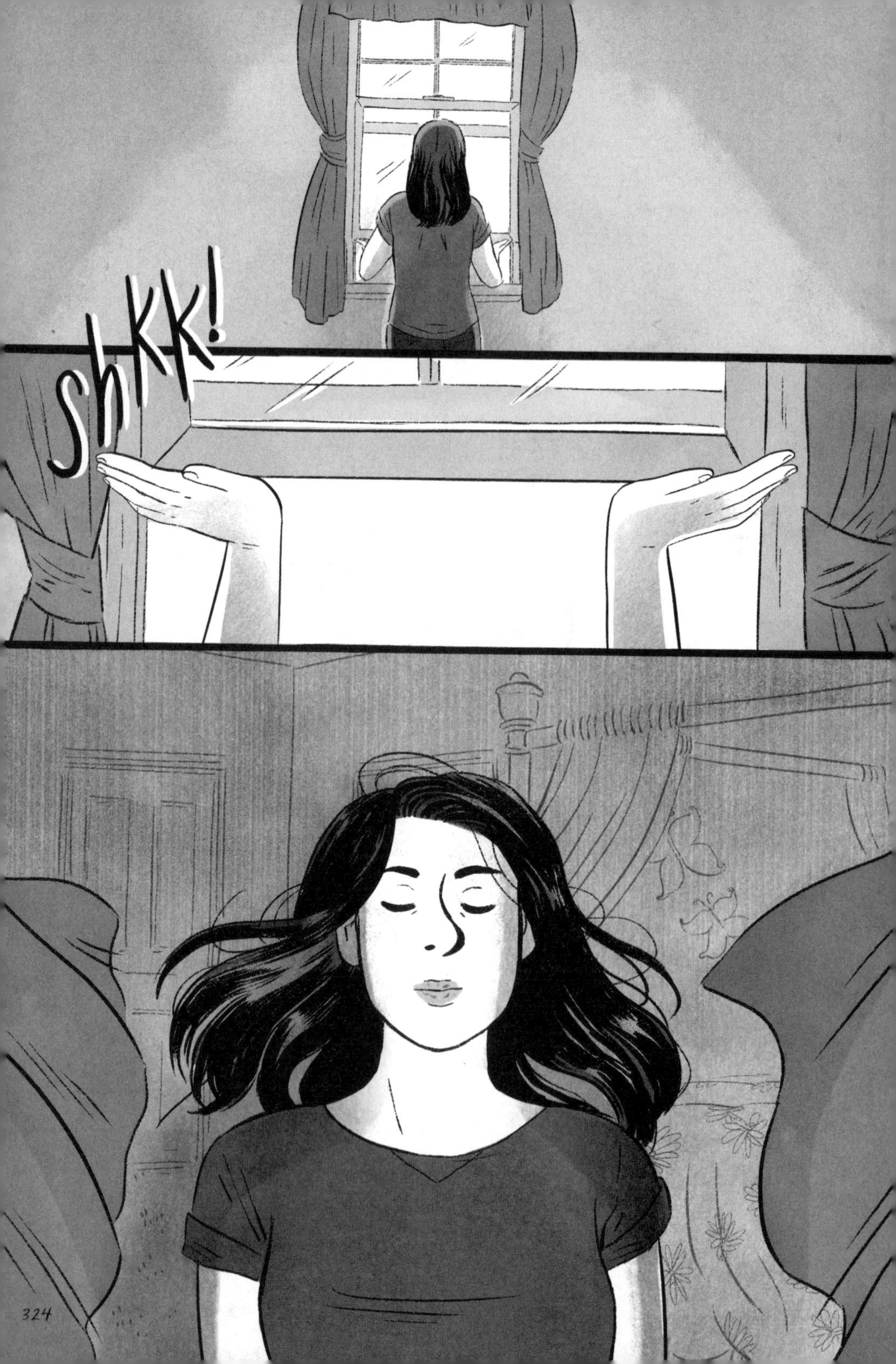
ShKK!

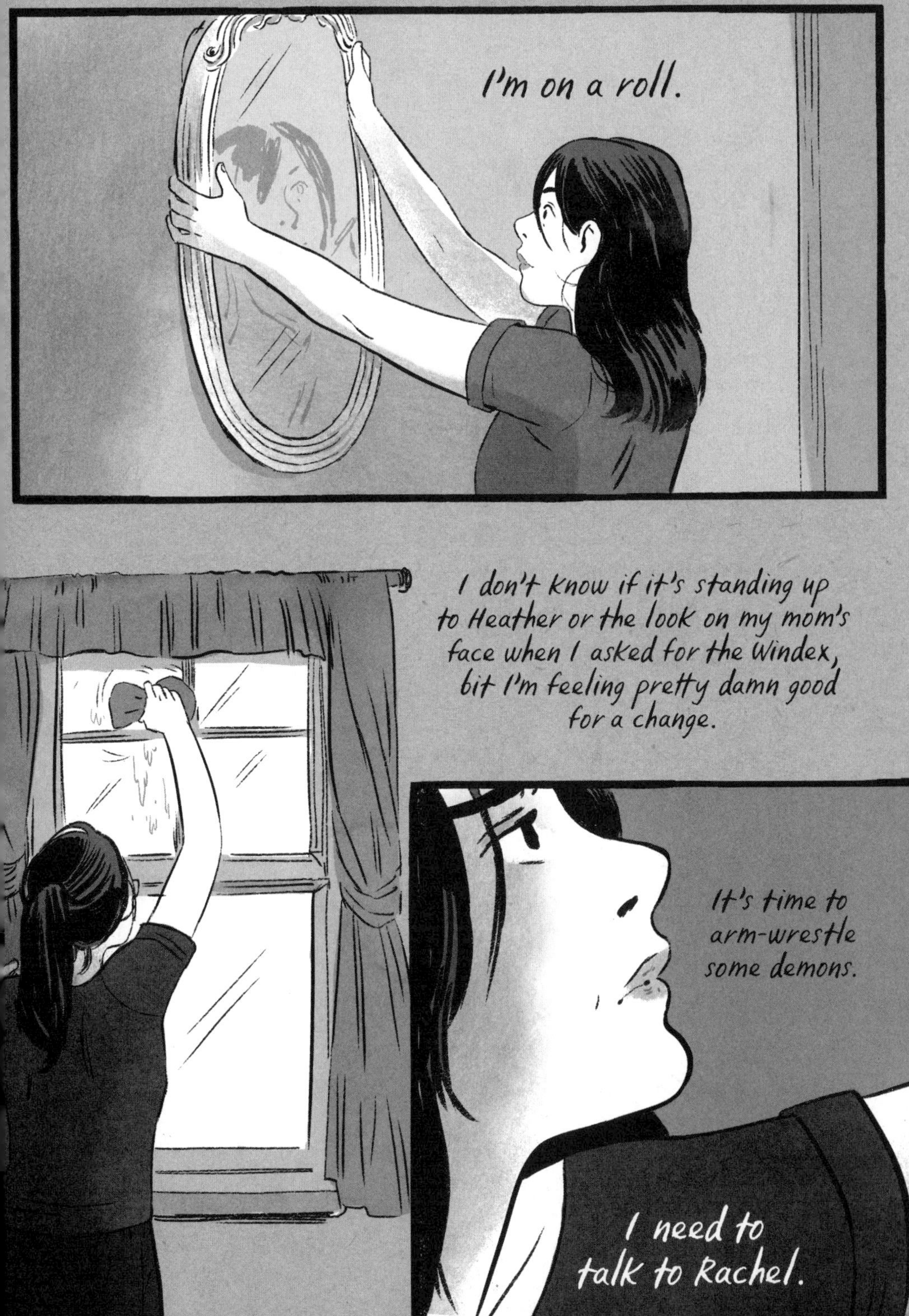
I'm on a roll.
I don't know if it's standing up to Heather or the look on my mom's face when I asked for the Windex, bit I'm feeling pretty damn good for a change.
It's time to arm-wrestle some demons.
I need to talk to Rachel.

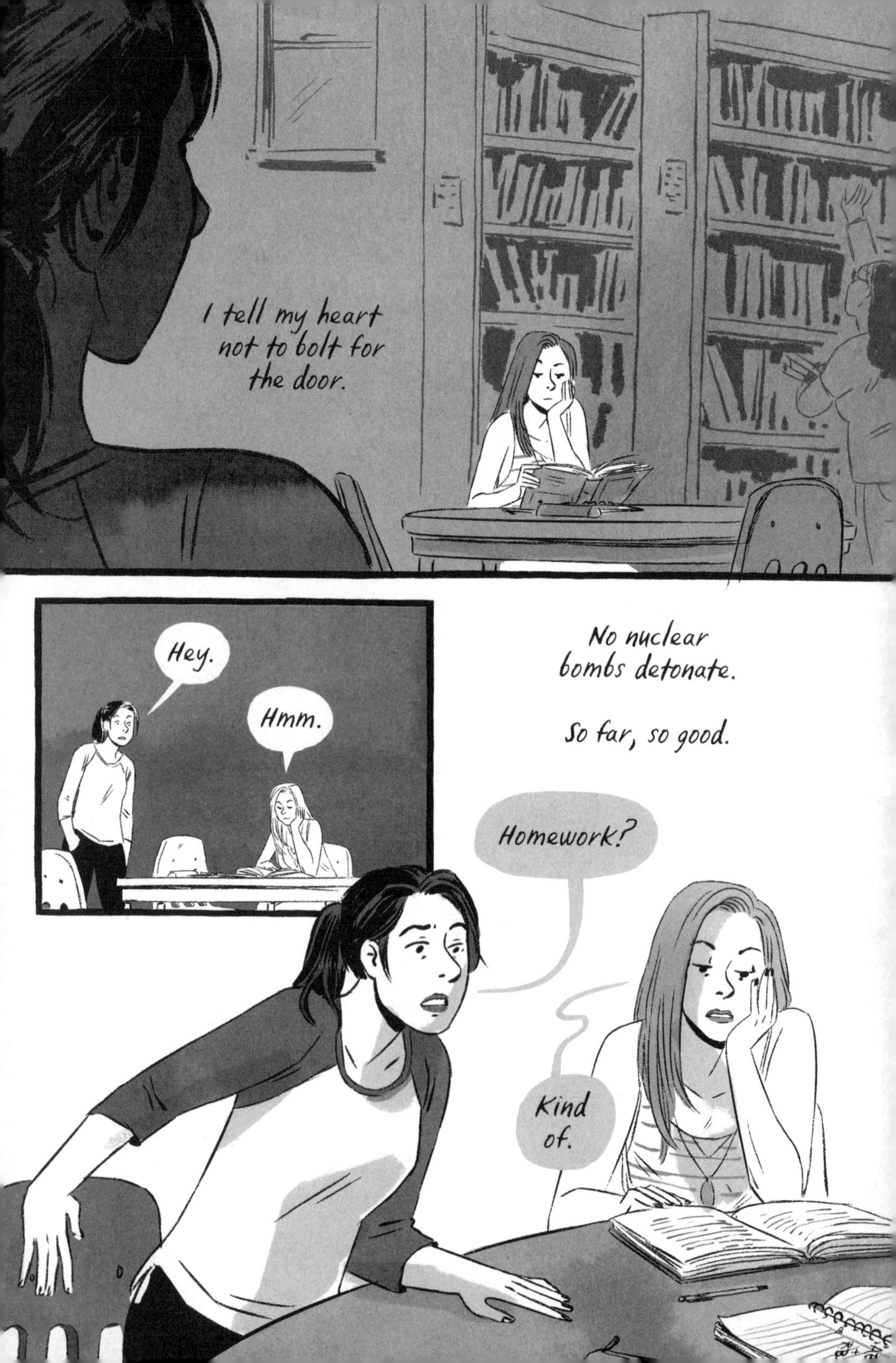
I tell my heart not to bolt for the door.
Hey.
Hmm.
No nuclear bombs detonate.
So far, so good.
Homework?
Kind of.

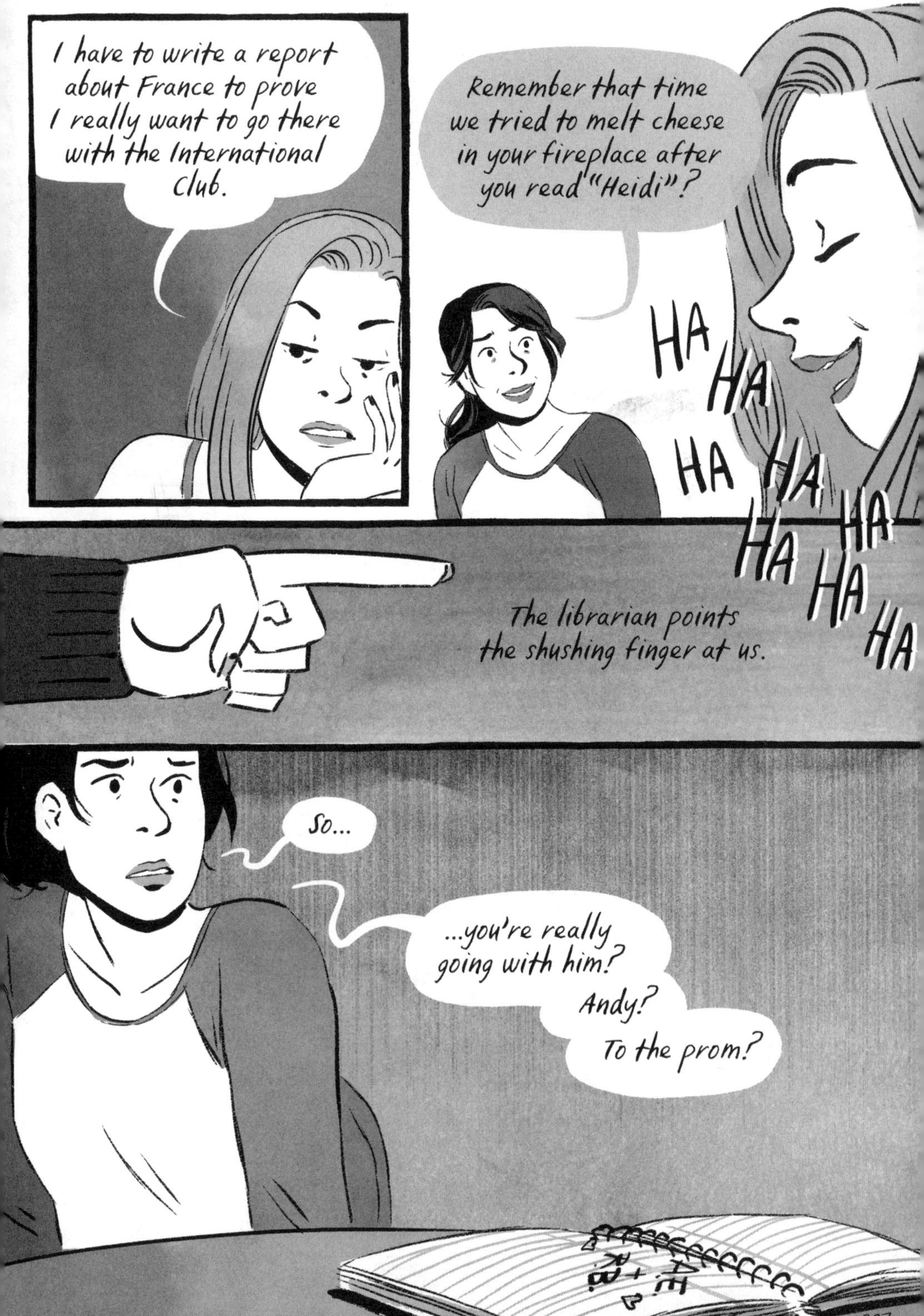

I have to write a report about France to prove I really want to go there with the International Club.
Remember that time we tried to melt cheese in your fireplace after you read "Heidi"?
HA HA HA HA HA HA HA HA HA
The librarian points the shushing finger at us.
So...
...you're really going with him?
Andy?
To the prom?

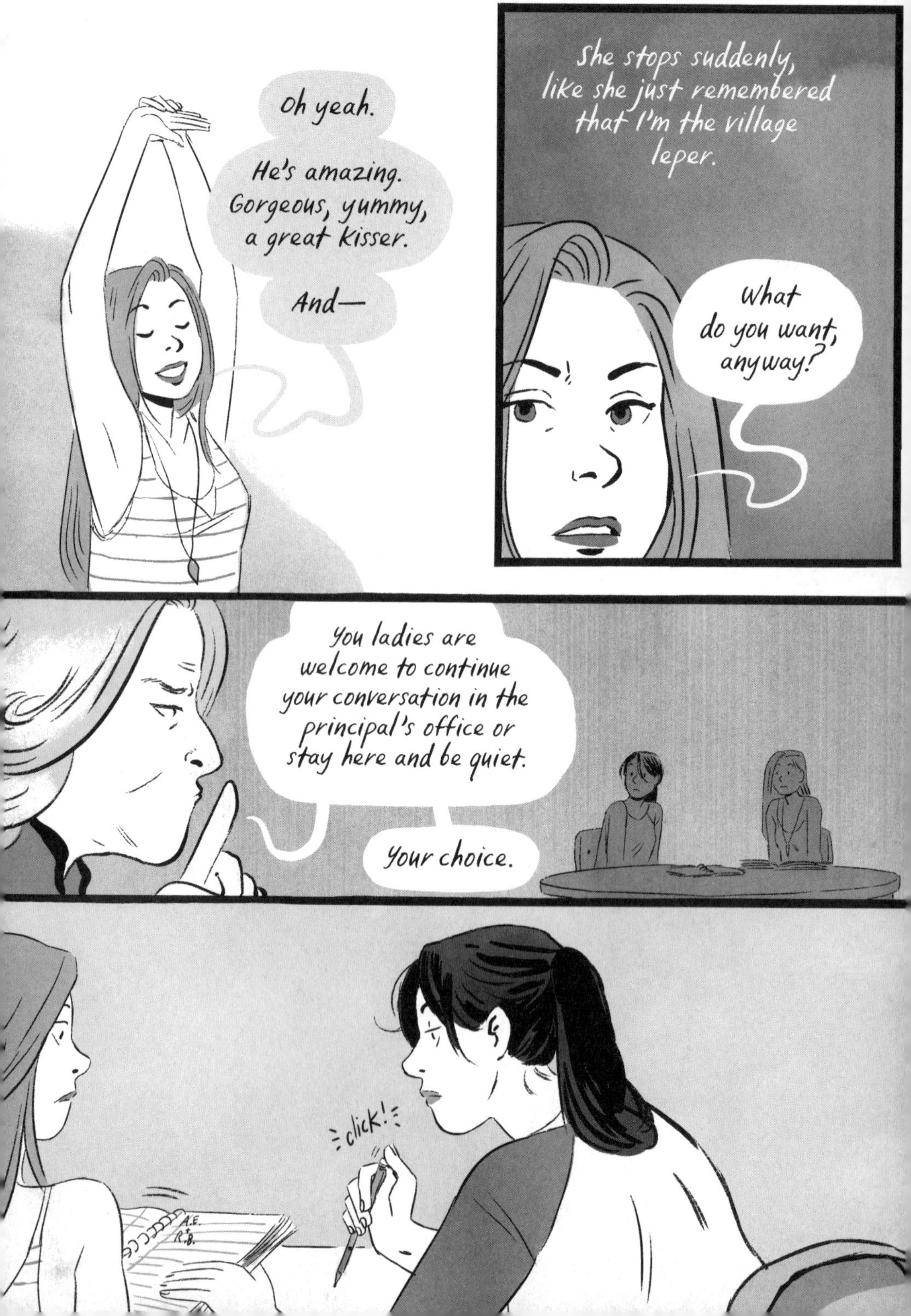
Oh yeah.
He's amazing. Gorgeous, yummy, a great kisser.
And—
She stops suddenly, like she just remembered that I'm the village leper.
What do you want, anyway?
You ladies are welcome to continue your conversation in the principal's office or stay here and be quiet.
Your choice.
click!
A.E. + R.B.

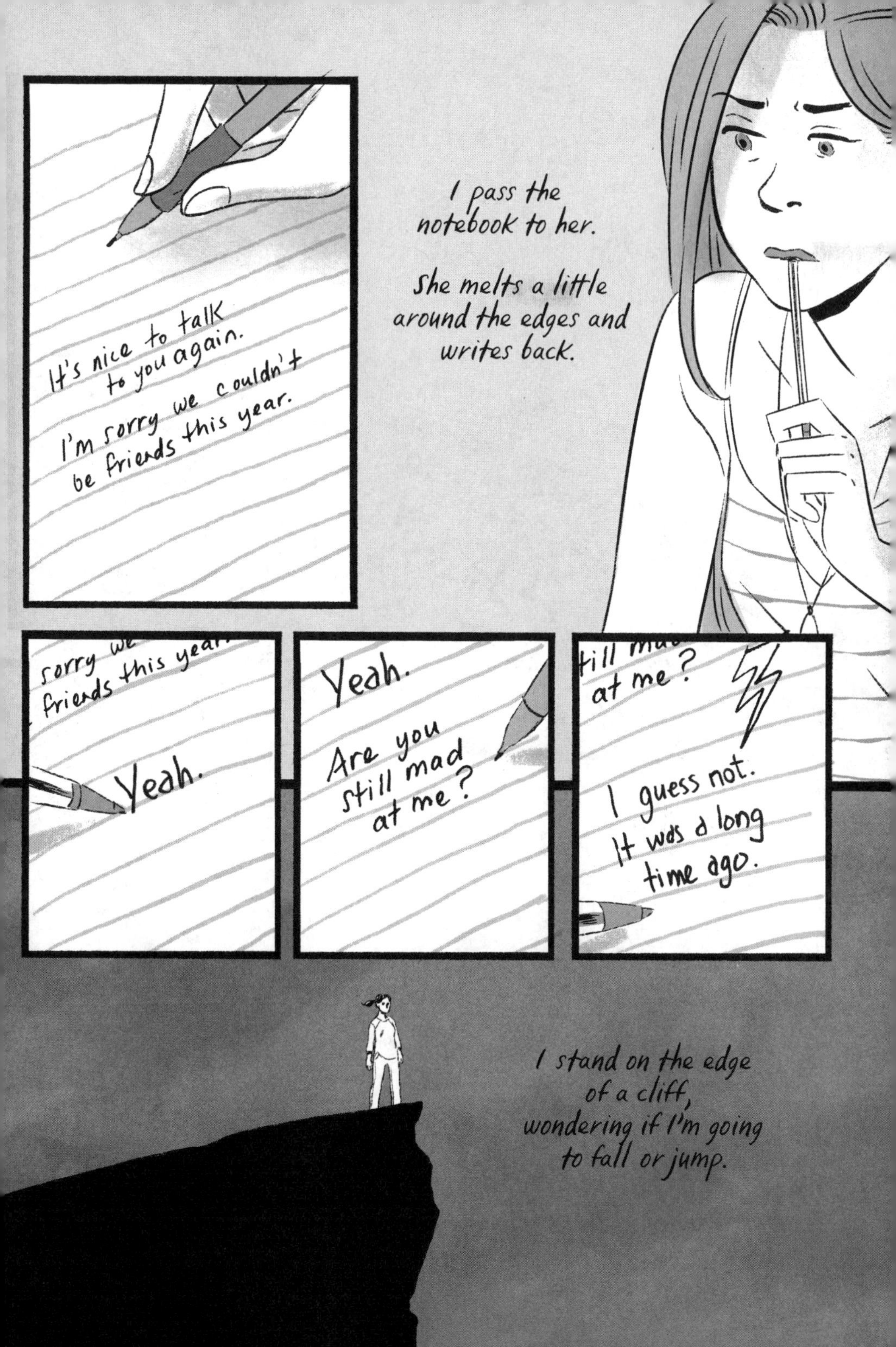

It's nice to talk to you again.
I'm sorry we couldn't be friends this year.
I pass the notebook to her.
She melts a little around the edges and writes back.
sorry we
friends this year.
Yeah.
Yeah.
Are you still mad at me?
at me?
I guess not. It was a long time ago.
I stand on the edge of a cliff, wondering if I'm going to fall or jump.

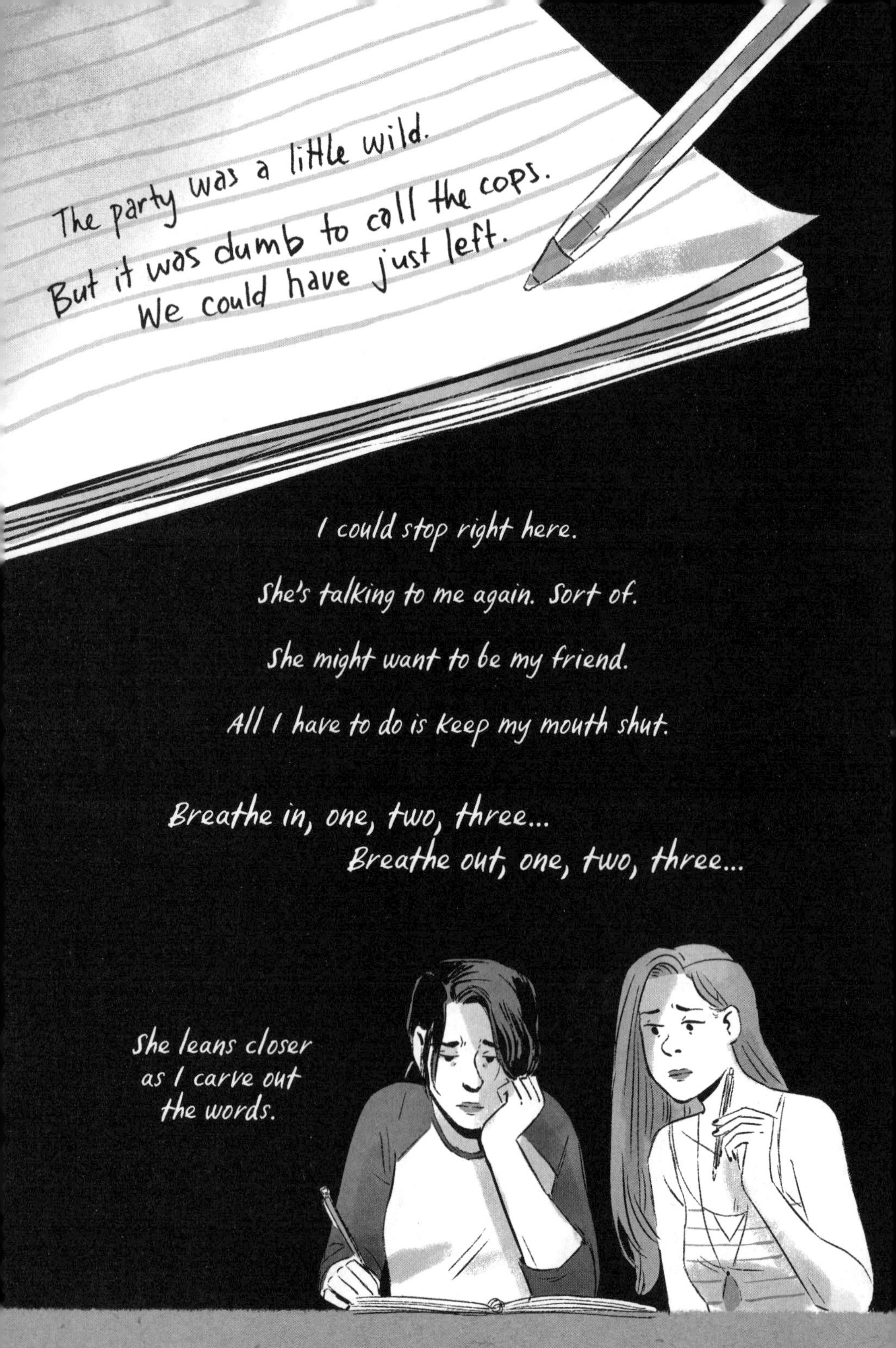
The party was a little wild.
But it was dumb to call the cops.
We could have just left.
I could stop right here.
She's talking to me again. Sort of.
She might want to be my friend.
All I have to do is keep my mouth shut.
Breathe in, one, two, three...
Breathe out, one, two, three...
She leans closer as I carve out the words.

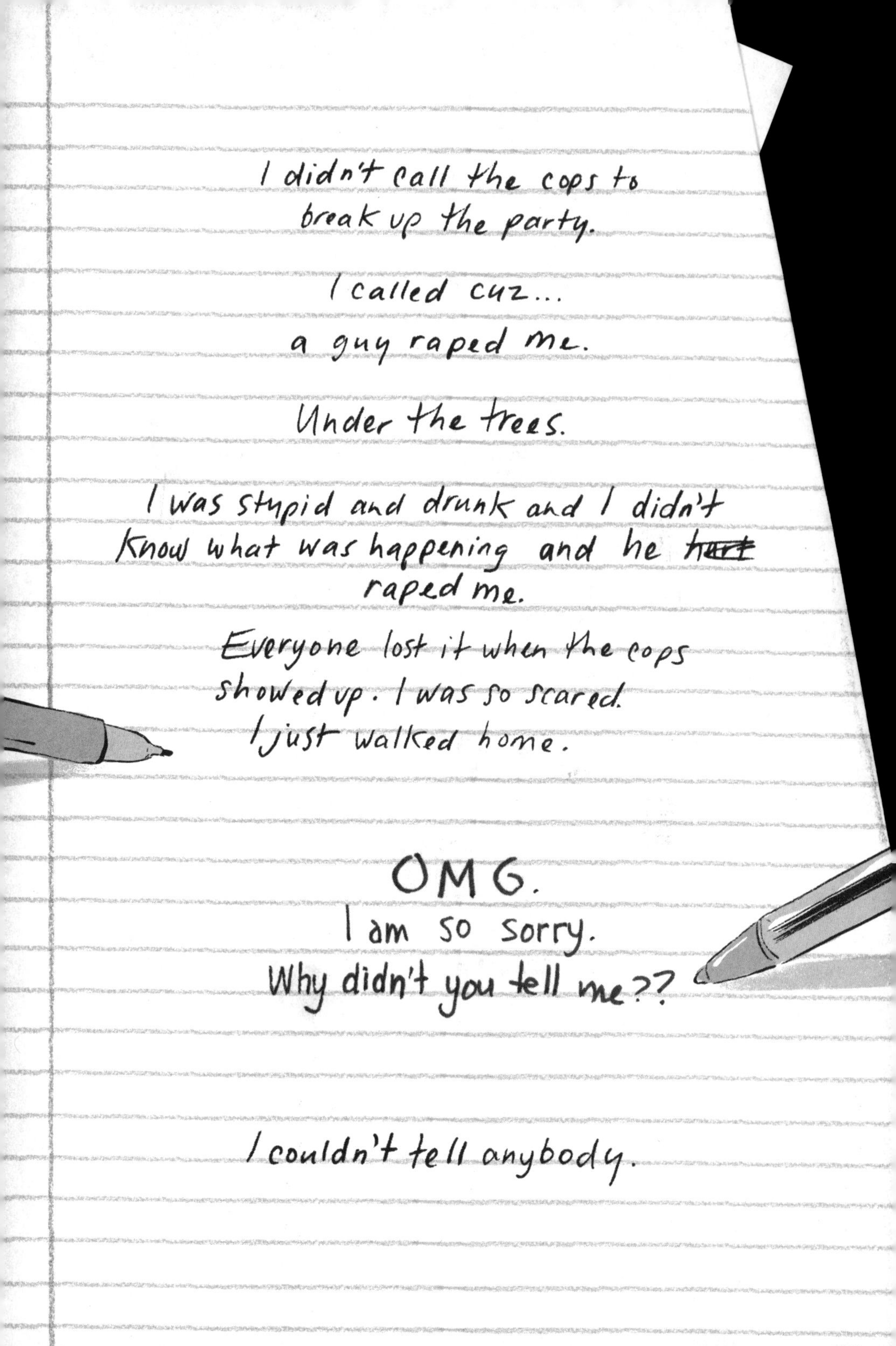
I didn't call the cops to break up the party.
I called cuz...
a guy raped me.
Under the trees.
I was stupid and drunk and I didn't know what was happening and he ~~hurt~~ raped me.
Everyone lost it when the cops showed up. I was so scared. I just walked home.
OMG.
I am so sorry.
Why didn't you tell me??
I couldn't tell anybody.

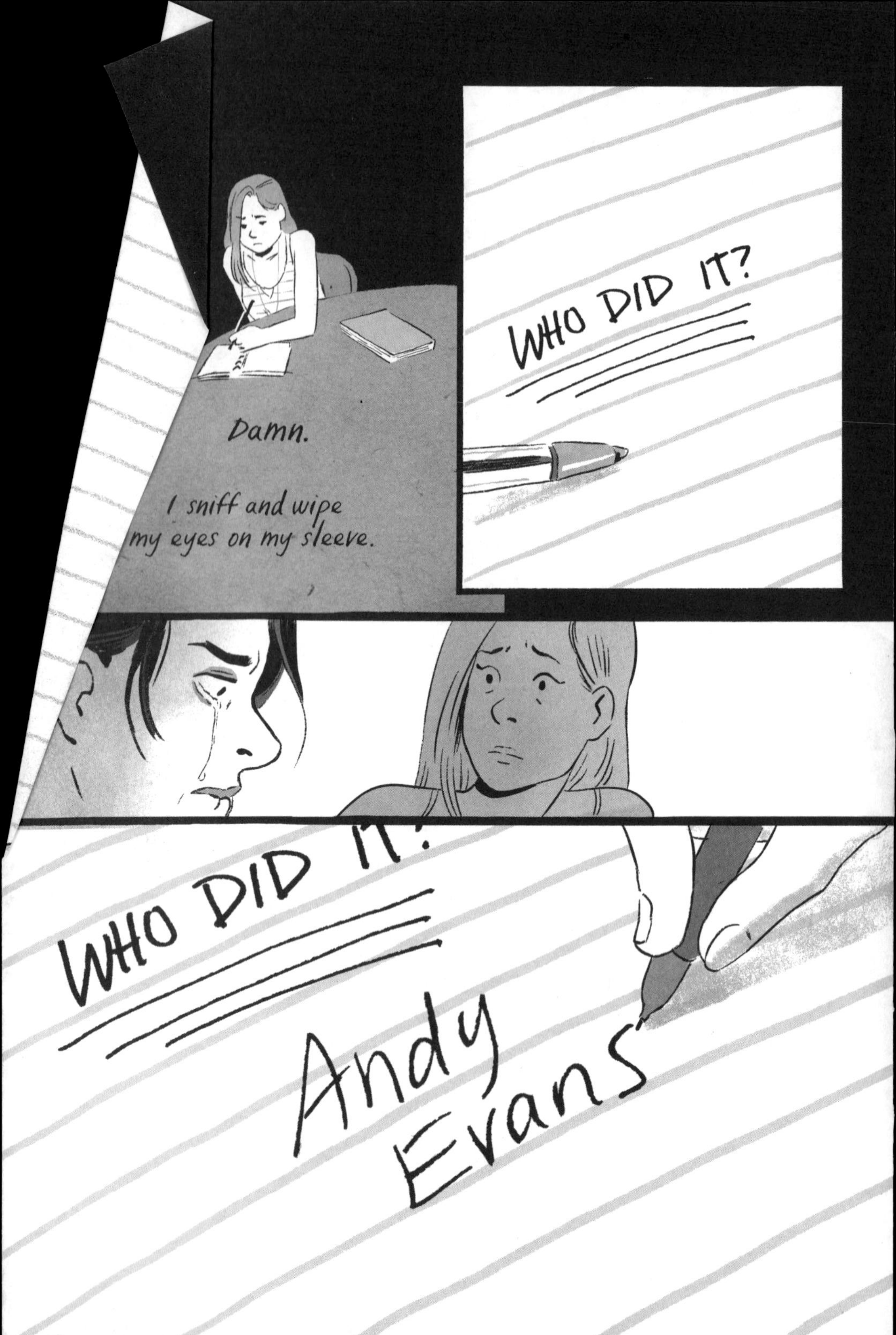
Damn.
I sniff and wipe my eyes on my sleeve.
WHO DID IT?
WHO DID IT?
Andy Evans

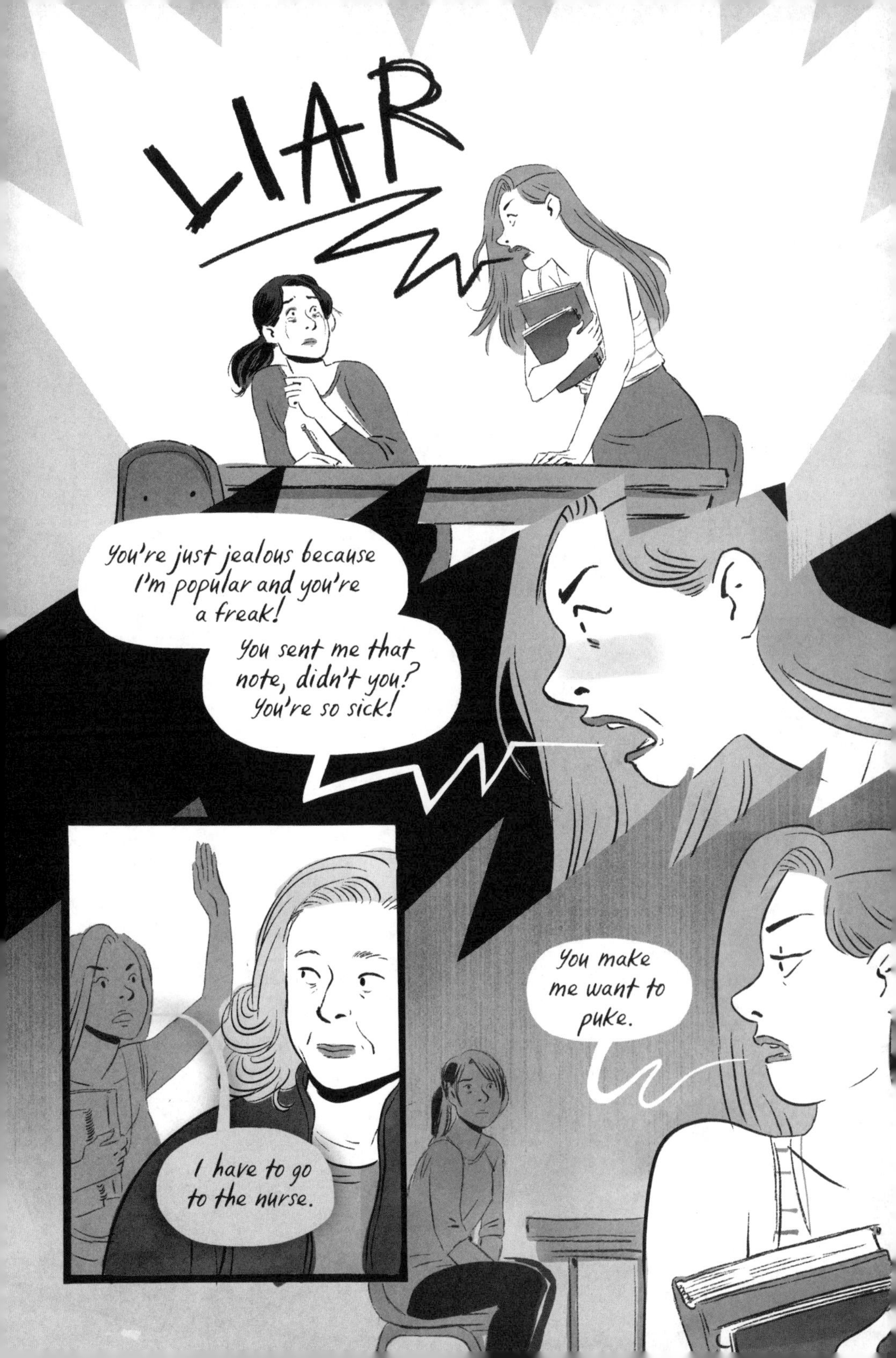
LIAR
You're just jealous because I'm popular and you're a freak!
You sent me that note, didn't you? You're so sick!
You make me want to puke.
I have to go to the nurse.

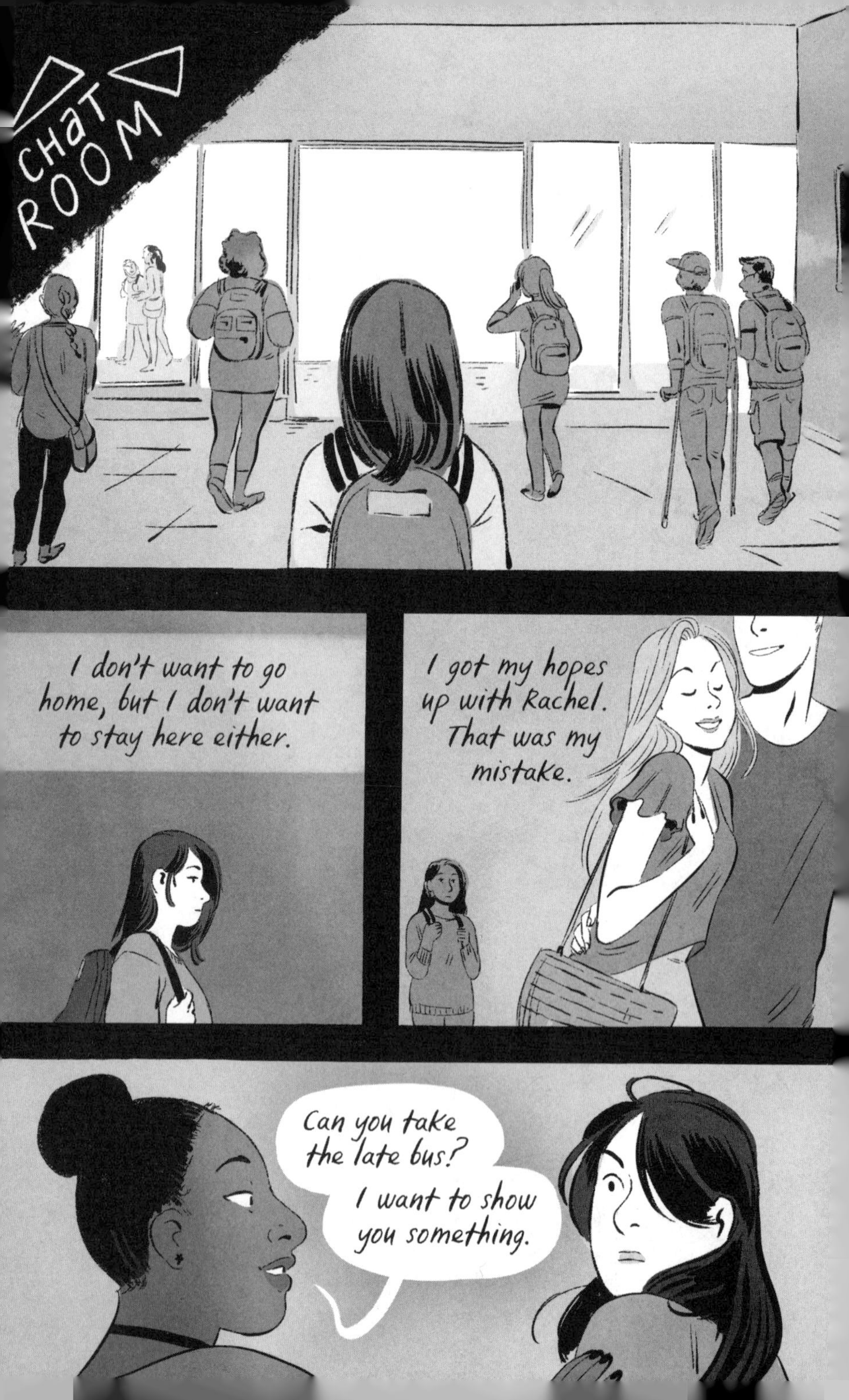
CHAT ROOM
I don't want to go home, but I don't want to stay here either.
I got my hopes up with Rachel. That was my mistake.
Can you take the late bus?
I want to show you something.

KC
4evr
i luv DEREK
C.J. is Hott
omG YES
I hate this place
he's a BASTARD
GUYS TO STAY AWAY FROM
Creep
stay away..!!!!!!
ANDY EVANS
!!!
SHOULD B LOCKED UP
I went to the movies w/ him and he put his hands down my pants during PREVIEWS
CALL THE COPS
he needs that drug they give perverts so they can't get it UP
he needs it 24/7
I feel like I can fly.

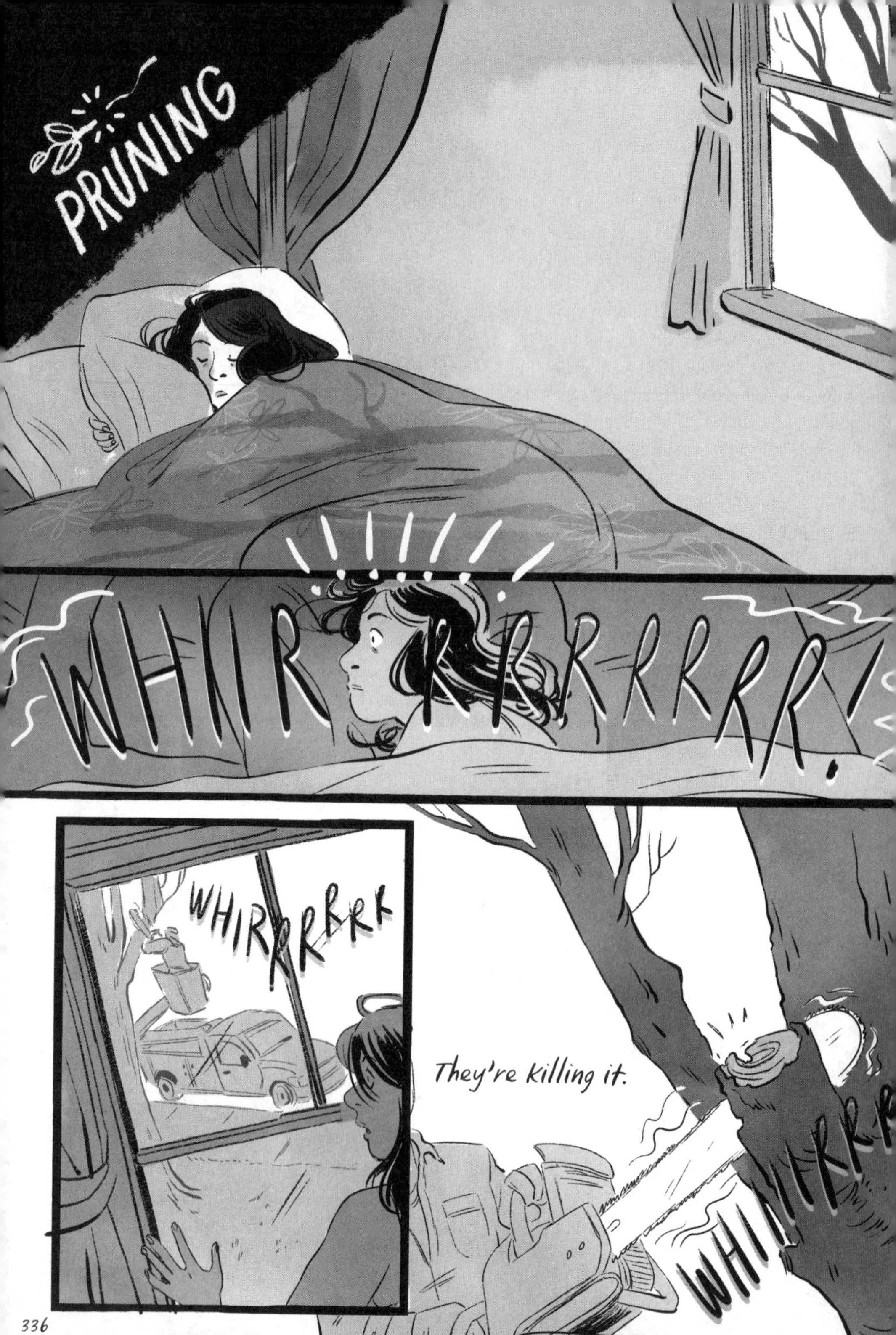
PRUNING
WHIIRRRRRRRR!
WHIRRRRRR
They're killing it.
WHIIRRR

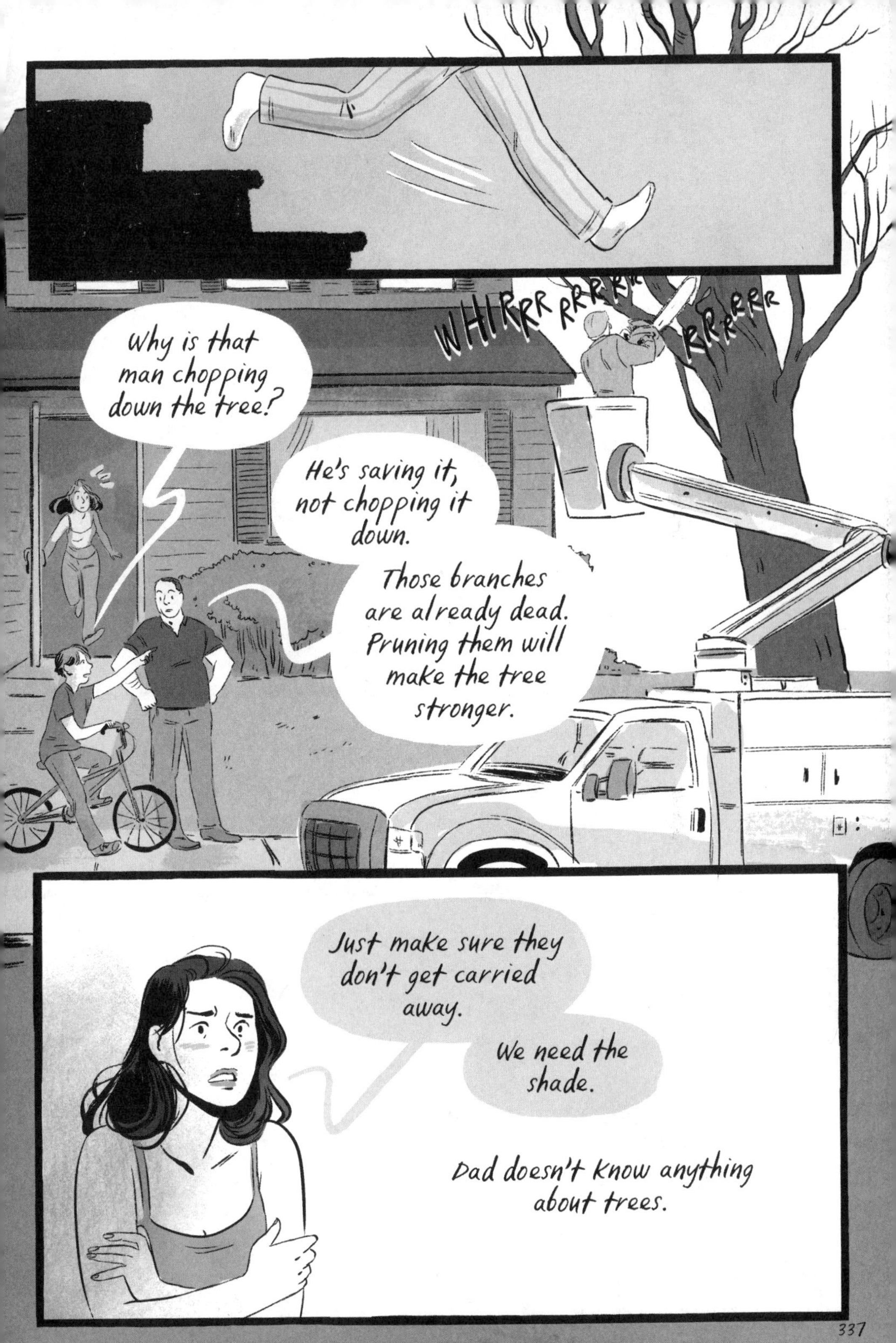
WHIRRRRRRRR RRRRRRR
Why is that man chopping down the tree?
He's saving it, not chopping it down.
Those branches are already dead. Pruning them will make the tree stronger.
Just make sure they don't get carried away.
We need the shade.
Dad doesn't know anything about trees.

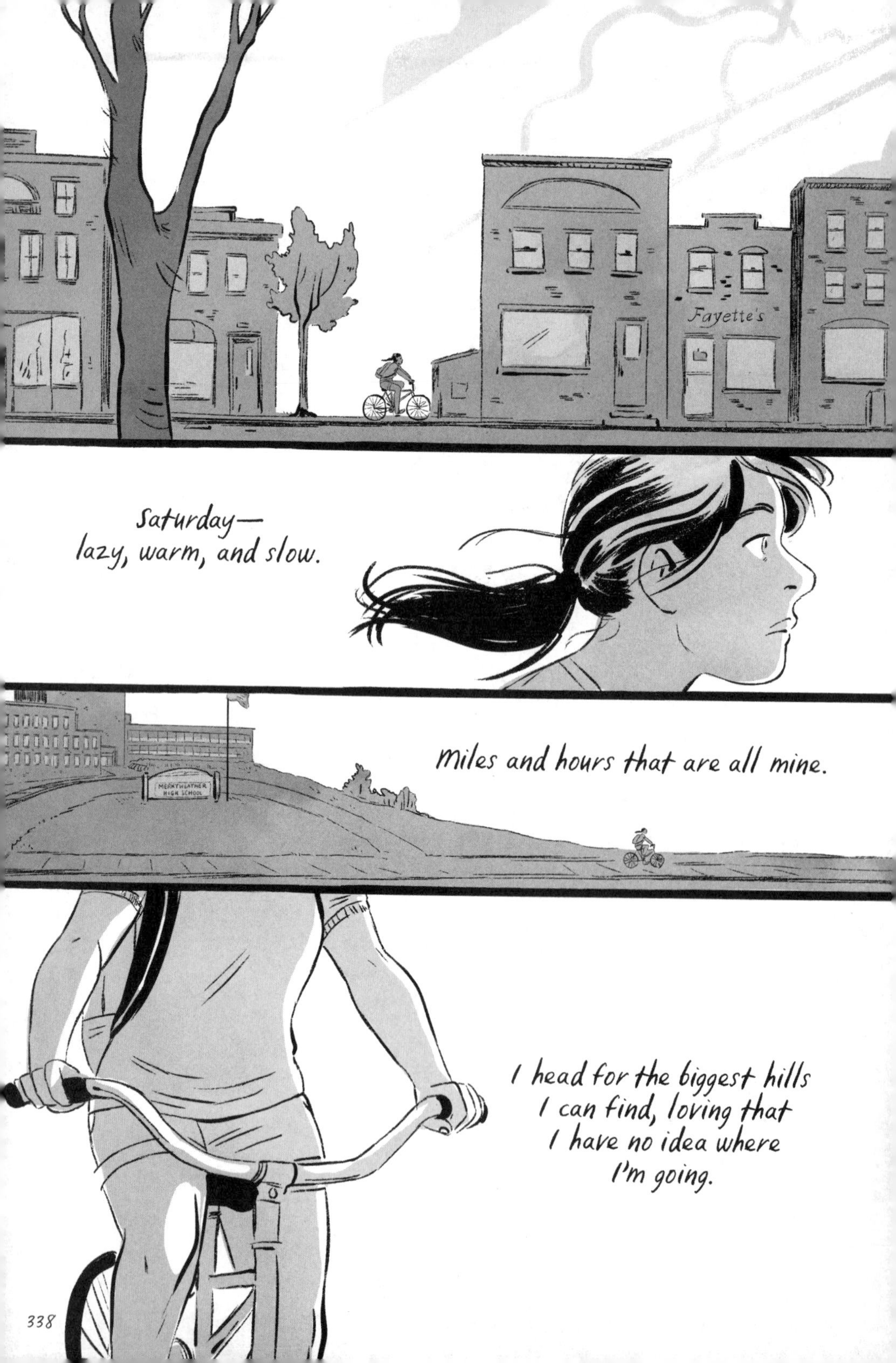
Fayette's
Saturday—
lazy, warm, and slow.
MERRYWEATHER
HIGH SCHOOL
Miles and hours that are all mine.
I head for the biggest hills
I can find, loving that
I have no idea where
I'm going.

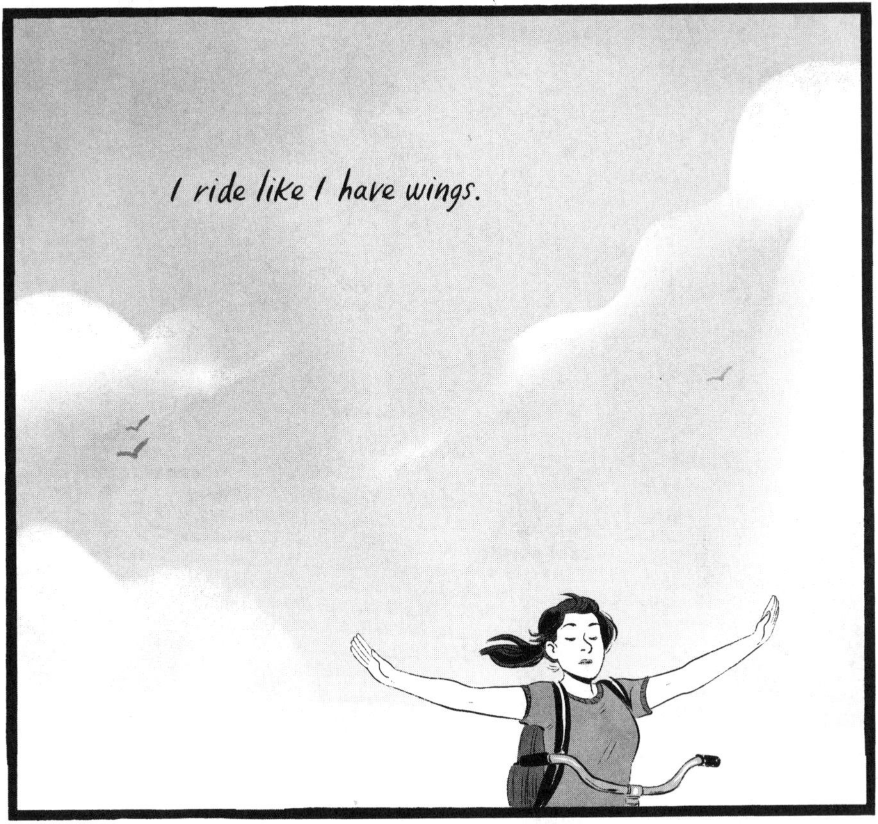
I ride like I have wings.

Almost.

Some devious internal compass brought me back.

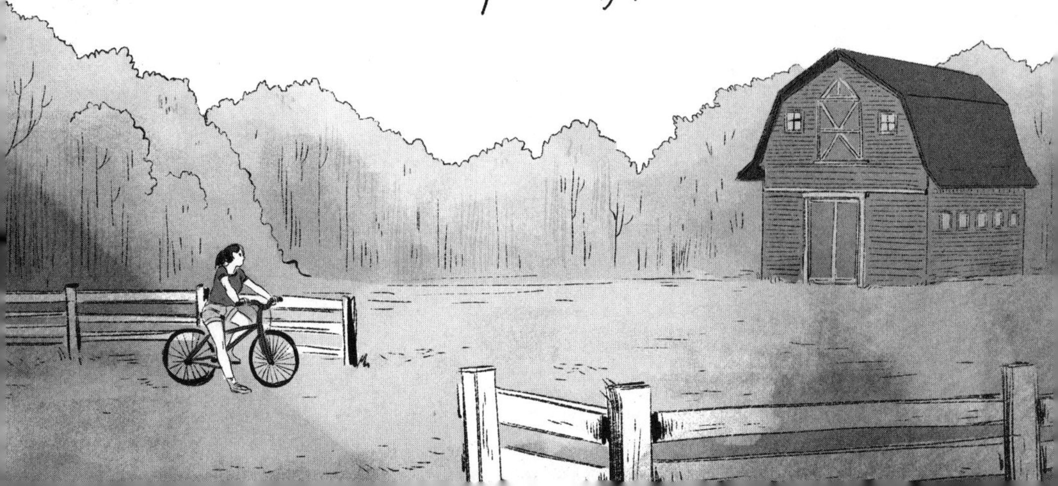

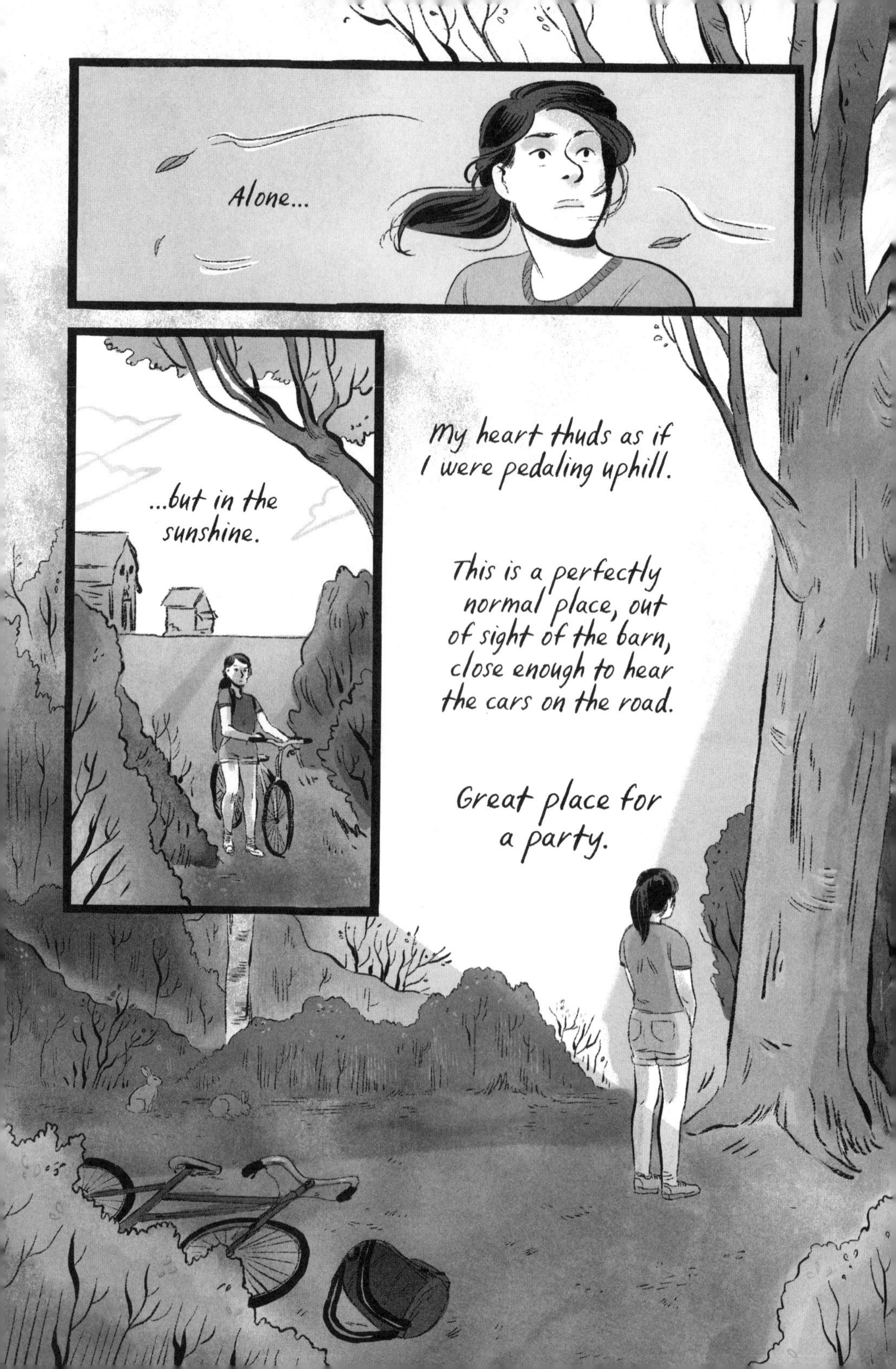
Alone...
...but in the sunshine.
My heart thuds as if I were pedaling uphill.
This is a perfectly normal place, out of sight of the barn, close enough to hear the cars on the road.
Great place for a party.

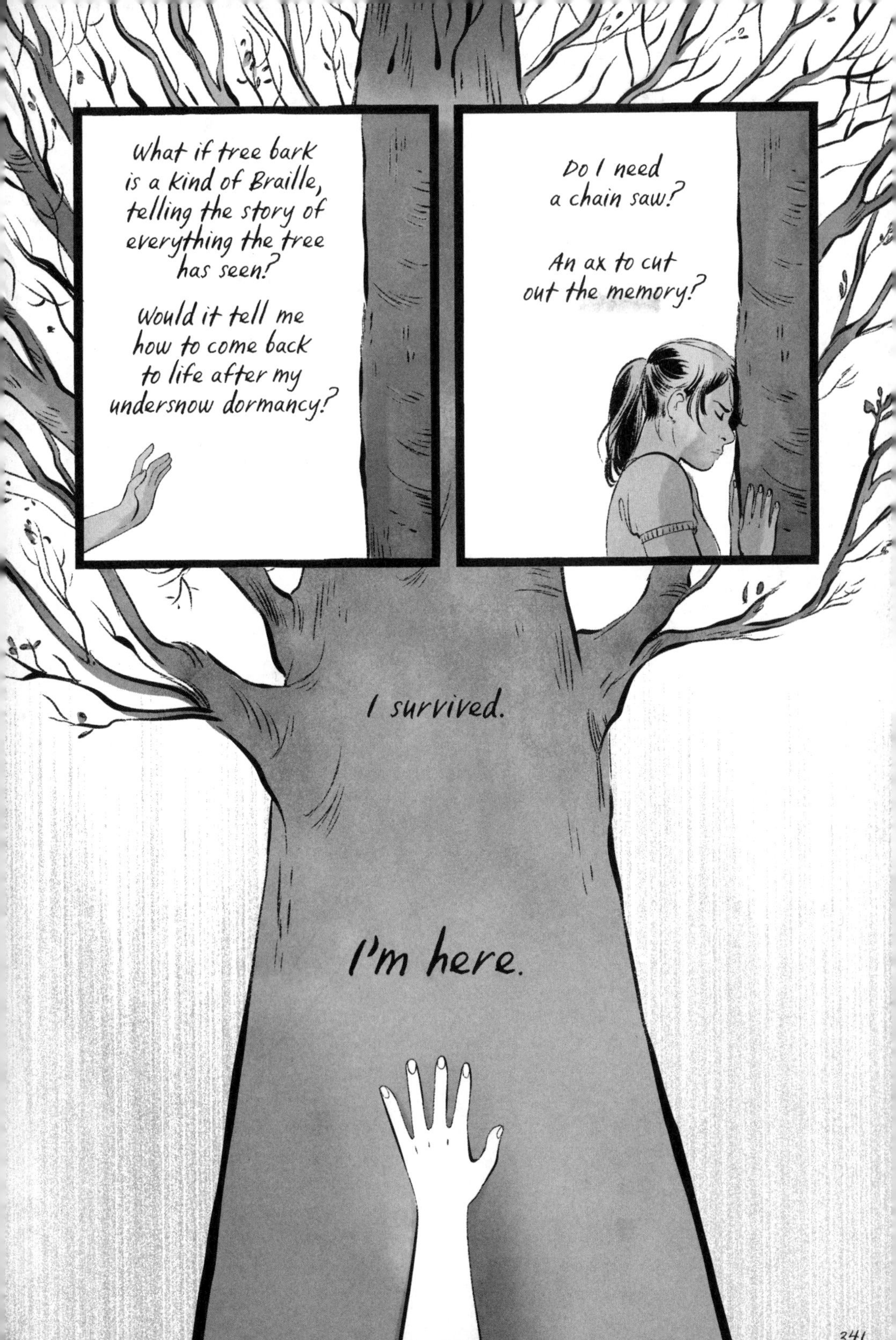
What if tree bark is a kind of Braille, telling the story of everything the tree has seen?
Would it tell me how to come back to life after my undersnow dormancy?
Do I need a chain saw?
An ax to cut out the memory?
I survived.
I'm here.

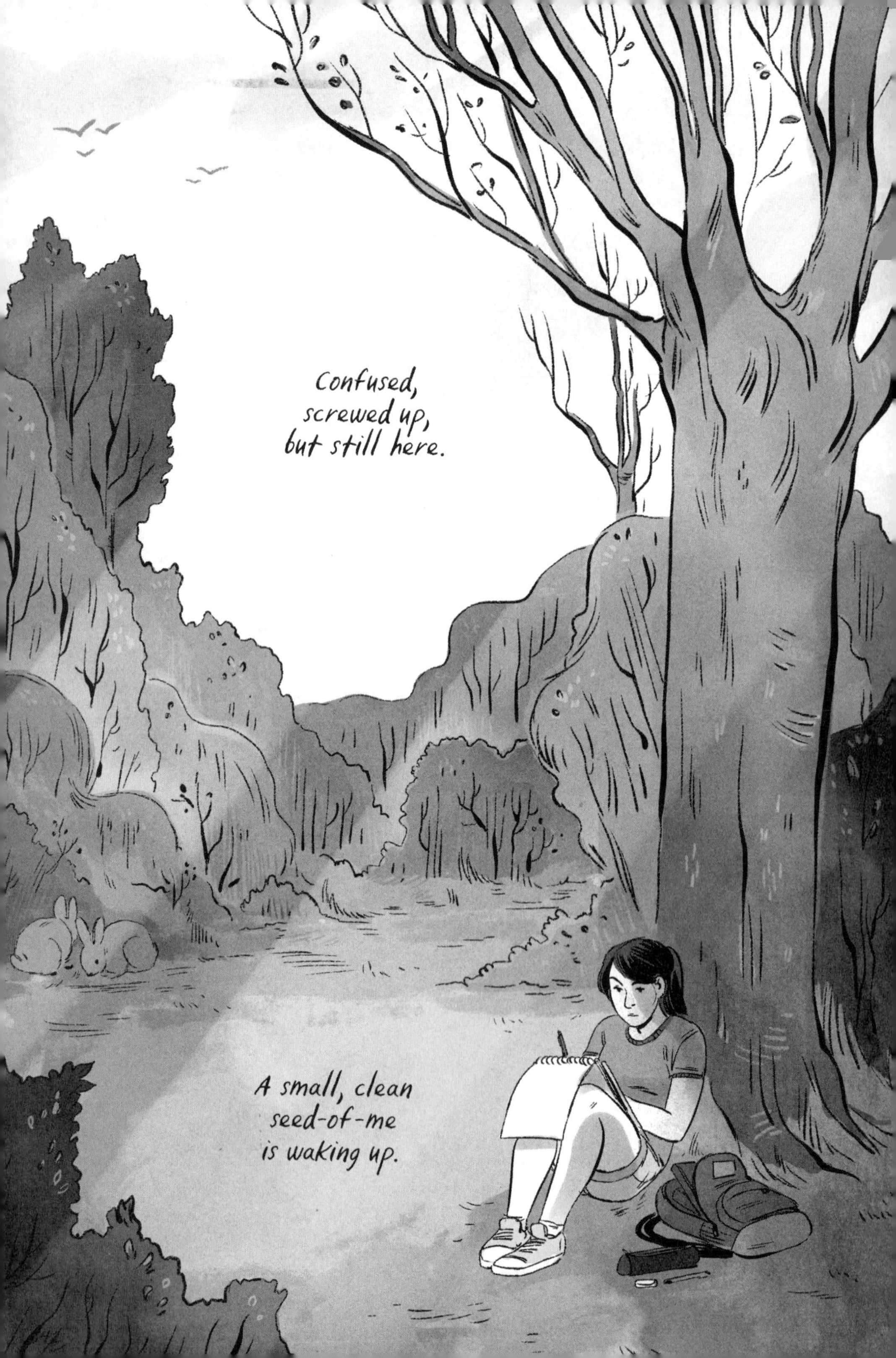
Confused,
screwed up,
but still here.
A small, clean
seed-of-me
is waking up.

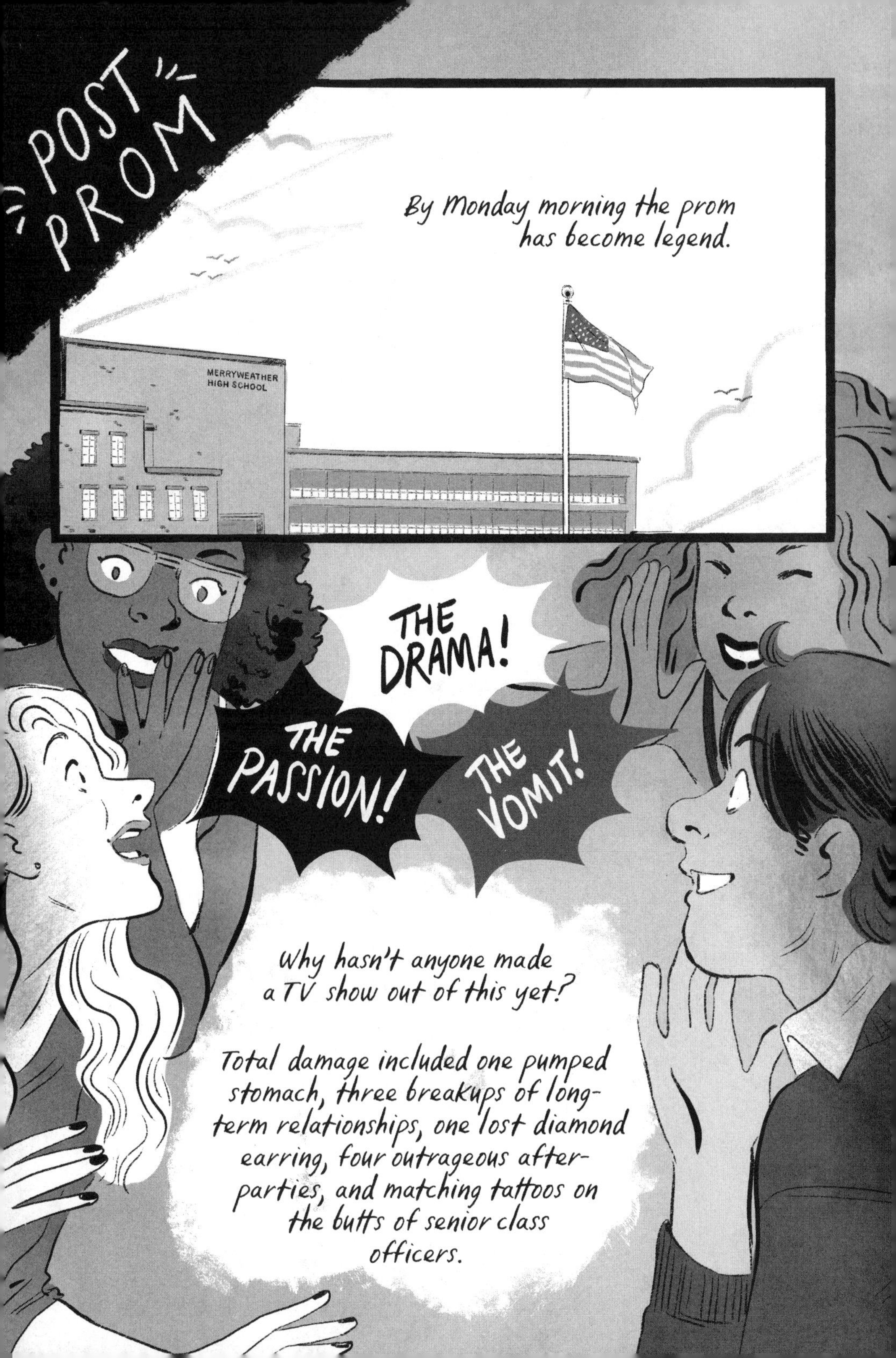
POST PROM
By Monday morning the prom has become legend.
MERRYWEATHER HIGH SCHOOL
THE DRAMA!
THE PASSION!
THE VOMIT!
Why hasn't anyone made a TV show out of this yet?
Total damage included one pumped stomach, three breakups of long-term relationships, one lost diamond earring, four outrageous after-parties, and matching tattoos on the butts of senior class officers.

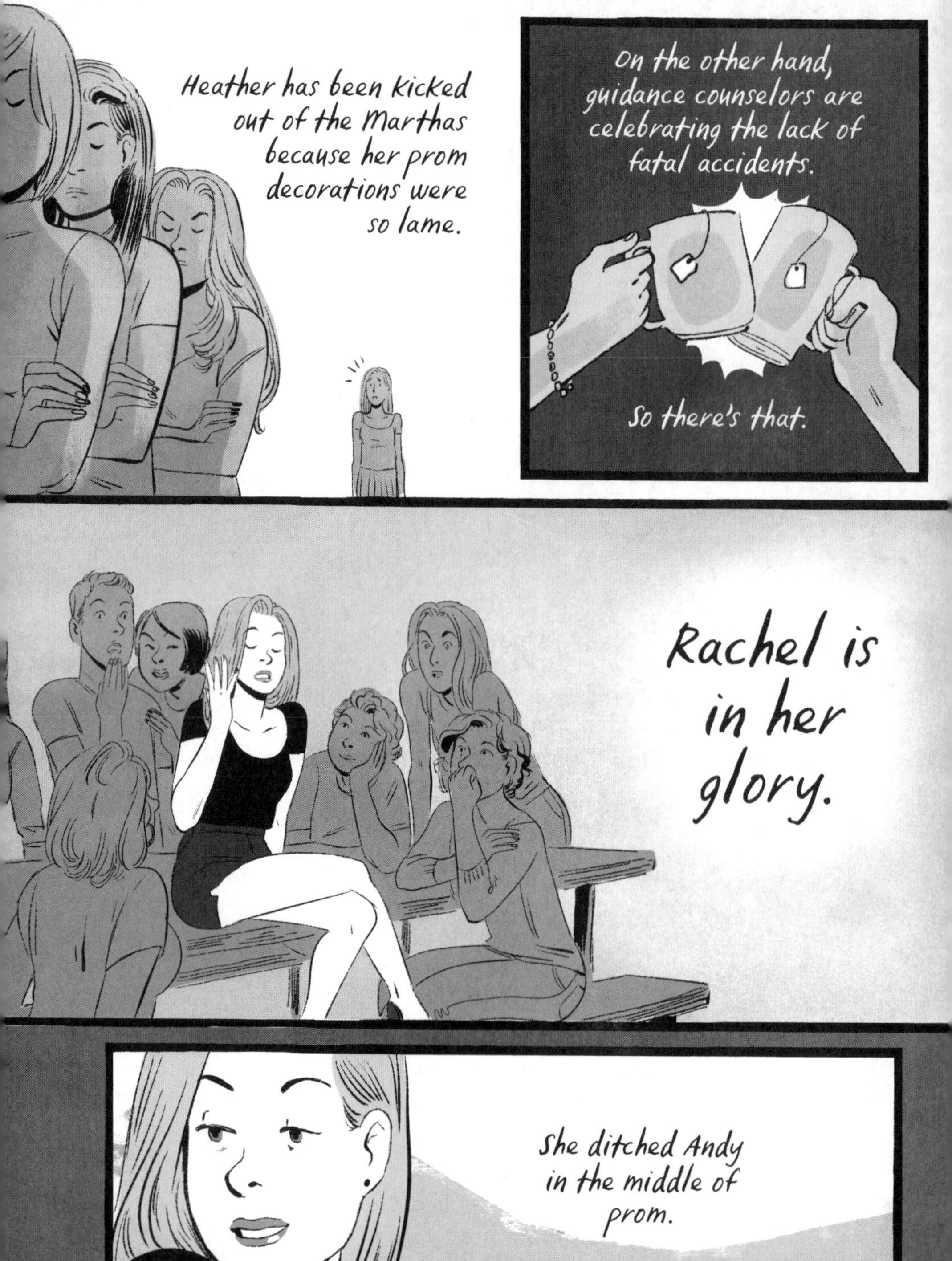
Heather has been kicked out of the Marthas because her prom decorations were so lame.
On the other hand, guidance counselors are celebrating the lack of fatal accidents.
So there's that.
Rachel is in her glory.
She ditched Andy in the middle of prom.

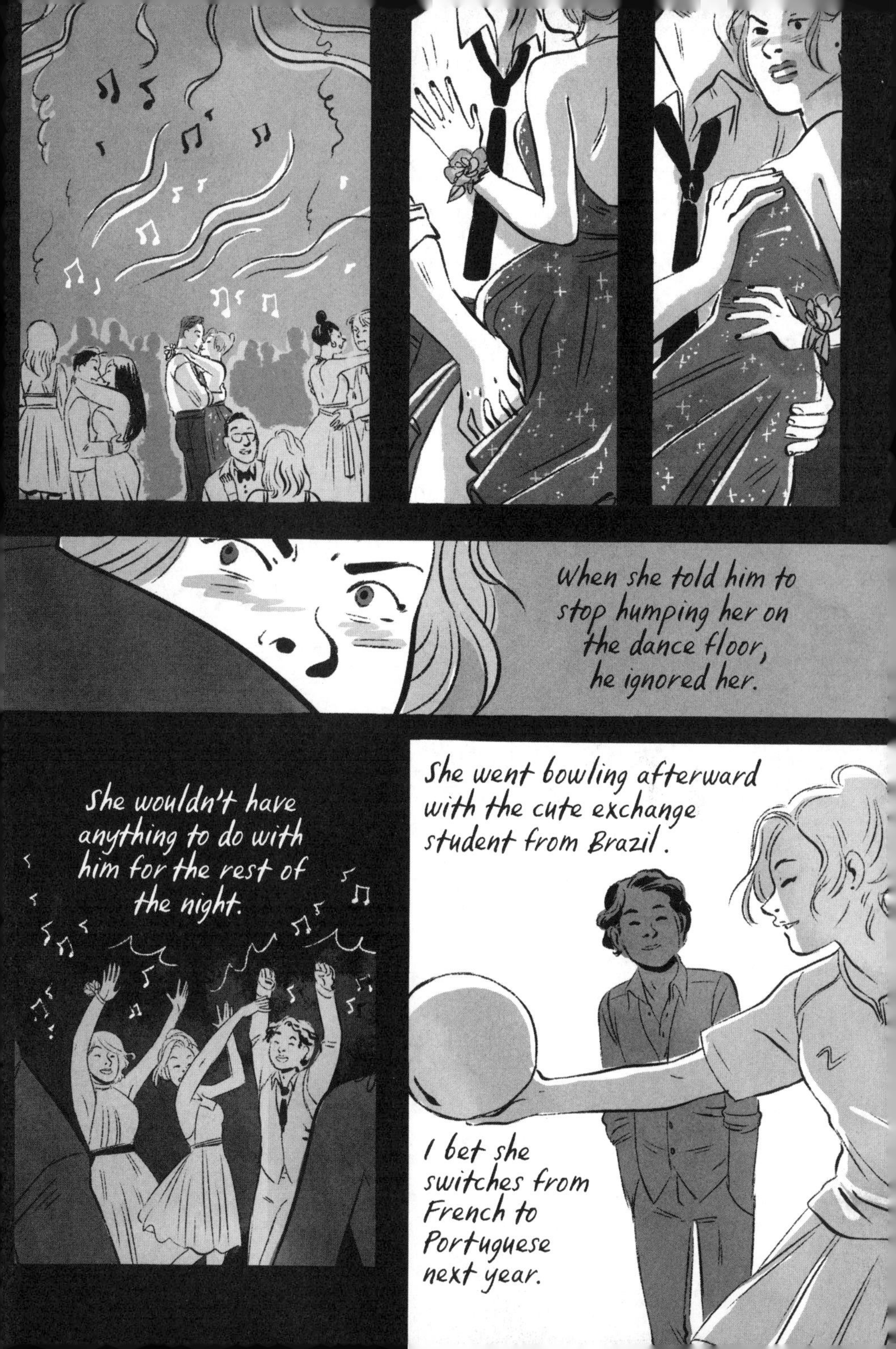
When she told him to stop humping her on the dance floor, he ignored her.
She wouldn't have anything to do with him for the rest of the night.
She went bowling afterward with the cute exchange student from Brazil.
I bet she switches from French to Portuguese next year.

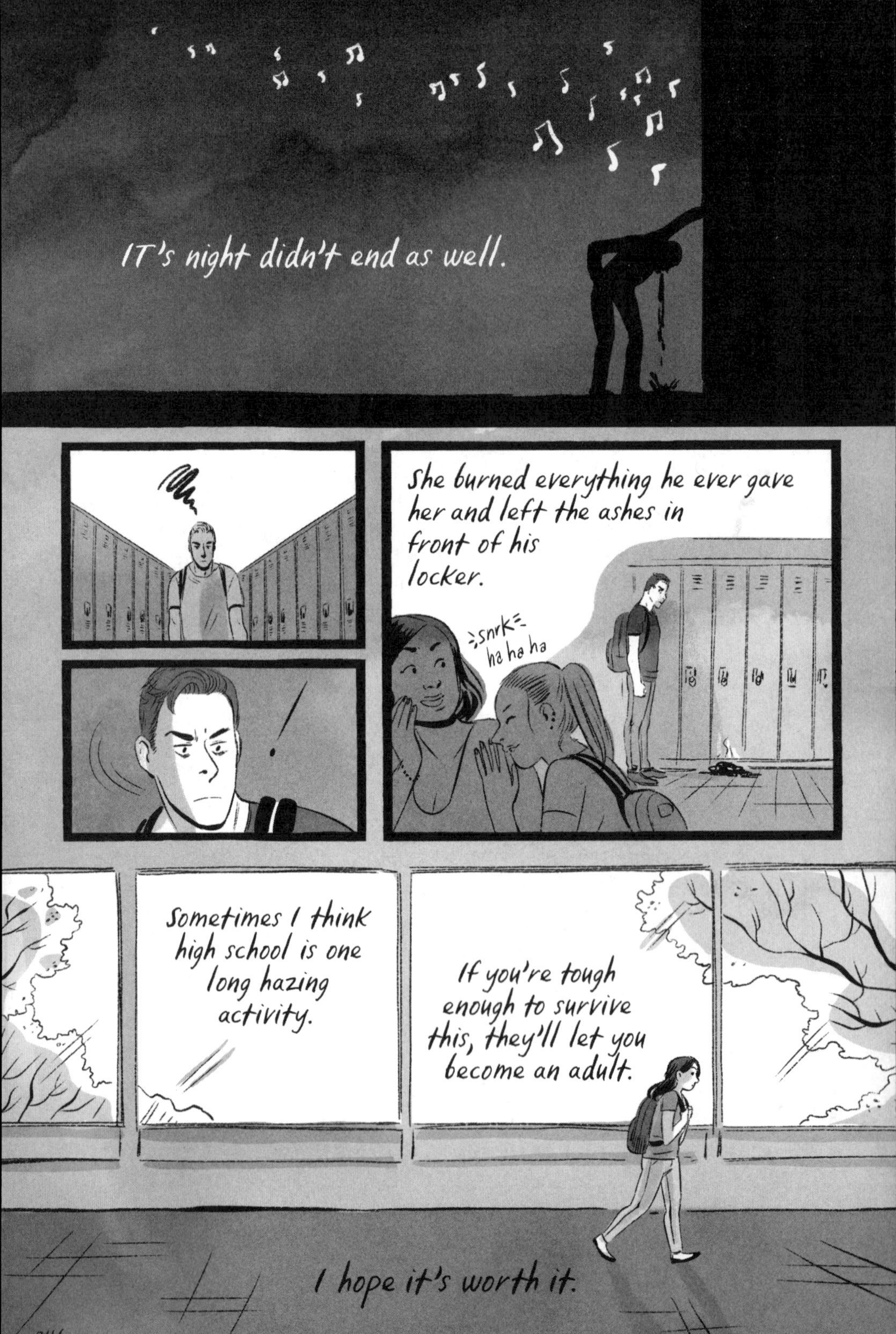

IT's night didn't end as well.
She burned everything he ever gave her and left the ashes in front of his locker.
snrk
ha ha ha
Sometimes I think high school is one long hazing activity.
If you're tough enough to survive this, they'll let you become an adult.
I hope it's worth it.

I don't want to hang out in my little hidey-hole anymore.

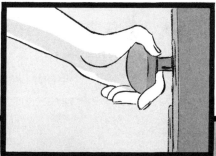

click

But I want to take home my Maya Angelou poster, a couple drawings, and the weird turkey-bone sculpture.

It's grown on me.

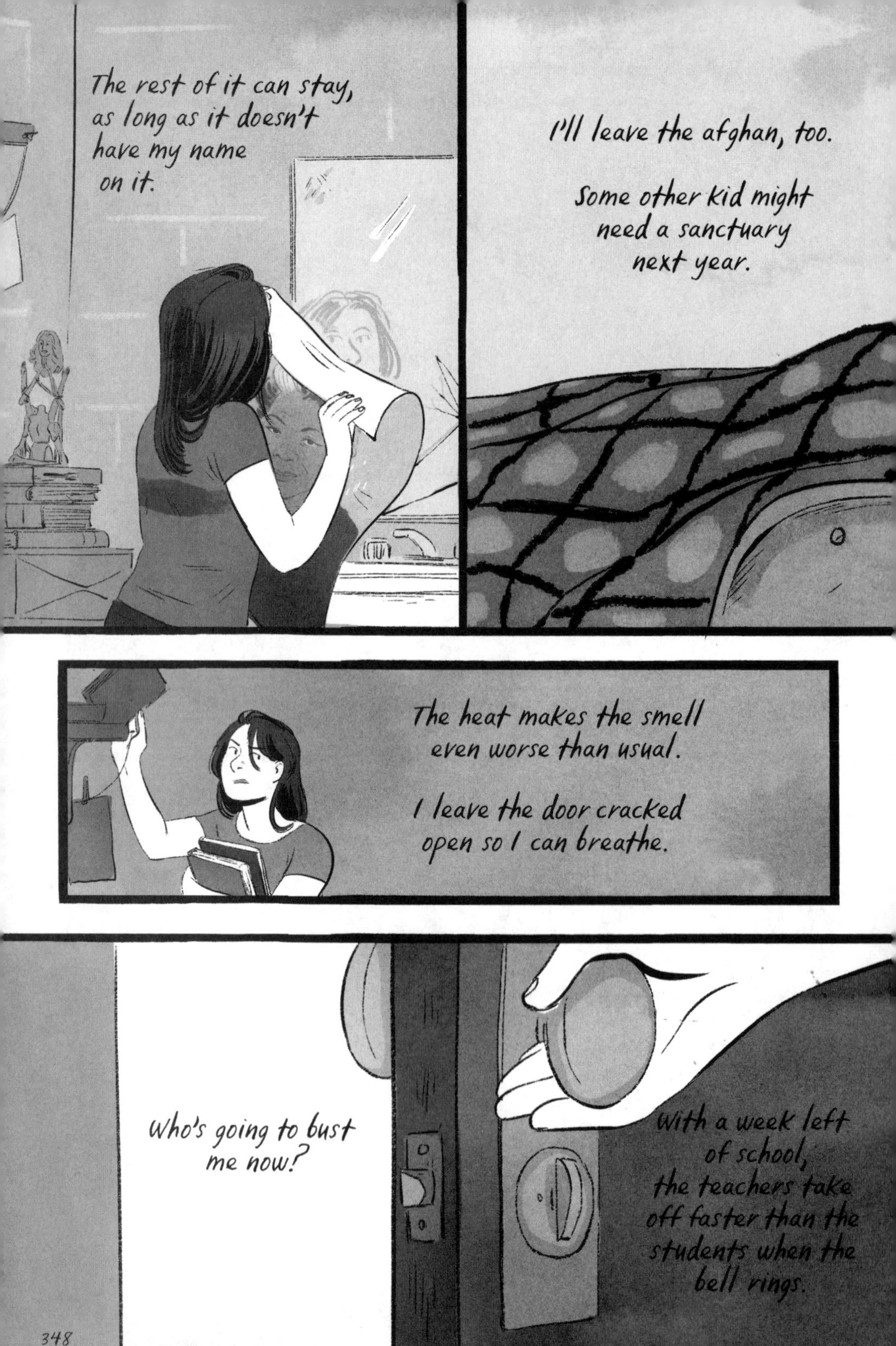
The rest of it can stay, as long as it doesn't have my name on it.
I'll leave the afghan, too.
Some other kid might need a sanctuary next year.
The heat makes the smell even worse than usual.
I leave the door cracked open so I can breathe.
Who's going to bust me now?
With a week left of school, the teachers take off faster than the students when the bell rings.

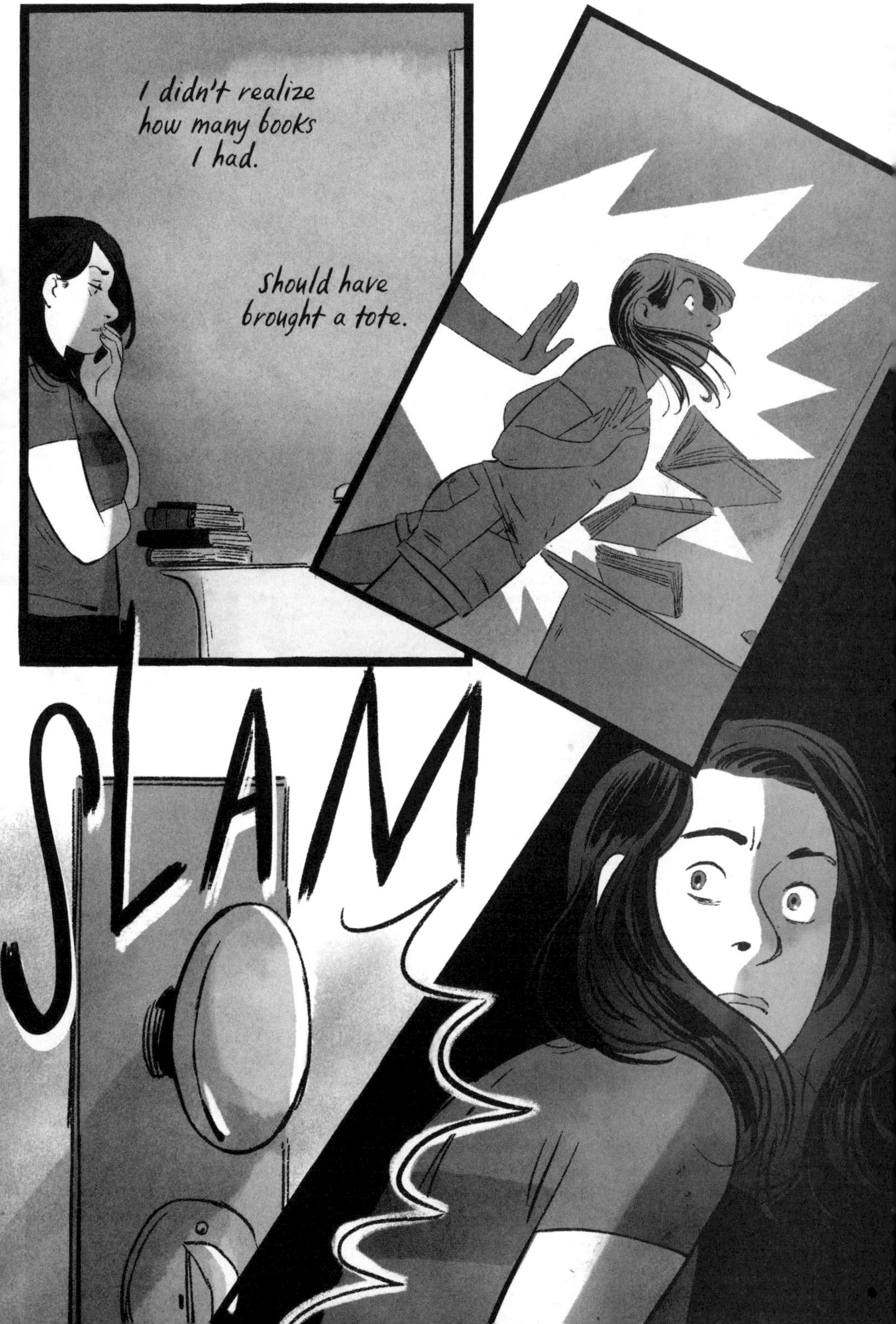

I didn't realize how many books I had.
Should have brought a tote.
SLAM

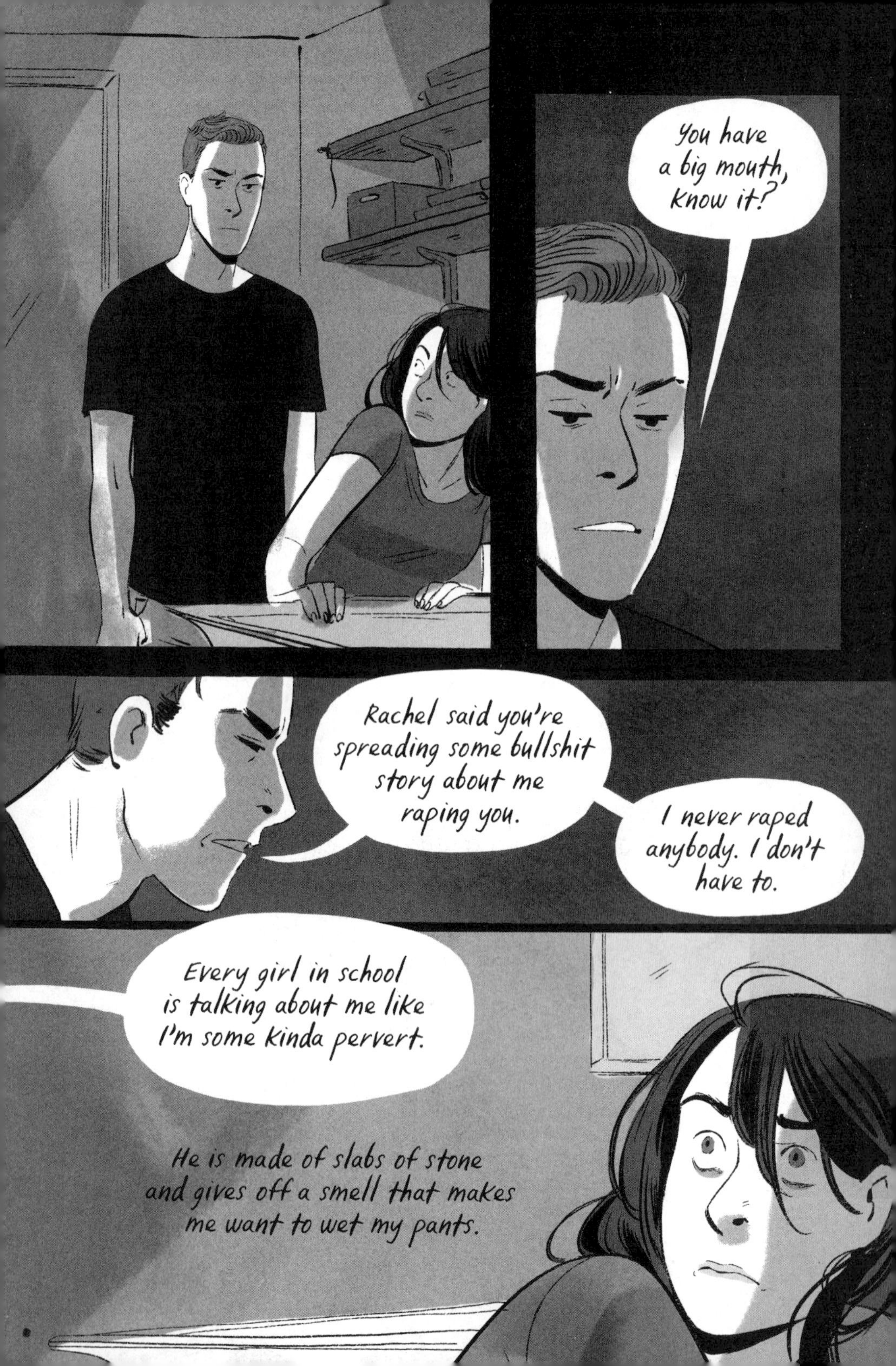
You have a big mouth, know it?
Rachel said you're spreading some bullshit story about me raping you.
I never raped anybody. I don't have to.
Every girl in school is talking about me like I'm some kinda pervert.
He is made of slabs of stone and gives off a smell that makes me want to wet my pants.

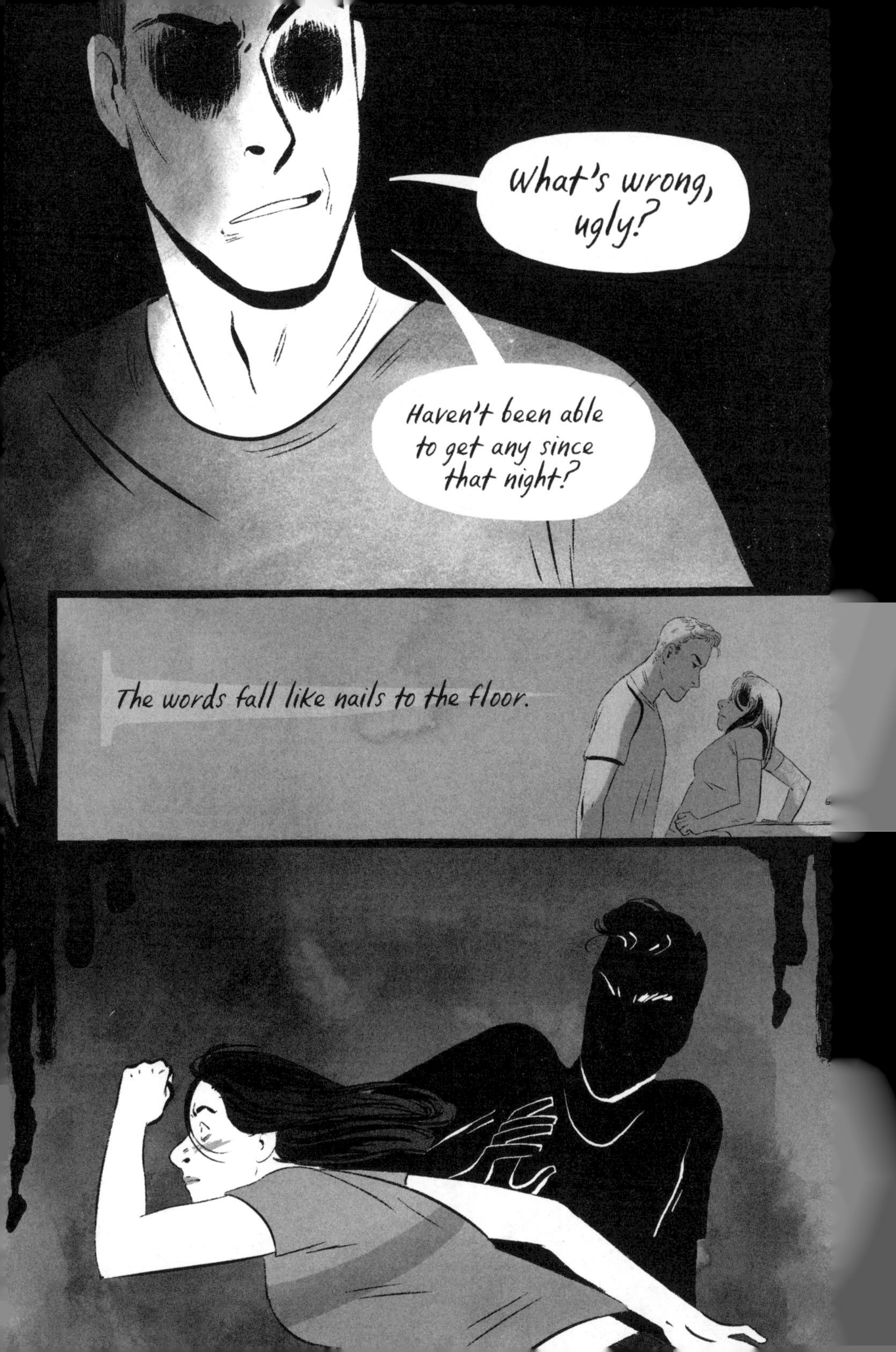
What's wrong, ugly?
Haven't been able to get any since that night?
The words fall like nails to the floor.

Oh no.
You're not going anywhere.
You really screwed things up for me.
You are one strange bitch.
I can't believe anyone listens to you.
CLICK!

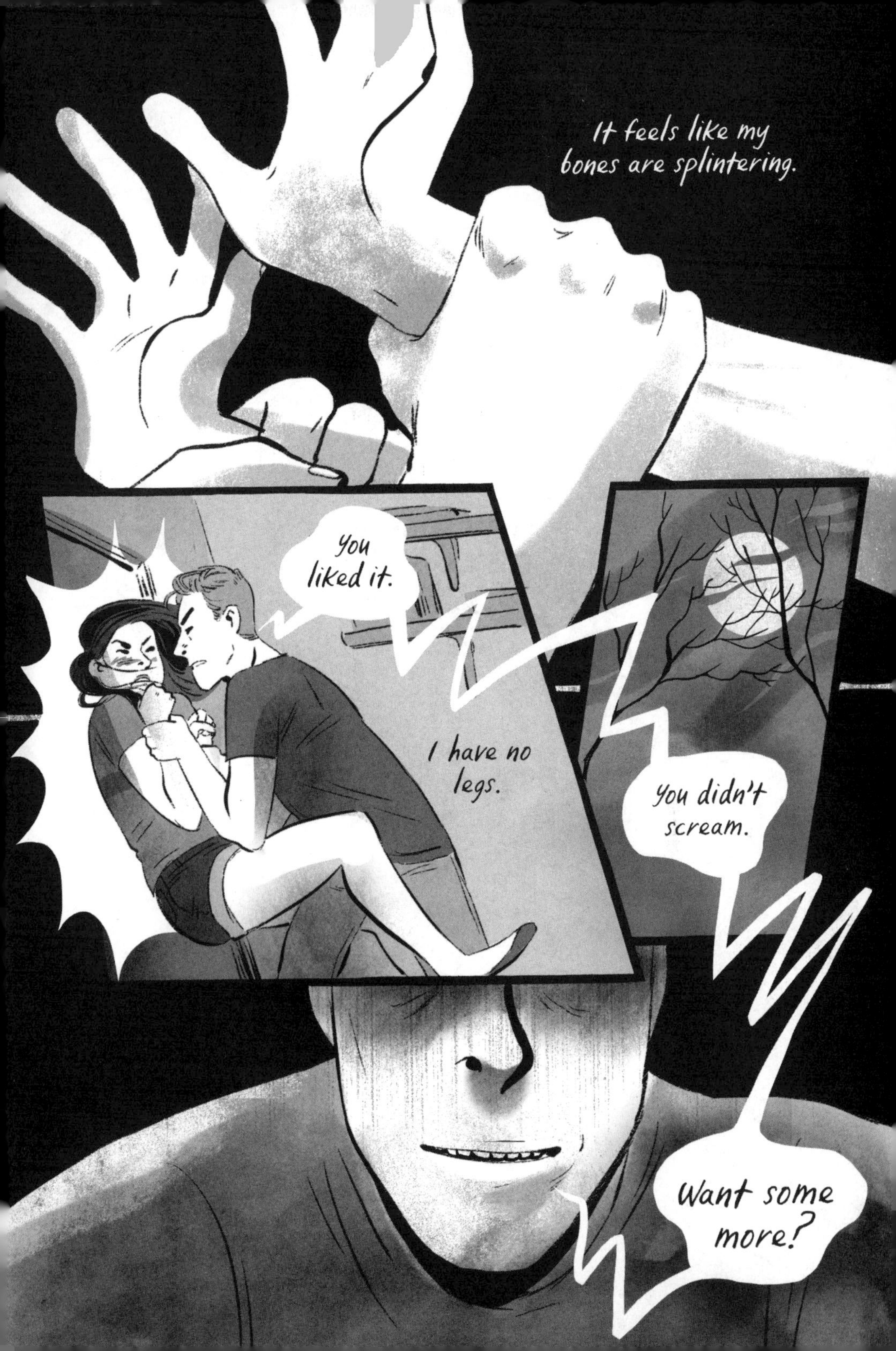
It feels like my bones are splintering.
You liked it.
I have no legs.
You didn't scream.
Want some more?

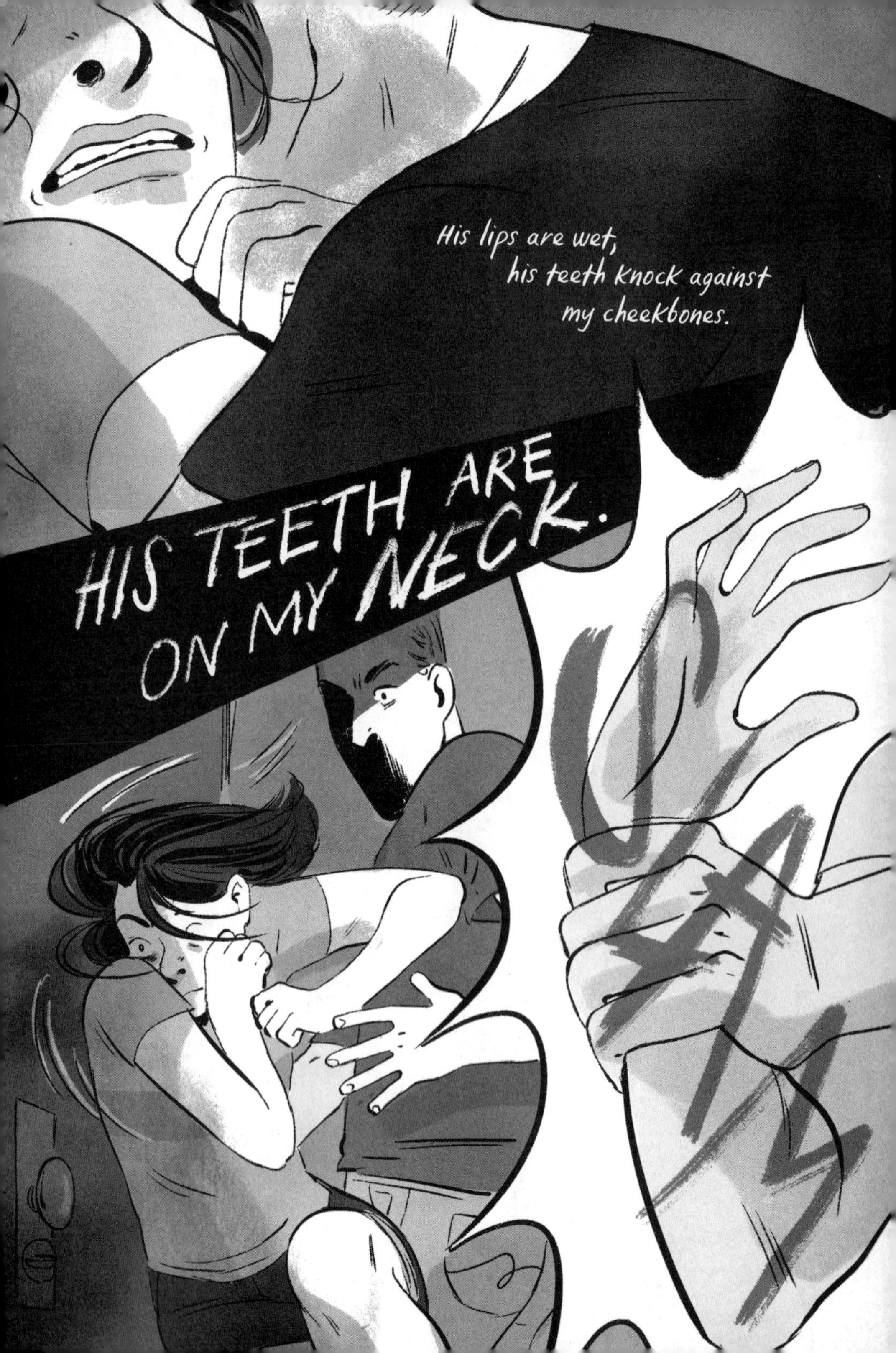
His lips are wet,
his teeth knock against
my cheekbones.
HIS TEETH ARE ON MY NECK.

He's trying to get both wrists in one hand.
He needs a free hand.
I REMEMBER
I REMEMBER
METAL HANDS
HOT KNIFE HANDS
A sound explodes from me.

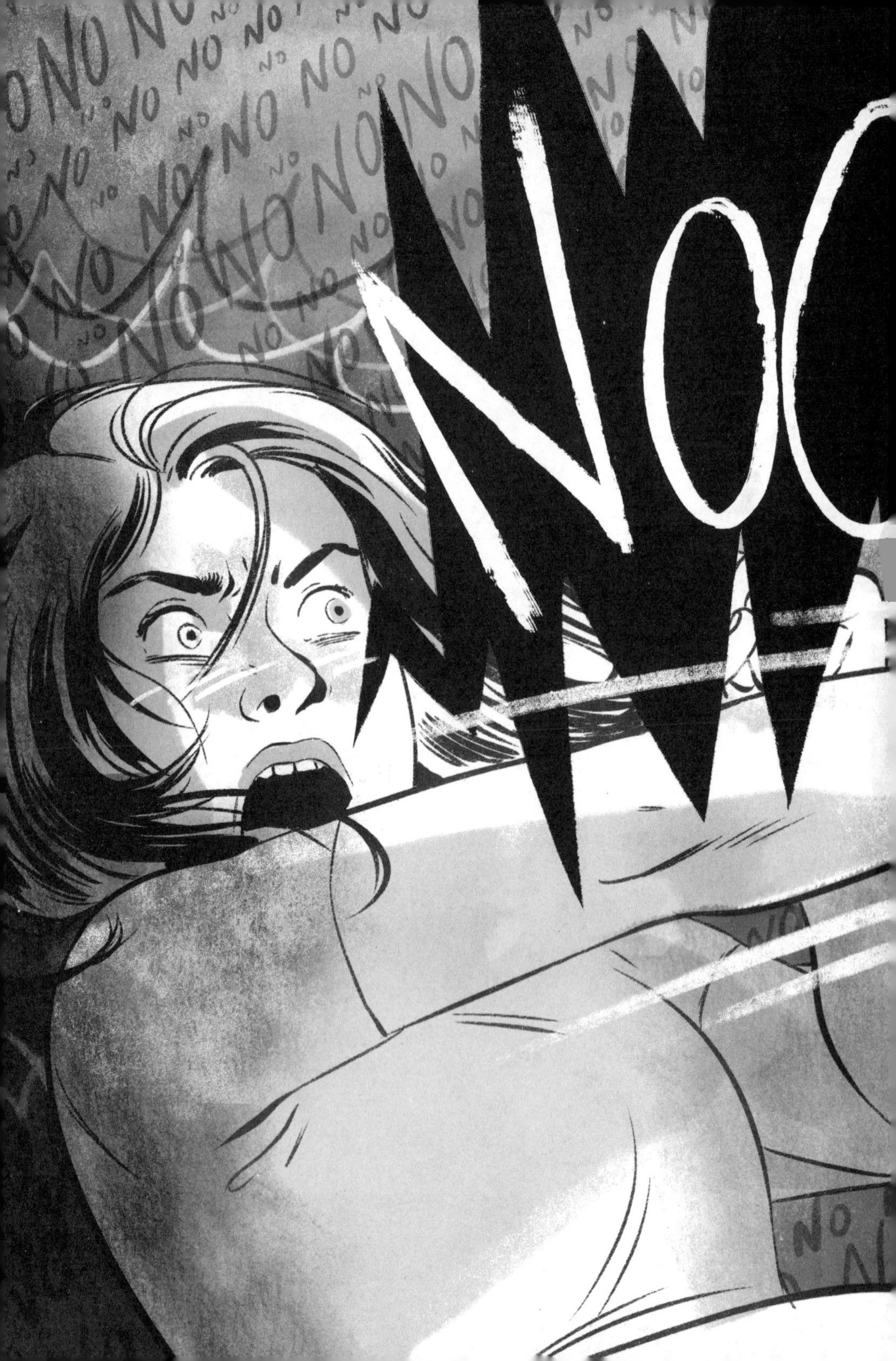
NO
NOO

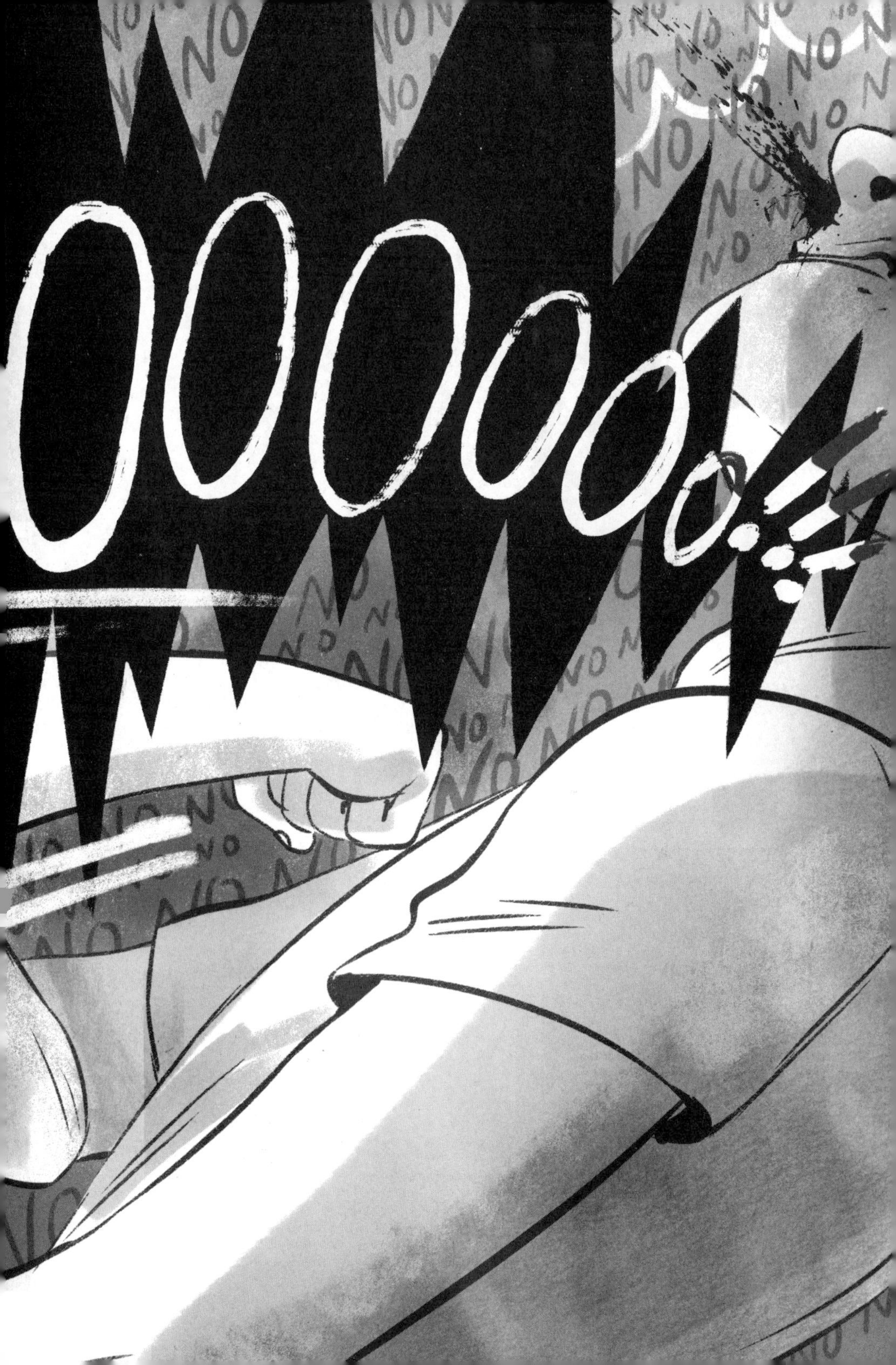
OOOOOO!!!
NO NO NO

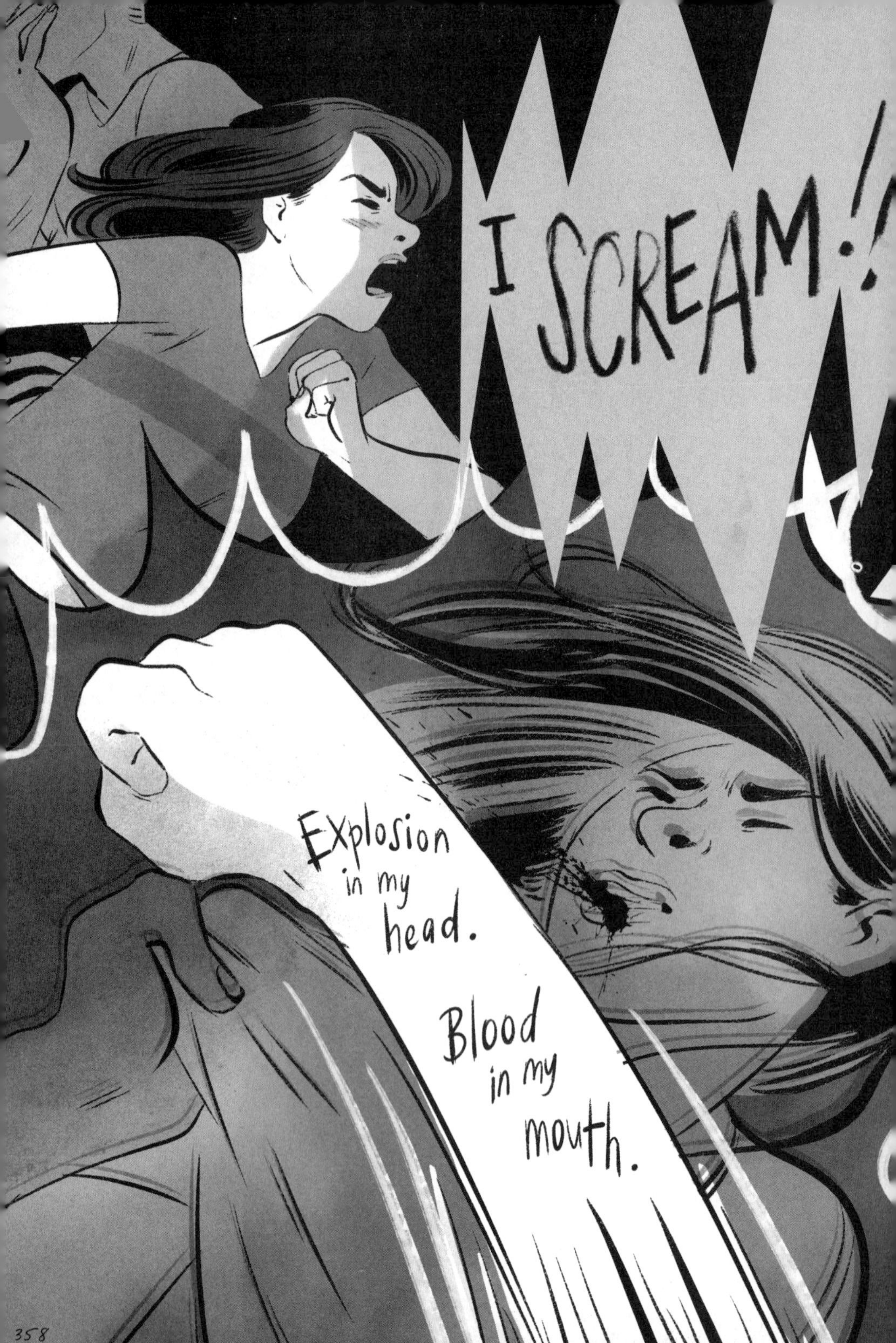
I SCREAM!!
Explosion in my head.
Blood in my mouth.

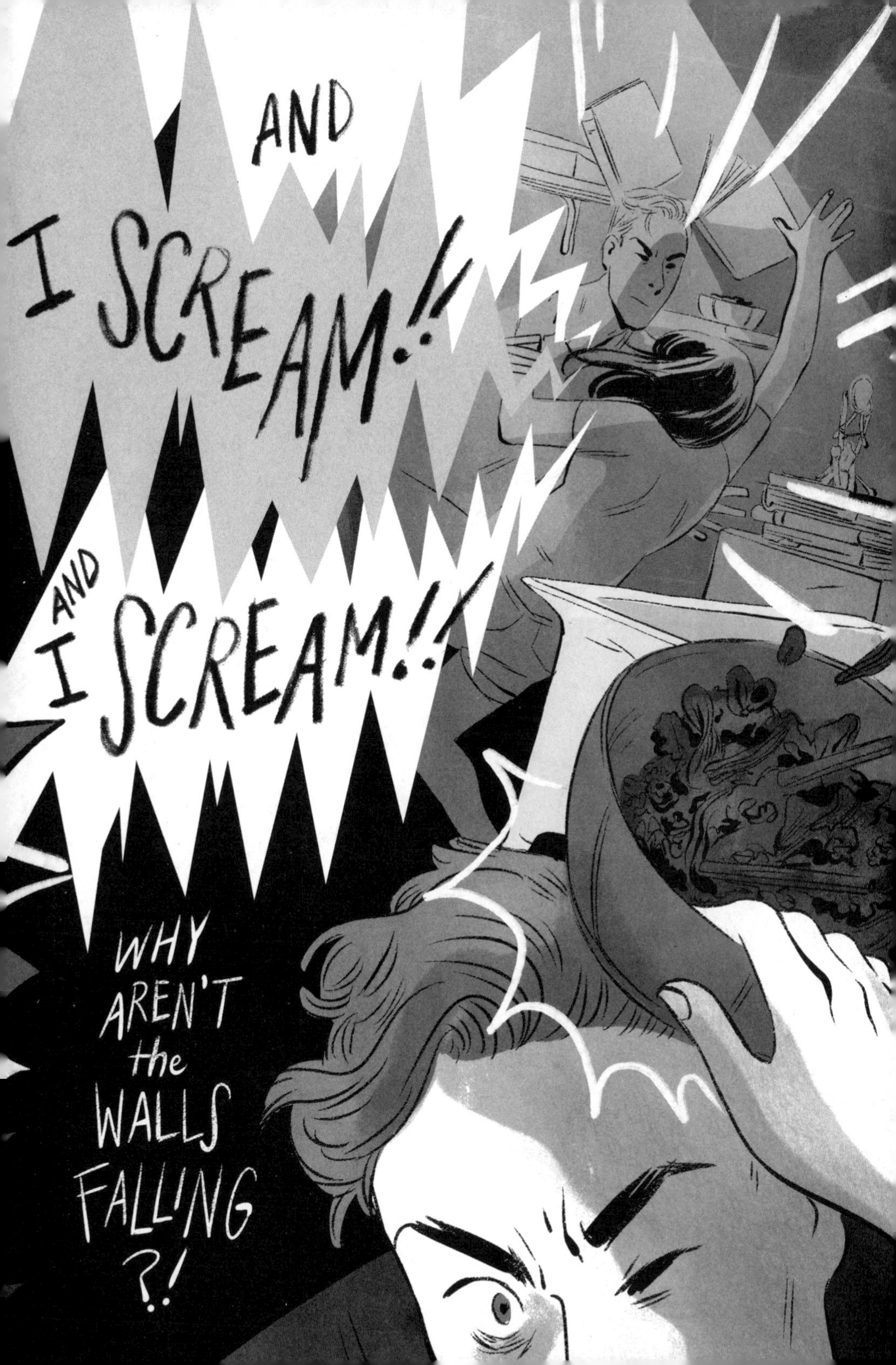
AND
I SCREAM!!
AND
I SCREAM!!
WHY AREN'T the WALLS FALLING ?!

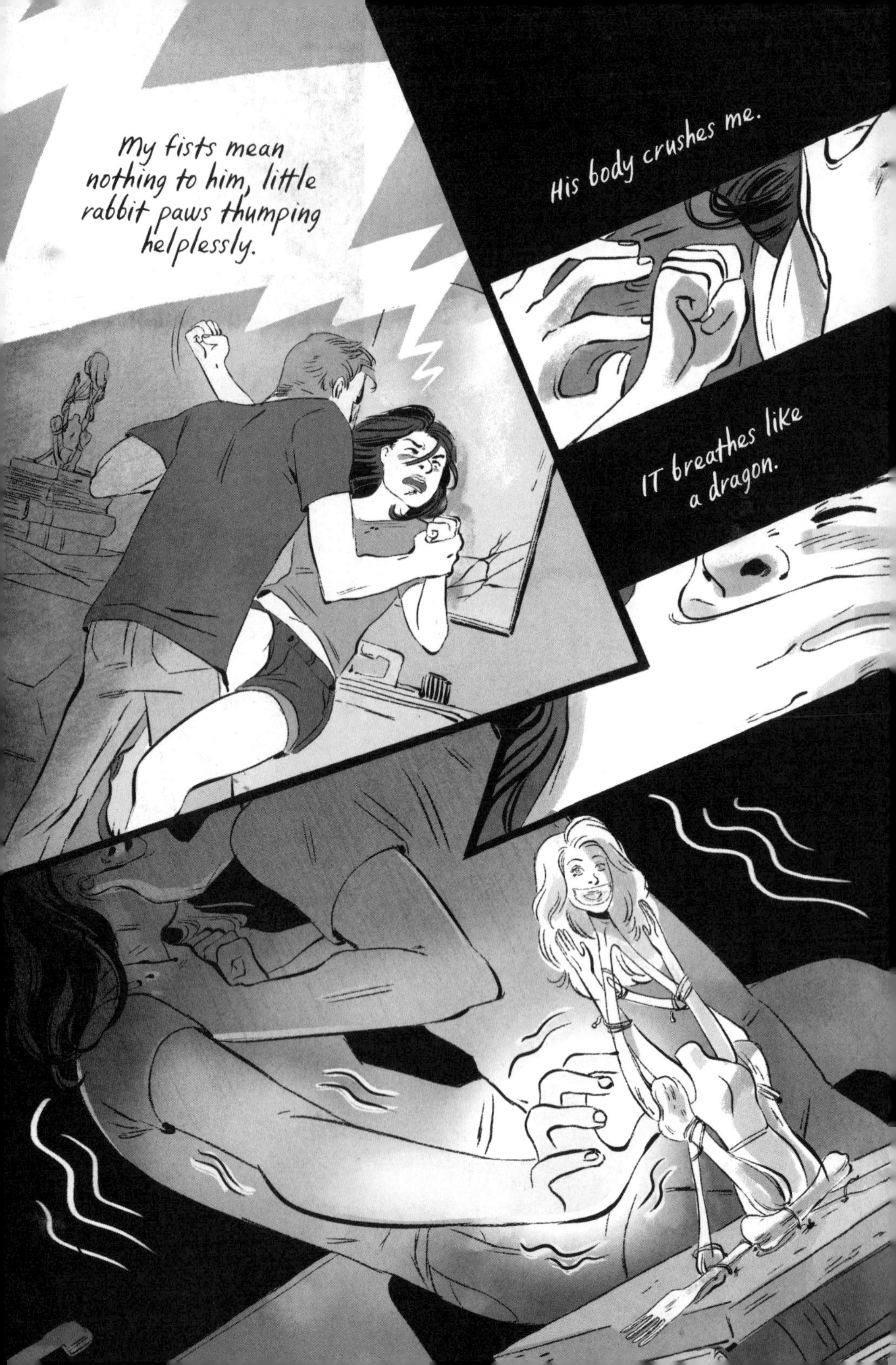
My fists mean nothing to him, little rabbit paws thumping helplessly.
His body crushes me.
IT breathes like a dragon.

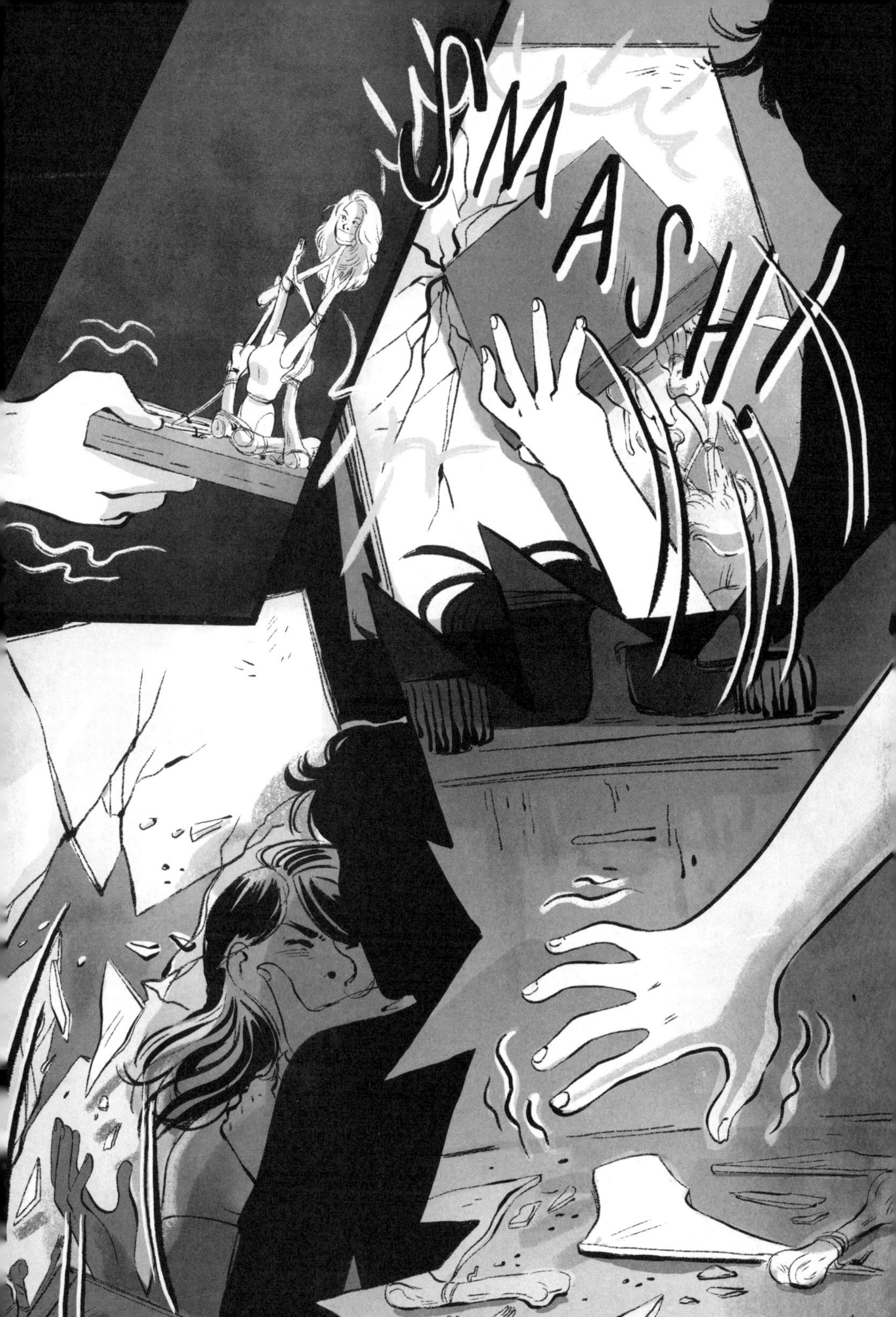
SMASH!

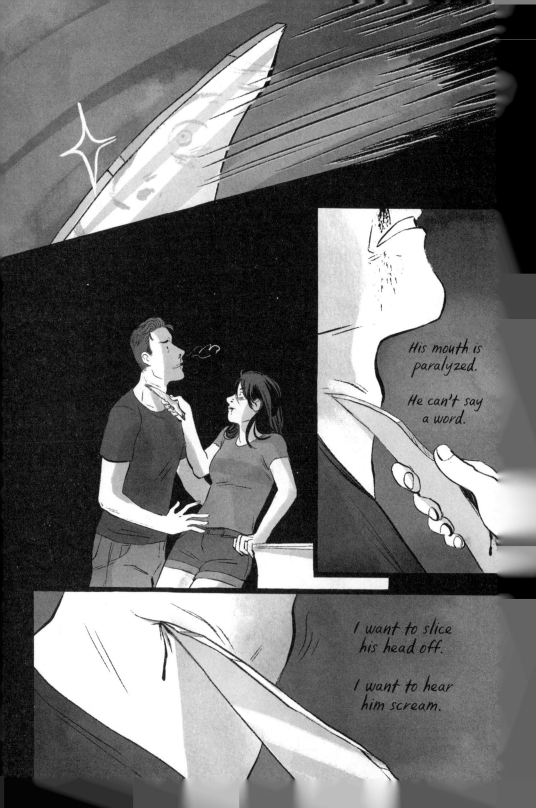

His mouth is
paralyzed.

He can't say
a word.

I want to slice
his head off.

I want to hear
him scream.

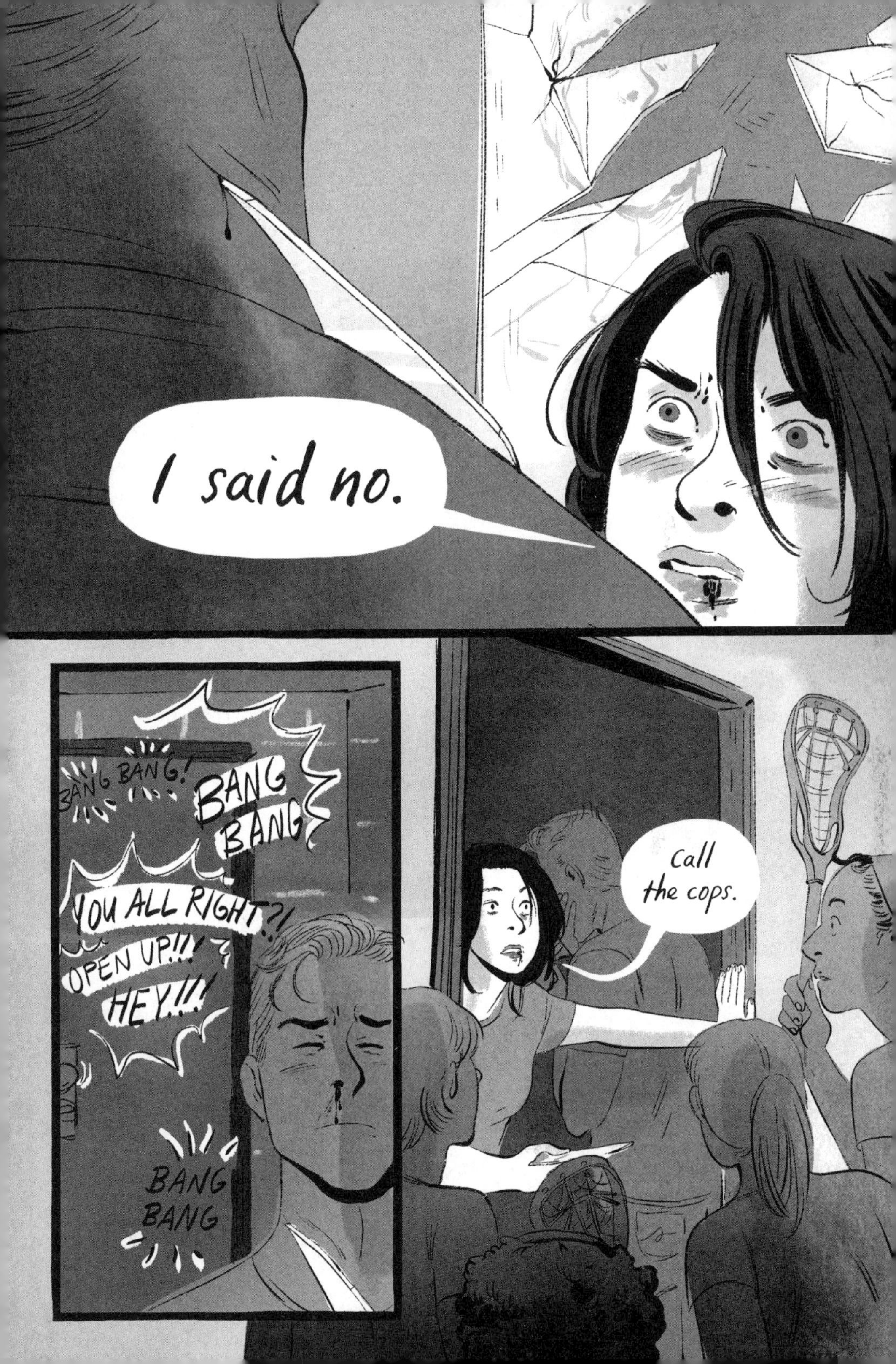
I said no.
BANG BANG!
BANG BANG
YOU ALL RIGHT?!
OPEN UP!!
HEY!!!
BANG BANG
Call the cops.

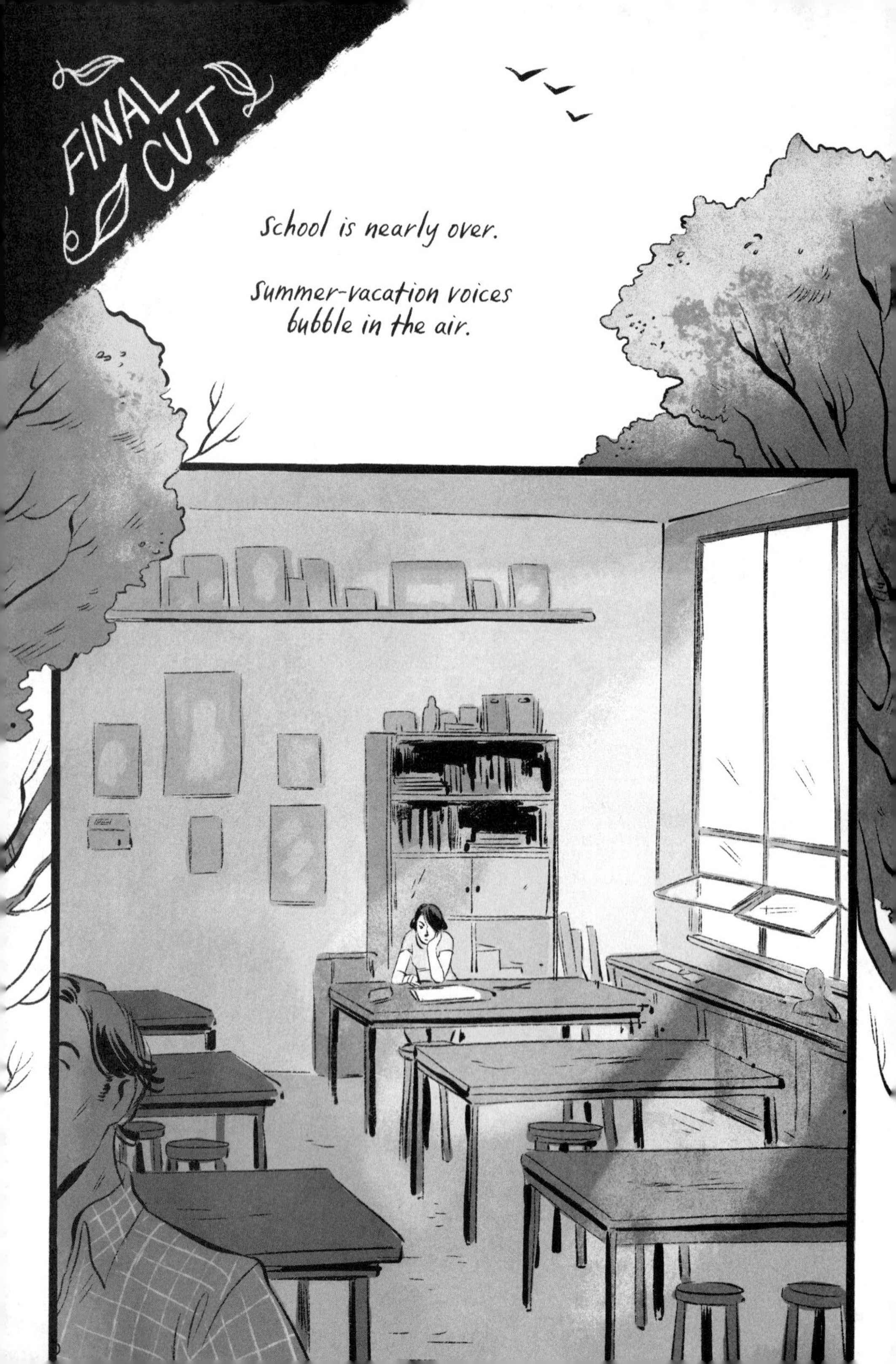
FINAL CUT
School is nearly over.
Summer-vacation voices
bubble in the air.

NAME	GRADE
MELINDA	?

MELINDA | ?

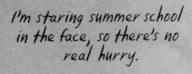

I'm staring summer school in the face, so there's no real hurry.

But I want to finish this tree.

Lilac flows through the open windows with a few lazy bees.

Tires squeal out of the parking lot, another sober student farewell.

The seniors are going to New York City to study art or graphic design.

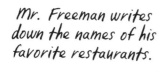

Mr. Freeman writes down the names of his favorite restaurants.

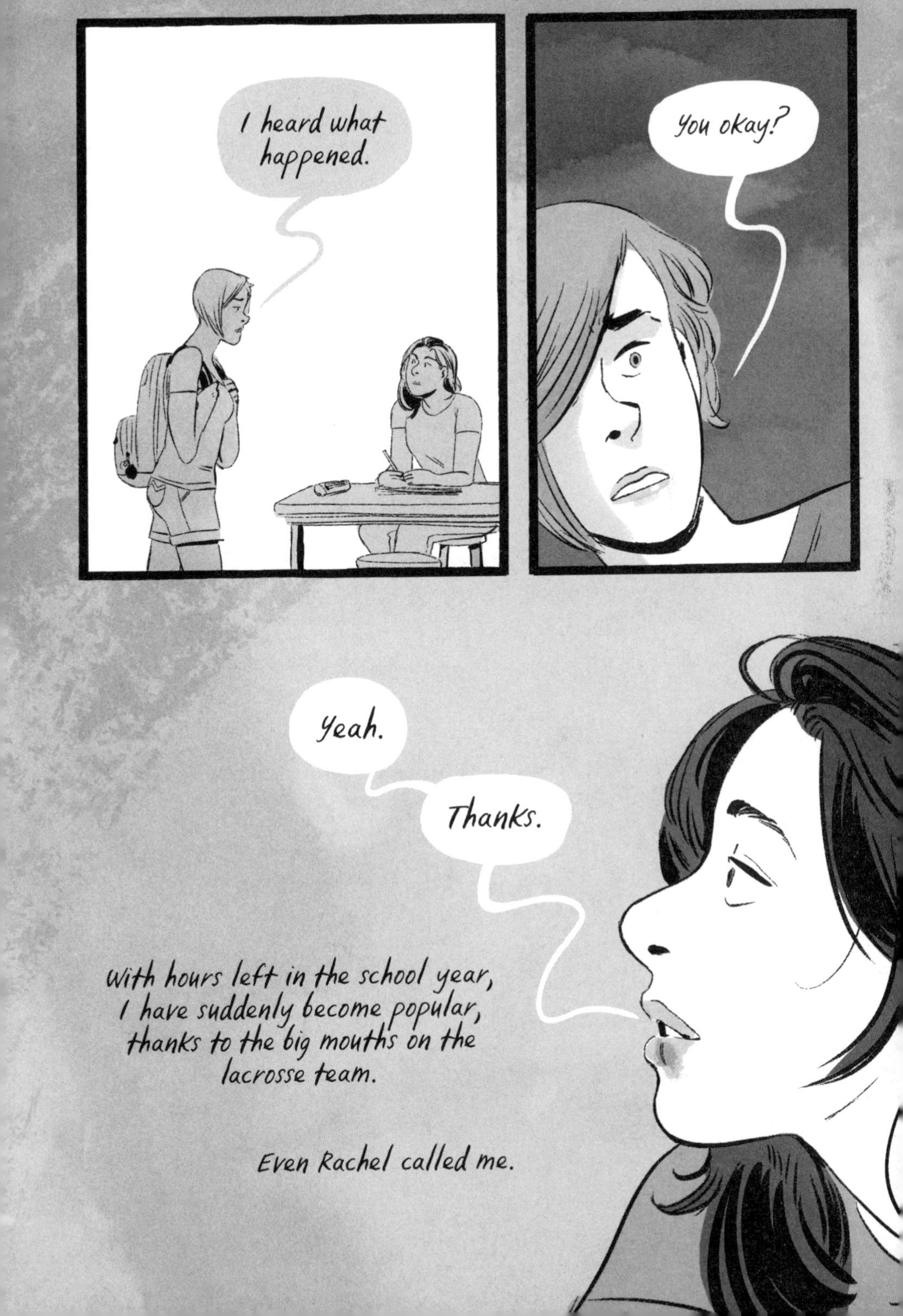
I heard what happened.
You okay?
Yeah.
Thanks.
With hours left in the school year, I have suddenly become popular, thanks to the big mouths on the lacrosse team.
Even Rachel called me.

IT happened.

There is no avoiding it,
no forgetting it.

No running away,
or flying,
or burying,
or hiding.

Andy Evans raped me in August.

It wasn't my fault.

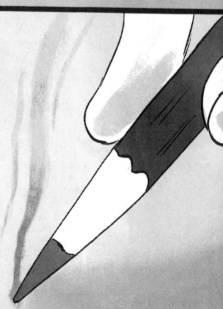

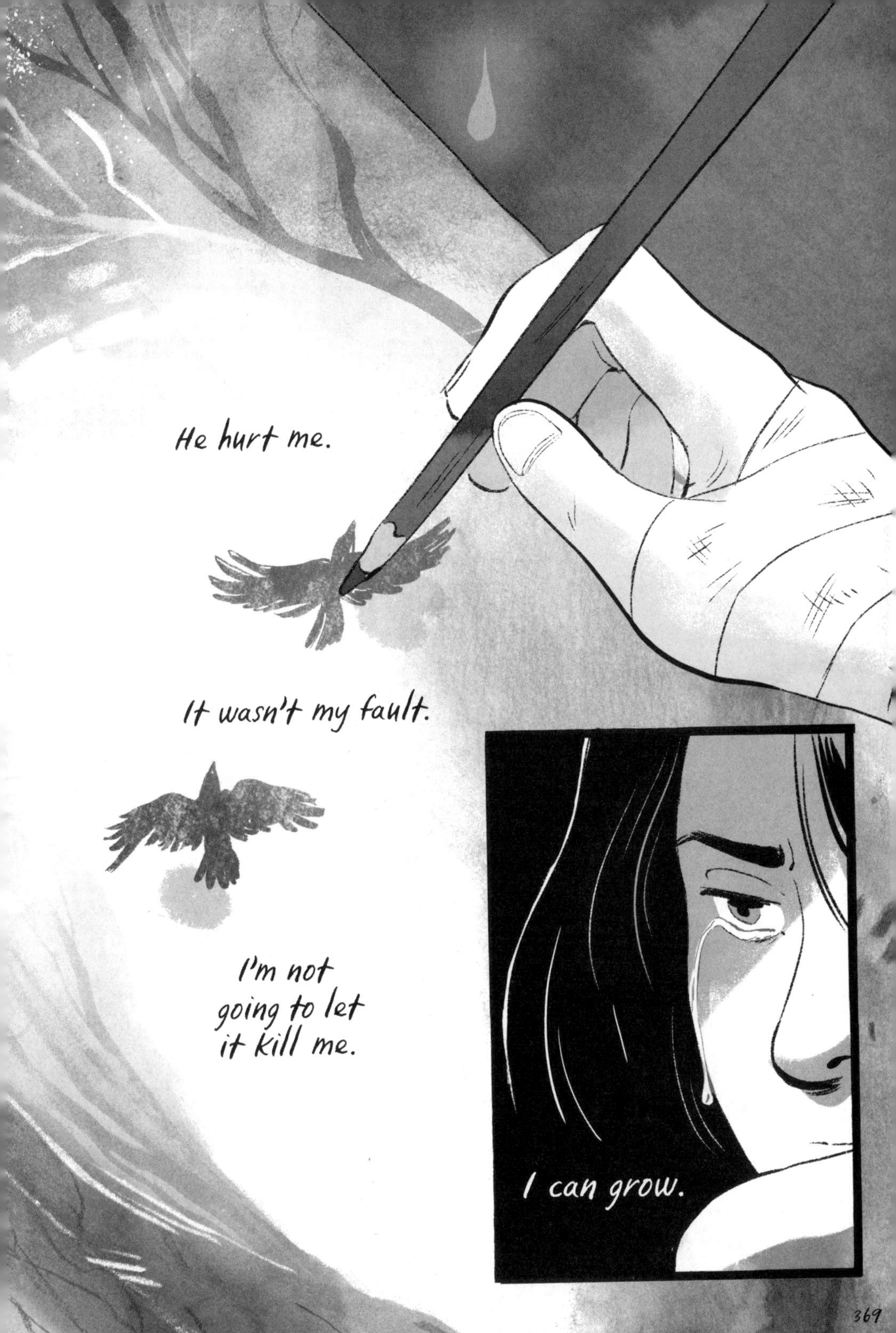
He hurt me.
It wasn't my fault.
I'm not going to let it kill me.
I can grow.

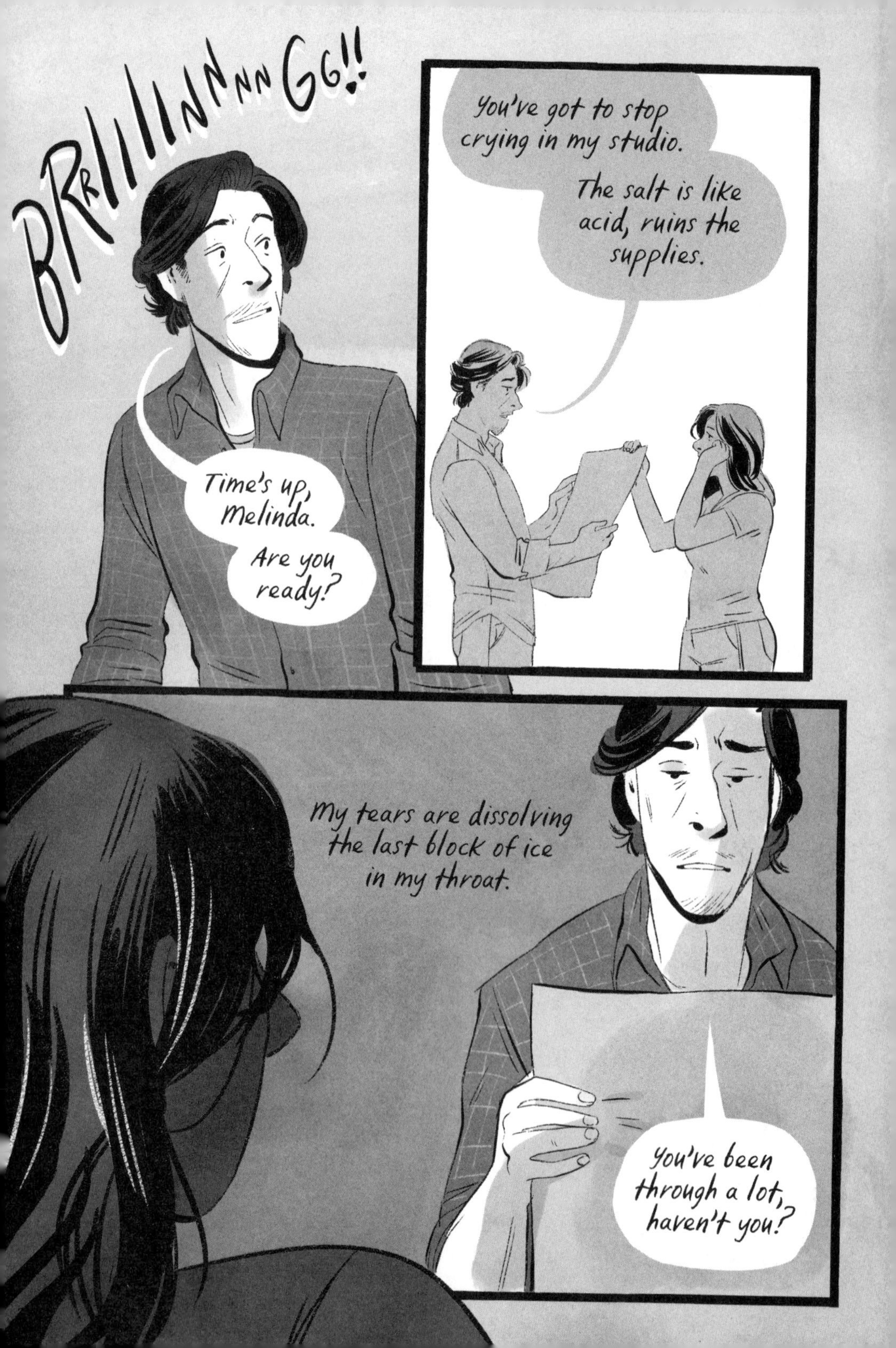
BRRRIIIINNNNGG!!
You've got to stop crying in my studio.
The salt is like acid, ruins the supplies.
Time's up, Melinda.
Are you ready?
My tears are dissolving the last block of ice in my throat.
You've been through a lot, haven't you?

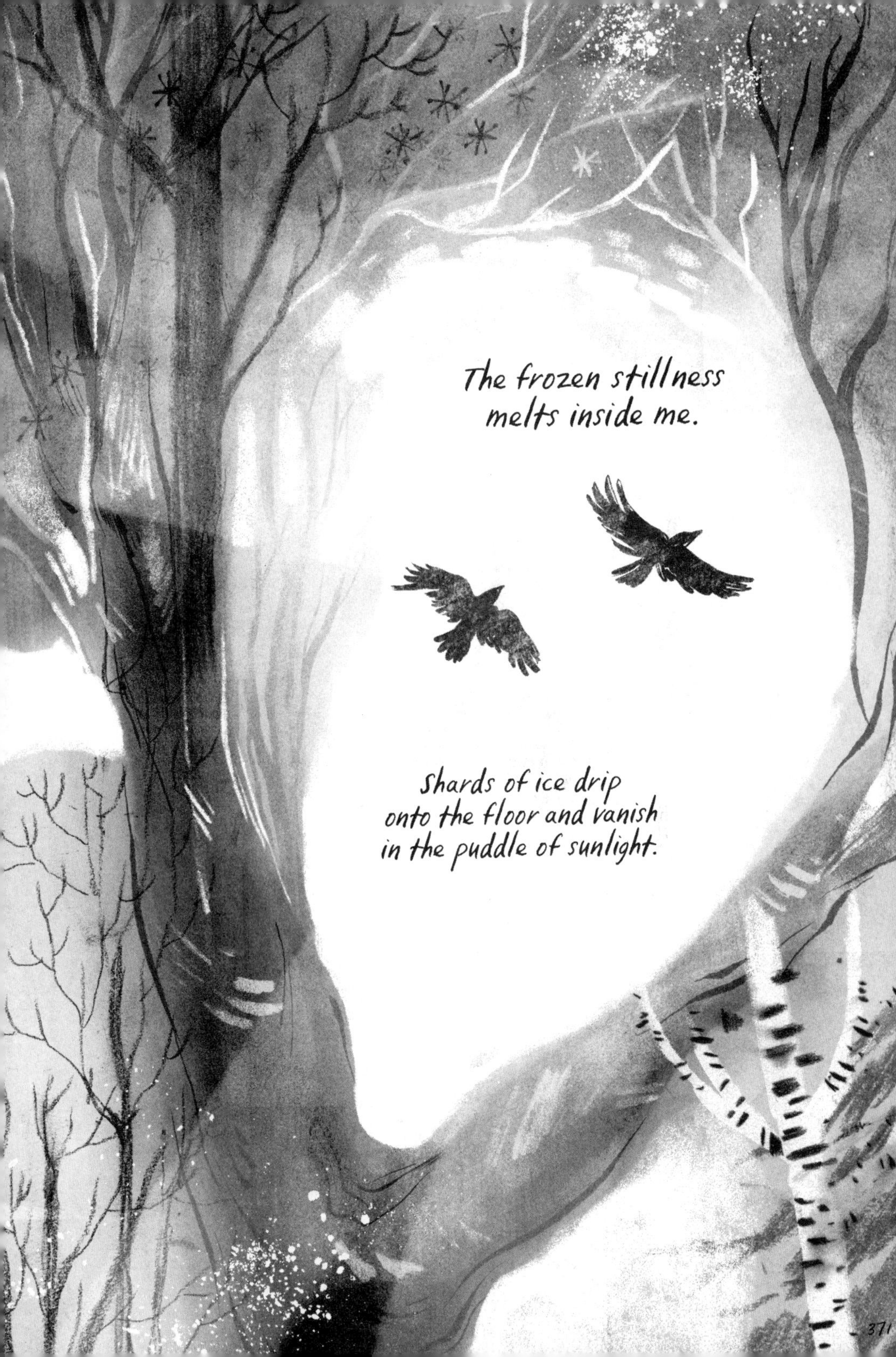
The frozen stillness melts inside me.
Shards of ice drip onto the floor and vanish in the puddle of sunlight.

Let me tell you about it.

Resource List:

Here is a list of organizations that offer support and services to survivors of sexual assault. The description of each is taken from that group's website.

RAINN – https://www.rainn.org/ – "RAINN (Rape, Abuse & Incest National Network) is the nation's largest anti-sexual violence organization. RAINN created and operates the National Sexual Assault Hotline (800.656.HOPE, online.rainn.org) in partnership with more than 1,000 local sexual assault service providers across the country. RAINN also carries out programs to prevent sexual violence, help survivors, and ensure that perpetrators are brought to justice."

National Sexual Violence Resource Center – https://www.nsvrc.org/ – "The NSVRC staff collects and disseminates a wide range of resources on sexual violence, including statistics, research, position statements, statutes, training curricula, prevention initiatives, and program information. With these resources, the NSVRC assists coalitions, advocates, and others interested in understanding and eliminating sexual violence."

SurvJustice – http://www.survjustice.org/ – "SurvJustice is a D.C.-based national not-for-profit organization that increases the prospect of justice for all survivors through effective legal assistance that enforces victim rights and holds both perpetrators and enablers of sexual violence accountable in campus, criminal, and civil systems."

End Rape On Campus – http://endrapeoncampus.org/ – "End Rape on Campus (EROC) works to end campus sexual violence through direct support for survivors and their communities; prevention through education; and policy reform at the campus, local, state, and federal levels."

Farrar Straus Giroux Books for Young Readers
An imprint of Macmillan Publishing Group, LLC
175 Fifth Avenue, New York, NY 10010

Text copyright © 1999 by Laurie Halse Anderson
Pictures copyright © 2018 by Emily Carroll
All rights reserved
Printed in the United States of America
Designed by Emily Carroll and Andrew Arnold
First edition, 2018
1 3 5 7 9 10 8 6 4 2

fiercereads.com

Library of Congress Control Number: 2017933387
ISBN: 978-0-374-30028-9

Our books may be purchased in bulk for promotional, educational,
or business use. Please contact your local bookseller or the Macmillan
Corporate and Premium Sales Department at (800) 221-7945 ext. 5442
or by email at MacmillanSpecialMarkets@macmillan.com.